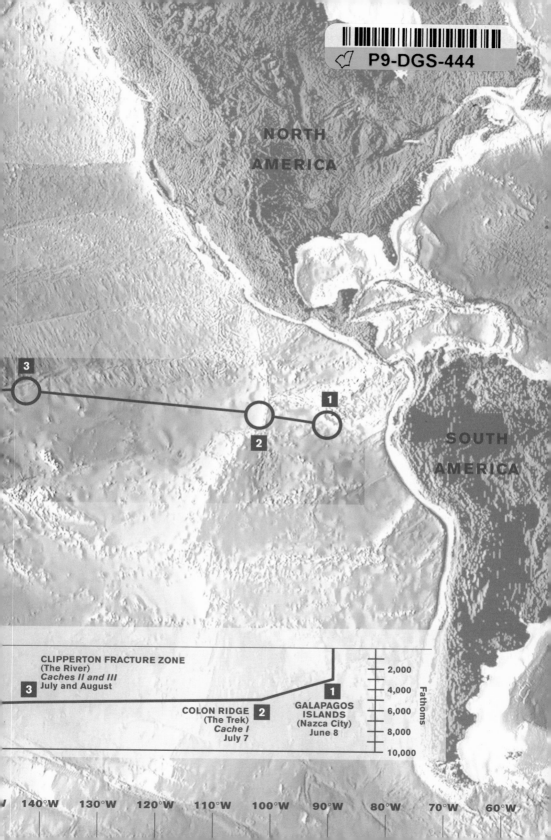

NORTH
AMERICA

SOUTH
AMERICA

3

1

2

CLIPPERTON FRACTURE ZONE
(The River)
Caches II and III
July and August

3

COLON RIDGE
(The Trek)
Cache I
July 7

2

**GALAPAGOS
ISLANDS**
(Nazca City)
June 8

1

2,000

4,000

6,000

8,000

10,000

Fathoms

140°W   130°W   120°W   110°W   100°W   90°W   80°W   70°W   60°W

THE
DESCENT

THE
DESCENT

JEFF LONG

A NOVEL

CROWN PUBLISHERS
New York

Endpaper map by Steve Long and Mapping Specialists Ltd.

Published by Crown Publishers, 201 East 50th Street, New York, New York 10022. Member of the Crown Publishing Group.

Random House, Inc. New York, Toronto, London, Sydney, Auckland
www.randomhouse.com

CROWN is a trademark and the Crown colophon is a registered trademark of Random House, Inc.

Printed in the United States of America

Design by Deborah Kerner

Library of Congress Cataloging-in-Publication Data

Long, Jeff.
The descent / Jeff Long.—1st ed.
p.   cm.
I. Title.
PS3562.04943D47 1999
813'.54—dc21   98-46829
                                                        CIP
ISBN 0-609-60293-4
10 9 8 7 6 5 4 3 2 1
First Edition

FOR MY HELENAS,
A CHAIN UNBROKEN.

ACKNOWLEDGMENTS

It is a fairy tale that writers are recluses quietly cohabiting with their muse. This writer, anyway, benefited from a world of other people's ideas and support. Ironically, ascent informed important moments in *The Descent*'s genesis. The book began as an idea that I presented to a climber, my friend and manager, Bill Gross, who spent the next fifteen months helping me refine the story. His genius and encouragement fueled every page. Early on he shared the project with two other creative spirits in the film world, Bruce Berman and Kevin McMahon at Village Roadshow Pictures. Their support made possible my "re-entry" into New York publishing. There a mountaineer and writer named Jon Waterman introduced me to the talents of another climber, literary agent Susan Golomb. She labored to make the story presentable, cohesive, and true to itself. With her sharp eye and memory of terrain, she would make a great sniper. I thank my editors: Karen Rinaldi for her literary candor and electricity, Richard Marek for his dedicated grasp and professionalism, and Panagiotis Gianopoulos, a rising luminary in the publishing world. I want to add special thanks to my nameless, faceless copy editor. This is my seventh book, and I only learned now that, for professional reasons, copy editors are never revealed to writers. Like monks, they toil in anonymity. I specifically requested the best copy editor in the country, and whoever he or she is, my wish was granted. My deep appreciation to Jim Walsh, another of the hidden minds behind the book.

I am not a spelunker, nor an epic poet. In other words, I needed guides to penetrate my imaginary hell. It was my father, the geologist, who set me roaming in childhood mazes, from old mines to honey-combed sandstone structures, from Pennsylvania to Mesa Verde and Arches national monuments. Besides the obvious and well-used inspirations for my poetic license, I'm obliged to several contemporary works. Alice K. Turner's *The History of Hell* (Harcourt Brace) was stunning in its scope, scholarship, and wicked humor. Dante had his Virgil; I had my Turner. Another instructor of the underworld was the indispensable *Atlas of the Great Caves of the World*, by Paul Courbon. "Lechuguilla Restoration: Techniques Learned in the Southwest Focus," by Val Hildreth-Werker and Jim C. Werker, gave me a "deeper" appreciation of cave environments. Donald Dale Jackson's *Underground Worlds* (Time-Life Books) never quit amazing me with the beauty of subterranean places. Finally, it was my friend Steve Harrigan's remarkable novel about cave diving, *Jacob's Well* (Simon and Schuster), that truly anchored my nightmares about dark, deep, tubular realms.

The Descent was informed by many other people's work and ideas, too many to list without a bibliography. However, *Turin Shroud*, by Lynn Picknett and Clive Prince (HarperCollins), provided the basis for my own Shroud chapter. "Egil's Bones," by Jesse L. Byock (*Scientific American*, January 1995), provided me a disease to go with my masks. *Unveiled: Nuns Talking*, by Mary Loudon (Templegate Publishers), gave me a peek behind the veil. Stephen S. Hall's *Mapping the Next Millennium* (Vintage) opened my mind to the world of cartography. Peter Sloss, of the Marine Geology and Geophysics Computer Graphics at the National Oceanic and Atmospheric Administration, generously displayed his state-of-the-art mapmaking. Philip Lieberman's *The Biology and Evolution of Language* (Harvard) helped me backward into the origins of speech, as did Dr. Rende, a speech language pathologist at the University of Colorado. Michael D. Coe's *Breaking the Maya Code* (Thames and Hudson), David Roberts's "The Decipherment of Ancient Maya" (*Atlantic Monthly*, September 1991), Colin Renfrew's "The Origins of Indo-European Languages" (*Scientific American*, October 1989), and especially Robert Wright's "The Quest for the Mother Tongue" (*Atlantic Monthly*, April 1991) gave me a window on linguistic discovery. "Unusual Unity" by Stephen Jay Gould (*Natural History*, April 1997) and "The African Emergence and Early Asian Dispersals of the Genus Homo" by Roy Larick and Russell L. Ciochon (*American Scientist*, November–December 1996) got my wheels seriously spinning and led me to further readings. Cliff Watts, yet another climber and friend, guided me to an internet article on prions, by Stanley B. Prusiner, and gave medical advice about everything from altitude to vision. Another climber, Jim Gleason, tried his damnedest to keep my junk science to a minimum, all in vain I'm afraid he'll feel. I only hope that my plundering and mangling of fact may pave some amused diversion.

Early on, Graham Henderson, a fellow Tibet traveler, gave my journey direction with his observations about *The Inferno*. Throughout, Steve Long helped map the journey, both on paper and in countless conversations. Pam Novotny loaned me her Zen-like patience and calm, in addition to editorial assistance. Angela Thieman, Melissa Ward, and Margo Timmins provided constant inspiration. I am grateful to Elizabeth Crook, Craig Blockwick, Arthur Lindquist-Kliessler, and Cindy Butler for their crucial reminders of a light at the end of the tunnel.

Finally, thank you, Barbara and Helena, for putting up with the chaos that finally came to order. Love may not conquer all, but happily it conquers us.

A
C
K
N
O
W
L
E
D
G
M
E
N
T
S

BOOK ONE

DISCOVERY

*It is easy to go down into
Hell . . . ; but to climb back
again, to retrace one's steps
to the upper air—there's
the rub. . . .*

—VIRGIL, *Aeneid*

1
IKE

In the beginning was the word.

Or words.

Whatever these were.

They kept their lights turned off. The exhausted trekkers huddled in the dark cave and faced the peculiar writing. Scrawled with a twig, possibly, dipped in liquid radium or some other radioactive paint, the fluorescent pictographs floated in the black recesses. Ike let them savor the distraction. None of them seemed quite ready to focus on the storm beating against the mountainside outside.

With night descending and the trail erased by snow and wind and their yak herders in mutinous flight with most of the gear and food, Ike was relieved to have shelter of any kind. He was still pretending for them that this was part of their trip. In fact they were off the map. He'd never heard of this hole-in-the-wall hideout. Nor seen glow-in-the-dark caveman graffiti.

"Runes," gushed a knowing female voice. "Sacred runes left by a wandering monk."

The alien calligraphy glowed with soft violet light in the cave's cold bowels. The luminous hieroglyphics reminded Ike of his old dorm wall with its black-light posters. All he needed was a lash of Hendrix plundering Dylan's anthem, say, and a whiff of plump Hawaiian red sinsemilla. Anything to vanquish the howl of awful wind. *Outside in the cold distance, a wildcat did growl. . . .*

"Those are no runes," said a man. "It's Bonpo." A Brooklyn beat, the accent meant Owen. Ike had nine clients here, only two of them male. They were easy to keep straight.

"Bonpo!" one of the women barked at Owen. The coven seemed to take collective delight in savaging Owen and Bernard, the other man. Ike had been spared so far. They treated him as a harmless Himalayan hillbilly. Fine with him.

"But the Bonpo were pre-Buddhist," the woman expounded.

The women were mostly Buddhist students from a New Age university. These things mattered very much to them.

Their goal was—or had been—Mount Kailash, the pyramidal giant just east of the Indian border. "A Canterbury Tale for the World Pilgrim" was how he'd advertised the trip. A *kor*—a Tibetan walkabout—to and around the holiest mountain in the world. Eight thousand per head, incense included. The problem was, somewhere along the trail he'd managed to misplace the mountain. It galled him. They were lost. Beginning at dawn today, the sky had changed from blue to milky gray. The herders had quietly bolted with the yaks. He had yet to announce that their tents and food were history. The first sloppy snowflakes had started kissing their Gore-Tex hoods just an hour ago, and Ike had taken this cave for shelter. It was a good call. He was the only one who knew it, but they were now about to get sodomized by an old-fashioned Himalayan tempest.

Ike felt his jacket being tugged to one side, and knew it would be Kora, wanting a private word. "How bad is it?" she whispered. Depending on the hour and day, Kora was his lover, base-camp shotgun, or business associate. Of late, it was a challenge estimating which came first for her, the business of adventure or the adventure of business. Either way, their little trekking company was no longer charming to her.

Ike saw no reason to front-load it with negatives. "We've got a great cave," he said.

"Gee."

"We're still in the black, head-count-wise."

"The itinerary's in ruins. We were behind as it was."

"We're fine. We'll take it out of the Siddhartha's Birthplace segment." He kept the worry out of his voice, but for once his sixth sense, or whatever it was, had come up short, and that bothered him. "Besides, getting a little lost will give them bragging rights."

"They don't want bragging rights. They want schedule. You don't know these people. They're not your friends. We'll get sued if they don't make their Thai Air flight on the nineteenth."

"These are the mountains," said Ike. "They'll understand." People forgot. Up here, it was a mistake to take even your next breath for granted.

"No, Ike. They won't understand. They have real jobs. Real obligations. Families." That was the rub. Again. Kora wanted more from life. She wanted more from her pathless Pathfinder.

"I'm doing the best I can," Ike said.

Outside, the storm went on horsewhipping the cave mouth. Barely May, it wasn't supposed to be this way. There should have been plenty of time to get his bunch to, around, and back from Kailash. The bane of mountaineers, the monsoon normally didn't spill across the mountains this far north. But as a former Everester himself, Ike should have known better than to believe in rain shadows or in schedules. Or in luck. They were in for it this time. The snow would seal their pass shut until late August. That meant he was going to have to buy space on a Chinese truck and shuttle them home via Lhasa—and that came out of his land costs. He tried calculating in his head, but their quarrel overcame him.

"You *do* know what I mean by Bonpo," a woman said. Nineteen days into the trip, and Ike still couldn't link their spirit nicknames with the names in their passports. One woman, was it Ethel or Winifred, now preferred Green Tara, mother deity of Tibet. A pert Doris Day look-alike swore she was special friends with the Dalai Lama. For weeks now Ike had been listening to them celebrate the life of cavewomen. Well, he thought, here's your cave, ladies. Slum away.

They were sure his name—Dwight David Crockett—was an invention like their own. Nothing could convince them he wasn't one of them, a dabbler in past lives. One evening around a campfire in northern Nepal, he'd regaled them with tales of Andrew Jackson, pirates on the Mississippi, and his own legendary death at the Alamo. He'd meant it as a joke, but only Kora got it.

"You should know perfectly well," the woman went on, "there was no written language in Tibet before the late fifth century."

"No written language that we *know* about," Owen said.

"Next you'll be saying this is Yeti language."

It had been like this for days. You'd think they'd run out of air. But the higher they went, the more they argued.

"This is what we get for pandering to civilians," Kora muttered to Ike. Civilians was her catch-all: eco-tourists, pantheist charlatans, trust funders, the overeducated. She was a street girl at heart.

"They're not so bad," he said. "They're just looking for a way into Oz, same as us."

"Civilians."

Ike sighed. At times like this, he questioned his self-imposed exile. Living apart from the world was not easy. There was a price to be paid for choosing the less-traveled road. Little things, bigger ones. He was no longer that rosy-cheeked lad who had come with the Peace Corps. He still had the cheekbones and cowled brow and careless mane. But a dermatologist on one of his treks had advised him to stay out of the high-altitude sun before his face turned to boot leather. Ike had never considered himself God's gift to women, but he saw no reason to trash what looks he still had. He'd lost two of his back molars to Nepal's dearth of dentists, and another tooth to a falling rock on the backside of Everest. And not so long ago, in his Johnnie Walker Black and Camels days, he'd taken to serious self-abuse, even flirting with the lethal west face of Makalu. He'd quit the smoke and booze cold when some British nurse told him his voice sounded like a Rudyard Kipling punchline. Makalu still needed slaying, of course. Though many mornings he even wondered about that.

Exile went deeper than the cosmetics or even prime health, of course. Self-doubt came with the territory, a wondering about what might have been, had he stayed the course back in Jackson. Rig work. Stone masonry. Maybe mountain guiding in the Tetons, or outfitting for hunters. No telling. He'd spent the last eight years in Nepal and Tibet watching himself slowly devolve from the Golden Boy of the Himalayas into one more forgotten surrogate of the American empire. He'd grown old inside. Even now there were days when Ike felt eighty. Next week was his thirty-first birthday.

"Would you look at this?" rose a cry. "What kind of mandala is that? The lines are all twisty."

Ike looked at the circle. It was hanging on the wall like a luminous moon. Mandalas were meditation aids, blueprints for divinity's palaces. Normally they consisted of circles within circles containing squared lines. By visualizing it just so, a 3-D architecture was supposed to appear above the mandala's flat surface. This one, though, looked like scrambled snakes.

Ike turned on his light. End of mystery, he congratulated himself. Even he was stunned by the sight.

"My God," said Kora.

Where, a moment before, the fluorescent words had hung in magical suspense, a nude corpse stood rigidly propped upon a stone shelf along the back wall. The words weren't written on stone. They were written on him. The mandala was separate, painted on the wall to his right side.

A set of rocks formed a crude stairway up to his stage, and various passersby had attached *katas*—long white prayer scarves—to cracks in the stone ceiling. The *katas* sucked back and forth in the draft like gently disturbed ghosts.

The man's grimace was slightly bucktoothed from mummification, and his eyes were calcified to chalky blue marbles. Otherwise the extreme cold and high altitude had left him perfectly preserved. Under the harsh beam of Ike's headlamp, the lettering was faint and red upon his emaciated limbs and belly and chest.

That he was a traveler was self-evident. In these regions, everyone was a pilgrim or a nomad or a salt trader or a refugee. But, judging from his scars and unhealed wounds and a metal collar around his neck and a warped, badly mended broken left arm, this particular Marco Polo had endured a journey beyond imagination. If flesh is memory, his body cried out a whole history of abuse and enslavement.

They stood beneath the shelf and goggled at the suffering. Three of the women—and Owen—began weeping. Ike alone approached. Probing here and there with his light beam, he reached out to touch one shin with his ice ax: hard as fossil wood.

Of all the obvious insults, the one that stood out most was his partial castration. One of the man's testicles had been yanked away, not cut, not even bitten—the edges of the tear were too ragged—and the wound had been cauterized with fire. The burn scars radiated out from his groin in a hairless keloid starburst. Ike couldn't get over the raw scorn of it. Man's tenderest part, mutilated, then doctored with a torch.

"Look," someone whimpered. "What did they do to his nose?"

Midcenter on the battered face was a ring unlike anything he'd ever seen before. This was no silvery Gen-X body piercing. The ring, three inches across and crusted with blood, was plugged deep in his septum, almost up into the skull. It hung to his bottom lip, as black as his beard. It was, thought Ike, utilitarian, large enough to control cattle.

Then he got a little closer and his repulsion altered. The ring was brutal. Blood and smoke and filth had coated it almost black, but Ike could plainly see the dull gleam of solid gold.

Ike turned to his people and saw nine pairs of frightened eyes beseeching him from beneath hoods and visors. Everyone had their lights on now. No one was arguing.

"Why?" wept one of the women.

A couple of the Buddhists had reverted to Christianity and were on their knees, crossing themselves. Owen was rocking from side to side, murmuring Kaddish.

Kora came close. "You beautiful bastard." She giggled. Ike started. She was talking to the corpse.

"What did you say?"

"We're off the hook. They're not going to hit us up for refunds after all. We don't have to provide their holy mountain anymore. They've got something better."

"Let up, Kora. Give them some credit. They're not ghouls."

"No? Look around, Ike."

Sure enough, cameras were stealing into view in ones and twos. There was a flash, then another. Their shock gave way to tabloid voyeurism.

In no time the entire cast was blazing away with eight-hundred-dollar point-and-shoots. Motor drives made an insect hum. The lifeless flesh flared in their artificial lightning. Ike moved out of frame, and welcomed the corpse like a savior. It was unbelievable. Famished, cold, and lost, they couldn't have been happier.

One of the women had climbed the stepping-stones and was kneeling to one side of the nude, her head tilted sideways.

She looked down at them. "But he's one of us," she said.

"What's that supposed to mean?"

"Us. You and me. A white man."

Someone else framed it in less vulgar terms. "A Caucasian male?"

"That's crazy," someone objected. "Here? In the middle of nowhere?"

Ike knew she was right. The white flesh, the hair on its forearms and chest, the blue eyes, the cheekbones so obviously non-Mongoloid. But the woman wasn't pointing to his hairy arms or blue eyes or slender cheekbones. She was pointing at the hieroglyphics painted on his thigh. Ike aimed his light at the other thigh. And froze.

The text was in English. Modern English. Only upside down.

It came to him. The body hadn't been written upon after death. The man had written upon himself in life. He'd used his own body as a blank page. Upside down. He'd inscribed his journal notes on the only parchment guaranteed to travel with him. Now Ike saw how the lettering wasn't just painted on, but crudely tattooed.

Wherever he could reach, the man had jotted bits of testimony.

Abrasions and filth obscured some of the writing, particularly below the knees and around his ankles. The rest of it could easily have been dismissed as random and lunatic. Numbers mixed with words and phrases, especially on the outer edges of each thigh, where he'd apparently decided there was extra room for new entries. The clearest passage lay across his lower stomach.

"'All the world will be in love with night,'" Ike read aloud, "'and pay no worship to the garish sun.'"

"Gibberish," snapped Owen, badly spooked.

"Bible talk," Ike sympathized.

"No, it's not," piped up Kora. "That's not from the Bible. It's Shakespeare. *Romeo and Juliet.*"

Ike felt the group's repugnance. Indeed, why would this tortured creature choose for his obituary the most famous love story ever written? A story about opposing clans. A tale of love transcending violence. The poor stiff had been out of his gourd on thin air and solitude. It was no coincidence that in the highest monasteries on earth, men endlessly obsessed about delusion. Hallucinations were a given up here. Even the Dalai Lama joked about it.

"And so," Ike said, "he's white. He knew his Shakespeare. That makes him no older than two or three hundred years."

It was becoming a parlor game. Their fear was shifting to morbid delight. Forensics as recreation.

"Who *is* this guy?" one woman asked.

"A slave?"

"An escaped prisoner?"

Ike said nothing. He went nose-to-nose with the gaunt face, hunting for clues. *Tell your journey,* he thought. *Speak your escape. Who shackled you with gold?* Nothing. The marble eyes ignored their curiosity. The grimace enjoyed its voiceless riddles.

Owen had joined them on the shelf, reading from the opposite shoulder. "RAF."

Sure enough, the left deltoid bore a tattoo with the letters RAF beneath an eagle. It was right side up and of commercial quality. Ike grasped the cold arm.

"Royal Air Force," he translated.

The puzzle assembled. It even half-explained the Shakespeare, if not the chosen lines.

"He was a pilot?" asked the Paris bob. She seemed charmed.

"Pilot. Navigator. Bombardier." Ike shrugged. "Who knows?"

Like a cryptographer, he bent to inspect the words and numbers twining the flesh. Line after line, he traced each clue to its dead end. Here and there he punctuated complete thoughts with a jab of his fingertip. The trekkers backed away, letting him work through the cyphers. He seemed to know what he was doing.

Ike circled back and tried a string in reverse. It made sense this time. Yet it made no sense. He got out his topographical map of the Himalayan chain and found the longitude and latitude, but snorted at their nexus. No way, he thought, and lifted his gaze across the wreckage of a human body. He looked back at the map. Could it be?

"Have some." The smell of French-pressed gourmet coffee made him blink. A plastic mug slid into view. Ike glanced up. Kora's blue eyes were forgiving. That warmed him more than the coffee. He took the cup with murmured thanks and realized he had a terrific headache. Hours had passed. Shadows lay pooled in the deeper cave like wet sewage.

Ike saw a small group squatting Neanderthal-style around a small Bluet gas stove, melting snow and brewing joe. The clearest proof of their miracle was that Owen had broken down and was actually sharing his private stock of coffee. There was one hand-grinding the beans in a plastic machine, another squeezing the filter press, yet another grating a bit of cinnamon on top of each cupful. They were actually cooperating. For the first time in a month, Ike almost liked them.

"You okay?" Kora asked.

"Me?" It sounded strange, someone asking after his well-being. Especially her.

As if he needed any more to ponder, Ike suspected Kora was going to leave him. Before setting off from Kathmandu, she'd announced this was her final trek for the company. And since Himalayan High Journeys was nothing more than her and him, it implied a larger dissatisfaction. He would have minded less if her reason was another man, another country, better profits, or higher risks. But her reason was him. Ike had broken her heart because he was Ike, full of dreams and childlike naïveté. A drifter on life's stream. What had attracted her to him in the first place now disturbed her, his lone wolf/high mountains way. She thought he knew nothing about the way people really worked, like this notion of a lawsuit, and maybe there was some truth to that. He'd been hoping the trek would somehow bridge their gap, that it would draw her back to the magic that drew him. Over the past two years she'd grown weary, though. Storms and bankruptcy no longer spelled magic for her.

"I've been studying this mandala," she said, indicating the painted circle filled with squirming lines. In the darkness, its colors had been brilliant and alive. In their light, the drawing was bland. "I've seen hundreds of mandalas, but I can't make heads or tails out of this one. It looks like chaos, all those lines and squiggles. It does seem to have a center, though." She glanced up at the mummy, then at Ike's notes. "How about you? Getting anywhere?"

He'd drawn the oddest sketch, pinning words and text in cartoon balloons to different positions on the body and linking them with a mess of arrows and lines.

Ike sipped at the coffee. Where to begin? The flesh declared a maze, both in the way it told the story and in the story it told. The man had written his evidence as it occurred to him, apparently, adding and revising and contradicting himself, wandering with his truths. He was like a shipwrecked diarist who had suddenly found a pen and couldn't quit filling in old details.

"First of all," he began, "his name was Isaac."

"Isaac?" asked Darlene from the assembly line of coffee makers. They had stopped what they were doing to listen to him.

Ike ran his finger from nipple to nipple. The declaration was clear. Partially clear. *I am Isaac*, it said, followed by *In my exile/In my agony of Light.*

"See these numbers?" said Ike. "I figure this must be a serial number. And 10/03/23 could be his birthday, right?"

"*Nineteen* twenty-three?" someone asked. Their disappointment verged on childlike. Seventy-five years old evidently didn't qualify as a genuine antique.

"Sorry," he said, then continued. "See this other date here?" He brushed aside what remained of the pubic patch. "4/7/44. The day of his shoot-down, I'm guessing."

"Shoot-down?"

"Or crash."

They were bewildered. He started over, this time telling them the story he was piecing together. "Look at him. Once upon a time, he was a kid. Twenty-one years old. World War II was on. He signed up or got drafted. That's the RAF tattoo. They sent him to India. His job was to fly the Hump."

"Hump?" someone echoed. It was Bernard. He was furiously tapping the news into his laptop.

"That's what pilots called it when they flew supplies to bases in Tibet and China," Ike said. "The Himalayan chain. Back then, this whole region was part of an Oriental Western Front. It was a rough go. Every now and then a plane went down. The crews rarely survived."

"A fallen angel," sighed Owen. He wasn't alone. They were all becoming infatuated.

"I don't see how you've drawn all that from a couple of strands of numbers," said Bernard. He aimed his pencil at Ike's latter set of numbers. "You call that the date of his shoot-down. Why not the date of his marriage, or his graduation from Oxford, or the date he lost his virginity? What I mean is, this guy's no kid. He looks forty. If you ask me, he wandered away from some scientific or mountain-climbing expedition within the last couple years. He sure as snow didn't die in 1944 at the age of twenty-one."

"I agree," Ike said, and Bernard looked instantly deflated. "He refers to a period of captivity. A long stretch. Darkness. Starvation. Hard labor." *The sacred deep.*

"A prisoner of war. Of the Japanese?"

"I don't know about that," Ike said.

"Chinese Communists, maybe?"

"Russians?" someone else tried.

"Nazis?"

"Drug lords?"

"Tibetan bandits!"

The guesses weren't so wild. Tibet had long been a chessboard for the Great Game.

"We saw you checking the map. You were looking for something."

"Origins," Ike said. "A starting point."

"And?"

With both hands, Ike smoothed down the thigh hair and exposed another set of numbers. "These are map coordinates."

"For where he got shot down. It makes perfect sense." Bernard was with him now.

"You mean his airplane might be somewhere close?"

Mount Kailash was forgotten. The prospect of a crash site thrilled them.

"Not exactly," Ike said.

"Spit it out, man. Where did he go down?"

Here's where it got a little fantastic. Mildly, Ike said, "East of here."

"How far east?"

"Just above Burma."

"Burma!" Bernard and Cleopatra registered the incredibility. The rest sat mute, perplexed within their own ignorance.

"On the north side of the range," said Ike, "slightly inside Tibet."

"But that's over a thousand miles away."

"I know."

It was well past midnight. Between their cafe lattes and adrenaline, sleep was unlikely for hours to come. They sat erect or stood in the cave while the enormity of this character's journey sank in.

"How did he get here?"

"I don't know."

"I thought you said he was a prisoner."

Ike exhaled cautiously. "Something like that."

"Something?"

"Well." He cleared his throat softly. "More like a pet."

"What!"

"I don't know. It's a phrase he uses, right here: 'favored cosset.' That's a pet calf or something, isn't it?"

"Ah, get out, Ike. If you don't know, don't make it up."

He hunched. It sounded like crazed drivel to him, too.

"Actually it's a French term," a voice interjected. It was Cleo, the librarian. "*Cosset* means lamb, not calf. Ike's right, though. It does refer to a pet. One that is fondled and enjoyed."

"Lamb?" someone objected, as if Cleo—or the dead man, or both—were insulting their pooled intelligence.

"Yes," Cleo answered, "lamb. But that bothers me less than the other word, 'favored.' That's a pretty provocative term, don't you think?"

By the group's silence, they clearly had not thought about it.

"This?" she asked them, and almost touched the body with her fingers. "This is favored? Favored over what others? And above all, favored by whom? In my mind, anyway, it suggests some sort of master."

"You're inventing," a woman said. They didn't want it to be true.

"I wish I were," said Cleo. "But there is this, too."

Ike had to squint at the faint lettering where she was pointing. *Corvée*, it said.

"What's that?"

"More of the same," she answered. "Subjugation. Maybe he *was* a prisoner of the Japanese. It sounds like *The Bridge on the River Kwai* or something."

"Except I never heard of the Japanese putting nose rings in their prisoners," Ike said.

"The history of domination is complex."

"But nose rings?"

"All kinds of unspeakable things have been done."

Ike made it more emphatic. "*Gold* nose rings?"

"Gold?" She blinked as he played his light on the dull gleam.

"You said it yourself. A favored lamb. And you asked the question, Who favored this lamb?"

"You know?"

"Put it this way. He thought he did. See this?" Ike pushed at one ice-cold leg. It was a single word almost hidden on the left quadricep.

"Satan," she lip-read to herself.

"There's more," he said, and gently rotated the skin.

Exists, it said.

"This is part of it, too." He showed her. It was assembled on the flesh like a prayer or a poem. *Bone of my bones / flesh of my flesh.* "From Genesis, right? The Garden of Eden."

He could sense Kora struggling to orchestrate some sort of rebuttal. "He was a prisoner," she tried. "He was writing about evil. In general. It's nothing. He hated his captors. He called them Satan. The worst name he knew."

"You're doing what I did," Ike said. "You're fighting the evidence."

"I don't think so."

"What happened to him was evil. But he didn't hate it."

"Of course he did."

"And yet there's something here," Ike said.

"I'm not so sure," Kora said.

"It's in between the words. A tone. Don't you feel it?"

Kora did—her frown was clear—but she refused to admit it. Her wariness seemed more than academic.

"There are no warnings here," Ike said. "No 'Beware.' No 'Keep Out.'"

"What's your point."

"Doesn't it bother you that he quotes *Romeo and Juliet*? And talks about Satan the way Adam talked about Eve?"

Kora winced.

"He didn't mind the slavery."

"How can you say that?" she whispered.

"Kora." She looked at him. A tear was starting in one eye. "He was grateful. It was written all over his body."

She shook her head in denial.

"You know it's true."

"No, I don't know what you're talking about."

"Yes, you do," Ike said. "He was in love."

Cabin fever set in.

On the second morning, Ike found that the snow had drifted to basketball-rim heights outside the cave's entryway. By then the tattooed corpse had lost its novelty, and the group was getting dangerous in its boredom. One by one, the batteries of their Walkmans winked out, leaving them bereft of the music and words of angels, dragons, earth drums, and spiritual surgeons. Then the gas stove ran out of fuel, meaning several addicts went into caffeine withdrawal. It did not help matters when the supply of toilet paper ran out.

Ike did what he could. As possibly the only kid in Wyoming to take classical flute lessons, he'd scorned his mother's assurances that someday it would come in handy. Now she was proved right. He had a plastic recorder, and the notes were quite beautiful in the cave. At the end of some Mozart snatches, they applauded, then petered off into their earlier moroseness.

On the morning of the third day, Owen went missing. Ike was not surprised. He'd seen mountain expeditions get high-centered on storms just like this, and knew how twisted the dynamics could get. Chances were Owen had wandered off to get exactly this kind of attention. Kora thought so, too.

"He's faking it," she said. She was lying in his arms, their sleeping bags zipped together. Even the weeks of sweat had not worn away the smell of her coconut shampoo. At his recommendation, most of the others had buddied up for warmth, too, even Bernard. Owen was the one who had apparently gotten left out in the cold.

"He must have been heading for the front door," Ike said. "I'll go take a look." Reluctantly he unzipped his and Kora's paired bags and felt their body heat vanish into the chill air.

He looked around the cave's chamber. It was dark and freezing. The naked corpse towering above them made the cave feel like a crypt. On his feet now, blood moving again, Ike didn't like the look of their entropy. It was too soon to be lying around dying.

"I'll come with you," Kora said.

It took them three minutes to reach the entranceway.

"I don't hear the wind anymore," Kora said. "Maybe the storm's stopped."

But the entry was plugged by a ten-foot-high drift, complete with a wicked cornice curling in at the crown. It allowed no light or sound from the outer world. "I don't believe it," Kora said.

Ike kick-stepped his boot toes into the hard crust and climbed to where his head bumped the ceiling. With one hand he karate-chopped the snow and managed a thin view. The light was gray out there, and hurricane-force winds were skinning the surface with a freight-train roar. Even as he watched, his little opening sealed shut again. They were bottled up.

He slid back to the base of the snow. For the moment he forgot about the missing client.

"Now what?" Kora asked behind him.

Her faith in him was a gift. Ike took it. She—they—needed him to be strong.

"One thing's certain," he said. "Our missing man didn't come this way. No footprints, and he couldn't have gotten out through that snow anyway."

"But where could he have gone?"

"There might be some other exit." Firmly he added, "We may need one."

He had suspected the existence of a secondary feeder tunnel. Their dead RAF pilot had written about being reborn from a "mineral womb" and climbing into an "agony of light." On the one hand, Isaac could have been describing every ascetic's reentry into reality after prolonged meditation. But Ike was beginning to think the words were more than spiritual metaphor. Isaac had been a warrior, after all, trained for hardship. Everything about him declared the literal physical world. At any rate, Ike wanted to believe that the dead man might have been talking about some subterranean passage. If he could escape through it to *here*, maybe they could escape through it to *there*, wherever that might be.

Back in the central chamber, he prodded the group to life. "Folks," he announced, "we could use a hand."

A camper's groan emitted from one cluster of Gore-Tex and fiberfill. "Don't tell me," someone complained, "we have to go save him."

"If he found a way out of here," Ike retorted, "then *he's* saved *us*. But first we have to find him."

Grumbling, they rose. Bags unzipped. By the light of his headlamp, Ike watched their pockets of body heat drift off in vaporous bursts, like souls. From here on, it was imperative to keep them on their feet. He led them to the back of the cave. There were a dozen portals honeycombing the chamber's walls, though only two were man-sized. With all the authority he could muster, Ike formed two teams: them all together, and him. Alone. "This way we can cover twice the distance," he explained.

"He's leaving us," Cleo despaired. "He's saving himself."

"You don't know Ike," Kora said.

"You won't leave us?" Cleo asked him.

Ike looked at her, hard. "I won't."

Their relief showed in long streams of exhaled frost.

"You need to stick together," he instructed them solemnly. "Move slowly. Stay in flashlight range at all times. Take no chances. I don't want any sprained ankles. If you get tired and need to sit down for a while, make sure a buddy stays with you. Questions? None? Good. Now let's synchronize watches. . . ."

He gave the group three plastic "candles," six-inch tubes of luminescent chemicals that could be activated with a twist. The green glow didn't light much space and only lasted two or three hours. But they would serve as beacons every few hundred yards: crumbs upon the forest floor.

"Let me go with you," Kora murmured to him. Her yearning surprised him.

"You're the only one I trust with them," he said. "You take the right tunnel, I'll take the left. Meet me back here in an hour." He turned to go. But they didn't move. He realized they weren't just watching him and Kora, but waiting for his blessing. "*Vaya con Dios,*" he said gruffly.

Then, in full view of the others, he kissed Kora. One from the heart, broad, a breath-taker. For a moment, Kora held on tight, and he knew things were going to be all right between them, they were going to find a way.

Ike had never had much stomach for caving. The enclosure made him claustrophobic. Just the same, he had good instincts for it. On the face of it, ascending a mountain was the exact reverse of descending into a cave. A mountain gave freedoms that could be equally horrifying and liberating. In Ike's experience, caves took away freedom in the same proportions. Their darkness and sheer gravity were tyrants. They compressed the imagination and deformed the spirit. And yet both mountains and caves involved climbing. And when you came right down to it, there was no difference between ascent and descent. It was all the same circle. And so he made swift progress.

Five minutes deep, he heard a sound and paused. "Owen?"

His senses were in flux, not just heightened by the darkness and silence, but also subtly changed. It was hard to put words to, the clean dry scent of dust rendered by mountains still in birth, the scaly touch of lichen that had never seen sunshine. The visuals were not completely trustworthy. You saw like this on very dark nights on a mountain, a headlight view of the world, one beam wide, truncated, partial.

A muffled voice reached him. He wanted it to be Owen so the search could be over and he could return to Kora. But the tunnels apparently shared a common wall. Ike put his head against the stone—chill, but not bitterly cold—and could hear Bernard calling for Owen.

Farther on, Ike's tunnel became a slot at shoulder height. "Hello?" he called into the slot. For some reason, he felt his animal core bristle. It was like standing at the mouth of a deep, dark alleyway. Nothing was out of place. Yet the very ordinariness of the walls and empty stone seemed to promise menace.

Ike shone his headlamp through the slot. As he stood peering into the depths at a tube of fractured limestone identical to the one he was already occupying, he saw nothing in itself to fear. Yet the air was so . . . inhuman. The smells were so faint and unadulterated that they verged on no smell, Zen-like, clear as water. It was almost refreshing. That made him more afraid.

The corridor extended in a straight line into darkness. He checked his watch: thirty-two minutes had passed. It was time to backtrack and meet the group. That was the arrangement, one hour, round trip. But then, at the far edge of his light beam, something glittered.

Ike couldn't resist. It was like a tiny fallen star in there. And if he was quick, the whole exercise wouldn't last more than a minute. He found a foothold and pulled himself in. The slot was just big enough to squeeze through, feetfirst.

On the other side of the wall, nothing had changed. This part of the tunnel looked no different from the other. His light ahead picked out the same gleam twinkling in the far darkness.

Slowly he brought his light down to his feet. Beside one boot, he found another reflection identical to the one glinting in the distance. It gave the same dull gleam.

He lifted his boot.

It was a gold coin.

Carefully, blood knocking through his veins, Ike stopped. A tiny voice warned him not to pick it up. But there was no way . . .

The coin's antiquity was sensuous. Its lettering had worn away long ago, and the shape was asymmetrical, nothing stamped by any machine. Only a vague, amorphous bust of some king or deity still showed.

Ike shone his light down the tunnel. Past the next coin he saw a third one winking in the blackness. Could it be? The naked Isaac had fled from some precious underground reserve, even dropping his pilfered fortune along the way.

The coins blinked like feral eyes. Otherwise the stone throat lay bare, too bright in the foreground, too dark in the back. Too neatly appointed with one coin, then another.

What if the coins had not been dropped? What if they'd been placed? The thought knifed him. *Like bait.*

He slugged his back against the cold stone.

The coins were a trap.

He swallowed hard, forced himself to think it through.

The coin was cold as ice. With one fingernail he scraped away a veneer of encrusted glacier dust. It had been lying here for years, even decades or centuries. The more he thought about it, the more his horror mounted.

The trap was nothing personal. It had nothing to do with drawing him, Ike Crockett, into the depths. To the contrary, this was just random opportunism. Time was not a consideration. Even patience had nothing to do with it. The way trash fishermen did, someone was chumming the occasional traveler. You threw down a handful of scraps and maybe something came, and maybe it didn't. But who came here? That was easy. People like him: monks, traders, lost souls. But why lure them? To where?

His bait analogy evolved. This was less like trash fishing than bear-baiting. Ike's dad used to do it in the Wind River Range for Texans who paid to sit in a blind and "hunt" browns and blacks. All the outfitters did it, standard operating procedure, like working cattle. You cultivated a garbage heap maybe ten minutes by horse from the cabins, so that the bears got used to regular feeding. As the season neared, you started putting out tastier tidbits. In an effort at making them feel included, Ike and his sister were called upon each Easter to surrender their marsh-mallow bunnies. As he neared ten, Ike was required to accompany his father, and that was when he saw where his candy went.

The images cascaded. A child's pink candy left in the silent woods. Dead bears hanging in the autumn light, skins falling heavily as by magic where the knives traced lines. And underneath, bodies like men almost, as slick as swimmers.

Out, thought Ike. Get out.

Not daring to take his light off the inner mountain, Ike climbed back through the slot, cursing his loud jacket, cursing the rocks that shifted underfoot, cursing his greed. He heard noises that he knew didn't exist. Jumped at shadows, he cast himself. The dread wouldn't leave him. All he could think of was exit.

He got back to the main chamber out of breath, skin still crawling. His return couldn't have taken more than fifteen minutes. Without checking his watch, he guessed his round trip at less than an hour.

The chamber was pitch black. He was alone. He stopped to listen as his heartbeat slowed, and there was not a sound, not a shuffle. He could see the fluorescent writing hovering at the far edge of the chamber. It entwined the dark corpse like some lovely exotic serpent. He lashed his light across the chamber. The gold nose ring glinted. And something else. As if returning to a thought, he pulled his light back to the face.

The dead man was smiling.

Ike wiggled his light, jimmied the shadows. It had to be an optical trick, that or his memory was failing. He remembered a tight grimace, nothing like this wild smile. Where before he'd seen only the tips of a few teeth, joy—open glee—now played in his light. *Get a grip, Crockett.*

His mind wouldn't quit racing. What if the corpse itself was bait? Suddenly the text took on a grotesque clarity. *I am Isaac.* The son who gave himself to sacrifice. For love of the Father. *In exile. In my agony of Light.* But what could this all mean?

He'd done his share of hardcore rescues and knew the drill—not that there was much of a drill for this one. Ike grabbed his coil of 9-mm rope and stuffed his last four AA batteries into a pocket, then looked around. What else? Two protein bars, a Velcro ankle brace, his med kit. It seemed as if there should have been more to carry. The cupboard was pretty much bare, though.

Just before departing the main chamber, Ike cast his light across the room. Sleeping bags lay scattered on the floor like empty cocoons. He entered the right-hand tunnel. The passage snaked downward at an even pitch, left, then right, then became steeper. What a mistake, sending them off, even all together. Ike couldn't believe he'd put his little flock at this kind of risk. For that matter, he couldn't believe the risk they'd taken. But of course they'd taken it. They didn't know better.

"Hello!" he called. His guilt deepened by the vertical foot. Was it his fault they'd put their faith in a counterculture buccaneer?

The going slowed. The walls and ceiling grew corrupt with long sheets of delaminating rock. Pull the wrong piece, and the whole mass might slide. Ike pendulumed from admiration to resentment. His pilgrims were brave. His pilgrims were foolhardy. And he was in danger.

If not for Kora, he would have talked himself out of further descent. In a sense, she became a scapegoat for his courage. He wanted to turn around and flee. The same foreboding that had paralyzed him in the other tunnel flared up again. His very bones seemed ready to lock in rebellion, limb by limb, joint by joint. He forced himself deeper.

At last he reached a plunging shaft and came to a halt. Like an invisible waterfall, a column of freezing air streamed past from reaches too high for his flashlight beam. He held his hand out, and the cold current poured through his fingers.

At the very edge of the precipice, Ike looked down around his feet and found one of his six-inch chemical candles. The green glow was so faint he had almost missed it.

He lifted the plastic tube by one end and turned off his headlamp, trying to judge how long ago they had activated the mixture. More than three hours, less than six. Time was racing out of his control. On the off-chance, he sniffed the plastic. Impossibly, it seemed to hold a trace of her coconut scent.

"Kora!" he bellowed into the tube of air.

Where outcrops disturbed the flow of wind, a tiny symphony of whistles and sirens and bird cries answered back, a music of stone. Ike stuffed the candle into one pocket.

The air smelled fresh, like the outside of a mountain. Ike filled his lungs with it. A rush of instincts collided in what could only be called heartache. In that instant, he wanted what he had never really missed. He wanted the sun.

He searched the sides of the shaft with his light—up and down—for signs that his group had gone this way. Here and there he spotted a possible handhold or a shelf to rest upon, though no one—not even Ike in his prime—could have climbed down into the shaft and survived.

The shaft's difficulties exceeded even his group's talent for blind faith. They must have turned around and gone some other way. Ike started out.

A hundred meters farther back, he found their detour.

He had walked right past the opening on his way down. On the return, the hole was practically blatant—especially the green glow ebbing from its canted throat. He had to take his pack off in order to get through the small aperture. Just inside lay the second of his chemical candles.

By comparing the two candles—this one was much brighter—Ike fixed the group's chronology. Here indeed was their deviation. He tried to imagine which pioneer spirit had piloted the group into this side tunnel, and knew it could only have been one person.

"Kora," he whispered. She would not have left Owen for dead any more than he. It was she who would be insisting on probing deeper and deeper into the tunnel system.

The detour led to others. Ike followed the side tunnel to one fork, then another, then another. The unfolding network horrified him. Kora had unwittingly led them—him, too—deep into an underground maze.

"Wait!" he shouted.

At first the group had taken the time to mark their choices. Some of the branches were marked with a simple arrow arranged with rocks. A few showed the right way or the left way with a big X scratched on the wall. But soon the marks ended. No doubt emboldened by their progress, the group had quit blazing its path. Ike had few clues other than a black scuff mark or a fresh patch of rock where someone had pulled loose a handhold.

Second-guessing their choices devoured the time. Ike checked his watch. Well past midnight. He'd been hunting Kora and the lost pilgrims for over nine hours now. That meant they were desperately lost.

His head hurt. He was tired. The adrenaline was long gone. The air no longer had the smell of summits or jetstream. This was an interior scent, the inside of the mountain's lungs, the smell of darkness. He made himself chew and swallow a protein bar. Ike wasn't sure he could find his way out again.

Yet he kept his mountaineer's presence of mind. Thousands of physical details clamored for his attention. Some he absorbed, most he simply passed between. The trick was to see simply.

He came upon a glory hole, a huge, unlikely void within the mountain. His light beam withered in the depths and towering height of it.

Even worn down, he was awed. Great columns of buttery limestone dangled from the arched ceiling. A huge *Om* had been carved into one wall. And dozens, maybe hundreds, of suits of ancient Mongolian armor hung from rawhide thongs knotted to knobs and outcrops. It looked like an entire army of ghosts. A vanquished army.

The wheat-colored stone was gorgeous in his headlamp. The armor twisted in a slight breeze and fractured the light into a million points.

Ike admired the soft leather *thangka* paintings pinned to the walls, then lifted a fringed corner and discovered that the fringe was made of human fingers. He dropped it, horrified. The leather was flayed human skins. He backed away, counting the *thangkas*. Fifty at least. Could they have belonged to the Mongolian horde?

He looked down. His boots had tracked halfway across yet another mandala, this one twenty feet across and made of colored sand. He'd seen some of these in Tibetan monasteries before, but never so large. Like the one beside Isaac in the cave chamber, it held details that looked less architectural than like organic worms. His were not the only footprints spoiling the artwork. Others had trampled it, and recently. Kora and the gang had come this way.

At one junction he ran out of signs altogether. Ike faced the branching tunnels and, from somewhere in his childhood, remembered the answer to all labyrinths: consistency. Go to your left or to your right, but always stay true. This being Tibet—the land of clockwise circumambulation around sacred temples and mountains—he chose left. It was the correct choice. He found the first of them ten minutes later.

Ike had entered a stratum of limestone so pure and slick it practically swallowed the shadows. The walls curved without angles. There were no cracks or ledging in the rock, only rugosities and gentle waves. Nothing caught at the light, nothing cast darkness. The result was unadulterated light. Wherever Ike turned his lamp beam, he was surrounded by radiance the color of milk.

Cleopatra was there. Ike rounded the wing and her light joined with his. She was sitting in a lotus position in the center of the luminous passage. With ten gold coins spread before her, she could have been a beggar.

"Are you hurt?" Ike asked her.

"Just my ankle," Cleo replied, smiling. Her eyes had that holy gleam they all aspired to, part wisdom, part soul. Ike wasn't fooled.

"Let's go," he ordered.

"You go ahead," Cleo breathed with her angel voice. "I'll stay a bit longer."

Some people can handle solitude. Most just think they can. Ike had seen its victims in the mountains and monasteries, and once in a jail. Sometimes it was the isolation that undid them. Sometimes it was the cold or famine or even amateur meditation. With Cleo it was a little of all of the above.

Ike checked his watch: 3:00 A.M. "What about the rest of you? Where did they go?"

"Not much farther," she said. Good news. And bad news. "They went to find you."

"Find me?"

"You kept calling for help. We weren't going to leave you alone."

"But I didn't call for help."

She patted his leg. "All for one," she assured him.

Ike picked up one of the coins. "Where'd you find these?"

"Everywhere," she said. "More and more, the deeper we got. Isn't it wonderful?"

"I'm going for the others. Then we'll all come back for you," Ike said. He changed the fading batteries in his headlamp while he talked, replacing them with the last of his new ones. "Promise you won't move from here."

"I like it here very much."

He left Cleo in a sea of alabaster radiance.

The limestone tube sped him deeper. The decline was even, the footing uncomplicated. Ike jogged, sure he could catch them. The air took on a coppery tang, nameless, yet distantly familiar. Not much farther, Cleo had said.

The blood streaks started at 3:47 A.M.

Because they first appeared as several dozen crimson handprints upon the white stone, and because the stone was so porous that it practically inhaled the liquid, Ike mistook them for primitive art. He should have known better.

Ike slowed. The effect was lovely in its playful randomness. Ike liked his image: slap-happy cavemen.

Then his foot hit a puddle not yet absorbed into the stone. The dark liquid splashed up. It sluiced in bright streaks across the wall, red on white. Blood, he realized.

"God!" he yelled, and vaulted wide in instant evasion. A tiptoe, then the same bloody sole landed again, skidded, torqued sideways. The momentum drove him facefirst into the wall and then sent him tumbling around the bend.

His headlamp flew off. The light blinked out. He came to a halt against cold stone.

It was like being clubbed unconscious. The blackness stopped all control, all motion, all place in the world. Ike even quit breathing. As much as he wanted to hide from consciousness, he was wide awake.

Abruptly the thought of lying still became unbearable. He rolled away from the wall and let gravity guide him onto his hands and knees. Hands bare, he felt about for the headlamp in widening circles, torn between disgust and terror at the viscous curd layering the floor. He could even taste the stuff, cold upon his teeth. He pressed his lips shut, but the smell was gamy, and there was no game in here, only his people. It was a monstrous thought.

At last he snagged the headlamp by its connecting wire, rocked back onto his heels, fumbled with the switch. There was a sound, distant or near, he couldn't tell. "Hey?" he challenged. He paused, listened, heard nothing.

Laboring against his own panic, Ike flipped the switch on and off and on. It was like trying to spark a fire with wolves closing in. The sound again. He caught it this time. Nails scratching rock? Rats? The blood scent surged. What was going on here?

He muttered a curse at the dead light. With his fingertips he stroked the lens, searching for cracks. Gently he shook it, dreading the rattle of a shattered lightbulb. Nothing.

Was blind, but now I see. . . . The words drifted into his consciousness, and he was uncertain whether they were a song or his memory of it. The sound came more distinctly. *'Twas grace that taught my heart to fear.* It washed in from far away, a woman's lush voice singing "Amazing

Grace." Something about its brave syllables suggested less a hymn than an anthem. A last stand.

It was Kora's voice. She had never sung for him. But this was she. Singing for them all, it seemed.

Her presence, even in the far depths, steadied him. "Kora," he called. On his knees, eyes wide in the utter blackness, Ike disciplined himself. If it wasn't the switch or the bulb . . . he tried the wire. Tight at the ends, no lacerations. He opened the battery case, wiped his fingers clean and dry, and carefully removed each slender battery, counting in a whisper, "One, two, three, four." One at a time, he cleaned the tips against his T-shirt, then swabbed each contact in the case and replaced the batteries. Head up, head down, up, down. There was an order to things. He obeyed.

He snapped the plate back onto the case, drew gently at the wire, palmed the lamp. And flicked the switch.

Nothing.

The scratch-scratch noise rose louder. It seemed very close. He wanted to bolt away, any direction, any cost, just flee.

"Stick," he instructed himself. He said it out loud. It was something like a mantra, his own, something he told himself when the walls got steep or the holds thin or the storms mean. *Stick*, as in *hang*. As in *no surrender*.

Ike clenched his teeth. He slowed his lungs. Again he removed the batteries. This time he replaced them with the batch of nearly dead batteries in his pocket. He flipped the switch.

Light. Sweet light.

He breathed it in.

In an abattoir of white stone.

The image of butchery lasted one instant. Then his light flickered out.

"No!" he cried in the darkness, and shook the headlamp.

The light came on again, what little there was of it. The bulb glowed rusty orange, grew weaker, then suddenly brightened, relatively speaking. It was less than a quarter-strength. More than enough. Ike took his eyes from the little bulb and dared to look around once more.

The passageway was a horror.

In his small circle of jaundiced light, Ike stood up. He was very careful. All around, the walls were zebra-striped with crimson streaks. The bodies had been arranged in a row.

You don't spend years in Asia without seeing a fair share of the dead. Many times, Ike had sat by the burning ghats at Pashaputanath, watching the fires peel flesh from bone. And no one climbed the South Col of

Everest these days without passing a certain South African dreamer, or on the north side a French gentleman sitting silently by the trail at 28,000 feet. And then there had been that time the king's army opened fire on Social Democrats revolting in the streets of Kathmandu and Ike had gone to Bir Hospital to identify the body of a BBC cameraman and seen the corpses hastily lined side by side on the tile floor. This reminded him of that.

It rose in him again, the silence of birds. And how, for days afterward, the dogs had limped about from bits of glass broken out of windows. And above all else, how, in being dragged, a human body gets undressed.

They lay before him, his people. He had viewed them in life as fools. In death, half-naked, they were pathetic. Not foolishly so. Just terribly. The smell of opened bowels and raw meat was nearly enough to panic him.

Their wounds . . . Ike could not see at first without seeing past the horrible wounds. He focused on their undress. He felt ashamed for these poor people and for himself. It seemed like sin itself to see their jumble of pubic patches and lolling thighs and randomly exposed breasts and stomachs that could no longer be held in or chests held high. In his shock, Ike stood above them, and the details swarmed up: here a faint tattoo of a rose, there a cesarean scar, the marks of surgeries and accidents, the edges of a bikini tan scribed upon a Mexican beach. Some of this was meant to be hidden, even to lovers, some to be revealed. None of it was meant to be seen this way.

Ike made himself get on with it. There were five of them, one male, Bernard. He started to identify the women, but with a rush of fatigue he suddenly forgot their names altogether. At the moment, only one of them mattered to him, and she was not here.

The snapped ends of very white bone stood from lawnmower-like gashes. Body cavities gaped empty. Some fingers were crooked, some missing at the root. Bitten off? A woman's head had been crushed to a thick, panlike sac. Even her hair was anonymous with gore, but the pubis was blond. She was, poor creature, thank God, not Kora.

That familiarity one reaches with victims began. Ike put one hand to the ache behind his eyes, then started over again. His light was failing. The massacre had no answer. Whatever had happened to them could happen to him.

"Stick, Crockett," he commanded.

First things first. He counted on his fingers: six here, Cleo up the tunnel, Kora somewhere. That left Owen still at large.

Ike stepped among the bodies, searching for clues. He had little experience with such extremes of trauma, but there were a few things he could tell. Judging by the blood trails, it looked like an ambush. And it had been done without a gun. There were no bullet holes. Ordinary knives were out of the question, too. The lacerations were much too deep and massed so strangely, here upon the upper body, there at the backs of the legs, that Ike could only imagine a pack of men with machetes. It looked more like an attack by wild animals, especially the way a thigh had been stripped to the bone.

But what animal lived miles inside a mountain? What animal collected its prey in a neat row? What animal showed this kind of savagery, then conformity? Such frenzy, then such method. The extremes were psychotic. All too human.

Maybe one man could have done all this, but Owen? He was smaller than most of these women. And slower. Yet these poor people had all been caught and mutilated within a few meters of one another. Ike tried to imagine himself as the killer, to conceive the speed and strength necessary to commit such an act.

There were more mysteries. Only now did Ike notice the gold coins scattered like confetti around them. It looked almost like a payoff, he now recognized, an exchange for the theft of *their* wealth. For the dead were missing rings and bracelets and necklaces and watches. Everything was gone. Wrists, fingers, and throats were bare. Earrings had been torn from lobes. Bernard's eyebrow ring had been plucked away.

The jewelry had been little more than baubles and crystals and cheap knickknacks; Ike had specifically instructed the trekkers to leave their valuables in the States or in the hotel safe. But someone had gone to the trouble of pilfering the stuff. And then to pay for it in gold coins worth a thousand times what had been taken.

It made no sense. It made even less sense to stand here and try to make it make sense. He was not normally the type who couldn't think what to do, and so his confusion now was all the more intense. His code said *Stay*, like a sea captain, stay to sort through the crime and bring back, if not his wayfarers, then at least a full accounting of their demise. The economy of fear said *Run*. Save what life could be saved. But run which way and save which life? That was the excruciating choice. Cleopatra waited in one direction in her lotus position and white light. Kora waited in the other, perhaps not as surely. But hadn't he just heard her song?

His light ebbed to brown. Ike forced himself to rifle the pockets of his dead passengers. Surely someone had batteries or another flashlight or some food. But the pockets had been slashed and emptied.

The frenzy of it struck him. Why shred the pockets and even the flesh beneath them? This was no ordinary robbery. Stopping down his loathing, he tried to summarize the incident: a crime of rage, to judge by the mutilations, yet a crime of want, to judge by the thievery. Again it made no sense.

His light blinked out and the blackness jumped up around him. The weight of the mountain seemed to press down. A breeze Ike had not felt before brought to mind vast mineral respiration, as if a juggernaut were waking. It carried an undertone of gases, not noxious but rare, distant.

And then his imagination became unnecessary. That scratching sound of nails on stone returned. This time there was no question of its reality. It was approaching from the upper passageway. And this time Kora's voice was part of the mix.

She sounded in ecstasy, very near to orgasm. Or like his sister that time, in that instant just as her infant daughter came out of her womb. That, Ike conceded, or this was a sound of agony so deep it verged on the forbidden. The moan or low or animal petition, whatever it was, begged for an ending.

He almost called to her. But that other sound kept him mute. The climber in him had registered it as fingernails scraping for purchase, but the torn flesh lying in the darkness now evoked claws or talons. He resisted the logic, then embraced it in a hurry. Fine. Claws. A beast. Yeti. This was it. What now?

The dreadful opera of woman and beast drew closer.

Fight or flight? Ike asked himself.

Neither. Both were futile. He did what he had to do, the survivor's trick. He hid in plain sight. Like a mountain man pulling himself into a womb of warm buffalo meat, Ike lay down among the bodies on the cold floor and dragged the dead upon him.

It was an act so heinous it was sin. In lying down between the corpses in utter blackness and in bringing a smooth naked thigh across his and draping a cold arm across his chest, Ike felt the weight of damnation. In disguising himself as dead, he let go part of his soul. Fully sane, he gave up all aspects of his life in order to preserve it. His one anchor to believing this was happening to him was that he could not believe it was happening to him. "Dear God," he whispered.

The sounds became louder.

There was only one last choice to make: to keep open or to close his eyes to sights he could not see anyway. He closed them.

Kora's smell reached him upon that subterranean breeze. He heard her groan.

Ike held his breath. He'd never been afraid like this, and his cowardice was a revelation.

They—Kora and her captor—came around the corner. Her breathing was tortured. She was dying. Her pain was epic, beyond words.

Ike felt tears running down his face. He was weeping for her. Weeping for her pain. Weeping, too, for his lost courage. To lie unmoving and not give aid. He was no different from those climbers who had left him for dead once upon a mountain. Even as he inhaled and exhaled in tiny beadlike drops and listened to his heart's hammering pump and felt the dead close him in their embrace, he was giving Kora up for himself. Moment by moment he was forsaking her. Damned, he was damned.

Ike blinked at his tears, despised them, reviled his self-pity. Then he opened his eyes to take it like a man. And almost choked on his surprise.

The blackness was full, but no longer infinite. There were words written in the darkness. They were fluorescent and coiled like snakes and they moved.

It was him.

Isaac had resurrected.

*Have you ever been at sea in
a dense fog, when it seemed
as if a tangible white
darkness shut you in, and
the great ship, tense and
anxious, groped her way
toward the shore . . . and you
waited with beating heart
for something to happen?*

—HELEN KELLER, *The Story of My Life*

2

ALI

NORTH OF ASKAM,
THE KALAHARI DESERT, SOUTH AFRICA
1995

"Mother?"

The girl's voice entered Ali's hut softly.

Here was how ghosts must sing, thought Ali, this Bantu lilt, the melody searching melody. She looked up from her suitcase.

In the doorway stood a Zulu girl with the frozen, wide-eyed grin of advanced leprosy: lips, eyelids, and nose eaten away.

"Kokie," said Ali. Kokie Madiba. Fourteen years old. She was called a witch.

Over the girl's shoulder, Ali caught sight of herself and Kokie in a small mirror on the wall. The contrast did not please her. Ali had let her hair grow out over the past year. Next to the black girl's ruined flesh, her golden hair looked like harvest wheat beside a salted field. Her beauty was obscene to her. Ali moved to one side to erase her own image. For a while she had even tried taking the small mirror off her wall. Finally she'd hung it back on the nail, despairing that abnegation could be more vain than vanity.

"We've talked about this many times," she said. "I am Sister, not Mother."

"We have talked about this, ya'as, mum," the orphan said. "Sister, Mother."

Some of them thought she was a holy woman, or a queen. Or a witch. The concept of a single woman, much less a nun, was very odd out here in the bush. For once the offbeat had served her well. Deciding she must be in exile like them, the colony had taken her in.

"Did you want something, Kokie?"

"I bring you this." The girl held out a necklace with a small shrunken pouch embroidered with beadwork. The leather looked fresh, hastily tanned, with small hairs still attached. Clearly they had been in a hurry to finish this for her. "Wear this. The evil stays away."

Ali lifted it from Kokie's dusty palm and admired the geometric designs formed by red, white, and green beads. "Here," she said, setting it back in Kokie's grip, "you put it on me."

Ali bent and held her hair up so that the leper girl could get the necklace placed. She copied Kokie's solemnity. This was no tourist trinket. It was part of Kokie's beliefs. If anyone knew about evil, it had to be this poor child.

With the spread of post-apartheid chaos and a surge in AIDS brought south by Zimbabweans and Mozambiquans imported to work the gold and diamond mines, hysteria had been unleashed among the poor. Old superstitions had risen up. It was no longer news that sexual organs and fingers and ears—even handfuls of human fat—were being stolen from morgues and used for fetishes, or that corpses lay unburied because family members were convinced the bodies would come to life again.

The worst of it by far was the witch-hunting. People said that evil was coming up from the earth. So far as Ali was concerned, people had been saying such things since the beginning of man. Every generation had its terrors. She was convinced this one had been started by diamond miners seeking to deflect public hatred away from themselves. They spoke of reaching depths in the earth where strange beings lurked. The populace had turned this nonsense into a campaign against witches. Hundreds of innocent people had been necklaced, macheted, or stoned by superstitious mobs throughout the country.

"Have you taken your vitamin pill?" Ali asked.

"Oh, ya'as."

"And you will continue taking your vitamins after I'm gone?"

Kokie's eyes shifted to the dirt floor. Ali's departure was a terrible pain for her. Again, Ali could not believe the suddenness of what was happening. It was only two days ago that she had received the letter informing her of the change.

"The vitamins are important for the baby, Kokie."

The leper girl touched her belly. "Ya'as, the baby," she whispered joyfully. "Every day. Sun come up. The vitamin pill."

Ali loved this girl, because God's mystery was so profound in its cruelty toward her. Twice Kokie had attempted suicide and both times Ali had saved her. Eight months ago the suicide attempts had stopped. That was when Kokie had learned she was pregnant.

It still surprised Ali when the sounds of lovers wafted to her in the night. The lessons were simple and yet profound. These lepers were not horrible in one another's sight. They were blessed, beautiful, even dressed in their poor skin.

With the new life growing inside her, Kokie's bones had taken on flesh. She had begun talking again. Mornings, Ali heard her murmuring tunes in a hybrid dialect of Siswati and Zulu, more beautiful than birdsong.

Ali, too, felt reborn. She wondered if this, perhaps, was why she'd ended up in Africa. It was as if God were speaking to her through Kokie and all the other lepers and refugees. For months now, she had been anticipating the birth of Kokie's child. On a rare trip to Jo'burg, she'd purchased Kokie's vitamins with her own allowance and borrowed several books on midwifery. A hospital was out of the question for Kokie, and Ali wanted to be ready.

Lately, Ali had begun dreaming about it. The delivery would be in a hut with a tin roof surrounded by thorn brush, maybe this hut, this bed. Into her hands a healthy infant would emerge to nullify the world's corruption and sorrows. In one act, innocence would triumph.

But this morning Ali's realization was bitter. *I will never see the child of this child.*

For Ali was being transferred. Thrown back into the wind. Yet again. It didn't matter that she had not finished here, that she had actually begun drawing close to the truth. Bastards. That was in the masculine, as in *bishoprick*.

Ali folded a white blouse and laid it in her suitcase. *Excuse my French, O Lord.* But they were beginning to make her feel like a letter with no address.

From the moment she'd taken her vows, this powder blue Samsonite suitcase had been her faithful companion. First to Baltimore for some ghetto work, then to Taos for a little monastic "airing out," then to Columbia University to blitzkrieg her dissertation. After that, Winnipeg for more street-angel work. Then a year of postdoc at the Vatican Archives, "the memory of the Church." Then the plum assignment, nine months in Europe as an attaché—an *addetti di nunziatura*—assisting the papal diplomatic delegation at NATO nuclear nonproliferation talks. For a twenty-seven-year-old country girl from west Texas, it was heady stuff. She'd been selected as much for her longtime connection with U.S. Senator Cordelia January as for her training in linguistics. They'd played her like a pawn, of course. "Get used to it," January had counseled her one evening. "You're going places." That was for sure, Ali thought, looking around the hut.

Very obviously the Church had been grooming her—formation, it was called—though for what she couldn't precisely say. Until a year ago, her CV had showed nothing but steady ascent. Blue sky, right up to her fall from grace. Abruptly, no explanations offered, no second chances offered, they'd sent her to this refugee colony tucked in the wilds of San—or Bushman—country. From the glittering capitals of Western civilization straight into the Stone Age, they had drop-kicked her to the rump of the planet, to cool her heels in the Kalahari desert with a bogus mission.

Being Ali, she had made the most of it. It had been a terrible year, in truth. But she was tough. She'd coped. Adapted. Flourished, by God. She'd even started to peel away the folklore of an "elder" tribe said to be hiding in the backcountry.

At first, like everyone else, Ali had dismissed the notion of an undiscovered Neolithic tribe existing on the cusp of the twenty-first century. The region was wild, all right, but these days it was crisscrossed by farmers, truckers, bush planes, and field scientists—people who would have spied evidence before now. It had been three months before Ali had started taking the native rumors seriously.

What was most exciting to her was that such a tribe did seem to exist, and that its evidence was mostly linguistic. Wherever this strange tribe was hiding, there seemed to be a protolanguage alive in the bush! And day by day she was closing in on it.

For the most part, her hunt had to do with the Khoisan, or Click, language spoken by the San. She had no illusions about ever mastering their language herself, especially the system of clicks that could be dental, palatal, or labial, voiced, voiceless, or nasal. But with the help of a

San ¡Kung translator, she'd begun assembling a set of words and sounds they only expressed in a certain tone. The tone was deferential and religious and ancient, and the words and sounds were different from anything else in Khoisan. They hinted at a reality that was both old and new. Someone was out there, or had been long ago. Or had recently returned. And whoever they were, they spoke a language that pre-dated the prehistoric language of the San.

But now—like that—the midsummer night's dream was over. They were taking her away from her monsters. Her refugees. Her evidence.

Kokie had begun singing softly to herself. Ali returned to her packing, using the suitcase to shield her expression from the girl. Who would watch out for them now? What would they do without her in their daily lives? What would she do without them?

". . . *uphondo lwayo/yizwa imithandazo yethu/Nkosi sikelela/Thina lusapho iwayo . . .*"

The words crowded through Ali's frustration. Over the past year, she had dipped hard into the stew of languages spoken in South Africa, especially Nguni, which included Zulu. Parts of Kokie's song opened to her: Lord bless us children / Come spirit, come holy spirit / Lord bless us children.

"*O feditse dintwa/Le matswenyecho. . . .*" Do away with wars and troubles. . . .

Ali sighed. All these people wanted was peace and a little happiness. When she first showed up, they had looked like the morning after a hurricane, sleeping in the open, drinking fouled water, waiting to die. With her help, they now had rudimentary shelter and a well for water and the start of a cottage industry that used towering anthills as forges for making simple farm tools like hoes and shovels. They had not welcomed her coming; that had taken some time. But her departure was causing real anguish, for she had brought a little light into their darkness, or at least a little medicine and diversion.

It wasn't fair. Her coming had meant good things for them. And now they were being punished for her sins. There was no possible way to explain that. They would not have understood that this was the Church's way of breaking her down.

It made her mad. Maybe she was a bit too proud. And profane at times. With a temper, yes. And indiscreet, certainly. She'd made a few mistakes. Who hadn't? She was sure her transfer out of Africa had to do with some problem she'd caused somebody somewhere. Or maybe her past was catching up with her again.

Fingers trembling, Ali smoothed out a pair of khaki bush shorts and the old monologue rolled around in her head. It was like a broken record, her *mea culpas*. The fact was, when she dove, she dove deep. Controversy be damned. She was forever running ahead of the pack.

Maybe she should have thought twice before writing that op-ed piece for the *Times* suggesting the Pope recuse himself from all matters relating to abortion, birth control, and the female body. Or writing her essay on Agatha of Aragon, the mystic virgin who wrote love poems and preached tolerance: never a popular subject among the good old boys. And it had been sheer folly to get caught practicing Mass in the Taos chapel four years ago. Even empty, even at three in the morning, church walls had eyes and ears. She'd been more foolish still, once caught, to defy her Mother Superior—in front of the archbishop—by insisting women had a liturgical right to consecrate the Host. To serve as priests. Bishops. Cardinals. And she would have gone on to include the Pope in her litany, too, but the archbishop had frozen her with a word.

Ali had come within a hair of official censure. But close calls seemed a perpetual state for her. Controversy followed her like a starving dog. After the Taos incident, she'd tried to "go orthodox." But that was before the Manhattans. Sometimes a girl just lost control.

It had been just a little over a year ago, a grand cocktail gathering with generals and diplomats from a dozen nations in the historic part of The Hague. The occasion was the signing of some obscure NATO document, and the Papal nuncio was there. There was no forgetting the place, a wing of the thirteenth-century Binnerhoef Palace known as the Hall of Knights, a room loaded with delicious Renaissance goodies, even a Rembrandt. Just as vividly she recalled the Manhattans that a handsome colonel, urged on by her wicked mentor January, kept bringing to her.

Ali had never tasted such a concoction, and it had been years since such chivalry had laid siege to her. The net effect had been a loose tongue. She'd strayed badly in a discussion about Spinoza and somehow ended up sermonizing passionately about glass ceilings in patriarchal institutions and the ballistic throw-weight of a humble chunk of rock. Ali blushed at the memory, the dead silence through the entire room. Luckily January had been there to rescue her, laughing that deep laugh, sweeping her off first to the ladies' room, then to the hotel and a cold shower. Maybe God had forgiven her, but the Vatican had not. Within days, Ali had been delivered a one-way air ticket to Pretoria and the bush.

"They coming, look, Mother, see." With a lack of self-consciousness that was a miracle in itself, Kokie was pointing out the window with the remains of her hand.

Ali glanced up, then finished closing the suitcase. "Peter's *bakkie*?" she asked. Peter was a Boer widower who liked to do favors for her. It was always he who drove her to town in his tiny van, what locals called a *bakkie*.

"No, mum." Her voice got very small. "Casper's comin'."

Ali joined Kokie at the window. It was indeed an armored troop carrier at the head of a long rooster tail of red dust. Casspirs were feared by the black populace as juggernauts that brought destruction. She had no idea why they had sent military transport to fetch her, and chalked it up to more mindless intimidation. "Never mind," she said to the frightened girl.

The Casspir churned across the plain. It was still miles away and the road got more corrugated on this side of the dry lakebed. Ali guessed there were still ten minutes or so before it got here.

"Is everyone ready?" she asked Kokie.

"They ready, mum."

"Let's see about our picture, then."

Ali lifted her small camera from the cot, praying the winter heat had not spoiled her one roll of Fuji Velvia. Kokie eyed the camera with delight. She'd never seen a photograph of herself.

Despite her sadness about leaving, there were reasons to be thankful she was getting transferred. It made her feel selfish, but Ali was not going to miss the tick fever and poison snakes and walls of mud mixed with dung. She was not going to miss the crushing ignorance of these dying peasants, or the pig-eyed hatreds of the Afrikaaners with their fire-engine-red Nazi flag and their brutal, man-eating Calvinism. And she was not going to miss the heat.

Ali ducked through the low doorway into the morning light. The scent surged across to her even before the colors. She drew the air deep into her lungs, tasting the wild riot of blue hues on her tongue.

She raised her eyes.

Acres of bluebonnets spread in a blanket around the village.

This was her doing. Maybe she was no priest. But here was a sacrament she could give. Shortly after the camp well was drilled, Ali had ordered a special mix of wildflower seed and planted it herself. The fields had bloomed. The harvest was joy. And pride, rare among these outcasts. The bluebonnets had become a small legend. Farmers—Boer and English both—had driven with their families for hundreds of kilometers to see this sea of flowers. A tiny band of primeval Bushmen had visited and reacted with shock and whispers, wondering if a piece of sky had landed here. A minister with the Zionist Christian Church had conducted an outdoor ceremony. Soon enough, the flowers would die off.

The legend was fixed, though. In a way, Ali had exorcised what was grotesque and established these lepers' claim to humanity.

The refugees were waiting for her at the irrigation ditch that led from the well and watered their crop of maize and vegetables. When she first mentioned a group photo, they immediately agreed that this was where it should be taken. Here was their garden, their food, their future.

"Good morning," Ali greeted them.

"*Goot morgan, Fundi,*" a woman solemnly returned. *Fundi* was an abbreviation of *umfundisi.* It meant "teacher" and was, for Ali's tastes, the highest compliment.

Sticklike children raced out from the group and Ali knelt to embrace them. They smelled good to her, particularly this morning, fresh, washed by their mothers.

"Look at you," she said to them, "so pretty. So handsome. Now who wants to help me?"

"Me, me. I am, mum."

Ali employed all the children in putting a few rocks together and tying some sticks into a crude tripod. "Now step back or it will fall," she said.

She worked quickly now. The Casspir's approach was beginning to alarm the adults, and she wanted the picture to show them happy. She balanced the camera atop her tripod and looked through the viewfinder.

"Closer," she gestured to them, "get closer together."

The light was just right, angling sidelong and slightly diffuse. It would be a kind picture. There was no way to hide the ravages of disease and ostracism, but this would highlight their smiles and eyes at least.

As she focused, she counted. Then recounted. They were missing someone.

For a while after first coming here, it had not occurred to her to count them from day to day. She had been too busy teaching hygiene and caring for the ill and distributing food and arranging the drill for a well and the tin sheeting for roofs. But after a couple of months she had grown more sensitive to the dwindling numbers. When she asked, it was explained with a shrug that people came and people went.

It was not until she had caught them red-handed that the terrible truth surfaced.

When she first had come upon them in the bush one day, Ali had thought it was hyenas working over a springbok. Perhaps she should have guessed before. Certainly it seemed that someone else could have told her.

Without thinking, Ali had pulled the two skeletal men away from the old woman they were strangling. She had struck one with a stick and driven them away. She had misunderstood everything, the men's motive, the old lady's tears.

This was a colony of very sick and miserable human beings. But even reduced to desperation, they were not without mercy.

The fact was, the lepers practiced euthanasia.

It was one of the hardest things Ali had ever wrestled with. It had nothing to do with justice, for they did have the luxury of justice. These lepers—hunted, hounded, tortured, terrorized—were living out their days on the edge of a wasteland. With little left to do but die off, there were few ways left to show love or grant dignity. Murder, she had finally accepted, was one of them.

They only terminated a person who was already dying and who asked. It was always done away from camp, and it was always carried out by two or more people, as quickly as possible. Ali had crafted a sort of truce with the practice. She tried not to see the exhausted souls walking off into the bush, never to return. She tried not to count their numbers. But disappearance had a way of pronouncing a person, even the silent ones you barely noticed otherwise.

She went through the faces again. It was Jimmy Shako, the elder, they were missing. Ali hadn't realized Jimmy Shako was so ill or so generous as to unburden the community of his presence. "Mr. Shako is gone," she said matter-of-factly.

"He gone," Kokie readily agreed.

"May he rest in peace," Ali said, mostly for her own benefit.

"Don't t'ink so, Mother. No rest for him. We trade him off."

"You what?" This was a new one.

"This for that. We give him away."

Suddenly Ali wasn't sure she wanted to know what Kokie meant. There were times when it seemed Africa had opened to her and she knew its secrets. Then times like this, when the secrets had no bottom. She asked just the same: "What are you talking about, Kokie?"

"Him. For you."

"For me." Ali's voice sounded tiny in her ears.

"Ya'as, mum. That man no good. He saying come get you and give you down. But we give him, see." The girl reached out and gently touched the beaded necklace around Ali's neck. "Ever'ting okay now. We take care of you, Mother."

"But who did you give Jimmy to?"

Something was roaring in the background. Ali realized it was bluebonnets stirring in the soft breeze. The rustle of stems was thunderous. She swallowed to slake her dry throat.

Kokie's answer was simple. "Him," she said.

"Him?"

The bluebonnets' sea roar elided into the engine noise of the nearing Casspir. Ali's time had arrived.

"Older-than-Old, Mother. Him." Then she said a name, and it contained several clicks and a whisper in that elevated tone.

Ali looked more closely at her. Kokie had just spoken a short phrase in proto-Khoisan. Ali tried it aloud. "No, like this," Kokie said, and repeated the words and clicks. Ali got it right this time, and committed it to memory.

"What does it mean?" she asked.

"God, mum. The hungry God."

Ali had thought to know these people, but they were something else. They called her Mother and she had treated them as children, but they were not. She edged away from Kokie.

Ancestor worship was everything. Like ancient Romans or modern-day Shinto, the Khoikhoi deferred to their dead in spiritual matters. Even black evangelical Christians believed in ghosts, threw bones for divining the future, sacrificed animals, drank potions, wore amulets, and practiced *gei-xa*—magic. The Xhosa tribe pinned its genesis on a mythical race called *xhosa*—angry men. The Pedi worshiped Kgobe. The Lobedu had their Mujaji, a rain queen. For the Zulu, the world hinged upon an omnipotent being whose name translated as Older-than-Old. And Kokie had just spoken the name in that protolanguage. The mother tongue.

"Is Jimmy dead or not?"

"That depends, mum. He be good, they let him live down there. Long time."

"You killed Jimmy," Ali said. "For me?"

"Not kilt. Cut him some."

"You did what?"

"Not we," said Kokie.

"Older-than-Old?" Ali added the Click name.

"Oh ya'as. Trimmed that man. Then give to us the parts."

Ali didn't ask what Kokie meant. She'd heard too much as it was.

Kokie cocked her head and a delicate expression of pleasure appeared within her frozen smile. For an instant Ali saw standing before her the gawky teenaged girl she had grown to love, one with a special secret to tell. She told it. "Mother," Kokie said, "I watched. Watched it all."

Ali wanted to run. Innocent or not, the child was a fiend.

"Good-bye, Mother."

T
H
E

D
E
S
C
E
N
T

Get me away, she thought. As calmly as she could, tears stinging her eyes, Ali turned to walk from Kokie.

Immediately Ali was boxed in.

They were a wall of huge men. Blind with tears, Ali started to fight them, punching and gouging with her elbows. Someone very strong pinned her arms tight.

"Here, now," a man's voice demanded, "what's this crap?"

Ali looked up into the face of a white man with sunburned cheeks and a tan army bush cap. "Ali von Schade?" he said. In the background the Casspir sat idling, a brute machine with radio antennae waving in the air and a machine gun leveled. She quit struggling, amazed by their suddenness.

Abruptly the clearing filled with the carrier's wake of red dust, a momentary tempest. Ali swung around, but the lepers had already scattered into the thorn bush. Except for the soldiers, she was alone in the maelstrom.

"You're very lucky, Sister," the soldier said. "The kaffirs are washing their spears again."

"What?" she said.

"An uprising. Some kaffir sect thing. They hit your neighbor last night, and the next farm over, too. We came from them. All dead."

"This your bag?" another soldier asked. "Get in. We're in great danger out here."

In shock, Ali let them push and steer her into the sweltering armored bed of the vehicle. Soldiers crowded in and made their rifles safe and the doors closed shut. Their body odor was different from that of her lepers. Fear, that was the chemical. They were afraid in a way the lepers were not. Afraid like hunted animals.

The carrier rumbled off and Ali rocked hard against a big shoulder.

"Souvenir?" someone asked. He was pointing at her bead necklace.

"It was a gift," said Ali. She had forgotten it until now.

"Gift!" barked another soldier. "That's sweet."

Ali touched the necklace defensively. She ran her fingertips across the tiny beads framing the piece of dark leather. The small animal hairs in the leather prickled her touch.

"You don't know, do you?" said a man.

"What?"

"That skin."

"Yes."

"Male, don't you think, Roy?"

Roy answered, "It would be."

"Ouch," said a man.

"Ouch," another repeated, but in a falsetto.

Ali lost patience. "Quit smirking."

That drew more laughs. Their humor was rough and violent, no surprise.

A face reached in from the shadows. A bar of light from the gunport showed his eyes. Maybe he was a good Catholic boy. One way or another, he was not amused.

"That's privates, Sister. Human."

Ali's fingertips stopped moving across the hairs.

Then it was her turn to shock them.

They expected her to scream and rip the charm away. Instead, she sat back. Ali laid her head against the steel, closed her eyes, and let the charm against evil rock back and forth above her heart.

There were giants in the
earth in those days . . .
mighty men which were of
old, men of renown.

—GENESIS 6:4

3

BRANCH

0210 hours
1996

Rain.

Roads and bridges had washed away, rivers lay choked. Operations maps had to be reinvented. Convoys sat paralyzed. Landslides were carrying dormant mines onto lanes laboriously cleared. Land travel was at a standstill.

Like Noah beached upon his mountaintop, Camp Molly perched high above a confederacy of mud, its sinners stilled, the world at bay. Bosnia, cursed Branch. Poor Bosnia.

The major hurried through the stricken camp on a boardwalk laid frontier-style to keep boots above the mire. *We guard against eternal darkness, guided by our righteousness.* It was the great mystery in Branch's life, how twenty-two years after escaping from St. John's to fly helicopters, he could still believe in salvation.

Spotlights sluiced through messy concertina wire, past tank traps and claymores and more razor wire. The company's brute armor parked chin-out with cannon and machine guns leveled at distant hilltops.

Shadows turned multiple-rocket-launcher tubes into baroque cathedral organ pipes. Branch's helicopters glittered like precious dragonflies stilled by early winter.

Branch could feel the camp around him, its borders, its guardians. He knew the sentinels were suffering the foul night in body armor that was proof against bullets but not against rain. He wondered if Crusaders passing on their way to Jerusalem had hated chain mail as much as these Rangers hated Kevlar. *Every fortress a monastery*, their vigilance affirmed to him. *Every monastery a fortress.*

Surrounded by enemies, there were officially no enemies for them. With civilization at large trickling down shitholes like Mogadishu and Kigali and Port-au-Prince, the "new" Army was under strict orders: Thou shalt have no enemy. No casualties. No turf. You occupied high ground only long enough to let the politicos rattle sabers and get reelected, and then you moved on to the next bad place. The landscape changed; the hatreds did not.

Beirut. Iraq. Somalia. Haiti. His file read like some malediction. Now this. The Dayton Accords had designated this geographical artifice the ZOS—the zone of separation—between Muslims and Serbs and Croats. If this rain kept them separated, then he wished it would never stop.

Back in January, when the First Cav entered across the Drina on a pontoon bridge, they had found a land reminiscent of the great standoffs of World War I. Trenches laced the fields, which held scarecrows dressed like soldiers. Black ravens punctuated the white snow. Skeletons broke beneath their Humvee tires. People emerged from ruins bearing flintlocks, even crossbows and spears. Urban fighters had dug up their own plumbing pipes to make weapons. Branch did not want to save them, for they were savage and did not want to be saved.

He reached the command and communications bunker. For a moment in the dark rain, the earthen mound loomed like some half-made ziggurat, more primitive than the first Egyptian pyramid. He went up a few steps, then descended steeply between piled sandbags.

Inside, banks of electronics lined the back wall. Men and women in uniform sat at tables, their faces illuminated by laptop computers. The overhead lights were dim for screen reading.

There was an audience of maybe three dozen. It was early and cold for such waiting. Rain beat without pause against the rubber door flaps above and behind him.

"Hey, Major. Welcome back. Here, I knew this was for someone."

Branch saw the cup of hot chocolate coming, and crossed two fingers at it. "Back, fiend," he said, not altogether joking. Temptation lay in the minutiae. It was entirely possible to go soft in a combat zone, especially one as well fed as Bosnia. In the spirit of the Spartans, he declined the Doritos, too. "Anything started?" he asked.

"Not a peep." With a greedy sip, McDaniels made Branch's chocolate his own.

Branch checked his watch. "Maybe it's over and done with. Maybe it never happened."

"O ye of little faith," the skinny gunship pilot said. "I saw it with my own eyes. We all did."

All except Branch and his copilot, Ramada. Their last three days had been spent overflying the south in search of a missing Red Crescent convoy. They'd returned dog-tired to this midnight excitement. Ramada was here already, eagerly scanning his E-mail from home at a spare duty station.

"Wait'll you review the tapes," McDaniels said. "Strange shit. Three nights running. Same time. Same place. It's turning into a very popular draw. We ought to sell tickets."

It was standing-room only. Some were soldiers sitting behind laptop duty station computers hardwired into Eagle base down at Tuzla. But tonight the majority were civilians in ponytails or bad goatees or PX T-shirts that read I SURVIVED OPERATION JOINT ENDEAVOR or BEAT ALL THAT YOU CAN BEAT, with the mandatory "Meat" scrawled underneath in Magic Marker. Some of the civilians were old, but most were as young as the soldiers.

Branch scanned the crowd. He knew many of them. Few came with less than a Ph.D. or an M.D. stapled to their names. Not one did not smell like the grave. In keeping with Bosnia's general surreality, they had dubbed themselves Wizards, as in Oz. The UN War Crimes Tribunal had commissioned forensics digs at execution sites throughout Bosnia. The Wizards were their diggers. Day in, day out, their job was to make the dead speak.

Because the Serbs had hosted most of the genocide in the American-held sector and would have killed these professional snoops, Colonel Frederickson had decided to house the Wizards on base. The bodies themselves were stored at a former ball-bearing factory on the outskirts of Kalejsia.

It had proved a stretch, the First Cav accommodating this science tribe. For the first month or so, the Wizards' irreverence and antics and porno flicks had been a refreshing departure. But over the year, they'd degenerated into a tired *Animal House* schtick, sort of like *M*A*S*H* of the dead. They ate inedible Meals Ready to Eat with great relish and drank all the free Diet Cokes.

In keeping with the weather, when it rained, it poured. The scientists' numbers had tripled in the last two weeks. Now that the Bosnian elections were over, IFOR was scaling down its presence. Troops were going home, bases were closing. The Wizards were losing their shotguns. Without protection, they knew they could not stay. A large number of massacre sites were going to go untouched.

Out of desperation, Christie Chambers, M.D., had issued an eleventh-hour call to arms over the Web. From Israel to Spain to Australia to Canyon de Chelly and Seattle, archaeologists had dropped their shovels, lab techs had taken leave without pay, physicians had sacrificed tennis holidays, and professors had donated grad students so that the exhumation might go on. Their hastily issued ID badges read like a Who's Who of the necro sciences. All in all, Branch had to admit they weren't such bad company if you were going to be stranded on an island like Molly.

"Contact," Sergeant Jefferson announced at one screen.

The entire room seemed to draw a breath. The throng massed behind her to see what KH-12, the polar-orbiting Keyhole satellite, was seeing. Right and left, six screens showed the identical image. McDaniels and Ramada and three other pilots hogged a screen for themselves. "Branch," one said, and they made room for him.

The screen was gorgeous with lime-green geography. A computer overlaid the satellite image and radar data with a ghostly map.

"Zulu Four," Ramada helpfully pinpointed with his Bic.

Right beneath his pen, it happened again.

The satellite image flowered with a pink heat burst.

The sergeant tagged the image and keyed a different remote sensor on her computer, this one fed from a Predator drone circling at five thousand feet. The view shifted from thermal to other radiations. Same coordinates, different colors. She methodically worked more variations on the theme. Along one border of the screen, images stacked in a neat row. These were PowerPoint slides, visual situation reports from previous nights. Center-screen was real time. "SLR. Now UV," she enunciated. She had a rich bass voice. She could have been singing gospel. "Spectro, here. Gamma."

"Stop! See it?"

A pool of bright light was spilling amorphously from Zulu Four.

"So what am I seeing here, please?" one of the Wizards bawled at the screen next to Branch. "What's the signature here? Radiation, chemical, what?"

"Mostly nitrogen," said his fat companion. "Same as last night. And the night before that. The oxygen comes and goes. It's a hydrocarbon soup down there."

Branch listened.

Another of the kids whistled. "Look at this concentration. Normal atmosphere's what, eighty percent nitrogen?"

"Seventy-eight-point-two."

"This has to be near ninety."

"It fluctuates. Last two nights, it went almost ninety-six. But then it just tapers off. By sunrise, back to a trace above norm."

Branch noticed he wasn't the only one eavesdropping. His pilots were dropping in, too. Like him, their eyes were fixed on their own screens.

"I don't get it," a boy with acne scars said. "What gives this kind of surge? Where's all the nitrogen coming from?"

Branch waited through their collective pause. Maybe the Wizards had answers.

"I keep telling you, guys."

"Stop. Spare us, Barry."

"You don't want to hear it. But I'm telling you . . ."

"Tell me," said Branch. Three pairs of eyeglasses turned toward him.

The kid named Barry looked uncomfortable. "I know it sounds crazy. But it's the dead. There's no big mystery here. Animal matter decays. Dead tissue ammonifies. That's nitrogen, in case you forgot."

"And then *Nitrosomonas* oxidizes the ammonia to nitrate. And *Nitrobacter* oxidizes the nitrate to other nitrates." The fat man was using a broken-record tone. "The nitrates get taken up by green plants. In other words, the nitrogen never appears aboveground. This ain't that."

"You're talking about nitrifying bacteria. There's *de*nitrifying bacteria, too, you know. And that *does* leak aboveground."

"Let's just say the nitrogen does come from decay." Branch addressed the one called Barry. "That still doesn't account for this concentration, does it?"

Barry was circuitous. "There were survivors," he explained. "There always are. That's how we knew where to dig. Three of them testified that this was a major terminus. It was in use over a period of eleven months."

"I'm listening," Branch said, not sure where this was going.

"We've documented three hundred bodies, but there's more. Maybe a thousand. Maybe a whole lot more. Five to seven thousand are still unaccounted for from Srebrenica alone. Who knows what we'll find underneath this primary layer? We were just opening Zulu Four when the rain shut us down."

"Fucking rain," the eyeglasses to his left muttered.

"A lot of bodies," Branch coaxed.

"Right. A lot of bodies. A lot of decay. A lot of nitrogen release."

"Delete." The fat man was playing to Branch now, shaking his head with pity. "Barry's playing with his food again. The human body only contains three percent nitrogen. Let's call it three kilograms per body, times five thousand bodies. Fifteen thousand kgs. Convert it to liters, then meters. That's only enough nitrogen to fill a thirty-meter cube. Once. But this is a lot more nitrogen, and it disperses every day, then returns every night. It's not the bodies, but something associated with them."

Branch didn't smile. For months he'd been watching the forensics guys bait one another with monkey play, from planting a skull in the AT&T telephone tent to verbal wit like this cannibalism jive. His disapproval had less to do with their mental health than with his own troops' sense of right and wrong. Death was never a joke.

He locked eyes with Barry. The kid wasn't stupid. He'd been thinking about this. "What about the fluctuations?" Branch asked him. "How does decay explain the nitrogen coming and going?"

"What if the cause is periodic?"

Branch was patient.

"What if the remains are being disturbed? But only during certain hours."

"Delete."

"Middle-of-the-night hours."

"Delete."

"When they logically think we can't see them."

As if to confirm him, the pile moved again.

"What the fuck!"

"Impossible."

Branch let go of Barry's earnest eyes and took a look.

"Give us some close-up," a voice called from the end of the line.

The telephoto jacked closer in peristaltic increments. "That's as tight as it gets," the captain said. "That's a ten-meter square."

You could see the jumbled bones in negative. Hundreds of human skeletons floated in a giant tangled embrace.

"Wait . . ." McDaniels murmured. "Watch."

Branch focused on the screen.

"There."

From beneath, it appeared, the pile of dead stirred.

Branch blinked.

As if getting comfortable, the bones rustled again.

"Fucking Serbs," McDaniels cursed.

No one disputed the indictment.

Of late, the Serbs had a way of making themselves the theory of choice.

Those tales of children being forced to eat their fathers' livers, of women being raped for months on end, of every perversion . . . they were true. Every side had committed atrocities in the name of God or history or boundaries or revenge.

But of all the factions, the Serbs were the best known for trying to erase their sins. Until the First Cav put a stop to it, the Serbs had raced about excavating mass graves and dumping the remains down mine shafts or grating them to fertilizer with heavy machinery.

Strangely, their terrible industry gave Branch hope. In destroying evidence of their crime, the Serbs were trying to escape punishment or blame. But on top of that—or within it—what if evil could not exist without guilt? What if this *was* their punishment? What if this was penance?

"So what's it going to be, Bob?"

Branch looked up, less at the voice than at its liberty in front of subordinates.

For Bob was the colonel. Which meant his inquisitor could only be Maria-Christina Chambers, queen of the ghouls, formidable in her own right. Branch had not seen her when he came into the room.

A pathology prof on sabbatical from OU, Chambers had the gray hair and pedigree to mix with whomever she wanted. As a nurse, she'd seen more combat in Vietnam than most Green Beanies. Legend had it, she'd even taken up a rifle during Tet. She despised microbrew, swore by Coors, and was forever kicking dirt clods or talking crops like a Kansas farmboy. Soldiers liked her, including Branch. As well, the Colonel—Bob—and Christie had grown to be friends. But not over this particular issue.

"We going to dodge the bastards again?"

The room fell to such quiet, Branch could hear the captain pressing keys on her keyboard.

"Dr. Chambers . . ." A corporal tried heading her off.

Chambers cut him short. "Piss off, I'm talking to your boss."

"Christie," the colonel pleaded.

Chambers was having none of it this morning, though. To her credit, she was unarmed this time, not a flask in sight. She glared.

The colonel said, "Dodge?"

"Yes."

"What more do you want us to do, Christie?"

Every bulletin board in camp dutifully carried NATO's Wanted poster. Fifty-four men charged with the worst war crimes graced the poster. IFOR, the Implementation Forces, was tasked with apprehending every man it found. Miraculously, despite nine months in country and an extensive intelligence setup, IFOR had found not one of them. On several notorious occasions, IFOR had literally turned its head in order to not see what was right in front of them.

The lesson had been learned in Somalia. While hunting a tyrant, twenty-four Rangers had been trapped, slaughtered, and dragged by their heels behind the armed trucks called Technicals. Branch himself had missed dying in that alley by a matter of minutes.

Here the idea was to return every troop home—alive and well—by Christmas. Self-preservation was a very popular idea. Even over testimony. Even over justice.

"You know what they're up to," Chambers said.

The mass of bones danced within the shimmering nitrogen bloom.

"Actually I don't."

Chambers was undaunted. She was downright grand. "'I will allow no atrocity to occur in my presence,'" she quoted to the colonel.

It was a clever bit of insubordination, her way of declaring that she and her scientists were not alone in their disgust. The quote came from the colonel's very own Rangers. During their first month in Bosnia, a patrol had stumbled upon a rape in progress, only to be ordered to stand back and not intervene. Word had spread of the incident. Outraged, mere privates in this and other camps had taken it upon themselves to author their own code of conduct. A hundred years ago, any army in the world would have taken a whip to such impudence. Twenty years ago, JAG would have fried some ass. But in the modern volunteer Army, it was allowed to be called a bottom-up initiative. Rule Six, they called it.

"I see no atrocity," the colonel said. "I see no Serbs at work. No human actor at all. It could be animals."

"Goddammit, Bob." They'd been through it a dozen times, though never in public this way.

"In the name of decency," Chambers said, "if we can't raise our sword against evil . . ." She heard the cliché coming together out of her own mouth and abandoned it.

"Look." She started over. "My people located Zulu Four, opened it, spent five valuable days excavating the top layer of bodies. That was before this goddam rain shut us down. This is by far the largest massacre site. There's at least another eight hundred bodies in there. So far, our documentation has been impeccable. The evidence that comes out of Zulu Four is going to convict the worst of the bad guys, if we can just finish the job. I'm not willing to see it all destroyed by goddam human wolverines. It's bad enough they engineered a massacre, but then to despoil the dead? It's your job to guard that site."

"It is *not* our job," said the colonel. "Guarding graves is not our job."

"Human rights depends—"

"Human rights is not our job."

A burst of radio static eddied, became words, became silence.

"I see a grave settling beneath ten days of rain," the colonel said. "I see nature at work. Nothing more."

"For once, let's be certain," Chambers said. "That's all I'm asking."

"No."

"One helicopter. One hour."

"In this weather? At night? And look at the area, flooded with nitrogen."

In a line, the six screens pulsed with electric coloration. Rest in peace, thought Branch. But the bones shifted again.

"Right in front of our eyes . . ." muttered Christie.

Branch felt suddenly overwhelmed. It struck him as obscene that these dead men and boys should be cheated of their only concealment. Because of the awful way they had died, these dead were destined to be hauled back into the light by one party or another—if not by the Serbs, then by Chambers and her pack of hounds, perhaps over and over again. In this gruesome condition they would be seen by their mothers and wives and sons and daughters and the sight would haunt their loved ones forever.

"I'll go," he heard himself say.

When the colonel saw it was Branch who had spoken, his face collapsed. "Major?" he said. *Et tu?*

In that instant, the universe revealed depths Branch had failed to estimate or even dream. For the first time he realized that he was a favorite son and that the colonel had hoped in his heart to hand on the division to him someday. Too late, Branch comprehended the magnitude of his betrayal.

Branch wondered what had made him do it. Like the colonel, he was a soldier's soldier. He knew the meaning of duty, cared for his men, understood war as a trade rather than a calling, shirked no hardship, and was as brave as wisdom and rank allowed. He had measured his shadow under foreign suns, had buried friends, taken wounds, caused grief among his enemies.

For all that, Branch did not see himself as a champion. He didn't believe in champions. The age was too complicated.

And yet he found himself, Elias Branch, advocating the proposition. "Someone's got to start it," he stated with awful self-consciousness.

"It," monotoned the colonel.

Not quite sure even what he meant after all, Branch did not try to define himself. "Sir," he said, "yes, sir."

"You find this so necessary?"

"It's just that we have come so far."

"I like to believe that, too. What is it you hope to accomplish, though?"

"Maybe," said Branch, "maybe this time we can look into their eyes."

"And then?"

Branch felt naked and foolish and alone. "Make them answer."

"But their answer will be false," said the colonel. "It always is. What then?"

Branch was confused.

"Make them quit, sir." He swallowed.

Unbidden, Ramada came to Branch's rescue. "With permission, sir," he said. "I'll volunteer to go with the major, sir."

"And me," said McDaniels.

From around the room, three other crews volunteered also. Without asking, Branch had himself an entire expeditionary force of gunships. It was a terrible deed, a show of support very close to patricide. Branch bowed his head.

In the great sigh that followed, Branch felt himself released forever from the old man's heart. It was a lonely freedom and he did not want it, but now it was his.

"Go, then," spoke the colonel.

0410

Branch led low, lights doused, blades cleaving the foul ceiling.

The other two Apaches prowled his wings, lupine, ferocious.

He gave the bird its head of steam: 145 kph. Get this thing over with. By dawn, flapjacks with bacon for his gang of paladins, some rack time for himself, then start it all over. Keeping the peace. Staying alive.

Branch guided them through the darkness by instruments he hated. As far as he was concerned, night-vision technology was an act of faith that did not deserve him. But tonight, with the sky empty of all but his platoon, and because the strange peril—this cloud of nitrogen—was invisible to the human eye, Branch chose to rely on what his flight helmet's target-acquisition monocle and the optics pod were displaying.

The seat screen and their monocles were showing a virtual Bosnia transmitted from base. There a software program called PowerScene was translating all the current images of their area from satellites, maps, a Boeing 707 Night Stalker at high altitude, and daytime photos. The result was a 3-D simulation of almost real time. Ahead lay the Drina as it had been just moments before.

On their virtual map, Branch and Ramada would not arrive at Zulu Four until after they had actually arrived there. It took some getting to used to. The 3-D visuals were so good, you wanted to believe in them. But the maps were never true maps of where you were going. They were only true to where you'd been, like a memory of your future.

Zulu Four lay ten klicks southeast of Kalejsia in the direction of Srebrenica and other killing fields bordering the Drina River. Much of the worst destruction was clustered along this river on the border of Serbia.

From the backseat of the gunship, Ramada murmured, "Glory," as it came into view.

Branch flicked his attention from PowerScene to their real-time night scan. Up ahead, he saw what Ramada meant.

Zulu Four's dome of gases was crimson and forbidding. It was like biblical evidence of a crack in the cosmos. Closer still, the nitrogen had the appearance of a huge flower, petals curling beneath the nimbostratus canopy as gases hit the cold air and sheared down again. Even as they caught up with it, the deadly flower appeared on their PowerScene with a bank of unfolding information in LCD overprint. The scene shifted. Branch saw the satellite view of his Apaches just now arriving at where they had already passed. *Good morning,* Branch greeted his tardy image.

"You guys smell it? Over." That would be McDaniels, the eight-o'clock shotgun.

"Smells like a bucket of Mr. Clean." Branch knew the voice: Teague, back in the rear pocket.

Someone began humming the TV tune.

"Smells like piss." Ramada. Blunt as iron. Quit horsing around, he meant.

Branch caught the front edge of the odor. Immediately he exhaled.

Ammonia. The nitrogen spinoff from Zulu Four. It did smell like piss, rotten morning piss, ten days old. Sewage.

"Masks," he said, and seated his own tight against the bones of his face. Why take chances? The oxygen surged cool and clean in his sinuses.

The plume crouched, squat, wide, a quarter-mile high.

Branch tried to assess the dangers with his instruments and artificial light filters. Screw this stuff. They said little to him. He opted for caution.

"Listen up," he said. "Lovey, Mac, Teague, Schulbe, all of you. I want you to take position one klick out from the edge. Hold there while Ram and I take a wide circle around the beast, clockwise." He made it up as he went along. Why not counterclockwise? Why not up and over?

"I'll keep the spiral loose and high and return to your grouping. Let's not mess with the bastard until it makes more sense."

"Music to my ear, *jefe*," Ramada approved, navigator to pilot. "No adventures. No heroes."

Except for a snapshot he had shown Branch, Ramada had yet to lay eyes upon his brand-new baby boy, back in Norman, Oklahoma. He should not have come on this ride, but would not stay back. His vote of confidence only made Branch feel worse. At times like this, Branch detested his own charisma. More than one soldier had died following him into the path of evil.

"Questions?" Branch waited. None.

He broke left, banking hard away from the platoon.

Branch wound clockwise. He started the spiral wide and teased closer. The plume was roughly two kilometers in circumference.

Bristling with minigun and rockets, he made the full revolution at high speed, just in case some harebrain might be lurking on the forest floor with a SAM on one shoulder and slivovitz for blood. He wasn't here to provoke a war, just to configure the strangeness. Something was going on out here. But what?

At the end of his circle, Branch flared to a halt and spied his gunships waiting in a dark cluster in the distance, their red lights twinkling. "It doesn't look like anyone's home," he said. "Anybody see anything?"

"Nada," spoke Lovey.

"Negative here," McDaniels said.

Back at Molly, the assemblage was sharing Branch's electronically enhanced view. "Your visibility sucks, Elias." Maria-Christina Chambers herself.

"Dr. Chambers?" he said. What was she doing on the net?

"It's the old chestnut, Elias. Can't see the forest for the trees. We're way too saturated with the fancy optics. The cameras are cued to the nitrogen, so all we're getting is nitrogen. Any chance you might snug in and give it the old eyeball?"

Much as Branch liked her, much as he wanted to go in and do precisely that—eyeball the hell out of it—the old woman had no business in his chain of command. "That needs to come from the colonel, over," he said.

"The colonel has stepped out. My distinct impression was that you were being given, ah, total discretion."

The fact that Christie Chambers was putting the request directly over military airwaves could only mean that the colonel had indeed departed the command center. The message was clear: Since Branch was so all-fired independent, he had been cut loose to fend for himself. In archaic terms, it was something close to banishment. Branch had fragged himself.

"Roger that," Branch said, idling. Now what? Go? Stay? *Search on for the golden apples of the sun . . .*

"Am assessing conditions," he radioed. "Will inform of my decision. Out."

He hovered just beyond reach of the dense opaque mass and panned with the nose-mounted camera and sensors. It was like standing face-to-face before the first atomic mushroom.

If only he could see. Impatient with the technology, Branch abruptly killed the infrared night vision and pushed the eyepiece away. He flipped on the undercarriage headlights.

Instantly the specter of a giant purple cloud vanished.

Spread before them, Branch saw a forest—with trees. Stark shadows cast long and bleak. Near the center, the trees were leafless. The nitrogen release on previous nights had blighted them.

"Good God!" Chambers's voice hurt his ears.

Pandemonium erupted over the airwaves. "What the hell was that?" someone yelled.

Branch didn't know the voice, but from the background it sounded like a small riot breaking out at Molly.

Branch tensed. "Say again. Over," he said.

Chambers came back on. "Don't tell me you didn't see that. When you turned your lights on . . ."

The comm room noised like a flock of tropical birds in panic. Someone was yelling, "Get the colonel, get him now!" Another voice boomed, "Give me replay, give me replay!"

"What the fuck?" McDaniels wondered from the floating huddle. "Over."

Branch waited with his pilots, listening to the chaos at base.

A military voice came on. It was Master Sergeant Jefferson at her console. "Echo Tango, do you read? Over." Her radio discipline was a miracle to hear.

"This is Echo Tango, Base," Branch replied. "You are loud and clear. Is there a situation in development? Over."

"Big motion on the KH-12 feed, Echo Tango. Something's going on in there. Infrared just showed multiple bogeys. You say you see nothing? Over."

Branch squinted through the canopy. The rain lay plasticized on his Plexiglas, smearing his vision. He angled down to give Ramada an unobstructed view. From this distance, the site looked toxic but peaceful.

"Ram?" he said quietly, at a loss.

"Beats me," Ramada said.

"Any better?" he spoke into his mouthpiece.

"Better," breathed Chambers. "Hard to see, though."

Branch moved laterally for vantage and trained the lights on ground zero. Zulu Four lay not far ahead, nestled among stark spears of killed forest.

"There it is," Chambers said.

You had to know what to look for. It was a large pit, open and flooded with rainwater. Sticks floated on top of the pool. Bones, Branch knew instinctively.

"Can we get any more magnification?" Chambers asked.

Branch held his position while specialists fiddled with the image back at camp. There beyond his Plexiglas lay the apocalypse: Pestilence, Death, War. All but that final horseman, Famine. *What in creation are you doing here, Elias?*

"Not good enough," Chambers complained over his headset. "All we're doing is magnifying the distortion."

She was going to repeat her request, Branch knew. It was the logical next step. But she never got the chance.

"There again, sir," the master sergeant reported over the radio. "I'm counting three, correction, four thermal shapes, Echo Tango. Very distinct. Very alive. Still nothing on your end? Over."

"Nothing. What kind of shapes, Base? Over."

"They look to be human-sized. Otherwise, no detail. The KH-12 just doesn't have the resolution. Repeat. We're imaging multiple shapes, in motion at or in the site. Beyond that, no definition."

Branch sat there with the cyclic shoving at his hand.

At or in? Branch slipped right, searching for better vantage, sideways, then higher, not venturing one inch closer. Ramada toggled the light, hunting. They rose high above the dead trees.

"Hold it," Ramada said.

From above, the water's surface was clearly agitated. It was not a wild agitation. But neither was it the kind of smooth rippling caused by falling leaves, say. The pattern was too arrhythmic. Too animate.

"We're observing some kind of movement down there," Branch radioed. "Are you picking any of this up on our camera, Base? Over."

"Very mixed results, Major. Nothing definite. You're too far away."

Branch scowled at the pool of water. He tried to fashion a logical explanation. Nothing above ground clarified the phenomenon. No people, no wolves, no scavengers. Except for the motion breaking the water's surface, the area was lifeless.

Whatever was causing the disturbance had to be in the water. Fish? It was not impossible, with the overflowing rivers and creeks reaching through the forest. Catfish, maybe? Eels? Bottom feeders, whatever they were? And large enough to show up on a satellite infrared.

There was not a need to know. No more so than, say, the need to unravel a good mystery novel. It would have been reason enough for Branch, if he were alone. He yearned to get close and wrestle the answer out of that water. But he was not free to obey his impulses. He had men under his command. He had a new father in the backseat. As he was trained to do, Branch let his curiosity wither in obedience to duty.

Abruptly the grave reached out to him.

A man reared up from the water.

"Jesus," Ramada hissed.

The Apache shied with Branch's startle reflex. He steadied the chopper even as he watched the unearthly sight.

"Echo Tango One?" The corporal was shaken.

The man had been dead for many months. To the waist, what was left of him slowly lifted above the surface, head back, wrists wired together. For a moment he seemed to stare up at the helicopter. At Branch himself.

Even from their distance, Branch could tell a story about the man. He was dressed like a schoolteacher or an accountant, definitely not a soldier. The baling wire around his wrists they'd seen on other prisoners from the Serbs' holding camp at Kalejsia. The bullet's exit cavity gaped prominently at the left rear of his skull.

For maybe twenty seconds the human carrion bobbed in place, a ridiculous mannequin. Then the fabrication twisted to one side and dropped heavily onto the bank of the grave pit, half in, half out. It was almost as if a prop were being discarded, its shock effect spent.

"Elias?" Ramada wondered in a whisper.

Branch did not respond. *You asked for it,* he was thinking to himself. *You got it.*

Rule Six echoed. *I will permit no atrocity to occur in my presence.* The atrocity had already occurred, the killing, the mass burial. All in the past tense. But this—this desecration—was in his presence. His *present* presence.

"Ram?" he asked.

Ramada knew his meaning. "Absolutely," he answered.

And still Branch did not enter. He was a careful man. There were a few last details.

"I need some clarification, Base," he radioed. "My turbine breathes air. Can it breathe this nitrogen atmosphere?"

"Sorry, Echo Tango," Jefferson said, "I have no information on that."

Chambers came on the air, excited. "I might be able to help answer that. Just a sec, I'll consult one of our people."

Your people? thought Branch with annoyance. Things were slipping out of order. She had no place whatsoever in this decision. A minute later she returned. "You might as well get it straight from the horse's mouth, Elias. This is Cox, forensic chemistry, Stanford."

A new voice came on. "Heard your question," the Stanford man said. "Will an air-breather breathe your adulterated concentrate?"

"Something like that," Branch said.

"Ah hmm," Stanford said. "I'm looking at the chemical spectrograph downloaded from the Predator drone five minutes ago. That's as close to current as we're going to get. The plume is showing eighty-nine percent nitrogen. Your oxygen's down to thirteen percent, nowhere close to normal. Looks like your hydrogen quota took the biggest hit. Big deal. So here's your answer, okay?"

He paused. Branch said, "We're all ears."

Stanford said, "Yes."

"Yes, what?" said Branch.

"Yes. You can go in. You don't want to breathe this mix, but your turbine can. *Nema problema.*"

The universal shrug had entered Serbo-Croatian, too. "Tell me one thing," Branch said. "If there's no problem, how come I don't want to breathe this mix?"

"Because," said the forensic chemist, "that probably wouldn't be, ah, circumspect."

"My meter's running, Mr. Cox," Branch said. Fuck circumspect.

He could hear the Stanford hotshot swallow. "Look, don't mistake me," the man said. "Nitrogen's very good stuff. Most of what we breathe is nitrogen. Life wouldn't exist without it. Out in California, people pay big bucks to enhance it. Ever hear of blue-green algae? The idea is to bond nitrogen organically. Supposed to make your memory last forever."

Branch stopped him. "Is it safe?"

"I wouldn't land, sir. Don't touch down, definitely. I mean unless you've been immunized against cholera and all the hepatitises and probably bubonic plague. The biohazard's got to be off the scale down there, with all that sepsis in the water. The whole helicopter would have to be quarantined."

"Bottom line," Branch tried again, voice pinched tight. "Will my machine fly in there?"

"Bottom line," the chemist finally summarized, "yes."

The pit of fetid water curdled beneath them. Bones rocked on the surface. Bubbles breached like primordial boil. Like a thousand pairs of lungs exhaling. Telling tales.

Branch decided.

"Sergeant Jefferson?" he radioed. "Do you have your handgun?"

"Yes sir, of course, sir," she said. They were required to carry a firearm at all times on base.

"You will chamber one round, Sergeant."

"Sir?" They were also required never to load a weapon on base unless under direct attack.

Branch didn't drag his joke out any longer. "The man who was just on the radio," he said. "If he proves wrong, Sergeant, I want you to shoot him."

Over the airwaves, Branch heard McDaniels snort his approval.

"Leg or head, sir?"

He liked that.

Branch took a minute to get the other gunships positioned at the edges of the gas cloud, and to double-check his armament and snug his oxygen mask hard and tight.

"All right, then," he said. "Let's get some answers."

0425

He entered from on high with his faithful navigator at his back, meaning to descend at his own pace. To go slowly. To winnow out the perils one by one. With his three gunships poised at the rear like wrathful archangels, Branch meant to own this blighted real estate from the top down.

But the Stanford forensic chemistry specialist was wrong.

Apaches did not breathe this gaseous broth.

He was no more than ten seconds in when the acid haze began sparking furiously. The sparks killed the pilot flame already burning in the turbine, then, sparking more, relit the engine with a small explosion beneath the rotors. The exhaust-gas temperature gauge went into the red. The pilot flame became a two-foot wildfire.

It was Branch's job to be ready for all emergencies. Part of your training as a pilot involved hubris, and part of it involved preparing for your own downfall. This particular mechanical bankruptcy had never happened to him before, but he had reflexes for it anyway.

When the rotors surged, he corrected for it. When the machine started into failure and instruments shorted out, he did not panic. The power cut out on him.

"I've got a hot start," Branch declared calmly. Fed by an oxygen surge, the bushing above their heads held a fiery bluish globe, like St. Elmo's fire.

"Autorote," he announced next when the machine—logically—failed altogether.

Autorotation was a state of mechanical paralysis.

"Going down," he announced. No emotion. No blame. Here was here.

"Are you hit, Major?" Count on Mac. The Avenger.

"Negative," Branch reassured. "No contact. Our turbine's blown."

Autorotation, Branch could handle. It was one of his oldest instincts, to shove the collective down and find that long, steep, safe glide that imitated flight. Even with the engine dead, the rotor blades would continue spinning with the centrifugal force, allowing for a short, steep forced landing. That was the theory. At a plunging speed of 1,700 feet per minute, it all translated into thirty seconds of alternative.

Branch had practiced autorotations a thousand times, but never in the middle of night, in the middle of a toxic forest. With the power cut, his headlights died. The darkness leaped out at him. He was startled by its quickness. There was no time for his eyes to adjust. No time to flip on the monocle's artificial night vision. *Damn instruments.* That was his downfall. Should have been relying on his own eyes. For the first time he felt fear.

"I'm blind," Branch reported in a monotone.

He fought away the image of trees waiting to gut them. He reached for the faith of his wings. *Hold the pitch flat, the rotors will spin.*

The dead forest rushed at his imagination like switchblades in an alley. He knew better than to think the trees might cushion them. He wanted to apologize to Ramada, the father who was young enough to be his son. *Where have I brought us?*

Only now did he admit his loss of control. "Mayday," he reported.

They entered the treeline with a metallic shriek, limbs raking the aluminum, breaking the skids, reaching to skin their souls out of the machine.

For a few seconds more their descent was more glide than plummet.

The blades sheared treetops, then the trees sheared his blades.

The forest caught them.

The Apache braked in a mangle.

The noise quit.

Wrapped nose-down against a tree, the machine rocked gently like a cradle in rain. Branch lifted his fists from the controls. He let go. It was done.

Despite himself, he passed out.

He woke gagging. His mask was filled with vomit. In darkness and smoke, he clawed at the straps, freed the facepiece, dragged hard at the air.

Instantly he tasted and smelled the poison reach into his lungs and blood. It seared his throat. He felt diseased, anciently diseased, plagued into his very bones. *Mask,* he thought with alarm.

One arm would not work. It dangled before him. With his good hand he fumbled to find the mask again. He emptied the mess, pressed the rubber to his face.

The oxygen burned cold across the nitrogen wounds in his throat.

"Ram?" he croaked.

No answer.

"Ram?"

He could feel the emptiness behind him.

Strapped facedown, bones broken, wings clipped, Branch did the only other thing he was able to do, the one thing he had come to do. He had entered this dark forest to witness great evil. And so he made himself see. He refused delirium. He looked. He watched. He waited.

The darkness eased.

It was not dawn arriving. Rather, it was his own vision binding with the blackness. Shapes surfaced. A horizon of gray tones.

He noticed now a strange, taut lightning flickering on the far side of his Plexiglas. At first he thought it was the storm igniting thin strands of gas. The hits of light penciled in various objects on the forest floor, less with actual illumination than through brief flashes of silhouette.

Branch struggled to make sense of the clues spread all around him, but apprehended only that he had fallen from the sky.

"Mac," he called on his radio. He traced the communications cord to his helmet, and it was severed. He was alone.

His instrument panel still showed aspects of vitality. Various green and red lights twinkled, fed by batteries here and there. They signified only that the ship was still dying.

He saw that the crash had cast him among a tangle of fallen trees close to Zulu Four. He peered through Plexiglas sprayed with a fine spiderweb. A gracile crucifix loomed in the near distance. It was a vast, fragile icon, and he wondered—hoped—that some Serb warrior might have erected it as penance for this mass grave. But then Branch saw that it was one of his broken rotor blades caught at a right angle in a tree.

Bits of wreckage smoldered on the floor of soaked needles and leaves. The soak could be rain. Rather late, it came to him that the soak could also be his own spilled fuel.

What alarmed him was how sluggish his alarm was. From far away, it seemed, he registered that the fuel could ignite and that he should extricate himself and his partner—dead or alive—and get away from his ship. It was imperative, but did not feel so. He wanted to sleep. *No.*

He hyperventilated with the oxygen. He tried to steel himself to the pain about to come, jock stuff mostly, when the going gets tough . . .

He reared up, shouldering high against the side canopy, and bones grated upon bones. The dislocated knee popped in, then out again. He roared.

Branch sank down into his seat, shocked alive by the crescendo of nerve endings. Everything hurt. He laid his head back, found the mask.

The canopy flapped up, gently.

He drew hard at the oxygen, as if it might make him forget how much more pain was left to come. But the oxygen only made him more lucid. In the back of his mind, the names of broken bones flooded in helpfully. Horribly. Strange, this diagnosis. His wounds were eloquent. Each wanted to announce itself precisely, all at the same time. The pain was thunderous.

He raised a wild stare at the bygone sky. No stars up there. No sky. Clouds upon clouds. A ceiling without end. He felt claustrophobic. *Get out.*

He took a final lungful, let go of the mask, shed his useless helmet.

With his one good arm, Branch grappled himself free of the cockpit. He fell upon the earth. Gravity despised him. He felt crushed smaller and smaller into himself.

Within the pain, a distant ecstasy opened its strange flower. The dislocated knee popped back into place, and the relief was almost sexual. "God," he groaned. "Thank God."

He rested, panting rapidly, cheek upon the mud. He focused on the ecstasy. It was tiny among all the other savage sensations. He imagined a doorway. If only he could enter, all the pain would end.

After a few minutes, Branch felt stronger. The good news was that his limbs were numbing from the gas saturation in his bloodstream. The bad news was the gas. The nitrogen reeked. It tasted like aftermath.

". . . Tango One . . ." he heard.

Branch looked up at the caved-in hull of his Apache. The electronic voice was coming from the backseat. "Echo . . . read me . . ."

He stood away from the earth's flat seduction. It was beyond his comprehension that he could function at all. But he had to tend to Ramada. And they had to know the dangers.

He climbed to a standing position against the chill aluminum body. The ship lay tilted upon one side, more ravaged than he had realized. Hanging on to a handhold, Branch looked into the rear cavity. He braced for the worst.

But the backseat was empty.

Ramada's helmet lay on the seat. The voice came again, tiny, now distinct. "Echo Tango One . . ."

Branch lifted the helmet and pulled it onto his own head. He remembered that there was a photograph of the newborn son in its crown.

"This is Echo Tango One," he said. His voice sounded ridiculous in his own ears, elastic and high, cartoonish.

"Ramada?" It was Mac, angry in his relief. "Quit screwing around and report. Are you guys okay? Over."

"Branch here," Elias identified with his absurd voice. He was concussed. The crash had messed up his hearing.

"Major? Is that you?" Mac's voice practically reached for him. "This is Echo Tango Two. What is your condition, please? Over."

"Ramada is missing," Branch said. "The ship is totaled."

Mac took a half-minute to absorb the information. He came back on, all business. "We've got a fix on you on the thermal scan, Major. Right beside your bird. Just hold your position. We're coming in to provide assistance. Over."

"No," Branch quacked with his bird voice. "Negative. Do you read me?"

Mac and the other gunships did not respond.

"Do not, repeat, do *not* attempt approach. Your engines will not breathe this air."

They accepted his explanation reluctantly. "Ah, roger that," Schulbe said.

Mac came on. "Major. What is *your* condition, please?"

"My condition?" Beyond suffering and loss, he didn't know. Human? "Never mind."

"Major." Mac paused awkwardly. "What's with the voice, Major?"

They could hear it, too?

Christie Chambers, M.D., was listening back at Base. "It's the nitrogen," she diagnosed. Of course, thought Branch. "Is there any way you can get back on oxygen, Elias? You must."

Feebly, Branch rummaged for Ramada's oxygen mask, but it must have been torn away in the crash. "Up front," he said dully.

"Go up there," Chambers told him.

"Can't," said Branch. It meant moving again. Worse, it meant giving up Ramada's helmet and losing his contact with the outside world. No, he would take the radio link over oxygen. Communication was information. Information was duty. Duty was salvation.

"Are you injured?"

He looked down at his limbs. Strange darts of electric color were scribbling along his thighs, and he realized that the beams of light were lasers. His gunships were painting the region, defining targets for their weapons systems.

"Must find Ramada," he said. "Can't you see him on your scan?"

Mac was fixed on him. "Are you mobile, sir?"

What were they saying? Branch leaned against the ship, exhausted.

"Are you able to walk, Major? Can you evacuate yourself from the region?"

Branch judged himself. He judged the night. "Negative."

"Rest, Major. Stay put. A bio-chem team is on its way from Molly. We will insert them by cable. Help is on the way, sir."

"But Ramada . . ."

"Not your concern, Major. We'll find him. Maybe you should just sit down."

How could a man just disappear? Even dead, his body would go on emitting a heat signature for hours more. Branch raised his eyes and tried to find Ramada wedged in the trees. Maybe he'd been thrown into the funeral waters.

Now another voice entered. "Echo Tango One, this is Base." It was Master Sergeant Jefferson; Branch wanted to lay his head against that resonant bosom.

"You are not alone," Jefferson said. "Please be advised, Major. The KH-12 is showing unidentified movement to your north-northwest."

North-northwest? His instruments were dead. He had no compass, even. But Branch did not complain. "It's Ramada," he predicted confidently. Who else could it be out there? His navigator was alive after all.

"Major," cautioned Jefferson, "the image carries no combat tag. This is not confirmed friendly. Repeat, we have no idea who is approaching you."

"It's Ramada," Branch insisted. The navigator must have climbed from the broken craft to do what navigators do: orient.

"Major." Jefferson's tone had changed. With all the world listening, this was just for him. "Get out of there."

Branch hung to the side of the wreckage. Get out of here? He could barely stand.

Mac came on. "I'm picking it up now, too. Fifteen yards out. Coming straight for you. But where the fuck did he come from?"

Branch looked over his shoulder.

The dense atmosphere opened like a mirage. The interloper staggered out from the brush and trees.

Lasers twitched frenetically across the figure's chest, shoulders, and legs. The intruder looked netted with modern art.

"I've got a lock," Mac clipped.

"Me too." Teague's monotone.

"Roger that," Schulbe said. It was like listening to sharks speak.

"Say go, Major, he's smoke."

"Disengage," Branch radioed urgently, aghast at their lights. *So this is how it is to be my enemy.* "It's Ramada. Don't shoot."

"I'm vectoring more presence," Master Sergeant Jefferson reported. "Two, four, five more heat images, two hundred meters southeast, coordinates Charlie Mike eight three . . ."

Mac cut through. "You sure, Major? Be sure."

The lasers did not desist. They went on scrawling twitchy designs on the lost soldier. Even with the help of their neurotic doodles, even with the stark clarity of his nearness, Branch was not sure he wanted to be sure this was his navigator.

He ascertained the man by what was left of him. His rejoicing died.

"It's him," Branch said mournfully. "It is."

Except for his boots, Ramada was naked and bleeding from head to foot. He looked like a runaway slave, freshly flayed. Flesh trailed in rags from his ankles. Serbs? Branch wondered in awe.

He remembered the mob in Mogadishu, the dead Rangers dragged behind Technicals. But that kind of savagery took time, and they couldn't have crashed more than ten or fifteen minutes ago. The crash, he considered, perhaps the Plexiglas. What else could have shredded him like this?

"Bobby," he called softly.

Roberto Ramada lifted his head.

"No," whispered Branch.

"What's going on down there, Major? Over."

"His eyes," said Branch.

They had taken his eyes.

"You're breaking up . . . Tango . . ."

"Say again, say again . . ."

"His eyes are gone."

"Say again, eyes are . . ."

"The bastards took his eyes."

Schulbe: "His eyes?"

Teague: "But why?"

There was a moment's pause.

Then Base registered. ". . . new sighting, Echo Tango One. Do you copy . . ."

Mac came on with his cyber-voice. "We're picking up a new set of bogeys, Major. Five thermal shapes. On foot. They are closing on your position."

Branch barely heard him.

Ramada stumbled as if burdened by their laser beams. Branch realized the truth.

Ramada had tried to flee through the forest. But it was not Serbs who had turned him back. The forest itself had refused to let him pass.

"Animals," Branch murmured.

"Say again, Major."

Wild animals. On the edge of the twenty-first century, Branch's navigator had just been eaten by wild animals.

The war had created wild animals out of domestic pets. It had freed beasts from zoos and circuses and sent them into the wilderness. Branch was not shocked by the presence of animals. The abandoned coal tunnels would have made an ideal niche for them. But what kind of animal took your eyes? Crows, perhaps, though not at night, not that Branch had ever heard of. Owls, maybe? But surely not while the prey was still alive?

"Echo Tango One . . ."

"Bobby," Branch said again.

Ramada turned toward his name and opened his mouth in reply. What emerged was more blood than vowel. His tongue, too, was gone.

And now Branch saw the arm. Ramada's left arm had been stripped of all flesh below the elbow. The forearm was fresh bone.

The blinded navigator beseeched his savior. All that emerged was a mewl.

"Echo Tango One, please be apprised . . ."

Branch shucked the helmet and let it hang by the cord outside the cockpit. Mac and Master Sergeant Jefferson and Christie Chambers would have to wait. He had mercy to perform. If he did not bring Ramada in, the man would blunder on into the wilderness. He would drown in the mass grave, or the carnivores would take him down for good.

Summoning all his Appalachian strength, Branch forced himself upright and pressed away from the ship. He stepped toward his poor navigator.

"Everything will be okay," he spoke to his friend. "Can you come closer to me?"

Ramada was at the far edge of his sanity. But he responded. He turned in Branch's direction. Forgetful, the hideous bone lifted to take Branch's hand, even though it lacked a hand itself.

Branch avoided the amputation and got one arm around Ramada's waist and hoisted him closer. They both collapsed against the ruins of their helicopter.

It was a blessing of sorts, Ramada's horrible condition. Branch felt freed by comparison. Now he could dwell on wounds far worse than his own. He laid the navigator across his lap and palmed away the gore and mud on his face.

While he held his friend, Branch listened to the dangling helmet.

". . . One, Echo Tango One . . ." The mantra went on.

He sat in the mud with his back against the ship, clutching his fallen angel: *Pietà* in the mire. Ramada's limbs fell mercifully limp.

"Major," Jefferson sang in the near silence. "You are in danger. Do you copy?"

"Branch." Mac sounded violent and exhausted and full of worries high above. "They're coming for you. If you can hear me, take cover. You must take cover."

They didn't understand. Everything was okay now. He wanted to sleep.

Mac went on yelling. ". . . thirty yards out. Can you see them?"

If he could have reached the helmet radio, Branch would have asked them to calm down. Their commotion was agitating Ramada. He could hear them, obviously. The more they yelled, the more poor Ramada moaned and howled.

"Hush, Bobby." Branch stroked his bloody head.

"Twenty yards out. Dead ahead, Major. Do you see them? Do you copy?"

Branch indulged Mac. He squinted into the nitrous mirage enveloping them. It was little different from looking through a glass of water. Visibility was twenty feet, not yards, beyond which the forest stood warped and dreamlike. It made his head ache. He nearly gave up. Then he caught a movement.

The motion was peripheral. It pronounced the depths, a bit of pallor in the dark woods. He glanced to the side, but it was gone.

"They're fanning out, Major. Hunter-killer style. If you copy, get away. Repeat, begin escape and evasion."

Ramada was grunting idiotically. Branch tried to quiet him, but the navigator was in a panic. He pushed Branch's hand away and hooted fearfully at the dead forest.

"Be quiet," Branch whispered.

"We see you on the infrared, Major. Presume you are unable to move. If you copy, get your ass down."

Ramada was going to give them away with his noise.

Branch looked around and there, close at hand, his oxygen mask was dangling against the ship. Branch took it. He held it to Ramada's face.

It worked. Ramada quit hooting. He took several unabated pulls at the oxygen.

Seizures followed a moment later.

Later, people would not blame Branch for the death. Even after Army coroners determined that Ramada's death was accidental, few believed Branch had not meant to kill him. Some felt it showed his compassion toward this mutilated victim. Others said it demonstrated a warrior's self-preservation, that Branch had no choice under the circumstances.

Ramada writhed in Branch's embrace. The oxygen mask was ripped away. Ramada's agony burst out in a howl.

"It will be okay," Branch told him, and pushed the mask back into place.

Ramada's spine arched. His cheeks sucked in and out. He clawed at Branch.

Branch held on. He forced the oxygen into Ramada like it was morphine.

Slowly, Ramada quit fighting. Branch was sure it signified sleep.

Rain pattered against the Apache.

Ramada went limp.

Branch heard footsteps. The sound faded. He lifted the mask.

Ramada was dead.

In shock, Branch felt for a pulse.

He shook the body, no longer in torment.

"What have I done?" Branch asked aloud. He rocked the navigator in his arms.

The helmet spoke in tongues. ". . . down . . . all around . . ."

"Locked. Ready on . . ."

"Major, forgive me . . . cover . . . on my command . . ."

Master Sergeant Jefferson delivered last rites. "In the name of the Father, and of the Son . . ."

The footsteps returned, too heavy for human, too fast.

Branch looked up barely in time. The nitrous screen gashed open.

He was wrong. What sprang from the mirage were not animals like any on earth. And yet he recognized them.

"God," he uttered, eyes wide.

"Fire," spoke Mac.

Branch had known battle, but never like this. This was not combat. It was the end of time.

The rain turned to metal. Their electric miniguns harrowed the earth, chopped under the rich soil, evaporated the leaves and mushrooms and roots. Trees fell in columns, like a castle breaking to pieces. His enemy turned to roadkill.

The gunships drifted invisibly a kilometer out, and so for the first few seconds Branch saw the world turn inside out in complete silence. The ground boiled with bullets.

The thunder caught up just as their rockets reached in.

Darkness vanished utterly.

No man was meant to survive such light.

It went on for eternity.

They found Branch still sitting against his shipwreck, holding his navigator across his lap. The metal skin was scorched black and hot to the touch. Like a shadow in reverse, the aluminum behind his back bore his pale outline. The metal was immaculate, protected by his flesh and spirit.

After that, Branch was never the same.

4
PERINDE AC CADAVER

JAVA
1998

It was a lovers' meal, raspberries plucked from the summit slopes of Gunung Merapi, a lush volcano towering beneath the crescent moon. You would not know the old blind man was dying, his enthusiasm for the raspberries was so complete. No sugar, certainly not, or cream. De l'Orme's joy in the ripe berries was a thing to see. Berry by berry, Santos kept replenishing the old man's bowl from his own.

De l'Orme paused, turned his head. "That would be him," he said.

Santos had heard nothing, but cleaned his fingers with a napkin. "Excuse me," he said, and rose swiftly to open the door.

He peered into the night. The electricity was out, and he had ordered a brazier to be lit upon the path. Seeing no one, he thought de l'Orme's keen ears were wrong for a change. Then he saw the traveler.

The man was bent before him on one knee in the darkness, wiping mud from his black shoes with a fistful of leaves. He had the large hands of a stonemason. His hair was white.

"Please, come in," Santos said. "Let me help." But he did not offer a hand to assist.

The old Jesuit noticed such things, the chasm between a word and a deed. He quit swabbing at the mud. "Ah, well," he said, "I'm not done walking tonight anyway."

"Leave your shoes outside," Santos insisted, then tried to change his scold into a generosity. "I will wake the boy to clean them."

The Jesuit said nothing, judging him. It made the young man more awkward. "He is a good boy."

"As you wish," the Jesuit said. He gave his shoelace a tug, and the knot let go with a pop. He undid the other and stood.

Santos stepped back, not expecting such height, or bones so raw and sturdy. With his rough angles and boxer's jaw, the Jesuit looked built by a shipwright to withstand long voyages.

"Thomas." De l'Orme was standing in the penumbra of a whaler's lamp, eyes shrouded behind small blackened spectacles. "You're late. I was beginning to think the leopards must have gotten you. And now look, we've finished dinner without you."

Thomas advanced upon the spare banquet of fruits and vegetables and saw the tiny bones of a dove, the local delicacy. "My taxi broke down," he explained. "The walk was longer than I expected."

"You must be exhausted. I would have sent Santos to the city for you, but you told me you knew Java."

Candles upon the sill backlit his bald skull with a buttery halo. Thomas heard a small, rattling noise at the window, like *rupiah* coins being thrown against the glass. Closer, he saw giant moths and sticklike insects, working furiously to get at the light.

"It's been a long time," Thomas said.

"A very long time." De l'Orme smiled. "How many years? But now we are reunited."

Thomas looked about. It was a large room for a rural *pastoran*—the Dutch Catholic equivalent of a rectory—to offer a guest, even one as distinguished as de l'Orme. Thomas guessed one wall had been demolished to double de l'Orme's workspace. Mildly surprised, he noted the charts and tools and books. Except for a well-polished colonial-era secretary desk bursting with papers, the room did not look like de l'Orme at all.

There was the usual aggregation of temple statuary, fossils, and artifacts that every field ethnologist decorates "home" with. But beneath that, anchoring these bits and pieces of daily finds, was an organizing principle that displayed de l'Orme, the genius, as much as his subject matter. De l'Orme was not particularly self-effacing, but neither was he the sort to occupy one entire shelf with his published poems and two-volume memoir and another with his yardage of monographs on kinship, paleoteleology, ethnic medicine, botany, comparative religions, et cetera. Nor would he have arranged, shrinelike and alone upon the uppermost shelf, his infamous *La Matière de le Coeur (The Matter of the Heart)*, his Marxist defense of Teilhard de Chardin's Socialist *Le Coeur de la Matière*. At the Pope's express demand, de Chardin had recanted, thus destroying his reputation among fellow scientists. De l'Orme had not recanted, forcing the Pope to expel his prodigal son into darkness. There could be only one explanation for this prideful show of works, Thomas decided: the lover. De l'Orme possibly did not know the books were set out.

"Of course I would find you here, a heretic among priests," Thomas chastised his old friend. He waved a hand toward Santos. "And in a state of sin. Or, tell me, is he one of us?"

"You see?" de l'Orme addressed Santos with a laugh. "Blunt as pig iron, didn't I say? But don't let that fool you."

Santos was not mollified. "One of whom, if you please? One of you? Certainly not. I am a scientist."

So, thought Thomas, this proud fellow was not just another seeing-eye dog. De l'Orme had finally decided to take on a protégé. He searched the young man for a second impression, and it was little better than the first. He wore long hair and a goatee and a fresh white peasant shirt. There was not even dirt beneath his nails.

De l'Orme went on chuckling. "But Thomas is a scientist also," he teased his young companion.

"So you say," Santos retorted.

De l'Orme's grin vanished. "I do say so," he pronounced. "A fine scientist. Seasoned. Proven. The Vatican is lucky to have him. As their science liaison, he brings the only credibility they have in the modern age."

Thomas was not flattered by the defense. De l'Orme took personally the prejudice that a priest could not be a thinker in the natural world, for in defying the Church and renouncing the cloth, he had, in a sense, borne his Church out. And so he was speaking to his own tragedy.

Santos turned his head aside. In profile, his fashionable goatee was a flourish upon his exquisite Michelangelo chin. Like all of de l'Orme's acquisitions, he was so physically perfect you wondered if the blind man was really blind. Perhaps, Thomas reflected, beauty had a spirit all its own.

From far away, Thomas recognized the unearthly Indonesian music called gamelan. They said it took a lifetime to develop an appreciation for the five-note chords. Gamelan had never been soothing to him. It only made him uncomfortable. Java was not an easy place to drop in on like this.

"Forgive me," he said, "but my itinerary is compressed this time. They have me scheduled to fly out of Jakarta at five tomorrow afternoon. That means I must return to Yogya by dawn. And I've already wasted enough of our time by being so late."

"We'll be up all night," de l'Orme grumbled. "You'd think they would allow two old men a little time to socialize."

"Then we should drink one of these." Thomas opened his satchel. "But quickly."

De l'Orme actually clapped his hands. "The Chardonnay? My '62?" But he knew it would be. It always was. "The corkscrew, Santos. Just wait until you taste this. And some *gudeg* for our vagabond. A local specialty, Thomas, jackfruit and chicken and tofu simmered in coconut milk . . ."

With a long-suffering look, Santos went off to find the corkscrew and warm the food.

De l'Orme cradled two of three bottles Thomas carefully produced. "Atlanta?"

"The Centers for Disease Control," Thomas identified. "There have been several new strains of virus reported in the Horn region. . . ."

For the next hour, tended by Santos, the two men sat at the table and circled through their "recent" adventures. In fact, they had not seen each other in seventeen years. Finally they came around to the work at hand.

"You're not supposed to be excavating down there," Thomas said.

Santos was sitting to de l'Orme's right, and he leaned his elbows on the table. He had been waiting all evening for this. "Surely you don't call this an excavation," he said. "Terrorists planted a bomb. We're merely passersby looking into an open wound."

Thomas dismissed the argument. "Bordubur is off limits to all field archaeology now. These lower regions within the hillside were especially not to be disturbed. UNESCO mandated that none of the hidden footer wall was to be exposed or dismantled. The Indonesian government forbade any and all subsurface exploration. There were to be no trenches. No digging at all."

"Pardon me, but again, we're not digging. A bomb went off. We're simply looking into the hole."

De l'Orme attempted a distraction. "Some people think the bomb was the work of Muslim fundamentalists. But I believe it's the old problem. *Transmigrai*. The government's population policy. It is very unpopular.

They forcibly relocate people from overcrowded islands to less crowded ones. Tyranny at its worst."

Thomas did not accept his detour. "You're not supposed to be down there," he repeated. "You're trespassing. You'll make it impossible for any other investigation to occur here."

Santos, too, was not distracted. "Monsieur Thomas, is it not true that it was the Church that persuaded UNESCO and the Indonesians to forbid work at these depths? And that you personally were the agent in charge of halting the UNESCO restoration?"

De l'Orme smiled innocently, as if wondering how his henchman had learned such facts.

"Half of what you say is true," Thomas said.

"The orders did come from you?"

"Through me. The restoration was complete."

"The restoration, perhaps, but not the investigation, obviously. Scholars have counted eight great civilizations piled here. Now, in the space of three weeks, we've found evidence of two more civilizations beneath those."

"At any rate," Thomas said, "I'm here to seal the dig. As of tonight, it's finished."

Santos slapped his palm on the wood. "Disgraceful. Say something," he appealed to de l'Orme.

The response was practically a whisper. *"Perinde ac cadaver."*

"What?"

"'Like a corpse,'" said de l'Orme. "The *perinde* is the first rule of Jesuit obedience. 'I belong not to myself but to Him who made me and to His representative. I must behave like a corpse possessing neither will nor understanding.'"

The young man paled. "Is this true?" he asked.

"Oh yes," said de l'Orme.

The *perinde* seemed to explain much. Thomas watched Santos turn pitying eyes upon de l'Orme, clearly shaken by the terrible ethic that had once bound his frail mentor. "Well," Santos finally said to Thomas, "it's not for us."

"No?" said Thomas.

"We require the freedom of our views. Absolutely. Your obedience is not for us."

Us, not me. Thomas was starting to warm to this young man.

"But someone invited me here to see an image carved in stone," said Thomas. "Is that not obedience?"

"That was not Santos, I assure you." De l'Orme smiled. "No, he argued for hours against telling you. He even threatened me when I sent you the fax."

"And why is that?" asked Thomas.

"Because the image is natural," Santos replied. "And now you'll try to make it supernatural."

"The face of pure evil?" said Thomas. "That is how de l'Orme described it to me. I don't know if it's natural or not."

"It's not the true face. Only a representation. A sculptor's nightmare."

"But what if it does represent a real face? A face familiar to us from other artifacts and sites? How is that anything other than natural?"

"There," complained Santos. "Inverting my words doesn't change what you're after. A look into the devil's own eyes. Even if they're the eyes of a man."

"Man or demon, that's for me to decide. It is part of my job. To assemble what has been recorded throughout human time and to make it into a coherent picture. To verify the evidence of souls. Have you taken any photos?"

Santos had fallen silent.

"Twice," de l'Orme answered. "But the first set of pictures was ruined by water. And Santos tells me the second set is too dark to see. And the video camera's battery is dead. Our electricity has been out for days."

"A plaster casting, then? The carving is in high relief, isn't it?"

"There's been no time. The dirt keeps collapsing, or the hole fills with water. It's not a proper trench, and this monsoon is a plague."

"You mean to say there's no record whatsoever? Even after three weeks?"

Santos looked embarrassed. De l'Orme came to the rescue. "After tomorrow there will be abundant record. Santos has vowed not to return from the depths until he has recorded the image altogether. After which the pit may be sealed, of course."

Thomas shrugged in the face of the inevitable. It was not his place to physically stop de l'Orme and Santos. The archaeologists didn't know it yet, but they were in a race against more than time. Tomorrow, Indonesian army soldiers were arriving to close the dig down and bury the mysterious stone columns beneath tons of volcanic soil. Thomas was glad he would be gone by then. He did not relish the sight of a blind man arguing with bayonets.

It was nearly one in the morning. In the far distance, the gamelan drifted between volcanoes, married the moon, seduced the sea. "I'd like to see the fresco itself, then," said Thomas.

"Now?" barked Santos.

"I expected as much," de l'Orme said. "He's come nine thousand miles for his peek. Let us go."

"Very well," Santos said. "But I will take him. You need to get your rest, Bernard."

Thomas saw the tenderness. For an instant he was almost envious.

"Nonsense," de l'Orme said. "I'm going also."

They walked up the path by flashlight, carrying musty umbrellas wrapped against their bamboo handles. The air was so heavy with water it was almost not air. Any instant now, it seemed, the sky must open up and turn to flood. You could not call these Javanese monsoons rain. They were a phenomenon more like the eruption of volcanoes, as regular as clockwork, as humbling as Jehovah.

"Thomas," said de l'Orme, "this pre-dates everything. It's so very old. Man was still foraging in the trees at this time. Inventing fire, finger-painting on cave walls. That is what frightens me. These people, who-ever they were, should not have had the tools to knap flint, much less carve stone. Or do portraiture or erect columns. This should not exist."

Thomas considered. Few places on earth had more human antiquity than Java. Java Man—*Pithecanthropus erectus*, better known as *Homo erectus*—had been found only a few kilometers from here, at Trinil and Sangiran on the Solo River. For a quarter-million years, man's ancestors had been sampling fruit from these trees. And killing and eating one another, too. The fossil evidence was clear about that as well.

"You mentioned a frieze with grotesques."

"Monstrous beings," de l'Orme said. "That is where I'm taking you now. To the base of Column C."

"Could it be self-portraiture? Perhaps these were hominids. Perhaps they had talents far beyond what we've given them credit for."

"Perhaps," said de l'Orme. "But then there is the face."

It was the face that had brought Thomas so far. "You said it's horrible."

"Oh, the face is not horrible at all. That's the problem. It's a common face. A human face."

"Human?"

"It could be your face." Thomas looked sharply at the blind man. "Or mine," de l'Orme added. "What's horrible is its context. This ordinary face looks upon scenes of savagery and degradation and monstrosity."

"And?"

"That's all. He's looking. And you can tell he will never look away. I don't know, he seems content. I've felt the carving," de l'Orme said. "Even its touch is unsavory. It's most unusual, this juxtaposition of normalcy and chaos. And it's so banal, so prosaic. That's the most intriguing thing. It's completely out of sync with its age, whatever age that may be."

Firecrackers and drums echoed from scattered villages. Ramadan, the month of Muslim fasting, had just ended yesterday. Thomas saw the crescent of the new moon threading between the mountains. Families would be feasting. Whole villages would stay up until dawn watching the shadow plays called *wayang*, with two-dimensional puppets making love and doing battle as shadows thrown upon a sheet. By dawn, good would triumph over evil, light over darkness: the usual fairy tale.

One of the mountains beneath the moon separated in the middle distance, and became the ruins of Bordubur. The enormous stupa was supposed to be a depiction of Mount Meru, a cosmic Everest. Buried for over a thousand years by an eruption of Gunung Merapi, Bordubur was the greatest of the ruins. In that sense, it was death's palace and cathedral all in one, a pyramid for Southeast Asia.

The ticket for admission was death, at least symbolically. You entered through the jaws of a ferocious devouring beast garlanded with human skulls—the goddess Kali. Immediately you were in a mazelike afterworld. Nearly ten thousand square meters—five square kilometers—of carved "story wall" accompanied each traveler. It told a tale almost identical to Dante's *Inferno* and *Paradiso*. At the bottom the carved panels showed humanity trapped in sin, and depicted hideous punishment by hellish demons. By the time you "climbed" onto a plateau of rounded stupas, Buddha had guided humanity out of his state of *samsara* and into enlightenment. No time for that tonight. It was going on two-thirty.

"Pram?" Santos called into the darkness ahead. "*Asalamu alaikum.*" Thomas knew the greeting. Peace unto you. But there was no reply.

"Pram is an armed guard I hired to watch over the site," de l'Orme explained. "He was a famous guerrilla once. As you might imagine, he's rather old. And probably drunk."

"Odd," Santos whispered. "Stay here." He moved up the path and out of sight.

"Why all the drama?" commented Thomas.

"Santos? He means well. He wanted to make a good impression on you. But you make him nervous. He has nothing left tonight but his bravado, I'm sorry to say."

De l'Orme set one hand upon Thomas's forearm. "Shall we?" They continued their promenade. There was no getting lost. The path lay before them like a ghost serpent. The festooned "mountain" of Bordubur towered to their north.

"Where do you go from here?" Thomas asked.

"Sumatra. I've found an island, Nias. They say it is the place Sinbad the Sailor met the Old Man of the Sea. I'm happy among the aborigines, and Santos stays occupied with some fourth-century ruins he located among the jungle."

"And the cancer?"

De l'Orme didn't even make one of his jokes.

Santos came running down the trail with an old Japanese carbine in one hand. He was covered in mud and out of breath. "Gone," he announced. "And he left our gun in a pile of dirt. But first he shot off all the bullets."

"Off to celebrate with his grandchildren would be my guess," de l'Orme said.

"I'm not so sure."

"Don't tell me tigers got him?"

Santos lowered the barrel. "Of course not."

"If it will make you feel more secure, reload," said de l'Orme.

"We have no more bullets."

"Then we're that much safer. Now let's continue."

Near the Kali mouth at the base of the monument, they veered right off the path, passing a small lean-to made of banana leaves, where old Pram must have taken his naps.

"You see?" Santos said. The mud was torn as if in a struggle.

Thomas spied the dig site. It looked more like a mud fight. There was a hole sunk into the jungle floor, and a big pile of dirt and roots. To one side lay the stone plates, as large as manhole covers, that de l'Orme had referred to.

"What a mess," said Thomas. "You've been fighting the jungle it-self here."

"In fact I'll be glad to be done with it," Santos said.

"Is the frieze down there?"

"Ten meters deep."

"May I?"

"Certainly."

Thomas gripped the bamboo ladder and carefully let himself down. The rungs were slick and his soles were made for streets, not climbing. "Be careful," de l'Orme called down to him.

"There, I'm down."

Thomas looked up. It was like peering out of a deep grave. Mud was oozing between the bamboo flooring, and the back wall—saturated with rainwater—bulged against its bamboo shoring. The place looked ready to collapse upon itself.

De l'Orme was next. Years spent clambering around dig scaffolding made this second nature. His slight bulk scarcely jostled the handmade ladder.

"You still move like a monkey," Thomas complained.

"Gravity." De l'Orme grinned. "Wait until you see me struggle to get back up." He cocked his head back. "All right, then," he called to Santos. "All clear on the ladder. You may join us."

"In a moment. I want to look around."

"So what do you think?" de l'Orme asked Thomas, unaware that Thomas was standing in darkness. Thomas had been waiting for the more powerful torch that Santos had. Now he took out his pocket light and turned it on.

The column was of thick igneous rock, and extraordinarily free of the usual jungle ravaging. "Clean, very clean," he said. "The preservation reminds me of a desert environment."

Sans peur et sans reproche," de l'Orme said. Without fear and without reproach. "It's perfect."

Thomas appraised it professionally, the material before the subject. He moved the light to the edge of a carving: the detailing was fresh and uncorroded. This original architecture must have been buried deep, and within a century of its creation.

De l'Orme reached out one hand and laid his fingertips upon the carving to orient himself. He had memorized the entire surface by touch, and now began searching for something. Thomas walked his light behind the thin fingers.

"Excuse me, Richard," de l'Orme spoke to the stone, and now Thomas saw a monstrosity, perhaps four inches high, holding up its own bowels in offering. Blood was spilling upon the ground, and a flower sprang from the earth.

"Richard?"

"Oh, I have names for all my children," de l'Orme said.

Richard became one of many such creatures. The column was so densely crowded with deformity and torment that an unsophisticated eye would have had trouble separating one from the other.

"Suzanne, here, she's lost her children." De l'Orme introduced a female dangling an infant in each hand. "And these three gentlemen, the Musketeers I call them." He pointed at a gruesome trio cannibalizing one another. "All for one, one for all."

It went much deeper than perversion. Every manner of suffering showed here. The creatures were bipedal and had opposing thumbs and, here and there, wore animal skins or horns. Otherwise they could have been baboons.

"Your hunch may be right," de l'Orme said. "At first I thought these creatures were either depictions of mutation or birth defects. But now I wonder if they are not a window upon hominids now extinct."

"Could it be a display of psychosexual imagination?" Thomas asked. "Perhaps the nightmare of that face you mentioned?"

"One almost wishes it were so," de l'Orme said. "But I think not. Let us suppose our master sculptor here somehow tapped into his subconscious. That might inform some of these figures. But this isn't the work of a single hand. It would have taken an entire school of artisans generations to carve this and other columns. Other sculptors would have added their own realities or even their own subconscious. There should be scenes of farming or hunting or court life or the gods, don't you think? But all we have here is a picture of the damned."

"But surely you don't think it's a picture of reality."

"In fact I do. It's all too realistic and unredemptive not to be reality." De l'Orme found a place near the center of the stone. "And then there's the face itself," he said. "It's not sleeping or dreaming or meditating. It's wide awake."

"Yes, the face," Thomas encouraged.

"See for yourself." With a flourish, de l'Orme placed the flat of his hand on the center of the column at head level.

But even as his palm lighted upon the stone, de l'Orme's expression changed. He looked imbalanced, like a man who had leaned too far forward.

"What is it?" asked Thomas.

De l'Orme lifted his hand, and there was nothing beneath it. "How can this be?" he cried.

"What?" said Thomas.

"The face. This is it. Where it was. Someone's destroyed the face!"

At de l'Orme's fingertip, there was a crude circle gouged into the carvings. At the edges, one could still make out some carved hair and beneath that a neck. "This was the face?" Thomas asked.

"Someone's vandalized it."

Thomas scanned the surrounding carvings. "And left the rest untouched. But why?"

"This is abominable," howled de l'Orme. "And us without any record of the image. How could this happen? Santos was here all day yesterday. And Pram was on duty until . . . until he abandoned his post, curse him."

"Could it have been Pram?"

"Pram? Why?"

"Who else even knows of this?"

"That's the question."

"Bernard," said Thomas. "This is very serious. It's almost as if some-one were trying to keep the face from my view."

The notion jolted de l'Orme. "Oh, that's too much. Why would anyone destroy an artifact simply to—"

"My Church sees through my eyes," Thomas said. "And now they'll never see what there was to see here."

As if distracted, de l'Orme brought his nose to the stone. "The defac-ing is no more than a few hours old," he announced. "You can still smell the fresh rock."

Thomas studied the mark. "Curious. There are no chisel marks. In fact, these furrows look more like the marks of animal claws."

"Absurd. What kind of animal would do this?"

"I agree. It must have been a knife used to tear it away. Or an awl."

"This is a crime," de l'Orme seethed.

From high above, a light fell upon the two old men deep in the pit. "You're still down there," said Santos.

Thomas held his hand up to shade the beam from his eyes. Santos kept his light trained directly upon them. Thomas felt strangely trapped and vulnerable. Challenged. It made him angry, the man's disrespect. De l'Orme, of course, had no inkling of the silent provocation. "What are you doing?" Thomas demanded.

"Yes," said de l'Orme. "While you go wandering about, we've made a terrible discovery."

Santos moved his light. "I heard noises and thought it might be Pram."

"Forget Pram. The dig's been sabotaged, the face mutilated."

Santos descended in powerful, looping steps. The ladder shook under his weight. Thomas stepped to the rear of the pit to make room.

"Thieves," shouted Santos. "Temple thieves. The black market."

"Control yourself," de l'Orme said. "This has nothing to do with theft."

"Oh, I knew we shouldn't trust Pram," Santos raged.

"It wasn't Pram," Thomas said.

"No? How do you know that?"

Thomas was shining his light into a corner behind the column. "I'm presuming, mind you. It could be someone else. Hard to recognize who this is. And of course I've never met the man."

Santos surged into the corner and stabbed his light into the crack and upon the remains. "Pram." He gagged, then was sick into the mud.

It looked like an industrial accident involving heavy machinery. The body had been rammed into a six-inch-wide crevice between one column and another. The dynamic force necessary to break the bones and squeeze the skull and pack all the flesh and meat and clothing into that narrow space was beyond comprehension.

Thomas made the sign of the cross.

We are quick to flare up, we
races of men on the earth.

—HOMER, *The Odyssey*

5

BREAKING NEWS

On these wide plains, seared in summer, harrowed by December winds, they had conceived Elias Branch as a warrior. To here he was returned, dead yet not dead, a riddle. Locked from sight, the man in Ward G turned to legend.

Seasons turned. Christmas came. Two-hundred-pound Rangers at the officers' club toasted the major's unearthly tenacity. The hammer of God, that man. One of us. Word of his wild story leaked out: cannibals with breasts. No one believed it, of course.

One midnight, Branch climbed from bed by himself. There were no mirrors. Next morning they knew he'd been looking by the bloody footprints, knew what he'd seen through the mesh grille covering his window: virgin snow.

Cottonwoods came to green glory. School hit summer. Ten-year-old Army brats racing past the hospital on their way to fish and swim pointed at the razor wire surrounding Ward G. They had their horror tale exactly backward: in fact, the medical staff was trying to *unmake* a monster.

There was nothing to be done about Branch's disfigurement. The artificial skin had saved his life, not his looks. There was so much tissue damage that when it healed, even he could not find the shrapnel wounds for all the burn scars. Even his own body had trouble understanding the regeneration.

His bones healed so quickly the doctors did not have the chance to straighten them. Scar tissue colonized his burns with such speed that sutures and plastic tubing were integrated into his new flesh. Pieces of rocket metal fused into his organs and skeleton. His entire body was a shell of cicatrix.

Branch's survival, then his metamorphosis, confounded them. They openly talked about his changes in front of him, as if he were a lab experiment gone awry. His cellular "bounce" resembled cancer in certain respects, though that did not explain the thickening of joints, the new muscle mass, the mottling in his skin pigment, the small, calcium-rich ridges ribbing his fingernails. Calcium growths knobbed his skull. His circadian rhythms had tripped out of synch. His heart was enlarged. He was carrying twice the normal number of red blood cells.

Sunlight—even moonbeams—were an agony to him. His eyes had developed tapetum, a reflective surface that magnified low light. Until now, science had known only one higher primate that was nocturnal, the aotus, or night monkey. His night vision neared triple the aotus norm.

His strength-to-weight ratio soared to twice an ordinary man's. He had double the endurance of recruits half his age, sensory skills that wouldn't quit, and the VO_2 max of a cheetah. Something had turned him into their long-sought super soldier.

The med wonks tried blaming it all on a combination of steroids or adulterated drugs or congenital defects. Someone raised the possibility that his mutations might be the residual effect of nerve agents encountered during past wars. One even accused him of autosuggestion.

In a sense, because he was a witness to unholy evidence, *he* had become the enemy. Because he was inexplicable, he was the threat from within. It was not just their need for orthodoxy. Ever since that night in the Bosnian woods, Branch had become their chaos.

Psychiatrists went to work on him. They scoffed at his tale of terrible furies with women's breasts rising up among the Bosnian dead, explaining patiently that he had suffered gross psychic trauma from the rocketing. One termed his story a "coalition fantasy" of childhood nuclear nightmares and sci-fi movies and all the killing he had directly seen or taken part in, a sort of all-American wet dream. Another pointed at similar stories of "wild people" in the forest legends of medieval Europe, and suggested that Branch was plagiarizing myth.

At last he realized they simply wanted him to recant. Branch pleasantly conceded. Yes, he said, it was just a bad fantasy. A state of mind. Zulu Four never happened. But they didn't believe his retraction.

Not everyone was so dedicated to studying his aberrations. An unruly physician named Clifford insisted that healing came first. Against the researchers' wishes, he tried flushing Branch's system with oxygen, and irradiated him with ultraviolet light. At last Branch's metamorphosis eased. His metabolism and strength tapered to human levels. The calcium outgrowths on his head atrophied. His senses reverted to normal. He could see in sunshine. To be sure, Branch was still monstrous. There was little they could do about his burn scars and nightmares. But he was better.

One morning, eleven months after arriving, ill with daylight and the open air, Branch was told to pack up. He was leaving. They would have discharged him, but the Army didn't like freaks with combat medals bumming around the streets of America. Posting him back to Bosnia, they at least knew where to find him.

Bosnia was changed. Branch's unit was long gone. Camp Molly was a memory on a hilltop. Down at Eagle Base near Tuzla, they didn't know what to do with a helicopter pilot who couldn't fly anymore, so they gave Branch some foot soldiers and essentially told him to go find himself. Self-discovery in camouflage: there were worse fates. With the carte blanche of an exile, he headed back to Zulu Four with his platoon of happy-go-lucky gunners.

They were kids who'd given up shredding or grunge or the 'hood or Net surfing. Not one had seen combat. When word went out that Branch was going armed into the earth, these eight clamored to go. Action at last.

Zulu Four had returned to as much normalcy as a massacre site could. The gases had cleared. The mass grave had been bulldozed flat. A concrete marker with an Islamic crescent and star marked the site. You had to look hard to still find pieces of Branch's gunship.

The walls and gullies around the site were cored with coal mines. Branch picked one at random and they followed him in. In later histories, their spontaneous exploration would become known as the first probe by a national military. It marked the beginning of what came to be called the Descent.

They had come as prepared as one did in those early days, with handheld flashlights and a single coil of rope. Following a coal miner's footpath, they walked upright—safeties off—through neat tunnels trimmed with wood pillars and roof supports. In the third hour they came to a rupture in the walls. From the rock debris spilled onto the floor, it seemed someone had carved his way *out* from the rock.

Following a hunch, Branch led them into this secondary tunnel. Beyond all reckoning, the network went deeper. No miner had mined this. The passage was raw but ancient, a natural fissure winding down. Occasionally the way had been improved: narrow sections had been clawed wider, unstable ceilings had been buttressed with stacked rock. There was a Roman quality to some of the stonework, crude keystones in some of the arches. In other places the drip of mineral water had created limestone bars from top to bottom.

An hour deeper, the GIs began to find bones where body parts had been dragged in. Bits and pieces of cheap jewelry and cheaper Eastern European wristwatches lay on the trail. The grave robbers had been sloppy and hurried. The ghoulish litter reminded Branch of a kid's Halloween bag with a rip in it.

They went on, flashing their lights at side galleries, grumbling about the dangers. Branch told them to go back, but they stuck with him. In deeper tunnels they found still deeper tunnels. At the bottom of those, they found yet more tunnels.

They had no idea how deep it was before they quit descending. It felt like the belly of the whale.

They did not know the history of man's meanderings underground, the lore of his tentative exploration. They hadn't entered this Bosnian maw for love of caving. These were normal enough men in normal enough times, none obsessed with climbing the highest mountain or soloing an ocean. Not one saw himself as a Columbus or a Balboa or a Magellan or a Cook or a Galileo, discovering new lands, new pathways, a new planet. They didn't mean to go where they went. And yet they opened this hadal door.

After two days in the strange winding corridor, Branch's platoon reached its limit. They grew afraid. For where the tunnels forked for the hundredth time and plunged still lower, they came upon a footprint. And it was not exactly human. Someone took a Polaroid photo and then they *di-di mau*'ed it back to the surface.

The footprint in that GI's Polaroid photo entered the special state of paranoia usually reserved for nuclear accidents and other military slips. It was designated a Black Op. The National Security Council convened. The next morning, NATO commanders met near Brussels. In top secrecy, the armed forces of ten countries poised to explore the rest of Branch's nightmare.

Branch stood before the council of generals. "I don't know what they were," he said, once more describing his night of the crash in Bosnia. "But they were feeding on the dead, and they were not like us."

The generals passed around the photo of that animal track. It showed a bare foot, wide and flat, with the big toe separate, like a thumb. "Are those horns growing on your head, Major?" one asked.

"The doctors call them osteophytes." Branch fingered his skull. He could have been the bastard child of an accidental mating between species. "They started coming back when we went down."

There was, the generals finally accepted, more to this than just a coal hole in the Balkans. Suddenly, Branch found himself being treated not like damaged goods, but like an accidental prophet. He was magically restored to his command and given free rein to go wherever his senses led him. His eight troops became eight hundred. Soon other armies joined in. The eight hundred became eighty thousand, then more.

Beginning with the coal mines at Zulu Four, NATO recon patrols went deeper and wider and began to piece together a whole network of tunnels thousands of meters below Europe. Every path connected another, however intricately. Enter Italy and you might exit in Slovakia or Spain or Macedonia or southern France. But there was no mistaking a more central direction to the system. The caves and pathways and sinkholes all led down.

Secrecy remained tight. There were injuries, to be sure, and a few fatalities. But the casualties were all caused by roofs collapsing or ropes breaking or soldiers tripping into holes: occupational hazards and human error. Every learning curve has its price.

The secret held, even after a civilian cave diver by the name of Harrigan penetrated a limestone sinkhole called Jacob's Well in south Texas, which supposedly transected the Edwards Aquifer. He claimed to have found a series of feeder passages at a depth of minus five thousand feet, which went deeper still. Further, he swore the walls contained paintings by Mayan or Aztec hands. A mile deep! The media picked it up, checked around, and promptly cast it aside as either a hoax or narcosis. A day after the Texan was made a fool in public, he disappeared. Locals reckoned the embarrassment had been too much for him. In fact, Harrigan had just been shanghaied by the SEALs, handed a juicy consultant's fee, sworn to national secrecy, and put to work unraveling sub-America.

The hunt was on. Once the psychological barrier of "minus-five" was broken—that magical five-thousand-foot level that intimidated cavers the way eight thousand meters once did Himalayan mountaineers—the progress plunged quickly. One of Branch's long-range patrols of Army Rangers hit minus-seven within a week after Harrigan went public. By month five, the military penetration had logged a harrowing minus-fifteen. The underworld was ubiquitous and surprisingly accessible. Every continent harbored systems. Every city.

The armies fanned deeper, acquiring a vast and complex sub-geography beneath the iron mines of West Cumberland in South Wales and the Holloch in Switzerland and Epos Chasm in Greece and the Picos Mountains in Basque country and the coal pits in Kentucky and the *cenotes* of Yucatán and the diamond mines in South Africa and dozens of other places. The northern hemisphere was exceptionally rich in limestone, which fused at lower levels into warm marble and beerstone and eventually, much deeper, into basalt. This bedrock was so heavy it underlay the entire surface world. Because man had rarely burrowed into it—a few exploratory probes for petroleum and the long-abandoned Moho project—geologists had always assumed that basalt was a solid compressed mass. What man now found was a planetary labyrinth. Geological capillaries stretched for thousands of miles. It was rumored they might even reach out beneath the oceans.

Nine months passed. Every day the armies pushed their collective knowledge a little further, a little deeper. The Army Corps of Engineers and the Seabees saw their budgets soar. They were tasked to reinforce tunnels, devise new transport systems, drill shafts, build elevators, bore channels, and erect whole camps underground. They even paved parking lots—three thousand feet beneath the surface. Roadways were constructed through the mouths of caves. Tanks and Humvees and deuce-and-a-half trucks pouring ordnance, troops, and supplies into the inner earth.

By the hundreds, international patrols descended into the earth's recesses for more than half a year. Boot camps shifted their theater training. Jarheads sat through films from the United Mine Workers about basic techniques for shoring walls and maintaining a carbide lamp. Drill instructors began taking recruits to the rifle ranges at midnight for point-and-fire practice and blindfolded rappels. Physician assistants and medics learned about Weill's disease and histoplasmosis, fungal infections of the lungs contracted from bat guano, and Mulu foot, a tropical cave disease. None were told what practical use any of this had. Then one day they would find themselves shipped into the womb.

Every week the mass of 3-D, four-color worm lines expanded laterally and vertically beneath their maps of Europe and Asia and the United States. Junior officers took to comparing the adventure to Dungeons and Dragons without, exactly, the dragons or dungeons. Wrinkled noncoms couldn't believe their luck: Vietnam without the Vietnamese. The enemy was turning out to be a figment of one very disfigured major's

THE DESCENT

imagination. No one but Branch could claim to have seen demons with fish-white skin.

Not that there weren't "enemies." The signs of habitation were intriguing, sometimes gruesome. At those depths, tracks suggested a surprising spectrum of species, everything from centipedes and fish to a human-sized biped. One leathery wing fragment stirred images of sub-terannean flight, temporarily reviving Saint Jerome's visions of batlike dark angels.

In the absence of an actual specimen, scientists had named the enemy *Homo hadalis,* though they were the first to admit they didn't know if it was even hominid. The secular term became *hadal,* rhyming with *cradle.* Middens indicated that these ape creatures were communal, if semino-madic. A picture of harsh, grinding, sunless subsistence emerged. It made the brute life of human peasantry look charming by comparison.

But whoever lived down here—and the evidence of primitive occupa-tion at the deeper levels was undeniable—had been scared off. They encountered no resistance. No contact. No live sightings. Just lots of caveman souvenirs: knapped flint points, carved animal bones, cave paintings, and piles of trinkets stolen from the surface: broken pencils, empty Coke cans and beer bottles, dead spark plugs, coins, lightbulbs. Their cowardice was officially excused as an aversion to light. Troops couldn't wait to engage them.

The military occupation went deeper and wider in breathless secrecy. Intelligence agencies triumphed in embargoing soldiers' mail home, confining units to base, and derailing the media.

The military exploration entered its tenth month. It seemed that the new world was empty after all, and that the nation-states had only to set-tle into their basements, catalog their holdings, and fine-tune new sub-borders. The conquest became a downright promenade. Branch kept urging caution. But soldiers quit carrying their weapons. Patrols resem-bled picnics or arrowhead hunts. There were a few broken bones, a few bat bites. Every now and then a ceiling collapsed or someone drove off an abyssal roadway. Overall, however, safety stats were actually better than normal. Keep your guard up, Branch preached to his Rangers. But he had begun to sound like a nag, even to himself.

The hammer dropped. Beginning on November 24, 1999, soldiers throughout the subplanet did not return to their cave camps. Search parties were sent down. Few came out. Carefully laid communications lines went dead. Tunnels collapsed.

It was as if the entire subplanet had flushed the toilet. From Norway to

Bolivia, from Australia to Labrador, from wilderness bases to within thirty feet of sunshine, armies vanished. Later it would be called a decimation, which means the death of one in ten. What happened on November 24 was its opposite. Fewer than one of every ten would survive.

It was the oldest trick in the history of warfare. You lull your enemy. You draw him in. You cut off his head. Literally.

A tunnel at minus-six in sub-Poland was found with the skulls of three thousand Russian, German, and British NATO troops. Eight teams of LRRPs and Navy SEALs were found crucified in a cavern nine thousand feet beneath Crete. They had been captured alive at scattered sites, herded together, and tortured to death.

Random slaughter was one thing. This was something else. Clearly a larger intelligence was at work. System-wide, the acts were planned and executed upon a single clockwork command. Someone—or some group—had orchestrated a magnificent slaughter over a twenty-thousand-square-mile region.

It was as if a race of aliens had just breached upon man's shores.

Branch lived, but only because he was laid up with a recurring malarial fever. While his troops forged deeper below the surface, he lay in an infirmary, packed in ice bags and hallucinating. He thought it was his delirium speaking as CNN broke the terrible news.

Half raving, Branch watched his President address the nation in prime time on December 2. No makeup tonight. He had been weeping. "My fellow Americans," he announced. "It is my painful duty . . ." In somber tones the patriarch enunciated the American military losses incurred over the past week: in all, 29,543 missing. The worst was feared. In the course of three terrible days, the United States had just suffered half as many American dead as the entire Vietnam War total. He avoided all mention of the global military toll, an unbelievable quarter of a million soldiers. He paused. He cleared his throat uncomfortably, shuffled papers, then pushed them aside.

"Hell exists." He lifted his chin. "It is real. A geological, historical place beneath our very feet. And it is inhabited. Savagely." His lips thinned. "Savagely," he repeated, and for a moment you could see his great anger.

"For the last year, in consultation and alliance with other nations, the United States has initiated a systematic reconnaisance of the edges of this vast subterranean territory. At my command, 43,000 American military personnel were committed to searching this place. Our probe into this frontier revealed that it is inhabited by unknown life-forms. There is nothing supernatural about it. Over the next days and weeks you will probably be asking how it is that if there are beings down there, we have never seen them before now. The answer is this: we have seen them. From the beginning of human time, we have suspected their presence among us. We have feared them, written poems about them, built religions against them. Until very recently, we did not know how much we really knew. Now we are learning how much we don't know. Until several days ago, it was assumed these creatures were either extinct or had retreated from our military advance. We know differently now."

The President stopped talking. The cameraman started back for the fade-out. Suddenly he began again. "Make no mistake," he said. "We will seize this dark empire. We will beat this ancient enemy. We will loose our terrible swift sword upon the forces of darkness. And we will prevail. In the name of God and freedom, we will."

The picture immediately switched to the Press Room downstairs. The White House spokesman and a Pentagon bull stood before the roomful of stunned journalists. Even in his fever, Branch recognized General Sandwell, four stars and a barrel chest. Son of a bitch, he muttered at the TV.

A woman from the *L.A. Times* stood, shaken. "We're at war?"

"There has been no declaration of war," the spokesman said.

"War with hell?" the *Miami Herald* asked.

"Not war."

"But hell?"

"An upper lithospheric environment. An abyssal region riddled with holes."

General Sandwell shouldered the spokesman aside. "Forget what you think you know," he told them. "It's just a place. But without light. Without a sky. Without a moon. Time is different down there." Sandy always had been a showboat, thought Branch.

"Have you sent reinforcements down?"

"For now, we are in a wait-and-see mode. No one goes down."

"Are we about to be invaded, General?"

"Negative." He was firm. "Every entrance is secured."

"But creatures, General?" The *New York Times* reporter seemed affronted. "Are we talking about devils with pitchforks and pincers? Do the enemy have hooves and horns on their heads and tails, and fly on wings? How would you describe these monsters, sir?"

"That's classified," Sandwell spoke into the mike. But he was pleased with the "monsters" remark. Already the media was demonizing the enemy. "Last question?"

"Do you believe in Satan, General?"

"I believe in winning." The general pushed the mike away. He strode from the room.

Branch slid in and out of fever dreams. A kid with a broken leg in the next bed channel-surfed endlessly. All night, every time Branch opened his eyes, the TV showed a different state of surreality. Day came. Local news anchors had been prepped. They knew to keep the hysteria out of their voices, to stick with the script. *We have very little information at this time. Please stay tuned for further information. Please remain calm.* An unbroken stream of text played across the bottom of the TV screen listing churches and synagogues open to the public. A government Web page was set up to advise families of the missing soldiers. The stock market plunged. There was an unholy mix of grief and terror and grim exuberance.

Survivors began trickling upward. Suddenly the military hospitals were taking in bloodied soldiers raving childishly about beasts, vampires, ghouls, gargoyles. Lacking a vocabulary for the dark monstrosity below, they tapped into the Bible legends, horror novels, and childhood fantasies. Chinese soldiers saw dragons and Buddhist demons. Kids from Arkansas saw Beelzebub and *Alien.*

Gravity won out over human ritual. In the days following the great decimation, there was simply no way to transport all the bodies up to the surface just so they could be lowered six feet back into the ground. There wasn't even time to dig mass graves in the cave floors. Instead, bodies were piled into side tunnels and sealed away with plastic explosives and the armies retreated. The few funeral services with an actual body featured closed caskets, screwed shut beneath the Stars and Stripes: NOT TO BE VIEWED.

The Federal Emergency Management Agency was put in charge of civil defense education. Lacking any real information about the threat, FEMA dusted off its antiquated literature from the seventies about what to do in case of nuclear attack, and handed it out to governors, mayors, and town councils. Turn on your radio. Lay in a supply of food. Stock up on water. Keep away from windows. Stay in your basement. Pray.

Foreboding emptied grocery stores and gun shops. As the sun went down on the second night, TV crews tracked national guardsmen taking up lines along highways and ringing ghettos. Detours led to roadblocks where motorists were searched and relieved of their weapons and liquor. Dusk closed in. Police and military helicopters prowled the skies, spotlighting potential trouble spots.

South Central Los Angeles went up first, no surprise there. Atlanta was next. Fire and looting. Shootings. Rape. Mob violence. The works.

Detroit and Houston. Miami. Baltimore. The national guard watched with orders to contain the mobs inside their own neighborhoods, and not to interfere.

Then the suburbs lit up, and no one was prepared for that. From Silicon Valley to Highlands Ranch to Silver Spring, bedroom commuters went rampaging. Out came the guns, the repressed envy, the hate. The middle class blew wide open. It started with phone calls from house to house, shocked disbelief twisting into realization that death lurked beneath their sprinkler systems. Strangely, suddenly, they had a lot to get out. They put the ghettos to shame with their fires and violence. In the aftermath, the national guard commanders could only say that they had not expected such savagery from people with lawns to call their own.

On Branch's TV, it looked like the last night on earth. For many people it was. When the sun rose, it illuminated a landscape America had been fearing since the Bomb. Six-lane highways were choked with mangled, burned cars and trucks that had tried to flee. Pitched battles had ensued. Gangs had swept through the traffic jams, shooting and knifing whole families. Survivors meandered in shock, crying for water. Dirty smoke poured into the urban skies. It was a day of sirens. Weather copters and roving news vans cruised the fringes of destroyed cities. Every channel showed havoc.

From the floor of the U.S. Senate, the majority leader, C.C. Cooper, a self-made billionaire with his eye on the White House, clamored for martial law. He wanted ninety days, a cooling-off period. He was opposed by a lone black woman, the formidable Cordelia January. Branch listened to her rich Texas vowels cow Cooper's notion.

"*Just* ninety days?" she thundered from the podium. "No, sir. Not on my watch. Martial law is a serpent, Senator. The seed of tyranny. I urge my distinguished colleagues to oppose this measure." The vote was ninety-nine in favor, one opposed. The President, haggard and sleepless, snatched at the political cover and declared martial law.

At 1:00 P.M. EST, the generals locked America down. Curfew began Friday at sunset and lasted until dawn on Monday. It was pure coincidence, but the cooling-off period landed on the ecclesiastical day of rest. Not since the Puritans had the Old Testament held such power in America: observe the Sabbath or be shot on sight.

It worked. The first great spasm of terror passed over.

Oddly enough, America was grateful to the generals. The highways got cleared. Looters were gunned down. By Monday, supermarkets were allowed to reopen. On Wednesday, children went back to school.

Factories reopened. The idea was to jump-start normalcy, to put yellow school buses back on the street, get money flowing, make the country feel returned to itself.

People cautiously emerged from their houses and cleaned their yards of riot debris. In the suburbs, neighbors who had been at one another's throats or on top of each other's wives now helped rake up the broken glass or scoop out ashes with snow shovels. Processions of garbage trucks came through. The weather was glorious for December. America looked just fine on the network news.

Suddenly, man no longer looked out to the stars. Astronomers fell from grace. It became a time to look inward. All through that first winter, great armies—hastily buttressed with veterans, police, security guards, even mercenaries—poised at the scattered mouths of the underworld, their guns pointed at the darkness, waiting while governments and industries scraped together conscripts and arsenals to create an overwhelming force.

For a month, no one went down. CEOs, boards of directors, and religious institutions badgered them to get on with the *Reconquista*, anxious to launch their explorations. But the death toll was well over a million now, including the entire Afghani Taliban army, which had practically jumped into the abyss in pursuit of their Islamic Satan. Generals cautiously declined to send in further troops.

A small legion of robots was commandeered from NASA's Mars project and put to use investigating the planet within their own planet. Creeping along on metal spider legs, the machines bore arrays of sensors and video equipment designed for the harshest conditions of a world far away. There were thirteen, each valued at five million dollars, and the Mars crew wanted them back intact.

The robots were released in pairs—plus one soloist—at seven different sites around the globe. Scores of scientists monitored each one around the clock. The "spiders" held up quite well. As they crept deeper into the earth, communication became difficult. Electronic signals meant to flash unimpeded from the Martian poles and alluvial plains were hampered by thick layers of stone. In a sense, the labyrinth underfoot was light-years more distant than Mars itself. The signals had to be computer-enhanced, interpreted, and coalesced. Sometimes it took many hours for a transmission to reach the top, and many hours or days to untangle the electronic jumble. More and more often, transmissions simply didn't surface.

What did come up showed an interior so fantastic that the planetologists and geologists refused to believe their instruments. It took a week for the electronic spiders to find the first human images. Deep within the limestone wilderness of Terbil Tem, beneath Papua New Guinea, their bones showed as ultraviolet sticks on the computer scan. Estimates ranged from five to twelve sets of remains at a depth of twelve hundred feet. A day later, miles inside the volcanic honeycombs around Japan's Akiyoshi-dai, they found evidence that bands of humans had been driven to depths lower than any explored, and there slaughtered. Deep inside Algeria's Djurdjura massif and the Nanxu River sink in China's Guanxi province, far below the caves under Mt. Carmel and Jerusalem, other robots located the carnage of battles fought in cubbyholes and crawl spaces and immense chambers.

"Bad, very bad," breathed hardened viewers. The bodies of soldiers had been stripped, mutilated, degraded. Heads were missing or arranged like masses of bowling balls. Worse, their weapons were gone. Place after place, all that remained were nude bodies, anonymous, turning to bone. You could not tell who these men and women had been.

One by one, their spiders ceased to transmit. It was too soon for their batteries to go dead. And not all of them had reached their signal threshold. "They're killing our robots," the scientists reported. By the end of December, only one was left, a solitary satellite creeping on legs into regions so deep it seemed nothing could live.

Far beneath Copenhagen, the robot eye picked up a strange detail, a close-up of a fisherman's net. The computer cowboys fiddled with their machinery, trying to resolve the image, but it remained the same, oversized links of thread or thin rope. They keyed in commands for the spider to back up slightly for a wider perspective.

Almost a full day passed before the spider transmitted back, and it was as dramatic as the first picture sent from the back of the moon. What had looked like thread or rope was iron circlets linked together. The net was in fact chain mail, the armor of an early Scandinavian warrior. The Viking skeleton inside had long ago fallen to dust. Where there had been a desperate black struggle, the armor itself was pinned to the wall with an iron spear.

"Bullshit," someone said.

But the spider rotated on command, and the den was filled with Iron Age weaponry and broken helmets. The NATO troops and Afghani Taliban and soldiers of a dozen other modern armies were not, then, the first to invade this abyssal world and raise arms against man's demons.

"What's going on down there?" the mission control chief demanded.

After another week, the transmission bursts conveyed nothing more than earth noise and electromagnetic pulses of random tremors. Finally the spider quit sending. They waited three days, then began to dismantle the station, only to hear a transmission beep. They hastily jacked the monitor in, and at long last got their face.

The static parted. Something moved on screen, and in the next instant the screen went black. They replayed the tape in slow motion and sweated out electronic bits of an image. The creature had, seemingly, a rack of horns, a stub of vestigial tail. Red eyes, or green, depending on the camera filter. And a mouth that must have been crying out with fury and damnation—or possibly maternal alarm—as it bore down on the robot.

It was Branch who broke the impasse. His fever spiked and he resumed command of what had become a ghost battalion. He leaned over the maps and tried to plot where his platoons had been that fateful day. "I need to find my people," he radioed his superiors, but they would have none of it. Stay put, they ordered.

"That's not right," Branch said, but did not argue. He turned from the radios, shouldered his Alice pack, and grabbed his rifle. He walked between the German armored column parked at the mouth of the Leoganger Steinberge cave system in the Bavarian Alps, deaf to the officers shouting to him to halt. The last of his Rangers, twelve men, followed like black wraiths, and the Leopard tank crews crossed themselves.

For the first four days the tunnels were strangely vacant, not a trace of violence, not a whiff of cordite, not a bullet scar. Even the highlights strung along walls and ceilings worked. Abruptly, at a depth of 4,150 meters, the lights ceased. They turned on their headlamps. The going slowed.

Finally, seven camps down, they solved the mystery of Company A. The tunnel dilated into a high chamber. They rounded left onto a sprawled battlefield.

It was like a lake of drowned swimmers that had been drained. The dead had settled atop one another and dried in a tangle. Here and there, bodies had been propped upright to continue their combat in the afterlife. Branch led on, barely recognizing them. They found 7.62-mm rounds for M-16s, a few gas masks, some broken Friz helmets. There were also plenty of primitive artifacts.

The combatants had slowly dried on the bone, constricting into tight rawhide sacks. The bowed spines and open jaws and mutilations seemed to bark and howl at the rubberneckers passing among them. Here was the hell Branch had been taught. Goya and Blake had done their homework well. The impaled and butchered were horrible.

The platoon wandered through the grim scene, their lights wagging. "Major," whispered their chain gunner. "Their eyes."

"I see," said Branch. He glanced around at the rearing, plunging remains. On every face, the eyes had been stabbed and mutilated. And he understood. "After Little Bighorn," he said, "the Sioux women came and punctured the cavalry soldiers' ears. The soldiers had been warned not to follow the tribes, and the women were opening their ears so they could hear better next time."

"I don't see no survivors," moaned a boy.

"I don't see no haddie, either," said another. Haddie was the hadal, whoever that was.

"Keep looking," Branch said. "And while you're at it, collect tags. At least we can bring their names out with us."

Some were covered with masses of translucent beetles and albino flies. On others a fast-acting fungus had reduced the remains to bone. In one trough, the dead soldiers were glazed over with mineral liquid and becoming part of the floor. The earth itself was consuming them.

"Major," a voice said, "you need to see this."

Branch followed the man to a steep overhang where the dead had been laid neatly side by side in a long row. Under their dozen light beams, the platoon saw the bodies had been dusted in bright red ochre powder, and then sprinkled with brilliant white confetti. It was a rather beautiful sight.

"Haddie?" breathed a soldier.

Beneath the layers of ochre, the bodies were indeed those of their enemy. Branch climbed across to the overhang. Close up now, he saw that the white confetti was teeth. There were hundreds of them, thousands, and they were human. He picked one up, a canine, and it had chip marks where a rock had hammered it from some GI's mouth. He gently set it back on the ground.

The hadal warriors' heads were pillowed on human skulls. At their feet were offerings.

"Mice?" said Sergeant Dornan. "Dried-up mice?" There were scores of them.

"No," said Branch. "Genitals."

The bodies differed in size. Some were bigger than the soldiers. They had the shoulders of Masai, and looked freakish next to their comrades with bandy legs. A few had peculiar talons in place of fingernails and toenails. If not for what they'd done to their teeth, and their penis sheaths made of carved bone, they would have looked quasi-human, like five-foot-tall pro linebackers.

Also scattered among the hadal corpses were five slender figures, gracile, delicate, almost feminine, but definitely male. At first glance, Branch expected them to be teenagers, but under the red ochre their faces were every bit as aged as the rest. All five of the gracile hadals had shaped skulls, flattened on back from binding in infancy. It was among these smallest specimens that the outside canines were most pronounced, some as long as baboon canines.

"We need to take some of these bodies up with us," Branch said.

"What we want to do that for, Major?" a boy asked. "They're the bad guys."

"Yeah. And dead," said his buddy.

"Proof positive. It will begin our knowledge about them," Branch said. "We're fighting something we've never really seen. Our own nightmares." To date, the U.S. military had not acquired a single specimen. The Hezbollah in southern Lebanon claimed to have taken one alive, but no one believed it.

"I'm not touching those things. No, that's the devil, look at him."

They did look like devils, not men. Like animals steeped in cancers. A lot like me, thought Branch. It was hard for him to reconcile their humanlike forms with the coral horns that had bloomed from their heads. Some looked ready to claw their way back to life. He didn't blame his troops for being superstitious.

They all heard the radio at the same time. A scratchy sound issued from a pile of trophies, and Branch carefully rooted through the photographs and wristwatches and wedding and high school graduation rings, and pulled out the walkie-talkie. He clicked the transmit button three times. Three clicks answered.

"Someone's down there," said a Ranger.

"Yeah. But who?" That gave them pause. Human teeth crackled under their boots.

"Identify yourself, over," Branch spoke into the radio.

They waited. The voice that replied was American. "It's so dark in here," he groaned. "Don't leave us, man."

Branch placed the radio on the ground and backed away.

"Wait a minute," said the chain gunner. "That sounded like Scoop D. I know him. But we didn't get his location, Major."

"Quiet," Branch whispered to his troops. "They know we're here."
They fled.

Like worker ants, the soldiers scurried through the dark vein, each bearing before him one large white egg. Except these were not eggs, but balls of illumination, cast round and individual by each man's headlamp. Of the thirteen yesterday, there were just eight left. Like souls extinguished, those other men and lights were lost, their weapons fallen into enemy hands. One who remained, Sergeant Dornan, had broken ribs.

They had not stopped moving in fifty hours, except to lay fire into the pitch blackness behind them. Now, from the deepest point, came Branch's whispered command: "Make the line here." It passed, man by man, from the strongest to the stricken up the chain. The Rangers came to a halt in a forking passage. It was a place they had visited before.

The three stripes of fluorescent orange spray paint upon the Neolithic wall images were a welcome sight. They were blaze marks made by this same platoon, three to indicate their third camp on the way down. The exit was no more than three days up.

Sergeant Dornan's tiny moan of relief filled the limestone silence. The wounded man sat, cradled his weapon, laid his head against the stone. The rest of them went to work prepping their last stand.

Ambush was their only hope. Failing here, not one would reach the light of day, which had taken on all the King James connotations they had ever known. The glory of the light of day.

Two dead, three missing, and Dornan's broken ribs. And their chain gun, for chrissake. The General Electric gun with all its ammo. Snatched whole from their midst. You don't lose a weapon like that. Not only did it leave their platoon without suppressing fire, but someday some bravo like themselves was going to meet its solid wall of machine-gun fire made in America.

Now a large party was closing fast upon their rear. They could clearly hear the approach on their radio as *things,* whatever they were, passed by the remote mikes they'd placed on their retreat. Even amplified, the enemy moved softly, with serpentine ease, but quickly, too. Now and then one brushed against the walls. When they spoke, it was not in language any of these grunts knew.

One nineteen-year-old spec 4 hunkered by his ruck, fingers trembling. Branch went to him. "Don't listen, Washington," he said. "Don't try to understand."

The frightened kid looked up. And there was Frankenstein. *Their* Frankenstein. Branch knew the look.

"They're close."

"No distractions," Branch said.

"No sir."

"We're going to turn this thing around. We're going to own it."

"Yes sir."

"Now those claymores, son. How many in your ruck?"

"Three. Everything I got, Major."

"Can't ask for anything more than that, can we? One here, I'd say. One there. They'll do just fine."

"Yes sir."

"We stop them here." Branch raised his volume slightly for the other Rangers. "This is the line. Then it's over. Then we go home. We're almost out, boys. Get your sunscreen ready."

They liked that. Except for the major, they were all black. Sunscreen, right.

He moved up the line from man to man, spacing the mines, assigning their fields of fire, weaving his ambush. It was a spooky arena down here. Even if you could put aside these bursts of cave paintings and strange carved shapes and the sudden rockfall and flash floods and the mineralized skeletons and the booby traps. Even if you made this place at peace with itself, the space itself was horror. The tunnel walls compressed their universe into a tiny ball. The darkness threw it into free-fall. Close your eyes, and the mix could drive you mad.

Branch saw the weariness in them. They had been without radio contact with the surface for two weeks. Even with communications, they couldn't have called in artillery or reinforcements or evacuation. They were deep and alone and beset by bogeymen, some imagined, some not.

Branch paused beside the prehistoric bison painted on the wall. The animal had spears bristling from its shoulders, and its entrails were trampled underneath. It was dying, but so was the hunter who had killed it. The stick figure of a man was toppling over backward, gored by the long horns. Hunter and hunted, one in spirit. Branch set the last of his claymores at the feet of the bison and tilted it upon little wire tripod legs.

"They're getting closer, Major."

Branch looked around. It was the radioman, with a pair of headphones on. One last time he perused his ambush, saw in advance how the mines would flower, where the shot would fly true, where it would skip with terminal velocity, and which niches might escape their explosion of light and metal. "On my word," he said. "Not until."

"I know." They all knew. Three weeks in the field with Branch was enough time to learn his lessons.

The radioman cut his light. Around the fork, other soldiers doused their headlamps, too. Branch felt the blackness flood them over.

They had pre-sighted their rifles. Branch knew that in the terrible darkness, each soldier in his lonely post was mentally rehearsing the same left-to-right burst. Blind without light, they were about to be blinded with it. Their muzzle flash would ruin their low-light vision. The best thing was to pretend you were seeing and let your imagination take care of the target. Close your eyes. Wake up when it was over.

"Closer," whispered the radioman.

"I hear them now," Branch said. He heard the radioman gently switch off his radio and set aside his headphones and shoulder his weapon.

The pack advanced single file, of course. It was a tubular fork, man-wide. One, then two passed the bison. Branch tracked them in his head. They were shoeless, and the second slowed when the first did.

Can they smell us? Branch worried. Still he did not give the word. The game was nerves. You had to let them all come in before you shut the door. Part of him was ready with the claymores in case one of his soldiers startled and opened fire.

The creatures stank of body grease and rare minerals and animal heat and encrusted feces. Something bony scratched a wall. Branch sensed that the fork was filling. His sense had less to do with sound than with the feel of the air. However slight, the current was altered. Their mass respiration and the motion of bodies had created tiny eddies in the space. Twenty, Branch estimated. Maybe thirty. God's children, perhaps. *Mine now.*

"Now," he uttered. He twisted the detonator.

The claymores blossomed in a single colorless buck of shot. Pellets rattled against the stone, a fatal squall. Eight rifles joined, walking their bursts back and forth among the demon pack.

The bursts of muzzle flash seared between Branch's fingertips as he held them before his glasses. He rolled his eyes up into his skull to protect his vision. But the lightning streaks of auto-fire still reached in. Unblind and yet not seeing, he aimed by staccato stroke.

Confined by the corridors, the stink of powder filled their lungs. Branch's heart surged. He recognized one yell of the many yelling voices as his own. *God help me,* he prayed at his rifle stock.

In all the thunder of gunfire, Branch knew his rifle ran empty only when it quit hunching at the meat of his shoulder. He switched clips twice. On the third switch, he paused to gauge the killing.

To his right and left, his boys went on machining the darkness with their gunfire. Maybe he wanted to hear the enemy beg for mercy. Or howl for it. Instead what he heard was laughter. *Laughter?*

"Cease fire," he called.

They didn't. Blood up, they strafed, pulled dry, fresh-clipped, strafed again.

He shouted once more. One by one, his men stopped firing. The echoes pulsed off into the arterials.

The smell of blood and freshly chipped stone was pungent. You could practically spit it out of your mouth. That laughter went on, strange in its purity.

"Lights," said Branch, trying to keep the momentum theirs. "Reload. Be ready. Shoot first. Sort it out later. Total control, lads."

Their headlamps came alive. The corridor drifted in white smoke. Fresh blood spoiled the cave paintings. Closer in, the carnage was absolute. Bodies lay tangled in a foggy distant mass. The heat of their blood steamed, adding to the humidity of this place.

"Dead. Dead. Dead," said a troop. Someone giggled. It was that or weep. They had done this thing. A massacre of their very own.

Rifles twitching side to side, the spellbound Rangers closed in on their vaporous kill. At last, thought Branch, behold the eyes of dead angels. He finished refilling his spare clips, scanned the upper tunnel for latent intruders, then got to his feet.

Ever cautious, he circled the chamber, threw light down the left fork, then the right. Empty. Empty. They'd taken out the whole contingent. No stragglers. No blood trails leading away. One hundred percent payback.

They gathered in a semicircle at the edge of the dead. Over by the heaped kill, his men stood frozen, their lights casting downward in a collection pool. Branch shouldered in among them. Like them, he froze.

"No fucking way," a troop darkly muttered.

His neighbor refused the sight, too. "What's these doing here? What the fuck these doing here?"

Now Branch saw why his enemy had died so meekly.

"Christ," he breathed. There were two dozen or more upon the floor. They were nude and pathetic. And human. They were civilians. Unarmed.

Even mauled by the shrapnel and gunfire, you could see their awful gauntness. Their decorated skin stretched taut across meatless rib cages. The faces were a study in famine, cheeks parsed, eyes hollowed. Their feet and legs were ulcerated. The sinewy arms lay thin as a child's. Their loins were cased in old waste. Only one thing might explain them.

"Prisoners," said Spec 4 Washington.

"Prisoners? We didn't kill no prisoners."

"Yeah," said Washington. "They were prisoners."

"No," said Branch. "Slaves."

There was a silence.

"Slaves? There's no such thing. This is modern days, Major."

He showed them the brand marks, the stripes of paint, the ropes linking neck to neck.

"Makes 'em prisoners. Not slaves." The black kids acted like authorities on the subject.

"See those raw marks on their shoulders and backs?"

"So?"

"Abrasions. They've been humping loads. Prisoners, labor. Slaves."

Now they saw. Cued by Branch, they fanned out. This had just gotten very personal.

Spooked, high-stepping, the troops moved among the limbs and smoke. Most of the captives were male. Besides the neck-to-neck rope, many were shackled at the ankles with leather thongs. A few bore iron bracelets. Most had been ear-tagged, or their ears had been sliced or fringed the way cowboys jingle-bobbed cattle.

"Okay, they're slaves. Then where's their keepers?"

The consensus was immediate. "Gotta be a keeper. Gotta be a boss for the chain gang."

They went on looking through the pile, absorbing the atrocity, refusing the notion that slaves might keep themselves slaves. Body by body, though, they failed to find a demon master.

"I don't get it. No food. No water. How'd they keep alive?"

"We passed that stream."

"That's water, then. I didn't see no fish."

"Here we go, see here. Jerky." A Ranger held up a foot-long piece of dried meat. It looked more like a dried stick or shriveled leather. They found more pieces, mostly tucked into shackles or clutched in dead hands.

Branch examined a piece, bent it, smelled the meat. "I don't know what this could be," he said. Then he did. It was human.

It had been a caravan, they determined, though an empty one. No one could say what these captives had been hauling, but hauling they had been, and for long distances and recently. As Branch had noticed, the emaciated bodies had fresh sores on their shoulders and backs, the kind any soldier recognized, from a heavy load carried too long.

The Rangers were grave and angry as they made their way through the dead. At first glance, most of these people looked Central Asian. That explained the strange language. Afghanis, Branch guessed from the blue eyes. To his Lurps, though, these were brothers and sisters. That was enough for them to think about.

So the enemy had beasts of burden? All the way from Afghanistan? But this was sub-Bavaria. The twenty-first century. The implications were staggering. If the enemy was able to run strings of captives from so far away, it could also move armies . . . beneath humankind's feet. Screw the high ground. With this kind of low ground, the high ground was nothing but a blind man waiting to be robbed. Their enemy could surface anywhere, anytime, like prairie dogs or fire ants.

So what's new? Who was to say the children of hell hadn't been popping into mankind's midst from the start? Making slaves. Stealing souls. Raiding the garden of light. It was a concept too fundamental for Branch to accept easily.

"Here he is, I found him," the Spec 4 called near the back of the heap. Knee-deep in the torn mass, he had his rifle and light aimed at something on the ground. "Oh yeah, this one. Here's their boss man. I got the motherfucker."

Branch and the others hurried over. They clustered around the thing. Poked and kicked it a few times. "It's dead, all right," the medic said, wiping his fingers after hunting for a pulse. That made them more comfortable. They gathered closer.

"He's bigger than the rest."

"King of the apes."

Two arms, two legs: the body looked long and supple, lying tangled with its neighbors. It was soaked in gore, some its own, to judge by the wounds. They tried to figure it out, carefully, at gunpoint.

"That some kind of helmet?"

"He got snakes. Snakes growing out his head."

"Nah, look. That's dreadlocks. Full a' mud or something."

The long hair was indeed tangled and filthy, a Medusa's nest. Hard to tell if any of the muddy hair-tails on his head was bone or not, but he surely seemed demonic. And something in his aspect—the tattoos, the iron ring around his throat. This was taller than those furies he had seen in Bosnia, and immensely more powerful-looking than these other dead. And yet he was not what Branch had expected.

"Bag him," Branch said. "Let's get out of here."

The Spec 4 stayed as jumpy as a Thoroughbred. "I ought to shoot him again."

"What you want to do that for, Washington?"

"Just ought to. He's the one running the others. He's got to be evil."

"We've done enough," Branch said.

Muttering, Washington gave the creature a tight kick across the heart and turned away. Like an animal waking, the big rib cage drew a great breath, then another. Washington heard the respiration and dove among the bodies, shouting as he rolled.

"He's alive! He's come back to life."

"Hold your fire!" Branch yelled. "Don't shoot him."

"But they don't die, Major, look at it."

The creature was stirring among the bodies.

"Keep your heads on," Branch said. "Let's just walk in on this, one step at a time. Let's see what we see. I want him alive." They were getting closer to the surface. With luck, they might emerge with a live catch. If the going got complicated, they could always just cap their prisoner and keep running. He watched it in their light beams.

Somehow this one had missed the massed headshot woven into their ambush. The way Branch had set his claymores, everyone in the column was supposed to have taken it in the face. This one must have heard something the slaves hadn't, and managed to duck the lethal instant. With instincts this acute, the hadals could have avoided human detection for all of history.

"He's the boss, all right, he's the one," someone said. "Got to be. Who else?"

"Maybe," Branch said. They were fierce in their desire for retribution.

"You can tell. Look at him."

"Shoot him, Major," Washington asked. "He's dying anyhow."

All it would take was the word. Easier still, all it would take was his silence. Branch had only to turn his head, and it would be done.

"Dying?" said the thing, and opened its eyes and looked up at them. Branch alone did not jump away.

"Pleased to meet you," it said to him.

The lips peeled back upon white teeth. It was the grin of someone whose last sole possession was the grin itself.

And then he started laughing that laughter they had heard. The mirth was real. He was laughing at them. At himself. His suffering. His extremity. The universe. It was, Branch realized, the most audacious thing he'd ever seen.

"Shoot the thing," Sergeant Dornan said.

"Don't," Branch commanded.

"Ah, come on," said the creature. The nuance was pure Western. Wyoming or Montana. "Do," he said. And quit laughing.

In the silence, someone locked a load.

"No," said Branch. He knelt down. Monster to monster. Cradled the Medusa head in both hands. "Who are you?" he asked. "What's your name?" It was like taking confession.

"He's human? He's one of us?" a soldier murmured.

Branch brought the head closer, and saw a face younger than he'd thought. That was when they discovered something that had been inflicted on none of the other prisoners. Jutting from one vertebra at the base of his neck, an iron ring had been affixed to his spinal column. One yank on that ring, and he would be turned into a head atop a dead body. They were awed by that. Awed by the independence that needed such breaking.

"Who are you?" Branch said.

A tear streaked down from one eye. The man was remembering. He offered his name like surrendering his sword. He spoke so softly, Branch had to lean in.

"Ike," Branch told the others.

First you must conceive that
the earth . . . is everywhere
full of windy caves, and
bares in its bosom a
multitude of mirrors and
gulfs and beedling,
precipitous crags. You must
also picture that under the
earth's back, many buried
rivers with torrential force
roll their waters mingled
with sunken rocks.

—LUCRETIUS,
The Nature of the Universe (55 B.C.)

6

DIXIE CUPS

BENEATH ONTARIO
Three years later

The armored train car slowed to thirty kph as it exited the worm-
hole into a vast subterranean chamber containing Camp Helena. The
track arced along the canyon's ridgeline and descended to the chamber
floor. Inside the car, Ike roamed from end to end, stepping over
exhausted men and combat gear and the blood, tireless, shotgun ready.
Through the front window he saw the lights of man. Through the rear,

the strafed, fouled mouth to the depths fell behind. His heart felt pulled in two, into the future, into the past.

For seven dark weeks the platoon had been hunting Haddie, their horror, in a tunnel spoking off the deepest transit point. For four of those weeks they'd been living by the trigger. Corporate mercenaries were supposed to police the deep lines, but somehow the national militaries were back in the action. And taking the hits. Now they sat on brand-new cherry-red plastic seats in an automated train, with muddy field gear propped against their legs and a soldier dying on the floor.

"Home," one of the Rangers said to him.

"All yours," Ike replied. He added, "Lieutenant," and it was like passing the torch back to its original owner. They were back in the World now, and it was not his.

"Listen," Lieutenant Meadows said in a low voice, "what happened, maybe I don't have to report it all. A simple apology, in front of the men . . ."

"You're forgiving me?" Ike snorted. The tired men looked up. Meadows narrowed his eyes, and Ike pulled out a pair of glacier glasses with nearly black lenses. He hooked the wings on his ears and sealed the plastic against the wild tattooing that ran from forehead to cheekbones to chin.

He turned from the fool and squinted out the windows at the sprawling firebase below them. Helena's sky was a storm of man-made lights. From this vantage, the array of sabering lasers formed an angular canopy one mile wide. Strobes twinkled in the distance. His dreadlocks—slashed to shoulder length—helped shield his eyes, but not enough. So powerful in the lower darkness, Ike shied here in the ordinary.

In Ike's mind, these settlements were like shipwrecks in the Arctic with winter closing in, reminders that passage was swift and temporary. Down here, one did not belong in one place for long.

Every cavity, every tunnel, every hole along the chamber's soaring walls was saturated with light, and yet you could still see winged animals flitting about in the domelike "sky" extending a hundred meters above camp. Eventually the animals tired and spiraled down to rest or feed—and promptly got fried upon contact with the laser canopy. The work and living quarters in camp were protected from this bone and charcoal debris, as well as from the occasional fall of rocks, by steeply angled fifty-meter-tall rooftops with titanium-alloy superframes. The effect, from Ike's window, was a city of cathedrals inside a gigantic cave.

With conveyor belts spanning off into side holes and an elevator shaft and various ventilation chimneys jutting through the ceiling and a pall of petroleum smog, it looked like hell, and this was man's doing. A steady stream of food, supplies, and munitions churned down the belts. Ore churned back up.

The train car glided to a stop by the front gate and the Rangers unhorsed in a file, nearly bashful in the face of such safety, eager to get past the razor wire and lay into some cold beer and hot burgers and serious rack time. For his own part, a fresh platoon would do. Already Ike was ready to leave.

A tardy MASH team came rushing out with a stretcher, and as they passed through the gate, a panel of arc lights turned them as white as angels. Ike knelt beside his wounded man because it was the right thing to do, but also because he had to find his resolve again. The arc lights were arranged to saturate every thing that entered this way, and to kill whatever lights killed down here.

"We'll take him," the medics said, and Ike let go of the boy's hand. He was the last left in the car. One by one the Rangers had gone through the gate, turning into bursts of blinding radiance.

Ike faced the camp's gate, straining against the impulse to gallop back into the darkness. His urges were so raw they hurt like wounds. Few people understood. He had entered this Manichaean state: it was either darkness or light, and it seemed that all his gray scale was gone.

With a small cry, Ike cupped his hands to his eyes and leaped through the gate. The lights bleached him as immaculate as a rising soul. Like that, he made his way inside once again. It seemed more difficult each time.

Inside the razor wire and sandbags, Ike slowed his pulse and cleared his lungs. Following regulations, he shucked his clip, then dry-fired into the sandbox by the bunker, and showed his tags to the sentinels in their Kevlar armor.

CAMP HELENA, the sign read. HOME OF BLACKHORSE, 11TH ARMORED CAV, had been crossed out and replaced with WOLFHOUNDS, 27TH INFANTRY. In turn, that had been replaced with the names of a half-dozen more resident units. The one constant in the upper right corner was their altitude: Minus 16,232 Feet.

Hunched beneath his battle gear, Ike trudged past troops in their field "ninjas," the black camos issued for deep work, or off-duty in their Army sweats or gym trunks. Whether they were on their way to training or to the mess or the basketball cage or the PX to snarf some Zingers or Yoo-Hoos, one and all carried a rifle or pistol, ever mindful of the great massacre two years before.

From beneath his ropy hair, Ike cast side glances at the civilians starting to take over. Most were miners and construction workers, sprinkled with mercenaries and missionaries, the front wave of colonization. On his departure, two months ago, there had been just a few dozen of them. Now they seemed to outnumber the soldiers. Certainly they had the hauteur of a majority.

He heard bright laughter and was startled by the sight of three prostitutes in their late twenties. One had veritable volleyballs surgically affixed to her chest. She was even more surprised at the sight of Ike. The soda straw slid from her strawberry lips, and she stared in disbelief. Ike twisted his face from view and hurried on.

Helena was growing up. Fast. Like scores of other settlements around the world, it was evident not just in the explosion of new quadrants and settlers from the World. You could see it in the building materials. Concrete told the tale. Wood was a luxury down here, and sheet-metal production took time to develop and needed the right ores in close proximity to be cost-effective. Concrete, on the other hand, had only to be teased up from the ground and out from the walls. Cheap, quick to set, durable, concrete meant populism. It fed the frontier spirit.

Ike entered a quadrant that, two months ago, had been home to the local company of Rangers. But the obstacle course, rappeling tower, firing range, and primitive track had been usurped. A horde of squatters had invaded. Every manner of tent, lean-to, and gypsy shelter sprawled here. The din of voices, commerce, and dog-eat-dog music tracks hit him like a foul smell.

All that remained of unit headquarters were two office cubes taped together with duct tape. They had a ceiling made of cardboard. Ike parked his rucksack by the outer wall, then looked twice at the roughnecks and desperadoes wandering about, and brought it inside the doorway. A little foolishly, he knocked on the cardboard wall.

"Enter," a voice barked.

Branch was talking to a portable computer balanced on boxes of MREs, his helmet on one side, rifle on the other. "Elias," Ike greeted him.

Branch was not pleased to see him. His mask of scar tissue and cysts twisted into a snarl. "Ah, our prodigal son," he said, "we were just chatting about you."

He turned the laptop so that Ike could see the face on the little flat screen, and so the computer camera could see Ike. They were videolinked with Jump Lincoln, one of Branch's old Airborne buddies and presently the commanding officer in charge of Lieutenant Meadows.

"Have you lost your fucking mind?" Jump's image said to Ike. "I just got a field report slapped in front of me. It says you disobeyed a direct order. In front of my lieutenant's entire patrol. And that you drifted a weapon in his general direction in a threatening manner. Do you have anything at all to say, Crockett?"

Ike didn't play dumb, but he wasn't about to bend over, either. "The lieutenant writes a fast report," he commented. "We only pulled in twenty minutes ago."

"You threatened an officer?" Jump's bark was tinny over the computer speaker.

"Contradicted."

"In the field, in front of his men?"

Branch sat shaking his head in brotherly disgust.

"The man doesn't belong out there," Ike said. "He got one boy mangled on a wrong call. I saw no reason to keep feeding the lieutenant's version of reality. I finally got him to see reason."

Jump fumed as frames dropped on the computer. He finally said, "I thought it was a cleared region. This was supposed to be a shakedown cruise for Meadows. You're telling me you ran into hadals?"

"Booby traps," Ike said. "Old. Centuries old. I doubt there's been traffic through there since the Ice Age." He didn't bother addressing the issue of being sent to baby-sit a shake-and-bake ROTC student.

The computer image turned to a wall map. "Where have they all gone?" Jump wondered. "We haven't made physical contact with the enemy in months."

"Don't worry," Ike said. "They're down there somewhere."

"I'm not so sure. Some days I think they really are on the run. Or they've died off from disease or something."

Branch grabbed at the interlude. "It looks like a stalemate to me," he said to Jump. "My clown cancels out yours. I think we're agreed." The two majors knew Meadows was a disaster. And it was certain they'd never send him out with Ike again. That was good enough for Ike.

"Fuck it, then," Jump said. "I'm going to bury the report. This time."

Branch went on glaring at Ike. "I don't know, Jump," he said. "Maybe we ought to quit coddling him."

"Elias, I know he's a special project of yours," Jump said. "But I've told you before, don't get attached. There's a reason we treat the Dixie cups with such caution. I'm telling ya, they're heartbreakers."

"Thanks for the burial. I owe you." Branch punched the computer's off button and turned to Ike. "Nice work," he said. "Tell me, are you trying to hang yourself?"

If it was contrition he wanted, Ike offered none. Ike helped himself to some boxes and made a seat. "Dixie cups," he said. "That's a new one. More Army slang?"

"Spook, if you must know. It means 'use once, throw away.' The CIA used it to refer to their indigenous guerrilla ops. Now it includes the cowboys like you that we haul in from the deep and use for scout work."

Ike said, "It kind of grows on ya."

Branch's mood stayed foul. "Your sense of timing is unbelievable. Congress is closing the base on us. Selling it. To another pack of corporate hyenas. Every time you turn around, the government's caving in to another cartel. We do the dirty work, then the multinationals move in with their commercial militias and land developers and mining equipment. We bleed, they profit. I've been given three weeks to transfer the entire unit to temporary quarters two thousand feet below Camp Alison. I don't have a lot of time, Ike. I'm busting nuts to keep you alive down here. And you go and threaten an officer in the field?"

Ike raised two fingers and spread them. "Peace, dad."

Branch exhaled. He glanced around his tiny office space in disgust. Country-western loped in mega-decibels nearby. "Look at us," Branch said. "Pitiful. We bleed. The corporations profit. Where's the honor in it?"

"Honor?"

"Don't hand me that. Yeah, the honor. Not the money. Not the power. Not the possession. Just the bottom line for being true to the code. This." He pointed at his heart.

"Maybe you believe too much," Ike suggested.

"And you don't?"

"I'm not a lifer. You are."

"You're not anything," Branch said, and his shoulders sagged. "They've gone ahead with your court-martial up top. *In absentia*. While you were still in the field. One AWOL turns into a desertion-under-fire charge."

Ike was not particularly devastated. "So now I appeal."

"This was the appeal."

Ike didn't show the slightest distress.

"There's a ray of hope, Ike. You've been ordered to go up for the sentencing. I talked with JAG, and they think you can throw yourself on the mercy of the court. I've pulled all the strings I can up there. I told them what you did behind the lines. Some important people have promised to put a good word in for you. No promises, but it sounds to me like the court will show leniency. They by God ought to."

"That's my ray of hope?"

Branch didn't rise to it. "You can do worse, you know."

They'd argued this one into knots. Ike didn't retort. The Army had been less a family than a holding pen. It wasn't the Army that had broken his slavery and dragged him back to his own humanity and seen to it that his wounds were cleaned and shackles cut. It was Branch. Ike would never forget that.

"You could try anyway," Branch said.

"I don't need it," Ike softly replied. "I don't need ever to go up again."

"It's a dangerous place down here."

"It's worse up there."

"You can't be alone and survive."

"I can always join some outfit."

"What are you talking about? You're facing a dishonorable discharge, with possible brig time. You'll be an untouchable."

"There's other action."

"A soldier of fortune?" Branch looked sick. "You?"

Ike dropped it.

Both men fell silent. Finally Branch got it out, barely a whisper. "For me," he swallowed.

If it wasn't so obviously hard for him to have said it, Ike would have refused. He would have set his rifle in one corner and shoved his ruck into the room and stripped his encrusted ninjas off and walked naked from the Rangers and their Army forever. But Branch had just done what Branch never did. And because this man who had saved his life and nurtured him back to sanity and been like a father to him had laid his pride in the dirt before Ike's feet, Ike did what he had sworn never to do again. He submitted.

"So where do I go?" he asked.

Both of them tried to ignore Branch's happiness.

"You won't regret it," Branch promised.

"Sounds like a hanging," Ike cracked without a smile.

WASHINGTON, D.C.

Midway up the escalator as steep as an Aztec staircase, Ike could take no more. It was not just the unbearable light. His journey from the earth's bowels had become a gruesome siege. His senses were in havoc. The world seemed inside out.

Now as the stainless-steel escalator rose to ground zero and the howl of traffic poured down, Ike clung to the rubber handrail. At the top, he was belched onto a city sidewalk. The crowd jostled and drove him farther away from the Metro entrance. Ike was carried by noises and accidental nudges into the middle of Independence Avenue.

Ike had known vertigo in his day, but never anything like this. The sky plummeted overhead. The boulevard spilled every which way. Nauseated, he staggered into a blare of car horns. He fought the terrifying sense of open space. Through a tiny aperture of tunnel vision, he struggled to a wall bathed in sunlight.

"Get off, you," a Hindi accent scolded him. Then the shopkeeper saw his face and retreated back inside.

Ike laid his cheek against the brick. "Eighteenth and C streets," he begged a passerby. It was a woman in heels. Her staccato abruptly hurried in a wide arc around him. Ike forced himself away from the wall.

Across the street, he began the awful climb up a hillock girdled by American flags at full mast. He lifted his head to find the Washington Monument gutting the sheer blue belly of day. It was the cherry blossom season, that was evident. He could barely breathe for the pollen.

A flock of clouds drifted overhead, gave mercy, then vanished. The sunlight was terrible. He moved on, flesh hot. Tulips shattered his vision with their musket fire of brilliant colors. The gym bag in his hand—his sole luggage—grew heavy. He was panting for air, and that stung his old pride, a Himalayan mountaineer in such a state at sea level.

Eyes squeezed tight behind his dark glacier glasses, Ike retreated to an alley with shade. At last the sun sank. His nausea lifted. He could bare his eyes. He roamed the darkest parts of the city by moonlight, urgent as a fugitive.

No prowling for him. He raced pell-mell. This was his first night aboveground since he was snowbound in Tibet long ago. No time to eat. Sleep could wait. There was everything to see.

Like a tourist with the thighs of an Olympic sprinter, he plunged tirelessly. There were ghettos and Parisian boulevards and bright restaurant districts and august gated embassies. Those he dodged, holding to the emptier places.

The night was gorgeous. Even dimmed by urban lights, the stars sprayed overhead. He breathed the brackish tidal air. Trees were budding.

It was April, all right. And yet, as he hurtled across the grass and pavement and leaped over fences and dodged cars, Ike felt only November in his soul. The night's very mercy condemned him. He was not long for this world, he knew. And so he memorized the moon and the marshes and the ganged oaks and the braid of currents on the slow Potomac.

He did not mean to, but he came upon the National Cathedral atop a lawned hill. It was like falling into the Dark Ages. An entrenched mob of thousands of faithful occupied the grounds, their squalid tent city unlit except for candles or lanterns. Ike hesitated, then went forward. It was obvious that families and whole congregations had come here and were living side by side with the poor and insane and sick and addicted.

Flying buttresses dangled huge Crusade-like banners with a red cross, and the twin Gothic towers flickered in the cast of great bonfires. There wasn't a cop in sight. It was as if the cathedral had been relinquished to the true believers. Peddlers hawked crucifixes, New Age angels, blue-green algae pills, Native American jewelry, animal parts, bullets sprinkled with holy water, and round-trip air travel to Jerusalem on charter jets.

A militia was signing up volunteers—"muscular Christians" for guerrilla strikes on hell. The muster table was piled with literature and *Soldier of Fortune* magazines, and manned by frauds with Gold's Gym biceps and expensive guns. A cheap training video showed Sunday-school flames and actors made up as damned souls pleading for help.

Right beside the TV stood a woman missing one arm and both her breasts, naked to the waist, daring them with her scars like glory. Her accent was Pentecostal, maybe Louisiana, and in her one hand she held a poisonous snake. "I was a captive of the devils," she was testifying. "But I was rescued. Only me, though, not my poor children, nor all the other good Christians down deeper in the House. Good Christians in need of righteous salvation. Go down, you brothers with strong arms. Bring up the weak. Carry the light of the Lord into that Stygian dark. Take the spirit of Jesus, and of the Father, and the Holy Spirit. . . ."

Ike backed away. How much was that snake woman being paid to show her flesh and proselytize and recruit these gullible men? Her wounds looked suspiciously like surgery scars, possibly from a double mastectomy. Regardless, she did not speak like a former captive. She was too certain of herself.

To be sure, there were human captives among the hadals. But they were not necessarily in need of rescue. The ones Ike had seen, the ones who had survived for any length of time among the hadals, tended to sound like a sum of zero. But once you'd been there, limbo could mean a kind of asylum from your own responsibilities. It was heresy to speak aloud, especially among liberty-preaching patriots like these tonight, but Ike himself had felt the forbidden rapture of losing himself to another creature's authority.

Ike made his way up the steps dense with humanity and entered the medieval transept. There were touches of the twentieth century: the floor was inlaid with state seals, and one stained-glass window bore the image of astronauts on the moon. Otherwise he might have been passing through the crest of a Black Plague. The air was filled with smoke and incense and the smell of unwashed bodies and rotten fruit, and the stone walls echoed with prayers. Ike heard the Confiteor blend with the Kaddish. Appeals to Allah mixed with Appalachian hymns. Preachers railed about the Second Coming, the Age of Aquarius, the One True God, angels. The petition was general. The millennium wasn't turning out to be much fun, it seemed.

Before dawn, mindful of his debt to Branch, he returned to 18th and C streets, Northwest, where he had been told to report. He sat at one end of the granite steps and waited for nine o'clock. Despite his premonitions, Ike told himself there could be no turning back. His honor had come down to a matter of the mercy of strangers.

The sun arrived slowly, advancing down the canyon of office buildings like an imperial march. Ike watched his footprints melt in the lawn's frost. His heart sank at the erasure.

An overwhelming sadness swept him, a sense of deep betrayal. What right did he have to come back into the World? What right did the World have to come back into him? Suddenly his being here, trying to explain himself to strangers, seemed like a terrible indiscretion. Why give himself away? What if they judged him guilty?

For an instant, in his mind a small lifetime, he was returned to his captivity. It had no single image. A great howl. The feel of a mortally exhausted man's bones hard against his shoulder. The odor of minerals. And chains . . . like the edge of music, never quite in rhythm, never quite song. Would they do that to him again? Run, he thought.

"I didn't think you'd be here," a voice spoke to him. "I thought they would need to hunt you down."

Ike glanced up. A very wide man, perhaps fifty years old, was standing on the sidewalk in front of him. Despite the neat jeans and a designer parka, his carriage said military. Ike squinted left and right, but they were alone. "You're the lawyer?" he asked.

"Lawyer?"

Ike was confused. Did the man know him or not? "For the court-martial. I don't know what you're called. My advocate?"

The man nodded, understanding now. "Sure, you might call me that."

Ike stood. "Let's get it over with, then," he said. He was full of dread, but saw no alternative to what was in motion.

The man seemed bemused. "Haven't you noticed the empty streets? There's no one around. The buildings are all closed. It's Sunday."

"Then what are we doing here?" he asked. It sounded foolish to him. Lost.

"Taking care of business."

Ike coiled inside himself. Something wasn't right. Branch had told him to report here, at this time. "You're not my lawyer."

"My name is Sandwell."

Ike could not fill the man's pause with any recognition. When the man realized Ike had never heard of him, he smiled with something like sympathy.

"I commanded your friend Branch for a time," Sandwell said. "It was in Bosnia, before his accident, before he changed. He was a decent man." He added, "I doubt that changed."

Ike agreed. Some things did not change.

"I heard about your troubles," Sandwell said. "I've read your file. You've served us well over the past three years. Everyone sings your praises. Tracker. Scout. Hunter-killer. Once Branch got you tamed, we've made good use of you. And you've made good use of us, gotten your pound of flesh back from Haddie, haven't you?"

Ike waited. Sandwell's "us" gave an impression that he was still active with the military. But something about him—not his country laird's clothes, but something in his manner—suggested he had other meat on his plate, too.

Ike's silences were starting to annoy Sandwell. Ike could tell, because the next question was meant to put him on the spot. "You were piloting slaves when Branch found you. Isn't that correct? You were a kapo. A warder. You were one of them."

"Whatever you want to call it," Ike said. It was like slapping a rock to accuse him of his past.

"Your answer matters. Did you cross over to the hadals, or didn't you?"

Sandwell was wrong. It didn't matter what Ike said. In his experience, people made their own judgments, regardless of the truth, even when the truth was clear.

"This is why people can never trust you recaptures," Sandwell said. "I've read enough psych evaluations. You're like twilight animals. You live between worlds, between light and darkness. No right or wrong. Mildly psychotic at best. Under ordinary circumstances, it would have been folly for the military to rely on people like you in the field."

Ike knew the fear and contempt. Precious few humans had been repossessed from hadal captivity, and most went straight into padded cells. A few dozen had been rehabbed and put to work, mostly as seeing-eye dogs for miners and religious colonies.

"I don't like you, is my point," Sandwell continued. "But I don't believe you went AWOL eighteen months ago. I read Branch's report of the siege at Albuquerque 10. I believe you went behind enemy lines. But it wasn't some grand act, to save your comrades in the camp. It was to kill the ones that did this to you." Sandwell gestured at the markings and scars on Ike's face and hands. "Hate makes sense to me."

Since Sandwell appeared so satisfied, Ike did not contradict him. It was the automatic assumption that he led soldiers against his former captor for the revenge. Ike had quit trying to explain that to him the Army was a captor, too. Hate didn't enter the equation at all. It couldn't, or he would have destroyed himself long ago. Curiosity, that was his fire.

Unawares, Ike had edged from the creep of sunbeams. He saw Sandwell looking. Ike caught himself, stopped.

"You don't belong up here." Sandwell smiled. "I think you know that."

This guy was a regular Welcome Wagon. "I'll leave the minute they let me. I came to clear my name. Then it's back to work."

"You sound like Branch. But it's not that simple, Ike. This is a hanging court. The hadal threat is over. They're gone."

"Don't be so sure."

"Everything is perception. People want the dragon to be slain. What that means is we don't have any more need for the misfits and rebels. We don't need the trouble and embarrassment and worry. You scare us. You look like them. We don't want the reminder. A year or two ago, the court would have considered your talents and value in the field. These days they want a tight ship. Discipline. Order."

Sandwell kept the fascism casual. "In short, you're dead. Don't take it personally. Yours isn't the only court-martial. The armies are about to purge the ranks of all the rawness and unpleasantry. You repos are finished. The scouts and guerrillas go. It happens at the end of every war. Spring cleaning."

Dixie cups. Branch's words echoed. He must have known about, or sensed, this coming purge. These were simple truths. But Ike was not ready to hear them. He felt hurt, and it was a revelation that he could feel anything at all.

"Branch talked you into throwing yourself on the mercy of the court," Sandwell stated.

"What else did he tell you?" Ike felt as weightless as a dead leaf.

"Branch? We haven't spoken since Bosnia. I arranged this little discussion through one of my aides. Branch thinks you're meeting an attorney who's a friend of a friend. A fixer."

Why the duplicity? Ike wondered.

"It takes no great stretch of the imagination," Sandwell went on. "Why else would you put yourself through this, if not for mercy? As I've said, it's beyond that. They've already decided your case."

His tone—not derisive but unsentimental—told Ike there was no hope. He didn't waste time asking the verdict. He simply asked what the punishment was.

"Twelve years," Sandwell said. "Brig time. Leavenworth."

Ike felt the sky coming to pieces overhead. Don't think, he warned himself. Don't feel. But the sun rose and strangled him with his own shadow. His dark image lay broken on the steps beneath him.

He was aware of Sandwell watching him patiently. "You came here to see me bleed?" he ventured.

"I came to give you a chance." Sandwell handed him a business card. It bore the name Montgomery Shoat. There was no title or address. "Call this man. He has work for you."

"What kind of work?"

"Mr. Shoat can tell you himself. The important thing is that it will take you deeper than the reach of any law. There are zones where extradition doesn't exist. They won't be able to touch you, down that far. But you need to act immediately."

"You work for him?" Ike asked. Slow this thing down, he was telling himself. Find its footprints, backtrack a bit, get some origin. Sandwell gave nothing.

"I was asked to find someone with certain qualifications. It was pure luck to find you in such delicate straits." That was information of a kind. It told him that Sandwell and Shoat were up to something illicit or oblique, or maybe just unhealthy, but something that needed the anonymity of a Sunday morning for its introduction.

"You've kept this from Branch," Ike said. He didn't like that. It wasn't an issue of having Branch's permission, but of a promise. Running away would seal the Army out of his life forever.

Sandwell was unapologetic. "You need to be careful," he said. "If you decide to do this, they'll mount a search for you. And the first people they'll interrogate are the ones closest to you. My advice: Don't compromise them. Don't call Branch. He's got enough problems."

"I should just disappear?"

Sandwell smiled. "You never really existed anyway," he said.

There is nothing more
powerful than this
attraction toward an abyss.

—JULES VERNE,
Journey to the Center of the Earth

7
THE MISSION

Ali entered in sandals and a sundress, as if they were a magic spell to hold back the winter. The guard ticked her name off a list and complained she was early and without her party, but passed her through the station. He gave some rapid-fire directions. Then she was alone, with the Metropolitan Museum of Art to herself.

It was like being the last person on earth. Ali paused by a small Picasso. A vast Bierstadt Yellowstone. Then she came to a banner for the main exhibit declaring THE HARVEST OF HELL. The subtitle read "Twice Reaped Art." Devoted to artifacts of the underworld, most of the exhibit's objects had been brought back to the surface by GIs and miners. All but a few had been stolen from humans and brought into the subplanet to begin with, thus "twice reaped."

Ali had come well ahead of her engagement with January, in part to enjoy the building, but mostly to see for herself what *Homo hadalis* was capable of. Or, in this case, what he was not capable of. The show's gist was this: *H. hadalis* was a man-sized packrat. The creatures of the subplanet had been plundering human inventions for eons. From ancient pottery to plastic Coke bottles, from voodoo fetishes to Han Dynasty ceramic tigers, to an Archimedean-type water screw, to a sculpture by Michelangelo long thought destroyed.

Among the artifacts made *by* humans were several made *from* them. She came to the notorious "Beachball" made of different-colored human skins. No one knew its purpose, but the sac—once inflated, now fossilized as a perfect sphere—was especially offensive to people because it so coldly exploited the races as mere fabric.

By far the most intriguing artifact was a chunk of rock that had been pried from some subterranean wall. It was inscribed with mysterious hieroglyphics that verged on calligraphy. Obviously, because it was included in this "twice reaped" display, the curators had judged it to be human graffiti that had been taken down into the abyss. But as Ali stood pondering the slab of rock, she wondered. It did not look like any writing she had ever seen.

A voice found her. "There you are, child."

"Rebecca?" she said, and turned.

The woman facing her was like a stranger. January had always been invincible, an Amazon with that ample embrace and taut black skin. This person looked deflated, suddenly old. With one hand locked upon her cane, the senator could only open one arm to her. Ali swiftly bent to hug her, and felt the ribs in her back.

"Oh, child," January whispered happily, and Ali laid her cheek against the hair cropped short and gone white. She breathed in the smell of her.

"The guards told us you've been here an hour," January said, then spoke to a tall man who had trailed behind her. "Isn't it what I predicted, Thomas? Always charging out ahead of the cavalry, ever since she was a child. It's not for nothing they called her Mustang Ali. She was a legend in Kerr County. And you see how beautiful she is?"

"Rebecca," Ali rebuked her. January was the most modest woman on earth, yet the worst braggart. Childless herself, she had adopted several orphans over the years, and they had all learned to endure these explosions of pride.

"Oblivious, I'm telling you," January went on. "Never looked in a mirror. And when she entered the convent, it was a dark day. Strong Texas boys, she had them weeping like widows under a Goliad moon." And January, too, Ali recalled of that day. She had wept while she drove, apologizing again and again for not understanding Ali's calling. The truth was that Ali no longer understood it herself.

Thomas stayed out of it. For the moment, this was the reunion of two women, and he kept himself incidental. Ali acquired him with a single glance. He was a tall, rangy man in his late sixties, with a scholar's eyes and yet a hard-beaten frame. He was unfamiliar to Ali, and though he was not wearing a collar, she knew he was a Jesuit: she had a sense for them. Perhaps it was their shared oddity.

"You must forgive me, Ali," January said. "I told you this would be a private meeting. But I've brought some friends. Of necessity."

Now Ali saw two more people circulating through the far end of the exhibit, a slight blind man attended by a large younger man. Several more elderly people entered a far door.

"Blame me, this was my doing." Thomas offered his hand. Apparently, Ali's reunion was at an end. She had thought the entire day belonged to her and January, but there was business looming. "I've wanted to meet you, more than you know. Especially now, before you started out for the Arabian sands."

"Your sabbatical," the senator said. "I didn't think you'd mind my telling."

"Saudi Arabia," Thomas added. "Not the most comfortable place for a young woman these days. The *sharia* is in full enforcement since the fundamentalists took over and slaughtered the royal family. I don't envy you, a full year draped in *abaya*."

"I'm not thrilled with the prospect of being dressed like a nun," Ali agreed.

January laughed. "I'll never understand you," she said to Ali. "They give you a year off, and back you go to your deserts."

"But I know the feeling," Thomas said. "You must be eager to see the glyphs." Ali grew more wary. This was not something she had written or told to January. To January, Thomas explained, "The southern regions near Yemen are especially rich. Proto-Semitic pictograms from the Saudis' *ahl al-jahiliya*, their Age of Ignorance."

Ali shrugged as if it were common enough knowledge, but her radar was up now. The Jesuit knew things about her. What more? Could he know of her other reason for this year away, the step back she had taken from her final vows? It was a hesitation the order took seriously, and the desert was as much a stage for her faith as for her science. She wondered if the mother superior had sent this man covertly to guide her, then dismissed the thought. They would never dare. It was her choice to make, not some Jesuit's.

Thomas seemed to read her misgivings. "You see, I've followed your career," he said. "I've dabbled in the anthropology of linguistics myself. Your work on Neolithic inscriptions and mother languages is—how to put this?—elegant beyond your years."

He was being careful not to flatter her, which was wise. She was not easily courted.

"I've read everything I could find by you," he said. "Daring stuff, especially for an American. Most of the protolanguage work is being done by Russian Jews in Israel. Eccentrics with nowhere to go. But you're young and have opportunities everywhere, yet still you choose this radical inquiry. The beginning of language."

"Why do people see it as so radical?" Ali asked. He had spoken to her heart. "By finding our way back to the first words, we reach back to our own genesis. It takes us that much closer to the voice of God."

There, she thought. In all its naïveté. The core of her search, mind and soul. Thomas seemed deeply satisfied. Not that she needed to satisfy him.

"Tell me, as a professional," he asked, "what do you make of this exhibit?"

She was being tested, and January was in on it. Ali went along with them for the moment, cautiously. "I'm a little surprised," she ventured, "by their taste for sacred relics." She pointed at strands of prayer beads originally from Tibet, China, Sierra Leone, Peru, Byzantium, Viking Denmark, and Palestine. Next to them was a display case with crucifixes and calligrams and chalices made of gold and silver. "Who would think they'd collect such exquisitely delicate work? This is more what I would expect."

She passed a suit of twelfth-century Mongolian armor, pierced and still stained with blood. Elsewhere there were brutally used weapons and armor, and devices of torture . . . though the display literature reminded viewers that the devices had been human to begin with.

They stopped in front of a blow-up of the famous photo of a hadal about to destroy an early reconnaissance robot with a club. It represented modern mankind's first public contact with "them," one of those events people remember ever after by where they were standing or what they were doing at the moment. The creature looked berserk and demonic, with hornlike growths on his albino skull.

"The pity is," Ali said, "we may never know who the hadals really were before it's too late."

"It may already be too late," January offered.

"I don't believe that," Ali said.

Thomas and January traded a look. He made up his mind. "I wonder if we might discuss a certain matter with you," he said. Immediately, Ali knew this was the purpose of her entire visit to New York, which January had arranged and paid for.

"We belong to a society," January now started to explain. "Thomas has been collecting us from around the world for years. We call ourselves the Beowulf Circle. It is quite informal, and our meetings are infrequent. We come together at various places to share our revelations with one another and to—"

Before she could say more, a guard barked, "Put that down."

There was a sudden commotion as guards rushed down. At the center of their alarm were two of those people who had come in behind Thomas and January. It was the younger man with long hair. He was hefting an iron sword from one of the displays.

"It is for me," his blind companion apologized, and accepted the heavy sword into his open palms. "I asked my companion, Santos—"

"It's all right, gentlemen," January told the guards. "Dr. de l'Orme is a renowned specialist."

"*Bernard* de l'Orme?" Ali whispered. He had parted jungles and rivers to uncover sites throughout Asia. Reading about him, she had always thought of him as a physical giant.

Unconcerned, de l'Orme went on touching the early Saxon blade and leather-wrapped handle, seeing it with his fingertips. He smelled the leather, licked the iron.

"Marvelous," he pronounced.

"What are you doing?" January asked him.

"Remembering a story," he answered. "An Argentine poet once told of two gauchos who entered a deadly knife fight because the knife itself compelled them."

The blind man held up the ancient sword used by man and his demon both. "I was just wondering about the memory of iron," he said.

"My friends," Thomas welcomed his sleuths, "we should begin."

Ali watched them materialize from the darkened library stacks. Suddenly, Ali felt only half dressed. In Vatican City, winter was still scourging the brick streets with sleet. By contrast, her little Christmas holiday in New York City was feeling downright Roman, as balmy as late summer. But her sundress served to emphasize these old people's fragility, for they were cold despite the warmth outside. Some wore fashionable ski parkas, while others shivered in layers of wool or tweed.

They gathered around a table made of English oak, cut and polished before the era of great cathedrals. It had survived wars and terrors, kings, popes, and bourgeoisie, and even researchers. The walls were massed with nautical charts drawn before America was a word.

Here was the set of gleaming instruments Captain Bligh had used to guide his castaways back to civilization. A glass case held a stick-and-shell map used by Micronesian fishermen to follow ocean currents between islands. In the corner stood the complicated Ptolemaic astrolabe that had been used in Galileo's inquisition. Columbus's map of the New World occupied a corner of one wall, raw, exotic; painted upon a sheepskin, its legs used to indicate the cardinal directions.

There was also a large blow-up of Bud Parsifal's famous snapshot from the moon showing the great blue pearl in space. Rather immodestly, the former astronaut took a position immediately beneath his photo, and Ali recognized him. January stayed by her side, now and then whispering names, and Ali was grateful for her presence.

As they seated themselves, the door opened and a final addition limped in. Ali at first thought he was a hadal. He had melted plastic for skin, it seemed. Darkened ski goggles were strapped to his misshapen head, sealing out the room light. The sight startled her, and she recoiled, never having seen a hadal, alive or dead. He took the chair next to her, and she could hear him panting heavily.

"I didn't think you were going to make it," January said to him across Ali.

"A little trouble with my stomach," he replied. "The water, maybe. It always takes me a few weeks to adjust."

He was human, Ali realized. His shortness of breath was a common symptom of veterans freshly returning to higher altitudes. She'd never seen one so physically marauded by the depths.

"Ali, meet Major Branch. He's something of a secret. He's with the Army, sort of an informal liaison with us. An old friend. I found him in a military hospital years ago."

"Sometimes I think you should have left me there," he bantered, and offered his hand to Ali. "Elias will do." He grimaced at her, then she saw it was a smile—without lips. The hand was like a rock. Despite the bull-like muscles, it was impossible to tell his age. Fire and wounds had erased the normal landmarks.

Besides Thomas and January, Ali counted eleven of them, including de l'Orme's protégé, Santos. Except for her and Santos and this character beside her, they were old. All told, they combined almost seven hundred years of life experience and genius—not to mention a working memory of all recorded history. They were venerable, if somewhat forgotten. Most had left the universities or companies or governments where they had distinguished themselves. Their awards and reputations were no longer useful. Nowadays they lived lives of the mind, helped along by their daily medicines. Their bones were brittle.

The Beowulf Circle was a strange gang of paladins. Ali surveyed the chilly bunch, placing faces, remembering names. With little overlap, they represented more disciplines than most universities had colleges to contain.

Again, Ali wished for something besides this sundress. It hung upon her like an albatross. Her long hair tickled her spine. She could feel her body beneath the cloth.

"You might have told us you would be taking us from our families," grumbled a man whose face Ali knew from old *Time* magazines. Desmond Lynch, the medievalist and peacenik. He had earned a Nobel Prize for his 1952 biography of Duns Scotus, the thirteenth-century philosopher, then had used the prize as a bully pulpit to condemn everything from the McCarthy witch-hunts to the Bomb and, later, the war in Vietnam. Ancient history. "So far from home," he said. "Into such weather. And at Christmas!"

Thomas smiled at him. "Is it so bad?"

Lynch made himself look deadly behind his briarwood cane. "Don't be taking us for granted," he warned.

"You have my oath on that," said Thomas more soberly. "I'm old enough not to take one heartbeat for granted."

They were listening, all of them. Thomas moved from face to face around the table. "If the moment were not so critical," he said, "I would never trespass upon you with a mission so dangerous. But it is. And I must. And so we are here."

"But here?" a tiny woman asked from a child's wheelchair. "And in this season? It does seem so . . . un-Christian of you, Father."

Vera Wallach, Ali recalled. The New Zealand physician. She had single-handedly defeated the Church and banana republicans in Nicaragua, introducing birth control during the Sandinista revolution. She had faced bayonets and crucifixes, and still managed to bring her sacrament to the poor: condoms.

"Yes," growled a thin man. "The hour is godforsaken. Why now?" He was Hoaks, the mathematician. Ali had noticed him toying with a map that inverted the continental shelves and gave a view of the surface from inside the globe.

"But it's always this way," said January, countering the ill humor. "It's Thomas's way of imposing his mysteries on us."

"It could be worse," commented Rau, the untouchable, another Nobel winner. Born to the lowest caste in Uttar Pradesh, he had still managed the climb to India's lower house of Parliament. There he had served as his party's speaker for many years. Later, Ali would learn, Rau had been on the verge of renouncing the world, shedding his clothes and name, and throwing himself onto the pathway of saddhus living day to day by gifts of rice.

Thomas gave them several more minutes to greet one another and curse him. In whispers to Ali, January went on describing various characters. There was the Alexandrian, Mustafah, of a Coptic family that extended on his mother's side to Caesars. Though Christian, he was an expert on *sharia*, or Islamic law, one of the few to ever be able to explain it to westerners. Saddled with emphysema, he could speak only in short bursts.

Across the table sat an industrialist named Foley, who had made several side fortunes, one in penicillin during the Korean War, another in the blood and plasma industry, before going on to "dabble" in civil rights and underwrite numerous martyrs. He was arguing with the astronaut Bud Parsifal. Ali recollected his tale: after teeing off on the moon, Parsifal had gone searching for Noah's Ark upon Mount Ararat, discovered geological evidence of the Red Sea parting, and pursued a legion of other crazy riddles. Clearly the Beowulf Circle was a crew of misfits and anarchists.

Finally they had gone full circle. It was Thomas's turn. "I am lucky to have such friends," he said to her. Ali was astonished. The others were listening, but his words were for her. "Such souls. Over many years, during my travels, I've enjoyed their company. Each of them has labored to bend mankind away from its most destructive ideas. Their reward"—he wryly smiled—"has been this calling."

He used that word, *calling*. It was no coincidence. Somehow he had learned that this nun was faltering in her vows. The calling had not faded, but changed.

"We've lived long enough to recognize that evil is real, and not accidental," Thomas went on. "And over the years we've attempted to address it. We've done this by supporting one another, and by joining our various powers and observations. It's that simple."

It sounded too simple. In their spare time, these old people fought evil.

"Our greatest weapon has always been scholarship," Thomas added.

"You're an academic society, then," Ali stated.

"Oh, more like a round table of knights," Thomas said. There were a few smiles. "I wish to find Satan, you see." His eyes met Ali's, and she saw that he was serious. They all were.

Ali couldn't help herself. "The Devil?" This group of Nobel laureates and scholars had made evil incarnate into a game of hide-and-seek.

"The Devil," Mustafah, the Egyptian, wheezed. "That old wives' tale."

"Satan," January corrected, for Ali's benefit.

They were all concentrating on Ali now. No one questioned her presence among them, which suggested she was already well known to them. Now Thomas's recitation of her Saudi plans and the pre-Islamic glyphs and her protolanguage quest took on force. These people had been studying her. She was getting head-hunted. What was going on here? Why had January brought her into this? "Satan?" she said.

"Absolutely," January affirmed. "We're dedicated to the idea. The reality."

"Which reality would that be?" Ali asked. "The nightmarish demon of malnourished, sleep-deprived monks? Or the heroic rebel of Milton?"

"Hush," said January. "We may be old, but we're not silly. Satan is a catchall term. It gives identity to our theory of a centralized leadership. Call him what you want, a maximum leader, a *caudillo*. A Genghis Khan or Sitting Bull. Or a council of wise men, or warlords. The concept is sound. Logical."

Ali retreated into silence.

"It's a word, no more, a name," Thomas said to her. "The term *Satan* signifies a historical character. A missing link between our fairy tale of hell and the geological fact of it. Think about it. If there can be a historical Christ, why not a historical Satan? Consider hell. Recent history tells us that the fairy tales had it all wrong, and yet right. The underworld is not full of dead souls and demons, yet it has human captives and an indigenous population that was—until recently—savagely defending its territory. Now, despite thousands and thousands of years of being damned and demonized in human folklore, the hadals seem very much like us. They have a written language, you know," he said. "At least they did, once upon a time. The ruins suggest they had a remarkable civilization. They may even have souls."

Ali couldn't believe a priest was saying such things. Human rights were one thing; the ability to know grace was something entirely different. Even if the hadals proved to have some genetic link with humans, their capacity for souls was theologically unlikely. The Church did not acknowledge souls in animals, not even among the higher primates. Only man qualified for salvation. "Let me understand," she said. "You're looking for a creature named Satan?"

No one denied it.

"But why?"

"Peace," said Lynch. "If he is a great leader, and if we can come to understand him, we may forge a lasting peace."

"Knowledge," said Rau. "Think what he might know, where he might lead us."

"And if he's merely the equivalent of an ancient war criminal," said the soldier Elias, "then we can seek justice. And punishment."

"One way or another," said January, "we're striving to bring light to the darkness. Or darkness to the light."

It sounded so naïve. So youthful. So seductive and abundant with hope. Almost, thought Ali, plausible—hypothetically. And yet, a Nuremberg trial for the king of hell? Then she saddened. Of course they would be attracted to tilting at windmills. Thomas had drawn them back into the world, just as they were dying out from it.

"And how do you propose to find this creature—being, entity—whatever he is?" she asked. It was meant to be a rhetorical question. "What chance do you have of finding an individual fugitive when the armies can't seem to find any hadals at all? I keep hearing that they may even be extinct."

"You're skeptical," Vera said. "We wouldn't have it any other way. Your skepticism is crucial. You'd be useless to us without it. Believe me, we were just like you when Thomas first presented his idea. But here we are, years later, still coming together when Thomas calls."

Thomas spoke. "You asked how do we hope to locate the historical Satan? Like reaching into mud, we must feel around and then pull him loose."

"Scholarship," said the mathematician Hoaks. "By revisiting excavations and reexamining the evidence, we compile a more careful picture. Like a behavioral profile."

"I call it a unified theory of Satan," said Foley. He had a businessman's mind, given to strategy and output. "Some of us visit libraries or archaeological sites or science centers around the world. Others conduct interviews, debrief survivors, cultivate leads. In this way we hope to outline psychological patterns and identify any weaknesses that might be useful in a summit conference. Who knows, we may even be able to construct a physical description of the creature."

"It sounds like such . . . an adventure," said Ali. She didn't want to offend anyone.

"Look at me," Thomas said. There was a trick of light. Something. Suddenly he seemed a thousand years old. "He's down there. Year after year, I've failed to locate him. We can no longer afford that."

Ali wavered.

"That's the dilemma," said de l'Orme. "Life's too short for doubt, and yet too long for faith."

Ali recalled his excommunication, and guessed it had been excruciating.

"Our problem is that Satan hides in plain view," de l'Orme said. "He always has. He hides within our reality. Even our virtual reality. The trick, we're learning, is to enter the illusion. In that way, we hope to find him out. Would you please show Mademoiselle von Schade our little photo?" he asked his assistant.

Santos spread out a long roll of glossy Kodak paper. It showed an image of an old map. Ali had to stand to see its details. Most of the group gathered around.

"The others have had the benefit of several weeks to examine this photo," de l'Orme explained. "It's a route map known as the Peutinger Table. Twenty-one feet long by one foot high in the original. It details a medieval network of roads seventy thousand miles long that ran from the British Isles to India. Along the road were stage stops, spas, bridges, rivers, and seas. Latitude and longitude were irrelevant. The road itself was everything."

The archaeologist paused. "I had asked you all to try to find anything out of the ordinary on the photo. I particularly directed your attention to the Latin phrase 'Here be dragons,' midcenter on the map. Did anyone notice anything unusual in that region?"

"It's seven-thirty in the morning," someone said. "Please teach us our lesson so we may eat our breakfast."

"If you please," de l'Orme said to his aide.

Santos lifted a wooden box onto the table, brought out from it a thick scroll, and began to unroll it delicately. "Here is the original table," said de l'Orme. "It is housed here in the museum."

"This is why we were brought to New York?" complained Parsifal.

"Please, compare for yourselves," said de l'Orme. "As you can see, the photo duplicates the original at a scale of one-to-one. What I wish to demonstrate is that seeing is not believing. Santos?"

The young man drew on a pair of latex gloves, produced a surgical scalpel, and bent over the original.

"What are you doing?" an emaciated man squeaked in alarm. His name was Gault, and Ali would later learn that he was an encyclopedist of the old Diderot school, which believed that all things could be known and arranged alphabetically. "That map is irreplaceable," he protested.

"It's all right," de l'Orme said. "He's simply exposing an incision we've already made."

The excitement of an act of vandalism in front of their eyes woke them up. Everyone came close to the table. "It is a secret the cartographer built into his map," de l'Orme said. "A well-kept secret. If not for a blind man's bare fingertips, it might never have been discovered. There is something quite wicked about our reverence for antiquity. We've come to treat the thing itself with such care that it has lost its original truth."

"But what's this?" someone gasped.

Santos was inserting his scalpel into the parchment where the cartographer had painted a small forested mountain with a river issuing from its base.

"Because of my blindness, I'm allowed certain dispensations," de l'Orme said. "I touch things most other people may not. Several months ago, I felt a slight bump at this place on the map. We had the parchment X-rayed, and there seemed to be a ghost image underneath the pigment. At that point we performed surgery."

Santos opened a tiny hidden door. The mountain lifted upon hinges made of thread. Underneath lay a crude but coherent dragon. Its claws embraced the letter *B*.

"The *B* stands for *Beliar*," said de l'Orme. "Latin for 'Worthless.' Another name for Satan. This was the manifestation of Satan concurrent with the making of the Peutinger Table. In the Gospel of Bartholomew, a third-century tract, Beliar is dragged up from the depths and interrogated. He gives an autobiography of the fallen angel."

The scholars marveled at the mapmaker's ingenuity and craft. They congratulated de l'Orme on his detective work.

"This is insignificant. Trivial. The mountain on this doorway lies in the karst country of the former Yugoslavia. The river coming from its base is probably the Pivka, which emerges from a Slovenian cave known today as Postojna Jama."

"The Postojna Jama?" Gault barked in recognition. "But that was Dante's cave."

"Yes," said de l'Orme, and let Gault tell them himself.

"It's a large cave," Gault explained. "It became a famous tourist attraction in the thirteenth century. Nobles and landowners would tour with local guides. Dante visited while researching—"

"My God," said Mustafah. "For a thousand years the legend of Satan was located right here. But how can you call this trivial?"

"Because it leads us nowhere we've not already been," said de l'Orme. "The Postojna Jama is now a major portal for traffic going in and out of the abyss. The river has been dynamited. An asphalt road leads into the mouth. And the dragon has fled. For a thousand years this map told us where he once resided, or possibly where one of his doorways into the subplanet lay. But now Satan has gone elsewhere."

Thomas took over again.

"Here before us is another example of why we can't stay in our homes, believing we know the truth. We must unlearn our instincts, even as we depend on them. We must put our hands on what is untouchable. Listen for his motion. He's out there, in old books and ruins and artifacts. Inside our language and dreams. And now, you see, the evidence will not come to us. We must go to it, wherever it is. Otherwise we're merely looking into mirrors of our own invention. Do you understand? We must learn *his* language. We must learn *his* dreams. And perhaps bring him into the family of man."

Thomas leaned on the table. It gave a slight groan beneath his weight. He looked at Ali. "The truth is, we must go out into the world. We must risk everything. And we must not return without the prize."

Even if I believed in your historical Satan," Ali said, "it's not my fight."

The meeting had adjourned. Hours had passed. The Beowulf scholars had gone off, leaving her alone with January and Thomas. She felt weary and electrified at the same time, but tried to show only a smooth face. Thomas was a cipher to her. He was making her a cipher to herself.

"I agree," Thomas replied. "But your passion for the mother tongue helps us in our fight, you see. And so our interests marry."

She glanced at January. Something was different in her eyes. Ali wanted an ally, but what she saw was obligation and urgency. "What is it you want from me?"

What Thomas next told her went beyond daring. He was toying with a yellowed globe, and now let it spin to a halt. He pointed at the Galápagos Islands. "Seven weeks from now, a science expedition is to be inserted through the Pacific floor into the Nazca Plate tunnel system. It will consist of roughly fifty scientists and researchers who have been recruited mostly from American universities and laboratories. For the next year, they'll be operating out of a state-of-the-art research institute based on the Woods Hole model. It's said to be located at a remote mining town. We're still working to learn which mining town, and if the science station even exists. Major Branch has been helpful, but even military intelligence can't make heads or tails out of why Helios is underwriting the project and what they're really up to."

"Helios?" Ali said. "The corporation?"

"It's actually a multinational cartel comprising dozens of major businesses, totally diversified," January said. "Arms manufacture to tampons to computers. Baby formula, real estate, car assembly plants, recycled plastics, publishing, plus television and film production, and an airline. They're untouchable. Now, thanks to their founder, C.C. Cooper, their agenda has taken a sharp turn. Downward into the subplanet."

"The presidential candidate," Ali said. "You served in the Senate with him."

"Mostly against him," January said. "He is a brilliant man. A true visionary. A closet fascist. And now a bitter and paranoid loser. His own party still blames him for the humiliation of that election. The Supreme Court eventually tossed out his charges of election fraud. As a result, he sincerely believes the world's out to get him."

"I haven't heard a thing about him since his defeat," said Ali.

"He quit the Senate and returned to Helios," January said. "We were sure that was the end of him, that Cooper would quietly go back to making money. Even the people who watch such things didn't notice for a while. C.C. was using shells and proxies and dummy corporations to snap up access rights and tunneling equipment and subsurface technology. He was cutting deals with governments of nine different Pacific Rim nations to joint-venture the drilling operations and provide labor, again hidden behind numerous layers. The result is that while we've been pacifying the regions underneath our cities and continents, Helios has gotten the jump on everyone else in suboceanic exploration and development."

"I thought the colonization was under international auspices," said Ali.

"It is," said January, "within the boundaries of international law. But international law hasn't caught up with nonsovereign territories. Offshore, the law is still catching up with subterranean discoveries."

"I didn't understand this either," said Thomas. "It turns out that subterranean territory beneath the oceans is still like the Wild West, subject to the whims of whoever occupies it. Recall the British tea company in India. The fur companies in North America. The American land companies in Texas. In the case of the Pacific Ocean, that means a huge expanse of country beyond international reach."

"Which translates as opportunity for a man like C.C. Cooper," said January. "Today Helios owns more seafloor drill holes than any other entity, governmental or otherwise. They lead in hydroponic agricultural methods. They own the latest technology for enhanced communications through rock. Their labs have created new drugs to help them push the depths. They've approached the subplanet the way America approached manned landings on the moon forty years ago, as a mission requiring life support systems, modes of transportation and access, and logistics. While the rest of the world's been tiptoeing into their planetary basements, Helios has spent billions on research and development, and is poised to exploit the frontier."

"In other words," Thomas said, "Helios isn't sending these scientists down out of the goodness of its heart. The expedition is top-loaded with earth sciences and biology. The object of the expedition is to expand knowledge about the lithosphere and learn more about its resources and life-forms, especially those that can be exploited commercially for energy, metallurgy, medicine, and other practical uses. Helios has no interest in humanizing our perception of the hadals, and so the anthropology component is very small."

At the mention of anthropology, Ali started. "You want me to go? Down there?"

"We're much too old," January said.

Ali was stunned. How could they ask such a thing of her? She had duties, plans, desires.

"You should know," Thomas said to Ali, "the senator didn't choose you. I did. I've been watching you for years, following your work. Your talents are exactly what we need."

"But down there . . ." She had never conceived herself on such a journey. She hated the darkness. A year without sun?

"You would thrive," said Thomas.

"You've been there," Ali said. He spoke with such authority.

"No," said Thomas. "But I've traveled among the hadals by visiting their evidence in ruins and museums. My task has been complicated by eons of human superstition and ignorance. But if you go back far enough in the human record, there are glimpses of what the hadals were like thousands of years ago. Once upon a time they were more than these degraded, inbred creatures we reckon with today."

Her pulse was hammering. She wanted not to be excited. "You want me to locate the hadals' leader?"

"Not at all."

"Then what?"

"Language is everything."

"Decipher their writings? But only fragments exist."

"Down there, I'm told, glyphs are abundant. Miners blow up whole galleries of them every day."

Hadal glyphs! Where could this lead?

"A lot of people think the hadals have died off. That doesn't matter," said January. "We still have to live with what they were. And if they're merely in hiding somewhere, then we've got to know what they're capable of—not just their savagery, but the greatness they once aspired to.

It's clear they were once civilized. And if the legend is true, they fell from their own grace. Why? Could such a fall be lying in wait for mankind?"

"Restore their ancient memory to us," Thomas said to Ali. "Do that, and we can truly know Satan."

It came back to that, their king of hell.

"No one has managed to decode their writings," Thomas said. "It's a lost language, possibly—probably—lost even to these remnant creatures. They've forgotten their own glory. And you're the only person I can think of who might find the language locked within hadal hieroglyphics and script. Unlock that dead language, and we may have a chance to understand who they once were. Unlock that language, and you may just find the secret of your mother tongue."

"All that said, I want to be perfectly clear." January searched her face. "You can say no, Ali."

But of course she could not.

BOOK TWO

INQUISITION

Canst thou draw out
leviathan with an hook?

—Job 41:1

8

INTO THE STONE

June 08

It seemed the helicopter was bound west forever across the cobalt blue water, landless, stained red by the sunset. Night chased her across the infinite Pacific. Childishly, Ali wished they could stay ahead of the darkness.

The islands were all but covered with intricate scaffolding and decks, miles and miles of it, ten stories high in some places. Expecting amorphous lava piles, Ali was affronted by the neat geometry. They'd been busy out here. Nazca Depot—named for the geological plate it fed to— was nothing but a vast parking garage anchored on pylons. Supertankers floated alongside, mouths open, taking on small symmetrical mountains of raw ore conveyed by belts. Trucks hauled containers from one level to another.

The helicopter sliced between skeletal towers, landing briefly to disgorge Ali, who recoiled at the stench of gases curdling into mists. She had been forewarned. Nazca Depot was a work zone. There were barracks for workers, but no facilities, not even cots or a Coke machine, for passengers in transit. By chance, a man appeared on foot among the vehicles and noises. "Excuse me," Ali yelled above the roar of the helicopter. "How do I get to Nine-Bay?"

The man's eyes ran down her long arms and legs, and he pointed with no enthusiasm. She dodged among the beams and diesel fumes, down three flights to reach a freight elevator with doors that opened up and down like jaws. Some wag had written *Lasciate ogni speranza, voi ch'entrate* over the gate, Dante's welcoming injunction in the original.

Ali got into the cage and pressed her number. She felt a strange sense of grief, but couldn't figure out why.

The cage released her onto a deck thronged with other passengers. There were hundreds of people down here, mostly men, all heading in one direction. Even with the sea breeze brooming through, the air was rank with their odor, a force in itself. In Israel and Ethiopia and the African bush, she had done her share of traveling among masses of soldiers and workers, and they smelled the same worldwide. It was the smell of aggression.

With loudspeakers hammering at them to queue, to present tickets, to show passports, Ali was swept into the current. "Loaded weapons are not permitted. Violators will be disarmed and their weapons confiscated." There was no mention of arrest or punishment. It was enough, then, that violators would be sent down without their guns.

The crowd bore her past a bulletin board fifty feet long. It was divided alphabetically, A–G, H–P, Q–Z. Thousands of messages had been pinned for others to find: equipment for sale, services for hire, dates and locations for rendezvous, E-mail addresses, curses. TRAVELER'S ADVISORY, a Red Cross sign warned. PREGNANT WOMEN ARE STRONGLY ADVISED AGAINST DESCENT. FETAL DAMAGE AND/OR DEATH DUE TO . . ."

A Department of Health poster listed a Hit Parade of the top twenty "depth drugs" and their side effects. Ali wasn't pleased to find listed two of the drugs in her personal med kit. The last six weeks had been a whirlwind of preparation, with inoculations and Helios paperwork and physical training consuming every hour. Day by day, she was learning how little man really knew about life in the subplanet.

"Declare your explosives," the loudspeaker boomed. "All explosives must be clearly marked. All explosives must be shipped down Tunnel K. Violators will be . . ."

The crowd movement was peristaltic, full of muscular starts and stops. In contrast to Ali's daypack, normal luggage here tended toward metal cases and stenciled footlockers and hundred-pound duffel bags with bulletproof locks. Ali had never seen so many gun cases in her life. It looked like a convention of safari guides, with every variety of camouflage and body armor, bandolier, holster, and sheath. Body hair and neck veins were de rigueur. She was glad for their numbers, because some of the men frightened her with their glances.

In truth, she was frightening herself. She felt out of balance. This voyage was purely of her own volition, of course. All she had to do was stop walking and the journey could stop. But something was started here.

Passing through the security and passport and ticket checks, Ali neared a great edifice made of glistening steel. Rooted in solid black stone, the enormous steel and titanium and platinum gateway looked immovable. This was one of Nazca Depot's five elevator shafts connecting with the upper interior, three miles beneath their feet. The complex of shafts and vents had cost over $4 billion—and several hundred lives—to drill. As a public transportation project, it was no different from a new airport, say, or the American railway system a hundred and fifty years ago. It was meant to service colonization for decades to come.

Out of necessity, the press of soldiers, settlers, laborers, runaways, convicts, paupers, addicts, fanatics, and dreamers grew orderly, even mannerly. They realized at last that there was going to be room for everyone. Ali walked toward a bank of stainless-steel doors side by side. Three were already shut. A fourth closed slowly as she drew near. The last stood open.

Ali headed for the farthest, least crowded entrance. Inside, the chamber was like a small amphitheater, with concentric rows of plastic seats descending toward an empty center. It was dark and cool, a relief from the press of hot bodies outside. She headed for the far side, opposite the door. After a minute her eyes adjusted to the dim lighting and she chose a seat. Except for a man at the end of the row, she was temporarily alone. Ali set her daypack on the floor, took a deep breath, and let her muscles unwind.

The seat was ergonomic, with a curved spine rest and a harness that adjusted for your shoulders and snapped across your chest. Each seat had a fold-up table, a deep bin for possessions, and an oxygen mask. There was an LCD screen built into every seatback. Hers showed an altimeter reading of 0000 feet. The clock alternated between real time and their departure in minus-minutes. The elevator was scheduled to leave in twenty-four minutes. Muzak soothed the interim.

A tall curved window bordered the walkway above, much like an aquarium wall. Water lapped against the upper rim. Ali was about to walk up for a peek, then got sidetracked with a magazine nestled in the pocket beside her. It was called *The Nazca News,* and its cover bore an imaginative painting of a thin tube rising from a range of ocean-floor mountains, an artist's rendition of the Nazca Depot elevator shaft. The shaft looked fragile.

Ali tried reading. Her mind wouldn't focus. She felt barraged with details: G forces, compression rates, temperature zones. "Ocean water reaches its coldest temperature—35 degrees—at 12,000 feet below the surface. Below that depth, it gradually heats. Water on the ocean floor averages 36.5 degrees."

"Welcome to the moho," a sidebar opened. "Located at the edge of the East Pacific Rise, Nazca Depot accesses the subplanet at a depth of just 3,066 fathoms."

There were nuggets and sidebars scattered throughout. A quote from Albert Einstein: "Something deeply hidden had to be behind things." There was a table of residual gases and their effect on various human tissues. Another article featured Rock Vision™, which produced images of geologic anomalies hundreds of feet ahead of a mining face. Ali closed the magazine.

The back page advertised Helios, the winged sun on a black backdrop.

She noticed her neighbor. He was only a few seats away, but she could barely make out his silhouette in the dim light.

He was not looking at her, yet some instinct told Ali she was being observed. Faced forward, he was wearing dark goggles, the sort welders use. That made him a worker, she decided, then saw his camouflage pants. A soldier, she amended. The jawline was striking. His haircut—definitely self-inflicted—was atrocious.

She realized the man was delicately sniffing the air. He was smelling her.

Several figures appeared at the doorway, and the presence of more passengers emboldened her. "Excuse me?" she challenged the man.

He faced her fully. The goggles were so darkly tinted and the lenses so scratched and small, she wondered how much of anything he could really see. A moment later, Ali discovered the markings on his face. Even in the dim light, she could tell the tattoos were not just ink printed into flesh. Whoever had decorated him had taken a knife to the task. His big cheekbones were incised and scarified. The rawness of it jolted her.

"Do you mind?" he asked, and came a seat closer. For a better smell? Ali wondered. She looked quickly at the doorway. More passengers were filing through.

"Speak up," she snapped.

Unbelievably, the goggles were aimed at her chest. He even bent to improve his view. He seemed to squint, reckoning.

"What are you doing?" she demanded.

"It's been a long while," he said. "I used to know these things. . . ."

His audacity astounded her. Any closer, and she'd lay her open palm across his face.

"What are those?" He was pointing right at her breasts.

"Are you for real?" Ali whispered.

He didn't react. It was as if he hadn't heard her. He went on wagging his fingertip. "Bluebells?" he asked.

Ali drew into herself. He was examining her dress? "Periwinkles," she said, then doubted him again. His face was too monstrous. He had to be trespassing against her. And if he was not? She made a note to say a quick act of contrition some other time.

"That's what they are," the man said to himself, then went back to his seat, and faced forward again.

Ali remembered a sweatshirt in her daypack, and put it on.

Now the chamber filled quickly. Several men took the seats between Ali and that stranger. When there were no more seats, the doors gently kissed shut. The LCD said seven minutes.

There was not another woman or child in the chamber. Ali was glad for her sweatshirt. Some were hyperventilating and eyeing the door, full of second thoughts. Several had a sedated slackness and looked at peace. Others clenched their hands or opened portable computers or scratched at crossword puzzles or huddled shoulder-to-shoulder for earnest scheming.

The man to her left had lowered a seatback tray and was quietly laying out two plastic syringes. One had a baby-blue cap over the needle, the other a pink cap. He held the baby-blue syringe up for her observation. "Sylobane," he said. "It suppresses the retinal cones and magnifies your retinal rods. Achromatopsia. In plain English, it creates a supersensitivity to light. Night vision. Only problem is, once you start you have to keep doing it. Lots of soldiers with cataracts up top. Didn't keep up."

"What about that one?" she asked.

"Bro," he said. "Russian steroid. For acclimation. The Soviets used to dose their soldiers with it in Afghanistan. Can't hurt, right?"

He held up a white pill. "And this little angel's just to let me sleep." He swallowed it.

That sadness washed over her again, and suddenly she remembered. The sun! She had forgotten to get a final look at the sun. Too late now.

Ali felt a nudge at her right. "Here, this is for you," a slight man offered. He was holding out an orange. Ali accepted the gift with hesitant thanks.

"Thank that guy." He pointed down the row to the stranger with tattoos. She leaned forward to get his attention, but the man didn't look at her.

Ali frowned at the orange. Was it a peace offering? A come-on? Did he mean for her to peel and eat it, or save it for later? Ali had the orphan's habit of attaching great meaning to gifts, especially simple gifts. But the more she contemplated it, the less this orange made sense to her.

"Well, I don't know what to do with this," she complained quietly to her neighbor, the messenger. He looked up from a thick manual of computer codes, took a moment to recollect. "It's an orange," he said.

Far more than seemed right, it irritated her, the messenger's indifference, the idea of a gift, the fruit itself. Ali was keyed up, and knew it. She was frightened. For weeks her dreams had been filled with awful images of hell. She dreaded her own superstitions. With each step of the journey, she was certain her fears would ease. If only it weren't too late to change her mind! The temptation to retreat—to allow herself to be weak—was terrible. And prayer was not the crutch it had once been for her. That was concerning.

She was not the only anxious one. The chamber took on a moment-to-moment tension. Eyes met, then darted away. Men licked their lips, rubbed their whiskers, took bites at the air. She collected the tiny gestures into her own anxiety.

Ali wanted to put the orange down, but it would have rolled on the tray. The floor was too dirty. The orange had become a responsibility. She laid it in her lap, and its weight seemed too intimate. Following the instructions on the LCD, she buckled into the seat rig, and her fingers were trembling. She picked up the orange again and cupped her fingers around it and the trembling eased.

The wall display ticked down to three minutes.

As if signaled, the passengers began their final rites. A number of men tied rubber tubing around their biceps and gently slid needles into their veins. Those taking pills looked like birds swallowing worms. Ali heard a hissing sound, men sucking hard at aerosol dispensers. Others drank from small bottles. Each had his own compression ritual. All she had was this orange.

Its skin glistened in the darkness in her cupped hands. Light bent upon its color. Her focus changed. Suddenly it became a small round center of gravity for her.

A tiny chime sounded. Ali looked up just as the time display dissolved to zero.

The chamber fell silent.

Ali felt a slight motion. The chamber slid backward on a track and stopped. She heard a metallic snap underfoot. Then the chamber moved down perhaps ten feet, stopped again, and there was another snap, this time overhead. They moved down again, stopped.

She knew from a diagram in *The Nazca News* what was happening. The chambers were coupling like freight cars, one atop another. Joined in that fashion, the entire assembly was about to be lowered upon a cushion of air, with no cables attached. She had no idea how the pods got hoisted back to the surface again. But with discoveries of vast new petroleum reserves in the bowels of the subplanet, energy was no longer an issue.

She craned to see through the big curved window. As they lowered one pod at a time, the window slowly acquired a view. The LCD said they were twenty feet underwater. The water turned dark turquoise, illuminated by spotlights. Then Ali saw the moon. Right through the water, a full white moon. It was the most beautiful sight.

They dropped another twenty feet. The moon warped. It vanished. She held the round orange in her palms.

They dropped twenty feet more. The water turned darker. Ali peered through the window. Something was out there. Mantas. Giant manta rays were circling the shaft, drafting on strange muscular wings.

Twenty feet lower, the Plexiglas was replaced by solid metal. The window went black, a curved mirror. She looked down into her hands and breathed out. And suddenly her fear was gone. The center of gravity was right there, in her grasp. Could that be his gift? She looked down the row. The stranger had laid his head back against the chair. His goggles were lifted onto his forehead. His smile was small and contented. Sensing her, he turned his head. And gave her a wink.

They dropped.

Plunged.

The initial surge of gravity made Ali grab for purchase. She grasped the armrests and slugged her head against the back of the seat. The sudden lightness set off biological alarms. Her nausea was instantaneous. A headache blossomed.

According to the LCD, they didn't slow. Their speed remained a constant, uncompromising 1,850 feet per minute. But the sensation started to even out. Ali started to feel her way inside the plummet. She managed to plant her feet and relax her grip and look around. The headache eased. The nausea she could handle.

Half the chamber had dropped asleep or into drugged semiconsciousness. Men's heads lolled upon their chests. Bodies dangled loosely against seat harnesses. Most looked pale, punch-drunk, or sick. The tattooed soldier seemed to be meditating. Or praying.

She made a rough calculation in her head. This wasn't adding up. At 1,850 feet per minute and a depth of 3.4 miles, the commute should have taken no more than ten or eleven minutes. But the literature described "touchdown" as seven hours away. Seven hours of this?

The LCD altimeter soared into the minus thousands, then decelerated. At minus 14,347 feet, they braked to a halt. Ali waited for an explanation over the intercom, but none came. She glanced around at the asylum of half-dead fellow travelers and decided that information was pretty unnecessary, so long as they got where they were going.

The window came alive again. Outside the shaft's Plexiglas wall, powerful lights illuminated the blackness. To Ali's awe, she was looking out upon the ocean floor. It might as well have been the moon out there.

The lights cut sharply at the permanent night. No mountains here. The floor was flat, white, scribbled with long odd script, tracks left by bottom-dwellers. Ali saw a creature treading delicately above the sediment upon stiltlike legs. It left tiny dots upon the blankness.

Farther out, another set of lights came on. The plain was littered with hundreds of inert cannonballs. Manganese nodules, Ali knew from her reading. There was a fortune in manganese out there, and yet it had been bypassed for the sake of far greater fortune deeper down.

The vista was like a dream. Ali kept trying to make sense of her place in this inhuman geography. But with each further step, she belonged less and less.

A gruesome fish with fangs and a greenish light bud for bait steered past the window. Otherwise it was lonely out there. Dreamless. She held the orange.

After an hour, the pod started down again, this time slower. As it descended, the ocean floor rose to eye and ceiling level, then was gone. There was a brief lighted glimpse of cored stone through the window. Then quickly the glass fell black and she was looking at herself again.

Now it begins, thought Ali, the edge of the earth. And it was like passing inside herself.

INCIDENT AT PIEDRAS NEGRAS

MEXICO

Osprey crossed the bridge like a *turista,* on foot, wearing a daypack. He left the sunburned GIs behind their sandbags in Texas. On the Mexico side, nothing suggested an international border, no barricade, no soldiers, not even a flag.

By arrangement with the local university, a van was waiting. To Osprey's great surprise, his driver was the most beautiful woman he'd ever seen. She had skin like dark fruit, and brilliant red lipstick. "You are the butterfly man?" she asked. Her accent was like a musical gift.

"Osprey," he stammered.

"It's hot," she said. "I brought you a Coca-Cola." She offered him a bottle. Hers was beaded with condensation. Lipstick circled the tip.

While she drove, he learned her name. She was an economics student. "Why are you chasing the *mariposa?*" she asked. *Mariposa* was the Mexican term for the monarch butterfly.

"It's my life," he answered.

"Your whole life?"

"From childhood. Butterflies. I was drawn by their movements and colors. And their names. Painted Ladies! Red Admirals! Question Marks! Ever since, I've followed them. Wherever the *mariposas* migrate, I go with them."

Her smile made his heart squeeze.

They passed a shantytown overlooking the river. "You go south," she said, "they go north. Nicaraguans, Guatemalans, Hondurans. And my own people, too."

"They'll try to cross over tonight?" Osprey asked. He looked past their white cotton pants and decaying tennis shoes and cheap sunglasses to glean hints of ancient tribes, Mayan, Aztec, Olmec. Once upon a time, their ancestors might have been warriors or kings. Now they were paupers, driftwood aiming for land.

"They kill themselves trying to leave their origins. How can they resist?"

Osprey glanced across the Rio Grande's coil of brown, poisoned water at the butt side of America. Heated to mirage, the buildings and billboards and power lines did seem to offer hope—provided you could factor out the necklace of razor wire glittering in the middle distance, and the sparkle of binoculars and video lenses overseeing the passage. The van continued along the river.

"Where are you going?" she asked.

"To the highlands around Mexico City. They roost in the mountain fir stands through the winter. In the spring they'll return this way to lay their eggs."

"I mean today, Mr. Osprey."

"Today. Yes." He fumbled with his maps.

She stopped suddenly. They had reached a place overcome by orange and black wings. "Incredible," Ada murmured.

"It's their rest stop for the night," Osprey said. "Tomorrow they'll be gone. They travel fifty miles every day. In another month, all of the masses of monarchs will reach their roost."

"They don't fly at night?"

"They can't see in the darkness." He opened the van door. "I may take an hour," he apologized. "Perhaps you should return later."

"I'll wait for you, Mr. Osprey. Take your time. When you're finished, we can have dinner, if you'd like."

If I'd like? Dazed, Osprey took his rucksack and gently closed the door behind him.

Remembering his purpose, he headed west into the sinking sun. His inquiry dealt with the monarchs' age-old migration path. *Danaus plexippus* laid its eggs in North America, then died. The young emerged with no parents to guide it, and yet each year flew thousands of miles along the same ancestral route to the same destination in Mexico. How could this be? How could a creature that weighed less than half a gram have a memory? Surely memory weighed something. What was memory? There was no bottom to the mystery for Osprey. Year after year, he collected them alive. While they wintered, he studied them in his laboratory.

Osprey unzipped his daypack and took out a bundle of folded white boxes, the same kind that Chinese food comes in. He assembled twelve, leaving their tops open. His task was simple. He approached a cluster of hundreds, held a box out, and two or three alighted inside. He closed the box.

After forty minutes, Osprey had eleven boxes dangling by their wire handles from a string around his neck. Hurrying, badly distracted by the girl in the van, he trotted across a sagging depression toward the final cluster. The depression gave way. With monarchs clinging to his arms and head, he plunged through a hole in the ground.

The fall registered as a clatter of rocks, then sudden darkness.

Consciousness returned in bits. Osprey struggled to take stock. He was in pain, but could move. The hole was very deep, or else night had arrived. Luckily he hadn't lost his rucksack. He opened it and found his flashlight.

The beam was a source of both comfort and distress. He found himself lying at the pit of a limestone sinkhole, battered but unbroken. There was no sign of the hole he'd fallen through. And his landing had crushed several boxes of his beloved monarchs. For a moment, that was more defeating than the fall itself.

"Hello," he called out several times. There was no one down here to hear him, but Osprey hoped his voice might carry through the hole somewhere overhead. Perhaps the Mexican woman would be looking for him. He had a momentary fantasy that she might fall through the hole and they could be trapped together for a night or two. At any rate, there was no response.

Finally he pulled himself together, stood up, dusted himself off, and got on with trying to find an exit. The sinkhole was cavernous, its walls riddled with tubular openings. He poked his light into a few, thinking one of them must surely lead to the surface. He chose the largest.

The tube snaked sideways. At first he was able to crawl on his knees. But it narrowed, forcing him to leave his daypack. At last he was reduced to muscling forward on elbows and belly, careful to scoot his flashlight and the remaining five boxes of live butterflies ahead of him.

The porous walls kept tearing his clothing and hooking his trouser cuffs. The rock cut his arms. He knocked his head, and sweat stung his eyes. He was going to emerge in tatters, reeking, farcical. So much for dinner, he thought.

The tube grew tighter. A wave of claustrophobia took his breath. What if he got wedged inside this place? Trapped alive! He calmed himself. There was no room to turn around, of course. He could only hope the artery led somewhere more reasonable.

After an awkward, ten-foot wrestling match, with both arms above his head and pushing mightily with his toes, Osprey emerged into a larger tunnel.

His spirits soared. A faint footpath was worn into the rock. All he had to do was follow it out. "Hello," he called to his left and right. He heard a slight rattling noise in the distance. "Hello?" he tried again. The noise stopped. Seismic goblins, he shrugged, and started off in the opposite direction.

Another hour passed, and still the path had not led him out. Osprey was tired, aching, and hungry. Finally he decided to reverse course and explore the path's other end. The trail went up and down, then came to a series of forks he hadn't seen before. He went one way, then another, with increasing frustration. At last he reached a tubular opening similar to the one that had brought him here. On the chance it might return him to the original chamber, Osprey set his butterflies and light on the ledge and crawled inside.

He'd gotten only a short distance when, to his great annoyance, the rock snagged his ankle again. He yanked to free himself, but the ankle stayed caught. He tried to see behind him, but his body filled the opening.

That was when he felt the tube move. It seemed to slip forward an inch or so, though he knew it was his body sliding backward. The disturbing thing was, he hadn't moved a muscle.

Now he felt a second motion, this time a tug at his ankle. It was no longer possible to blame the rock for catching his cuff. This was something organic. He could feel it getting a better grip on his leg. The animal, whatever it was, suddenly began pulling him back.

Osprey desperately tried holding on to the rock, but it was like falling down a slippery chimney. His hands slid across the surface. He had enough presence of mind to hold on to his light and the boxes of butterflies. Then his legs cleared the tube, and in the next instant his body and head popped free. He dropped to the tunnel floor in a heap. One of his boxes fell open and three butterflies escaped, drifting erratically through his light beam.

He whipped the flashlight around to fend off the animal. There in his cone of light stood a live hadal. Osprey shouted his alarm just as it fled from his light. Its whiteness startled him most of all. The bulging eyes gave it an aspect of enormous hunger, or curiosity.

The hadal ran one way, Osprey the other. He covered fifty yards before his light beam illuminated three more hadals crouching in the tunnel's far depths. They turned their heads from his light, but didn't budge.

Osprey cast his flashlight back the way he'd come. Not far enough away prowled four or five more of the white creatures. He swung his head back and forth, awestruck by his predicament. He took his Swiss Army knife from a pocket and opened its longer blade. But they came no closer, repulsed by his light.

It seemed utterly fantastic. He was a lepidopterist. He dealt with animals whose existence depended on sunshine. The subplanet had nothing to do with him. Yet here he was, caged beneath the ground, faced with hadals. The terrible fact bore down on him. The weight of it exhausted him. Finally, unable to move in either direction, Osprey sat down.

Thirty yards to his right and left, the hadals settled in, too. He flipped his light from side to side for a while, thinking that was keeping them at bay. At last it became apparent the hadals weren't interested in coming any closer for the time being. He positioned the flashlight so that its beam cast a ball of light around him. While the three monarchs that had escaped from his box fluttered in the light, Osprey began calculating how long his battery might last.

He stayed awake as long as possible. But the combination of fatigue, his fall, and adrenaline hangover finally mastered him. He dozed, bathed in light, clutching his pocketknife.

He woke dreaming of raindrops. They were pebbles thrown by the hadals. His first thought was that the pebbles were meant to torment him. Then he realized the hadals were trying to break his lightbulb. Osprey grabbed the flashlight to shield it. He had another thought. If they could throw pebbles, they could probably throw rocks big enough to hurt or kill him—but they hadn't. That was when he understood they meant to capture him alive.

The waiting went on. They sat at the edges of his light. Their patience was depressing. It was so utterly unmodern, a primitive's patience, unbeatable. They were going to outlast him, he had no doubt at all about that.

Hours turned into a day, then two. His stomach rumbled with hunger. His tongue dried in his mouth. He told himself it would be better this way. Without food or water, he might start hallucinating. The last thing he wanted was to be lucid in the end.

As time passed, Osprey did his best not to look at the hadals, but eventually his curiosity took over. He turned his light on one group or the other, and gathered their details. Several were naked except for rawhide loin strings. A few wore ragged vests made of some kind of leather. All were male, as he could tell by their penis sheaths. Each sported a sheath made from an animal horn, jutting from his groin, and tied erect with twine, like those worn by New Guinea natives.

It was easy to anticipate the end. His battery began to fail. To either side, the hadals had moved closer. The light faded to a dim ball. Osprey shook the flashlight hard, and the beam brightened momentarily, and the hadals withdrew another five or ten yards. He sighed. It was time. *C'est la vie.* He chuckled, and laid the blade along his wrist.

He could have waited until the last instant of light before making the cuts, but feared they might not be done well. Too shallow, and it would simply be a painful nip at the nerves. Too deep, and the veins might convulse and close off. He needed to get the strokes right, while he could still see.

T

H

E

D

E

S

C

E

N

T

He pulled evenly. Blood jumped from the steel. It leaped out of him. In the shadows, he heard the hadals murmur.

Carefully he switched the knife to his left hand and did the opposite wrist. The knife fell from his grip. After a minute he felt cold. The pain at the end of each arm turned to a dull ache. His blood spread on the stone floor. It was impossible to separate the dying light from his fading vision.

Osprey laid his head back against the wall. His thoughts settled. Increasingly, a vision of the beautiful Mexican woman had begun visiting him. Her face had come to replace his butterflies, all of whom had died because his light was not enough. He had arranged each monarch beside him, and as he slumped sideways, their wings lay like orange and black tissue on the ground.

Off in the distance, the hadals were chirping and clicking to one another. Their agitation was obvious. He smiled. They'd won, but they'd lost.

The light shrank. It died. Her face rose in the darkness. Osprey let out a low moan. The blackness pillowed him.

On the brink of unconsciousness, he felt the hadals pounce on him. He smelled them. Felt them grabbing at him. Tying his arms with rope. Too late, he realized they were binding tourniquets above his wounds. They were saving his life. He tried to fight, but was too weak.

In the weeks ahead, Osprey returned to life slowly. The stronger he got, the more pain he had to endure. He was carried sometimes. Occasionally they forced him to walk blindly down the tunnels. In pitch darkness, he had to rely on every sense but sight. Some days they simply tortured him. He could not imagine what they were doing to him. Captivity tales swirled in his head. He began to rave, and so they cut his tongue out. That was near the end of his sanity.

It was beyond Osprey's comprehension that the hadals summoned one of their finest artisans to peel the upper layers of skin, no more, from tip to tip of each shoulder and down to the base of his spine. Under the artisan's direction, the wound was salted to prepare his canvas. Its seasoning took days, requiring more abrasion, more salt. Finally an outline of veins and border was applied in black, and left to grow over. After another three days, a rare blend of bright ochre powder was laid on.

By that time, Osprey's wish had come true. He was mad from pain and deprivation. His insanity had nothing to do with the hadals freeing him to roam in their tunnels. If madness was the password, then most of their human captives would have been free. Who could understand such creatures? Human quirks and fallibilities were a constant source of puzzlement.

Osprey's freedom was a special case. He was allowed to go wherever his whim took him. No matter which band he strayed behind, they made sure to feed him, and it was considered meritorious to protect him from dangers and guide him along the trail. He was never given supplies to carry. He carried no claim mark or brand. No one owned him. He belonged to everyone, a creature of great beauty.

Children were brought to see him. His legend spread quickly. Wherever he went, it was known that this was a holy man, captured with small houses of souls around his neck.

Osprey would never know what the hadals had painted into the flesh of his back. It would have pleased him no end. For, every time he moved, with every breath he took, it seemed the man was carried along by iridescent orange and black wings.

> The frontier is the outer edge
> of the wave—the meeting-
> point between savagery
> and civilization . . . the
> line of most rapid and
> effective Americanization.
> The wilderness masters
> the colonist.
>
> —FREDERICK JACKSON TURNER,
> *The Significance of the Frontier in American History*

9

LA FRONTERA

**THE GALÁPAGOS RIFT SYSTEM,
LATITUDE 0.55°N**

Promptly at 1700 hours, the expeditionaries boarded their electric buses. They were loaded with handouts and booklets and notebooks numbered and marked Classified, and were sporting pieces of Helios clothing. The black SWAT-style caps had proved especially popular, very menacing. Ali contented herself with a T-shirt with the Helios winged-sun logo printed on the back. With scarcely a purr, the buses eased from the walled compound out onto the street.

Nazca City reminded Ali of Beijing, with its hordes of bicyclists. At rush hour in a boomtown with streets so narrow, the bikes were faster than their buses. They had jobs to get to. Through her window, Ali took in their faces, their Pacific Rim races, their humanity. What a feast of souls!

Declassified maps showed boom cities like Nazca as veritable nerve cells reaching tendrils out into the surrounding space. The attractions were simple: cheap land, mother lodes of precious minerals and petroleum, freedom from authority, a chance to start over. Ali had come expecting glum fugitives and desperadoes with no other place to go. But these were the faces of college-educated office workers, bankers, entrepreneurs, a motivated service sector. As a port city of the future, Nazca City was said to have the potential of San Francisco or Singapore. In four years it had become the major link between the equatorial subplanet and coastal cities up and down the western side of the Americas.

Ali was relieved to see that the people of Nazca City looked normal and healthy. Indeed, because the subplanet attracted younger, stronger workers, the population abounded in good health. Most of the station cities like Nazca had been retrofitted with lamps that simulated sunlight, and so these bicyclists were as tan as beachcombers. Practically everyone had seen soldiers or workers who had returned to the surface several years ago suffering bone growths and enlarged eyes or strange cancers, even vestigial tails. For a while, religious groups had blamed hell itself for the physical spoliation, calling it proof of God's plan, a vast gulag where contact meant punishment. But as she looked around, it seemed the research labs and drug companies really had mastered the prophylaxis for hell. Certainly these people exhibited no deformities. Ali realized that her subconscious fears of turning into a toad, monkey, or goat had been for nothing.

The city was a vast indoor mall with potted trees and flowering bushes, clean, with the latest brand names. There were restaurants and coffee bars, along with brightly lit stores selling everything from work clothes and plumbing supplies to assault rifles. The neatness was slightly marred by beggars missing limbs and sidewalk merchants hawking contraband.

At one intersection an old Asian woman was selling miserable puppies lashed alive to sticks. "Stew meat," one of the scientists told Ali. "They sell it by the catty, 500 grams, a little more than a pound. Beef, chicken, pork, dog."

"Thanks," said Ali.

Obviously it intrigued him. "I went exploring yesterday. Anything that moves goes into the pot. Crickets, worms, slugs. They even eat dragons, *xiao long,* their snakes."

Ali peered out. A long gossamer sausage stretched beside the road, twenty feet high, a football field in length. The plastic had bold *hangul* lettering along the front. Ali didn't read Korean, but knew a greenhouse when she saw one. There were more, lying end to end like gigantic plump pupae. Through their opaque walls she saw fieldworkers tending crops, climbing little ladders propped in orchards. Parrots and macaws soared alongside the convoy of buses. A monkey scampered past. The subsere—the secondary population of invader species—was thriving down here.

In the far distance a detonation rumbled gently. She'd felt similar vibrations through her bedsprings all night. The incessant construction work was evident everywhere. It didn't take long to detect the man-made edges of this place. The neat right angles abutted raw rock. Pressure fissures spiderwebbed the asphalt. A patch of moss had grown heavy and peeled from the ceiling, exposing mesh and barbed wire and surging lasers overhead.

They reached a newly cut ring road girdling the city, and left behind the traffic jam of cyclists and workers. Picking up speed, they gained a view of the enormous hollow salt dome containing the colony. It was life in a bell jar here. The entire vault, measuring three miles across and probably a thousand feet high, was brightly lit. Up in the World, it would be approaching sunset. Down here, night never came. Nazca City's artificial sunlight burned twenty-four hours a day, Prometheus on a caffeine jag.

Except for a catnap, sleep had been impossible last night. The group's collective excitement verged on the childlike, and she was caught up in their spirit of adventure. This morning, exhausted with their imagining, they were ready for the real thing.

Ali found her fellow travelers' last-minute preparations touching. She watched one rough-and-ready fellow across the aisle bent over his fingernails, clipping them just so, as if his mortal being depended on it. Last night, several of the youngest women, meeting for the first time, had spent the wee hours of the morning fixing one another's hair. A little enviously, Ali had listened to people placing calls to their spouses or lovers or parents, assuring them the subplanet was safe. Ali said a silent prayer for them all.

The buses stopped near a train platform and the passengers disembarked. If it hadn't been brand new, the train would have seemed old-fashioned. There was a boarding platform trimmed with iron rails painted black and teal. Farther along the track, the train was mostly freight and ore cars. Heavily armed soldiers patrolled the landings while workers loaded supplies onto flatcars at the rear.

The three front cars were elegant sleepers with aluminum panels on the outside and simulated cherrywood and oak in the hallways. Ali was surprised again at how much money was being plowed into development down here. Just five or six years ago, this had presumably been hadal grounds. The sleeper cars, on glistening tracks, declared how confident the corporate boards were of human occupation.

"Where are they taking us now?" someone grumbled publicly. He wasn't the only one. People had begun complaining that Helios was cloaking each stage of their journey in unnecessary mystery. No one could say where their science station lay.

"Point Z-3," answered Montgomery Shoat.

"I've never heard of that," a woman said. One of the planetologists, Ali placed her.

"It's a Helios holding," Shoat replied. "On the outskirts of things."

A geologist started to unfold a survey map to locate Point Z-3. "You won't find it on any maps," Shoat added with a helpful smile. "But you'll see, that really doesn't matter."

His nonchalance drew mutters, which he ignored.

Last evening, at a catered Helios banquet for the freshly arrived scientists, Shoat had been introduced as their expedition leader. He was a superbly fit character with bulging arm veins and great social energy, but he was curiously off-putting. It was more than the unfortunate face, pinched with ambition and spoiled with unruly teeth. It was a manner, Ali thought. A disregard. He traded on a thin repertoire of charm, yet didn't care if you were charmed. According to gossip Ali heard afterward, he was the stepson of C.C. Cooper, the Helios magnate. There was another son by blood, a legitimate heir to the Cooper fortunes, and that seemed to leave Shoat to take on more hazardous duties such as escorting scientists to places at the remote edges of the Helios empire. It sounded almost Shakespearean.

"This is our venue for the next three days," he announced to them. "Brand-new cars. Maiden voyage. Take your pick, any room. Single occupancy if you like. There's plenty of room." He had the magnanimity of a man used to sharing with friends a house not really his. "Spread out. Shower, take a nap, relax. Dinner is up to you. There's a dining car one back. Or you can order room service and catch a flick. We've spared no expense. Helios's way of wishing you—and me—bon voyage."

No one pressed the issue of their destination any further. At 1730 a pleasant chime announced their departure. As if casting loose on a raft upon a gentle stream, the Helios expedition soundlessly coasted into the depths. The track looked level but was not, sloping almost secretly downward. As it turned out, gravity was the workhorse. Their engine was attached to the rear and would only be used to pull the cars back to this station. One by one, drawn by the earth itself, the cars left behind the sparkling lights of Nazca City.

They approached a portal titled Route 6. An extra, nostalgic 6 had been added with Magic Marker. In a different ink, someone else had attached a third 6. At the last minute a young biologist hopped down from the train and took a final quick snapshot, then ran to catch up again while the others cheered him. That made them all feel well launched. The train slid through a brief wall of forced air, a climate lock, and they passed inside.

Immediately the temperature and humidity dropped. Nazca City's tropical environment vanished. It was ten degrees colder in the rail tunnel, and the air was as dry as a desert. At last, Ali realized, they were entering the unabridged hell. No fire and brimstone here. It felt more like high chaparral, like Taos.

The tracks glittered as if someone had taken a polishing rag to them. The train began to pick up speed, and they all went to their rooms. In her berth, Ali found a wicker basket with fresh oranges, Tobler chocolate, and Pepperidge Farm cookies. The little refrigerator was stocked. Her bunk had a single red rose on the pillow. When she lay down, there was a video monitor overhead for watching any of hundreds of films. Old monster movies were her vice. She said her prayers, then fell asleep to *Them* and the hiss of tracks.

In the morning, Ali squeezed into the small shower and let the hot water run through her hair. She could not believe the amenities. Her timing with room service was just right, and she sat by the tiny window with her omelette and toast and coffee. The window was round and small, like a cabin port on a ship. She saw only blackness out there, and thought that explained the compressed view. Then she noticed ELLIS BULLETPROOF GLASS etched in small letters on the glass, and realized the whole train was probably reinforced against attack.

At 0900 their training resumed in the dining car. The first morning on the train was given to refresher courses in things like emergency medicine, climbing techniques, basic gun craft, and other general information they were supposed to have learned over the past few months. Most had actually done their homework, and the session was more like an icebreaker.

That afternoon, Shoat escalated their teachings. Slide projectors and a large video monitor were set up at one end of the dining car. He announced a series of presentations by expedition members on their various specialties and theories. Ali was enjoying herself. Show-and-tell, with iced shrimp and nachos.

The first two speakers were a biologist and a microbotanist. Their topic was the difference between troglobite, trogloxene, and troglophile. The first category truly lived in the troglo—or "hole"—environment. Hell was their biological niche. The second, xenes, adapted to it, like eyeless salamanders. The third, troglophiles like bats and other nocturnal animals, simply visited the subterranean world on a regular basis, or exploited it for food or shelter.

The two scientists began arguing the merits of preadaptation, the "predestination to darkness." Shoat stepped to the front and thanked them. His manner was crisp, yet random. They were here on Helios's nickel. This was his show.

Through the remainder of the afternoon, various specialists were introduced and gave their remarks. Ali was impressed by the group's relative youth. Most had their doctorates. Few were older than forty, and some were barely twenty-five. People wandered in and out of the dining car as the hours wound on, but Ali sat through it all, fixing faces with names, drinking in the esoterica of sciences she'd never studied.

After a patio-type supper of hamburgers and cold beer, they had been promised a just-released Hollywood movie. But the machine would not work, and that was when Shoat stumbled. To this point, his day of orientation had featured scientists who were practiced speakers, or at least in command of their topics. Seeking to enliven the evening with a change of entertainment, Shoat tried something different.

"Since we're getting to know each other," he announced, "I wanted to introduce a guy we'll all come to depend on. We are extremely fortunate to have obtained him from the U.S. Army, where he was a famous scout and tracker. He has the reputation of being a Ranger's Ranger, a true veteran of the deep. Dwight," he called. "Dwight Crockett. I see you back there. Come on up. Don't be shy."

Shoat's tracker was apparently not prepared for this attention. He balked, whoever he was, and after a minute Ali turned to see him. Of all people, the reluctant Dwight was that very same stranger she'd insulted on the Galápagos elevator yesterday. What on earth was he doing here? she wondered.

With all eyes on him now, Dwight let go of the wall and stood straight. He was dressed in new Levi's and a white shirt closed to the throat and buttoned at each wrist. His dark glacier glasses glittered like insect eyes. Sporting that awful Frankenstein haircut, he looked completely out of place, like those ranch hands Ali had sometimes seen in the hill country, troubled in human company, better left in their remote line shacks. The tattooing and scars on his face and scalp encouraged a healthy distance.

"Was I supposed to say something?" he asked from the back of the car.

"Come up here where everyone can see you," Shoat insisted.

"Unreal," someone whispered next to Ali. "I've heard of this guy. An outlaw."

Dwight kept his displeasure economical, the slightest shake of his head. When he finally came forward, the crowd parted. "Dwight's the one you really want to hear from," Shoat said. "He never got around to graduate school, he doesn't have an academic specialty. But talk about authority in the field. He spent eleven years in hadal captivity. The last three years he's been hunting Haddie for the Rangers and Special Forces and SEALs. Now I've read your résumés, folks. Few of our group have ever visited the subterranean world. None of us has ever gone beyond the electrified zones. But Ike here can tell us what it's like. Out there." Shoat sat down. It was Ike's stage.

He stood before their patter of applause, and his awkwardness seemed endearing, a little pathetic. Ali caught a few of the murmured remarks about his scars and exploits. Deserter, she heard. Berserker. Cannibal. Slave runner. Animal. It was all traded breathlessly, in the superlative. Strange, she thought, how legends grew. They made him sound like a sociopath, and yet they were drawn to him, excited by the romance of his imagined deeds.

Dwight let them have their curiosity. The tracks sibilated in their growing silence, and people turned uncomfortable. Ali had seen it a hundred times, how Americans and Europeans chafed at silence. In contrast, Dwight was downright primal with his patience. Finally his reticence proved too much. "Don't you have anything to say?" Shoat said.

Dwight shrugged. "You know, I haven't had such an interesting day in a long time. You people know your stuff." Ali wasn't prepared for that. None of them were. This odd brute had been sitting in the rear all afternoon, deliberately unremarkable, quietly getting educated. By them! It was enchanting.

Shoat was annoyed. Maybe this was supposed to have been a freak show. "How about questions. Any questions?"

"Mr. Crockett," a woman from MIT started. "Or is it Captain, or some other rank?"

"No," he said, "they busted me out. I don't have any rank. And don't bother with the 'mister,' either."

"Very well. Dwight, then," the woman went on. "I wanted to ask—"

"Not Dwight," he interrupted. "Ike."

"Ike?"

"Go on."

"The hadals have disappeared," she said. "Every day civilization pushes the night back a little further. My question, sir, is whether it's really so dangerous out there?"

"Things have a way of flying apart," Ike said.

"Not that we'll be going out in harm's way," the woman said.

Ike looked at Shoat. "Is that what this man told you?"

Ali felt uneasy. He knew something they didn't. On second thought, that wasn't saying much.

Shoat moved them along. "Question?" he said.

Ali stood. "You were their prisoner," she said. "Can you share a little about your experience? What did they do to you? What are the hadals like?"

The dining car fell silent. Here was a campfire story they could listen to all night. What a resource Ike could be to her, with his insights into the hadals' habits and culture. Why, he might even speak their language.

Ike smiled at her. "I don't have a lot to say about those days."

There was disappointment.

"Do you think they're still out there somewhere? Is there any chance we might see one?" someone else asked.

"Where we're going?" Ike said. Unless Ali was wrong, he was provoking Shoat on purpose, dancing on the edge of information they were not yet supposed to have.

Shoat's annoyance built.

"Where are we going?" a man asked.

"No comment," Shoat answered for Ike.

"Have you been in our particular territory yourself?"

"Never," Ike said. "I used to hear rumors, of course. But I never believed they could be true."

"Rumors of what?"

Shoat was checking his watch.

The train gave a soft lurch. They braked to a slow halt. People went to look through the small windows and Ike was forgotten, momentarily. Shoat stood on a chair. "Grab your bags and personal effects, folks. We're changing trains."

Ali shared an open flatcar with three men and freight, mostly heavy equipment parts. She sat against a John Deere crate labeled PLANE-TARIES, DIFFERENTIALS. One of the men had bad gas and kept grimacing in apology.

The ride was smooth. The artery was man-made, bored to a uniform twenty-foot diameter. The trackbed was crushed gravel sprayed with black oil. Overhead, bare bulbs bled down rusty light. Ali kept thinking of a Siberian gulag. Wires and pipes and cables veined the walls.

Cavities opened to the sides. They didn't see any people, just crawlers and loaders and excavators and pipe layers, piled rubber tires, and cement ties. The track made a slithery sound under their wheels, seamless. Ali missed the click-clack of rail joints. She remembered a train journey with her parents, falling asleep to the rhythm while the world passed by.

Ali gave one of her fresh apples to the man who was still awake. They'd been grown in the hydroponic gardens at Nazca City. He said, "My daughter loves apples," and showed her a picture.

"What a beautiful girl," Ali said.

"Kids?" he asked.

Ali pulled a jacket over her knees. "Oh, I don't think I could bear to leave a child," she answered too quickly. The man winced. Ali said, "I didn't mean it that way."

The train was relentlessly gentle. It never slowed, never stopped. Ali and her neighbors improvised a latrine with privacy by pushing some of the crates together. They had a communal supper, each contributing some food.

At midnight the walls brightened from cinnamon to tan. Her companions were all sleeping when the train entered a band of marine fossils. Here exoskeletons, there ancient seaweeds, there a spray of tiny brachiopods. The bore-cutter had sheared the rich find with impunity.

"Did you see that, Mapes!" a voice yelled from a car ahead. "Arthropoda!"

"Trilobitomorpha!" Mapes shrieked in ecstatic response from behind.

"Check those dorsal grooves! Pinch me!"

"Look at this one coming up, Mapes! Early Ordovician!"

"Ordovician, hell!" Mapes bellowed. "Cambrian, man. Early. Very early. Look at that rock. Shit, maybe even late Precam!"

The fossils jumped and writhed and wove like a miles-long tapestry. Then the walls went blank again.

At three in the morning, they came upon the remains of their first ambush. At first it seemed like nothing more than a car accident.

The clues began with a long scrape mark on the left wall where a vehicle of some sort had struck the stone. Abruptly the mark leaped to the right wall, where it became a gouge, then ricocheted to the opposite side and back again. Someone had lost control.

The evidence became more violent, more puzzling. Broken fragments of stone mixed with headlight glass, then a torn section of heavy steel mesh.

The gashes and scrapes went on and on, left, then right.

Miles farther, the crazy bounce ended. All that remained of the reckless ride was a tangle of metal. The destroyed backhoe had been torn open.

They drifted past. The stone was scorched, but furrowed, too. Ali had seen war zones in Africa, and recognized the starred splatter print of an explosion.

Around the bend, they came on two white crosses planted Latino-style in a grotto carved into the wall. Tufts of hair, rags, and animal bones had been nailed to the stone. The rags, she comprehended, were leather hides. Skins. Flayed skin. This was a memorial.

After that, miles passed in silence. Here it was at last—all their childhood legends of desperate fights waged against biblical mutants—before their eyes, unintended, where fate had given it. This was not a TV report that could be turned off. This was not a poet's inferno in a book that could be put back on the shelf. Here was the world they lived in now.

At around three, Ali fell asleep. When she woke, the stone was still in motion. The tunnel's smooth walls became less regular. Fractures appeared. Pressure cracks filigreed the ceiling. Crevices lurked like darkened closets. Ali saw a cardboard sign in the distance. WATTS GOLD, LTD. it announced. An arrow pointed at a secondary path branching off into the gloom. A few miles farther on, the wall breached upon another ragged hole. Ali looked inside, and lights sparkled far away in the darkness. BLOCKWICK CLAIM, a sign said. BEWARE OF DOG.

From there on, side roads and crude tunnels fed off every mile or so, sometimes identified as a camp or mining claim, anonymous and unwelcoming. A few were lit at their deepest points with tiny fires. Others were as dark as wells, forlorn. What kind of people gave themselves to such remoteness? H. G. Wells had gotten it right in his *Time Machine*. The underworld was peopled not with demons, but with proles.

Ali smelled the settlement long before they reached it. The smog was part petroleum, part unrefined sewage, part cordite and dust. Her eyes began watering. The air got thicker, then putrid. It was five o'clock in the morning.

The tunnel walls widened, then flew open upon a cavernous shaft steeping in pollution and overhung by bright turquoise cliffs lit, in a civic fashion, with several spotlights. Otherwise, Point Z-3, locally known as Esperanza, was dimly illuminated. The burden of darkness was evidently too much to overcome with their thin ration of electricity from Nazca City. Despite the cheerful Matisse-like cliffs, it did not look like a friendly home for the next year.

"Helios built a science institute here?" asked one of Ali's companions. "Why bother?"

"I was expecting something a little more modern," agreed another. "This place doesn't look like it's heard of the flush toilet."

The train coasted through an opening in a glittering briar patch of razor wire. It was like a city made of knife-sharp Slinkys. Concertina piled atop glittering concertina. The coils lay twenty feet high in places. The razor wire got more space than the settlement itself, which was simply a mob of tents on small platforms whittled into the descending hillside.

The train slowed upon a ridge that fell on the far side into a chasm.

Farther along the barrier, they saw a desiccated body suspended high on the outside section of an accordion snarl of wire. The creature's grimace was almost joyful. "Hadal," said a scientist. "Must have been attacking the settlement." They all craned to see. But the rags hanging from the body were American military. The soldier had been trying to climb his way in over the concertina. Something had been chasing him.

The railway ended in a bunker complex bristling with electric cannons. There was no question about its function. If the settlement came under attack, people were meant to come here. This train would be their last hope of exit.

A squalid settler in canvas pants made notes on a piece of paper as they rolled past. Except for the steel teeth, he might have been an extra in a hillbilly movie.

"How you doing?" one of Ali's companions called down.

The settler spat.

The train slid inside the bunker and stopped. Immediately it was set upon by gangs of men with huge hands and bare feet. The workers were degraded, some scarcely recognizable as anatomically modern humans. It wasn't just the Hulk muscles and Abe Lincoln brows and cheekbones and their guttural exchanges. They smelled different: a musk odor. And some of them had bone growing right through their flesh. Many had strips of burlap draped over their heads to protect them from the railyard's dim lighting. While Ali and the others climbed down from the flatcars, the yard workers cast off chains and straps and manually unloaded crates weighing hundreds of pounds. Ali was fascinated by their enormous strength and deformities. Several of the giants noticed her attention and smiled.

Ali walked along the flatcars between boxes and crates and earth-moving equipment. She joined a crowd on a flat landing dramatically perched at the rim of the great chasm. The landing was bordered with a stone rampart like those at Grand Canyon or Yosemite, but instead of viewing scopes along the wall, there were gun mounts and electric cannon. Far below, she saw the upper reaches of a path snaking back and forth along the ridge wall, sinking into pitch blackness.

Some of the locals were mingling with the expedition members. They had not washed in many months or years. The patches on their caked clothing looked more soldered on than sewn. They gaped with coal miners' eyes, brilliant white holes in their grime. Ali thought she saw mild insanity here, the sort that zoo animals fall into. The handles on their guns and machetes were shiny with use.

A famished-looking man with freshly scraped cheeks was delivering a welcome speech on behalf of the township. He was the mayor, Ali guessed. He proudly pointed out the turquoise cliffs, then launched upon a brief history of Esperanza, its first human habitation four years ago, the "coming" of the railroad a year later, how the last attack—"well over" two years ago—had been repulsed by local minutemen and about recent discoveries of gold, platinum, and iridium deposits. He then began a description of his town's future, the plans for cliff-front sky-scrapers, a nuclear generator, round-the-clock lighting for the entire chamber, a professional security force, another tunnel for a second rail line, and one day maybe even their own elevator tube to the surface.

"Excuse me," someone cut him off. "We've come a long way. We're tired. Can you just tell us where the science station is?"

The mayor looked helplessly at the notes for his speech. Bits of tissue stuck to his shaving nicks. "Science station?" he said.

"The research institute," someone shouted.

Shoat stepped in front of the mayor. "Go inside," he told the scientists. "We've arranged for hot food and clean water. In an hour, everything will be explained."

"There is no science station," Shoat told them.

A howl went up.

Shoat waved them quiet. "No station," he repeated. "No institute. No headquarters. No laboratories. Not even a base camp. It was all a fiction."

The auditorium, deep within the bunker, exploded with curses and shouts. Though appalled by the deception, Ali had to give Shoat credit. The group's outrage verged on the homicidal, but he didn't cower.

"Just what are you doing?" a woman cried out.

"On behalf of Helios, I am protecting the greatest trade secret of all time," Shoat responded. "It's a matter of intellectual property. A matter of geographical possession."

"What are you raving about?"

"Helios has spent vast sums to develop the information you're about to see. You've no idea how many other entities—corporations, foreign governments, armies—would kill for what will be revealed. This is the last great secret on earth."

"Gibberish," someone yelled. "Just tell us where you're hijacking us to."

Shoat never flinched. "Meet the chief of Helios's cartography department," he said, and opened a door on one wall.

The cartographer was a diminutive man with leg braces. His head was large for his body. He smiled automatically. Ali had not seen him on the train, and presumed he had arrived earlier to prepare for them. He cut the lights.

"Forget the moon," he told them. "Forget Mars. You're about to walk on the planet inside our planet."

A video screen lit up. The first image was a still of a yellowed Mercator map. "Here was the world in 1587," he said. The cartographer's silhouette bobbed across the bottom of the large screen. "Lacking facts, young Mercator plundered the accounts of Marco Polo, which were themselves based on plundered hearsay and folklore. Here, for instance"—he pointed at a misshapen Australia—"was a total fabrication. A medieval hypothesis. Logic suggested that the continents in the north must be counterweighted by continents in the south, and so a mythical place called Terra Australis Incognita was invented. Mercator incorporated it on this map. And here's the marvel of it. Using this map, sailors found Australia."

The cartographer pointed his pencil high. "Up there is another landmark invented out of Mercator's imagination. They named it Polus Arcticus. Again, explorers discovered the Arctic by relying on the fiction of it. A hundred and fifty years later, the French cartographer Philippe Buache drew a gigantic—and equally imaginary—Antarctic Pole to counterweight Mercator's imaginary Arctic. And once again, explorers discovered it by using a map made of myth. So it is with hell and what you are about to see. You might say my mapping department has invented a reality for you to explore."

Ali looked around. The one figure in the audience that struck her was Ike. Her fascination with him was becoming something of an enigma. At the moment he looked singularly odd, wearing sunglasses in a darkened room.

The old map became a large globe slowly revolving behind the cartographer. It was a satellite view, real-time. Clouds flocked against mountain ranges or moved across the blue oceans. On the night side, city lights flared like forest fires.

"We call this Level 1," said the cartographer. The globe froze still with the vast Pacific facing them. "Until World War II, we were sure the ocean floor was a huge flat surface, covered with a uniform thickness of sea mud. Then radar was invented, and there was quite a shock in store."

The video image flickered.

"Lo and behold, it wasn't smooth."

A trillion gallons of water vanished in an instant. They were left staring at the seafloor, drained of all water, its trenches and faults and seamounts like so many wrinkles and warts.

"At great cost, Helios has peeled the onion even deeper. We've consolidated an aerial-seismic mosaic of overlapping earth images. We took every piece of information from earthquake stations and sonic sleds towed behind ships and from oil drillers' seismographs and from earth tomographies collected over a ninety-five-year period. Then we combined it with satellite data measuring the heights of the ocean surface, reverse-albedo, gravity fields, geo-magnetics, and atmospheric gases. The methods have all been used before, but never all in combination. Here's the result, a series of delaminated views of the Pacific region, layer by layer."

"Now we're getting somewhere," one of the scientists grunted. Ali felt it herself. This was big.

"You've seen seafloor topographies before," the cartographer said. "But the scale was, at best, one to twenty-nine million. What our department has produced for Level 2 is almost equivalent to walking on the ocean bottom. One to sixteen."

He tapped a button on his palm mouse, and the image magnified. Ali felt herself shrinking like Alice in Wonderland. A colored dot in the mid-Pacific soared and became a towering volcano.

"This is the Isakov Seamount, east of Japan. Depth 1,698 fathoms. A fathom, as you know, equals six feet. We use fathoms for depth readings, feet for elevations. You'll be using both. Fathoms for your position relative to sea level, and feet to measure the heights of cave ceilings and other subterranean features. Just remember to convert to fathoms when you're down there."

Down there? thought Ali. *Aren't we already?*

The cartographer moved his mouse. Ali felt flung between canyon walls. Then the image threw them onto a plain of flattened sediment.

They sped across it. "Ahead lies the Challenger Deep, part of the Mariana Trench."

Suddenly they were plunging off the plain into a vertical chasm. They fell. "Five thousand nine hundred seventy-one fathoms," he said. "That's 35,827 feet. Six-point-eight miles deep. The deepest known point on earth. Until now."

The image flickered again. A simple drawing showed a cross-section of the earth's crust. "Beneath the continents, the abyssal cavities are not exceptionally deep. They mostly exploit surficial limestone, which is readily eroded by water into such traditional features as sinkholes and caves. These have been the focus of public attention lately because they're close to home, underneath cities and suburbs. At last count, the combined military estimate of continental tunnels ran to 463,000 linear miles, with an average depth of only three hundred fathoms.

"Where you're going is considerably deeper. Beneath the ocean crust, we're dealing with a whole different rock from limestone, much newer in geological terms than the continental rock. Until a few years ago, it was presumed that the interior of ocean rock was nonporous and much too hot and pressurized to sustain life. Now we know better.

"The abyss beneath the Pacific is basalt, which gets attacked every few hundred thousand years by huge plumes of hydrogen-sulfide brine, or sulfuric acid, which snake up from deeper layers. This acid brine eats through the basalt like worms through an apple. We now believe there may be as many as six million miles of naturally occurring cavities in the rock beneath the Pacific, at an average depth of 6,100 fathoms. That's 36,600 feet below sea level, or six-point-nine miles."

"Six *million* miles?" someone said.

"Correct," said the cartographer. "Very little of that is passable for human beings, naturally. But what is passable is more than enough. Indeed, what is passable seems to have been in use for thousands of years."

Hadals, thought Ali, and heard the stillness all around her.

The screen filled with gray, shot through with squiggles and holes. The overall effect was of worms burrowing through a block of mud, surfacing and diving into the nether zone.

"The Pacific floor covers roughly 64,186,000 square miles. As you can see, it's riddled with these cavities, hundreds and thousands of miles of them. From Level 15, roughly four miles down, the density of rock and our limited technology drop our scale to 1:120,000. But we've still managed to count some eighteen thousand significant subterranean branches.

"They seem to dead-end or circle on themselves and go nowhere. All except one. We think this particular tunnel was carved by an acid plume relatively recently, less than a hundred thousand years ago, just moments in geological time. It appears to have welled up from beneath the Mariana Trench system, then corkscrewed east into younger and younger basalt. This tunnel goes from Point A—where we sit this morning—all the way across to Point B." He walked from east to west across the front of the screen, pulling his pencil point across the entire Pacific territory. "Point B lies at point-seven degrees north by 145.23 degrees east, just this side of the Mariana Trench system. There it dips deeper, beneath the Trench.

"Where it goes, we're not quite sure. It probably links with the Carolinian system west of the Philippines. A profusion of tunnels shoots throughout the Asian plate systems, giving access to the basements of Australia, the Indonesian archipelago, China, and so on. You name it, there are doorways to the surface everywhere. We believe these connect with the sub-Pacific network here at Point B, but our scan is still in progress. It's a cartographic missing link for the moment, as the source of the Nile once was. But not for long. In less than a year, you are going to tell me where it leads."

It took Ali and the others a minute to catch up.

"You're sending us out there?" someone gasped.

Ali was staggered. She couldn't begin to grasp the enormity of the endeavor. Nothing January or Thomas had told her was preparation for this. She heard people breathing hard all around her. What could this mean, she wondered, a journey so audacious? Why send them all the way across to Asia? It was a stratagem of some sort, a geopolitical chess move. It reminded her less of Lewis and Clark's traverse than of the great expeditions of discovery once launched by Spain and England and Portugal.

It struck her. Their journey was meant to be a declaration, a *pronunciamento*. Wherever the expedition went, Helios would be asserting its domain. And the cartographer had just told them where they were going, beneath the equator, from South America all the way to China.

In a flash, Ali saw the grand design.

Helios—Cooper, the failed President—intended to lay claim to the entire subbasement of the oceanic bowl. He was going to create a nation for himself. But a nation the size of the Pacific Ocean? She had to relay this information to January.

Ali sat in the darkness, gaping at the screen. It would be larger than all the nations on earth put together! Helios would own almost half the globe. What could you possibly do with such immense space? How could you manifest such power?

She was awed by the grandeur of it. Such imperial vision: it was virtually psychotic. And she and these scientists were to be the agents in gaining it.

Her neighbors were lodged in their own thoughts. Most were probably weighing the risks, adjusting their search goals, adapting to the vastness of the challenge, reckoning the odds.

"Shoat!" a man bellowed.

Shoat's face obligingly appeared at the podium light.

"No one said anything about this," the man said.

"You did sign on for a year," Shoat pointed out.

"You expect us to traverse the Pacific Ocean? A mile to three miles beneath the ocean floor? Through unexplored territory? Hadal territory?"

"I'll be with you every step of the way," Shoat said.

"But no one's ever gone west of the Nazca Plate."

"That's true. We'll be the first."

"You're talking about being on the move for an entire year."

"Precisely our reason for sending you a workout schedule over the last six months. All those climbing walls and StairMasters and heavy squats weren't for your cosmetic enhancement."

Ali could sense the group calculating.

"You have no idea what's out there," someone said.

"That's not exactly true," Shoat said. "We have *some* idea. Two years ago, a military reconnaisance probed some of the path. Basically they found the remains of a prehistoric passageway, a network of tunnels and chambers that are well marked and have been improved and maintained over a period of several thousand years. We think it may have been a kind of Silk Road for the Pacific abyss."

"How far did the soldiers get?"

"Twenty-three miles," Shoat answered. "Then they turned around and came back."

"Armed soldiers."

Shoat was unflappable. "They weren't prepared. We are."

"What about hadals?"

"There hasn't been a sighting in over two years," Shoat said. "But just to be safe, Helios has hired a security force. They will accompany us every step of the way."

A gentleman stood. He had Isaac Asimov muttonchops and black horn-rims, and had X'ed out the word "Hi" on his name tag. Ali knew his face from the dust jackets of his numerous books: Donald Spurrier, a renowned primatologist. "What about human limitations? Your projected route must be five thousand miles long."

The cartographer turned to the glowing map. His finger traced a set of lines that ambled back and forth across the equatorial rhumb. "In fact, with all the bends and turns and vertical loss and gain, a better estimate is eight thousand miles, plus or minus a thousand."

"Eight thousand miles?" said Spurrier. "In a single year? On foot?"

"For what it's worth, our train ride just gave us an easy thirteen hundred miles without a step."

"Leaving a mere 6,700 miles. Are we supposed to run nonstop for a year?"

"Mother Nature is lending a hand," the cartographer said.

"We've detected significant motion along the route," Shoat said. "We believe it's a river."

"A river?"

"Moving from east to west. Thousands of miles long."

"A theoretical river. You haven't seen it."

"We'll be the first."

Spurrier was no longer resisting. "We won't go thirsty, then."

"Don't you see?" Shoat said. "It means we can float."

They were dazzled.

"What about supplies? How can we hope to carry enough for a year?"

"We start with porters. Every four to six weeks thereafter, we will be supplied by drill hole. Helios has already begun drilling supply holes for us at selected points. They will drill straight through the ocean floor to intersect our route, and lower food and gear. At those points, by the way, we'll have brief contact with the World. You'll be able to communicate with your families. We'll even be able to evacuate the sick or injured."

It all sounded reasonable.

"It's radical. It's daring," Shoat said. "It's one year out of your lives. We could have spent it sitting on our butts in a hole like this. Instead, one year from now, we'll go down in history. You'll be writing papers and publishing books about this for the rest of your lives. It will cement your tenure, gain you chairs of departments, win you prizes and acclaim. Your children and grandchildren will beg you for the tale of what you're about to do."

"This is a huge decision," a man said. "I need to consult my wife." A general murmur agreed.

"I'm afraid the communications line is down." It was a blatant lie, Ali could see it. But that was part of the price. He was drawing a line for them to step across. "You may, of course, post mail. The next train back to Nazca City leaves two months from now." Helios was playing hardball, a total embargo on information.

Shoat surveyed them with reptilian coolness. "I don't expect everyone here tonight to be with us in the morning. You're free to return home, of course." In two months' time, on the train. The expedition would have a tremendous head start on any leaks to the media. He looked at his watch.

"It's late," he said. "The expedition departs at 0600. That leaves only a few hours for you to sleep on your choices. That's enough, though. I'm a firm believer that each of us comes into this world with our decisions already made."

The lights came up. Ali blinked. Everywhere, people were leaning forward onto seatbacks, rubbing their hands, making calculations. Faces were lit with excitement. Thinking fast, she looked for Ike's reaction to judge the proposition. But he had left while the lights were still off.

He who fights with monsters
might take care lest he
thereby become a monster.
And if you gaze for long into
an abyss, the abyss gazes
also into you.

—FRIEDRICH NIETZSCHE,
Beyond Good and Evil

10

DIGITAL SATAN

"She was caught in a nursing home near Bartlesville, Oklahoma," Dr. Yamamoto explained to them. Thomas and Vera Wallach and Foley, the industrialist, followed the physician from her office. Branch came last, eyes protected by dark ski goggles, sleeves buttoned at each wrist to hide his burn scars.

"It was one of those homes that give adult children nightmares," Dr. Yamamoto went on. She couldn't have been more than twenty-seven. Her lab coat was unbuttoned. Underneath it, a T-shirt read THE LAKE CITY 50-MILE ENDURANCE RUN. She exuded vitality and happiness, Branch thought. The wedding ring on her finger looked only a few weeks old.

They took an elevator up. A sign, supplemented with Braille, listed the floors by specialty. Primates occupied the basement. The upper floors were Psychiatry and Neurophysiology. They got off on the top floor, which bore no title, and started down another hallway.

"It turns out the administrator at this Bartlesville scam had served time for a variety of frauds and forgeries," Dr. Yamamoto said. "He's back in, I guess. I hope. A real prince. His so-called facility advertised itself as specializing in Alzheimer's patients. Behind the scenes, he kept the patients just barely alive in order to keep the Medicare/Medicaid checks coming in. Bed restraints, horrific conditions. No medical personnel whatsoever. Apparently our little intruder was able to hide there for over a month before a janitor finally noticed."

The young doctor halted at a door with a keypad. "Here we are," she said, and gently entered the code. Long fingers. A soft, sure touch.

"You play violin," Thomas guessed.

She was delighted. "Guitar," she confessed. "Electric. Bass. I have a band, Girl Talk. All guys, and me."

She held the door for them. Immediately, Branch sensed the change in light and sound. No windows in here. No spill of sunbeams. The slight whistle of wind against brick quit. These walls were thick.

To the right and left, doorways opened onto rooms orbiting computer screens. A plaque read DIGITAL ADAM PROJECT, NATIONAL LIBRARY OF MEDICINE. Branch didn't see a single book.

Yamamoto's voice adjusted to the new quiet. "Lucky for us it was the janitor who noticed," she continued. "The administrator and his gang of thieves would never have called the police. To make a long story short, the cops came. They were suitably horrified. At first they were sure it was animals. One of the cops used to trap coyotes and bobcats. He set out some old rusty leg traps."

They reached a set of double doors. Another keypad. Different numbers, Branch noticed. They entered in stages: first a guard, then a scrub room, where Yamamoto helped them put on disposable green gowns and surgical masks and double pairs of latex gloves, then a main room with biotechs at work over test tubes and keyboards. She led them around gleaming banks of equipment and picked up her narrative.

"That night she came back for more. One of the traps caught her leg. The cops came roaring in. She was a complete surprise. They were not at all prepared. Barely four feet high and, even with her tibia and fibula broken in half, she still almost beat five grown men. She came very close to escaping, but they got her. We would have preferred a live specimen, of course."

They came to a door labeled NIPPLES ALERT on a handwritten sheet.

"Nipples?" asked Vera.

Yamamoto noticed the sign and snatched it down. "A joke," she said. "It's cold in there. The room is refrigerated. We call it the pit and the pendulums."

Branch was gratified by her blush. She was a professional. What's more, she wanted to look professional to them. She led them through the door.

Inside, it was not as cold as Branch had expected. A wall thermometer read thirty-one degrees Fahrenheit. Very bearable for an hour or two of work. Not that anyone was in here. The work was all being done automatically.

Machinery susurrated, a steady rhythm. Shh. Shh. Shh. As though to quiet an infant. A number of lights pulsed with each hush.

"They killed her?" Vera asked.

"No, it wasn't that," Yamamoto said. "She was alive after they got the nets and rope on. But the trap was rusty. Sepsis set in. Tetanus. She died before we arrived. I brought her here in a footlocker packed with dry ice."

There were four stainless-steel autopsy tables. Each held a block of blue gelatin. Each block was positioned against a machine. Each machine flashed a light every five seconds.

"We named her Dawn," said Yamamoto.

They looked into the blue gelatin and there she was, her cadaver frozen and suspended in gel and cut crosswise into four sections.

"We were halfway through computerizing our digital Eve when the hadal came our way." Yamamoto indicated a dozen freezer drawers along one wall. "We put Eve back into storage and immediately went to work on Dawn. As you can see, we've quartered her body and bedded the four sections in gelatin. These machines are called cryomacrotomes. Glorified meat shavers. Every few seconds they cut a half-millimeter off the bottom of each gelatin block, and a synchronized camera photographs the new layer."

"How long has it been here?" Foley asked.

It, not *she,* Branch noticed. Foley was keeping things impersonal. For his own part, Branch felt a connection. How could you not? The small hand had four fingers and a thumb.

"Two weeks. It's just a function of the blades and cameras. In another few months we'll have a computer bank with over twelve thousand images. She'll end up as forty billion bytes of information stored on seventy CD-ROM disks. Using a mouse, you will be able to travel through a 3-D image of Dawn's interior."

"And your purpose?"

"Hadal physiology," Dr. Yamamoto said. "We want to know how it differs from human."

"Is there any way to accelerate your inquiry?" asked Thomas.

"We don't know what we're looking for, or even what questions to ask. As it is, we don't dare miss anything. There's no telling what might lie in the smallest detail."

They separated and went to different tables. Through the translucent gel, Branch saw a pair of lower legs and feet. There was the place the trap had snapped her bones. The skin was fish white.

He found the head-and-shoulders section. It was like a bust in alabaster. The lids were half shut, exposing bleached blue irises. The mouth was slightly open. Working from the neck upward, the machine's pendulum was still at throat level.

"You've probably seen a lot like her," Dr. Yamamoto spoke at his shoulder. Her voice was severe.

Branch cocked his head and looked closer, almost affectionately. "They're all different," he said. "Kind of like us."

He could tell she'd expected something coarse or stormy from him. Most people took one look at him and assumed he couldn't get enough of Haddie's blood.

The physician's voice softened. "Judging by her teeth and the immaturity of her pelvic girdle," she said, "Dawn was probably twelve or thirteen years old. We could be way off on that, of course. We have nothing to compare her with, so we're simply guessing. Specimens have been very hard to get. You'd think after so much contact, so many killings, we'd be swimming in bodies."

"That is odd," said Vera. "Do they decompose faster than normal mammal remains?"

"Depending on the exposure to direct sunlight. But the scarcity of good specimens has more to do with desecration." Branch noticed that she did not look at him.

"You mean mutilation?"

"It's more than that."

"Desecration, then," said Thomas. "That's a strong term."

Yamamoto went over to the storage drawers and pulled out a long tray on rollers. "I don't know, what do you call it?" A hideous animal lay on the metal, scorched black, teeth bared, dismembered, mutilated. It could have been eight thousand years old.

"Caught and burned one week ago," she said.

"Soldiers?" asked Vera.

"Actually, no. This came from Orlando, Florida. A regular neighborhood. People are scared. Maybe it's a form of racial catharsis. There's this revulsion or anger or terror. People seem to feel they have to lay waste to these things, even after they've killed them. Maybe they think they're destroying evil."

"Do you?" asked Thomas.

Her almond eyes were sad. Then disciplined. Either way, compassion or science, she did not.

"We offer rewards for undamaged specimens," she told them. "But this is about the best that comes in. This guy, for instance. He was captured alive by a group of middle-aged accountants and software engineers playing touch football at a suburban soccer field. By the time they got finished with him, he was a piece of charcoal."

Branch had seen far worse.

"All around the country. All around the world," she said. "We know they're coming up into our midst. There are sightings and killings every hour, somewhere in metro and rural America. Try to get a whole, undamaged cadaver in the lab, though. It's a real problem. It makes research very slow."

"Why do you think they're coming up, Doctor? Seems like everyone has a theory."

"None of us here has a clue," Yamamoto said. "Frankly, I'm not convinced the hadals are coming up in any greater numbers than they have historically. But it's safe to say that humans are more sensitized to the hadals' presence these days, and so we're seeing them more clearly. The majority of sightings are false, as with UFOs. A great number have been sightings of transients and freight riders and animals, even tree branches scratching at the window, not hadals."

"Ah," said Vera, "it's all in our imagination?"

"Not at all. They're definitely here, hiding in our landfills, our suburban basements, our zoos, warehouses, national parks. In our underbelly. But nowhere near the numbers the politicians and journalists want us to believe. As far as invading us, come on. Who's invading who here? We're the ones sinking shafts and colonizing caves."

"Dangerous talk," said Foley.

"At a certain point, our hate and fear change us," the young woman said. "I mean, what kind of world do we want to raise our children in? That's important, too."

"But if they're not appearing in any greater numbers than before," argued Thomas, "doesn't that throw out all the catastrophe theories we keep hearing, that a great famine or plague or environmental disaster is to blame for their coming among us?"

"That's one more thing our research may help answer. A people's history speaks through their bones and tissue," said Yamamoto. "But until we collect more specimens and expand our database, I can't tell you anything more than what the bodies of Dawn and a few of her brothers and sisters have told us."

"Then we know almost nothing about their motivation?"

"Scientifically speaking, no. Not yet. But sometimes we—the staff and I—sit around and invent life stories for them." The young doctor indicated her stainless-steel mausoleum. "We give them names and a past. We try to understand how it must have been to be them."

She touched the side of the cutting table with the hadal female's head. "Dawn is easily our group's favorite."

"This?" said Vera. But clearly she was charmed by the staff's humanity.

"Her youth, I guess. And the hard life she led."

"Tell us her story, if you don't mind," said Thomas. Branch looked at the Jesuit. Like Branch, he had a raw exterior that people misjudged. But Thomas felt an affinity for the creatures that was unfashionable at the moment. Branch thought it perfectly in character. Weren't all Jesuits liberation theologists?

The young woman looked uncomfortable. "It's not really my place," she said. "The specialists haven't gone over the data yet, and anything we've made up is pure conjecture."

"Just the same," Vera said, "we want to hear."

"All right, then. She came from very deep, from an atmosphere rich in oxygen, judging by the relatively small rib cage. Her DNA shows a relevant difference from samples sent to us from other regions around the world. The consensus is that these hadals all evolved from *Homo erectus*, our own ancestor. It's common knowledge that we shared a mother and father long ago. But then the same can be said about us and orangutans, or lemurs, or even frogs. At some point we all share genesis.

"One surprise is how alike the hadals are to us. Another is how unalike they are to one another. Have you ever heard of Donald Spurrier?"

"The primatologist?" said Thomas. "He was here?"

"Now I'm really embarrassed," Yamamoto said. "I'd never heard of him, but people told me later he's world-famous. Anyway, he stopped up to see our little girl one afternoon and essentially conducted an impromptu seminar for us. He told us that *Homo erectus* spun off more variations than any other hominid group. We're one of the spinoffs. Hadals may be another. *Erectus* apparently migrated from Africa to Asia hundreds of thousands of years ago, and the splinter groups possibly evolved into different forms around the world, before going into the interior. Again, I'm not an expert on such things."

To Branch, Yamamoto's modesty was engaging, but a distraction. They were here today on business, to glean every possible clue that she and her colleagues had harvested from this hadal corpse. "In great part," Thomas said, "you have just stated our purpose, to understand why we turn out the way we do. What more can you tell us?"

"There's a high concentration of radioisotopes in her tissue, but that's to be expected, coming from the subplanet, a stone cavity bombarded by mineral radiation from all directions. My own hunch is that radiation may help explain the mutations in their population. But please don't quote me on that. Who really knows why any of us turn out the way we do?"

Yamamoto passed a hand over the block of blue gel, as if stroking the monstrous face. "To our eye, Dawn looks so primitive. Some of our visitors have remarked on what a throwback she is. They think she's so much closer to *erectus* and the Australopithecenes than we are. In fact, she is every bit as evolved as we are, just in a different direction."

That had been one surprise for Branch. You expected stereotypes and racism and prejudices from the ordinary masses. But it was turning out that the sciences were just as rife with it. Indeed, intellectual biases—academic arrogance—helped explain why hell had gone undiscovered for so long.

"Dawn's dental formula is identical to yours and mine—and to hominid fossils three million years old: two incisors, one canine, two premolars, three molars." Yamamoto turned to another table. "The lower limbs are similar to ours, though hadal joints have more sponge in the bone, which suggests Dawn might have been even more efficient at walking than *Homo sapiens sapiens*. And she did a lot of that, walking. It's tough to see through the gel, but if you look hard, she put a lot of miles on those feet. The calluses are thicker than my thumbnail. Her arches have fallen. Somebody measured her: size eleven, quadruple wide."

She moved to the next table, the thorax and upper arms. "So far, few surprises here, either. The cardiovascular system is robust, if not perfectly healthy. The heart's enlarged, meaning she probably came up rapidly from minus four or five miles. Her lungs show chemical scarring, probably from breathing gases vented from the deeper earth. That's an old animal bite there."

Yamamoto turned to the final table. It held the abdomen and lower arms. One hand was clenched, the other graceful. "Again, it's hard to get a clear view. But the finger bones have a significant crook, midway between ape and human digits. That helps explain the stories we hear about hadals scaling walls and pulling themselves through underground nooks and crannies."

Yamamoto gestured at the abdominal chunk. The blade had begun at the top and was shaving back and forth toward the pelvic area. The pubis had scant black hair, the start of womanhood.

"We did nail down part of her short, savage history. Before mounting her in gel and starting the cuts, we reviewed the MRI and CT images. Something about the pelvic saddle didn't look right, and I got the head of our Ob/Gyn department up for a look. He recognized the trauma right away. Rape. Gang rape."

"What's this you're saying?" Foley asked.

"Twelve years old," said Vera. "Can you imagine? That explains why she came up, though."

"How do you mean?" asked Yamamoto.

"The poor thing must have fled from the creatures that did this to her."

"I didn't mean to suggest it was hadals who did this to her. We typed the sperm. It was all human. The injuries were very recent. We contacted the sheriff's department in Bartlesville, and they suggested we talk to the male attendants at the nursing home. The attendants denied it. We could take samples from them, but it wouldn't change anything. This kind of thing's not a crime. One group or another helped themselves to her. They had her locked in a refrigerated meat locker for several days."

Again, Branch had seen worse.

"What a remarkable conceit civilization is," said Thomas. His face looked neither angry nor sad, but seasoned. "This child's suffering is ended. Yet, even as we speak, similar evil plays out in a hundred different places, ours upon them, theirs upon us. Until we can bring some sense of order to bear, the evil will continue to have a hiding place."

He was speaking to the child's body, it seemed, perhaps reminding himself.

"What else?" Yamamoto asked herself aloud. She looked around at the body parts. They were at the abdominal quadrant. "Her stool," Yamamoto started again, "was hard and dark and rank-smelling. A typical carnivore's stool."

"What *was* her diet then?"

"In the last month before death?" said Yamamoto.

"I would have thought oat-bran muffins and fruit juices and whatever else one might scavenge in a geriatric kitchen. Foods with fiber and roughage, easy to digest," suggested Vera.

"Not this gal. She was a meat-eater, no two ways about it. The police report was clear. The stool sample only confirmed it. Exclusively meat."

"But where—"

"Mostly from the feet and calves," said Yamamoto. "That's how she went undetected for so long. The staff thought it was rats or a feral cat, and just applied ointments and bandages. Then Dawn would come back the next night and feed some more."

Vera was silent. Yamamoto's little "gal" had not exactly lent herself to cuddling.

"Not pretty, I know," Yamamoto continued. "But then she didn't have a pretty life."

The blade hissed, the block moved imperceptibly.

"Don't get me wrong. I'm not justifying predation. I'm just not condemning it. Some people call it cannibalism. But if we're going to insist they're not *sapiens,* then technically it's no different from what mountain lions do to us. But these incidents do help explain why people are so scared. Which makes good, undamaged specimens that much harder to obtain. And deadlines impossible to meet. We're way behind."

"Way behind whom?" asked Vera.

"Ourselves," said Yamamoto. "We've been handed deadlines. And we haven't made one yet."

"Who's setting your deadlines?"

"That's the grand mystery. At first we thought it was the military. We kept getting raw computer models for developing new weapons. We were supposed to fill in the blanks—you know, tissue density, positions of organs. Generally provide distinctions between our species and theirs. Then we started getting memos from corporations. But the corporations keep changing. Now we're not even sure about them. For our purposes, it really doesn't matter. The light bill's getting paid."

"I have a question," Thomas said. "You sound a little uncertain about whether Dawn and her kind are really a separate species. What did Spurrier have to say?"

"He was adamant that hadals are a different species, some kind of primate. Taxonomy's a sensitive subject. Right now Dawn is classified as *Homo erectus hadalis.* He got upset when I mentioned the move to rename them *Homo sapiens hadalis.* In other words, an evolutionary branch of us. He said the *erectus* taxon is wastebasket science. Like I said, there's a lot of fear out there."

"Fear of what?"

"It runs against the current orthodoxy. You could get your funding cut. Lose your tenure. Not get hired or published. It's subtle. Everyone's playing it very safe for now."

"What about you?" Thomas asked. "You've handled this girl. Followed her dissection. What do you think?"

"That's not fair," Vera scolded Thomas. "She just got through saying how dangerous the times are."

"It's okay," Yamamoto said to Vera. She looked at Thomas. *"Erectus* or *sapiens?* Let me put it this way. If this were a live subject, if this were a vivisection, I wouldn't do it."

"So you're saying she's human?" asked Foley.

"No. I'm saying she's similar enough, perhaps, not to be *erectus.*"

"Call me a devil's advocate, certainly a layman," Foley said. "But she doesn't look similar to me."

Yamamoto went over to her wall of drawers and pulled a lower tray out. It held a carcass even more grotesque than the ones they'd seen. The skin was wildly scarified. Body hair had grown rampant. The face was all but hooded with a cabbage-like dome of fleshy calcium deposits. Something close to a ram's horn had grown from the middle of the forehead.

She rested one gloved hand on the creature's rib cage. "As I said, the idea was to find differences between our two species. We know there are differences. Those are obvious to the naked eye. Or seem to be. But so far all we've found are physiological similarities."

"How can you say he's similar?" asked Foley.

"That's exactly the point. We were sent this specimen by our lab chief. Sort of a double-blind test to see what we'd come up with. Ten of us worked on the autopsy for a week. We compiled a list of almost forty distinctions from the average *Homo sapiens sapiens*. Everything from blood gases to bone structure to ophthalmic deformities to diet. We found traces of rare minerals in his stomach. He'd been eating clay and various fluorescents. His intestines glowed in the dark. Only then did the lab chief tell us."

"Tell you what?"

"That this was a German soldier from one of the NATO task forces."

Branch had known it was human from the start, but he let Yamamoto make her point.

"That can't be." Vera began lifting and opening surgical cavities and pressing at the bony helmet. "What about this?" she said. "And this?"

"All residuals from his tour of duty. Side effects from the drugs he was told to take or from the geochemical environment in which he was serving."

Foley was shocked. "I've heard of some amount of modification. But never anything like this disfigurement." Suddenly remembering Branch, he stopped himself.

"He does look demonic," Branch commented.

"All in all, it was an instructive anatomy lesson," Yamamoto said. "Very humbling. I came away with one abiding thought. It doesn't matter if Dawn stems from *erectus* or *sapiens*. Go back far enough and *sapiens* is *erectus*."

"Are there no differences, then?" Thomas asked.

"Many. Many. But now we've seen how many incongruities there are between one human and another. It's become an epistemological issue. How to know what we think we know." She slid the drawer shut.

"You sound demoralized."

"No. Distracted, perhaps. Derailed. Off track. But I'm convinced we'll start hitting real discrepancy in three to five months."

"Oh?" said Thomas.

She went back to the table where Dawn's head and shoulders were slowly, very slowly feeding into the pendulum. "That's when we'll begin entering the brain."

11

LOSING THE LIGHT

BETWEEN THE CLIPPERTON AND
GALÁPAGOS FRACTURE ZONES

In groups of four, they were winched into the depths off the
cliffs of Esperanza. Like great naval guns, a battery of five winches faced
out along the chasm rim, motors roaring, their great spools of wire cable
winding out. Freight and humanity alike rode the nets and platforms
down. The chasm was over four thousand feet deep. There were no seat
belts or safety instructions, only frayed come-along straps and oily
chains and floor bolts to secure crates and machinery. The live cargo
managed for itself.

The massive winch arms creaked and groaned. Ali got her pack nestled behind her, and hitched herself to the low railing with carabiners
and a knot. Shoat came over with a clipboard in hand. "Good morning,"
she yelled into the roar and exhaust fumes.

As he had predicted, a number of them had quit the game overnight.
Five or six so far, but given Shoat's and Helios's manner, Ali had
expected more to resign. Judging by Shoat's pleased grin, it seemed he
had, too. She had never spoken with him. A sudden fear flashed through
her other fears, that he might suddenly remove her from the expedition.

"You're the nun," he said. You could never call the pinched face and hungry eyes disarming, but he was personable enough. He offered his hand, which was surprisingly thin, given the pumped biceps and thighs.

"I'm here as an epigrapher and linguist."

"We need one of those? You kind of came out of nowhere," he said.

"I didn't hear about the opportunity until late."

He studied her. "Last chance."

Ali looked around the deck and saw some of those who were staying. They looked ferocious, but forlorn, too. It had been a night of tears and rage and vows of a class-action suit against Helios. There had even been a fistfight. Part of the resentment, Ali realized, was that these people had made their minds up once, and Shoat had forced them to do it again. "I've made my peace," Ali assured him.

"That's one way of putting it." Shoat checked her name on the list.

The cables came taut overhead. The platform lifted. Shoat gave it a hearty shove and walked away as they went swinging into the abyss. One of Ali's companions shouted good-bye to the group of scientists staying behind.

The sound of the winch engines vanished high overhead. It was as if the lights of Esperanza had been flicked off. Suspended by a wire, they sank into blackness, slowly spinning. The overhang was stupendous. Sometimes the cliff wall was so far away their flashlights barely reached it.

"Live worm on a hook," one of her neighbors said after the first hour. "Now I know how it feels."

That was it. Not another word was uttered by any of them all the way down.

Ali had never known such emptiness.

Hours later, they neared the floor. Chemical runoff and human sewage had pooled in a foul marsh stretching along the base and extending beyond the light across the floor. The stench cut through Ali's dust mask. She gasped, then dumped the stench with disgust. Closer still, her skin prickled with the acidity.

The winch landed them with a bump on the edge of the beach of poisons. A hand—something meaty, but gnarled and missing two fingers—grabbed the railing in front of her. *"Bajarse, rapido,"* the man barked. Rags hung from his head, perhaps to soak up his sweat or to shield him from their lights.

Ali unhooked herself and clambered off, and the character threw her pack off. Their platform started to rise. The last of her neighbors had to hop to the ground.

She looked around at this first wave of explorers. There were fifteen or twenty of them, standing in a clump and shining their flashlights. One man had drawn a big handgun and was aiming it vaguely toward the remoteness.

"Bad place to stand. Better move before something falls on your heads," a voice said. They turned toward a niche in the rock. Inside sat a man, his assault rifle parked to one side. He had night glasses. "Follow that trail." He pointed. "Keep going for about an hour. The rest of your people will catch up soon enough. And you, *pendejo*, the gunslinger. Put it back in your pants before someone gets shot."

They did as he said. Lights wagging, they followed a trail that meandered around the cliff base. There was no chance of getting lost. It was the only trail.

A bleak fog hung across the floor. Rags of gas drifted at their knees. Small toxic clouds swirled at head level, blinding white in their headlamps. Here and there, licks of flame sprang up like St. Elmo's fire, then extinguished.

It was a swamp, deathly quiet. Animals had come here by the tens of thousands. Drawn by the spillage or non-native nutrients or, after a while, by the meat of earlier visiting animals, they had eaten and drunk here. Now their bones and decay spoiled among the rocks mile after mile.

Ali paused where two of the biologists were conversing by a pile of liquefying flesh and spiny bones. "We know that spines and protective armor are the proof of expanding numbers of predators in an environment," one explained to her. "When predators begin devouring predators, evolution starts building body defenses. Protein is not a perpetual-motion machine. It has to begin somewhere. But no one's ever found where the hadal food chain begins." At least to date, no one had found evidence of plants down here. Without plants, you had no herbivores; what you ended up with was an entire ecology based on meat.

His friend pried the jaws open to examine the teeth. Something scaly and clawed came crawling out, another invader species from the surface. "Just the way I expected," the friend said. "Everything is hungry down here. Starved."

Ali moved on and saw at least a dozen different sizes and shapes of skulls and rib cages, a brand-new menagerie that was not entirely new to her imagination. One set of bones had the dimensions of a short snake with a large head. Something else had once transported itself on two legs. Another animal could have been a small frog with wings. None of it moved.

Soon Ali was sweating and breathing hard. She'd known there would be a period of adaptation to the trail, that it was going to take time to acclimate to the depths, to build up their quadriceps and adjust to new circadian rhythms. The stench of animal carcasses and the mining network's sewage didn't help. And an obstacle course of rusting cables, twisted rails, sudden ladders, and staircases made progress more difficult.

Ali reached a clearing. A group of scientists was resting at a stone bench. She got out of her pack and joined them. Farther on, the trail dropped in a deep, winding staircase. The masonry seemed old, fused with accretions. Ali looked around for carved inscriptions or other signs of hadal culture, but there was none.

"That's got to be the last of our people coming down," a trekker said.

Ali followed his pointing finger. Like tiny comets, three points of light slowly descended in the darkness with silvery filaments for tails. Ali was surprised. For all the walking they'd done, the platforms were not so far away, maybe just a mile. Higher, at the edge of the rim, the town of Esperanza was visible against the black night, a dim bulb indeed. For a moment she saw the boomtown's painted cliffs. The bright blue color twinkled in the toxic mist like a wishing star, and so she made a wish.

After their rest, the trail changed. The swamp receded. The reek of death fell away. The trail rose at a pleasant incline. They came to a ledge overlooking a flat plateau.

"More animals," someone said.

"They're not animals."

Once upon a time, in Palestine, people had made human sacrifices in the valley of Hinnon, later using the valley as a dumping ground for dead animals and executed prisoners. Cremation fires could be seen burning there night and day. With time Hinnon became Gehenna, which became the Hebrew name for the land of the dead. Ali had become something of a student of the literature of hell, and could not help wondering if they had stumbled upon some modern equivalent of Hinnon.

As they trekked onto the plateau, the image resolved itself. The bodies were simply men lying in an open-air camp. "They must be our porters," Ali said. She estimated a hundred or more men gathered here. Cigarette smoke mixed with their pungent body odor. Dozens of blue plastic drums shaped on one side to fit the human spine gave her a clue.

They had reached the rendezvous point. From here the expedition would truly launch. Like uninvited guests, the scientists waited at the edge of the encampment, not quite sure what came next. The porters did nothing to accommodate them. They went on lying about, sharing cigarettes and cups of hot drinks or sleeping on the bare ground. "They look . . . tell me they didn't hire hadals," a woman said.

"How could they hire hadals?" someone asked. "We're not even sure they exist anymore."

The porters' incipient horns and beetling brows and their body art, almost defective in its jailhouse shabbiness, had a certain pathos to it. Not that anyone would have pitied these men to their faces. They had the bricklike stare and keloid scars of a street gang. Their clothing was a mishmash of L.A. ghetto and the jungle. Some wore Patagonia shorts and Raiders caps, others wore loincloths with hip-hop jackets. Most carried knives. Ali saw machetes—but no vines. The blades were for protection, from the animals she'd been passing for the last hour, and possibly from any stray hostiles, but above all from one another.

They had fresh white plastic collars around their necks. She'd heard of convict labor and chain gangs in the subplanet, and maybe the collars were some sort of electronic shackles. But these men looked too physically similar, too familiar, to be a collection of prisoners. They must have come from the same tribe, the front end of a migration. They were *indios*, though Ali could not say from which region. Possibly Andean. Their cheekbones were broad and monumental, their black eyes almost Oriental.

A huge young black soldier appeared at their side. "If you'll come this way," he said, "the colonel has hot coffee prepared. We just received a radio update. The rest of your group has touched down. They'll be here soon."

Attached to his dogtag chain was a small steel Maltese cross, the official emblem of the Knights Templar. Recently revived through the largesse of a sports shoe manufacturer, the military religious order had become famous for employing former high school and college athletes with little other future. The recruitment had started at Promise Keepers and Million Man March rallies, and snowballed into a well-trained, tightly disciplined mercenary army for hire to corporations and governments.

In passing a knot of the *indios*, she saw a head rise; it was Ike. His glance at her lasted barely a second. She still owed him thanks for that orange in the Nazca elevator. But he returned his attention to the circle of porters, hunkering among them like Marco Polo.

Ali saw lines and arcs drawn on the stone in their midst, and Ike was shifting pebbles and bits of bone from one place to another. She thought they must be playing a game, then realized he was querying the *indios*, getting directions or gathering information. One other thing she saw, too. Near one foot, Ike had a small pile of carefully stacked leaves, clearly a last-minute purchase. She recognized them. He was a chewer of coca leaves.

Ali moved on to the soldiers' part of the camp. All was in motion here, men in camouflage uniforms bustling around, checking weapons. There were at least thirty of them, even quieter than the *indios,* and she decided the legend must be true about the mercenaries' vows of silence. Except for prayer or essential communication, speech was considered an extravagance among themselves.

Drawn by coffee fumes, the scientists found a stove perched on rocks and helped themselves, then started poking through the neatly arranged crates and plastic drums, looking for their equipment.

"You don't belong here," the black soldier said. "Please vacate the depot." He moved to block them. They went around him and rooted deeper.

"It's okay," someone told him, "it's our stuff."

The hunt turned unruly. "My spectroscope!" someone announced triumphantly.

"Ladies and gentlemen," a voice requested.

Ali barely heard him over the shouting and jostle of equipment.

A single gunshot cracked the air. The bullet had been aimed out from camp, angled toward the ground. Where it struck the bare bedrock fifty feet out, the round blossomed into a shower of splintered light.

Everyone stopped.

"What was that?" a scientist said.

"That," announced the shooter, "was a Remington Lucifer." He was a tall man, clean-shaven, slim in the fashion of field officers. He wore a chest rig with a shoulder holster for his modest-sized pistol. He had black and charcoal-gray camouflaged SWAT pants bloused into light-weight boots. His black T-shirt looked clean. A pair of night glasses dangled at his throat.

"It is an ammunition specially developed for use in the subplanet. It is a .25-caliber round, made of hardened plastic with a uranium tip. Different levels of heat and sonic vibration shape its functional capabilities. It can create a devastating wound, break up into multiple fléchettes, or simply create a blinding distraction. This expedition marks the official debut for the Lucifer and other technologies." The accent was Tennessee aristocracy.

Spurrier approached the soldier, muttonchops fluffed, hand outstretched. He had delegated himself the scientists' spokesman. "You must be Colonel Walker."

Walker bypassed Spurrier's outstretched hand. "We have two problems, people. First, those loads you have looted were packed by weight and balanced for carrying. Their contents have been carefully inventoried. I have a list of every item in every load. Every load is numbered. You have now set our departure back by a half hour while the loads are repacked.

"Problem two, one of my men made a request. You ignored it." He met their eyes. "In the future, you will please treat such requests as direct orders. From me." He shut his holster case with a snap.

"Looting?" a scientist protested. "It's our equipment. How can we loot ourselves? Just who's in charge here?"

Still wearing his pack, Shoat arrived. "I see you've met," he said, and turned to the group. "As you know, Colonel Walker will be our chief of security. From here on out, he'll be in charge of our defense and logistics."

"We have to ask him for permission to do science?" a man objected.

"This is an expedition, not your personal office," said Shoat. "The answer is yes. From now on, you'll need to coordinate your needs with the colonel's man, who will direct you to the proper shipment."

"We're a group," said Walker. With his uniform and trappings and his lean height, he had undeniable presence. In one hand he carried a Bible bound in matching camouflage. "The group takes priority. You simply need to anticipate your individual requirements, and my quartermaster will assist you. For the sake of order, you'll have to speak with him at the end of each day. Not in the morning while we are packing, not in the middle of the day while we are on the trail."

"I have to ask permission to get my own equipment?"

"We'll sort it out." Shoat sighed. "Colonel, is there anything else you'd like to add?"

Walker sat on the edge of a rock with one boot planted. "My job is hired gun," he said. "Helios brought me on to provide preservation for this enterprise." He unfolded a sheaf of pages and held it up. "My contract," he said, skimming the clauses. "It's got some rather unique features."

"Colonel," Shoat warned. Walker ignored him.

"Here, for instance, is a list of bonus payments that I get for each one of you who survives the journey."

The colonel had their fullest attention. Shoat didn't dare interrupt.

"It reminds me a lot of a bounty," said Walker. "According to this, I get so much for every hand, foot, limb, ear, and/or eye that I deliver intact and healthy. That's your hands, your feet, your eyes." He found the part. "Let's see, at three hundred dollars per eye, that's six hundred per pair. But they're only offering five hundred per mind. Go figure."

The outcry went up. "This is outrageous."

Walker waved the contract like a white flag. "You need to know something else," he boomed out. They stilled, somewhat. "I've put my time in down here, and it's time to smell the roses, if you will. Dabble in politics, maybe. Do some consulting work. Spend some downtime with my wife and kids. And that's where you come in."

They drew quiet.

"You see," said Walker, "my aim is to get filthy rich off you people. I mean to collect every penny of this entire schedule of bonuses. Every eyeball, every testicle, every toe. Do you ever ask yourselves who you can really trust?"

Walker folded his contract and closed it in his daybook. "Let me submit that the one thing in this world you can always trust is self-interest. And now you know mine."

Shoat was paying painful attention. The colonel had just threatened the expedition's union—and saved it. But why? wondered Ali. What was Walker's game?

He clapped the King James against his thigh. "We are beginning a great journey into the unknown. From now on, this expedition will operate within guidelines and the protection of my judgment. Our best protection will be a common set of ideas. A law. That law, people, is mine. From here on, we will observe tenets of military jurisprudence. In return, I will restore you to your families."

Shoat's neck made a slow extension, turtle-like. His soldier of fortune had just declared himself the ultimate legal authority over the Helios expedition for the next year. It was the most audacious thing Ali had ever seen. She waited for the scientists to raise the roof with their protests.

But there was silence. Not one objection. Then Ali understood.

The mercenary had just promised them their lives.

Like any expedition, they settled into themselves by inches.

A pace developed.

Camp broke at 0800. Walker would read a prayer to his troops—usually something grim from Revelation or Job or his favorite, Paul to the Corinthians—*The night is far spent, the day is at hand: let us therefore cast off the works of darkness, and let us put on the armor of light*—before sending a half-dozen ahead to audit the risks. The scientists would follow. The porters brought up the rear, protected—driven, it was becoming evident—by the silent soldiers. The division of labor was succinct, the lines uncrossable.

The porters spoke Quechua, once the language of the Incas. None of the Americans spoke it, and their attempts to use Spanish were rebuffed. Ali tried her hand at it, but the *indios* were not disposed to fraternizing. At night the mercenaries patrolled their perimeter in three shifts, guarding less against hadal adversaries than against the flight of their own porters.

In those first weeks they rarely saw their scout. Ike had vaulted into the night of tunneling, and kept himself a day or two ahead of them. His absence created an odd yearning among the scientists. When they asked about his welfare, Walker was dismissive. The man knows his duty, he would say.

Ali had presumed the scout was part of Walker's paramilitary, but learned otherwise. He was not exactly a free agent, if that was the term. Apparently Shoat had purchased him from the U.S. Army. He was essentially chattel, little different from his hadal days. Ike's mystery mounted, in part, Ali suspected, because people were able to attach their fantasies to him. She limited her own desires to eventually interviewing him about hadal ethnography, and possibly assembling a root glossary, though she could not get that orange out of her mind.

For the time being, Ike did what Walker termed his duty. He found them the path. He led them into the darkness. They all knew his blaze mark, a one-foot-high cross spray-painted on the walls in bright blue.

Shoat informed them the paint would begin degrading after a week. Again, it was an issue of his trade secrets. Helios was determined to throw any competitors off their scent. As one scientist pointed out, the disappearing paint would also throw them off their own scent. They would have no way of retracing their own footsteps.

To reassure them, Shoat held up a small capsule he described as a miniature radio transmitter. It was one of many he would be planting along the way, and would lie dormant until he triggered it to life with his remote control. He compared it to Hansel and Gretel's trail of crumbs, then someone pointed out that the crumbs Hansel dropped had all been eaten by birds. "Always negative," he griped at them.

In twelve-hour cycles, the team moved, then rested, then moved again. The men sprouted whiskers. Among the women, roots began to grow out, eyeliner and lipstick fell from daily fashion. Dr. Scholl's adhesive pads for blisters became the currency of choice, even more valuable than M&M's.

Ali had never been part of an expedition, but felt herself immersed in the tradition of what they were doing. They could have been whalers setting sail, or a wagon train moving west. She felt as if she knew it all by heart.

For the first ten days their joints and muscles were in shock. Even those hardy athletes among them groaned in their sleep and struggled with leg cramps. A small cult built around ibuprofen, the anti-inflammatory pain tablet. But each day their packs got a little lighter as they ate food or discarded books that no longer seemed so essential. One morning, Ali woke up with her head on a rock and actually felt refreshed.

Their farewell tans faded. Their feet hardened. More and more, they could see in quarter-light and less. Ali liked the smell of herself at night, her honest sweat.

Helios chemists had infused their protein bars with extra vitamin D to substitute for lost sunshine. The bars were dense with other additives, too, boosters Ali had never heard of. Among other things, her night vision grew richer by the hour. She felt stronger. Someone wondered if the food bars might not contain steroids, too, eliciting a playful round of science nerds flexing their imaginary new musculatures for one another.

Ali liked the scientists. She understood them in a way Shoat and Walker never could. They were here because they had answered their hearts. They felt compelled by reasons outside themselves, for knowledge, for reductionism, for simplicity, in a sense for God.

Inevitably, someone came up with a nickname for their expedition. It turned out to be Jules Verne who most appealed to this bunch, and so they became the Jules Verne Society, soon shortened to the JV. The name stuck. It helped that for his *Journey to the Center of the Earth*, Verne had chosen two scientists for his heroes, rather than epic warriors or poets. Above all, the JV liked the fact that Verne's small party of scientists had emerged miraculously intact.

The tunnels were ample. Their path looked groomed. Someone—apparently long ago—had cleared loose stones and chiseled corners to form walls and benches alongside the trail. It was hypothesized that the stonecutting might have been accomplished centuries ago by Andean slaves, for the joints and massive blocks were identical to masonry at Machu Picchu and in Cuzco. At any rate, their porters seemed to know exactly what the benches were for as they backed their heavy loads onto the old shelves.

Ali couldn't get over it. Miles went by, as flat as a sidewalk, looping right and left in easy bends, a pedestrian's delight. The geologists, especially, were astounded. The lithosphere was supposed to be solid basalt at these depths. Unbearably hot. A dead zone. But here was a virtual subway tunnel. You could sell tickets to this, one remarked. Don't worry, said his pal, Helios will.

One night they camped next to a translucent quartz forest. Ali heard tiny underworld creatures rustling, and the sound of water trickling through deep fissures. This was their first good encounter with indigenous animals. The expedition's lights kept the animals in hiding. But one of the biologists set out a recording device, and in the morning he played for them the rhythm of two- and three-chambered hearts: subterranean fish and amphibians and reptiles.

The nocturnal sounds were unsettling for some, raising the specter of hadal predators or of bugs or snakes with deadly venoms. For Ali, the nearness of life was a balm. It was life she had come in search of, hadal life. Lying on her back in the blackness, she couldn't wait to actually see the animals.

For the most part, their fields were sufficiently diverse to forestall professional competition. That meant they shared more than they bickered. They listened to one another's hypotheses with saintly patience. They put on skits at night. A harmonica player performed John Mayall songs. Three geologists started a barbershop routine, calling themselves the Tectonics. Hell was turning out to be fun.

Ali estimated they were making 7.2 miles per day on foot. At mile fifty they held a celebration, with Kool-Aid and dancing. Ali did the twist and the two-step. A paleobiologist got her into a complicated tango, and it was like being drunk under a full moon.

Ali was a riddle to them. She was a scholar, and yet this other thing, a nun. Despite her dancing, some of the women told her they feared she was deprived. She never gossiped, never joined in the girl talk when the going got raw. They knew nothing about her past lovers, but presumed at least a few. They declared their intention of finding out. You make me sound like a social disease, Ali said, laughing.

Don't worry, they said, you can still be repaired.

Inhibitions receded. Clothing opened. Wedding bands started to vanish.

The affairs unfolded in full view of the group, and sometimes the sex, too. There were some initial attempts at privacy. Grown men and women passed notes back and forth, held hands in secret, or pretended to discuss important business. Late at night Ali could hear people grunting like hippies among the stones and heaped packs.

In their second week, they came upon cave art that might have been lifted from Paleolithic sites at Altamira. The walls held beautifully rendered animals and shapes and geometric doodles, some no larger than postage stamps. They were alive with color. Color! In a world of darkness.

"Look at that detail," breathed Ali.

There were crickets and orchids and reptiles, and nightmare concoctions that looked like something the geographer Ptolemy or Bosch might have drawn, beasts that were part fish or salamander, part bird and man, part goat. Some of the depictions used natural knobs in the rock for eye stems or gonads, or spalled divots for a hollow in the stomach, or mineral veins for horns or antennae.

"Turn off your light," Ali told her companions. "Here's how it would have looked by the flame of a torch." She swam her hand back and forth across her headlamp, and in the flickering light the animals seemed to move.

"Some of these species have been extinct for ten thousand years," a paleobiologist said. "Some I never knew existed."

"Who were the artists, do you think?" someone wondered.

"Not hadals," said Gitner, whose specialty was petrology, the history and classification of rocks. He had lost a brother in the national guard several years ago, and hated the hadals. "They're vermin who have burrowed into the earth. That's their nature, like snakes or insects."

One of the volcano people spoke. With her shaved head and long thighs, Molly was a figure of awe to the porters and mercenaries. "There might be another explanation here," she said. "Look at this." They gathered beneath a broad section of ceiling she had been studying.

"Okay," Gitner said, "a bunch of stick figures and boobie dolls. So what?"

At first glance, that did seem to be the extent of it. Wielding spears and bows, warriors mounted wild attacks on one another. Some had trunks and heads made of twin triangles. Others were just lines. Crowded into one corner stood several dozen Venuses loaded with vast breasts and obese buttocks.

"These look like prisoners." Molly pointed at a file of stick figures roped together.

Ali pointed at a figure with one hand on the chest of another. "Is that a shaman healing people?"

"Human sacrifice," muttered Molly. "Look at his other hand." The figure was holding something red in one outstretched hand. His hand was resting not on top of the figure's chest, but inside it. He was displaying a heart.

That evening, Ali transferred some of her sketches of the cave art onto her day map. She had conceived the maps as a private journal. But, once discovered, her maps quickly became expedition property, a reference point for them all.

From her work on digs near Haifa and in Iceland, Ali came armed with the trappings of the trade. She had schooled herself in grids and contours and scale, and went nowhere without her leather tube for rolls of paper. She could wield a protractor with command, cobble together a legend from scratch. They were less maps than a timetable with places, a chronography. Down here, far beneath the reach of the GPS satellite, longitude and latitude and direction were impossible to determine. Their compasses were rendered useless by electromagnetic corruption. And so she made the days of the month her true north. They were entering territory without human names, encountering locations that no one knew existed. As they advanced, she began to describe the indescribable and to name the unnamed.

By day she kept notes. In the evening, while the camp settled, Ali would open her leather tube of paper and lay out her pens and watercolors. She made two types of maps, one an overview, or blueprint, of hell, which corresponded to the Helios computer projection of their route. It had dates with the corresponding altitudes and approximate locations beneath various features on the surface or the ocean floor.

But it was her day maps, the second type, that were her pride. These were charts of each day's particular progress. The expedition's photographs would be developed on the surface someday, but for now her small watercolors and line drawings and written marginalia were their memory. She drew and painted things that attracted her eye, like the cave art, or the green calcite lily pads veined with cherry-red minerals that floated in pools of still water, or the cave pearls rolled together like nests of hummingbird eggs. She tried to convey how it was like traveling through the inside of a living body at times, the joints and folds of the earth, the liver-smooth flowstone, the helictites threading upward like synapses in search of a connection. She found it beautiful. Surely God would not have invented such a place as His spiritual gulag.

Even the mercenaries and porters liked to look at her maps. People enjoyed watching their voyage come alive beneath her pen and brush. Her maps comforted them. They saw themselves in the minutiae. Looking at her work, they felt a sense of control over this unexplored world.

On June 22, her day map included a major piece of excitement. "0955, 4,506 fathoms," it read. "Radio signals."

They had not yet broken camp that morning when Walker's communications specialist picked up the signals. The entire expedition had waited while more sensors were laid out and the long-wave transmission was patiently harvested. It took four hours to capture a message that was a mere forty-five seconds long when played at normal speed. Everyone listened. To their disappointment, it was not for them.

Luckily, one woman was fluent in Mandarin. It was a distress signal sent from a People's Republic of China submarine. "Get this," she told them. "The message was sent nine years ago."

It got stranger.

"June 25," Ali recorded, "1840, 4,618 fathoms: More radio signals."

This time, after waiting for the long waves to pulse in through the basalt and mineral zones, what they received was a transmission from themselves. It was encrypted in their unique expedition code. Once they finished translating it, the message spoke of desperate starvation. "Mayday . . . is Wayne Gitner . . . dead . . . am alone . . . assist . . ." The eerie part was that the dispatch was digitally dated five months in the *future*.

Gitner stepped forward and identified the voice on the tape as his own. He was a no-nonsense fellow, and indignantly demanded an explanation. One sci-fi buff suggested that a time warp might have been caused by the shifting geomagnetics, and suggested the message was a prophecy of sorts. Gitner said bullshit. "Even if it was a time distortion, time only travels in one direction."

"Yeah," said the buff, "but which direction? And what if time's circular?" However it had been done, people agreed it made for a good ghost story. Ali's map legend for that day included a tiny Casper ghost with the description "Phantom Voice."

Her maps noted their first genuine, live hadal life-form. Two planetologists spied it in a crevice and came racing to camp with their capture. It was a bacterial fuzz barely half an inch in diameter, a subsurface lithoautotrophic microbial ecosystem, or SLIME in the parlance. A rock-eater.

"So?" said Shoat.

The discovery of a bacterium that ate basalt impeached the need for sunlight. It meant the abyss was self-sustaining. Hell was perfectly capable of feeding on itself.

On June 29 they reached a fossilized warrior. He was human and probably dated to the sixteenth century. His flesh had turned to limestone. His armor was intact. They guessed he had come here from Peru, a Cortés or Don Quixote who had penetrated this eternal darkness for Church, glory, or gold. Those with camcorders and still cameras documented the lost knight. One of the geologists tried to sample the sheath of rock encrusting the body, only to chip an entire leg off.

The geologist's accidental vandalism was soon exceeded by the group's very presence. In the space of three hours, the biochemicals of their combined respiration spontaneously generated a grape-green moss. It was like watching fire. The vegetation, spawned by the air from inside their bodies, rapidly colonized the walls and coated the conquistador. Even as they stood there, the hall was consumed with it. They fled as if fleeing themselves.

Ali wondered if, in passing this lost knight, Ike had seen himself.

INCIDENT IN GUANGDONG PROVINCE

PEOPLE'S REPUBLIC OF CHINA

It was getting dark, and this so-called "miracle" city didn't exist on any maps.

Holly Ann wished Mr. Li would drive a little faster. The adoption agency's guide wasn't much of a driver, or, for that matter, much of a guide. Eight cities, fifteen orphanages, twenty-two thousand dollars, and still no baby.

Her husband, Wade, rode with his nose plastered to the opposite window. Over the past ten days they'd crisscrossed the southern provinces, enduring floods, disease, pestilence, and the edges of a famine. His patience was in rags.

It was odd, everywhere the same. Wherever they visited, the orphanages had all been empty of children. Here and there they'd found wizened little deformities—hydrocephalic, mongoloid, or genetically doomed—a few breaths short of dying. Otherwise, China suddenly, inexplicably, had no orphans.

It wasn't supposed to be this way. The adoption agency had advertised that China was jammed with foundlings. *Female* foundlings, hundreds of thousands of them, tiny girls exiled from one-child families that wanted a son. Holly Ann had read that female orphans were still sold as servants or as *tongyangxi*, child brides. If it was a baby girl you wanted, no one went home empty. Until us, thought Holly Ann. It was as if the Pied Piper had come through and cleaned the place out. And more than just orphans were missing. Children altogether. You saw evidence of them—toys, kites, streetside chalkboards. But the streets were barren of children under the age of ten.

"Where could they have gone?" Holly Ann asked each night.

Wade had come up with a theory. "They think we've come to steal their kids. They must be hiding them."

Out of that observation had grown today's guerrilla raid. Surprisingly, Mr. Li had agreed to it. They would drop in on an orphanage that was out of the way, and with no prior warning of their visit.

As night descended, Mr. Li drove deeper through the alleyways. Holly Ann hadn't come exactly expecting pandas in rain forests and kung fu temples beneath the Great Wall, but this was like a madman's blueprint, with detours and dead ends all held together by electric wires and rusty rebar and bamboo scaffolding. South China had to be the ugliest place on earth. Mountains were being leveled to fill in the paddies and lakes. Rivers were being dammed. Strangely, even as these people leveled the earth, they were crowding the sky. It was like robbing the sun to feed the night.

Acid rain started hitting the windshield in sloppy kisses, yellowish and festering like spit. Deep coal mines honeycombed the hills in this district, and everyone burned the mines' product. The air reeked.

The asphalt turned to dirt. The sun dropped. This was the witching hour. They'd seen it in other cities. The policemen in green uniforms vanished. From doorways and windows and niches in the towering alley, eyes tracked the *gweilo*—white devils—and passed them on to more eyes.

The darkness congealed. Mr. Li slowed, obviously lost. He rolled down his window and waved a man over from the sidewalk and gave him a cigarette. They talked. After a minute, the man got a bicycle and Mr. Li started off again, with his guide holding on to the door. Here and there the bicyclist issued a command and Mr. Li would turn down another street. Rain sprayed through the window into the back.

Side by side, the car and the bicyclist made turns for another five minutes. Then the man grunted and patted the rooftop. He detached from them and pedaled away.

"Here," Mr. Li announced.

"You're joking," Wade said.

Holly Ann craned her neck to see through the windshield. Surrounded by barbed wire, the gray walls of a factory complex squatted before them in their harsh headlights. Bits of ominous black thread had been tied to the barbed wire, and the walls carried huge, ugly characters in stark red paint. Half-finished skyscrapers blocked her view to the rear. They had reached some sort of dead epicenter. In every direction, the stone-stillness radiated out from here.

"Let's get this over with," Wade said, and got out of the car. He pulled at the gate. Concertina wire wobbled like quicksilver. Holly Ann's first impression gave way to another. This looked less like a factory than a prison. The barbed wire and inscriptions appeared to have one purpose: enclosure. "What kind of orphanage is this?" she asked Mr. Li.

"Good place, no problem," he said. But he seemed nervous.

Wade banged at the industrial-style door. The brick-and-pig-iron decor dwarfed him. When no one answered, he simply turned the handle and the metal door opened. He didn't turn around to gesture yes or no. He just went inside. "Great, Wade," Holly Ann muttered.

Holly Ann got out. Mr. Li's door stayed closed. She looked through the windshield and rapped on the glass. He looked up at her through his little cloud of tobacco smoke, eyes wishing her from his life, then reached under to turn off the ignition. The windshield wipers quit knocking back and forth. His image blurred with rain. He got out.

On second thought, she reached into the back and grabbed a packet of disposable diapers. Mr. Li left the headlights on, but locked all the doors. "Bandits," he said.

Holly Ann led. The viciously stroked words loomed on either side of them. Now she saw the scorch marks where flames had lapped at the brick. The foot of the wall was coated with charred glass from Molotov cocktails. Who would assault an orphanage?

The metal door was cold. Mr. Li brushed past her and went into the blackness. "Wait," she said to him. But his footsteps receded down the hallway.

Reminding herself of her mission, Holly Ann stepped inside. She drew in a deep breath, smelling for evidence. Babies. She looked for cartoon figures or crayon squiggles or smudges of little handprints on the lower walls. Instead, long staccato patterns of holes and chips violated the plaster. Termites, she thought with disgust.

"Wade?" she tried again. "Mr. Li?" She continued down the hallway. Moss flowered in cracks. The doors were all gone. Each room yawned black. If there were windows, they had been bricked up. The place was sealed tight. Then she came to a string of Christmas lights.

It was the strangest sight. Someone had strung hundreds of Christmas lights—red and green and little white flashing lights, and even red chili-pepper lights and green frog lights and turquoise trout lights like those found in margarita restaurants back home. Maybe the orphans liked it.

The air changed. An odor infiltrated. The ammonia of urine. The smell of baby poop. There was no mistaking it. There were babies in here. For the first time in weeks, Holly Ann smiled. She almost hugged herself.

"Hello?" she called.

An infant voice bubbled in the darkness. Holly Ann's head jerked up. The tiny soul might as well have called her by name.

She followed the sound into a side room reeking of human waste and garbage. The twinkle of Christmas lights did not reach this far. Holly Ann steeled herself, then got down on her hands and knees, advancing through the pile by touch. The garbage was cold. It took all her self-control not to think about what she was feeling. Vegetable matter. Rice. Discarded flesh. Above all, she tried not to think about someone throwing away a live infant.

The floor canted down toward the rear. Maybe there had been an earthquake. She felt a slight current of air against her face. It seemed to be coming up from some deeper place. She remembered the coal mines around here. It was possible they'd built their city upon ancient tunnels that were now collapsing under the weight.

She found the baby by its warmth.

As if it had always been her own, as if she were collecting it from a cradle, she scooped up the bundle. The little creature was sour-smelling. So tiny. Holly Ann brushed her fingertips across the baby's belly: the umbilical cord was ragged and soft, as if freshly bitten. It was a girl, no more than a few days old. Holly Ann held the little body to her shoulder and listened. Her heart sank. Instantly she knew. The baby was ill. She was dying.

"Oh, darling," she whispered.

Her heart was failing. Her lungs were filling. You could hear it. Not long now.

Holly Ann wrapped the infant in her sweater and knelt in the pile of putrid garbage, rocking her baby. Maybe this was how it was meant to be, a motherhood that lasted only a few minutes. Better than never at all, she thought. She stood and started back toward the hallway and Christmas lights.

A small noise stopped her. The sound had several parts, like a metal scorpion lifting its tail, poising to strike. Slowly Holly Ann turned.

At first the rifle and military uniform didn't register. She was a very tall and sturdy woman who had not smiled for many years. The woman's nose had been broken sideways long ago. Her hair must have been cut with a knife. She looked like someone who had been fighting—and losing—her entire life.

The woman hissed something at Holly Ann in a burst of Chinese. She made an angry gesture, pointing at the bundle inside Holly Ann's sweater. There was no mistaking her demand. She wanted the infant returned to the sewage pile in that horrible room.

Holly Ann recoiled, clutching the baby tighter. Slowly she raised the packet of disposable diapers. "It's okay," she assured the tall woman.

Like two different species, the women studied each other. Holly Ann wondered if this might be the infant's mother, and decided it couldn't possibly be.

Suddenly the Chinese woman scowled, and batted aside the diapers with her rifle barrel. She reached for the infant. Her peasant hand was thick and callused and manly.

In her entire life, Holly Ann had never made a fist in real anger, to say nothing of swinging one. Her first ever connected on the woman's thin mouth. It wasn't much of a punch, but it drew blood.

Holly Ann stepped back from her violence and wrapped both arms around the baby.

The Chinese woman wiped the bead of blood from her mouth and thrust the rifle barrel out. Holly Ann was terrified. But for whatever reason, the woman relented with a whispered oath, and motioned with her rifle.

Holly Ann set off in the direction indicated. Surely Wade would appear at any minute. Money would change hands. They would leave this terrible place.

With the gun at her back, Holly Ann climbed over a pile of bricks and torn sandbags. They reached a set of stairs and started up. Something crunched underfoot like metal beetles. Holly Ann saw a deep layer of hundreds of bullet casings coated with wet verdigris.

They went higher, three stories, then five. Holding the child, Holly Ann managed to keep up the pace. She didn't have much choice. Suddenly the woman caught at Holly Ann's arm. They stopped. This time the rifle was aimed back down the stair shaft.

Far below, something was moving. It sounded like eels coiling in mud. The two women shared a look. For an instant they actually had something in common, their fear. Holly Ann softly armored the infant with her hand. After another minute the Chinese woman got them on the move again, faster this time.

They reached the top floor. The roof gaped open in violent patches, and Holly Ann caught snatches of stars. She smelled fresh air. They clambered over a small landslide of scorched wood and cinder blocks and approached a brightly lit doorway.

Bags of cement had been piled like sandbags as a barricade. The fronts had been slashed open and rainwater had soaked the spillage, turning it to hard knuckles of concrete. It was like climbing folds of lava.

Holly Ann struggled, one arm clutching the infant. Near the top, her head knocked against a cold cannon barrel pointing where they'd come from. Hands with broken fingernails reached down for her from the electric brilliance.

All the dramatics changed. It was like entering a besieged camp: soldiers everywhere, guns, blasted architecture, rain cutting naked through great wounds in the roof. To Holly Ann's enormous relief, Wade was there, sitting in a corner, holding his head.

Once the room might have been a small auditorium, or a cafeteria. Now the space was illuminated with Stalinist klieg lights and looked like

Custer's Last Stand. Soldiers from the People's Liberation Army, mostly men in pea-green uniforms or black-striped camouflage, were all business among their weapons. They gave wide berth to Holly Ann. Several elites pointed at the baby inside her sweater.

In the distance, Mr. Li was appealing to an officer who carried himself with the iron spine of a hero of the people. His crewcut was gray. He looked weary.

She went over to Wade. He was bleeding into both eyes from a laceration across the scalp line. "Wade," she said.

"Holly Ann?" he said. "Thank God. Mr. Li told them you were still below. They sent someone to find you."

She avoided his bear hug. "I have something to show you," she announced quietly.

"It's very dangerous here," Wade said. "Something's going on. A revolution or something. I gave Li all our cash. I told him to pay anything, just get us out of here."

"Wade," she snapped. He wasn't listening to her.

A voice suddenly boomed in the back, where Mr. Li stood. It was the officer. He was shouting at Holly Ann's rescuer, the tall woman. All around her, soldiers looked angry or ashamed for her. Obviously she had allowed some terrible breach. Holly Ann knew it had to do with this baby.

The officer unsnapped his leather holster and looked at her. He drew his pistol out.

"Good Lord," Holly Ann murmured.

"What?" said Wade. He stood there like some bewildered monster. Useless.

It was her call. Holly Ann astonished herself. As the officer approached her, she started off to meet him halfway. They met in the center of the rubble-strewn room.

"Mr. Li," Holly Ann commanded.

Mr. Li glared at her, but came forward.

"Tell this man I have selected my child," she said. "I have medicine in the car. I wish to go home now."

Mr. Li started to translate, but the officer abruptly chambered a round. Mr. Li blinked rapidly. He was very pale. The officer said something to him.

"Put on floor," Mr. Li said to her.

"We have all the necessary permits," she explained quite evenly. She said it directly to the officer. "Out in our car, permits, understand? Passports. Documents."

"Please you put on floor," Mr. Li repeated very softly. He pointed at her baby. "That," he said, as if it were a dirty thing.

Holly Ann despised him. Despised China. Despised the God that allowed such things.

"She," said Holly Ann. "This girl goes with me."

"Not good," Mr. Li softly pleaded.

"She will die otherwise."

"Yes."

"Holly Ann?" Wade loomed behind her.

"It's a baby, Wade. *Our* baby. I found her. On a pile of garbage. And now they want to kill her." Holly Ann felt the infant stirring. The tiny fingernails pulled at her blouse.

"A baby?"

"No," Mr. Li said.

"I'm taking her home with us."

Mr. Li shook his head emphatically.

"Give them the money," she instructed him.

Wade blustered foolishly. "We're American citizens. You did tell them, didn't you?"

"This isn't for you," Mr. Li said. "It's a trade. This for that."

She could feel the infant's hunger, miniature lips groping for a nipple. "A trade?" she demanded. "Who are you trading with?"

Mr. Li glanced nervously at the soldiers.

"Who?" she insisted.

Mr. Li pointed at the ground. Through it. "Them."

Holly Ann felt faint. "What?"

"Our babies. Their babies. Trade."

The infant made a tiny sound.

Over Mr. Li's shoulder, Holly Ann saw the officer aiming his gun. She saw a puff of color spit from the barrel.

Holly Ann barely felt the bullet. Her fall to earth was more like floating. All the way down, she held the child in safety.

Above her, violent shadows thundered. More guns went off. Her name roared out.

She smiled and rested her head gently against the bundle at her shoulder. Little no-name. No-luck. *I belong to you.* Before they could reach her, Holly Ann did the only thing left to do. She unveiled the daughter China had refused. Time to say good-bye.

In her search around the world for a child, Holly Ann had seen babies of every race and color. Her search had changed her forever, she thought. Black eyes or blue, kinky hair or straight, chocolate skin or yellow or brown or white, crooked, blind, or straight: none of that mattered.

As she opened the sweater wrapping the baby, Holly Ann fully expected to recognize her common humanity in this tiny being. Every infant was a chalice. That was her conviction. Until now.

Even dying, Holly Ann was able to kick the thing away from her.

Oh God, she cursed, and closed her eyes.

A sound like giants walking wakened her. She looked. It was not footsteps, but the old man carefully planting one shot at a time as he tracked the foundling.

Finally it was done.

And she was glad.

> *. . . nature hath adapted*
> *the eyes of the Lilliputians*
> *to all objects proper for*
> *their view . . .*

—JONATHAN SWIFT, *Gulliver's Travels*

12
ANIMALS

THE JULY TUNNELS

In a gut of coiled granite, the mortal fed.

The meat was still warm from life. It was more than food, less than sacrament. Flesh is a landmark, if you know its flavor. The trick was setting your clock, so to speak, then categorically marking the shifts in tone or odor, or changes in the skin and muscle and blood, as you moved through the territory. Memorize the particulars, and you could begin to orient yourself in a cartography based on raw flesh. In terms of taste, the liver was often most distinct, sometimes the heart.

He crouched in the pocket of darkness with this creature squeezed between his thighs, the chest cavity opened. He rummaged. Like a mariner finding north, he committed to memory the organs, their relative position and size and smell. He sampled different pieces, just a taste. Palmed the skull, lifted the limbs, ran his hands along the limbs.

He'd never encountered a beast quite like this one. Its uniqueness did not register as a new phylum or species. The kill barely registered at the level of language. And yet it would permanently acquaint him. He would remember this creature in every detail.

Head held high to listen for intruders, he inserted his hands in the animal's hide and let his wonder run. He was utterly respectful. He was a student, no more. The animal was his teacher.

It was not just a matter of locating yourself east or south. Depth was sometimes far more consequential, and the consistency of flesh could serve as an altimeter of sorts. In the deep seas, such bathypelagic monsters as anglerfish were slow moving, with a metabolic rate as low as one percent of fish living near the surface. Their body tissue was watery, with little muscle and no fat. So it was at certain depths in the subplanet. Down some channels, you found reptiles or fish that were little more than vegetables with teeth. Even the ones that weren't poisonous weren't worth eating. Their food value verged on plain air. Even them he'd eaten.

Again, there were more reasons to hunt than filling your belly. With care you could plot a course, find a destination, locate water, avoid—or track—enemies. It made simple survival something more, a journey. A destiny.

The body spoke to him. He felt for eyes, found stems, tried to thumb open the lids, but they were sealed. Blind. The talons were a raptor's, with an opposing thumb. He had caught it drafting on the tunnel's breeze, but the wings were much too small for real flight.

He started at the top again. The snout. Milk teeth, but sharp as needles. The way the joints moved. The genitals, this one a male. The hip bones were abraded from scraping along the stone. He squeezed the bladder, and its liquid smelled sharp. He took one foot and pressed it against the dirt and felt the print.

All of this was done in darkness.

Finally, Ike was done. He laid the parts back inside the cavity and folded the arms across and pressed the body into a cleft in the wall.

They entered a series of deep trenches that resembled terrestrial canyons, but which had not been cut by the flow of water. These were instead the remains of seafloor spreading, fossilized here. They had found an ocean bottom—bone dry—2,650 fathoms beneath the Pacific Ocean floor.

That night they made camp near a huge coral bed stretching right and left into the darkness. It was like a Sherwood Forest made of calcified polyps. Great, oaklike branches reached up and out with green and blue and pink pastels and deep reds secreted, according to their geobotanist, by an ancestor of the gorgonian *Corallium nobile*. There were desiccated sea fans under their spreading limbs, so old their colors had leached to transparency. Ancient marine animals lay at their feet, turned to stone.

The expedition had been on its feet for over four weeks, and Shoat and Walker granted the scientists' request for an extra two days here. The scientists got hardly any sleep during their stay at the coral site. They would never pass this way again. Perhaps no human ever would. Frantically they harvested these traces of an alternate evolution. In lieu of carrying it with them, they arranged the material for digital storage on their hard disks, and the video cameras whirred night and day.

Walker brought in two winged animals. Still alive.

"Fallen angels," he announced.

They were upside down, strung with parachute cord, still half-poisoned from sedative. A soldier had been bitten by one, and lay sick with dry heaves. You could tell which animal had delivered the bite; its left wing had been crushed by a boot.

They weren't really fallen angels, of course. They were demons. Gargoyles.

The scientists clustered around, goggling at the feeble beasts. The animals twitched. One shot a cherubic arc of urine.

"How did you manage this, Walker? Where did you get them?"

"I had my troops dope their kill. They were eating a third one of these things. All we had to do was wait for them to return and eat some more, and then go collect them."

"Are there more?"

"Two or three dozen. Maybe hundreds. A flock. Or a hatch. Like bats. Or monkeys."

"A rookery," said one of the biologists.

"I've ordered my men to keep their distance. We've set a kill zone at the mouth of the subtunnel. We're in no danger."

Shoat had apparently been in on it. "You should smell their dung," he said.

Several of the porters, on seeing the animals, murmured and crossed themselves. Walker's soldiers brusquely directed them away.

Live specimens of an unknown species, especially warm-blooded higher vertebrates, were not something that came walking into a naturalist's camp. The scientists moved in with tape measures and Bic pens and flashlights.

The longest one measured twenty-two rapturously colored inches. The rich orchid hues—purple mottling into turquoise and beige—was one more of those paradoxes of nature: what use was such coloration in the darkness?

The big one had lactating teats—someone squeezed out a trickle of milk—and engorged crimson labia. At first glance, the other seemed to have similar genitalia, but a Bic tip opened the folds to expose a surprise.

"What am I seeing here?"

"It's a penis, all right."

"Not much of one."

"Reminds me of a guy I used to date," said one of the women.

But even as they bantered and joked, they were intently gleaning data from these bodies. The tall one was a nursing female, in heat. The other was a male with eroded three-cusp molars, callused foot pads and chipped claws, and ulcerated patches where his elbows and knees and shoulder bones had abraded against rock. That and other evidence of aging eliminated him as the female's "son." Perhaps they were mates. The female, at any rate, probably had one or more infants waiting for her to come home.

The two animals revived from Walker's sedative in trembling bursts. They surfaced into full consciousness only to hit the shock of the humans' lights and sink into stupor again.

"Keep those ropes tight, they bite," Walker said as the creatures shivered and struggled and lapsed back into semiconsciousness. They were diminutive. It didn't seem possible these could be the hadals who had slaughtered armies and left cave art and cowed eons of humans.

"They're not King Kong," Ali said. "Look at them, barely thirty pounds apiece. You'll kill them with those ropes."

"I can't believe you destroyed her wing," a biologist said to Walker. "She was probably just defending her nest."

"What's this," Shoat retorted, "Animal Rights Week?"

"I have a question," Ali said. "We're supposed to leave in the morning. What then? They're not house pets. Do we take them with us? Should we even have them here?"

Walker's expression, pleased to begin with, drew in on itself. Clearly he thought her ungrateful. Shoat saw the change, and nodded at Ali as if to say *Good work.*

"Well, we've got them here now," a geologist said with a shrug. "We can't pass up an opportunity like this."

They had no nets, cages, or restraining devices. While the animals were still relatively immobile, the biologists muzzled them with string and tied each to a pack frame with wings and arms outstretched, and feet wired together at the bottom. Their wingspread was modest, less than their height.

"Do they possess true flight?" someone asked. "Or are they just aerial opportunists, drafting down from high perches?"

Over the next hour, such details were debated with great passion. One way or another, everyone agreed they were prosimians that had some-how tumbled from the family tree of primates.

"Look at that face, almost human, like one of those shrunken heads you see in the anthro exhibits. What's the cranial measurement on this guy?"

"Relative to body size, Miocene ape, at best."

"Nocturnal extremists, just as I thought," said Spurrier. "And look at the rhinarium, this wet patch of skin. Like the tip of a dog's nose. I'm thinking lemuriforms here. An accidental colonizer. The subterranean eco-niche must have been wide open to them. They proliferated. Their adaptation radiated wildly. Species diversified. It only takes one preg-nant female, you know, wandering off."

"But frigging wings, for Pete's sake."

The gargoyles had begun struggling again. It was a slow, blind writhing. One made a noise midway between a bark and a peep.

"What do you suppose they eat?"

"Insects," one hazarded.

"Could be carnivorous—look at those incisors."

"Are you going to talk all day? Or find out?" It was Shoat.

Before anyone could stop him, he pulled his combat knife, with its blood gutter and double-edged tip, and in one motion cut the male's head off.

They were stunned.

Ali reacted first. She pushed Shoat. He didn't have the size of Walker's athlete-warriors, but he was solid enough. She put more weight into her second shove, and this time got him backed off a step. He returned the push, openhanded against her shoulder. Ali staggered. Quickly, Shoat made a show of holding the knife out and away, like she might hurt herself on the blade. They faced each other. "Calm yourself," he said.

Later Ali would say her contrition. For the moment she was too full of fury at him and just wanted to knock him over. It took an effort to turn away from him. She went over to the beheaded animal. Surprisingly little blood came out of the neck stem. Next to it, the other one was bucking wildly, curved claws grabbing at the air.

The group's protest was mild. "You're a wart, Montgomery," one said.

"Get on with it," Shoat said. "Open the thing up. Take your pictures. Boil the skull. Get your answers. Then pack." He started humming Willie Nelson: "'We're on the road again.'"

"Barbaric," someone muttered.

"Spare me," said Shoat. He pointed his knife at Ali. "Our Good

Samaritan said it herself. They're not house pets. We can't bring them with us."

"You knew what I meant," Ali said to Shoat. "We have to let them go. The one that's left."

The remaining creature had quit struggling. It lifted its head and was attentively smelling them and listening to their voices. The concentration was unsettling.

Ali waited for the group to ratify her. No one did. It was her show alone.

All at once, Ali felt powerfully isolated from these people, estranged and peculiar. It was not a new feeling. She had always been a little different, from her classmates as a child, from the novitiates at St. Mary's, from the world. For some reason, she hadn't expected it here, though.

She felt foolish. Then it came to her. They had separated themselves from her because they thought it was *her* business. The business of a nun. Of course she would champion mercy. It made her ridiculous.

Now what? she asked herself. Apologize? Walk away? She glanced over at Shoat, who was standing beside Walker, grinning. Damned if she was going to lose to him.

Ali took out her Swiss Army knife and tried picking open a blade.

"What are you doing?" a biologist asked.

She cleared her throat. "I'm letting her go," she said.

"Ah, Ali, I don't think that's the best thing right now. I mean, the animal's got a broken wing."

"We shouldn't have caught it in the first place," she said, and went on picking at the knife. But the blade was stuck. Her fingernail broke on the little slot. This was going completely against her. She felt the tears welling in her eyes, and lowered her head so the hair would at least curtain out their view.

"You're in my way," a voice said behind the crowd. There was an initial jostling, and then the circle abruptly opened up. Ali was even more surprised than the rest of them. It was Ike who stepped up beside her.

They had not seen him in over three weeks. He had changed. His hair was getting shaggy and the clean white shirt was gone, replaced with a filthy gray camo top. A half-healed wound marked one arm, and he had packed the ugly tear with red ochre. Ali stared at his arms, both of them covered with scars and markings and—along the inside of one forearm—printed text, like cheat notes.

He had lost or hidden his pack, but the shotgun and knife were in place, along with a pistol that had a silencer on it. He was wearing the bug-eyed glacier glasses, and smelled like a hunter. His shoulder came against her, and the skin was cool. In her relief, ever so slightly, Ali leaned against that sureness.

"We were starting to wonder if you'd gone country again," Colonel Walker said.

Ike didn't answer him. He took the pocketknife from Ali's hand and flipped the blade open. "She's right," he said.

He bent over the remaining animal and, in an undertone that only Ali could hear, he said something soothing, but also formal, an address of some sort. Almost a prayer. The animal grew still, and Ali pried up a piece of the cord for Ike to cut.

Someone said, "Now we'll see if these things can really fly."

But Ike didn't cut the cord. He gave a quick nick to the animal's jugular vein. Gagged with wire, the small mouth gulped for air. Then it was dead.

Ike straightened and faced the group. "No live catches."

Without a second thought, Ali balled her fist and clipped him on the shoulder, for all the good it did. It was like slugging a horse, he was so hard. The tears were streaking her face. "Why?" she demanded.

He folded her knife and solemnly returned it. "I'm sorry," she heard him whisper, but not to her. To Ali's astonishment, he was speaking to what he'd just killed. Then he straightened and faced the group.

"That was a waste of life," he said to them.

"Spare me," said Walker.

Ike looked directly at him. "I thought you knew some things."

Walker flushed. Ike turned to the rest of them. "You can't stay here anymore," he said. "The others will come looking now. We need to keep going."

"Ike," said Ali, as the group dispersed. He faced her, and she slapped him.

Thus is the Devil ever
God's ape.

—MARTIN LUTHER, *Table Talke* (1569)

13
THE SHROUD

VENICE, ITALY

"Ali has gone deeper," January reported gravely, while the group waited in the vault. She had lost a great deal of weight, and her neck veins were taut, like strings holding her head to her bones. She sat on a chair, drinking mineral water. Branch crouched beside her, quietly thumbing through a Baedeker's guide to Venice.

This was the Beowulf Circle first meeting in months. Some had been busy in libraries or museums; others had been hard at work in the field, interviewing journalists, soldiers, missionaries, anyone with experience of the depths. The quest had engaged them.

They were delighted to be in this city. Venice's winding canals led to a thousand secret places. The Renaissance spirit pleasantly haunted these sun-gorged plazas. The irony was that on a Sunday spilling over with light and church bells, they had come together in a bank vault.

Most of them looked younger, tanned, more limber. The spark was back in their eyes again. They were eager to share their findings with one another. January made hers first.

She had received Ali's letter only yesterday, delivered by one of the seven scientists who had quit the expedition and finally gotten free of Point Z-3. The scientist's tale, and Ali's dispatch, were disturbing. After Shoat and his expedition had departed, the dissidents had sulked for weeks, stranded among violent misfits. Male and female alike had been beaten and raped and robbed. At last a train had brought them back to Nazca City. Now aboveground, they were undergoing treatment for an exotic lithospheric fungus and various venereal diseases, plus the usual compression problems. But their misadventures paled next to the larger news they had brought out.

January summarized the Helios stratagem. Reading excerpts from Ali's letter, written right up to the hour of her descent from Point Z-3, she sketched out the plan to traverse beneath the Pacific floor and exit somewhere near Asia. "And Ali has gone with them," she groaned. "For me. What have I done?"

"Can't blame yourself." Desmond Lynch popped his briarwood cane against the tile floor. "She got herself into it. We all did."

"Thank you for the consolation, Desmond."

"What can be the meaning of this?" someone asked. "The cost must be prodigious, even for Helios."

"I know C.C. Cooper," January said, "and so I fear the worst. He seems to be carving out a nation-state all his own." She paused. "I've had my staff investigating, and Helios is definitely preparing for a full-scale occupation of the area."

"But his own country?" said Thomas.

"Don't forget," January said, "this is a man who believes the presidency was stolen from him by a conspiracy. He seems to have decided a fresh start is best. In a place where he can write all the rules."

"A tyranny. A plutocracy," said one of the scholars.

"He won't call it that, of course."

"But he can't do this. It violates international laws. Surely—"

"Possession is everything," January said. "Recall the conquistadores in the New World. Once they got an ocean between them and their king, they decided to set themselves up in their own little kingdoms. It threatened the entire balance of power."

Thomas was grim. "Major Branch, surely you can intercept the expedition. Take your soldiers. Turn these invaders back before they spark more war."

Branch closed his book. "I'm afraid I have no authority to do that, Father."

Thomas appealed to January. "He's your soldier. Order him. Give him the authority."

"It doesn't work that way, Thomas. Elias is not *my* soldier. He's a friend. As for authority, I've already spoken with the commander in charge of operational affairs, General Sandwell. But the expedition's crossed beyond the military frontier. And, as you pointed out, he doesn't want to provoke the war all over again."

"What are all your commandos and specialists good for? Helios can slip some mercenaries into the wilderness, but not the U.S. Army?"

Branch nodded. "You're sounding like some of the officers I know. The corporations are running amok down there. We have to play by the rules. They don't."

"We must stop them," Thomas said. "The repercussions could be devastating."

"Even if we had the green light, it's probably too late," January said. "They have a two-month head start. And since their departure, we've heard nothing from them. We have no idea where they are exactly. Helios isn't sharing any information. I'm sick with worry. They could be in great danger. They could be walking into a nation of hadals."

This led them to a discussion of where the hadals might be hiding, how many might still be alive, what their threat really was. In Desmond Lynch's opinion, the hadal population was sparse and scattered and probably in a third or fourth generation of die-off. He estimated their worldwide numbers at no more than a hundred thousand. "They're an endangered species," he declared.

"Maybe the population's retreated," Mustafah, the Egyptian, ventured.

"Retreated? To where? Where is there to go?"

"I don't know. Deeper, perhaps? Is that possible? How deep does the underworld go?"

"I've been thinking," said Thomas. "What if their aim was to come out from the underworld? To make their place in the light?"

"You think Satan's looking for an invitation?" Mustafah asked. "I can't think of many neighborhoods that would welcome such a family."

"It would need to be a place no one else wants, or a place no one dares to go. A desert, perhaps. A jungle. Real estate with a negative value."

"Thomas and I have been talking," Lynch said. "After a certain point, where else can a fugitive hide, except in plain sight? And there may be evidence he's up to just that."

Branch was listening carefully.

"We've learned of a Karen warlord in the south of Burma, close to Khmer Rouge country," Lynch said. "It's said he was visited by the devil. He may have spoken with our elusive Satan."

"The rumors may be nothing more than a forest legend," Thomas qualified. "But there's also a chance that Satan is attempting to find a new sanctuary."

"If it's true, it would almost be wonderful," said Mustafah. "Satan bringing his tribes out from the depths, like Moses leading his people into Israel."

"But how can we learn more?" said January.

"As you might imagine, the warlord will never come out of his jungle for us to interview," said Thomas. "And there are no cable links, no phone lines. The region has been gutted by atrocity and famine. It's one of those genocide zones, apocalyptic. Supposedly this warlord has turned the clock back to Year Zero."

"Then his information is lost to us."

"Actually," Lynch said, "I've decided to go into the jungle."

January and Mustafah and Rau reacted with one voice. "But you mustn't. Desmond, it's much too dangerous."

If discovery was part of Lynch's goal, the adventure was another. "My mind's made up," he said, relishing their concern.

They were standing in a virtual cage, with a massive steel door and gleaming bars. Farther in, Thomas could make out walls of safe deposit boxes and more doors with complex lock mechanisms. Their discussion went on as they waited.

The scholars began presenting evidence. "He would be like Kublai Khan or Attila," Mustafah stated. "Or a warrior king like Richard the First, summoning all of Christendom to march upon the infidel. A character of immense ambition. An Alexander or a Mao or a Caesar."

"I disagree," said Lynch. "Why a great warrior emperor? What we're seeing is almost exclusively defensive and guerrilla. I'd say, at best, our Satan is someone more like Geronimo than Mao."

"More like Lon Chaney than Geronimo, I should say," a voice spoke. "A character capable of many disguises." It was de l'Orme.

Unlike the others, de l'Orme had not been restored by his months of detective work. The cancer was a flame in him, licking the flesh and bone away. The left side of his face was practically melting, the eye socket sinking behind his dark glasses. He belonged in a hospital bed. Yet because he looked so weak beside these marble pillars and metal bars, he seemed that much stronger, a one-lung, one-kidney Samson.

At his side stood Bud Parsifal and two Dominican friars, along with five *carabinieri* carrying rifles and machine guns. "This way, please," said Parsifal. "We have little time. Our opportunity with the image lasts only an hour."

The two Dominicans began whispering with great concern, obviously about Branch. One of the *carabinieri* set his rifle to the side and unlocked a door made of bars. As the group passed through, a Dominican said something to the *carabinieri*, and they blocked Branch's entrance. He stood before them, a virtual ogre dressed in a worn sports jacket.

"This man's with us," January said to the Dominican.

"Excuse me, but we are the custodians of a holy relic," the friar said. "And he does not look like a man."

"You have my oath he is a righteous man," Thomas interrupted.

"Please understand," the friar said. "These are days of disquiet. We must suspect everyone."

"You have my oath," Thomas repeated.

The Dominican considered the Jesuit, his order's enemy. He smiled. His power was explicit now. He gestured with his chin, and the *carabinieri* let Branch through.

The troupe filed deeper into the vault, following Parsifal and the two friars into an even larger room. The room was kept dark until everyone was inside. Then the lights blazed on.

The Shroud hung before them, almost five meters high. From darkness to radiant display, it made a dramatic first impression. Just the same, even knowing its significance, the relic appeared to be little more than a long, unlaundered tablecloth that had seen too many dinner parties.

It was singed and scorched and patched and yellowed. Occupying the center, in long blotches like spilled food, lay the faint image of a body. The image was hinged in the middle, at the top of the man's head, to show both his front and back. He was naked and bearded.

One of the *carabinieri* could not contain himself. He handed his weapon to an understanding comrade and knelt before the cloth. One beat his breast and mumbled mea culpas.

"As you know," the older Dominican began, "the Turin Cathedral suffered extensive damage from a fire in 1997. Only through the greatest heroism was the sacred artifact itself rescued from destruction. Until the cathedral's renovation is complete, the holy *sydoine* will reside in this place."

"But why here, if you don't mind?" Thomas asked lightly. Wickedly. "From a temple to a bank? A place of merchants?"

The older Dominican refused to be baited. "Sadly, the mafiosi and terrorists will stoop to any level, even kidnapping Church relics for ransom. The fire at Turin Cathedral was essentially an attempt to assassinate this very artifact. We decided a bank vault would be most secure."

"And not the Vatican itself?" Thomas persisted.

The Dominican betrayed his annoyance with a birdlike tapping of his thumb against thumb. He did not answer.

Bud Parsifal looked from the Dominicans to Thomas and back again. He considered himself today's master of ceremonies, and wanted everything to go just right.

"What are you driving at, Thomas?" asked Vera, equally mystified.

De l'Orme chose to answer. "The Church denied its shelter," he explained. "For a reason. The shroud is an interesting artifact. But no longer a credible one."

Parsifal was scandalized. As current president of STURP—the semi-scientific Shroud of Turin Research Project, Inc.—he had used his influence to obtain this showing. "What are you saying, de l'Orme?"

"That it's a hoax."

Parsifal looked like a man caught naked at the opera. "But if you don't believe in it, why did you ask me to arrange all of this? What are we doing in here? I thought—"

"Oh, I believe in it," de l'Orme reassured him. "But for what it is, not for what you would have it be."

"But it's a miracle," the younger Dominican blurted out. He crossed himself, incredulous at the blasphemy.

"A miracle, yes," de l'Orme said. "A miracle of fourteenth-century science and art."

"History tells us that the image is *achieropoietos,* not made by human hands. It is the sacred winding cloth." The Dominican quoted, "'And Joseph took the body and wrapped it in a clean linen shroud, and laid it in his own new tomb.'"

"That's your proof, a bit of scripture?"

"Proof?" interjected Parsifal. Nearly seventy, there was still plenty of the golden boy left in him. You could almost see him bulling through a hole in the line, forcing the play. "What proof do you need? I've been coming here for many years. The Shroud of Turin Research Project has subjected this artifact to dozens of tests, hundreds of thousands of hours, and millions of dollars of study. Scientists, including myself, have applied every manner of skepticism to it."

"But I thought your radiocarbon dating placed the linen's manufacture between the thirteenth and fifteenth centuries."

"Why are you testing me? I've told you about my flash theory," Parsifal said.

"That a burst of nuclear energy transfigured the body of Christ, leaving this image. Without burning the cloth to ash, of course."

"A moderate burst," Parsifal said. "Which, incidentally, explains the altered radiocarbon dating."

"A moderate burst of radiation that created a negative image with details of the face and body? How can that be? At best it would show a silhouette of a form. Or just a large blob of darkness."

These were old arguments. Parsifal made his standard replies. De l'Orme raised other difficulties. Parsifal gave complicated responses.

"All I'm saying," said de l'Orme, "is that before you kneel, it would be wise to know to whom you kneel." He placed himself beside the Shroud. "It's one thing to know who the shroud-man is not. But today we have a chance to know who he *is*. That's my reason for asking for this display."

"The Son of God in human form," said the younger Dominican.

The older Dominican cut a sideways glance at the relic. Suddenly his whole expression widened. His lips formed a thin O.

"As God is my Father," the younger one said.

Now Parsifal saw it, too. And the rest of them, as well. Thomas couldn't believe his eyes.

"What have you done?" Parsifal cried out.

The man in the Shroud was none other than de l'Orme.

"It's you!" Mustafah laughed. He was delighted.

De l'Orme's image was naked, hands modestly crossed over his genitals, eyes closed. Wearing a wig and a fake beard. Side by side, the man and his image on the cloth were the same size, had the same short nose, the same leprechaun shoulders.

"Dear Christ in heaven," the younger Dominican wailed.

"A Jesuit trick," hissed the older.

"Deceiver," howled the younger.

"De l'Orme, what in the world?" said Foley.

The *carabinieri* were excited by the sudden alarm. Then they compared man to image and put two and two together for themselves. Four promptly dropped to their knees in front of de l'Orme. One placed his forehead on the blind man's shoe. The fifth soldier, however, backed against the wall.

"Yes, it is me on this cloth," said de l'Orme. "Yes, a trick. But not of Jesuits. Of science. Alchemy, if you will."

"Seize this man," shouted the older Dominican. But the *carabinieri* were too busy adoring the man-god.

"Don't worry," de l'Orme said to the panicked Dominicans, "your original is in the next room, perfectly safe. I switched this one for the purpose of demonstration. Your reaction tells me the resemblance is all I'd hoped for."

The older Dominican swung his wrathful gaze around the room and fastened the look of Torquemada upon that fifth *carabiniere*, haplessly backed against the wall. "You," he said.

The *carabiniere* quailed. So, thought Thomas, de l'Orme had paid the soldier to help spring this practical joke. The man was right to be frightened. He had just embarrassed an entire order.

"Don't blame him," de l'Orme said. "Blame yourself. You were fooled. I fooled you just the way the other shroud has fooled so many."

"Where is it?" demanded the Dominican.

"This way, please," de l'Orme said.

They filed into the next chamber, and Vera was waiting there in her wheelchair. Behind her, the Shroud was identical to de l'Orme's fake, except for its image. Here the man was taller and younger. His nose was longer. The cheekbones were whole. The Dominicans hurried to their relic and alternated between scrutinizing the linen for damage and guarding it from the blind trickster.

De l'Orme became businesslike. "I think you'll agree," he spoke to them, "the same process produced both images."

"You've solved the mystery of its production?" someone exclaimed. "What did you use then, paint?"

"Acid," another suggested. "I've always suspected it. A weak solution. Just enough to etch the fibers."

De l'Orme had their attention. "I examined the reports issued by Bud's STURP. It became clear to me the hoax wasn't created with paint. There's only a trace of pigment, probably from painted images being held against the cloth to bless them. And it was not acid, or the coloration would have been different. No, it was something else entirely."

He gave it a dramatic pause.

"Photography."

"Nonsense," declared Parsifal. "We've examined that theory. Do you realize how sophisticated the process is? The chemicals involved? The steps of preparing a surface, focusing an image, timing an exposure, fixing the end product? Even if this were a medieval concoction, what mind could have grasped the principles of photography so long ago?"

"No ordinary mind, I'll grant you that."

"You're not the first, you know," Parsifal said. "There were a couple of kooks years ago. Cooked up some notion that it was Leonardo da Vinci's tomfoolery. We blew 'em out of the water. Amateurs."

"My approach was different," de l'Orme said. "Actually, you should be pleased, Bud. It is a confirmation of your own theory."

"What are you talking about?"

"Your flash theory," said de l'Orme. "Only it requires not quite a flash. More like a slow bath of radiation."

"Radiation?" said Parsifal. "Now we get to hear that Leonardo scooped Madame Curie?"

"This isn't Leonardo," de l'Orme said.

"No? Michelangelo then? Picasso?"

"Be nice, Bud," Vera interrupted mildly. "The rest of us want to hear it, even if you know it all already."

Parsifal fumed. But it was too late to roll up the image and kick everyone out.

"We have here the image of a real man," de l'Orme said. "A crucified man. He's too anatomically correct to have been created by an artist. Note the foreshortening of his legs, and the accuracy of these blood trickles, how they bend where there are wrinkles in the forehead. And the spike hole in the wrist. That wound is most interesting. According to studies done on cadavers, you can't crucify a man by nailing his palms to a cross. The weight of the body tears the meat right off your hand."

Vera, the physician, nodded. Rau, the vegetarian, shivered with distaste. These cults of the dead baffled him.

"The one place you can drive a nail in the human arm and hang all that weight is here." He held a finger to the center of his own wrist. "The space of Destot, a natural hole between all the bones of the wrist. More recently, forensic anthropologists have confirmed the presence of nail marks through precisely that place in known crucifixion victims.

"It is a crucial detail. If you examine medieval paintings around the time this cloth was created, Europeans had forgotten all about the space of Destot, too. Their art shows Christ nailed through the palms. The historical accuracy of this wound has been offered as proof that a medieval forger could not possibly have faked the Shroud."

"Well, there!" said Parsifal.

"There are two explanations," de l'Orme continued. "The father of forensic anthropology and anatomy was indeed Leonardo. He would have had ample time—and the body parts—to experiment with the techniques of crucifixion."

"Ridiculous," Parsifal said.

"The other explanation," de l'Orme said, "is that this represents the victim of an actual crucifixion." He paused. "But still alive at the time the Shroud was made."

"What?" said Mustafah.

"Yes," said de l'Orme. "With Vera's medical expertise, I've managed to determine that curious fact. There's no sign of necrotic decay here. To the contrary, Vera has told me how the rib cage details are blurred. By respiration."

"Heresy," the younger Dominican hissed.

"It's not heresy," said de l'Orme, "if this is not Jesus Christ."

"But it is."

"Then you are the heretic, gentle father. For you have been worshiping a giant."

The Dominican had probably never struck a blind man in his entire life. But you could tell by his grinding teeth how close he was now.

"Vera measured him. Twice. The man on the shroud measures six feet eight inches," de l'Orme continued.

"Look at that. He *is* a tall brute," someone commented. "How can that be?"

"Indeed," said de l'Orme. "Surely the Gospels would have mentioned Christ's enormous height."

The elder Dominican hissed at him.

"I think now would be a good time to show them our secret," de l'Orme said to Vera. He placed one hand on her wheelchair, and she led him to a nearby table. She held a cardboard box while he lifted out a small plastic statue of the Venus di Milo. It nearly slipped from his fingers.

"May I help?" asked Branch.

"Thank you, no. It would be better for you to stay back."

It was like watching two kids unpack a science fair project. De l'Orme drew out a glass jar and a paintbrush. Vera smoothed a cloth flat on the table and put on a pair of latex gloves.

"What are you doing?" demanded the older Dominican.

"Nothing that will harm your Shroud," de l'Orme answered.

Vera unscrewed the jar and dipped the brush in. "Our 'paint,'" she said.

The jar held dust, finely ground, a lackluster gray. While de l'Orme held the Venus by the head, she gently feathered on the dust.

"And now," de l'Orme said, addressing the Venus, "say cheese."

Vera grasped the statue by its waist and held it horizontally above the cloth. "It takes a minute," she said.

"Please tell me when it starts," de l'Orme said.

"There," said Mustafah. For the image of the Venus was beginning to materialize on the fabric. She was in negative. Each detail became more clarified.

"If that doesn't beat all," Foley said.

Parsifal refused to believe. He stood there shaking his head.

"The radiation heats and weakens the fabric on one side, creating an image. If I hold my statue here long enough, the cloth will turn dark. If

I hold it higher, the image will be larger. Hold it high enough, and my miniature Venus becomes a giantess. That explains our giant Christ."

"Our paint is a low-grade isotope, newtonium," said Vera. "It's found naturally."

"And you painted yourself with it—your own nude—to create the forgery out there?" asked Foley.

"Yes," said de l'Orme. "With Vera's help. She knows her male anatomy, I must say."

The older Dominican looked in danger of sucking the very enamel off his teeth.

"But it's radioactive!" Mustafah said.

"To tell the truth, the isotopes made my arthritis feel better for a few days after. I thought maybe I'd stumbled on to a cure for a while there."

"Nonsense," Parsifal stormed in, as if remembering his hat. "If this were the answer, we'd have detected radiation in our tests."

"You would detect it on this cloth," Vera admitted. "But only because we spilled dust onto it. If I'd been careful not to touch the cloth, all you would detect is the visual image itself."

"I've been to the moon and back," said Parsifal. Whenever Parsifal fell back on his lunar authority, he was near the end of his rope. "And I've never come across such a mineral phenomenon."

"The problem is that you have never been beneath the earth's surface," said de l'Orme. "I wish I could take credit for this. But miners have been talking about ghost images burnt onto boxes or the sides of their vehicles for years now. This is the explanation."

"Then you admit there are only traces of it on the surface," Parsifal declared. "You say that man only recently found enough of your powder there to have an effect. So how could a medieval con artist get his hands on enough to coat an entire human body and create this image?"

De l'Orme frowned at the question. "But I told you, this is not Leonardo."

"What I don't understand"—Desmond Lynch rapped with his cane, excited—"is why? Why go to such extremes? Is it all just a prank?"

"Again, it's all about power," de l'Orme answered. "A relic like this, in times so superstitious? Why, whole churches came into being around the drawing power of a single Cross splinter. In 1350, all of Europe was transfixed by the display of a supposed Veronica's veil. Do you know how many holy relics were floating around Christendom in those days? Crusaders were returning home with all manner of holy war loot. Besides bones and Bibles from martyrs and saints, there were the baby

Jesus' milk teeth, his foreskin—seven of them, to be precise—and enough splinters to make a forest of True Crosses. Obviously this was not the only forgery in circulation. But it was the most audacious and powerful.

"What if someone suddenly decided to tap into this benighted Christian gullibility? He could have been a pope, a king, or simply an ingenious artist. What could be more powerful than a life-size snapshot of the entire body of Christ, depicting him just after his great test on the Cross and just before his disappearance into the Godhead? Done artfully, wielded cynically, such an artifact would have the ability to change history, to create a fortune, to rule hearts and minds."

"Ah, come on," Parsifal complained.

"What if that was his game?" de l'Orme postulated. "What if he was attempting to infiltrate Christian culture through their own image?"

"He? His?" said Desmond Lynch. "Who are you talking about?"

"Why, the figure in the Shroud, of course."

"Very well," growled Lynch. "But who is the rascal?"

"Look at him," de l'Orme said.

"Yes, we're looking."

"It's a self-portrait."

"The portrait of a trickster," said Vera. "He covered himself with newtonium and stood before a linen sheet. He deliberately perpetrated this artful dodge. A primitive photocopy of the son of God."

"I give up. Are we supposed to recognize him?"

"He looks a little like you up there, Thomas," someone joked.

Thomas blew his cheeks out.

"Long hair, goatee. Looks more like your friend Santos," someone teased de l'Orme.

"Now that you mention it," de l'Orme mused, "I suppose it could be any one of us."

It was turning into a game.

"We give up," said Vera.

"But you were so close," said de l'Orme.

"Enough," barked Gault.

"Kublai Khan," de l'Orme said.

"What?"

"You said it yourselves."

"Said what?"

"Geronimo. Attila. Mao. A warrior king. Or a prophet. Or just a wanderer, little different from us."

"You're not serious."

"Why not? Why not the author of the Prester John letters? The author of a Christ hoax? Perhaps even the author of the legends of Christ and Buddha and Mohammed?"

"You're saying . . ."

"Yes," said de l'Orme. "Meet Satan."

*Those new regions which we
found and explored . . . we
may rightly call a New World
. . . a continent more densely
peopled and abounding in
animals than our Europe or
Asia or Africa.*

—AMERIGO VESPUCCI, on America

14

THE HOLE

THE COLON RIDGE ZONE

"July 7," Ali recorded. "Camp 39: 5,012 fathoms, 79 degrees F.
We reached Cache I today."

She looked up to gather in the scene. How to put this?

Mozart was flooding the chamber over Dolby speakers. Lights blazed
with the glut of cable-fed electricity. Wine bottles and chicken bones littered the floor. A conga line of filthy, trail-hardened scientists was
snaking across the tilted floor. To *The Magic Flute.*

"Joy!" she printed neatly.

The celebration rocked around her.

Until this afternoon it had been one vast, unspoken doubt that the
cache would be here. Geologists had muttered that the feat was impossible, suggesting that the tunnels shifted about down here, as dodgy as
snakes. But just as Shoat had promised, the penetrator capsules were
waiting for them. The surface crews had punched a drill hole through
the ocean floor and landed the cargo dead on target, at their exact elevation and place in the tunnels. A few meters to the right or left, or

higher or lower, and everything would have been socketed in solid bedrock and irretrievable. Their retreat to civilization would have been vexed, to say the least, for their food was running low.

But now they had all the provisions and gear and clothing necessary for the next eight weeks, plus tonight's wine and loudspeakers for the opera and a holographic "Bully for You" speech from C.C. Cooper himself. You are the beginning of history, his small laser ghost toasted them.

For the first time almost five weeks, Ali could write on her day map their precise coordinates: "107 degrees, 20 minutes W / 3 degrees, 50 minutes N." On a traditional map of the surface, they were somewhere south of Mexico in blue, islandless water. An ocean-floor map placed them beneath a feature called the Colon Ridge, near the western edge of the Nazca Plate.

Ali took a sip of the Chardonnay that Helios had sent. She closed her eyes while the Queen of the Night sang her brokenhearted aria. Someone up top had a sense of humor. Mozart's magical underworld? At least they hadn't sent *The Damnation of Faust*.

The three forty-foot cylinders lay on their sides among the drill rubble, like tipped-over rocket ships. Their discarded hatch doors set among cables tangled in a steel rat's nest, salt water trickling down from a mile overhead. Various lines hung from the three-foot-wide hole in the ceiling, one for communications, two to feed them voltage from the surface, another dedicated to downloading compressed vid-mail from home. One of the porters sat beside the second electric cable, recharging a small mountain of batteries for their headlamps and flashlights and lab equipment and laptop computers.

Walker's quartermaster and various helpers were working overtime, sorting the shipment, stockpiling boxes, shouting out numbers. Helios had also delivered them mail, twenty-four ounces per person.

As part of her vow of poverty, Ali had grown used to only small portions of home news. Yet she was disappointed at how little mail January had sent her. As always, the note was handwritten on Senate letterhead. It was dated two weeks earlier, and the envelope had been tampered with, which possibly explained the sparse information it contained. January had learned of their secret departure from Esperanza, and was heartsick that Ali had chosen to go deeper.

"You belong . . . Where? Not out there, not unseen, not beyond my reach. Ali, I feel like you've taken something from me. The world was big enough without you slipping away like a shadow in the night. Please call or write me at first chance. And please return. If others are turning back, go with them."

There was oblique mention of the Beowulf scholars' progress: "Work proceeds on the dam project." That was their code for the identification of Satan. "As of yet, no location, few specifics, perhaps new terrain." For some reason, January had included a few enhanced photographs of the Turin Shroud, with some three-dimensional computer images of the head. Ali didn't know what to make of that.

She looked around camp, and most had already rifled their care packages and eaten treats sent from home and shared the snapshots from their families and loved ones. Everyone had gotten something, it seemed, even the porters and soldiers. Only Ike appeared to have nothing. He kept busy with a new spool of candy-striped climbing rope, measuring it in coils and cutting and burning the tips.

Not all the news was good. In the far corner, a man was trying to talk Shoat into getting him extracted via the drill hole. Ali could hear him over the music. "But it's my wife," he kept saying. "Breast cancer."

Shoat wasn't buying it. "Then you shouldn't have come," he said. "Extractions are only for life-and-death emergencies."

"This *is* life and death."

"*Your* life and death," Shoat stated, and went back to uplinking with the surface, making his reports and getting instructions and feeding the expedition's collected data through a wet, dangling communications cable. They'd been promised a videophone line at each cache so people could call home, but so far Shoat and Walker had been monopolizing it. Shoat told them there was a hurricane on the surface and the drill rig was in jeopardy. "You'll get your chance, if there's still time," he said.

Despite the glitches and some serious homesickness, the expedition was in high spirits. Their resupply technology worked. They were loaded with food and supplies for the next stage. Two months down, ten to go.

Ali squinted into their holiday of lights. The scientists looked jubilant tonight, dancing, embracing, downing California wines sent as a token of C.C. Cooper's appreciation, howling at the invisible moon. They also looked different. Filthy. Hairy. Downright antediluvian.

She'd never seen them this way. Ali realized it was because, for over a month, she had not really *seen*. Since casting loose of Esperanza, they had been dwelling in a fraction of their normal light. Tonight their twilight was at bay. Under the bright light she could see them, freckles, warts, and all. They were gloriously unbarbered and bewhiskered and smeared with mud and oil, as pale as grubs. Men bore old food in their beards. Women had rat's nests. They had started doing a cowboy line dance—to the birdcatcher Papageno singing "Love's Sweet Emotion."

Just then someone ambushed the opera and plugged in a Cowboy

Junkies disc. The tempo slowed. Lovers rose, clenched, swayed on the rocky floor.

Ali's scanning arrived at Ike on the far side of the chamber.

His hair was growing out at last. With his cowlick and sawed-off shotgun, he reminded Ali of some farm kid hunting jackrabbits. The glacier glasses were a disconcerting touch; he was forever protecting what he called his "assets." Sometimes she thought the dark glasses simply protected his thoughts, a margin of privacy. She felt unreasonably glad he was there.

The moment her glance touched on him, Ike's head skated off to the other side, and she realized he'd been watching her. Molly and a few of Ali's other girlfriends had teased that he had his eye on her, and she'd called them wicked. But here was proof.

Fair's fair, she thought, and spurred herself forward. There was no telling when he might vanish into the darkness again.

The wine had an extra kick to it, or the depths had lowered her inhibitions. Whatever, she made herself bold. She went directly to him and said, "Wanna dance?"

He pretended to have just noticed her. "It's probably not a great idea," he said, and didn't move. "I'm rusty."

He was going to make her work for this? "Don't worry, I've had my tetanus shots."

"Seriously, I'm out of practice."

And I'm in practice? she didn't say. "Come on."

He tried one last gambit. "You don't understand," he said. "That's Margo Timmins singing."

"So?"

"Margo," he repeated. "Her voice does things to a person. It makes you forget yourself."

Ali relaxed. He wasn't rejecting her. He was flirting. "Is that right?" she said, and stayed right there in front of him. In the pale light of the tunnels, Ike's scars and markings had a way of blending with the rock. Here, lit brightly, they were terrible all over again.

"Maybe you would understand," he reconsidered. Ike stood up, and the shotgun came with him; it had pink climber's webbing for a sling. He parked it across his back, barrel down, and took her hand. It felt small in his.

They went to where the others had cleared away rocks for a makeshift dance floor. Ali felt eyes following them. Paired with partners of their own, Molly and some of the other women were grinning like maniacs at her. Oddly, Ike had been designated part of their Ten Most Wanted list.

He had an aura. It cut through the vandalized surface. People wondered about him. And here Ali was, getting first crack at him. She vamped like it was the prom, waving her fingers at them.

Ike acted smooth enough, but there was a young man's hesitation as he faced her and opened his arms. She hesitated, too. They got themselves arranged, and he was just as self-conscious about their physical touch as she was. He kept the bravado smile, but she heard his throat clear as their bodies came together.

"I've been meaning to talk with you," she said. "You owe me an explanation."

"The animal," he guessed. His disappointment was blunt. He stopped dancing.

"No," she said, and got them in motion again. "That orange. Do you remember? The one you gave me on the ride down from the Galápagos?"

He backed off a step to get a look. "That was you?"

She liked that. "Did I look so pathetic?"

"You mean like a rescue job?"

"If you want to put it that way."

"I used to climb," he said. "That was always the biggest nightmare, getting rescued. You do your best to stay in control. But sometimes things slip. You fall."

"I *was* in distress, then."

"Nah." Now he was lying.

"So how come the orange?"

There was no particular answer she wanted here. Yet the circle needed completing. Something about that orange demanded accounting for, the poetry in it, his intuition that she had needed just such a preoccupation at just that moment. It had become something of a riddle, this gift from a man so raw and brutalized. An orange? Where had that come from? Perhaps he'd read Flaubert in his previous life, before his captivity. Or Durrell, she thought. Or Anaïs Nin. Wishful thinking. She was inventing him.

"There it was," he said simply, and she got a sense he was delighting in her confusion. "It had your name on it."

"Look, I'm not trying to obsess here," she said. Immediately his words about staying in control came drifting in. She faltered. He'd pegged her problem, cold. Control. "It was just so right, that's all," she murmured. "It's been a mystery to me, and I never got a chance to say—"

"Strawberry blondes," he interrupted.

"What?"

"I confess," he said. "You're an old weakness of mine." He didn't qualify between the universe of blondes and the singularity of this one.

It took Ali's breath away. Sometimes, once men found out she was a nun, they would dare her in some way. What made Ike different was his abandon. He had a carelessness in his manner that was not reckless, but was full of risk. Winged. He was pursuing her, but not faster than she was pursuing him, and it made them like two ghosts circling.

"That's it, then," she said. "End of mystery."

"Why say that?" he said.

This was turning out to be a nice dance.

"I like her singing," she said.

He took in her long body. It was a quick glance. She saw it, and remembered his scrutiny of the periwinkles on her sundress. He said, "You do live dangerously."

"And you don't?"

"There's a difference. I'm not a dedicated, you know," he faltered, "a professional . . ."

"Virgin?" she boldly finished. The wine was talking. His back muscles reflexed.

"I was going to say 'recluse.'"

Ike pulled her tighter and stroked his front across hers, a languorous swipe that moved her breasts. It drew a small gasp out of her.

"Mister Crockett," she scolded, and started to pull away. Instantly he let go, and his release startled her more. There was no time for elaborate decisions. Scapegoating the wine, she scooped him close again, got his hand seated at the hollow of her spine.

They danced without words for another minute. Ali tried to let herself be taken away by the music. But eventually the songs would stop and they would have to leave the safety of this brightly lit floor and resume their investigation of the dark places.

"Now it's your turn to explain," he said. "Just how did you end up here?"

Unsure how much he really wanted to hear, she edited herself. He kept asking questions, and soon she found herself defining protolanguage and the mother tongue. "Water," she said, "in Old German is *wassar*, in Latin *aqua*. Go deeper into the daughter languages, and the root starts to appear. In Indo-European and Amerind, water is *hakw*, in Dene-Caucasian *kwa*. The furthest back is *haku*, a computer-simulated proto-word. Not that anyone uses it anymore. It's a buried word, a root. But you can see how a word gets reborn through time."

"Haku," Ike said, though differently than she had, with a glottal stress on the first syllable. "I know that word."

Ali glanced at him. "From them?" she asked. His hadal captors. Exactly as she'd hoped, he had a glossary in him.

He winced, as with a phantom pain, and she caught her breath. The memory passed, if that's what it was. She decided not to pursue it for the moment, and returned to her own tale, explaining how she had come to collect and decipher hadal glyphs and remnant text. "All we need is one translator who can read their writings," she said. "It could unlock their whole civilization to us."

Ike misunderstood. "Are you asking *me* to teach you?"

She kept her voice flat. "Do you know how to, Ike?"

He clicked his tongue in the negative. Ali instantly recognized the sound from her time among the San Bushmen in southern Africa. That, too? she wondered. Click language? Her excitement was building.

"Even hadals don't know how to read hadal," he said.

"Then you've never actually seen a hadal reading," she clarified. "The ones you met were illiterate."

"They can't read hadal writings," Ike repeated. "It's lost to them. I knew one once. He could read English and Japanese. But the old hadal writing was alien to him. It was a great frustration for him."

"Wait." Ali stopped, dumbfounded. No one had ever suggested such a thing. "You're saying the hadals read modern human languages? Do they speak our languages, too?"

"He did," said Ike. "He was a genius. A leader. The rest are . . . much less than him."

"You knew him?" Her pulse raced. Who else could he be speaking of except the historical Satan?

Ike stopped. He was looking at her, or through her, with those impenetrable glacier glasses. She couldn't begin to read his thoughts. "Ike?"

"Why are you doing this?"

"I have a secret." She wanted to trust him. They were still touching, and that seemed a good start. "What if I told you my purpose was to get a positive identification of that man, whatever he is? To get more information about him. A description of his face. Clues to his behavior. Even to meet him."

"You won't." Ike's voice sounded dead.

"But anything's possible."

"No," he said. "I mean *you* won't. By the time you ever got that close, it wouldn't be you anymore."

She brooded. He knew something, but wasn't telling. "You're making him up," she declared. It was peevish, a last resort.

The dancers flowed around them.

Ike held out one arm. Turned just so in the light, Ali could see the raised scars where a glyph had been branded in the flesh. To the naked eye, the scars lay hidden beneath more superficial markings. She touched them with her fingertips . . . the way a hadal might in complete darkness. "What does it mean?" she asked.

"It's a claim mark," he said. "The name they gave me. Beyond that, I don't have a clue. And the thing is, the hadals don't, either. They just imitate drawings their ancestors left a long time ago."

Ali traced her fingers across the scarring. "What do you mean by a claim mark?"

He shrugged, regarding the arm as if it belonged to someone else. "There's probably a better term for it. That's what I call them. Each clan has its own, and then each member his own." He looked at her. "I can show you others," he said.

Ali kept her expression calm. Inside, she was ready to shout. All this time, her quest had held Ike for its answer. Why had no one else asked this man these questions in years past? Perhaps they had, and he hadn't been ready.

"Wait, let me get my notebook." She could barely contain herself. Here was the beginning of her glossary. The start of a Rosetta stone. By cracking the hadal code, she would open a whole new language to human understanding.

"Notebook?" he said.

"To draw the markings."

"But I have them with me."

"You have what?"

He started to unbutton his pocket, then stopped. "You're sure about this?"

She stared impatiently at the pocket, willing it to fly open. "Yes."

He pulled out a small packet of leather patches, each roughly the size of a baseball card, and handed them to her. They had been sliced in a neat rectangle and tanned to stay soft. At first Ali thought the leather was vellum of some kind, and that Ike had used them to trace or write on. There were faint colored designs on one side. Then she saw that the colors came from tattooing, and the weltlike ridges were keloid scars, and there were tiny, pallid hairs. It was skin, all right. Human skin. Hadal skin. Whatever this was.

Ike did not see her misgivings; he was too busy arranging the strips on her still, cupped palms. He gave a running commentary, intent, even scholarly. "Two weeks old," he said of one. "Notice the twisted serpents. I've never come across that motif. You can feel them twining together, very skillful, whoever incised him."

He laid a pair of patches side by side. "These two I got off a fresh kill. You can tell from the linked circles, they'd been travelers from a long way off, from the same region. It's a pattern I used to see on Afghans and Pakis. Captures, you know. Down beneath the Karakoram."

Ali was staring as much at him as at the skin pieces. She had never been squeamish, but she was stilled by his collection.

"Now here's the shape of a beetle, can you make that out? See how the wings are just opening? That's a different clan from others I've known, closed wings, wings wide. And this one here has got me stumped, it's nothing but dots. Footprints, maybe? A counting of time? Seasons? I don't know.

"Obviously this is a cave-fish design. See the light stalks dangling in front of its mouth? I've eaten fish like that. They're easy to catch by hand in shallow pools. Wait for the light to flash, then grab them by the stalks. Like pulling carrots or onions."

He set down the last of his patches. "Here's some of the geometrics you see on the borders of their mandalas. They're pretty standard for down here, a way to ritually enclose the outer circle and hold in the mandala's information. You've seen them on the walls. I'm hoping someone in our bunch can figure them out. We've got a lot of smart people here."

"Ike." Ali stopped him. "What do you mean 'fresh kill'?"

Ike picked up the two patches she was referring to. "A day old. Maybe two."

"I mean, what. What was killed? A hadal?"

"One of the porters. I don't know his name."

"We're missing a porter?"

"More like ten or twelve," Ike said. "You haven't noticed? In twos and threes, over the past week. They're sick of Walker's bullying."

"Does anyone else know?" No one had remarked on this to her. It signified a whole other level of the expedition, one that was darker and more violent than she—or the other scientists—had comprehended.

"Of course. That's a lot of hands to lose." Ike could have been talking about animals in a mule train. "Walker's got more of his troops patrolling the rear than the front. He keeps sending them off to catch one of the runaways. He wants to make an example."

"To punish them? For quitting a job?"

Ike looked queerly at her. "When you're running a string of men," he said, "one runaway can turn you inside out. The whole bunch can come apart on you. Walker knows that. What he can't seem to get through his skull, though, is that by the time they run away, it's too late to keep them. If they were mine," he added frankly, "it would be different."

The stories about Ike's slaving were true then. In some capacity or another, he'd ruled over his fellow captives. She could try his dark alleys another time. "And so they caught one of the runaways," Ali stated.

"Walker's guys?" Ike stopped. "They're mercenaries. Herd mentality rules. They're not going to spread themselves out or search deep. They're afraid. They drop an hour behind, stay clustered, come back in again."

That left one option, as far as Ali could see. It made her sad. "You did it then?" she said.

He frowned, not understanding.

"Killed the porter," she said.

"Why would I do that?"

"You just said, to make an example. For Colonel Walker."

"Walker," Ike snorted. "He'll have to do his own killing."

She was relieved. For a moment.

"This poor fella didn't make it far," Ike said. "I doubt any of them did. I found him mostly rendered."

Rendered? That was something you did to slaughtered cattle. Again, Ike was matter-of-fact.

"What are you talking about?" she asked. Had one of the escaped porters turned psychotic?

"It's these two, I have no doubt," Ike said. He held up the paired leather patches with the linked circles of scar tissue. "I tracked *them* tracking *him*. They took him together, one from the front, one from above."

"And then you found them."

"Yes."

"And you couldn't bring them back to us?"

The absurdity shocked him. "Hadals?" he said.

Now she understood. This hadn't been a murder. He'd told her the first time. Fresh kill. It hit her. "Hadals?" she said. "There were hadals? Here?"

"Not anymore."

"Don't try to placate me," she said. "I want to know."

"We're in their house now. What do you expect?"

"But Shoat told us it was uninhabited through this tunnel."

"Blind faith."

"And you haven't told anybody?"

"I took care of the problem. Now we're clear again."

Part of her was glad. Live hadals! Dead now. "What did you do?" she asked quietly, not sure she really wanted the details.

He chose not to give any. "I left them in a way that will speak to any others. We won't have trouble."

"Then where do these come from?" she asked, pointing at his collection.

"Other places. Other times."

"But you think there may be more."

"Nothing organized. Not in any numbers. They're just drifters. Wanderers. Opportunists."

She was shaken. "Do you carry these around with you everywhere?" she asked.

"Think of it as taking their driver's license or dogtag. It helps me get the bigger picture. Movement. Migrations. I learn from them, almost like they were talking to me." He held one patch to his nose and smelled. Then he licked it. "This one came from very deep. You can tell by the cleanness of him."

"What are you talking about?"

He offered it to her, and she turned her head. "Have you ever eaten range-fed beef? It tastes different from a cow that's been eating grain and hormones. Same here. This guy had never eaten sunlight. He'd never been to the surface. Never eaten an animal that had gone up top. It was probably his first time away from the tribe."

"And you killed him," she said.

He looked at her.

"You have no idea how brutal this looks," she said. "Dear God. What did they do to you?"

He shrugged. In the span of one heartbeat, he had fallen a thousand miles away from her. "I'll find him," he said.

"Who?"

He pointed at the raised scars on his arm. "Him," he said.

"You said that was your name."

"It was. His name was my name. I had no name except for his."

"Whose?"

"The one who owned me."

Four days farther on, they found Shoat's river.

Ike had been sent ahead. He was waiting for the expedition at a chamber filled with thunder. They had been hearing it for days. In the center of the floor lay a great vertical shaft, shaped at top like a funnel. A city block wide, the hole roared up at them.

The walls sweated. Small streams sluiced into the maw. They girdled the rim, trying to see the bottom. Their lights illuminated a deep, polished throat. The stone was calcareous serpentine with green mottling. Ike lowered a headlamp on a rope. Two hundred meters down, the tiny light skipped and skidded sideways on an invisible current.

"I'll be damned," Shoat said. "The river."

"You didn't expect it to be here?" someone said.

Shoat grinned. "Nobody knew. Our cartography department gave it a one-in-three chance. On the other hand, it was the most logical way to explain the continuum in their data."

"We came all this way on a wild guess?"

Shoat gave a happy-go-lucky shrug. "Kick off your shoes," he said, "no more backpacks. No more hoofing it. From here, we float."

"I think we should first study the situation," one of the hydrologists said. "We have no idea what's down there. What's the river's profile? How fast does it run? Where does it go?"

"Study it from the boats," Shoat said.

The porters did not arrive for another three hours. Since leaving Cache I, they had been freighted with double loads for double pay, some carrying in excess of a hundred and fifty pounds. They deposited their cargo in a dry area and went over to a separate chamber, where Walker had arranged a hot meal for them.

Ali came across to Ike, where he was rigging lines into the hole. At their parting on the dance floor, she'd been drunk and brimming with curiosity and, ultimately, repulsion. Now she was as sober as a pebble, and the repulsion had abated. "What happens with them?" she asked, referring to the porters. "Everyone's wondering."

"End of the road," he said. "Shoat's retiring them."

"They're going home? The colonel's been hunting the runaways down, and now they're all being turned loose?"

"It's Shoat's show," Ike said.

"Will they be okay?"

This was no place to cut men, two months out from the nearest civilization. But Ike saw no reward in arousing her indignation all over again. "Sure," he said. "Why not?"

"I thought they'd been guaranteed employment for a year."

He hooked a coil of rope with one hand and busied himself with knots. "We've got worries of our own," he advised. "They're about to become a powder keg. Once they figure out we're ditching them, it's a matter of time before they go for us."

"For us?" she started. "For revenge?"

"It's more basic than that," Ike said. "They'll want our weapons. Our food. Everything. From a strictly military point of view—Walker's view—the expeditious thing would be to frag them and be done with it."

"He would never dare," Ali said.

"You don't see it?" he asked. "The porters are segregated from the rest of us now. That side cave is a cage with no door. They can only come out one at a time, and that makes them easy targets if they get tired of being cooped up."

Ali couldn't believe this other, meaner layer to the expedition. "He's not going to shoot them, is he?"

"No need. By the time they finally decide to poke their heads out, we'll probably be long gone down the river."

All over again, the quartermaster opened the loads and laid out the supplies from Cache I. One of his first tasks was to distribute specially made survival suits to the soldiers and scientists. Made by Jagged Edge Gear for NASA, the suits were constructed of a ripstop fabric that was waterproof but land-friendly. He issued the suits in sizes from small to extra large. A wiry mercenary ran them through the basics.

"You can walk in it, climb in it, sleep in it. If you fall overboard, pull this emergency ring and the suit will self-inflate. It preserves your body heat. It keeps you dry. And it's shark-proof."

Someone made a joke about a magic suit of armor.

The suits were a composite of rubbery shorts, sleeveless vests, and skintight oversuits. The fabric was night-striped with charcoal gray and cobalt blue. As the scientists tried on their elastic clothing, the unsettling effect was of tigers on two feet. There were a few wolf whistles, male and female.

They tried lowering a video camera to examine the lowest reaches of the shaft. When that didn't work, Walker sent down his crash dummy: Ike.

Not so many years before, a trail must have led from the chamber down to the river. Ike had already spent part of a day looking for it. But along the most likely tunnel, there was a boulder-choke triggered by recent tremors. Hadal evidence was everywhere—carved pillars, washed-out wall paintings, spouts to lift streamlets, rocks piled to divert them—but no suggestion that the hole had ever been used the way they were about to use it, to access the river from straight above.

Ike rappelled into the stone throat, feet braced against the veined rock. At the bottom of the first rope, a hundred meters down, he peeked upward through the falling water. They were watching him, waiting to see what would happen.

The shaft gave way to a void. Ike had no warning. His feet were suddenly pumping against the blackness. He halted, dangling in a vast, quiet bubble of night.

Casting around with his light beam, he found the river fifty feet below. He had descended into a long, winding geological cupola. Its vaulted ceiling hung above the flat river surface. Strangely, the thunderous noise stopped the moment he left the shaft. It was practically silent here. He could hear the water slithering past, little more.

If not for his rope leading up through it, the shaft hole might have disappeared among all the other gnarled features above and around him. The walls and ceiling were scaled with igneous puzzles. It was a complicated space with one logic—the river.

He let himself down the line and locked off within reach of the water. It ran smooth as black silk. Tentatively, Ike reached his fingertips against it. Nothing leaped up to bite him. The current was firm. The water felt cool and heavy. It had no smell. If it had come from the Pacific Ocean, it was no longer sea water; the journey inward had filtered any salt from it. It was delicious.

He made his report on a short-range radio that Walker had given him. "It looks fine to me," he said.

They lowered like spiders on silk threads. Some required coaxing for the rappel, including several of the soldiers. Clients, thought Ike.

The launch was tricky.

The rafts were roped down with their pontoons fully inflated and the seats and floor assembled. They reminded Ike of lifeboats descending from a doomed ship.

The river swept away their first attempt. Luckily, no one was in it.

At Ike's instruction, the next raft was suspended just above the water while a team of boatmen rappelled down on five other ropes. They might have been puppets on strings, all hanging in the air. On the count of three, the crew pendulumed into the dangling raft just as it touched the water. Two men didn't release from their ropes quickly enough, and ended up swinging back and forth above the river while the raft drifted on. The others grabbed paddles and began digging at the water toward a huge polished natural ramp not far downstream.

The operation smoothed out once a small motor was lowered and attached to one of the rafts. The motorized boat gave them the ability to circle in the water and collect passengers and bags of gear hanging on a dozen different ropes. Some of the scientists proved to be quite competent with the ropes and craft. Several of Walker's forbidding avengers looked seasick. Ike liked that. The playing field was growing more level.

It took five hours to convey their tons of supplies down the shaft. A small flotilla of rafts ferried the cargo to shore. Except for the one raft, and the sacrifice of their porters, the expedition had lost nothing. There was general contentment about their streamlining. The Jules Verne Society was feeling able and sanctioned, as though they could handle anything hell had to throw at them.

Ali dreamed of the porters that night. She saw their faces fading into blackness.

T
H
E

D
E
S
C
E
N
T

Send forth the best ye breed—
Go, bind your sons to exile
To serve your captives' need.

—RUDYARD KIPLING,
"The White Man's Burden"

15

MESSAGE IN A BOTTLE

LITTLE AMERICA, ANTARCTICA

January had expected a raging white hell with hurricanes and Quonset huts. But their landing strip was dry, the windsock limp. She had pulled a lot of strings to get them here today, but wasn't quite sure what to expect. Branch could only say that it had to do with the Helios expedition. Events were developing that could affect the entire sub-planet.

The plane parked swiftly. January and Thomas exited down the Globemaster's cargo ramp, past forklifts and bundled GIs. "They're waiting," an escort told them.

They entered an elevator. January hoped it meant an upper-story room with a view. She wanted to watch this immense land and eternal sun. Instead they went down. Ten stories deep, the doors opened.

The hallway led to a briefing room, dark and silent inside. She had thought the room empty. But a voice near the front said, "Lights." It was spoken like a warning. When the lights came on, the room was full. With monsters.

At first she thought they were hadals cupping hands over eyes. But one and all were American officers. In front of her, a captain's jarhead haircut revealed lumps and corrugations on a skull the shape and size of a football helmet.

As a congresswoman, she had chaired a subcommittee investigating the effects of prolonged tours of duty into the interior. Now, surrounded by officers of her own Army, she saw for herself what "skeletal warp" and *osteitis deformans* really meant: an exile among their peers. January reached for the term: Paget's disease. It sent skeletal tissue into an uncontrolled cycle of breakdown and growth. The cranial cavity was not affected, and motion and agility were uncompromised. But deformity was rampant. She quickly searched for Branch, but for once he was indistinguishable from the crowd.

"Welcome to our distinguished guests, Senator January and Father Thomas." At the podium stood a general named Sandwell, known to January as an intriguer of extraordinary energy. His reputation as a field commander was not good. In effect, he had just warned his men to beware the politician and priest now in their midst. "We were just beginning."

The lights went out. There was audible relief, men relaxing back into their chairs again. January's eyes adjusted to the darkness. A large video screen was glowing aqua blue on one wall. Maps came up, a seafloor topo, then a wire-frame view of the Pacific, then a close-up.

"To summarize," Sandwell said, "a situation has developed in our WestPac sector, at a border station numbered 1492. These are commanding officers of sub-Pacific bases, and they are gathered here to receive our latest intelligence and to take my orders."

January knew that was for her benefit. The general was declaring that he had determined a course of action. January was not annoyed. She could always influence the outcome, if need be. The fact that she and Thomas were even in this room was a testament to her powers.

"When one of our patrols was first reported missing, we assumed they had come under attack. We sent a rapid response unit to locate and assist the patrol. The rapid response unit went missing, too. And then the lost patrol's final dispatch reached us."

Regret pulled at January. Ali was out there, beyond the lost patrol. Concentrate, she commanded herself, and focused on the general.

"It's called a message in a bottle," Sandwell explained. "One patrol member, usually the radioman, carries a thermopylae box. It continuously gathers and digitizes video images. In case of an emergency, it can be triggered to transmit automatically. The information is thrown into geological space.

"The problem is, different subterranean phenomena retard our frequencies at different rates. In this case, the transmission bounced off the upper mantle and came back up through basalt that was folded. In short, the transmission was lost in stone for five weeks. Finally we intercepted the message wave at our base above the Mathematician Seamounts. The transmission was badly degraded with tectonic noise. It took us another two weeks to enhance with computers. As a consequence, fifty-seven days have passed since the initial incident. During that time we lost three more rapid response units. Now we know it was no attack. Our enemy is internal. He is one of us. Video, please."

"Final Dispatch—Green Falcon" a title read. A dateline jumped up, lower right. ClipGal/ML1492/7-03/2304:34.

Whispering, January translated for Thomas. "Whatever it is, we're about to see something from the McNamara Line station 1492 at the Clipperton/Galápagos tunnel on July 3, starting at fifty-six minutes before midnight."

Heat signatures pooled out from the blackness on screen. Seven souls. They looked disembodied.

"Here they are," said Sandwell. "SEALs. Based out of UDT Three, WestPac. A routine search-and-destroy."

The patrol's heat signatures resolved on screen. Hot-green souls metamorphosed into distinct human bodies. As they approached the cameras, the SEALs' faces took on individual personalities. There were a few white kids, a couple of blacks, a Chinese-American.

"These are edited clips taken from the lipstick video worn by the radio operator. They're putting on their light gear. The Line is very close now."

"The Line" was shorthand for a robot perimeter first conceived during the Vietnam War, an automatic Maginot Line that would serve as a countrywide tripwire. Here, in remote parts of the underworld, the technology seemed to be holding the peace. There had been next to no trespassing for over three years.

The screen flared to a lighter blue. Triggered by motion detectors, the first band of lights—or the last, depending on which direction one was traveling, inward or out—automatically flipped on from recesses in the tunnel walls. Even wearing their dark goggles, the SEALs hunched and turned their faces away. Had they been hadals, they would have fled. Or died. That was the idea.

"I'll fast-forward through the next two hundred yards," Sandwell said. "Our point of interest lies at the mouth."

As Sandwell fast-forwarded, the platoon seemed to speed through ribs of light. With each successive zone they entered, more lights snapped on, and the zone behind them went dark. It was like zebra stripes. The carefully woven combinations of light and other electromagnetic wavelengths were blinding and generally lethal to life-forms bred in darkness. As the subplanet was being pacified, choke points like this one had been outfitted with arrays of lights—infrared, ultraviolet, and other photon transmitters—plus sensor-guided lasers, to "keep the genie bottled." Evidence of the genie began to appear. Sandwell resumed normal speed.

Bones and bodies littered the deadly bright avenue, as if a vicious battle had been fought here. In full view, spotlit by the megawatt of electricity, the hadal remains were almost uninteresting. Few had any coloration to their skins and hides. Even their hair lacked color. It was not white, even, just a dead, parched hue similar to lard.

As the patrol neared the tunnel's far end—what Sandwell had termed the mouth—attempts at sabotage became obvious. Lights had been broken, or blocked with primitive tools, or plugged with stones. The hadal sappers had paid a high price for their efforts. The SEALs came to a halt. Just ahead, where the tunnel mouth turned black, lay true wilderness.

January swallowed her suspense. Something bad was about to happen.

"Anybody see it?" Sandwell asked the room. No one replied. "They walked right past it," he said. "Just the way they were supposed to."

Again he fast-forwarded. At high speed, the troops took off their packs and began their janitorial duties, replacing parts and lightbulbs in the walls and ceiling, and lubricating equipment and recalibrating lasers. The on-screen clock raced through seven minutes.

"Here's where they find it," Sandwell said. The video slowed.

A group of SEALs had clustered around a spur of rock, obviously discussing a curiosity. The radioman approached, and his lipstick video camera gave a view of a small cylinder the size of a little finger. It was lodged in a crevice in the rock. "There it is," Sandwell announced.

There was no soundtrack, no voices. One of the SEALs reached for the cylinder. A second tried to caution him. Abruptly, one man fell backward. The rest simply slumped to the ground. The lipstick camera spun madly, and came to rest—sideways—upon a view of someone's boot. The boot twitched once, no more.

"We've timed it," Sandwell said. "It took less than two seconds—one-point-eight, to be exact—for seven men to die. Of course, it was in its concentrated form at release. But even weeks later and three miles away, after dispersing on the air current, it took just over two seconds—two-point-two—to kill our rapid response units. In other words, it is nearly instantaneous. With a one-hundred-percent mortality rate."

"What is this?" Thomas hissed at January. "What is this man talking about?"

"I have no idea," she muttered.

"Here it is again, slower, with more detail."

Frame by frame, Sandwell showed them the death scene from the cylinder onward. This time, the finger-length of metal tube revealed its parts: a main body, a small glass hood, a tiny light. Magnified, the SEAL's fingers reached in. The tiny light bead changed colors. The cylinder delivered the faintest burst of an aerosol spray. Men fell to the ground, as slowly as drowned sailors. This time, January was able to see evidence of the biological violence. One of the black kids twisted his face to the camera, mouth gulping, and his eyes were gone. A man's hand swept past the lens, blood whipping from the nails. Once again the boot twitched and something, a human liquid, seeped from the lace holes.

Gas, January recognized. Or germs. But so fast-acting?

The officers caught up with the information in a single leap. CBW— chemical and biological warfare—was the part of their training they least wanted to engage in the field. But here it was.

"Once more," Sandwell said.

"Impossible, absolutely impossible," an officer said. "Haddie doesn't have anywhere near this kind of capability. They're Neolithic throwbacks. They barely have the sophistication to make fire. They acquire weaponry, they don't invent it. Spears and booby traps, that's their creative limit. You can't tell me they're manufacturing CBs."

"Since then," Sandwell continued, disregarding him, "we've found three more capsules just like it. They have detonators designed to be triggered by a coded radio command. Once placed, they can only be neutralized with the proper signal. Tamper with it, and you saw what happens. And so we leave them untouched. Here's a video of the most recent cylinder. It was discovered five days ago."

This time the players were dressed in biochem suits. They moved with the slowness of astronauts in zero gravity. The dateline was different. It said ClipGal/Rail/09-01/0732:12. The camera angle shifted to a fracture in the cave wall. One of the suited troops started to insert a shiny stick into the crack. It was a dental mirror, January saw.

The next angle focused on an image in the mirror. "This is the backside of one of the capsules," Sandwell said.

The lettering was complete this time, though upside down. There was a tiny bar code, and an identification in English script. Sandwell froze the image. "Right side up," he ordered. The camera angle pivoted. SP-9, the lettering said, followed by USDoD.

"It's one of ours?" a voice asked.

"The 'SP' designates a synthetic prion, manufactured in the laboratory. Nine is the generation number."

"Is that supposed to be good news or bad news?" someone said. "The hadals aren't manufacturing the contagion that's killing us. We are."

"The Prion-9 model has an accelerant built in. On contact with the skin, it colonizes almost instantly. The lab director compared it to a supersonic black plague." Sandwell paused. "Prion-9 was tailored for the theater in case things got out of hand down below. But once they built the prion, it was decided that nothing could get so out of hand to ever use it. Simply put, it's too deadly to be deployed. Because it reproduces, small amounts have the potential to expand and fill an environmental niche. In this case, that niche is the entire subplanet."

A hand closed on January's arm with the force of a trap. The pain of Thomas's grip traveled up her bone. He let go. "I'm sorry," he whispered, and took his hand away.

January knew better than to interrupt a military briefing. She did it anyway. "And what happens when this prion fills its niche and decides to jump to the next niche? What about our world?"

"Excellent question, Senator. There is some good news with the bad. Prion-9 was developed for use in the subplanet exclusively. It only lives—and only kills—in darkness. It dies in sunlight."

"In other words, it can't jump its niche. That's the theory?" She let her skepticism hang.

Sandwell added, "One other thing. The synthetic prion has been tested on captive hadals. Once exposed, they die twice as fast as we do."

"Now there's an edge for you," someone snorted. "Nine-tenths of a second."

Captive hadals? Tests? January had never heard of these things.

"Last of all," Sandwell said, "all remaining stocks of this generation have been destroyed."

"Are there other generations?"

"That's classified. Prion-9 was going to be destroyed anyway. The order arrived just days after the theft. Except for the contraband cylinders already in the subplanet, there are no more."

A question came from the dark room. "How did the hadals get their hands on our ordnance, General?"

"It's not the hadals who planted the prion in our ClipGal corridor," Sandwell snapped. "We have proof now. It was one of us."

The video screen came on again. January was certain he was replaying the first tape. It looked to be the same black tunnel, disgorging the same disembodied heat signatures. The hot green amoebas became bipedal. She checked the dateline. The images came from Line station number 1492. But the date was different. It read 6/18. This video had been shot two weeks earlier than the SEAL patrol.

"Who are these people?" a voice asked.

The heat signatures took on distinct faces. A dozen became two dozen, all strung out. They weren't soldiers. But with their night glasses on, it was impossible to say exactly who or what they were. The first array of tunnel lights automatically engaged. And suddenly the figures on screen could be seen yelling happily and stripping their glasses off and generally acting like civilians on a holiday.

Their Helios uniforms were dirty, but not tattered or badly worn. January made a quick calculation. At this point, the expedition had been in its second month of trekking.

"Look," she whispered to Thomas.

It was Ali. She had a pack on and looked healthy, if thin, and better fit than some of the men. Her smile was a thing of beauty. She passed the wall camera with no idea that it was taping her.

Without turning her head, January noticed a change in the soldiers around her. In some way, Ali's smile testified to their nobility.

"The Helios expedition," Sandwell said for those who did not know.

More and more people filled the screen. Sandwell let his commanders appreciate the whole potpourri. Someone said, "You mean to say one of *them* planted the cylinders?"

Again Sandwell set them straight. "I repeat, it was one of us." He paused. "Not them. Us. One of you."

January fastened upon Ali's image. On screen, the young woman knelt by her pack and unrolled a thin sleeping pad on the stone and shared a candy with a friend. Her small communion with her neighbors was endearing.

Ali finished her preparations, then sat on her pad and opened a foil packet with a folded washcloth and cleaned her face and neck. Finally she folded her hands and exhaled. You could not mistake her contentment. At the end of her day, she was satisfied with her lot. She was happy.

Ali glanced up, and January thought she was praying. But Ali was looking at the lights in the tunnel ceiling. It verged on worship. January felt touched and appalled at the same time. For Ali loved the light. It was that simple. She loved the light. And yet she had given it up. All for what? For me, thought January.

"I know that son of a bitch." It was one of the ClipGal commanders speaking.

At center screen, a lean mercenary was issuing orders to three other armed men. "His name's Walker," the commander said. "Ex–Air Force. Jockeyed F-16s, then quit to go into business for himself. He got a bunch of Baptists killed on that colony venture south of the Baja structure. The survivors sued him for breach of contract. Somehow he ended up in my neighborhood. I heard Helios was hiring muscle. They got themselves a cluster-fuck."

Sandwell let the tape run another minute without comment. Then he said, "It's not Walker who planted the prion capsules." He froze the image. "It's this man."

Thomas gave a start, all but imperceptible. January felt the shock of recognition. She looked at his face quizzically, and his eyes skipped to hers. He shook his head. Wrong man. She returned her attention to the image on screen, searching her memory. The vandalized figure was no one she knew.

"You're mistaken," a soldier stated matter-of-factly from the audience. January knew that voice.

"Major Branch?" Sandwell said. "Is that you, Elias?"

Branch stood up, blocking part of the screen. His silhouette was thick and warped and primitive. "Your information is incorrect. Sir."

"You do recognize him then?"

The image frozen on screen was a three-quarters profile, tattooed, hair trimmed with a knife. Again January sensed Thomas's recoil. A click of teeth, a shift in breathing. He was staring at the screen. "Do we know this man?" she whispered. Thomas lifted his fingers: No.

"You've made a mistake," Branch repeated.

"I wish we had," said Sandwell. "He's gone rogue, Elias. That's the fact."

"No sir," Branch declared.

"It's our own fault," Sandwell said. "We took him in. The Army gave him sanctuary. We presumed he had returned to us. But it's very possible he never quit identifying with the hadals who had captured him. You've all heard of the Stockholm syndrome."

Branch scoffed. At his superior officer. "You're saying he's working for the devil?"

"I'm saying he appears to be a psychological refugee. He's trapped between two species, preying on each. The way I look at it, he's killing my men. And taking aim at the whole subplanet."

"Him," breathed January. Now the shock was hers. "Thomas, he's the one Ali wrote us about just before leaving Point Z-3. The Helios scout."

"Who?" asked Thomas.

January drew the name from her mental bank. "Ike. Crockett," she whispered. "A recapture. He escaped from the hadals. Ali said she was hoping to interview him, get his remembrances of hadal life, enlist his knowledge. What have I gotten her involved with?"

"Judging by his work so far," Sandwell continued, "Crockett is attempting to lay a belt of contagion along the entire sub-Pacific equator. With one signal he can trigger a chain reaction that will wipe out every living thing in the interior, human, hadal, and otherwise."

"Give me your proof," Branch insisted stubbornly. "Show me one clip or one picture of Ike planting CBs." January heard heartbreak mixed in with his defiance. Branch had some connection with this character on screen.

"We have no pictures," Sandwell said. "But we've retraced the original batch of stolen Prion-9. It was stolen from our West Virginia chemical weapons depot. The theft occurred the same week that Crockett visited Washington, D.C. The same week he was to face a court-martial and a dishonorable discharge, and then fled. Now four of those cylinders have been discovered in the very same corridor he's guiding the Helios expedition through."

"If the contagion goes off, he dies too," said Branch. "That's not Ike. He wouldn't kill himself. Anyone who knows him can tell you. He's a survivor."

"In fact, that's our clue," Sandwell said. "Your protégé had himself immunized."

There was silence.

"We interviewed the physician who administered the vaccine," Sandwell went on. "He remembered the incident, and for good reason. Only one man has ever been immunized against Prion-9."

A photograph flashed on the screen. It showed a medical release form. Sandwell let them have a minute with it. There was a doctor's name and address at the top. And at the bottom, a plain signature. Sandwell read it aloud: "Dwight D. Crockett."

"Shit," grunted one of the commanders.

Branch was stubborn in his loyalty. "I dispute your proof."

"I know this is difficult," Sandwell said to him.

Men stirred uneasily, January noticed. Later she would learn that Ike had taught many of them, saved some of them.

"It's imperative that we find this traitor," Sandwell told them. "Ike has just made himself the most wanted man on earth."

January raised her voice. "Let me understand," she said. "The only person immune to this plague, today, is the man who is planting it?"

"Affirmative, Senator," Sandwell said. "But not for long. In order to contain the prion release, we've closed the entire ClipGal corridor with explosives. We're evacuating the subplanet within a two-hundred-mile radius, including Nazca City. No one goes back in again until they get vaccinated. We start with you, gentlemen. We have medics waiting for you in the next room. Senator, and Father Thomas, you're both welcome to be vaccinated too."

Before January could decline, Thomas accepted. He glanced at her. "In case," he said.

A map filled the screen. It zoomed in on a vein within the earth. "This is the Helios expedition's projected trajectory," the general continued. "There's probably no way we can catch them from behind, meaning we have to intercept them from the side or the front. The problem is, we know where they've been, but not exactly where they're going.

"The Helios cartel has agreed to share information about the expedition's projected course. Over the next months, we'll be working closely with their mapping department to try to pinpoint the explorers. Meanwhile, we hunt."

"We're going to commit all possible assets. I want squads sent out. Exit points covered. We'll flush him out. We'll lay traps. We'll wait for him. And when he's located, you're to shoot him dead. On sight. That order comes from the top. I repeat, kill on sight. Before this renegade can kill us."

Sandwell faced them. "Now is the time to ask yourselves, is there any man here who cannot deal with the mission as described?"

He was asking one man alone. They all knew it. Their silence waited for Branch to recuse himself. He did not.

NEW GUINEA

The phone call at 0330 woke Branch in his berth. He slept little anyway. Two days had passed since the commanders had returned to their bases and begun harrowing the depths to find Ike. Branch, however, was assigned to mission control at SouthPac's New Guinea headquarters. It had been dressed up as a humanitarian gesture, but was fundamentally a way to neutralize him. They wanted Branch's insights into their prey, but did not trust him to kill Ike. He didn't blame them.

"Major Branch," a voice said on the phone. "This is Father Thomas."

Ever since the briefing, Branch had been expecting a call from January. His connection was with her, not with her Jesuit confidant.

He'd been surprised when the senator brought the man to their Antarctic meeting, and was not pleased to hear his voice. "How did you find me?" he asked.

"January."

"This probably isn't the best phone line to be using," Branch rankled.

Thomas disregarded him. "I have information about your soldier Crockett."

Branch waited.

"Someone is using our friend."

Our friend? thought Branch.

"I've just returned from visiting the physician who administered the vaccine."

Branch listened. Hard.

"I showed him a photo of Mr. Crockett."

Branch screwed the phone tighter against his ear.

"I think we can agree he has a rather distinctive look. But the physician had never seen Crockett in his life. Someone forged his signature. Someone posed as him."

Branch eased his grip. "Is it Walker then?" That had been his first suspicion.

"No," said Thomas. "I showed him Walker's photo. And photos of each of his hired gunmen. The physician was adamant. It was none of them."

"Then who?"

"I don't know. But something isn't right here. I'm trying to obtain photos of all the expedition members to show him. The Helios corporation is proving less than accommodating. In fact, the Helios representative told me there's officially no such expedition."

Branch made himself sit on the edge of the fiberglass bed rack. It was difficult to be calm. What was this priest's game? Why was he playing detective with an Army physician? And placing phone calls in the middle of the night like this, trumpeting Ike's innocence? "I don't have photos, either," said Branch.

"It occurred to me that another source of images might be that video General Sandwell played for us. It seemed to have a lot of faces."

So that was it. "You want me to get it for you."

"Perhaps the physician could pick his man from the crowd."

"Then ask Sandwell."

"I have. He's no more forthcoming than the corporation itself. In fact, I suspect he's something other than what he pretends to be."

"I'll see what I can do," Branch said. He didn't commit himself to the theory.

"Is there any chance of stopping the search for Crockett, or at least stalling it?"

"Negative. Hunter-killer teams have been inserted. They're going deep, a month each. Beyond recall."

"Then we need to move quickly. Send that video to the senator's office."

After he hung up, Branch sat in the semidarkness. He could smell himself, the plasticized flesh, the stink of his doubt. He was useless here. That was their intent. He was supposed to stay quietly parked at the surface and wait while they took care of business. Now Branch could not wait.

Obtaining the ClipGal videos for the priest might have its value. But even if the physician put his finger on the culprit, it was too late to reverse Sandwell's decision. Most of the long-range patrols had already passed beyond communication. Every hour put them deeper into the stone.

Branch got to his feet. No more hesitation. He had a duty. To himself. To Ike, who had no way to know what they had in mind for him.

Branch stripped off his uniform. It was like taking off his own skin; it could never be put on again after this.

What a peculiar thing a life was. Nearly fifty-two, he had spent more than three decades with the Army. What he was about to do should have seemed more difficult than this. Perhaps his fellow officers would understand and forgive him this excess. Maybe they'd just think he'd finally gone off his nut. Freedom was like that.

Naked, he faced the mirror, a dark stain upon the dark glass. His ruined flesh glistened like a pitted gem. He was sorry, suddenly, never to have had a wife or children. It would have been nice to leave a letter for someone, a last phone message. Instead he had this terrible companion, a broken statue in his looking glass.

He dressed in civilian clothing that barely fit, and took his rifle.

Next morning, no one wanted to report Branch AWOL.

Finally, General Sandwell got the word. He was furious and did not hesitate to issue the order. Major Branch was in on the conspiracy with Ike, he declared. "They're both traitors. Shoot them on sight."

It was a monstrous big river down there.

—MARK TWAIN,
The Adventures of Huckleberry Finn

16
BLACK SILK

THE EQUATOR, WEST

The paladin chased along the river's paths, devouring great distances. He had learned of yet more invasion, but this time along the ancient camino and nearing their final asylum. And so he had come to investigate this trespass, or destroy it, on behalf of the People.

He fought all memory. Suffered privations. Shed desire. Cast off grief. In service to the group, he gladly effaced his heart.

Some give up the world. For others, the world is taken away. Either way, grace comes in the moment. And so the paladin ran, seeking to erase all thoughts of his great love.

In her lifetime, the woman had borne him a child and learned her station and rightful duties and become mastered. Captivity had broken her mind and spirit. It had created a blank table for the Way to be written upon. Like him, she had recovered from the mutilations and initiations. On the merits of her nature, she had risen up from her lowly bestial status. He had helped create her, and, as happens, had come to love his creation. Now Kora was dead.

Stripped of clan, with his woman dead, he was rootless now and the world was vast. There were so many new regions and species to investigate, so many destinations calling to him. He could have forsaken the hadal tribes and gone deeper into the planet, or even returned to the surface. But he had chosen his path a long time ago.

After many hours the ascetic tired. It became time to rest.

He left the trail racing. One hand touched the rock wall. With an intelligence all their own, his fingertips found random purchase. Part of his brain changed direction and told the hand to pull, and his feet went with him. He could have been running still, but suddenly he was climbing at a gallop. He scuttled diagonally up the arched sides to a cavity near mid-ceiling, alongside the river.

He smelled the cavity to know what else had burrowed here, and when. Satisfied, he drew himself into the stone bubble. He wedged his limbs tight, socketed his spine just so, and said in full his night prayer, part supplication, part superstition. Some of the words were in a language that parents and their parents and their parents had spoken. Words that Kora had taught their daughter. *Hallowed be Thy name*, he thought.

The paladin did not close his eyes. But all the while his heart was slowing. His breathing almost stopped. He grew still. *My soul to keep.* The river flowed beneath him. He went to sleep.

Voices woke him, ricocheting off the river's skin. Human.

The recognition came slowly. In recent years he had purposely tried to forget this sound. Even in the mouths of quiet ones, it had a jarring discord. Bone-breaking in its aggression. Barging everywhere, like sunlight itself. It was no wonder that more powerful animals ran from them. It shamed him that he had once been part of their race, even if it had been over a half-century ago.

Here, speech was different. To articulate was just that, to join things together. Every precious space—every tube, every burrow, every gap and hollow—relied on its connection to another space. Life in a maze depended upon linkage.

Listen to humans, and their very speech defiled the construct. Space addled them. With nothing above their heads, no stone to cap the world, their thoughts went flying off into a void more terrible than any chasm. No wonder they were invading willy-nilly. Man had lost his mind to heaven.

Gradually he filled his lungs, but the water smell was too powerful. No chance of scent. That left him echoes to reckon with. He could have left long before they arrived. He waited.

They arrived in boats. No point guards, no discipline, no caution, no protection for their women. Their lights were a river where a trickle would have sufficed. He squinted through a tiny hole between his fingers, insulted by their extravagance.

They poured beneath his cavity without a single glance up. Not one of them! They were so sure of themselves. He lay still in the ceiling in plain view, a coil of limbs, contemptuous of their self-assurance.

Their rafts strung through the tunnel in a long, random mass. He quit counting heads to focus instead on their weak and strays.

There was little to recommend them. They were slow, with dulled senses, and out of sync. Each conducted himself with little reference to the group. Over the next hour he watched different individuals imperil the group's safety by brushing the walls or casting aside bits of uneaten food. It was more than sign they were leaving to predators. They were leaving the taste of themselves. Every time one rambled his hand along the rock, he painted human grease on the wall. Their piss gave off a pungent signature. Short of opening their veins and lying down, they could have done nothing more to invite their own slaughter.

The ones with tiny hurts did nothing to disguise their pain. They advertised their vulnerabilities, offered themselves as the easiest quarry. Their heads were too big, and their joints were askew at the hips and knees. He couldn't believe that he had been born like them. One changed little bandages on her feet and threw the old bandages into the water, where they washed to shore. He could smell her details from up here.

There were many women among them. That was the unbelievable part. Chattering and oblivious. Unguarded. Ripe women. In such a fashion, Kora had come to him in the darkness, long ago.

After they had passed deeper with the river's current, he waited an hour for his eyes to recover from their lights. Muscle by muscle, he released himself from the cavity. He hung by one arm from its slight lip, listening not so much for stragglers as for other predators, for there would surely be those. Content, he let go and landed on the trail.

In darkness he moved among their refuse, sampling it. He licked the foil of a candy wrapper, sniffed the rock where they had rubbed against it. He nosed at the female's bandages, then took them into his mouth. This was the taste of humans. He chewed.

He trailed them again, running along old paths worn into the shore stone, reaching them as they camped. He watched.

Many of them talked or sang to themselves, and it was like hearing the inside of their minds. Sometimes his Kora had sung like that, especially to their daughter.

Repeatedly, individuals would wander from camp and place themselves within his reach. He sometimes wondered if they had sensed his presence and were attempting to sacrifice themselves to him. One night he stole through their camp while they slept. Their bodies glowed in the darkness. A lone female started as he slid past, and stared directly at him. His visage seemed horrifying to her. He backed away and she lost his image and sank back into sleep. He was nothing more than a fleeting nightmare.

It was difficult to keep from harvesting one. But the time wasn't right, and there was no sense in frightening them at this early stage. They were heading deeper into the sanctuary all on their own, and he didn't know their rationale for coming here yet. And so he ate beetles, careful to mash them with his tongue lest they crunch.

Day by day, the river became their fever.

They made a flotilla of twenty-two rafts roped together, some lashed side by side, others trailing singly far behind, for the sake of solitude or mental health or science experiments or clandestine lovemaking. The large pontoon boats had a ten-man capacity, including 1,500 pounds of cargo. The smaller boats they used as dinghies to transport passengers from one polyurethane island to another during the day, or for floating hospital beds when people got sick, or for ranger duty, rigged with a machine gun and one of the battery-powered motors. Ike was given the only sea kayak.

There was not supposed to be weather down here. There could be no wind, no rain, no seasons: scientifically unfeasible. The subplanet was hermetically sealed, a near vacuum, they'd been told, its thermostat locked at 84 degrees Fahrenheit, its atmosphere motionless.

No thousand-foot waterfalls. No dinosaurs, for christsake. Most of all, there was not supposed to be light.

But there was all of that. They passed a glacier calving small blue icebergs into the river. The ceilings sometimes rained with monsoon weight. One of the mercenaries was bitten by a plate-armored fish unchanged since the age of trilobites.

With increasing frequency, they entered caverns illuminated by a type of lichen that ate rock. In its reproductive stage, apparently, the lichen extended a fleshy stalk, or ascocarp, with a positive and negative electrical charge. The result was light, which attracted flatworms by the millions. These were eaten, in turn, by mollusks that traveled on to new, unlit regions. The mollusks excreted lichen spores from their guts. The spores matured to eat the new rock. Light spread by inches through the darkness.

Ali loved it. What excited the botanists was not just the production of light energy, but the decomposition of rock, a lichen by-product. Decomposed rock was soil, which meant vegetation, and animals. The land of the dead was very much alive.

The geologists were elated. The expedition was about to leave the Nazca Plate and traverse beneath the East Pacific Rise. Here the Pacific Plate was just being born as freshly extruded rock, which steadily migrated west with a conveyor-belt motion. It would take 180 million years for the rock to reach the Asian margin, there to be devoured—subducted—back into the earth's mantle. They were going to see the entire Pacific plate geology, from birth to death.

In the third week of August, they passed through the rise between the roots of a nameless seamount, an ocean-floor volcano. The seamount itself sat a mile overhead, serviced by these ganglia reaching deep into the mantle for supplies of live magma. The riverine walls became hot.

Faces flushed. Lips cracked. Those still carrying Chapstick even used it on their splitting cuticles. By the thirtieth hour, they knew what it was like to be roasted alive.

Head draped with a red-and-white checkered cotton scarf, Ike warned them to keep covered. The NASA survival suits were supposed to wick their sweat to a second layer to circulate and cool. But the humidity inside their suits became unbearable. Soon everyone had stripped to underwear, even Ike in his kayak. Appendix scars, moles, birthmarks all went on display; later the revelations would fuel new nicknames.

Ali had never known thirst like this.

"How much longer?" a voice croaked from the line.

Ike grinned. "Drink," he said.

They moved on, mouths open. The batteries of their boat motors had run down. They paddled listlessly, spooning at the river.

At one point the tunnel wall became so hot, it glowed dull red. They could see raw magma through a gash opened in the wall. It arched and seethed like gold and blood, roiling in the planetary womb. Ali dared one glance and darted her face away and stroked on. Its hush was like a great geological lullaby.

The river looped around and through the volcano's searing root system. There were, as always, forks and false paths. Somehow, Ike knew which way to go.

The tunnel began to close on them. Ali was near the end of the line. Suddenly screams issued from the very back. She thought they were under attack.

Ike appeared, his kayak scooting upriver like a water bug. He passed

Ali's raft, then stopped. The walls had plasticized and bulged in on the tunnel, confining the very last raft on its upriver side.

"Who are they?" Ike asked Ali and her boatload.

"Walker's guys," someone answered. "There were two of them."

The shouting on the far side of the opening was anonymous. The hemorrhaged stone made a noise like a ship's ribs cracking. The outer sheath of stone splintered, throwing shrapnel.

Walker and his boat of men came paddling from lower down. The colonel assessed the situation. "Leave them," he said.

"But those are your men," Ike said.

"There's nothing to be done. It's already too narrow to get their raft through. They know to retreat if they get cut off." The soldiers in Walker's boats were lockjawed with fear, veins snaky from wrist to shoulder.

"Well, that won't do," Ike said, and shot upriver.

"Get back here!" Walker shouted after him.

Ike darted his kayak through the narrowing channel. The walls were deforming by the minute. Part of his checkered scarf touched the walls and caught fire. The hair on his head smoked. He popped through the maw at full speed.

The sides bloated in behind him. The bottom ten feet of the opening fused shut with a kiss. A gap remained open near the ceiling, but it was easily nine hundred degrees Fahrenheit through there. No one could conceivably climb through.

"Ike?" called Ali.

It was as if he had just changed into solid rock.

The new wall quickly choked back the river. Even as Ali's boat of people sat there, the river's bottom grew more exposed, inch by inch. The corridor was filling with steam. It was going to be a race to keep ahead of the deprivation.

"We can't stay here," someone said.

"Wait," Ali commanded. She added, "Please."

They waited and the riverbed drained lower. In another few minutes their raft would be sitting upon bare stone.

Ali's cracked lips parted. God the Father, she prayed. Let this one go free.

It was not like her. True devotion was not quid pro quo. You never cut deals with God. Once, as a child, she had pleaded for her parents' return. Ever since, Ali had decided to let be what was. Thy will be done.

"Let him live," she murmured.

The walls did not open. This was not a fairy tale. The stone stayed welded.

"Let's go," said Ali.

Then they heard a different sound. Dammed on the far side, the river had built height. Abruptly, a jet of water shot through the molten aperture at the top.

"Look!"

Like Jonah being vomited from the whale, one, then two men came blasting from the hole. Sheathed in water, they were protected from the scalding rock and thrown clear into the lower river.

The two soldiers staggered downstream through the thigh-deep water, weaponless, burned, naked. But alive. The raft of scientists returned and pulled the two bleating, shocked men onto their floor. "Where's Ike?" Ali yelled to them, but their throats were too swollen to speak.

They looked to the hole of spouting water, and a shape sprang through the torrent. It was long and black with mottled gray, Ike's empty sea kayak. Next appeared his paddle. Ike came last.

He held onto the gunnel of his kayak, half cooked. When his strength returned, he emptied the craft of water and got himself in and came paddling down to them. He was burned, but whole, right down to his shotgun.

It had been the closest of calls, and he knew it. He took a deep breath, shook the water from his hair, and did his best to stop down the big grin. He looked each of them in the eye, last of all Ali.

"What are we waiting for?" he said.

Many hours later, the expedition finished its marathon beneath the seamount. They pulled onto a shoal of green basalt in cooling air. There was a small stream of clear water.

The two lucky soldiers were returned to Walker, naked. Their gratitude to Ike was obvious. The colonel's shame at abandoning them was like a dangerous cloud.

For the next twenty hours, people slept. When they woke, Ike had stacked some rocks to pool the stream for them to drink. Ali had never seen him so happy.

"You made them wait," he said to her.

In full view of the others, he kissed her on the lips. Maybe that was the safest way he could think to do it. She went along with it, even blushing.

By now, Ali was beginning to recognize the archangel inside Ike's sausage skin of scars and wild tattooing. The more she trusted him, the more she did not. He had an esprit, an air of immortality. She could see how each brush with great risk would serve to feed it, and how eventually even a kiss might destroy him.

Naturally, they called the river Styx.

The slow current lofted them. Some days they barely dipped a paddle, drifting with the flow. Hundreds of miles of shoreline stretched by with elastic monotony. They named some of the more prominent landmarks, and Ali jotted the names down to enter onto her maps each night.

After a month of acclimation, their circadian rhythms were finally synched to the changeless night. Sleep resembled hibernation, profound crashes into dream, REMs practically shaking them. Initially they lapsed into ten-hour stretches, then twelve. Each time they closed their eyes, it seemed they slept longer. Finally their bodies settled on a communal norm: fifteen hours. After that much sleep, they would usually be good for a thirty-hour "day."

Ike had to teach them how to pace such a long waking cycle, otherwise they would have destroyed themselves with exhaustion. It took stronger muscles and thicker calluses and constant attention to respiration and food to stay mobile for twenty-four hours or more at a time.

If not for their watches, they would have sworn their biological clocks were the same as on the surface. There were many advantages to this new regimen. They were able to cover vastly more territory. Also, without the sun and moon to cue them, they began to live, in a sense, longer.

Time dilated. You could finish a five-hundred-page novel in a single sitting. They developed a craving for Beethoven and Pink Floyd and James Joyce, anything of magnum-opus length.

Ike tried to instill in them new awareness. The shapes of rocks, the taste of minerals, the holes of silence in a cavern: memorize it all, he said. They humored him. He knew his stuff, which took the burden off them. It was his job, not theirs. He went on trying. Someday you won't have your instruments and maps, he said. Or me. You'll need to know where you are with your fingertips, by an echo receding. Some tried to emulate his quiet manner, others his unspoken authority with things violent. They liked how he spooked Walker's solemn gunmen.

That he had been a mountaineer was obvious in his economy and care. From his big stone walls in Yosemite and his Himalayan mountains, Ike had learned to take the journey one inch at a time. Long before the underworld ever came into his life, Ali realized, it was the climbing that had shaped Ike's tactile perceptions. It came naturally to him to read the world through his fingertips, and Ali liked to think it had given him an edge even on his first accidental descent from Tibet. The irony was that his talent for ascent had become his vehicle for the abyss.

Often, before the others woke each morning, Ali would see him flickering off upon the black water, not a riffle in his wake. At such times she wishfully imagined this was the real man within him. The sight of him slipping monklike into the wilderness made her think of the simple force of prayer.

He quit using paint and simply blazed the wall with a pair of chemical candles and went on. They would float past his cold blue crosses glowing above the waters like a neon JESUS SAVES. They followed him through the apertures and rock meatus. He would be waiting on a scarp of olivine or reefs of iron, or sitting in his night-colored kayak, holding on to an outcrop. Ali liked him at peace.

One day they drifted around a bend and heard an unearthly sound, part whistle, part wind. Ike had found a primitive musical instrument left by some hadal. Made of animal bone, it had three holes on top and one on the bottom. They beached, and some of the flute players took turns trying to make it work for them. One got a trickle of Bach out, another a bit of Jethro Tull.

Then they gave it back to Ike, and he played what the flute was meant for. It was a hadal song, with clots of melody and measured rhythm. The alien sound spellbound them, even the soldiers. This was what moved the hadals? The syncopation, the cheeps and trills and sudden grunts, and finally a muffled shout: it was an earth song, complete with animal and water sounds and the rumble of quakes.

Ali was mesmerized, but appalled, too. More than the tattoos and scars, the bone flute declared Ike's captivity. It was not just his proficiency and memory of the song, but also his obvious love for it. This alien music spoke to the heart of him.

When Ike was done, they clapped uncertainly.

Ike looked at the bone flute as if he'd never seen such a thing, then tossed it into the river. When the others had left, Ali fished along the bottom and retrieved the instrument.

They made a sport of sighting hadal footpaths. Where the caverns narrowed and the shore vanished, they spied foot- and handholds traversing above the waterline, linking the riverside beaches. They found strands of crude chains fixed to the walls, rusting away. One night, failing to find a shore to camp upon, they tied to the chains and slept on the rafts. Perhaps hadal boatmen had used the lengths of chain to haul upriver, or hadals had clambered barefoot across the links. One way or another, the ancient thoroughfare had clearly been connected.

Where the river widened, sometimes sprawling hundreds of meters across, the water seemed to stop and they sat nearly becalmed. At other times the river coursed powerfully. You could not call rapids what they occasionally ran. The water had a density to it, and the cascades poured with Amazon-like torpor. Portaging was seldom necessary.

At the end of each "day," the explorers relaxed by small "campfires" consisting of a single chemical candle laid on the ground. Five or six people would gather around to share its colored light. They would sit on rocks and tell stories or mull over their own thoughts.

The past became more explicit. They dreamed more vividly. Their storytelling grew richer. One evening, Ali was consumed by a memory. She saw three ripe lemons on the wooden cutting board in her mother's kitchen, right down to the sunlight spangling off their pores. She heard her mother singing while they rolled pie dough in a storm of flour. Such images occurred to her more frequently, more vividly. Quigley, the team's psychiatrist, thought the distracting intensity of their memories might be a form of dementia or mild psychotic episode.

The tunnels and caves were very quiet. You could hear the hungry flipping of pages as people read the paperback novels circulating among them like rumors. The tap-tap of laptop keyboards went on for hours as they recorded data or wrote letters for transmission at the next cache. Gradually the candles would dim and the camp would sleep.

Ali's map grew more dreamlike. In lieu of a definite east-west orientation, she resorted to what artists call a vanishing point. That way, all the features on her chart had the same reference point, even if it was arbitrary. Not that they were lost, in general. In very broad terms, they knew exactly where they were, a mile beneath the ocean floor, moving west by southwest between the Clipperton and Galápagos fracture zones. On maps showing seafloor topography, the region above was a blank plain.

On foot they had averaged less than ten miles a day. In their first two weeks on the river, they floated ten times that, almost 1,300 miles. At this rate, if the river continued, they would reach the underbelly of Asia within three months.

The dark water was not quite dark; it had a faint pastel phosphorescence. If they kept their lights off, the river would surface from the blackness as a phantom serpent, vaguely emerald. One of the geochemists opened his pants and demonstrated how, in drinking the water, they now pissed streams of faint light.

Aided by the river's subtle luminescence, the patient ones like Ali were able to see perfectly well in the surface equivalent of near-night. Light that had once seemed necessary now hurt her eyes. Even so, Walker insisted on strong lights for guarding their flanks, which tended to disrupt the scientists' experiments and observations.

The scientists took to floating their rafts as far as possible from the soldiers' spotlights. No one thought twice about their growing segregation from the mercenaries until the evening of their camp of the mandalas.

It had been a short day, eighteen easy hours with few features to remark on. The small armada of rafts rounded a bend, and a spotlight picked out a pale, lone figure on a beach in the distance. It could only be Ike at a campsite he had found for them, and yet he didn't answer their calls. As they drew closer, they saw he was sitting facing the rock wall in a classic lotus position. He was on a shelf above the obvious camp.

"What's this crap?" groused Shoat. "Hey, Buddha. Permission to land."

They came on shore like an invasion party, swarming from their rafts onto dry land, securing their hold. Ike was forgotten as people ran about claiming flat spots for their sleeping places, or helped unload the rafts. Only after the initial flurry did they return their attention to him.

Ali joined the growing crowd of onlookers. Ike's back was to them. He was naked. He hadn't moved.

"Ike?" Ali said. "Are you okay?"

His rib cage rose and fell so faintly, Ali could barely detect the movement. The fingers of one hand touched the floor. He was much thinner than Ali had imagined. He had the collarbones of a mendicant, not a warrior, but his nakedness was not the source of their awe.

He had once been tormented: whipped, carved, even shot. Long, thin lines of surgical scar tissue bracketed his upper spine where doctors had removed his famous vertebral ring. This whole canvas of pain had been decorated—vandalized—with ink. In their waving lights, the geometric patterns and animal images and glyphs and text were animated on his flesh.

"For pity's sake." A woman grimaced.

His wickerwork of ribs and embellished skin and scars looked like history itself, terrible events laid one over another. Ali could not get the thought out of her head: devils had handled him.

"How long's he been sitting like this?" someone asked. "What's he doing?"

The crowd was subdued. There was something immensely powerful about this outcast. He had suffered enclosure and poverty and deprivation in ways they could not fathom. And yet that spine was as straight as a reed, that mind intent on transcending it all. Clearly he was at prayer.

Now they saw that the wall he was facing contained rows of circles painted onto the rock. Their lights bleached the circles faint and colorless. "Hadal stuff," a soldier said dismissively.

Ali went closer. The circles were filled with lightly drawn lines and scrawls, mandalas of some kind. She suspected that in darkness they would glow. But trying to glean information from them with so many lights on was useless.

"Crockett," snapped Walker, "get control of yourself." Ike's strangeness was starting to frighten people, and Ali suspected the colonel was intimidated by the extent of Ike's mute suffering, as if it detracted further from his own authority.

When Ike did not move, he said, "Cover that man."

One of his men went forward and started to drape Ike's clothing over his shoulders. "Colonel," the soldier said, "I think he might be dead. Come feel how cold he is."

Over the next few minutes the physicians established that Ike had slowed his metabolism to a near standstill. His pulse registered less than twenty beats, his breathing less than three cycles per minute. "I've heard of monks doing this," someone said. "It's some kind of meditation technique."

The group drifted off to eat and sleep. Later that night, Ali went to check on him. It was just a courtesy, she told herself. She would have appreciated someone checking on her. She climbed the footholds to his shelf and he was still there, back erect, fingertips pressed to the ground. Keeping her light off, she approached him to drape his shirt across his shoulders, for it had fallen off. That was when she discovered the blood glazing his back. Someone else had visited Ike, and run a knife blade across the yoke of his shoulders.

Ali was outraged. "Who did this?" she demanded in an undertone. It could have been a soldier. Or Shoat. Or a group of them.

His lungs suddenly filled. She heard the air slowly release through his nose. As in a dream, he said, "It's all the same."

When the woman parted from her group and went up a side chute away from the river, he thought she had gone to defecate. It was a racial perversity that the humans always went alone like this. At their moment of greatest vulnerability, with their bowels open and ankles trapped by clothing and clouds of odor spreading through the tunnel, just when they most needed their comrades gathered around for protection, each insisted on solitude.

But to his surprise, the female didn't void her bowels. Rather, she bathed.

She started by shedding her clothing. By the light of her headlamp, she brought her pubis to a lather with the soap bar and sleeved her palms around each thigh and ran them up and down her legs. She didn't come close to the fatted Venuses so dear to certain tribes he had observed. But neither was she bony. There was muscle in her buttocks and thighs. The pelvic girdle flared, a solid cup for childbearing. She emptied a bottle over her shoulders and the water snaked along her contours.

Right then, he determined to breed her.

Perhaps, he reasoned, Kora had died in order to make way for this woman. Or she was a consolation for Kora's death, provided by his destiny. It was even possible she *was* Kora, passed from one vessel to this next. Who could say? In search of a new home, souls were said to dwell in the stone, hunting ways through the cracks.

She had the unblemished flesh of a newborn. Her frame and long limbs were not without promise. Daily life could be severe, but the legs, especially, suggested an ability to keep up. He imagined the body with rings and paint and scars, once he had his way. If she survived the initiation period, he would give her a hadal name that could be felt and seen but never spoken, just as he had given many others names. Just as he had himself been given a name.

The acquisition could occur in several ways. He could lure her. He could seize her. Or he could simply dislocate one of her legs and bear her off. If all else failed, she would make good meat.

In his experience, temptation was most preferable. He was adroit, even artistic about it, and his status among hadals reflected it. Several times, near the surface, he had managed to entice small groups into his handling. Ensnare one, and she—or he—could sometimes be used to draw others. If it was a wife, her husband sometimes followed. A child generally guaranteed at least one parent. Religious pilgrims were easy. It was a game for him.

He stayed inert in the shadows, listening for others who might have been drawn here, human or otherwise. Assured of their seclusion, he finally made his move. In English.

"Hello?" He lofted the words furtively. He did nothing to disguise his desire.

She had turned for a second bottle of water, and at his voice she paused. Her head rotated left and right. The word had come from behind, but she was judging more than its direction. He liked her quickness of mind, her ability to sift the opportunities as well as the dangers.

"What are you doing out there?" the woman demanded. She was sure of herself. She made no attempt to cover herself. She faced upslope, nude, overt, blazing white. Her nakedness and beauty were tools for her.

"Watching," he said. "I've been watching you."

Something in her carriage—the line of her neck, the arch of her spine—accepted the voyeurism. "What do you want?"

"What do I want?" What would she want to hear so deep in the earth? He was reminded of Kora. "The world," he said. "A life. You."

She took it in. "You're one of the soldiers."

He let her own desires pronounce her. She had been watching the soldiers watch her, he realized. She had fantasized about them, though probably no one of them in particular. For she had not asked his name, only his occupation. His anonymity appealed to her. It would be less complicating. Very probably she had gone off alone like this hoping to lure just such a one here.

"Yes," he said. He did not lie to her. "I was a soldier once."

"So, are you going to let me see you?" she asked, and he could tell it was not a great need. The unknown was more primary. Good lassie, he thought.

"No," he said. "Not yet. What if you told?"

"What if I told?" she asked.

He could smell her change. The potent smell of her sex was beginning to fill the small chamber.

"They would kill me," he said.

She turned out the light.

Ali could tell that hell was starting to get to them.

This was Jonah's vista, the beast's gut as hollowed earth. It was the basement of their souls. As children they had all learned it was forbidden to enter this place, short of God's damnation. Yet here they were, and it scared them.

Perhaps not unnaturally, it was her they began to turn to. Men and women, scientists and soldiers, began seeking her out to make their confessions. Freighted with myths, they wanted out from their burden of sins. It was a way of keeping their sanity. Strangely, she was not prepared for their need.

It was always done singly. One of them would drift back or catch her alone in camp. Sister, they would murmur. A minute before, they had called her Ali. But then they would say Sister, and she would know what they wanted of her: to become a stranger to them, a loving stranger, nameless, all-forgiving.

"I'm not a priest," Ali told them. "I can't absolve you."

"You're a nun," they would say, as if the distinction were meaningless. And then it would start, the recitation of fears and regrets, their weaknesses and rancor and vendettas, their appetites and perversions. Things they dared not speak aloud to one another, they spoke to her.

In ecumenical parlance, it was now called reconciliation. Their hunger for it astonished her. At times, she felt trapped by their autobiographies. They wanted her to protect them from their own monsters.

Ali first noticed Molly's condition during an afternoon poker game. It was just the two of them in a small raft. Molly showed a pair of aces. That was when Ali saw her hands.

"You're bleeding," she said.

Molly's smile wavered. "No big deal. It comes and goes."

"Since when?"

"I don't know." She was evasive. "A month ago."

"What happened? This looks terrible."

There was a hole scraped in the flesh of each palm. Some of the meat looked cored out. It wasn't an incision, but it wasn't an ulcer, either. It looked eaten by acid, except acid would have cauterized the wound.

"Blisters," said Molly. Her eyes had developed dark circles. She kept her scalp shaved short out of habit, but it no longer suggested bountiful good health.

"Maybe one of the docs should take a look," Ali said.

Molly closed her fists. "There's nothing wrong with me."

"I was just concerned," said Ali. "We don't have to talk about it."

"You were implying something's wrong."

Molly's eyes began to bleed.

Taking no chances, the team's physicians quarantined the two women in a raft tugged a hundred yards behind the rest.

Ali understood. The possibility of some exotic disease had the expedition in a state of terror. But she resented Walker's soldiers watching them with sniperscopes. She was not allowed a walkie-talkie to communicate with the group because Shoat said they would only use it to beg and wheedle. By the morning of the fourth day, Ali was exhausted.

A quarter-mile to the front, a dinghy detached from the flotilla and started back toward her. Time for the daily house call. The doctors were wearing respirators and paper scrubs and latex gloves. Ali had called them cowards yesterday, and was sorry now. They were doing their best.

They drifted close and nodded to Ali. One flashed his light on Molly. Her beautiful lips were cracked. Her lush body was withering. The ulcerations had spread over her body. She turned her head from their light.

One of the physicians came into Ali's boat. She got into theirs, and the other doctor paddled her a short distance away to talk.

"We can't make sense of it," he said. His voice was muffled by the respirator. "We did the blood test again. It could still turn out to be an insect venom, or an allergic reaction. Whatever it is, you don't have it. You don't have to be out here with her."

Ali ignored the temptation. No one else would volunteer, they were too frightened. And Molly could not be alone. "Another transfusion," Ali said. "She needs more blood."

"We've given her five pints already. She's like a sieve. We may as well pour it into the water."

"You've given up?"

"Of course not," the doctor said. "We'll all keep fighting for her."

The doctor paddled her back to the quarantine raft. Ali felt cold and wooden. Molly was going to die.

As they paddled away, the physicians discarded their protective garments. They tore the paper suits from their limbs, stripped away their latex gloves, and left them like skins floating on the current.

Molly's wounds deepened. She began to sweat a rank grease through her pores. They put her on antibiotics, but that didn't help. A fever set in. Ali could feel its heat just by leaning across her.

Another time, Ali opened her eyes and Ike was sitting in his gray and black kayak alongside the quarantine raft, for all the world a killer whale bobbing on slow currents. He was not wearing the requisite scrubs and respirator, and his disregard was a small miracle to Ali. He tied his kayak to them and slipped from it onto the raft.

"I came to see you," he said to her. Molly lay asleep between Ali's legs.

"It's in her lungs," Ali reported. "She's suffocating on fungus."

Ike slipped one hand beneath Molly's cropped head and raised it gently and bent down. Ali thought he meant to kiss her. Instead, he sniffed at her open mouth. Her teeth were stained red. "It won't be long," he said, as if that were a mercy. "You should say prayers for her."

"Oh, Ike," sighed Ali. Suddenly she wanted to be held, but could not bring herself to ask for it. "She's too young. And this isn't the right place. She asked me what will happen to her body."

"I know what to do," he said, and did not elaborate. "Has she told you how this happened?"

"No one knows," said Ali.

"She does," he said.

Later, Molly confessed. There was none of that Sister, Sister for her. At first it seemed like a joke. "Hey, Al," she opened. "Wanna hear something off the wall?"

Small spasms clenched and unclenched the woman's long body. She strained to get control, at least from the neck up.

"Only if it's good," Ali kidded. You had to be like that with Molly. They were holding hands.

"Well," said Molly, and her small grin flickered on, then off. "About a month ago, I guess, I started this thing."

"Thing?" said Ali.

"Yeah. You know, what do they call it? Sex."

"I'm listening." Ali waited for a punchline. But Molly's eyes were desperate.

"Yes," whispered Molly.

Now Ali understood.

"I thought he was a soldier," Molly said. "That first time."

Ali let Molly orchestrate the tale. Sin was burial. Salvation was excavation. If Molly needed help with the shovel work, Ali would step in.

"He was in the shadows," said Molly. "You know the colonel's rules against soldiers fraternizing with us infidels. I had no idea which one he was. I don't know what came over me. Pity, I guess. I pitied him. So I gave him darkness, I let him be anonymous. I let him have me."

Ali was not at all shocked. Taking a nameless soldier seemed perfectly Molly-like. Her bravado was legend. "You made love," said Ali.

"We fucked," Molly corrected. "Hard. Okay?"

Ali waited. Where was the guilt?

"It wasn't the only time," said Molly. "Night after night, I went out into the darkness, and he was always there, waiting for me."

"I understand," said Ali, but did not. She saw no sin here. Nothing to reconcile.

"Finally it was like curiosity killed the cat. Who's Prince Charming, right? I had to know." Molly paused. "So one night I turned on my light."

"Yes?"

"I shouldn't have done that."

Ali frowned.

"He wasn't one of Walker's soldiers."

"One of the scientists," said Ali.

"No."

"Well?" Whom did that leave?

Molly's jaw tightened with the fever. She began shivering.

After a minute, Molly opened her eyes. "I don't know," she said. "I've never seen him before."

Ali accepted that at the level of denial. If Molly was hiding from her lover's secret identity, then it seemed to be part of Ali's task as confessor, in this case, to ferret out the incubus. "You know, that's impossible," she said. "There are no strangers in this group. Not after four months."

"I know. That's what I'm saying." She was, Ali saw, horrified.

"Describe him to me," Ali said. "Before your light." Together they would build the character. And then turn on the light.

"He smelled . . . different. His skin. When he was in my mouth. He tasted different. You know how a man has this taste? White or black or brown, it doesn't matter. His juices. His tongue. The breath from his lungs. They have this . . . flavor."

Ali listened. Clinically.

"He didn't. My midnight man. It wasn't like he was a blank. But it was different. Like he had more earth in his blood. Darkness. I don't know."

That didn't help much. "What about his body? Was there anything that distinguished him? Body hair? The size of his muscles?"

"While I had him between my legs?" Molly said. "Yeah. I could feel his scars. He's been through the wringer. Old wounds. Broken bones. And someone had cut patterns into his back and arms."

There was only one among them like Molly had just described. It occurred to Ali that Molly might be trying to hide his identity from *her*. "And when you turned on the light—"

"My first thought was a wild animal. He had stripes and spots. And pictures and lettering."

"Tattoos," Ali said. Why prolong it? But this was Molly's confession.

Molly nodded yes. "It all happened in an instant. He knocked the light from my hand. Then he disappeared."

"He was afraid of your light?"

"That's what I thought. Later I remembered something. In that first second, I said a name out loud. Now I think it was the name that made him run. But he wasn't afraid."

"What name, Molly?"

"I was wrong, Ali. It was the wrong name. They just looked alike."

"Ike," stated Ali. "You said his name because it was him."

"No." Molly paused.

"Of course it was."

"It wasn't. But I wish to God it had been. Don't you see?"

"No. You thought it was him. You wanted it to be him."

"Yes," Molly whispered. "Because what if it wasn't?"

Ali hesitated.

"That's what I'm saying," Molly groaned. "What I had between my legs . . ." She winced at the memory. "Someone's out there."

Ali lifted her head back suddenly. "A hadal! But why didn't you tell us before now?"

Molly smiled. "So you could tell Ike?" she said. "And then he would have gone hunting."

"But look," said Ali. She swept her hand at the ruination. "Look what he gave to you."

"You don't get it, kid."

"Don't tell me. You fell in love."

"Why not? You have." Molly closed her eyes. "Anyway, he's gone. Safe from us. And now you can't tell anyone, can you, Sister?"

Ike was there for the end.

Molly gasped with birdlike breaths. Grease sweated from her pores. Ali kept washing her body with water scooped from the river.

"You should rest," Ike said. "You've done your best."

"I don't want to rest."

He took the cup from her. "Lie down," he said. "Sleep."

When she woke hours later, Molly was gone. Ali was groggy with fatigue. "Did the docs come for her?" she asked hopefully.

"No."

"What do you mean?"

"She's gone, Ali. I'm sorry."

Ali got quiet. "Where is she, Ike? What have you done?"

"I put her in the river."

"Molly? You didn't."

"I know what I'm doing."

For an instant, Ali suffered a dreadful loneliness. It should not have happened this way. Poor Molly! Doomed to drift forever in this world. No burial? No ceremony? No chance for the rest of us to say farewell? "Who gave you that choice?"

"I was trying to make things easier for you."

"Tell me one thing," she said coldly. "Was Molly dead when you put her in?"

She wanted to punish him for his strangeness, and the question genuinely shook him. "Murder?" he said. "Is that what you think?"

Before her eyes, Ike seemed to fall away from her. A look crossed his face, the horror of a freak faced with his own mirror.

"I didn't mean that," she said.

"You're tired," he said. "You've had enough."

He got into his kayak and took the paddle and pulled at the river. The darkness covered him. She wondered if this was how it felt to go mad.

"Please don't leave me alone," she murmured.

After a minute she felt a tug. The rope came taut. The raft began moving. Ike was towing her back to human society.

INCIDENT AT RED CLOUD

NEBRASKA

JEFF LONG

The third time the witches started fiddling with him, Evan didn't fight.

He just lay as still as he could, and tried not to smell them. One held him around the chest from behind while the others took turns working at him. She kept whispering something in his ear. It was mumbo-jumbo, in circles. He thought of old Miss Sands, with her rosary beads. But this one had breath that smelled like roadkill.

Evan locked his eyes on the stars spread above the cornfield. Fireflies meandered between constellations. With all his might, he fastened on the North Star. Whenever they let him loose, that would be his beacon home again. In his mind he saw the back door, the stairs, the door to his room, the quilt upon his bed. He would wake in the morning. This would be nothing but a bad dream.

The night lay as black as engine oil. There was no moon, and the yard lights lay a mile away, barely a twinkle between the stalks. The first half hour his kidnappers had been mere silhouettes, dark cutouts against the stars. They were naked. He could feel their flesh. Smell it. Their titties were long and tubular, like in the old *National Geographic*s lying boxed in the cellar. Their ratty hair moved like black snakes against the stars.

Evan was pretty sure they weren't American. Or Mexican. He knew a little Spanish from the seasonal workers, and the old lady's chant wasn't that. He decided they were witches. A cult. You heard about such things.

It was a comfort of sorts. He'd never given much thought to witches. Vampires, yes. And the winged monkeys in *The Wizard of Oz*, and were-wolves, and flesh-eating zombies. And hadals, of course, though this was Nebraska, so safe the militias had disbanded. But witches? Since when did witches hurt you?

And yet they scared him. He scared himself. In his whole eleven years of life, Evan had never imagined such feelings down there. What they were doing felt good. But it was forbidden. If his mom and dad ever found out, they'd bust.

Part of him felt this wasn't fair. He shouldn't have been so late bicycling home. Still, it wasn't his fault the witches had jumped up along the county road. He'd pedaled away as fast as a fox, but even afoot they'd run him down. It wasn't his fault they'd brought him to the middle of this field to do things to him.

The problem was, he'd been raised to be accountable. It was his plea-sure. And it was dirty. Sniggering about boobies and panties after school was one thing. This was different. Staying late after baseball was his fault. And taking pleasure, that was really his fault. They were gonna bust.

In the initial moments of stripping him bare, the witches had ripped his shirt, shredded it. Evan couldn't reconcile that. It was a new shirt, and the destruction scared him more than their animal strength or the hunger they'd gone at him with. His mom and sisters were forever mending clothes and ironing them. They would never have ripped a shirt to tatters and tossed it in the dirt. Or done these other things. Never.

He didn't know exactly what was happening to him. It was the dirty thing you weren't supposed to talk about, that was plain enough. Copulation. But what precisely the act consisted of, that was the mys-tery. In daylight, he could have seen what was involved. This was more like wrestling with a blindfold on. So far, most of his information had come through touch and smell and sounds. The newness and power of the sensation confused him. He was ashamed to have cried out in front of women, mortified that it involved his unit.

They'd done it twice now, like milking a cow. The first time, Evan had been alarmed. There was no fighting off the bodily release. It felt like heat shooting out of his spine. Afterward, the mess lay as hot and thick as blood on his belly and chest.

Afraid they'd be disgusted with him, Evan started to apologize. But the whole bunch of them had thronged around him, dipping their fin-gers into his wet spots. It was almost like church. But instead of cross-ing themselves, they smeared it between their legs. So that's how it's done, he thought.

It went beyond his whole world of knowledge. For some reason, Evan was reminded of a science video he'd seen, in which a praying mantis female ate her mate when the act was over. That was reproduction. Until now he'd been mystified by the terrible consequences of doing it. Now the notion of punishment following the sin made perfect sense. No won-der people did it in the darkness.

Evan wanted them to quit, but secretly he didn't, too. Certainly the cluster of night women wanted more. After the first time, thinking it was over, he'd asked, "Can I please go home now?" His words had agi-tated them. If grasshoppers or beetles could talk, this was how they'd sound, clicking and muttering and smacking their lips. It didn't make any sense to him, but he got the gist. He was staying. They went at him again. And again.

This third time was proving troublesome. Maybe an hour passed.

Their rubbing and yanking and spitting on him didn't seem to be working. He sensed their frustration.

The one holding him from behind went on with her singsong chanting and rocking. "I'll be a good boy," he assured her in an exhausted whisper. She patted his cheek with a callused palm. It was like being petted with a stick.

Evan genuinely wanted to help out. What they didn't know was that he had an arithmetic test in the morning. He was supposed to be studying.

Gradually his eyes adjusted to the night. Their pale skin took on a faint glow. He could begin to see them. He and his buddies had all seen TV shows with bikini girls, and several had big brothers with *Playboy*s. It wasn't as if he had no clue what a woman's body looked like. But these women had no sunshine in them, no joy. They were all business. Evan felt like he was the center of a farm task, like the cow. Or like the hogs his dad butchered each winter. Like a beast at harvesting. They'd been at him for hours.

There might have been five of them, or as many as a dozen. They kept leaving and returning. The witches moved with watery grace, close to the ground, as if the sky were a weight. The cornstalks rustled. They orbited him like bleached white moons. Their stench ebbed, then surged.

They took turns, arguing over him in insect syllables. Each seemed to have a different idea about manipulating him. Evan had grown used to the one by his head. She seemed to be the oldest. Her chest wall had the feel of a washboard against his ear. Evan grew passive against her, and the arm relaxed. She wasn't unkind, just firm. Her skinny arm was a marvel, a few sinews covered with skin, but as strong as baling wire. When some of the others slapped or prodded him, she clucked at them, annoyed.

One, smaller than the rest, was taking lessons from the others. Evan decided she was the youngest, maybe his own age. They urged her to mount him a couple of times, but she was awkward and Evan didn't know what was expected of him. She seemed as frightened as he was. He gravitated to her in his thoughts.

He couldn't see their faces exactly, and didn't want to. This way he could imagine himself surrounded by neighbor ladies and his teachers and some of the girls at school. He added the pretty waitress at the Surf and Turf downtown. He attached familiar masks to these benighted faces looming overhead, and it consoled him. It let him have names for each.

What ruined his conjuring was their smell. Even Mrs. Peterson, the halfwit who sat in the park all day, would never have let herself get foul like this. These women stank. They were rancid and unwashed, and smelled worse than a stockyard. The dung crusting their flanks had the grassy sweetness of cow manure. When they muttered at him, he could smell deep inside their throats.

He was greasy with their juices and saliva. That was another shock, how wet they were between their legs. Nothing in his friends' centerfolds had prepared him for that. Or for their greed and hunger. Periodically one dipped her head, and it felt warm and soft down there, like the hot compresses his grandma used to make.

Their hands and fingers were as dry as lizard skin. They'd rubbed him raw, but the hurt was largely numbed by his fatigue. He lay in their center, and it seemed the stars wheeled in a great circle over him.

Crickets sang. An owl swooped by. Evan suddenly wondered if the witches might be the reason so many dogs and cats had disappeared over the last month. Maybe the animals had run off. Another thought came to him. What if they'd been eaten? A gust of wind rattled the corn rows. He shivered.

The witches entered a rhythm around him. It was like a dance, though they were kneeling or hunkered down on their heels. He set himself adrift on the pulse of their motions, the chant, their hands and mouths. Evan grew hopeful when several whispered approvingly. All at once he found himself approaching that same loss of control as before. He tried not to grunt, but it was too much.

Abruptly the blood heat of liquid spattered across his chest. Evan winced at the salty spray. Tasted it. And frowned.

This time it was the heat of real blood.

In the same instant, a rifle shot ruptured the quiet. Something, a body, flopped heavily across Evan's thighs.

"Evan, boy," a voice commanded across the corn rows. His father! "Lie down."

The sky cracked open. A ragged volley of deer rifles, shotguns, varmint pistols, and old revolvers shattered the constellations. Bullets slapped apart the corn leaves. The gunfire rattled like popcorn.

Evan lay still on his back. It was like drifting on a raft. Staring up at the Milky Way. What he would remember most was not the shooting, or the men yelling, or the witches scattering. Not the headlights careening through the walls of green corn, or the pitchfork lifting that young hadal girl into the wildly lit, raddled sky, where he saw the slight stub of a tail on her rump and her grublike pallor and her face, the chimp's eyes, the yellow teeth. Not the rack-rack of shotgun shells getting chambered. Not his father standing high overhead and lifting his head up to the stars to bellow like a bull.

No. What he would remember was the old woman by his head, how just before they shot the bones from her face, she bent down and kissed him by the ear. It was the kind of thing a grandma did.

The Aztecs said that . . . as long as one of them was left he would die fighting, and that we would get nothing of theirs because they would burn everything or throw it into the water.

—HERNÁN CORTÉS,
Third Dispatch to King Charles V of Spain

17

FLESH

WEST BENEATH

THE CLIPPERTON FRACTURE ZONE

Following Molly's death, they cast lower on the river, anxious to resume their sense of scientific control. The banks narrowed, the water quickened. Because they moved faster, they had more time to reach their destination, which was the next cache in early September. They began to explore the littoral regions bordering the river, sometimes staying in one place for two or three days.

The region had once abounded with life. In a single day they discovered thirty new plants, including a type of grass that grew from quartz and a tree that looked like something out of Dr. Seuss, with a stem that drew gases from the ground and synthesized them into metallic cellulose. A new cave orchid was named for Molly. They found crystallized animal remains. The entomologists caught a monstrous cricket, twenty-seven inches long. The geologists located a vein of gold as thick as a finger.

In the name of Helios, who held the patent rights on all such discoveries, Shoat collected their reports on disc each evening. If the discovery had special value, like the gold, he would issue a chit for a bonus payment. The geologists got so many they started using them like currency among the others, buying pieces of clothing, food, or extra batteries from those who had extras.

For Ali, the most rewarding thing was further evidence of hadal civilization. They found an intricate system of *acequias* carved into the rock to transport water from miles upriver into the hanging valley. In an overhang partway up a cliff lay a drinking cup made from a Neanderthal cranium. Elsewhere, a giant skeleton—possibly a human freak—lay in shackles solid with rust. Ethan Troy, the forensic anthropologist, thought the deeply incised geometric patterns on the giant's skull had been made at least a year before the prisoner's death. Judging by the cut marks around the entire skull, it seemed the giant had been scalped and kept alive as a showcase for their artwork.

They collected around a central panel emblazoned with ochre and handprints. In the center was a representation of the sun and moon. The scientists were astonished. "You mean to say they worshiped the sun and moon? At fifty-six hundred fathoms!"

"We need to be cautious," Ali said. But what else could this mean? What glorious heresy, the children of darkness worshiping light.

Ali got one photo of the sun and moon iconography, no more. When her flash billowed, the entire wall of pictographs—its pigments and record—lost color, turned pale, then vanished. Ten thousand years of artwork turned to blank stone.

Yet with the animals and handprints and sun and moon images burned away, they discovered a deeper set of engraved script.

A two-foot-long patch of letters had been cut into the basalt. In the abyssal shadows, the incisions were dark lines upon dark stone. They approached the wall tentatively, as if this too might disappear.

Ali ran her fingers along the wall. "It might have been carved to be read. Like Braille."

"That's writing?"

"A word. A single word. See this character here." Ali traced a *y*-tailed mark, then a backward *E*. "And this. They're not capped. But look at the linear form. It's got the stance and the stroke of ancient Sanskrit or Hebrew. Paleo-Hebrew, possibly. Probably older. Old Hebrew. Phoenician, whatever you want to call it."

"Hebrew? Phoenician? What are we dealing with, the lost tribes of Israel?"

"Our ancestors taught hadals how to write?" someone said.

"Or else hadals taught us," Ali said.

She could not take her fingertips from the word. "Do you realize," she whispered, "man has been speaking for at least a hundred thousand years. But our writing goes back no further than the upper Neolithic. Hittite hieroglyphics. Australian aboriginal art. Seven, eight thousand years, tops.

"This writing has got to be at least fifteen or twenty thousand years old. That's two or three times older than any human writing ever found. These are linguistic fossils. We could be closing in on the Adam and Eve of language. The root origin of human speech. The first word."

Ali was enraptured. Looking around, she could tell the others didn't understand. This was big. Human or not, it doubled or tripled the time-line of the mind. And she had no one to celebrate it with! Settle down, she told herself. For all her travels, Ali's was a paper world of linguists and bishops, of library carrels and yellow legal pads. She had occupied a quiet place that didn't allow celebration. And yet, just once, Ali wanted someone to knock the head off a bottle of champagne and douse her with bubbles, someone to gather her up for a wet kiss.

"Hold up your pen beside the letters for scale," one of the photographers told her.

"I wonder what it says," someone said.

"Who knows?" Ali said. "If Ike's right, if this is a lost language, then even the hadals don't know. Look how they had it buried under more primitive images. I think it's lost all meaning to them."

Returning to their rafts, for some reason, the name circled around on her. Ike. Her slow dancer.

On September 5, they found their first hadals. Reaching a fossilized shore, they unloaded their rafts and hauled gear to high ground and started to prepare for night. Then one of the soldiers noticed shapes within the opaque folds of flowstone.

By shining their lights at a certain angle, they could see a virtual Pompeii of bodies laminated in several inches to several feet of translucent plastic stone. They lay in the positions they had died in, some curled, most sprawled. The scientists and soldiers fanned out across the acres of amber, slipping now and then on the slick face.

Pieces of flint still jutted from wounds. Some had been strangled with their own entrails or decapitated. Animals had worked through all of them. Limbs were missing, chest and belly walls had been plundered. No question, this had been the end of a whole tribe or township.

Under Ali's sweeping headlamp, their white skin glittered like quartz crystal. For all the heavy bone in their brows and cheeks, and despite the obvious violence of their end, they were remarkably delicate.

H. hadalis—this variety, at any rate—looked faintly apelike, but with very little body hair. They had wide negroid noses and full lips, somewhat like Australian aborigines, but were bleached albino by the perpetual night. There were a few slight beards, little more than wispy goatees. Most looked no older than thirty. Many were children.

The bodies were scarred in ways that had nothing to do with sports or surgery: no appendectomy scars in this group, no neat smile lines around the knees or shoulders. These had come from camp accidents or hunts or war. Broken bones had healed crookedly. Fingers had been lopped off. The women's breasts hung slack, thinned and stretched and unbeautiful, basic tools like their sharpened fingernails and teeth or their wide flattened feet or their splayed big toes for climbing.

Ali tried integrating them into the family of modern man. It did not help that they had horns and calcium folds and lumps distorting their skulls. She felt strangely bigoted. Their mutations or disease or evolutionary twist—whatever—kept her at arm's length. She was sorry to be walking on them, yet glad to have them safely encased in stone. Whatever had been done to them, she imagined they would have been capable of doing to her.

That night they discussed the bodies lying beneath their camp.

It was Ethan Troy who solved their mystery. He had managed to chip loose portions of the bodies, mostly of children, and held them out for the rest to see. "Their tooth enamel hasn't grown properly. It's been disrupted. And all the kids have rickets and other long-limb malformations. And you only have to look to see their swollen stomachs. Massive starvation. Famine. I saw this once in a refugee camp in Ethiopia. You never forget."

"You're suggesting these are refugees?" someone asked. "Refugees from who?"

"Us," said Troy.

"You're saying man killed them?"

"At least indirectly. Their food chain was ruptured. They were fleeing. From us."

"Nuts," scoffed Gitner, lying on his back on a sleeping pad. "In case you missed it, those are Stone Age points sticking out of them. We had nothing to do with it. These guys got killed by other hadals."

"That's beside the point," said Troy. "They were depleted. Famished. Easy prey."

"You're right," Ike said. He didn't often enter group discussions, but he had been following this one intently. "They're on the move. The whole world of them. This is their diaspora. They've scattered. Gone deep to avoid our coming."

"What's it matter?" said Gitner.

"They're hungry," said Ike. "Desperate. That matters."

"Ancient history. This bunch died a long time ago."

"Why do you say that?"

"The accretion of flowstone. They're covered in it. At least five hundred years' worth, probably more like five thousand. I haven't run my calculations yet."

Ike went over to him. "Let me borrow your rock hammer," he said.

Gitner shoved it into Ike's hand. These days he seemed chronically fed up. Their endless debate about hadal links to humanity gnawed at what little good humor he'd ever had. "Do I get it back?" he said.

"Just a loaner," Ike said, "while we sleep." He walked over and placed it flat next to the wall and walked away.

In the morning, Git had to borrow another hammer to cut his free. Overnight the hammer had been covered with a sixteenth of an inch of clear flowstone.

It was a matter of simple arithmetic. The refugees had been slain no more than five months ago. The expedition was following the trail of their flight. And it was very near to fresh.

Even the mercenaries had come to depend on Ike's infallible sense of danger. Somehow the word got around about his climbing days, and they nicknamed him El Cap for the monolith in Yosemite. It was a dangerous attachment, and it annoyed Ike even more than it annoyed their commander. Ike didn't want their trust. He dodged them. He stayed out of camp more and more. But Ali could see his effect, all the same. Some of the boys had tattooed their arms and faces like Ike's. A few started going barefoot or slinging their rifles across their backs. Walker did what he could to stem the erosion. When one of his ghetto warriors got caught sitting cross-legged at prayer, Walker put him on sentry duty for a week.

Ike resumed his habit of staying a day or so ahead of the expedition, and Ali missed his eccentricities. She woke early, as always, but no longer saw his kayak plying out into the tubular wilderness while the camp still slept. She had no proof he was growing more remote from them, or her. But his absences made her anxious, especially as she was falling asleep at night. He had opened a gap in her.

On September 9 they detected the signal for Cache II. They had crossed the international date line without knowing it. They reached the site, but there were no cylinders awaiting them. Instead they found a heavy steel sphere the size of a basketball lying on the ground. It was attached to a cable dangling from the ceiling a hundred feet overhead.

"Hey, Shoat," someone demanded. "Where's our food?"

"I'm sure there's an explanation," Shoat said, but was clearly baffled.

They unbolted the curved casing. Inside, seated in polyfoam, was a small keypad with a note. "To the Helios Expedition: Supply cylinders are ready for penetration at your prompt. Key in the first five numerals of pi, in reverse, then follow with pound sign." They guessed it was a precaution to safeguard their food and supplies from any possible hadal piracy.

Shoat needed someone to write down pi for him, then keyed it in. He tapped the pound key, and a small red light changed to green. "I guess we wait," he said.

They made camp on the bank and took turns spotlighting the underside of the drill hole. Shortly after midnight, one of Walker's sentinels called out. Ali heard the scraping of metal. Everyone gathered and shone their lights upward, and there it was, a silvery capsule sinking toward them on a glittering thread. It was like watching a rocketship land. The group cheered.

The cylinder sizzled on touching the river, then slowly lowered onto its side and the cable looped in a tangle in the water. Its metal sheath was blued with scorch marks. They mobbed it, only to fall back from its heat.

None of the penetrators at Cache I had been seared this way. It meant the cylinder had passed through some kind of volcanic zone, probably a tendril of the Magellan Seamounts. Ali could smell the sulfur smoking on its skin.

"Our supplies," someone lamented. "They're getting cooked inside."

They made a bucket brigade, passing plastic bottles up and down the line to splash on the cylinder. The metal steamed, colors pulsing from one thermal complexion to another. Gradually it cooled enough for them to cog off the bolts. They got their knives into the seams and pried the hatch loose and threw open the doorway.

"God, what's that stink?"

"Meat. They sent us meat?"

"The heat must have started a fire in there."

Lights stabbed at the interior. Ali looked over shoulders, and it was hard to see for the smoke and stench and heat pouring through the hatch.

"Good Lord, what have they sent us?"

"Are those people?" she asked.

"They look like hadals."

"How can you say that? They're too burned to tell," someone said.

Walker pushed to the front, Ike and Shoat right behind him.

"What is this, Shoat?" Walker demanded. "What is Helios up to?"

Shoat was rattled. "I have no idea," he said. For once Ali believed him.

There were three bodies inside, strapped one above the other in a makeshift cradle of nylon webbing. While the cylinder was vertical, they would have been suspended in the harnesses like smoke jumpers.

"Those are uniforms," someone said. "Look here, U.S. Army."

"What do we do? They're all dead."

"Unbuckle them. Get them out."

"The buckles are melted shut. We'll have to cut them out. Let it cool off some more."

"What were they doing in there?" one of the physicians wondered to Ali.

The dead limbs lolled. One man had bitten off his tongue, and the flap of muscle lay on his chin. Then they heard a moan. It came from below the hatch opening, where the third man hung suspended and out of their reach.

Without a word, Ike vaulted into the smoking interior. He straddled the bodies at hatch level and slashed at the webbing, clearing out the dead first. Crawling deeper, he got the third man cut free and dragged him to the hatch, where a dozen hands finished the extraction.

Ali and a few others were tending the dead, laying bits of burned clothing across their faces. The man uppermost in the cylinder, where the heat and fire would have been worst, had shot himself through the mouth. The middle man had strangled on a strap now fused into his neck. Their clothing had caught fire, leaving them dressed only in their harnesses and strapped with weapons. Each bore a pistol, a rifle, and a knife.

"Check these scopes out." A geologist was sweeping the river with one of the soldier's rifles. "These things are rigged for sniper work at night. What were they coming to hunt?"

"We'll take those," Walker said, and his mercenaries collected all the other weapons.

Ali helped lay the third man on the ground, then stood back. His lungs and throat had been seared. He was coughing up a clear serous fluid, and his temperature control was shot. He was dying. Ike knelt beside him, along with the doctors and Walker and Shoat. Everyone was watching.

Walker peeled back a piece of charred cloth. "'First Cavalry,'" he read, and looked at Ike. "These are your people. What are they sending Rangers down for?"

"I have no idea."

"You know this man?"

"I don't."

The doctors covered the burned man with a sleeping bag and gave him water to drink. The man opened his one good eye. "Crockett?" he rasped.

"Guess he knows you," Walker said. The whole camp stood breathless.

"Why did they send you?" Ike asked.

The man tried to form the words. He struggled beneath the sleeping bag. Ike gave him more water.

"Closer," said the soldier.

Ike leaned in. He bent to hear.

"Judas," the man hissed.

The knife drove straight up through the sleeping bag.

The fabric or pain spoiled the assassin's thrust. The blade skipped along Ike's rib cage but did not enter. The soldier had enough strength for a second slash across Ike's back, then Ike caught his wrist.

Walker and Shoat and the doctors fell back from the attack. One of the mercenaries reacted with three quick shots into the burned man's thorax. The body bounced with each round.

"Cease fire!" Walker yelled.

It was over that fast.

The only sound was the water flowing.

The expedition stared in disbelief. No one moved. They had seen the attack and heard the soldier's whispered word.

Ike knelt in their midst, dumbfounded. He still held the assassin's wrist in one hand, and the gash along his ribs flowed red. He looked around at them, bewildered.

Suddenly, a terrible keening noise rose up from him.

Ali didn't expect that. "Ike?" she said from the ring of onlookers. No one dared go closer.

Ali stepped out from the circle and went to him. "Stop it," she said. They had depended on his strength for so long that his frailty endangered them. Before their eyes, he was coming undone.

He looked at her, then fled.

"What was that all about?" someone muttered.

For lack of shovels, they drifted the bodies out into the river. Many hours later, two more cylinders were lowered to them, each filled with cargo. They ate. Helios had sent them a feast for a hundred people: smoked rainbow trout, veal in cognac, cheese fondue, and a dozen different kinds of bread, sausages, pasta, and fruit. The crisp green lettuce in the salad brought tears of joy. It was, said a note, meant to celebrate C.C. Cooper's birthday. Ali suspected otherwise. Ike was meant to be dead, and this banquet was in effect a wake.

The attempt on Ike's life had no explanation or context or justice. What made it all the more irrational was that Ike was their most valued member. Even the mercenaries would have voted for him. With him as scout, they had felt like the Chosen People, destined to exit the wilderness on the heels of their tattooed Moses. But now he had been labeled a traitor, and was inexplicably marked for death.

The communications cable to the surface had been fried by the magma zone overhead, and so the expedition had only conjecture and superstition to fall back upon. In a way they all felt targeted, for in their experience Ike had been the best of men, and he was being punished for sins they had never known. It felt as though a great storm had opened upon them. The group's response was a little worry, then a lot of denial and bravado.

"It was a matter of time," said Spurrier. "Ike was going to come unwrapped sooner or later. You could see it coming. I'm surprised he held up this long."

"What does that have to do with anything?" Ali snapped.

"I'm not saying he brought it down on himself. But the man's definitely in torment. He's got more ghosts than a graveyard."

"What do you do to get the U.S. Army on your case?" Quigley, the psychiatrist, wondered. "I mean that was a suicide mission. They don't throw good men away on nothing."

"And that 'Judas' stuff? I thought once the court-martial was over, they were finished with you. Talk about bad luck. The guy's a born outcast."

"It's like the whole world's against him."

"Don't worry about him, Ali," said Pia, for whom love had come in the form of Spurrier. "He'll be back."

"I'm not so sure," Ali said. She wanted to blame Shoat or Walker, but they seemed genuinely disoriented by the incident. If Helios had meant to kill Ike, why not use their own agents? Why involve the U.S. Army? And why would the Army involve itself with doing Helio's bidding? It made no sense.

While the rest slept, Ali walked from the light of their camp. Ike had not taken his kayak or his shotgun, so she searched on foot with her flashlight. His footprints loped along the bank's mud.

She was furious with the group's smugness. They had depended on

Ike for everything. Without him, they might be dead or lost. He had been true to them, but now, when he needed them, they were not true to him.

We were his ruin. She saw that now. They had doomed Ike with their dependence. He would have been a thousand miles away if not for their weakness and ignorance and pride. That's what had kept him bound to them. Guardian angels were like that. Doomed by their pathos.

But blaming the group was a dodge, Ali had to admit. For it was *her* weakness, *her* ignorance, *her* pride that had bound Ike—not to them, but to her. The group's well-being was merely a collateral benefit. The uncomfortable truth was that he had promised himself to her.

Ali sorted her thoughts as she picked her way along the river. In the beginning Ike's allegiance to her had been unwanted, a vexation. She had buried the fact of his devotion under a heap of her own fictions, satisfying herself that he pursued the depths for reasons of his own, for his fabled lost lover or for revenge. Maybe that had been so in the beginning, but it no longer was. She knew that. Ike was here for her.

She found him in a field of night, no light, no weapon. He was sitting faced toward the river in his lotus position, his back bare to any enemies. He had cast himself onto the mercy of this savage desert.

"Ike," she said.

His shaggy head stayed poised and still. Her light cast his shadow onto the black water, where it was immediately forfeit. What a place, she thought. Darkness so hungry it devoured other darkness.

She came closer and took off her backpack. "You missed your own funeral," she joked. "They sent a feast."

Not a motion. Even his lungs did not move. He was going deep. Escaping.

"Ike," she said. "I know you can hear me."

One of his hands rested in his lap; the fingertips of his other hand touched the ground with all the weight of an insect.

She felt like a trespasser. But this wasn't contemplation she was invading, it was the start of madness. He couldn't win, not by himself.

Ali approached from one side. From behind he looked at peace. Then she saw that his face was drawn. "I don't know what's going on," she said. He was resisting her within his statue stillness. His jaw was clenched.

"Enough," she said, and opened her pack and pulled out the medical kit. "I'm cleaning those cuts."

Ali started brusquely with the Betadine sponge. But she slowed. The flesh itself slowed her. She ran her fingers along his back, and the bone and muscle and hadal ink and scar tissue and the calluses from his pack straps astonished her. This was the body of a slave. He had been harrowed. Every mark was the mark of use.

It disconcerted her. She had known the damned in many of their incarnations, as prisoners and prostitutes and killers and banished lepers. But she had never met a slave. Such creatures weren't supposed to exist in this age.

Ali was surprised at how well his shoulder fit in her hand. Then she recovered herself with a tidy pat. "You'll survive," she told him.

She walked a little distance away and sat down. For the rest of that night, she lay curled in a ball with his shotgun, protecting Ike while he finished returning to the world.

Am not I

A fly like thee?

Or art not thou

A man like me?

—WILLIAM BLAKE, "The Fly"

18

GOOD MORNING

Yamamoto emerged from the elevator with a smile.

"Morning!" she sang to a janitor mopping up a roof leak.

"I don't see no sun," he grumbled.

They had an old-fashioned blizzard raging out there, four-foot drifts, minus nine degrees. They were under siege. She would have the lab to herself today.

Yamamoto found last night's guard still on duty, asleep. She sent him off to the dorm to get some rest and hot food. "And don't come back until this afternoon," she said. "I can hold down the fort myself. No one's coming in anyway."

She was like that these days, mother to the world. Her hair was thicker, her cheeks in constant bloom. She hummed to the Womb, as her husband called it. Three more months.

The Digital Satan project was nearing completion. The lab was getting downright gamy with fast-food wrappers, sixty-four-ounce soda cups recycled as pencil holders, and mummified birthday leftovers. The bulletin board was bushy with doctored snapshots of lab personnel, excerpts of articles, and, most recently, employment notices for positions here and abroad.

She entered without double-gloving or a surgical mask. All kinds of lab rituals had fallen by the wayside, yet another sign that the project was getting short. Vials lay couched on a Taco Bell box. Someone had made a mobile of the computer chips they'd fried over the months.

Machine Two pumped out its endless hush-hush-hush nursery-room rhythm.

Except for the head, a young hadal female had just disappeared from existence, bones and all. Yet now she could be resurrected with a CD-ROM and a mouse. She was about to become electronically immortal. Wherever there was a computer, there could be a physical manifestation of Dawn. In a sense, her soul was truly in the machine.

For several weeks now, Yamamoto had been beset with awful dreams of Dawn. The hadal girl would be falling off a cliff or getting swept out to sea, and she would be reaching for help. Others in the lab related similar nightmares. Separation anxiety, they self-diagnosed. Dawn had been part of the gang. They were all going to miss her.

All that remained was the upper two-thirds of the hadal's cranium. It was slow going. Machine Two was calibrated to make the finest slices possible. The brain offered their most interesting exploration. Hopes remained high that they might actually unravel the sensory and cognition process—in effect, making the dead mind speak. All they had to do for the next ten weeks was baby-sit a glorified bologna slicer. Patience was a matter of Diet Pepsi and ribald jokes.

Yamamoto approached the metal table. The top of the girl's cranium was pale white inside the block of frozen blue gel. It looked like a moon suspended in a square of outer space. Electrodes fed out from the top and sides of the gel. At the base, the blade sliced. The camera fired.

The machine had pared away the lower jaw, then worked back and forth across the upper teeth and into the nasal cavity. Externally, most of the flared, batlike nose and all of the stretched, fringed earlobes were gone now. In terms of internal structures, they'd shaved through most of the medulla oblongata leading up from the spinal cord, and reduced most of the cerebellum—which controlled motor skills—at the base of the skull to digital bits. No lesions or abnormalities so far. For a necrotic brain, all systems were remarkably intact, practically viable. Everyone was marveling. Hope I'm that healthy after I die, someone had joked.

Things were just starting to get interesting. From around the country, neurosurgeons and brain and cognition specialists had begun calling or

E-mailing on a daily basis to keep updated. Certain parts of the brain, like the cerebellum they'd just passed, were fairly standard mammalian anatomy. They explained what made the animal an animal, but did little to fill in what made the hadal a hadal.

No longer would Dawn be just so much subterranean animal carcass. From the limbic system upward, she would once again become her own person. A personality might emerge, a rational process, clues to her speech, her emotions, her habits and instincts. In short, they were about to peek out through Dawn's cranial window and glimpse her worldview. It was tantamount to landing a spacecraft on another planet. More than that, this was like interviewing an alien for the first time and asking for her thoughts.

Yamamoto feathered through the electrodes, sorting the right-side wires, laying them out neatly on the table. It was still a slight mystery why Dawn seemed to be generating a slight electrical pulse. Her chart should have showed a flatline, but every now and then an irregular spike would jump up. This had been going on for months. It was a fact that, if you waited long enough, electrodes would eventually detect vital signs even from a bowl of Jell-O.

Yamamoto moved around the table to the left side and fanned out the wires on her palm. It was almost like braiding a child's hair. She paused to peer down into the gel block at what was left of the hadal face.

"Good morning," she said.

The head opened its eyes.

Rau and Bud Parsifal found Vera in a western clothing store in Denver International terminal, trying on cowboy hats. One could not have invented a more perfect antidote to the darkness on everyone's mind. Everyone had an opinion, a fear, a solution. No one knew where any of it was going down there, what they might find, what kind of world their children were going to grow up in. But here, in this gigantic, sweeping, tentlike terminal saturated with sunlight and open space, you could forget all that and simply eat ice cream. Or try on cowboy hats.

"How do I look?" Vera asked.

Rau patted his briefcase in applause. Parsifal said, "Lord spare us."

"Did you come together?" she asked.

"London via Cincinnati," said Parsifal.

"Mexico City," said Rau. "We bumped into each other in the concourse."

"I was afraid no one was going to make it," Vera said. "As it is, we may be too late."

"You called, we came," said Parsifal. "Teamwork." His paunch and hated bifocals made the gallantry that much more charming.

Rau checked his watch. "Thomas arrives within the hour. And the others?"

"Elsewhere," said Vera, "in transit, incommunicado, occupied. You've heard about Branch, I suppose."

"Has he lost his mind?" Parsifal said. "Running off into the subplanet like that. Alone. Of all people, you'd think he'd know what the hadals are capable of."

"It's not them I'm worried about."

"Please not that 'the enemy is us' business."

"You don't know about the shoot-to-kill order then?" Vera asked. "All the armies got it. Interpol has it."

Parsifal squinted at her. "What's this? Shoot Branch?"

"January's done what she can to revoke it. But there's a certain General Sandwell who has a vindictive streak. It's peculiar. January's trying to find out more about this general."

"Thomas is furious," Rau added. "Branch was our eyes and ears in the military. Now we're left guessing what the armies may be up to."

"And who may be planting the virus capsules."

"Nasty business," muttered Parsifal.

They met Thomas at his gate, straight from Hong Kong. The gaunt cubic angles of his face formed a mass of shadows, deepening his Abe Lincoln features. Otherwise, for a man who'd just been expelled from China, he looked remarkably refreshed. He glanced around at his greeting party. "A cowboy hat?" he said to Rau.

"When in Rome . . ." Rau shrugged.

They proceeded to the exit, grouped around Vera's wheelchair, catching up on one another's news.

"Mustafah and Foley?" asked Vera. "They're okay?"

"Tired," said Thomas. "We were detained in Kashi for several days. In Xinjiang province. Our cameras and journals were confiscated, our visas revoked. We are officially personae non gratae."

"What in the world were you doing out there, Thomas?"

"I wanted to examine a set of Caucasian mummies and some of their writing fragments. Four millennia old. Germanic script. Tocharian, to be exact. In Asia!"

"Mummies in the Chinese outback," Parsifal fumed. "Cryptic writings. What will that tell us?"

"This time I have to agree with you," said Vera. "It does seem remote from our mission. Sometimes I wonder just what it is I'm really doing.

For the past three months you've had me reviewing abstracts on mitochondrial DNA and human evolution. Tell me how data on placental samples from New Guinea gets us any closer to identifying a primordial tyrant?"

"In this instance, the mummies and their Indo-European script would seem to prove that Caucasian nomads influenced Chinese civilization four thousand years ago," Thomas said.

"And they expelled you for that?" Parsifal said. He fogged the glass with his breath and drew a crucifix. "Or did the Commies catch you giving last rites to the mummies?"

"Something far more dangerous is my guess," Rau said to the group. "If I'm correct, Thomas, you were proving that Chinese civilization did not develop in isolation. The likelihood that early Europeans may have helped germinate their culture is extremely threatening to the Chinese. They're a very proud people, these children of the Middle Kingdom."

"But again, what does that have to do with us?" asked Vera.

"Everything, perhaps," Rau ventured. "The notion that a great civilization might be modified or even inspired by the enemy or by a lesser race or by barbarians is highly relevant."

"Plain English will do just fine, Rau," Parsifal grumbled.

Thomas remained silent. He seemed to be enjoying their guesswork.

"What if human civilization didn't develop in isolation? What if we had mentors?"

"What do you have in mind, Rau?" Parsifal said. "Martians?"

"A little more down to earth." Rau smiled. "Hadals."

"Hadals!" Parsifal said. "Our mentors?"

"What if the hadals helped create our civilization through the eons? What if they cultivated our benighted ancestors, exposed to mankind its own native intelligence?"

"Haddie was our nursemaid? Those savages?"

"Careful," said Rau. "You're starting to sound like the Chinese with their barbarians."

"Is that it?" Vera asked Thomas. "You were looking at China as a paradigm for early human civilization?"

"Something like that," Thomas said.

"And so you traveled ten thousand miles, and went to jail, all to prove a theory?"

"A bit more, actually. I had a hunch, and it bore out. As I suspected, the Caucasian texts in Xinjiang weren't written in Tocharian script. Nor in any other human language. The reports were all wrong. Mustafah and Foley and I took one look at the mummies and knew. You see, the mum-

J
E
F
F

L
O
N
G

mies were tattooed with hadal symbols. These Caucasian nomads were operating as agents. Or messengers. They were transporting documents into ancient China. Documents written in some form of hadal script. If only we could read it!"

"But again," Parsifal said, "so what? That was four thousand years ago. And we can't read it."

"Four thousand years ago, someone sent these people on a mission to China," Thomas said. "Aren't you a little curious? Who sent them?"

A van took them to the medical center. At the entrance to the Rende Research Wing, they entered into a crush of cops and television cameras. A phalanx of university representatives were taking turns offering themselves to the wolves. Frost billowed from every mouth. Apparently the logic behind an outdoor press conference in midwinter was that it would be brief.

"Again, I urge you to use common sense," a deanlike figure was soothing the lenses. "There's no such thing as possession."

A pretty news anchor, soaked from the thighs down with snowmelt, shouted from the crowd. "Dr. Yaron, are you denying reports that the university medical center is conducting exorcism as a treatment at the present time?"

A bearded man with a white grin leaned into the microphone. "We're waiting," he said. "The guy with the chicken and holy water still hasn't showed up."

The cops at the sliding glass doors weren't about to let anyone in. Vera's medical ID was no help. Finally Parsifal flashed some old NASA credentials. "Bud Parsifal!" one said. "Hell, yes, come in." They all wanted to shake his hand. Parsifal was radiant.

"Spacemen," Vera whispered to Rau.

Inside the lab wing, the activity was equally manic, if less frenzied. Specialists were studying charts, X rays, and film images or mousing at computer models. Portable phones lay trapped on shoulders as people read data from screens or clipboards. Business suits intermixed with shoulder holsters and surgical scrubs of various colors. The hubbub reminded Vera of the aftermath of a natural disaster, an emergency room stretched beyond capacity.

They paused by a group watching a video. On screen, a young woman was bent over a block of blue gel on a steel table. "That's Dr. Yamamoto," Vera whispered to Rau and Parsifal. "Thomas and I met her last time."

"Here she goes," a man in the group said. He had a stopwatch in one hand. "Three, two, one. And . . . boom." Yamamoto abruptly stiffened on screen, then sank to her knees. For a moment she sat on her heels, staring, then tumbled to one side and went into violent spasms. The Beowulf scholars continued walking.

Other rooms held other screens and images: the bottom of a skull seemed to blossom open; a cursor arrow navigated up arteries, strayed upon neural arms, a highway of dreams and impulses.

Vera knocked at an open door. A blond woman in a lab smock was hunched over a microscope. "I'm looking for a Dr. Koenig," Vera said. The woman looked over, then came rushing to Vera with arms wide.

"Vera, you're back. Yammie told me you visited months ago."

Vera introduced them. "Mary Kay was one of my star pupils, when I could get her attention. Always off on triathlons and rock climbs. We could never keep up with her."

"The old days," said Mary Kay, probably all of thirty years old. Judging by the place, medicine had become the exclusive domain of the young and fit.

"You picked a bad time to visit, though," she said. "The entire facility's up in arms. Government agencies all over the place. The FBI." The purple circles under the young doctor's eyes were her testimony. Whatever this emergency was, she'd been hard at it for many hours.

"Actually, we heard something was happening," Vera said. "We've come to learn everything possible. If you can spare a few minutes."

"Of course I can. Let me finish one thing. I was about to run through some of the early stuff."

"Put me to work," Vera insisted.

Grateful, Mary Kay handed Vera a folded EEG readout. "These are the charts for day one of our hadal prep, almost a year ago. I've synched the video to 2:34 P.M., when they first quartered the body. If you don't mind, track the graph while they make the cuts. There should be some activity when the saw goes through. I'll tell you when."

She tapped a button on her keyboard. The frozen image started playing. "Okay," said Mary Kay. "Ready? They're about to sever the legs. Now."

It looked like a butcher's bandsaw on screen. Workers manipulated the long rectangle of blue gel sideways. Two of them lifted away a section after it passed through the saw.

"Nothing," Vera said. "No response on the chart. Flat."

"Here goes the head section. Anything?"

"No response. Not a bump," said Vera.

"Just what is it we're supposed to be looking for?" Parsifal asked.

"Activity. A pain response. Anything."

"Mary Kay," said Vera, "why are you looking for life signs in a dead hadal?"

The physician looked helplessly at Vera. "We're considering certain possibilities," she said, and it was clear the possibilities were unorthodox.

She ushered them down the wing, talking as they went. "Over the past fifty-two weeks, our computer-anatomy division has been sectioning a hadal specimen for general study. The project leader was Dr. Yamamoto, a noted pathologist. She was working alone in the lab on Sunday morning when this happened."

They entered a large room that reeked of chemicals and dead tissue. Rau's first impression was that a bomb had exploded. Big machines lay tipped on their sides. Wires had been pulled from ceiling panels. Long strips of industrial carpet lay ripped from the floor. Crime scene people and scientists alike wanted answers from what was left.

"A security guard found Dr. Yamamoto crouching in the far corner. He called for help. That was his last radio dispatch. We located him hanging from the pipes above the ceiling. His esophagus was torn out. By hand. Yammie was lying in the corner. Naked. Bleeding. Unresponsive."

"What happened?"

"At first we thought someone had broken in to either burgle or sabotage the premises, and that Lindsey had been assaulted. But as you can see, there are no windows, and only the one door. The door wasn't tampered with, which raised concerns that some hadals might have climbed through the vent system with the aim of destroying our database. We were studying hadal anatomy, after all. The project was underwritten with DoD grants. Arms makers have been clamoring for our tissue information to refine their weapons and ammunition."

"Where's Branch when we need him?" Rau said. "I've never heard of hadals doing such a thing. An attack like this, it implies such sophistication."

"Anyway, that's what we thought at first," Mary Kay continued. "You can imagine the uproar. The police came. We started to transport Yammie on a gurney. Then she regained consciousness and escaped."

"Escaped?" said Parsifal. "She was still frightened of the intruder?"

"It was terrible. She was wrecking machines. She slashed two guards with a scalpel. They finally shot her with a dart gun. Like a wild animal. That's when she lost the child."

"Child?" Vera asked.

"Yammie was seven months pregnant. The sedative or stress or activity . . . she miscarried."

"How dreadful."

They reached an eight-foot-long autopsy table. Vera had seen the human body insulted in a hundred different ways, shattered by trauma, wasted with disease and famine. But she was unprepared for the slight young woman with Japanese features who lay stretched out, covered with blankets, her head a Medusa-like riot of electrode patches and wires. It looked like a torture in progress. Her hands and feet had been tied down with a makeshift arrangement of towels, rubber tubing, and duct tape. The autopsy table's usual occupants did not require such restraints.

"Finally, one of the detectives sorted out the fingerprints and identified our culprit," said Mary Kay. "Yammie did it."

"Did what?" murmured Vera.

"You mean it was her?" said Rau. "Dr. Yamamoto killed the guard?"

"Yes. His throat tissue was under her nails."

"This woman?" Parsifal snorted. "But those machines must weigh a ton each."

To one side, Thomas's face was shadowed with dark thoughts.

"Why would she do such a thing?" asked Rau.

"We're baffled. It may be related to a grand mal, though her husband said she has no history of epilepsy. It could be a psychotic rage no one ever suspected. The one video monitor she didn't manage to demolish shows her falling into unconsciousness, then getting up and destroying the machines used for cutting tissue. The target of her anger was very specific, these machines, as if she was avenging herself for a great wrong."

"And killing the guard?"

"We don't know. The killing took place off camera. According to the security guard's radio report, he found her in a fetal position. She was clutching *that*." Mary Kay pointed to a desktop.

"Good lord," said Vera.

Parsifal walked over to the desk. Here was the source of the stench. What remained of a hadal head had been positioned between a 7-Eleven Big Gulp cup and the Denver Yellow Pages. The blue gel that had once encased it was mostly thawed. The liquid seeped down into the desk's drawers.

The lower half of the face and skull had been lopped away by the machine's blades so cleanly that the creature seemed to be materializing from the flat desktop. Its black hair was smeared flat upon the misshapen skull. A dozen small burr holes sprouted electrode wires. After so many months preserved from air, it was now in a state of rapid decomposition.

More disconcerting than the decay and missing jaws were the eyes. The lids were wide open. The eyes bulged, pupils fixed in a seemingly furious stare. "He looks pissed," said Parsifal.

"She," commented the physician. "The protruding eyes are a symptom of hyperthyroidism. Not enough iodine in the diet. She probably came from a region deficient in basic minerals like salt. A lot of hadals look like that."

"What would prompt anyone to embrace such a thing?" asked Vera.

"That's what we asked ourselves. Had Yammie started to identify subconsciously with her specimen? Did something trigger a personality reaction? Identification, sublimation, conversion. We went through all the possibilities. But Yammie was always so even. And never happier than now. Pregnant, fulfilled, loved." Mary Kay tucked the blanket around Yamamoto's neck, brushed the hair back from her forehead. A long bruise was surfacing above her eyes. In her frenzy, the woman must have flung herself against the machines and walls.

"Then the seizures returned. We hooked her up to an EEG. You've never seen anything like it. A neurological storm, more like a tempest. We induced a coma."

"Good," said Vera.

"Except it didn't work. We keep getting activity. Something seems to be eating its way through the brain, short-circuiting tissue as it goes. It's like watching a lightning bolt in slow motion. The big difference here is that the electrical activity isn't general. You'd think an electrical overload would be brain-wide. But this is all being generated from the hippocampus, almost selectively."

"The hippocampus, what is that, please?" Rau asked.

"The memory center," Mary Kay answered.

"Memory," Rau repeated softly. "And had this hippocampus been dissected by your machine yet?"

They all looked at Rau. "No," said Mary Kay. "In fact, the blade was just approaching it. Why?"

"Just a question." Rau peered around the room. "Also, were you keeping laboratory animals in this room?"

"Absolutely not."

"I thought not."

"What do animals have to do with it?" Parsifal said.

But Rau had more questions. "In clinical terms, Dr. Koenig, at its most basic, what is memory?"

"Memory?" said Mary Kay. "In a nutshell, memory is electric charges exciting biochemicals along synaptic networks."

"Electric wires," Rau summarized. "That's what our past reduces to?"

"It's much more complicated than that."

"But essentially true?"

"Yes."

"Thank you," Rau said. They waited for his conclusion, but after a few moments it became clear he was deep in contemplation.

"What's strange," said Mary Kay, "is that Yammie's brain scans are showing nearly two hundred percent of the normal electrical stimulus in a human brain."

"No wonder she's short-circuiting," Vera said.

"There's something else," said Mary Kay. "At first it looked like a big jumble of brain activity. But we're starting to sort it all out. And it looks like we're tracking two distinct cognitive patterns."

"What?" said Vera. "That's impossible."

"I don't follow you," said Parsifal.

Mary Kay's voice grew small. "Yammie's not alone in there," she said.

"One more time, please," Parsifal demanded.

"You have to understand," Mary Kay said, "none of this is for public disclosure."

"You have our word," said Thomas.

She stroked Yamamoto's arm. "We couldn't make sense out of the two cognitive patterns. But then, a few hours ago, something happened. The seizures stopped. Completely. And Yammie began to speak. She was unconscious, but she started talking."

"Excellent," said Parsifal.

"It wasn't in English, though. It wasn't anything we'd ever heard."

"What?"

"We happened to have an intern in the room. He'd served as a Navy medic in sub-Mexico. Apparently the military plants microphones in remote recesses. He'd heard some of the recordings and thought he recognized the sound."

"Not hadal," said Parsifal. Confusion aggravated him.

"Yes."

"Rubbish." Parsifal's face was turning red.

"We obtained a tape of hadal voices from the DoD's library, top secret. Then we compared it with Yammie's speech. It wasn't identical, but it was close enough. Apparently, human vocal cords need practice to handle the consonants and trills and clicks. But Yammie was speaking their language."

"Where could she have learned to speak it?"

"That's exactly the point," said Mary Kay. "As far as humans go, there aren't more than a handful of recaptures that speak it in the world. But Yammie was. It's all on tape."

"She must have heard some recaptures then," Parsifal said.

"It's more than simple mimicry, though. See that wall over there?"

"Is that mud?" asked Vera.

"Feces. Her own. Yammie used it to fingerpaint those symbols."

They all recognized the symbols as hadal.

"We can't figure out what they represent," said Mary Kay. "I'm told that someone on a science expedition below the Pacific was starting to crack the code. An archaeologist. Van Scott or something. The expedition's supposed to be a big secret. But one of the mining colonies leaked bits of the story. Only now the expedition's disappeared."

"Van Scott. It wouldn't be a woman, would it?" Vera asked. "Von Schade? Ali?"

"That's it. Then you know of her work?"

"Not nearly enough," said Vera.

"She's a friend," Thomas explained. "We're deeply concerned."

"I still don't understand," Parsifal said. "How could this young lady be mimicking an alphabet that humans have only just discovered exists? And aping a language that humans don't speak?"

"But she's not mimicking or aping them."

"Are we to suppose the creatures of hell are channeling through this poor woman?"

"Of course not, Mr. Parsifal."

"What then?"

"This is going to sound awfully half-baked."

"After the nonsense we just witnessed out front?" said Parsifal. "Possession. Exorcism. I'm feeling pretty warmed up."

"In fact," Mary Kay said, "Yammie seems to have become her subject. More precisely, the hadal has become her."

Parsifal gaped, then started to growl.

"Listen." Vera stopped him. "Just listen for a minute."

"Bud's right," Thomas protested. "We came all this way to hear such nonsense?"

"We're just trying to go where the evidence points us," Mary Kay pleaded.

"Let me get this straight. The soul from that thing," said Parsifal, pointing at the decaying cranium, "jumped inside of this young woman?"

"Believe me," Mary Kay said, "none of us want to believe it, either. But something catastrophic happened to her. The charts spiked right before Yammie fell unconscious. We've gone over the video a thousand times. You see Yammie holding the EEG leads, and then she falls down. Maybe she conducted an electric current through her hands. Or the head conducted one into her. I know it sounds fantastic."

"Fantastic? Try lunatic," Parsifal said. "I've had enough of this." On his way out, he stopped by the sectioned skull. "You should clean your necropolis," he declared to the roomful of people. "It's no wonder you're hatching such medieval rubbish." He opened a magazine and dropped it over the hadal head, then stalked out. From the tent of glossy pages, the hadal eyes seemed to peer out at them.

Mary Kay was trembling, shaken by Parsifal's vehemence.

"Forgive us," Thomas said to her. "We're used to one another's passions and dramas. We sometimes forget ourselves in public."

"I think we should have some coffee," Vera declared. "Is there a place we can collect our thoughts?"

Mary Kay led them to a small conference room with a coffee machine. A monitor on the wall overlooked the laboratory. The smell of coffee was a welcome relief from the chemical and decay stench. Thomas got them all seated and insisted on serving them. He made sure Mary Kay got the first cup. "I know it sounds crazy," she said.

"Actually," Rau said quietly after Parsifal was gone, "we shouldn't be so surprised."

"And why not?" Thomas said.

"We're talking about old-fashioned reincarnation. If you go back in time, you find versions of the theory are almost universal. For twenty thousand years the Australian aborigines have tracked an unbroken chain of ancestors in their infants. You find it everywhere, in many peoples, from Indonesians to Bantus to Druids. You get thinkers like Plato and Empedocles and Pythagoras and Plotinus trying to describe it. The Orphic mysteries and the Jewish Cabala took a crack at it. Even modern science has investigated the activity. It's quite accepted where I come from, a perfectly natural phenomenon."

"But I just can't accept that, in a laboratory setting, this hadal's *soul* passed into another person?"

"Soul?" said Rau. "In Buddhism there's no such thing as soul. They talk about an undifferentiated stream of being that passes from one existence to another. *Samsara,* they call it."

In part goaded by Thomas's skepticism, Vera challenged the idea, too. "Since when does rebirth involve epileptic seizures, homicide, and cannibalism? You call this perfectly natural?"

"All I can say is that birth doesn't always happen without problems,"

Rau said. "Why should rebirth? As for the devastation"—and he gestured at the TV view of destruction—"that may have to do with man's limited capacity for memory. Perhaps, as Dr. Koenig described, memory is a matter of electrical wiring. But memory is also a maze. An abyss. Who knows where it goes?"

"What was your question about lab animals, Rau?"

"I was just trying to eliminate other possibilities," he answered. "Classically, the transfer occurs between a dying adult and an infant or animal. But in this case the hadal had only this young woman at hand. And it found an occupied house, so to speak. Now it's disabling Dr. Yamamoto's memory in order to make room for itself."

"But why now?" asked Mary Kay. "Why all of a sudden, like this?"

"I can only guess," Rau said. "You told me your mechanical blade was about to dissect the hippocampus. Maybe this was the hadal memory's way of defending itself. By invading new territory."

"It invaded her? That's an odd way of putting it."

"You westerners," said Rau, "you mistake reincarnation with a sociable act, like a handshake or a kiss. But rebirth is a matter of dominion. Of occupation. Of colonization, if you will. It's like one country seizing land from another, and interposing its own people and language and government. Before long, Aztecs are speaking Spanish, or Mohawks are speaking English. And they start to forget who they once were."

"You're substituting metaphors for common sense," said Thomas. "It doesn't get us any closer to our goal, I'm afraid."

"But think about it," said Rau. He was getting excited. "A passage of continuous memory. An unbroken strand of consciousness, eons long. It could help explain his longevity. From man's narrow historical perspective, it could make him seem eternal."

"Who's this you're talking about?" Mary Kay asked.

"Someone we're looking for," Thomas said. "No one."

"I didn't mean to pry." After all she'd shared with them, her hurt was evident.

"It's a game we play," Vera rushed to explain, "nothing more."

The video monitor on the wall behind them had no sound, or else they might have noticed the initial flurry of action in the laboratory. Mary Kay's pager beeped and she looked down at it, then suddenly whirled in her chair to see the screen. "Yammie," she groaned.

People were rushing through the laboratory. Someone shouted at the monitor, a soundless cry. "What?" said Vera.

"Code Blue." And Mary Kay flew out the door. A half-minute later, she reappeared on the monitor.

"What's happening?" asked Rau.

Vera turned her wheelchair to face the monitor. "They're losing the poor girl. She's in cardiac arrest. Look, here comes the crash wagon."

Thomas was on his feet, watching the screen intently. Rau joined him. "Now what?" he said.

"Those are the shock paddles," Vera said. "To jump-start her heart again."

"You mean she's dead?"

"There's a difference between biological and clinical death. It may not be too late."

Under Mary Kay's direction, several people were shoving aside tables and wrecked machinery, making room for the heavy crash wagon. Mary Kay reached for the paddles and held them upright. To the rear, a woman was waving the electric plug in one hand, frantically casting around for an outlet.

"But they mustn't do that!" Rau cried.

"They have to try," said Vera.

"Didn't anyone understand what I was talking about?"

"Where are you going, Rau?" Thomas barked. But Rau was already gone.

"There he is," said Vera, pointing at the screen.

"What does he think he's doing?" Thomas said.

Still wearing his cowboy hat, Rau shouldered aside a burly policeman and made a sprightly hop over a spilled chair. They watched as people backed away from the stainless-steel table, exposing Yamamoto to the camera. The frail young woman lay still, tied and taped to the table, with wires leading off to machines. As Rau approached, Mary Kay stood her ground on the far side, shock paddles poised. He was arguing with her.

"Oh, Rau!" Vera despaired. "Thomas, we have to get him out of there. This is a medical emergency."

Mary Kay said something to a nurse, who tried to lead Rau away by the arm. But Rau pushed her. A lab tech grabbed him by the waist, and Rau doggedly held on to the edge of the metal table. Mary Kay leaned to place the paddles. The last thing Vera saw on the monitor was the body arching.

With Thomas pushing the wheelchair, they hurried to the laboratory, dodging cops, firemen, and staff in the hallway. They encountered a gurney loaded with equipment, and that consumed another precious minute. By the time they reached the lab, the drama was over. People were leaving the room. A woman stood at the door with one hand to her eyes.

Inside, Vera and Thomas saw a man draped partway across the table, his head laid next to Yamamoto's, sobbing. The husband, Vera guessed. Still holding the shock paddles, Mary Kay stood to one side, staring vacantly. An attendant spoke to her. When she didn't respond, he simply took the paddles from her hands. Someone else patted her on the back, and still she didn't move.

"Good heavens, was Rau right?" whispered Vera. They wove through the wreckage as Yamamoto's body was covered and lifted onto a stretcher. They had to wait for the stream of people to pass. The husband followed the bearers out.

"Dr. Koenig?" said Thomas. Wires cluttered the gleaming table.

She flinched at his voice, and raised her eyes to him. "Father?" she said, dazed.

Vera and Thomas exchanged a concerned look.

"Mary Kay?" Vera said. "Are you all right?"

"Father Thomas? Vera?" said Mary Kay. "Now Yammie's gone, too? Where did we go wrong?"

Vera exhaled. "You had me scared," she said. "Come here, child. Come here." Mary Kay knelt by the wheelchair. She buried her face against Vera's shoulder.

"Rau?" Thomas asked, glancing around. "Now where did he go?"

Abruptly, Rau burst from his hiding place in a heap of readout paper and piled cables. He moved so quickly, they barely knew it was he. As he raced past Vera's wheelchair, one hand hooked wide, and Mary Kay grunted and bent backward in pain. Her lab jacket suddenly gaped open from shoulder to shoulder, and red marked the long slash wound. Rau had a scalpel.

Now they saw the lab tech who had tried to pry Rau loose from the table. He sat slumped with his entrails across his legs.

Thomas yelled something at Rau. It was a command of some kind, not a question. Vera didn't know Hindi, if that's what it was, and was too shocked to care.

Rau paused and looked at Thomas, his face distorted with anguish and bewilderment.

"Thomas!" cried Vera, falling from her chair with the wounded physician in her arms.

In the one instant Thomas took his eyes from the man, Rau vanished through the doorway.

The suicide was aired on national television that evening. Rau couldn't have timed it better, with national media already gathered for the university's press conference in the street below. It was simply a matter of training their cameras on the roofline eight stories above.

With a fiery Rocky Mountain sunset for a backdrop, the SWAT cops edged closer and closer to Rau's swaying form, guns leveled. Aiming their acoustic dishes, sound crews on the ground picked up every word of the negotiator's appeal to the cornered man. Telephoto lenses trained on his twisted face, tracked his leap. Several quick-thinking cameramen utilized the same bounce technique, a quick nudge up, to self-edit the impact.

There was no doubt the former head of India's parliament had gone insane. The hadal head cradled in his arms was all the proof anyone needed. That and the cowboy hat.

*Brother, thy tail hangs down
behind.*

—RUDYARD KIPLING, *The Jungle Book*

19

CONTACT

The camp woke to tremors on the last day of summer.

Like the rest, Ali was asleep on the ground. She felt the earthquake work deep inside her body. It seemed to move her bones.

For a full minute the scientists lay on the ground, some curling in fetal balls, some clutching their neighbors' hands or embracing. They waited in awful silence for the tunnel to close upon them or the floor to drop away.

Finally some wag yelled out, "All clear. It was just Shoat, damn him. Wanking again." They all laughed nervously. There were no more tremors, but they had been reminded of how minuscule they were. Ali braced for an onset of confessions from her fragile flock.

Later in the morning, several in a group of women she was rafting with could smell what was left of the earthquake in the faint dust hanging above the river. Pia, one of the planetologists, said it reminded her of a stonecutters' yard near her childhood home, the smell of cemetery markers being polished and sandblasted with the names of the dead.

"Tombstones? That's a pleasant thought," one of the women said.

To dispel the sense of omen, Ali said, "See how white the dust is?

Have you ever smelled fresh marble just after a chisel has cut it?" She recalled for them a sculptor's studio she had once visited in northern Italy. He had been working on a nude with little success, and had begged Ali to pose for him, to help draw the woman out from his block of stone. For a time he had pursued her with letters.

"He wanted you to pose naked?" Pia was delighted. "He didn't know you were a nun?"

"I was very clear."

"So? Did you?"

Suddenly, Ali felt sad. "Of course not."

Life in these dark tubes and veins had changed her. She had been trained to erase her identity in order to allow God's signature upon her. Now she wanted desperately to be remembered, if only as a piece of sculpted marble.

The underworld was having its effect on others, too. As an anthropologist Ali was naturally alive to the entire tribe's metamorphosis. Tracking their idiosyncrasies was like watching a garden slowly grow rampant. They adopted peculiar touches, odd ways of combing their hair, or rolling their survival suits up to the knee or shoulder. Many of the men had started going bareback, the upper half of their suits hanging from their waists like shed skin. Deodorant was a thing of the past, and you barely noticed the body smells, except for certain unfortunates. Shoat, particularly, was known for his foot odor. Some of the women braided each other's hair with beads or shells. It was just for fun, they said, but their concoctions got more elaborate each week.

Some of the soldiers lapsed into gang talk when Walker wasn't around, and their weapons suddenly flowered with scrimshaw. They carved animals or Bible quotes or girlfriends' names onto the plastic stocks and handles. Even Walker had let his beard grow into a great Mosaic bush that had to be a garden spot for the cave lice that plagued them.

Ike no longer looked so much different from the rest of them. After the incident at Cache II, he had made himself more scarce. Many nights they never saw him, only his little tripod of glowing green candles designating a good campsite. When he did surface, it was only for a matter of hours. He was retreating into himself, and Ali didn't know how to reach him, or why it should matter so much to her. Maybe it was that the one in their group who most needed reconciliation seemed most resistant to it. There was another possibility, that she had fallen in love. But that was unreasonable, she thought.

On one of Ike's rare overnights at camp, Ali took a meal to him and they sat by the water's edge. "What do you dream?" she asked. When his brow wrinkled, she added, "You don't have to tell me."

"You've been talking with the shrinks," he said. "They asked the same thing. It's supposed to be a measure of fluency, right? If I dream in hadal."

She was unsettled. They all wanted a piece of this man. "Yes, it's a measure. And no, I haven't talked with anyone about you."

"So what do you want?"

"What you dream about. You don't have to tell me."

"Okay."

They listened to the water. After a minute, she changed her mind. "No, you do have to tell me." She made it light.

"Ali," he said. "You don't want to hear it."

"Give," she coaxed.

"Ali," he said, and shook his head.

"Is it so bad?"

Suddenly he stood up and went over to the kayak.

"Where are you going?" This was so strange. "Look, just drop it. I was prying. I'm sorry."

"It's not your fault," he said, and dragged the boat to water.

As he cut his way down the river, it finally dawned on her. Ike dreamed of her.

On September 28 they homed in on Cache III.

They had been picking up increasingly strong signals for two days. Not sure what other surprises Helios might have in store, still uncertain what the Ranger assassins had been up to, Walker told Ike to stay behind while he sent his soldiers in advance. Ike made no objections, and drifted his kayak among the scientists' rafts, silent and chagrined to be off point for a change.

Where the cache was supposed to be towered a waterfall. Walker and his mercenaries had beached near its base and were searching the lower walls with the powerful spotlights mounted on their boats. The waterfall rifled down a shield of olive stone from heights too high to see, beating up a mist that threw rainbows in their lights. The scientists ran their rafts onto shore and disembarked. Some quirk in the cul-de-sac's acoustics rendered the roar into a wall of white noise.

Walker came over. "The rangefinder reads zero," he reported. "That means the cylinders are here somewhere. But all we've got is this waterfall."

Ali could taste sea salt in the mist, and looked up into the great throat of the sinkhole rising into darkness. They were by now two-thirds of the way across the Pacific Ocean system, at a depth of 5,866 fathoms, over six miles beneath sea level. There was nothing but water overhead, and it was leaking through the ocean floor.

"They've got to be here," said Shoat.

"You've been carrying your own rangefinder around," Walker said. "Let's see if that works any better."

Shoat backed away and grasped at the flat leather pouch strung around his neck. "It won't work for this kind of thing," he said. "It's a homing device, specially made for the transistor beacons I'm planting along the way. For an emergency only."

"Maybe the cylinders hung up on a shelf," someone suggested.

"We're looking," said Walker. "But these rangefinders are calibrated precisely. The cylinders should be within two hundred feet. We haven't seen a sign of them. No cables. No drill scars. Nothing."

"One thing's certain," said Spurrier. "We're not going anywhere until those supplies are found."

Ike took his kayak downriver to investigate smaller strands. "If you find them, leave them. Don't touch them. Come back and tell us," Walker instructed him. "Somebody's got you in their crosshairs, and I don't want you close to our cargo when they pull the trigger."

The expedition broke into search parties, but found nothing. Frustrated, Walker put some of his mercenaries to work shoveling at the coarse sand in case the cylinders had burrowed under. Nothing. Tempers began to fray, and few wanted to hear one fellow's calculations about how to ration what little food remained until they reached the next cache, five weeks farther on.

They suspended the search to have their meal and rejuvenate their perspective. Ali sat with a line of people, their backs against the rafts, facing the waterfall. Suddenly Troy said, "What about there?" He was pointing at the waterfall.

"Inside the water?" asked Ali.

"It's the one place we haven't looked."

They left their food and walked across to the edge of the tributary feeding from the waterfall's base, trying to see through the mist and plunging water. Troy's hunch spread, and others joined them.

"Someone has to go in," Spurrier said.

"I'll do it," said Troy.

By now Walker had come over. "We'll take it from here," he said.

It took another quarter-hour to prepare Walker's "volunteer," a huge, sullen teenager from San Antonio's West Side who'd lately started branding himself with hadal glyphs. Ali had heard the colonel tongue-lashing him for godlessness, and this scout duty was obviously a punishment. The kid was scared as they tied him to the end of a rope. "I don't do waterfalls," he kept saying. "Let El Cap do it."

"Crockett's gone," Walker shouted into the noise. "Just keep to the wall."

Hooded in his survival suit, wearing his night-vision glasses more as diving goggles than for the low lux boost, the boy started in, slowly atomizing in the mist. They kept feeding rope into the waterfall, but after a few minutes there was no more tow on the line. It went slack.

They tugged at the rope and ended pulling the whole fifty meters back out. Walker held the end up. "He untied himself," Walker shouted to a second "volunteer." "That means there's a hollow inside. This time, don't untie. Give three tugs when you reach the chamber, then attach it to a rock or something. The idea is to make a handline, got it?"

The second soldier set off more confidently. The rope wormed in, deeper than the first time. "Where's he going in there?" Walker said.

The line came taut, then seized harder. The belayer started to complain, but the rope suddenly yanked from his hands and its tail whipped off into the mist.

"This isn't tug-of-war," Walker lectured his third scout. "Just anchor your end. A few moderate pulls will signal us." In the background, several mercenaries were amused. Their comrades in the mist were having some fun at the colonel's expense. The tension relaxed.

Walker's third man stepped through the curtain of spray and they started to lose sight of him. Abruptly he returned. Still on his feet, he came hurtling from the mist, backpedaling in a frenzy.

It happened quickly. His arms flailed, beating at some unseen weight on his front, suggesting a seizure. Backward momentum drove him into the crowd. People spilled to the sand. He landed deep in their midst, among their legs, and he spun spine up and arched, heaving away from the ground. Ali couldn't see what happened next.

The soldier let loose a deep bellow. It came from his core, a visceral discharge. "Move away, move away," Walker yelled, pistol in hand, wading through the crowd.

The soldier sagged, facedown, but kept twitching. "Tommy?" called a troop.

Brutally, Tommy came erect, what was left of him, and they saw that his face and torso had been ripped to scraps. The body keeled over backward.

That was when they caught sight of the hadal.

She was squatting in the sand where Tommy had carried her, mouth and hands and dugs brilliant with blood and their lights, blinded, as white as the abyssal fish they had seen. Ali's view lasted just a fraction of a second. A thousand years old, that creature. How could such a withered thing accomplish the butchery they had just seen?

With a cry, the crowd fell away from the apparition. Ali was knocked to the ground and pummeled by the stampede. Above her, soldiers fumbled at their weapons. A boot glanced off her head. Overhead, Walker came crashing through the frantic herd, more shadow than man among the wheeling lights, his handgun blazing.

The hadal leaped—impossibly—twenty feet onto the shield of olive stone. In the strobing patchwork of lights, she was ghastly white and rimed, it seemed, with scales or filth. This was the repository for the mother tongue? Ali was confused. Over the past months they had humanized the hadals in their discussions, but the reality was more like a wild animal. Her skin was practically reptilian. Then Ali realized it was skin cancer, and the hadal's flesh was ulcerated and checkered with scabs.

Walker was fearless, running alongside the wall and firing at the scampering hadal. She was making for the waterfall, and Ali guessed it was the sound that was her compass. But the stone grew slick with spray or the holds were polished off or Walker's bullets were striking the mark. She fell. Walker and his men closed in around her, and all Ali could see were eruptions of light from muzzle flash.

Dazed from the kick, Ali crawled to her feet and started over to the cluster of excited soldiers. She understood from their jubilation that this was the first live hadal any of them had ever seen, much less fought. Walker's crack team of mercenaries were no more familiar with the enemy than she was.

"Back to the boats," Walker told her.

"What are you going to do?"

"They've taken our cylinders," he said.

"You're going in there?"

"Not until we've pacified the waterfall."

She saw soldiers prepping the bigger miniguns mounted to their rafts. They were eager and grim, and she dreaded their enthusiasm. From her passages through African civil wars, Ali knew firsthand that once the juggernaut got loose, it was irrevocable. This was happening too quickly. She wanted Ike here, someone who knew the territory and could measure the colonel's hot backlash. "But those two boys are still inside."

"Madam," Walker answered, "this is a military affair." He motioned, and one of the mercenaries escorted her by the arm to where the last of the scientists were entering their boats. Ali clambered aboard and they pushed off from shore and watched the show at a distance.

Walker trained all their spotlights on the waterfall, illuminating the tall column so that it looked like a vast glass dragon clinging to the rock, respirating. He directed them to open fire into the water itself.

Ali was reminded of the king who tried to order the ocean's waves to stop. The water swallowed their bullets. The white noise devoured their gunfire, turning it into strings of snapping firecrackers. They laid on with their gunfire, and the water tore open in liquid gouts, only to heal instantly. Some of the special uranium-tipped Lucifer rounds struck the surrounding walls, clawing divots in the stone. A soldier fired a rocket into the bowels of the fall, and the trunk belched outward, revealing a nebulous gap inside. Moments later the gap sealed shut as more water poured down.

Then the waterfall began to bleed.

Under potent spotlight beams, the waters hemorrhaged. The tributary bloomed red, and the color fanned unevenly to midriver and carried downstream. Ali thought that if the gunfire didn't draw Ike, surely the blood trail would. She was frightened by the magnitude of what Walker had done. Gunning down the murderous hadal was one thing. But he had, seemingly, just opened the veins of a force of nature. He had unleashed something here, she could feel it.

"What in God's name was inside there?" someone gasped.

Walker deployed his soldiers with hand signals. Sleek in their survival suits, they flanked the waterfall, scurrying like insects. The rifles in their hands were remarkably still and steady, and each soldier was little more than the moving parts of his weapon. Half of Walker's contingent entered the mist from each side of the tributary. While the scientists watched from bobbing rafts, the other half zeroed in on the waterfall, ready to pump more rounds into it.

Several minutes passed. A man reappeared, glistening in his amphibian neoprene. He shouted, "All clear!"

"What about the cylinders?" Walker yelled to him.

The soldier said, "In here," and Walker and the rest of his men got off their bellies and went into the waterfall without a word to their charges.

At last the scientists paddled back to shore. Some were terrified that more hadals might come leaping at them, or shied from the blood they'd seen and stayed in the rafts. A handful went to the dead hadal for a closer look, Ali included. Little remained. The bullets had all but turned the creature inside out.

Ali went with five others inside the waterfall. Since the spray had already soaked her hair, she didn't bother pulling her hood up. There was the slightest of trails hugging the wall, and as they squeezed along it above the pool of water, the waterfall became a veil backlit by the spotlights. Deeper, the spotlights turned to liquid orbs, and finally the waterfall was too thick to allow any light. Its noise muffled all sounds from the outside. Ali turned on her headlamp and kept edging between the water and rock. They reached a globular grotto inside.

All three of their missing cylinders lay by the entrance, heaped with hundreds of yards of thick cable. Fully loaded, each of the cylinders weighed over four tons; it must have taken enormous effort to drag them into this hiding place. Two of the cables, Ali saw, ran upward into the waterfall. That suggested their communications lines might be intact.

Under the badly abraded black stencil declaring HELIOS, the name NASA surfaced in ghostly letters along one cylinder's side. The outer sheathing was pitted and gashed with bullet and shrapnel tracks, but was unruptured. A soldier kept clearing his eyes of water spray as he worked on opening its hatch door. The hadals had tried to force entry with boulders and iron rods, but had only managed to break off many of the thick bolts. The hatches were all in place. Ali climbed around the mass of cables and saw that the first body she came across was Walker's volunteer, the big teenager from San Antonio. They had torn his throat out by hand. She braced herself for more carnage.

Deeper in, Walker's men had laid chemical lights on ledges and stuck them into niches in the wall, casting a green pall through the entire chamber. Smoke from explosions hung like wet fog. The soldiers were circulating among the dead. Ali blinked quickly at the dense piles of bone and flesh, and raised her eyes to quell her sickness. There were many bodies in here. In the green light, the walls appeared to be sweating with humidity, but the sheen was blood. It was everywhere.

"Watch the broken bone ends," one of the physicians warned her. "Poke yourself on one of those, you could get a nasty infection."

Ali forced herself to look down, if only to place her feet. Limbs lay scattered. The worst of it were the hands, beseeching.

Several soldiers glanced over at Ali with great hollows for eyes. Not a trace of their earlier zeal remained. She was drawn to their contrition, thinking they were appalled by their deed. But it was more awful than that.

"They're all females," muttered a soldier.

"And kids."

Ali had to look closer than she wanted to, past the painted flesh and the beetle-browed faces. Only minutes before, they had been a roomful of people outwaiting the humans outside. She had to look for their sex and their fragility, and what the soldiers said was true.

"Bitches and spawn," one jived, trying to vitiate the shame. But there were no takers. They didn't like this: no weapons, not a single male. A slaughter of innocents.

Above them, a soldier appeared at the mouth of a secondary chamber and began waving his arm and shouting. It was impossible to hear him with the waterfall behind them, but Ali overheard a nearby walkie-talkie. "Sierra Victor, this is Fox One. Colonel," an excited voice reported, "we got live ones. What you want us to do?"

Ali saw Walker straighten from among the dead and reach for his own walkie-talkie, and she guessed what his command would be. He had already lost three men. For the sake of conservation, he would simply order the soldiers to finish the job. Walker lifted the walkie-talkie to his mouth. "Wait!" she yelled, and rushed down to him.

She could tell he knew her intent. "Sister," he greeted.

"Don't do it," she said.

"You should go outside with the others," he told her.

"No."

Their impasse might have escalated. But at that moment a man bellowed from the entrance and everyone turned. It was Ike, standing on top of the cylinders, the water sheeting from him. "What have you done?"

Hands lifted in disbelief, he descended from the cylinders. They watched him come to a body, and kneel. He set his shotgun to one side. Grasping the shoulders, he lifted her partway from the ground and the head lolled, white hair kinky around the horns, teeth bared. The teeth had been filed to sharp points.

Ike was gentle. He brought the head upright and looked at the face and smelled behind her ear, then laid her flat again.

Next to her lay a hadal infant, and he carefully cradled it in his arms as if it were still alive. "You have no idea what you've done," he groaned to the mercenaries.

"This is Sierra Victor, Fox One," Walker murmured into the walkie-talkie. His hand was cupped to it, but Ali heard him. "Open fire."

"What are you doing?" she cried, and grabbed the radio from the colonel. Ali fumbled with the transmit button. "You hold your fire," she said, and added, "damn you."

She let go of the transmit button and they heard a small confused voice saying, "Colonel, repeat. Colonel?" Walker made no effort to wrestle back the walkie-talkie.

"We didn't know," one boy said to Ike.

"You weren't here, man," said another. "You didn't see what they done to Tommy. And look at A-Z. Tore his throat out."

"What did you expect?" Ike roared at them. They grew subdued. Ali had never seen him ferocious before. And where did this voice come from?

"Their babies?" Ike thundered.

They backed away from him.

"They were hadals," said Walker.

"Yes," Ike said. He held the shattered child at arm's length and searched the small face, then laid the body against his heart. He picked up his shotgun and stood.

"They're beasts, Crockett." Walker spoke loudly for everyone to hear. "They cost us three men. They stole our cylinders and would have opened them. If we hadn't attacked, they would have looted our supplies and that would have been our death."

"This," Ike said, clutching the dead child, "this is your death."

"We are deep beyond—" Walker started.

"You've killed yourselves," Ike said more quietly.

"Enough, Crockett. Join the human race. Or go back to them."

The walkie-talkie in Ali's hand spoke up again, and she held it up for Ike to hear as well. "They're starting to move around. Say again. Should we open fire or not?"

Walker snatched the walkie-talkie from her, but Ike was equally fast. Without hesitation, he pointed his sawed-off gun at the colonel's face. Walker's mouth twisted in his beard.

"Give me that baby," she said to Ike, and took the little body. "We have other things to do. Don't we, Colonel?"

Walker looked at her, eyes huge with rage. He made up his mind. "Hold your fire," he snarled into the walkie-talkie. "We're coming for a look."

The stone floor buckled underfoot, and she had to skirt deep plunge holes. They climbed a slick incline to the higher, smaller chamber. The deadly hail of gunfire had not reached this far except as ricochets, which had done damage enough. They passed several more bodies before gaining the high floor.

The survivors were huddled in a pocket, and they seemed able to feel the light beams against their skin. Ali counted seven of them, two very young. They were mute, moving only when someone trained a headlamp on them for too long. "No more?" Ike asked the soldiers guarding them.

"Them. They tried to get away." The man indicated another eleven or twelve, sprawled near a duct.

The hadals kept their faces away from the light, and the mothers sheltered their young. Their flesh gleamed. The markings and scars undulated as their muscles shifted.

"Are they fatties, or what?" a mercenary said to Walker.

Several of the females were indeed obese. More correctly, they were steatopygic, with enormous surpluses of fat in their buttocks and breasts. To Ali's eye, they were identical to Neolithic Venuses carved from stone or painted on walls. They were magnificent in their size and decoration, and their greased and plaited hair. Here and there, Ali caught sight of the apelike brows and low foreheads, and again it was hard to reconcile them as quite human.

"These are sacred," Ike said. "They're consecrated."

"You make them sound like vestal virgins," Walker scoffed.

"It's just the opposite. These are their breeders. The pregnant and new mothers. Their infants and children. They know their species is going extinct. These are their racial treasure. Once the women conceive, they're brought into communal coveys like this. It's like living in a harem." He added, "Or a nunnery. They're cared for and watched over and honored."

"Is there a point to this?"

"Hadals are nomadic. They make seasonal rounds. When they move, each tribe keeps its women in the center of the line for protection."

"Some protection," a soldier spoke up. "We just turned their next generation into hamburger."

Ike didn't reply.

"Wait," said Walker. "You're saying we intersected the middle of their line?"

Ike nodded.

"Which means the males are off to either end?"

"Luck," Ike said. "Bad luck. I don't think we want to be here when they catch up."

"All right," Walker said. "You've had your look. Let's get this over with."

Instead, Ike walked into the midst of the hadals.

Ali couldn't hear Ike's words distinctly, but heard the rise and fall of his tone and occasional tongue clicks. The females responded with surprise, and so did the soldiers aiming their rifles at them. Walker cut a glance at Ali, and suddenly she feared for Ike's life. "If even one tries to run," Walker told his men, "you are to open fire on the whole pack."

"But the Cap's in there," a boy said.

"Full auto," Walker warned grimly.

Ali left Walker's side and went out to Ike, placing herself in the line of fire. "Go back," Ike whispered.

"I'm not doing this for you," she lied. "It's for them."

Hands reached up to touch Ike and her. The palms were rough, the nails broken and encrusted. Ike hunkered among them, and Ali let different ones grab her hands and smell her. His claim mark was of special interest. One wall-eyed ancient held on to his arm. She stroked the scarified nodes and questioned him. When Ike answered her, she drew away with revulsion, it seemed. She whispered to the others, who grew agitated and scrambled to get distance from him. Still perched on his toes, Ike hung his head. He tried another few phrases, and their fright only increased.

"What are you doing?" Ali asked. "What did you tell them?"

"My hadal name," said Ike.

"But you said it was forbidden to speak it out loud."

"It was, until I left the People. I wanted to find out how bad things really are with me."

"They know you?"

"They know *about* me."

From the hadals' loathing, it was clear his reputation was odious. Even the children were afraid of him. "This isn't good," Ike said, eyeing the soldiers. "We can't stay here. And if we leave—"

The walkie-talkie announced that two of the cylinders had been opened and Shoat had a communications line in operation. Ali could see by his face that Walker wanted to be shed of this business. "Enough," Walker said.

"Just leave them," Ali said to him.

"I'm a man who lives by his word," Walker replied. "It was your friend Crockett who declared the policy. No live catches."

"Colonel," Ike said, "killing the hadal is one thing. But I've got a human in this bunch. Shoot her down, and that would be murder, wouldn't it?"

Ali thought he was bluffing to buy time, or else talking about her. But he reached among the hadals and grabbed the arm of a creature who had been hiding behind the others. She gave a shriek and bit him, but Ike dragged her out, pinning her arms and hoisting her free. Ali had no chance to see her. The others clutched at her legs, and Ike kicked at them and backed away. "Move," he grunted to Ali. "Run while we can."

The hadals set up a piercing wail. Ali was certain they were about to rush after Ike and whatever it was he'd just kidnapped from them. "Move," shouted Ike, and she ran to the soldiers, who opened a way for her and Ike and his catch. She tripped and fell. Ike stumbled across her.

"In the name of the Father," Walker intoned. "Light 'em up."

The soldiers opened fire on the survivors. The noise was deafening in the small chamber, and Ali closed her ears with both palms. The killing lasted less than twelve seconds. There were a few mop-up shots, then the gunfire was over and the room stank with gas vented from their guns. Ali heard a woman still screaming, and thought they'd wounded one or were torturing her.

"This way." A soldier grabbed her. He was taking care of her. She knew him from his confessions, Calvino, an Italian stallion. His sins had been a pregnant girlfriend, a theft, little more.

"But Ike—"

"The colonel said now," he said, and Ali saw a brawl in progress against the back wall, with Ike near the bottom of the pile. In the corner lay their little massacre. All for nothing, she thought, and let the soldier lead her away, back to the grotto floor, out through the waterfall.

For the next few hours, Ali waited by the mist. Each time a soldier came out, she questioned him about Ike. They avoided her eyes and gave no answer.

At last Walker emerged. Behind him—guarded by mercenaries—came Ike's save.

They had bound the female's arms with rope and taped her mouth shut. Her hands were covered with duct tape, and she had wire wrapped around her neck as a leash. Her legs were shackled with comm-line cable. She'd been cut and was smeared with gore.

For all that, she walked like a queen, as naked as blue sky.

She was not a hadal, Ali realized.

Below the neck, most *Homos* of the last hundred thousand years were virtually the same, Ali knew. She focused on the cranial shape. It was modern and *sapiens*. Except for that, there was little else to pronounce the girl's humanness.

Every eye watched the girl. She didn't care. They could look. They could touch. They could do anything. Every glance, every insult made her more superior to them.

Her tattoos put Ike's to shame. They were blinding, literally. You could barely see her body for the details. The pigment that had been worked into her skin all but obliterated its natural brown color. Her belly was round, and her breasts were fat, and she shook them at one soldier, who pumped his head in and out with a downtown rhythm. There was no indication she spoke English or any other human language.

From head to toe, she had been embellished and engraved and bejeweled and painted. Every toe was circled with a thin iron ring. Her feet were flat from a lifetime of walking barefoot. Ali guessed she was no more than fourteen.

"We have been advised by our scout," Walker said, "that this child may know what lies ahead. We leave. Immediately."

Excluding the loss of Walker's three mercenaries, it seemed they had escaped without consequence from Cache III. They had acquired another six weeks of food and batteries, and had made a hasty uplink with the surface to let Helios know they were still in motion.

There was no sign of pursuit, despite which Ike pushed them thirty hours without a camp. He scared them on. "We're being hunted," he warned.

Several of the scientists who wanted to resign and return the way they'd come, chief among them Gitner, accused Ike of collaborating with Shoat to force them deeper.

Ike shrugged and told them to do whatever they wanted.

No one dared cross that line.

On October 2, a pair of mercenaries bringing up the rear vanished. Their absence was not noticed for twelve hours. Convinced the men had stolen a raft and were making a renegade bid to return home, Walker ordered five soldiers to track and capture them. Ike argued with him. What caused the colonel to reverse his order was not Ike, but a message over the walkie-talkie. The camp stilled, thinking the missing pair might be reporting in.

"Maybe they just got lost," one of the scientists suggested.

Layers of rock garbled the transmission, but it was a British voice coming over the radio. "Someone made a mistake," he told them. "You took my daughter." The wild child made a noise in her throat.

"Who is this?" Walker demanded.

Ali knew. It was Molly's midnight lover.

Ike knew. It was the one who had led him into darkness once upon a time. Isaac had returned.

The radio went silent.

They cast downriver and did not make camp for a week.

Every lion comes from its den,

All the serpents bite;

Darkness hovers, earth is silent,

As their maker rests in lightland.

—"The Great Hymn to Aten," 1350 B.C.

20

DEAD SOULS

SAN FRANCISCO, CALIFORNIA

Headfirst, the hadal drew himself from the honeycomb of cave mouths. He panted feebly, starved, dizzy, rejecting his weakness. Rime coated the perfect round openings of concrete pipes. The fog was so cold.

He could hear the sick and dying in the pyramided tunnels. The illness was as lethal as a sweep of plague or a poisoned stream or the venting of some rare gas through their arterial habitat.

His eyes streamed pus. This air. This awful light. And the emptiness of these voices. The sounds were too far away and yet too close. There was too much space. Your thoughts had no resonance here. You imagined something and the idea vanished into nothingness.

Like a leper, he draped hides over his head. Hunched inside the tattered skin curtains, he felt better, more able to see. The tribe needed him. The other adult males had been killed off. It was up to him. Weapons. Food. Water. Their search for the messiah would have to wait.

Even given the strength to escape, he would not have tried, not while children and women still remained here alive. All together they would live. Or all together they would die. That was the way. It was up to him. Eighteen years old, and he was now their elder.

Who was left? Only one of his wives was still breathing. Three of his children. An image of his infant son rose up—as cold as a pebble. *Aiya*. He made the heartbreak into rage.

The bodies of his people lay where they had pitched or reeled or staggered. Their corruption was strange to see. It had to be something in this thin, strangling air. Or the light itself, like an acid. He had seen many corpses in his day, but none so quickly gone to rot this way. A single day had passed here, and not one could be salvaged for meat.

Every few steps, he rested his hands on his knees to gasp for breath. He was a warrior and hunter. The ground was as flat as a pond top. Yet he could scarcely stand on his feet! What a terrible place this was. He moved on, stepping over a set of bones.

He came to a ghostly white line and lifted his drape of rags, squinting into the fog. The line was too straight to be a game trail. The suggestion of a path raised his spirits. Maybe it led to water.

He followed the line, pausing to rest, not daring to sit down. Sit and he would lie, lie and he would sleep and never wake again. He tried sniffing the currents of air, but it was too fouled with stench and odors to detect animals or water. And you couldn't trust your ears for all the voices. It seemed like a legion of voices pouring down upon him. Not one word made sense. Dead souls, he decided.

At its end, the line hit another line that ran right and left into the fog. Left, he chose, the sacred way. It had to lead somewhere. He came to more lines. He made more turns, some right, some left . . . in violation of the Way.

At each turn he pissed his musk onto the ground. Just the same, he grew lost. How could this be? A labyrinth without walls? He berated himself. If only he had gone left at every turn as he had been taught, he would have inevitably circled to the source, or at least been able to retrace his path by backtracking right at every nexus. But now he had jumbled his directions. And in his weakened condition. And with the tribe's welfare dependent on him alone. It was precisely times like these that the teachings were for.

Still hopeful of finding water or meat or his own scents in the bizarre vegetation, he went on. His head throbbed. Nausea racked him. He tried licking the frost from the spiky vegetation, but the taste of salts and nitrogen overruled his thirst. The ground vibrated with constant movement.

He did everything in his power to focus on the moment, to pace his advance and curtail distracting thoughts. But the luminous white line repeated itself so relentlessly, and the altitude was so severe, that his attention naturally meandered. In that way, he failed to see the broken bottle until it was halfway through the meat of his bare foot.

He cut his shriek before it began. Not a sound came out. They'd schooled him well. He took the pain in. He accepted its presence like a gracious host. Pain could be his friend or it could be his enemy, depending on his self-control.

Glass! He had prayed for a weapon, and here it was. Lowering his foot, he held the slippery bottle in his palms and examined it.

It was an inferior grade, intended for commerce, not warfare. It didn't have the sharpness of black obsidian, which splintered into razor shards, or the durability of glass crafted by hadal artisans. But it would do.

Scarcely believing his good fortune, the young hadal threw back his rag-headdress and willed himself to see in the light. He opened to it, braced by the pain in his foot, marrying to the agony. Somehow he had to return to his tribe while there was still time. With his other senses scrambled by the foulness and tremors and voices in this place, he had to make himself see.

Something happened, something profound. In casting off the rags covering his misshapen head, it was as if he broke the fog. All illusion fell away and he was left with this. On the fifty-yard line of Candlestick Park, the hadal found himself in a dark chalice at the pit of a universe of stars.

The sight was a horror, even for one so brave.

Sky! Stars! The legendary moon!

He grunted, piglike, and twisted in circles. There were his caves in the near distance, and in them his people. There lay the skeletons of his kin. He started across the field, crippled, limping, eyes pinned to the ground, desperate. The vastness all around him sucked at his imagination and it seemed he must tumble upward into that vast cup spread overhead.

It got worse. Floating above his head he saw himself. He was gigantic. He raised his right hand to ward off the colossal image, and the image raised its right hand to ward him off.

In mortal terror, he howled. And the image howled.

Vertigo toppled him.

He writhed upon the cleated grass like a salted leech.

"For the love of Christ," General Sandwell said, turning from the stadium screen. "Now *he's* dying. We're going to end up with no males."

It was three in the morning and the air was rich with sea, even indoors. The creature's howl lingered in the room, piped in over an expensive set of stereo speakers.

Thomas and January and Foley, the industrialist, peered through night-vision binoculars at the sight. They looked like three captains as they stood at the broad plate-glass window of a skybox perched on the rim of Candlestick Park. The poor creature went on flopping about in the center of the arena far below them. De l'Orme politely sat to one side of Vera's wheelchair, gathering what he could from their conversation.

For the last ten minutes they'd been following the hadal's infrared image in the cold fog as he stole along the grid lines, left and right at ninety-degree angles, seduced by the linearity or chasing some primitive instinct or maybe gone mad. And then the fog had lifted and suddenly this. His actions made as little sense magnified on the live-action video screen as in the miniature reality below.

"Is this their normal behavior?" January asked the general.

"No. He's bold. The rest have stuck close to the sewer pipes. This buck's pushed the limit. All the way to the fifty."

"I've never seen one live."

"Look quick. Once the sun hits, he's history." The general was dressed tonight in a pair of pressed corduroys and a multi-blue flannel shirt. His Hush Puppies padded silently on the thick Berber. The Bulova was platinum. Retirement suited him, especially with Helios to land in.

"You say they surrendered to you?"

"First time we've seen anything like it. We had a patrol out at twenty-five hundred feet below the Sandias. Routine. Nothing ever comes up that high anymore. Then out of nowhere this bunch shows up. Several hundred of them."

"You told us there are only a couple dozen here."

"Correct. Like I said, we've never seen a mass surrender before. The troops reacted."

"Overreacted, wouldn't you say?" said Vera.

The general gave her his gallows dimple. "We had fifty-two when they first arrived. Less than twenty-nine at last count yesterday. Probably fewer by now."

"Twenty-five hundred feet?" said January. "But that's practically the surface. Was it an invasion party?"

"Nope. More like a herd movement. Females and young, mostly."

"But what were they doing up here?"

"Not a clue. There's no communicating with them. We've got the linguists and supercomputers working full speed, but it might not even be a real language they speak. For our purposes tonight, it's just glorified gibberish. Emotional signing. Nothing informational. But the patrol leader did say the group was definitely heading for the surface. They were barely armed. It was almost like they were looking for something. Or someone."

The Beowulf scholars paused. Their eyes passed the question around the skybox room. What if this hadal crawling across the frosty grass of Candlestick Park had been embarked on a quest identical to their own, to find Satan? What if this lost tribe really had been searching for its missing leader . . . on the surface?

For the past week they had been discussing a theory, and this seemed to fit. It was Gault and Mustafah's theory, the possibility that their Satanic majesty might actually be a wanderer who had made occasional forays to the surface, exploring human societies over the eons. Images—mostly carved in stone—and oral tradition from peoples around the world gave a remarkably standard portrait of this character. The explorer came and went. He popped up out of nowhere and disappeared just as readily. He could be seductive or violent. He lived by disguise and deception. He was intelligent, resourceful, and restless.

Gault and Mustafah had cobbled the theory together while in Egypt. Ever since, they had carried on a discreet phone campaign to convince their colleagues that the true Satan was unlikely to be found cowering in some dark hole in the subplanet, but was more apt to be studying his enemy from within their very midst. They argued that the historical Satan might spend half his time down below among hadals, and the other half among man. That had raised other questions. Was their Satan, for instance, the same man throughout the ages, undying, an immortal creature? Or might he be a series of explorers, or a lineage of rulers? If he traveled among man, it seemed likely he resembled man. Perhaps, as de l'Orme had proposed, he was the character in the Shroud. If so, what would he look like now? If it was true that Satan lived among man, what disguise would he be wearing? Beggar, thief, or despot? Scholar, soldier, or stockbroker?

Thomas rejected the theory. His skepticism was ironic at times like this. After all, it was he who had launched them on this convoluted whirlwind of counter-intuitions and upside-down explanations. He had enjoined them to go out into the world and locate new evidence, old evidence, all the evidence. We need to know this character, he had said. We need to know how he thinks, what his agenda consists of, his desires and needs, his vulnerabilities and strengths, what cycles he subconsciously follows, what paths he is likely to take. Otherwise we will never have an advantage over him. That's how they had left it, at a standstill, the group scattered.

Foley looked from Thomas to de l'Orme. The gnomelike face was a cipher. It was de l'Orme who had forced this meeting with Helios and dragged every Beowulf member on the continent in with him.

Something was up. He had promised it would affect the outcome of their work, though he refused to say how.

All of this went over Sandwell's head. They did not speak one word of Beowulf's business in front of him. They were still trying to judge how much damage the general had done to them since going over to Helios five months ago.

The skybox was serving as Sandwell's temporary office. The Stick, as he affectionately called it, was in serious makeover. Helios was creating a $500 million biotech research facility in the arena space. BioSphere without the sunshine, he quipped. Scientists from around the country were being recruited. Cracking the mysteries of *H. hadalis* had just entered a new phase. It was being compared to splitting the atom or landing on the moon. The hadal thrashing about on the dying grass and fading hash marks was part of the first batch to be processed.

Here, where Y.A. Tittle and Joe Montana had earned fame and fortune, where the Beatles and Stones had rocked, where the Pope had spoken on the virtues of poverty, taxpayers were funding an advanced concentration camp. Once completed, it was designed to house five hundred SAFs—Subterranean Animal Forms—at a time. At its far end, the playing field was beginning to look like the basement of the Roman Colosseum ruins. The holding pens were in progress. Alleyways wound between titanium cages. Ultimately the old arena surface and all its cages would be covered over with eight floors of laboratory space. There was even a smokeless incinerator, approved by the Environmental Protection Agency, for disposing of remains.

Down on the field, the hadal had begun crawling toward the stack of concrete culverts temporarily housing his comrades. The Stick wouldn't be ready for nonhuman tenants for another year.

"Truly a march of the damned," de l'Orme commented. "In the space of a week, several hundred hadals have become less than two dozen. Shameful."

"Live hadals are as rare as Martians," the general explained. "Getting them to the surface alive and intact—before their gut bacteria curdles or their lung tissues hemorrhage or a hundred other damn things—it's like growing hair on rock."

There had been isolated cases of individual hadals living in captivity on the surface. The record was an Israeli catch: eighty-three days. At their present rate, what was left of this group of fifty wasn't going to last the week.

"I don't see any water. Or food. What are they supposed to be living on?"

"We don't know. That's the whole problem. We filled a galvanized tub with clean water, and they wouldn't touch it. But see that Porta Potti for the construction workers? A few of the hadals broke in the first day and drank the sewage and chemicals. It took 'em hours to quit bucking and shrieking."

"They died, you're saying."

"They'll either adapt or die," the general said. "Around here, we call it seasoning."

"And those other bodies lying by the sidelines?"

"That's what's left of an escape attempt."

From this height the visitors could see the lower stands filled with soldiers and ringed with miniguns trained on the playing field. The soldiers wore bulky oversuits with hoods and oxygen tanks.

On the giant screen, the hadal male cast another glance at the night sky and promptly buried his face in the turf. They watched him clutch at the grass as if holding on to the side of a cliff.

"After our meeting, I want to go closer," said de l'Orme. "I want to hear him. I want to smell him."

"Out of the question," said Sandwell. "It's a health issue. Nobody goes in. We don't want them getting contaminated with human diseases."

The hadal crawled from the forty to the thirty-five. The pyramid of culvert pipes stood near the ten. Farther on, he began navigating between skeletons and rotting bodies.

"Why are the remains lying in the open like that?" Thomas asked. "I should think they constitute a health hazard."

"You want a burial? This isn't a pet cemetery, Father."

Vera turned her head at the tone. Sandwell had definitely crossed over. He belonged to Helios. "It's not a zoo, either, General. Why bring them here if you're just going to watch them fester and die?"

"I told you, old-fashioned R-and-D. We're building a truth machine. Now we'll get the facts on what really makes them tick."

"And what's your part in it?" Thomas asked him. "Why are you here? With them. Helios."

The general bridled. "Operational configuration," he growled.

"Ah," said January, as if she had been told something.

"Yes, I've left the Army. But I'm still manning the line," Sandwell said. "Still taking the fight to the enemy. Only now I'm doing it with real muscle behind me."

"You mean money," said January. "The Helios treasury."

"Whatever it takes to stop Haddie. After all those years of being ruled by globalists and warmed-over pacifists, I'm finally dealing with real patriots."

"Bullshit, General," January said. "You're a hireling. You're simply helping Helios help itself to the subplanet."

Sandwell reddened. "These rumors about a start-up nation underneath the Pacific? That's tabloid talk."

"When Thomas first described it, I thought he was being paranoid," said January. "I thought no one in their right mind would dare rip the map to shreds and glue the pieces together and declare it a country. But it's happening, and you're part of it, General."

"But your map is still intact," a new voice said. They turned. C.C. Cooper was standing in the doorway. "All we've done is lift it and expose the blank tabletop. And drawn a new land where there was no land before. We're making a map within the map. Out of view. You can go on with your affairs as if we never existed. And we can go on with our affairs. We're stepping off your merry-go-round, that's all."

Years ago, *Time* magazine had mythologized C.C. Cooper as a Reaganomic whiz kid, lauding his by-the-bootstraps rise through computer chips and biotech patents and television programming. The article had artfully neglected to mention his manipulation of hard currency and precious resources in the crumbling Soviet Union, or his sleight of hand with hydroelectric turbines for the Three Gorges dam project in China. His sponsorship of environmental and human-rights groups was constantly being shoveled before the public as proof that big money could have a big conscience, too.

In person, the entrepreneurial bangs and wire rims looked strained on a man his age. The former senator had a West Coast vitality that might have played well if he'd become President. At this early hour, it seemed excessive.

Cooper entered, followed by his son. Their resemblance was eerie, except that the son had better hair and wore contacts and had a quarterback's neck muscles. Also, he did not have his father's ease among the enemy. He was being groomed, but you could see that raw power did not come naturally to him. That he had been included in this morning's meeting—and that the meeting had been offered in the deep of night, while the city slept—said much to Vera and the others. It meant Cooper considered them dangerous, and that his son was now supposed to learn about dispatching one's opponents away from public view.

Behind the two Cooper men came a tall, attractive woman in her late forties, hair bobbed and jet black. She had invited herself along, that was clear. "Eva Shoat," Cooper said to the group. "My wife. And this is my son, Hamilton. Cooper." As distinct from Montgomery, Vera realized. The stepson, Shoat.

Cooper led his entourage to the table and joined the Beowulf scholars and Sandwell. He didn't ask their names. He didn't apologize for being late.

"Your country-in-progress is a renegade," said Foley. "No nation steps out of the international polity."

"Says who?" Cooper asked agreeably. "Forgive my pun. But the international polity may go to the devil. I'm going to hell."

"Do you realize the chaos this will bring?" January asked. "Your control of ocean shipping lanes alone. Your ability to operate without any oversight. To violate international standards. To penetrate national borders."

"But consider the order I'll bring by occupying the underworld. In one fell swoop, I return mankind to its innocence. This abyss beneath our feet will no longer be terrifying and unknown. It will no longer be dominated by creatures like *that*." He pointed at the stadium video. The hadal was lapping its own vomit from the turf. Eva Shoat shuddered.

"Once our colonial strategy begins, we can quit fearing the monsters. No more superstitions. No more midnight fears. Our children and their children will think of the underworld as just another piece of real estate. They'll take holidays to the natural wonders beneath our feet. They'll enjoy the fruits of our inventions. They'll own the untapped energy of the planet itself. They'll be free to work on utopia."

"That's not the abyss man fears," Vera protested. "It's the one in here." She touched the ribs above her heart.

"The abyss is the abyss," said Cooper. "Light one and you light the other. We'll all be better for this, you'll see."

"Propaganda." Vera turned her head in distaste.

"Your expedition," Thomas said. He was angry tonight. "Where have they gone?"

"I'm afraid the news isn't good," said Cooper. "We've lost contact with the expedition. You can imagine our concern. Ham, do you have our map?"

Cooper's son opened his briefcase and produced a folded bathymetric map showing the ocean floor. It was creased and marked with a dozen different pens and grease pencils. Cooper traced his finger helpfully across the latitudes and longitudes. "Their last known position was west-southwest of Tarawa, in the Gilbert Islands. That could change, of course. Every now and then we harvest dispatches from the bedrock."

"You're still hearing from them?" asked January.

"In a sense. For over three weeks now, the dispatches have been nothing but bits and pieces of older communications sent months ago. The
transmissions get mangled by the layers of stone. We end up with
echoes. Electromagnetic riddles. It only suggests where they were weeks
ago. Where they are today, who can say?"

"That's all you can tell us?" asked January.

"We'll find them." Eva Shoat suddenly spoke up. She was fierce. Her
eyes were bloodshot from crying. Cooper cut a glance at her.

"You must be worried sick," Vera sympathized. "Montgomery is your
only child?" Cooper narrowed his eyes at Vera. She nodded to him. Her
question had been phrased deliberately.

"Yes," said Eva, then looked at her husband's son. "I mean no. I'm
worried. I'd be worried if it were Hamilton down there. I should never
have allowed Monty to go."

"He chose it himself," Cooper tautly observed.

"Only because he was desperate," Eva snapped back. "How else could
he compete in this family?"

Vera saw Thomas across the table, rewarding her with the slightest
hint of a smile. She had done well.

"He wanted to be part of things," Cooper said.

"Yes, part of this," Eva said, throwing her hand at the skybox view.

"And I've told you, Eva, he *is* a part of it. You have no idea how important his contribution will be."

"My son had to risk his life to be important to you?"

Cooper disengaged. It was an old argument, obviously.

"What precisely is this, Mr. Cooper?" Foley asked.

"I told you," said Sandwell. "A research facility."

"Yes," said January, "a place to *season* your hadal captives. By the
way, General, are you aware the term was once used about African
slaves arriving in this country?"

"You'll have to excuse Sandy," Cooper said. "He's a recent acquisition,
still adapting to the language and life on campus. I assure you, we're not
creating a population of slaves."

Sandwell bristled, but kept silent.

"Then what do you need live hadals for? What is it you're researching?" Vera asked.

Cooper steepled his fingers gravely. "We're finally starting to collect
longer-term data on the colonization," he said. "Soldiers were the first
group to go down in any numbers. Six years later, they're the first to
show real side effects. Alterations."

"The bony growths and cataracts?" said Vera. "But we've seen those since the beginning. The problems go away with time."

"This is different. In the last four to ten months we've been monitoring an outbreak of symptoms. Enlarged hearts, high-altitude edemas, skeletal dysplasia, acute leukemia, sterility, skin cancer. The horning and bone cancers have come charging back. The most disturbing development is that we're starting to see these symptoms among the veterans' newborns. For five years we've had nothing but normal births. Now, suddenly, their newborns are displaying morbid defects. I'm talking about mutations. The infant mortality rate has soared."

"Why haven't I heard of this?" January asked suspiciously.

"For the same reason Helios is rushing to find a cure. Because once the public finds out, every human inside the planet is going to evacuate. The interior is going to be left without security forces, without a labor force, without colonists. You can imagine the setback. After so much effort and investment, we could lose the whole subplanet to whatever this is. Helios doesn't want that to happen."

"What's going on?"

"In twenty-five words or less? The subplanet is changing us." Cooper gestured at the creature on the stadium screen. "Into *that*."

Eva Shoat laid a hand upon her long throat. "You knew this, and you let my son go down?"

"The effects aren't universal," said Cooper. "In the veteran populations, the split is roughly fifty-fifty. Half show no effect. Half display these delayed mutations. Hadal physiologies. Enlarged hearts, pulmonary and cerebral edema, skin cancer: those are all symptoms that hadals develop when they come to the surface. Something is switching on and off at the DNA level. Altering the genetic code. Their bodies begin producing proteins, chimeric proteins, which alter tissues in radically different ways."

"You can't predict which half of the population will develop the problems?" asked Vera.

"We don't have a clue. But if it's happening to six-year veterans, it's eventually going to happen to four-month miners and settlers."

"And Helios has to find a solution," observed Foley. "Or else your empire beneath the sea will be a ghost town before it ever starts."

"In vulgar terms, precisely."

"Obviously, you think there's a solution in the hadal physiology itself," Vera said.

Cooper nodded. "Genetic engineers call it 'cutting the Gordian knot.'

We have to resolve the complexities. Sort out the viruses and retro-viruses, the genes and phenotypes. Examine the environmental factors. Map the chaos. And so Helios is building a multibillion-dollar research campus here, and importing live hadals for research purposes. To make the subplanet safe for humans."

"But I don't understand," said Vera. "It seems to me research and development would be a thousand times less complicated down below. Among other things, why stress your guinea pigs by transporting them to the surface? You could build this same facility at a subterranean station for a fraction of the cost. You'll need to pressurize the entire laboratory to subplanetary levels. Why not just study the hadals down there? There would be no transportation costs. The mortality rate would be far lower. And you could test your results on colonists in the field."

"That's not an option," de l'Orme said. "Or it won't be soon."

They all turned to him.

"Unless he brings up a sample population of hadals, there won't be any hadals to sample soon. Isn't that the idea, Mr. Cooper?"

"No idea what you're talking about," Cooper said.

"Perhaps you could tell us about the contagion," de l'Orme said. "Prion-9."

Cooper appraised the little archaeologist. "I know what you know. We've learned that prion capsules are being planted along the expedition's route. But Helios has nothing to do with it. I won't ask you to believe me. I don't care if you do or not. It's my people who are at risk down there. My expedition. Except for your spy," he added, "the von Schade woman."

January's expression hardened.

"What's this about a contagion?" Eva demanded.

"I didn't want to worry you any more," Cooper said to his wife. "A deranged ex-soldier has attached himself to the expedition. He's lacing the route with a synthetic virus."

"My God," his wife whispered.

"Despicable," hissed de l'Orme.

"What was that?" Cooper said.

De l'Orme smiled. "The individual planting this contagion is named Shoat. Your son, madam."

"My son?"

"He's being used to deliver a synthetic plague. And your husband sent him."

The assembly gawked at the archaeologist. Even Thomas was dismayed.

"Absurd," Cooper blustered.

De l'Orme pointed in the direction of Cooper's son. "He told me."

"I've never seen you in my life," Hamilton replied.

"True as it goes, no more than I've seen you." De l'Orme grinned. "But you told me."

"Lunatic," Hamilton said under his breath.

"Ach," chided de l'Orme. "We've talked about that sharp tongue before. No more humiliating the wife at cocktail parties. And no more fists with her. We agreed. You were to work on *governing* your anger, yes? *Containing your tide.*"

The young man drained gray beneath his Aspen tan.

De l'Orme addressed them all. "Over the years, I've noticed that the birth of a son sometimes tempers a wild young man. It can even mark his return to the faith. So when I heard of the baptism of Hamilton's son, your grandson, Mr. Cooper, I had an idea. Sure enough, it seems fatherhood changed our spoiled young sinner. He has thrown himself onto the Rock with that special fervor of a lost man found. For over a year now, Hamilton's kept away from his heroin chic and his expensive call girls and he has cleansed himself weekly."

"What are you talking about?" Cooper demanded.

"Young Cooper has developed a taste for the holy wafer," said de l'Orme. "And you know the rules. No Eucharist before confession."

Cooper turned to his son with horror. "You spoke to the Church?"

Hamilton looked afflicted. "I was speaking to God."

De l'Orme tipped his head with mock acknowledgment.

"But what about the confidence between penitent and confessor?" marveled Vera.

"I left the cloth long ago," de l'Orme explained. "But I kept my friendships and personal connections. It was simply a matter of anticipating this venal man's *mea culpa*, and then installing myself in a small booth on certain occasions. Oh, we've talked for hours, Hamilton and I. I've learned much about the House of Cooper. Much."

The elder Cooper sat back. He stared out the skybox window into the night, or at his own image in the glass.

De l'Orme continued. "The Helios strategy is this: for disease to rage through the interior in one vast hurricane of death. The corporate entity can then occupy a world conveniently sterilized of all its nasty lifeforms. Including hadals. That's why Helios is preserving a population up here. Because they're about to kill everything that breathes down below."

"But why?" Thomas asked.

De l'Orme gave the answer. "History," he said. "Mr. Cooper has read his history. Conquest is always the same. It's much easier to occupy an empty paradise."

Cooper gave a sulfurous glance at his foolish son.

De l'Orme continued. "Helios obtained the Prion-9 from a laboratory under contract to the Army. Who obtained it for Helios is blatantly obvious. General Sandwell, it was also you who recruited the soldier Dwight Crockett. That's how Montgomery Shoat could be immunized under a scapegoat's name."

"Monty's been immunized?" his mother said.

"Your son is safe," said de l'Orme. "At least from the disease."

"Who controls the release of the contagion?" Vera asked Cooper. "You?"

Cooper snorted.

"Montgomery Shoat," guessed Thomas. "But how? Are the capsules programmed to release automatically? Is there a remote control? A code? How does it happen?"

"You mean how can you stop it?"

"For God's sake, tell them," Eva said to her husband.

"It can't be stopped," Cooper said. "That's the whole truth. Montgomery coded the trigger device himself. He's the only one who knows what the electronic sequence is. It's a mutual safeguard. This way his mission can't be compromised by anyone. Not you," he said to Thomas, then added bitterly, "and not an indiscreet son. And we, in our haste, can't trigger the virus before he determines the time is ripe."

"Then we have to find him," said Vera. "Give us your map. Show us where the cylinders have been placed."

"This?" Cooper slapped at the map. "It's merely a projection. Only the people on the expedition know where they've been. Even if you could find him, I doubt Montgomery remembers where he placed the capsules along a ten-thousand-mile path."

"How many are there?"

"Several hundred. We mean to be thorough."

"And trigger devices?"

"Just the one."

Thomas studied Cooper's face.

"What is your calendar for genocide? When does Shoat mean to start the plague?"

"I told you. When he decides the time is ripe. Naturally, he'll need the expedition's services for as long as possible. They provide him transportation, food, company, protection. He's not suicidal. He's not a kamikaze. He insisted on being vaccinated. He has a strong sense of survival. And ambition. I'm sure, when the time comes, he won't hesitate to finish the job."

"Even if it means killing off the expedition. *Your* people. And every human colonist and miner and soldier down there."

Cooper did not answer.

"What have you made our son into?" Eva said.

Cooper looked at her. "*Your* son," he said.

"Monster," she whispered back.

Just then, Vera said, "Look."

She was staring at the video screen. The hadal had reached the piled sewer pipes. He was pulling himself upright before the dark, round openings. The video screen showed him forty feet tall. His bare rib cage, scored with old wounds and ritual markings, bucked in quick, pumping waves. The creature was vocalizing, that much was evident.

Sandwell went over and rotated the round button on the wall. The audio feed came over the speakers. It sounded like the hooting and huffing of a captured ape.

A face had appeared at the mouth of one sewer pipe. Then other faces surfaced at other openings. Crusted and wet with their own filth, they came out from their cement burrows and fell upon the ground at the hadal's feet. There were only nine or ten of them left.

The hadal's voice changed. He was singing now, or praying. Beseeching or offering. To his own image, of all things. To the video screen. The others, women and their young, began to ululate.

"What's he doing?"

Still singing, the hadal took a child from one of the females and cradled it in his arms. He made a sacramental motion, as if tracing ashes on its head or throat, it was hard to see. Then he set the child aside and took another that was held up to him and repeated his gesture. "He's cutting their throats," January realized.

"What!"

"Is that a knife?"

"Glass," said Foley.

"Where did he get glass?" Cooper roared at the general.

An emaciated female stood before the butcher hadal. She cast her head back and opened her arms wide and it took her killer a minute to find the artery and saw her throat open. A second female stood.

Voice by voice, their song was dying.

"Stop him," Cooper shouted at Sandwell. "The bastard's killing off my pack."

But it was too late.

Love is duty. He took in the crook of his arm his own son, as cold as a pebble. He cried out the name of the messiah. Weeping, he made the cut and held his final child while it bled down his breast. At last he was free to join his own blood with theirs.

BOOK THREE

GRACE

Inter Babiloniam et
Jerusalem nulla pax est sed
guerra continua. . . .
Between Babylon and
Jerusalem there is no peace,
but continual war. . . .

—ST. BERNARD, *The Sermons*

21

MAROONED

THE SEA, 6,000 FATHOMS

No one had ever dreamed such a place.

The geologists had spoken about ancient paleo-oceans buried beneath
the continents, but only as hypothetical explanations for the earth's
wandering poles and gravity anomalies. The paleo-oceans were mathe-
matical fancies. This was real.

Abruptly—on October 22—it was there, motionless, calm. Men and
women who had been racing downriver for their lives stopped. They
climbed from their rafts and joined comrades standing agape upon the
pewter-colored sand. The water spread before them, an enormous flat
crescent. The slightest of waves licked at the shore. The surface was
smooth. Their lights skimmed from it.

They had no idea the shape or size of the water body. They sent their
laser beams pulsing upward, searching for a ceiling that finally measured a half-mile overhead. As for the length of the sea, the surface bent.
All they could say with certainty was that the horizon lay twenty miles
distant, with no obstructions in between and no end in sight.

The path split right and left around the sea. No one knew which

led where. "There's Walker's footprints," someone said, and they followed them.

Farther down the beach, they found their fourth cache. Side by side,
the three cylinders lay as neat as merchandise. Walker's men had
reached the site hours earlier and stockpiled the contents within a
makeshift firebase. Sand had been heaped into a circular berm with
entrenching shovels. Machine guns were trained on fields of fire.

The scientists approached on foot. One of the mercenaries came out
and put a hand up. "That's close enough," he said.

"But it's us," a woman said.

Walker appeared. "The depot is off limits," he informed them.

"You can't do that," someone shouted.

"We're in a state of high alert," Walker said. "Our highest priority is
the protection of food and supplies. If we were attacked and you were
inside our perimeter, there would be chaos. This is the wisest course.
We've located a campsite for you on the opposite side of that rock fall
over there. The quartermaster has issued your rations and mail."

"I need to see the girl," Ali said.

"Off limits, I'm afraid," Walker said. "She's been classified a military
asset."

The way he said it was odd, even for Walker. "Who's classified her?"
Ali asked.

"Classified." Walker blinked. "She has valuable information about the
terrain."

"But she speaks hadal dialect."

"I plan to teach her English."

"That will take too long. We can help, Ike and me. I've assembled glos-
saries before." This was her chance to dig into the raw language.

"Thank you for your enthusiasm, Sister."

Walker pointed at twenty bubble-wrapped bottles lying in the sand.
"Helios sent whiskey. Drink it or pour it out. Either way, it stays here.
We're not taking liquid weight with us."

Only afterward would the scientists realize the whiskey was part of
Walker's plan. That night they sulked and drank. Their estrangement
from the mercenaries had been building for months. The massacre had
made the divide even wider. Now they were two camps. The bottles
passed freely.

"We're ninety-eight-pound weaklings down here," someone complained.

"How much more can we take?" a woman asked.

"By God, I'm ready to go home," Gitner announced.

Ali saw the mood and decided to stay clear of it. The group was pungent with fear and grief and confusion. She went looking for Ike to share thoughts, only to find him propped among the rocks with his own bottle. Walker had turned him loose, though without his guns. She was mildly disappointed in Ike. Stripped of his weapons, he seemed impotent, more dependent on his ability to commit mayhem than was right. "What are you drinking for?" she demanded. "Tonight of all nights."

"What's wrong with tonight?" he said.

"We're coming apart. Look around."

In the distance, Walker's militia had set up strobe lights to defend their walls. In the foreground, in staccato silhouette, drunken dancers were doing dance moves and shedding their clothes. But there was no music. You could hear arguing and despair and lovers grinding each other into the hard sand. It sounded like August in a ghetto.

"We were too big to start with," Ike commented.

Ali stared at him. "You're not concerned?"

He tipped the bottle, wiped his mouth. "Sometimes you just have to go with it," he said.

"Don't give up on us, Ike."

He looked away.

Ali wandered to an isolated spot midway between the two camps and went to sleep.

In the middle of the night, she was awakened by a hand clamped across her mouth.

"Sister," a man whispered.

She felt a heavy bundle thrust into her hands.

"Hide it."

He left before Ali could say a word.

Ali laid the bundle beside her and unfolded it. She felt through the contents with her hands: a rifle and pistol, three knives, a sawed-off shotgun that could only belong to Ike, and boxes of ammunition. Forbidden fruit. Her visitor could only have been a soldier, and she felt certain it was one of the burned ones Ike had brought to safety. But why the guns?

Fearful that Walker was putting her through some kind of test, Ali almost returned the bundle of weapons to the fire base. She went to ask Ike's opinion, but he had passed out. Finally she buried the shadowy inheritance beneath a cliff wall.

Early in the morning, Ali woke to a phosphorescent sea fog blanketing the beach. In the quiet, she felt, rather than heard, footsteps padding through the sand. She stood and made out figures stealing through the fog, specters hauling treasure. As one came close, she saw it was a soldier, who gestured for her to be quiet and sit down. She knew him slightly, and for him had copied a short verse from Saint Teresa of Avila, her favorite mystic. This morning he didn't meet her eyes.

She sat down and stayed mute as the last of them filed past. They were headed toward the water, but even then she didn't guess. It was only after a few minutes, when no one else appeared, that she got up and walked to the shoreline and saw their lights dwindling smoothly across the still black sea.

She thought Walker must have sent out a dawn reconnaissance of some kind. But there were no rafts left on the sand. Ali walked back and forth, looking for their boats, sure she had misplaced their location. The pontoon tracks were clear, though. The rafts had all been taken.

"Wait," she called after the lights. "Hello."

It was an absurd mistake. They had forgotten her.

But if it was a mistake, why had that soldier motioned her to sit down again? It was part of a plan, she realized. They had meant to leave her.

The shock emptied her.

She'd been left.

Marooned.

Ali's sense of loss was immediate and overpowering, similar to that time, long ago, when a sheriff's deputy had come to her house to break the news of her parents' accident.

The sound of coughing reached through the fog, and the full truth came to her. She had not been abandoned alone. Walker had forsaken everyone not under his immediate command.

Tripping in the sand, she rushed across the beach and found the scientists scattered where their debauch had dropped them, still asleep. They woke reluctantly, and refused to believe her. Five minutes later, as they stood on the edge of the sea, where their rafts had been lying, the awful fact seeped in.

"What's the meaning of this?" roared Gitner.

"They've stranded us? Where's Shoat? He'd better have an explanation."

But Shoat was gone, too. And the feral girl.

"This can't be happening."

Ali watched their reactions as extensions of herself. She felt numb. Enraged. Paralyzed. Like her friends and comrades, she wanted to shout and kick at the sand and fall on her back. The treachery was beyond belief.

"Why have they done this?" someone cried.

"They must have left a note. An explanation."

"Listen to you," Gitner jeered. "You sound like teenagers who just got jilted. This is business, people. A race for survival. Walker just jettisoned a bunch of empty stomachs. I'm surprised he didn't do it sooner."

Ike came over from the cache site with a piece of paper in one hand, and Ali saw a row of numbers on it. "Walker left a portion of the food and medicine. But the communications line is destroyed. And they took all their weapons."

"They've left us here like a speed bump," someone cried. "A sacrificial offering to the hadals."

Ali grabbed Ike's arm, and her expression made them pause. Suddenly her visitor in the middle of the night made sense. "Do you believe in karma?" she asked Ike, and they followed her to the buried blanket of guns and knives. It took less than a minute to dig it out. Then it took an hour to argue about who got which of the weapons.

"I don't get it," Gitner said. "Ike saves the guy. But then he gives the hardware to a nun?"

"It's not obvious?" said Pia. "Ike's nun." They all looked at Ali.

Ike detoured it. "Now we have our chance." He finished loading his sawed-off.

In the depot they picked through the boxes and cans. Walker had left more than expected, but less than they needed. Further, his men had plundered care packages sent down to the scientists by anxious families and friends. The interior of the sand fort was littered with little gifts and cards and snapshots. It added insult to the crime, and put the scientists into greater despair.

The scientists numbered forty-six. A careful accounting showed they had food for 1,124 man-days, or twenty-nine days at full rations. That could be stretched, it was agreed. By halving their daily intake, the food would last two months.

Their exploration was dead. All that remained was a race for survival. The expedition faced two choices. They could try to return to Z-3—Esperanza—on foot. Or they could continue in search of the next cache, more supplies, and an exit from the subplanet.

Gitner was adamant: Esperanza was their only hope. "That way, at least we're not dealing with a complete unknown," he said. With two months' rations, they would have time enough to reach what was left of Cache III, splice the comm line together, and call in more supplies. He called anyone who did not agree a fool. "We don't have a minute to waste," he kept saying.

"What do you think?" they asked Ike.

"It's a crapshoot," he said.

"But which way should we go?"

Ali could tell that Ike had made up his mind. But he wanted no responsibility for their decisions, and grew quiet.

"There's nothing but hole to the west," Gitner declared. "Anyone that wants to go east, go with me."

Ali was surprised when Ike turned crafty and bartered with Gitner over the weapons. He finally let go of the rifle and its ammunition and the radio and a knife for an extra fifty days' rations of MREs. "If you don't mind," he said, "we'll just take a stab around this water."

Now that he had the majority of the weapons, food, and followers, Gitner didn't mind at all. "You're off your nut," Gitner told Ike. "What about the rest of you?"

"New territory," said Troy, the young forensics expert.

"Ike's done okay so far," said Pia.

Ali didn't defend her choice.

"Then we'll remember you," Gitner said.

He quickly wrangled his crew together and got them packed for their journey, prodding them with the possibility that Walker might decide to reclaim what was left. There was little time for the two groups to say good-bye. People from each coalition were shaking hands, bidding one another to break a leg, promising to send rescue if they got out first.

Just before leaving, Gitner approached Ali with his new rifle. "I think it's only fair that you give us your maps," he said. "You don't need them. We do."

"My day maps?" Ali said. They were hers. She had created them with all the art in her, and saw them as an extension of herself.

"We need to remember all the landmarks possible."

It was the first time Ali actively wished Ike would stand up for her, but he didn't. With everyone watching, she gave the tube of maps to Gitner. "Promise to take care of them," she asked. "I'd like them back someday."

"Sure." Gitner offered no thanks, just hitched the tube into his back-pack and started up the trail beside the river. His people followed.

Besides Ali and Ike, only seven people stayed behind.

"Which way do we go?"

"Left," said Ike. He was so sure.

"But Walker went right with the boats, I saw him," Ali said.

"That could work," Ike allowed. "But it's backward."

"Backward?"

"Can't you feel it?" Ike asked. "This is a sacred space. You always walk to the left around sacred places. Mountains. Temples. Lakes. That's just how it's done. Clockwise."

"Isn't that some Buddhist thing?" said Pia.

"Dante," said Ike. "Ever read the *Inferno*? Each time they hit a fork, the party goes left. Always left. And he was no Buddhist."

"That's it?" marveled a burly geologist. "All these months we've been following a poem and your superstitions?"

Ike grinned. "You didn't know that?"

The first fifteen days they marched shoeless, like beachcombers. The sand was cool between their toes. They sweated under heavy packs. At night their thighs ached. Drifting on rafts had taken its toll.

Ike kept them in motion, but slowly, the pace of nomads. "No sense in racing," he said. "We're doing fine."

They learned the water. Ali dipped her headlamp underneath the surface, and she may as well have tried shining her light from the back of a mirror. She cupped the water in her palms and it was like holding time. The water was ancient.

"This water—it's been living here for over a half-million years," the hydrologist Chelsea told her. It had a scent like the deep earth.

Ike stirred the sea with his hand and let a few drops onto his tongue. "Different," he pronounced. After that, he drank from the sea without hesitation. He let the others make up their own minds, and knew they were watching closely to see if he sickened or his urine bled. Twiggs, the microbotanist, was especially attentive.

By the end of the second day, all were drinking the water without purifying it.

"It's delicious," said Ali. Voluptuous, she meant, but did not want to say it out loud. It was somehow different from plain water, the way it slid on the tongue, its cleanness. She scooped a handful to her face and pulled it across the bones of her cheeks, and the sense of it lingered. It was all in her head, she decided. It had to do with this place.

One day they saw small sulfurous flashes along the black horizon. Ike said it was gunfire, maybe as much as a hundred miles away, on the opposite side of the sea. Walker was either making trouble or having it.

The water was their north. For nearly six months they had advanced with no foresight, trusting no compass, trapped in blind veins. Now they had the sea. For once they could anticipate their geography. They could see tomorrow, and the day after that. It was not a straight destiny, there were bends and arcs, but for a change they could see as far as their vision reached, a welcome alternative to the maze of claustrophobic tunnels.

Although everyone was hungry, they were not famished, and the water was always there to comfort them. Two and three and four times a day, they would bathe away their sweat. They tied strings to their plastic cups and could scoop up a drink without bending or breaking stride. Ali's hair had grown long. She loosed it from its braid and let it hang, lush and clean.

They were pleased with Ike's regime. He did not drive them. If anyone tired, Ike took some of their load. Once when Ike went off to investigate a side canyon, some of them tried lifting his pack, and couldn't budge it. "What does he have in there?" Chelsea asked. No one dared look, of course. That would have been like tampering with good luck.

When they turned their last light off at night, the beach gleamed with Early Cretaceous phosphorescence. Ali watched for hours as the sand pulsed against the inky sea, holding back the darkness. She had taken to lying on her back and imagining stars and saying prayers. Anything not to sleep.

Ever since Walker had overseen the massacre, sleep meant terrible dreams. Eyeless women pursued her. In the name of the Father.

One night Ike woke her from a nightmare. "Ali?" he said.

Sand was sticking to her sweat. She was panting. She clung to his hand. "I'm okay," she gasped.

"It's not quite that easy," Ike breathed, "with you."

Stay, she almost said. But then what? What was she supposed to do with him now?

"Sleep," said Ike. "You let things get to you too much."

Another week passed. They were slowing. Their stomachs rumbled at night.

"How much longer?" they asked Ike.

"We're doing fine," he heartened them.

"We're so hungry."

Ike looked at them, judging. "Not that hungry," he said mildly, and it was cryptic. How hungry did they have to be? wondered Ali. And what was his relief?

"Where can Cache V be? We must be near."

"What's the date?" said Ike. He knew they knew the next cylinders were not scheduled to be lowered for another six days. That didn't keep them from trolling hopefully for the cache signals. All of them had tiny cache locators built into their Helios wristwatches. First Pia, then Chelsea, used up their watch batteries trying to get some signal. It was magical thinking. No one wanted to talk about what would happen if Walker and his pirates reached the cache before them.

The six days passed, and still they didn't find the cache. They were covering only a few miles a day. Ike took on more and more of their weight. Ali found herself struggling with barely fifteen pounds on her back.

Ike recommended they ration themselves. "Share one packet of MREs with two or three people," he suggested. "Or eat just one over a two-day period." He never took away their food and rationed it for them, though.

They never saw him eat.

"What's he living on?" Chelsea asked Ali.

For twenty-three days Gitner led his castaways with eroding success. It seemed impossible, but in their second week they had somehow misplaced the river. One day it was there. The next it was just gone.

Gitner blamed Ali's day maps. He pulled the rolls of parchment from her leather tube and threw them on the ground. "Good riddance," he said. "Nothing but science fiction."

With the river gone, they had no more use for their water gear. They abandoned their survival suits in a rubbery pile of neoprene.

By the end of the third week, people were falling behind, disappearing.

A salt arch they were using as a bridge collapsed, plunging five into the void. Unbelievably, both of the expedition's two physicians suffered compound fractures of their legs. It was Gitner's call to leave them. Physician, heal thyself. It was two days before their echoing pleas faded in the tunnels behind.

As their numbers dwindled, Gitner relied on three advantages: his rifle, his pistol, and the expedition's supply of amphetamines. Sleep was the enemy. He still believed they would find Cache III, and that the comm lines could be repaired. Food ran low. Two murders soon followed. In both cases, a chunk of rock had been used and the victims' packs had been plundered.

At a fork in the tunnel, Gitner overrode the group's vote. Without a clue, he led them straight into a tunnel formation known as a spongework maze, or boneyard. At first they thought little of it. The porous maze was filled with pockets and linked cavities and stone bubbles that spread in every direction, forward and down and up and to the rear. It was like climbing through a massive, petrified sponge.

"Now we're getting somewhere," Gitner enthused. "Obviously some gaseous dissolution ate upward from the interior. We can gain some elevation in a hurry now."

They roped up, those still left, and started moving vertically through the pores and oviducts. But they tangled their ropes by following through the wrong hole. Friction braked their progress. Holes tightened, then gaped. Packs had to be handed up and through and across the interstices. It was time-consuming.

"We have to go back," someone growled up to Gitner. He unroped so they could not pull on him, and kept climbing. The others unroped, too, and some became lost, to which Gitner said, "Now we're reaching fighting weight." They could hear voices at night as the lost ones tried to locate the group. Gitner just popped more speed and kept his light on.

Finally, Gitner was left with only one man. "You screwed up, boss," he rasped to Gitner.

Gitner shot him through the top of the head. He listened to the body slither and knock deeper and deeper, then turned and continued up, certain the spongework would lead him out of the underworld into the sun again. Somewhere along the way, he hung his rifle on an outcrop. A little farther on, he left his pistol.

At 0440 on November 15, the spongework stopped. Gitner reached a ceiling.

He pulled his pack around in front of him, and carefully assembled the radio. The battery level was near the red, but he figured it was good for one loud shout. With enormous exactitude he attached the transmission tendrils to various features in the spongework, then sat on a marble strut and cleared his thoughts and throat. He switched the radio on.

"Mayday, mayday," he said, and a vague sense of déjà vu tickled at the back of his mind. "This is Professor Wayne Gitner of the University of Pennsylvania, a member of the Helios Sub-Pacific Expedition. My party is dead. I am now alone and require assistance. I repeat, please assist."

The battery died. He laid the set aside and took up his hammer and began clawing away at the ceiling. A memory that wouldn't quite take shape kept nagging at him. He just hit harder.

In mid-swing, he stopped and lowered the hammer. Six months earlier, he had listened to his own voice enunciating the very distress signal he had just sent. He had circled to his own beginning.

For some, that might have meant a fresh start.

For a man like Gitner, it meant the end.

I sit leaning against the cliff while the years go by, till the green grass grows between my feet and the red dust settles on my head, and the men of the world, thinking me dead, come with offerings . . . to lay by my corpse.

—HAN SHAN, *Cold Mountain*, c. 640 C.E.

22
BAD WIND

THE DOLOMITE ALPS

The scholars had been building toward this day since their first night together. For seventeen months, their journeys—Thomas's *capriccios*—had cast them across the globe like a throw of dice. At last they stood together again, or sat, for de l'Orme's castle perched high atop a limestone precipice, and it took very little exertion to get out of breath.

For once, Mustafah's emphysema gave him the advantage: he had an oxygen set, and could merely crank the airflow higher. Foley and Vera were sharing an Italian aspirin powder for their headaches. Parsifal, the astronaut, was making a bluff show of his athletic nature, but looked a bit green, especially as de l'Orme took them on a tour of the curving battlements overlooking the stepped crags and far plains.

"Don't like neighbors?" Gault asked. His Parkinson's had stabilized. Couched in a large wheelchair, he looked like a Pinocchio manipulated by naughty children.

"Isn't it wonderful?" said de l'Orme. "Every morning I wake and thank God for paranoia." He had already explained the castle's origins: a German Crusader had gone mad outside the walls of Jerusalem, and was exiled atop these rocks.

It was rather small for a castle. Built in a perfect circle on the very edge of the cliff, it almost resembled a lighthouse. They finished their tour. January was sitting where they'd left her, depleted by malaria, facing south to the sun with Thomas. Down below, lining the dead-end road, were their hired cars. Their drivers and several nurses were enjoying a picnic among the early flowers.

"Let's go inside," said de l'Orme. "At these heights, the sun feels very warm. But the slightest cloud can send the temperature plunging. And there's a storm coming."

Thick logs blazing on the iron grate barely took away the room's chill. The dining hall was stark, walls bare, not even a tapestry or a boar's head. De l'Orme had no need for decorations.

They sat around a table, and a servant came in with bowls of thick, hot soup. There were no forks, just spoons for the soup and knives to cut the fruit and cheese and prosciutto. The servant poured wine and then retreated, closing the doors behind him.

De l'Orme proposed a toast to their generous hearts and even more generous appetites. He was the host, but it was not really his party. Thomas had called this meeting, though no one knew why. Thomas had been brooding ever since arriving. They got on with the meal.

The food revived them. For an hour they enjoyed the company of their comrades. Most had been strangers at the outset, and their paths had intersected only rarely since Thomas had scattered them to the winds in New York City. But they had come to share a common purpose so strongly that they might as well have been brothers and sisters. They were excited by one another's tales, glad for one another's safety.

January recounted her last hour with Desmond Lynch in the Phnom Penh airport. He had been heading to Rangoon, then south, in search of a Karen warlord who claimed to have met with Satan. Since then, no one had heard a word from him.

They waited for Thomas to add his own impressions, but he was distracted and melancholy. He had arrived late, bearing a square box, all but unapproachable.

"And where is Santos?" Mustafah asked de l'Orme. "I'm beginning to think he doesn't like us."

"Off to Johannesburg," de l'Orme said. "It seems another band of hadals has surrendered. To a group of unarmed diamond miners!"

"That's the third this month," said Parsifal. "One in the Urals. Another beneath the Yucatán."

"Meek as lambs," said de l'Orme, "chanting in unison. Like pilgrims entering Jerusalem."

"What a notion."

"You'd think it would be much safer to go deeper. Away from us. It's almost as if they were afraid of the depths beneath them. As afraid as we are of the depths beneath us."

"Let's begin," said Thomas.

They had been waiting a long time to synthesize their information. At last it began, knives in hand, grapes flying. It started cautiously, with a show-me-yours-and-I'll-show-you-mine prudence. In no time, the exchange turned into a highly democratic free-for-all. They psychoanalyzed Satan with the vigor of freshmen. The clues led off in a dozen directions. They knew better, but could not help egging on the wild theories with wilder theories of their own.

"I'm so relieved," Mustafah admitted. "I thought I was the only one coming to these extraordinary conclusions."

"We should stick to what we know," Foley prudishly reminded them.

"Okay," said Vera. And it only got wilder.

He was a he, they agreed. Except for the four-thousand-year-old Sumerian tale of Queen Ereshkigal, or Allatu in the Assyrian, the monarch of the underworld was mainly a masculine presence. Even if the contemporary Satan proved to be a council of leaders, it was likely to be dominated by a masculine sensibility, an urge toward domination, a willingness to shed blood.

They extrapolated from prevailing views of animal behavior about alpha males, territorial imperative, and reproductive tyranny. Diplomacy might or might not work with such a character. A clenched fist or an empty threat would probably just incite him. The hadal leader would not be stupid: to the contrary, his reputation for deception and masks and inventiveness and cunning bargains suggested real cross-cultural genius.

He had the economic instincts of a salt trader, the courage of a soloist crossing the Arctic. He was a traveler among mankind, conversant in human languages, a student of power, an observer able to blend in without notice, an adventurer who explored at random or for profit or, like the Beowulf scholars and the Helios expedition who were exploring his lands, out of scientific curiosity.

His anonymity was a skill, an art, but not infallible. He had never been caught. But he had been sighted. No one knew exactly what he looked like, which meant he did not look like what people expected. He probably didn't have red horns or cloven hooves or a tail with a spike at the tip. That he could be grotesque or animalistic at times, and seductive or voluptuary or even beautiful at other times, suggested a switch of disguises or of lieutenants or spies. Or a lineage of Satans.

The ability to transfer memory from one consciousness to another, now clinically proven, was significant, said Mustafah. Reincarnation made possible a "dynasty" similar to that of the Dalai Lama theocracy. That was a jolt, the notion of Satan as an ongoing religious monarchy.

"Buddhism with extreme prejudice," quipped Parsifal.

"Perhaps," de l'Orme proposed irreverently, "Satan would be better off just dying out and becoming an idea, rather than struggling to be a reality. By sniffing around man's camp all these years, the lion has degenerated into a hyena. The tempest has become just a puff of bad wind, a fart in the night."

Whether the literature and archaeological and linguistic evidence were describing Satan himself or rather his lieutenants and spies, the profile was consistent with an inquiring mentality. No doubt about it, the darkness wanted to know about the light. But to know what? Civilization? The human condition? The feel of sunbeams?

"The more I learn about hadal culture," Mustafah said, "the more I suspect a great culture in decline. It's as if a collective intellect had developed Alzheimer's and slowly begun to lose its reason."

"I think of autism, not Alzheimer's," said Vera. "A vast onset of self-centered presentness. An inability to recognize the outside world, and with that an inability to create. Look at the artifacts coming up from subplanetary hadal sites. Over the last three to five thousand years, the artifacts have been increasingly human in origin: coins, weapons, cave art, hand tools. That could mean that the hadals turned away from menial and artistic labor as they pursued higher arts, or that they jobbed the day-to-day minutiae out to human artisans whom they'd captured, or that they valued stolen possessions more than homemade ones.

"But match it with the decline in hadal population over the past several thousand years. Some demographic projections suggest they might have numbered over forty million individuals subglobally at the time Aristotle and Buddha lived. The figure is probably less than 300,000 at present. Something's gone terribly wrong down there. They haven't grown more sophisticated. They haven't pursued the higher arts. If anything, they've simply become packrats, storing their human knickknacks in tribal nests, increasingly unaware of what they have or where they are or even what they are."

"Vera and I have talked about this at length," said Mustafah. "There's a tremendous amount of fieldwork to be done, of course. But if you go back a million years in the fossil record, it appears the hadals were developing hand tools and even amalgamated metal artifacts far ahead of what humans were producing on the surface. While man was still figuring out how to pound two rocks together, the hadals were inventing musical instruments made of glass! Who knows? Maybe man never did discover fire. Maybe we were taught it! But now you have these grotesque creatures reduced to savagery, their tribes draining off into the deepest holes. It's sad, really."

"The question is," said Vera, "does this overall decline reflect in all the hadals?"

"Satan," said January. "Above all, does it affect him?"

"Without having met him, I can't say for sure. But there is always a dynamic between a people and their leader. He's a mirror image of them. Kind of like God in reverse. We're an image of Him? How about Him as an image of us?"

"You're saying the leader isn't leading? That he's following his benighted masses?"

"Of course," said Mustafah. "Even the most isolated despot reflects his people. Otherwise he's just a madman." He gestured at the space around them. "No different from the knight who built this castle on top of a mountain in a rocky wilderness."

"Maybe that's what he is," said Vera. "Isolated. Alienated. Segregated by his genius. Wandering the world, above and below, cut off from his own kind, trying to figure some way into our kind."

"Are we so attractive to them?" January wondered.

"Why not? What if our light and civilization and intellectual and physical health is their salvation, so to speak? What if we represent paradise to them—or him—the way their darkness and savagery and ignorance represent our hell?"

"And Satan's tired of being Satan?" asked Mustafah.

"But of course," Parsifal said. "What could be more in keeping? The ultimate traitor. The Judas of all time. A serpent ascending. The rat jumping off the ship."

"Or at least an intellect contemplating his own transformation," said Vera. "Anguishing over his direction. Trying to decide whether he really can bring himself to cut loose."

"What's so wrong with that?" asked Foley. "Wasn't that Christ's agony? Isn't that Buddha's conundrum? The savior hits his wall. He gets worn out being the savior. He gets tired of the suffering. It means our Satan is mortal, that's all."

January opened her palms to them like pink fruit. "Why get so fancy?" she asked. "The theory works perfectly fine with a much simpler explanation. What if Satan came up to cut a deal? What if he wants to find someone like us as badly as we want to find him?"

Foley's pencil fanned a nervous yellow wing in the air. "But that's what I've been thinking!" he said. "In fact, I think he's already found us."

"What?" three of them asked at once.

Even Thomas raised his eyes from his dark thoughts.

"If there's one thing I've learned as an entrepreneur, it is that ideas occur in waves. Ideas transcend intelligence. In different cultures. Different languages. Different dreams. Why should the idea of peace be any different? What if the notion of a treaty or a summit or a cease-fire occurred to our Satan even as it occurred to us?"

"But you conjecture he's found us."

"Why not? We're not invisible. The Beowulf endeavor has been globetrotting for a year and a half. If Satan is half as resourceful as you say, he's heard of us. And yes, located us. And perhaps even penetrated us."

"Absurd," they cried. But hungered for more.

"Speak from the evidence," said Thomas.

"Yes, the evidence," said Foley. "It's your own evidence, Thomas. Wasn't it you who proposed that Satan might contact a leader as desperate—and enigmatic and vilified—as himself? A leader like this jungle warlord Desmond Lynch went off to find. As I recall, you once suggested Satan might want to establish a colony of his own, on the surface, in plain sight as it were, in a country like Burma or Rwanda, a place so benighted and savage no one dares cross its borders."

"You're proposing that *I* am Satan?" Thomas drolly asked.

"No. Not at all."

"I'm relieved. Then who?"

Foley went for broke. "Desmond."

"Lynch?" belched Gault.

"I'm quite serious."

"What are you talking about?" January protested. "The poor man's vanished. He's probably been eaten by tigers."

"Perhaps. But what if he had secreted himself in our midst? Listened to our thoughts? Waited for an opportunity like this, a chance to meet a despot and make his pact? I doubt he'd bid us a fond adieu before disappearing forever."

"Absurd."

Foley laid his yellow pencil neatly alongside of his pad. "Look, we've agreed on several things. That Satan is a trickster. A master of anonymity. He survives through his disguises and deceptions. And he may have been trying to strike a bargain . . . for peace or a hiding place, it doesn't matter. All I know is that Senator January last saw Desmond alive, on his way into a jungle no one dares to enter."

"Do you realize what you're saying?" asked Thomas. "I chose the man myself. I've known him for decades."

"Satan is patient. He has loads of time."

"You're suggesting that Lynch played us along from the beginning? That he used us?"

"Absolutely."

Thomas looked sad. Sad and decided. "Accuse him yourself," he said. He set his box on the table amid the fruit and cheeses. Beneath FedEx paperwork, it bore diplomatic seals printed in broken wax.

"Thomas, is this necessary?" January said, guessing.

"This was delivered to me three days ago," said Thomas. "It came via Rangoon and Beijing. Here's why I convened this meeting with all of you."

Lynch's head had been dipped in shellac. He would not have been pleased with what it had done to his thick Scottish hair, normally parted at the right temple. Through the slightly parted lids they could see round pebbles.

"They scooped his eyes out and put in stones," said Thomas. "Probably while he was still alive. While he was alive, too, they probably made this." He drew out a necklace of human teeth. "There are plier marks on several."

"Why are you showing us this?" January whispered.

Mustafah looked down at his plate. Foley's arms were limp upon the chair rests. Parsifal was astounded: he and Lynch had clashed over socialism. Now the bleeding heart's mouth was locked tight, the bushy eyebrows plasticized, and Parsifal realized he would wonder to his death about the courage of his own convictions. What a brave bastard, he was thinking.

"One other thing," Thomas continued. "A set of genitals was found inside the mouth. A monkey's genitals."

"How dare you," whispered de l'Orme. He could smell the death, sense it in the other's pall. "Here, in my home, at our meal?"

"Yes. I've brought this into your home, at our meal. So that you will not doubt me." Thomas stood, his big knuckles flat on the oak plank, the insulted head between his fists.

"My friends," he said, "we have reached the end."

They could not have been more stunned if he had produced a second head.

"The end?" said Mustafah.

"We have failed."

"How can you say such a thing?" Vera objected. "After all we've accomplished."

"Do you not see poor Lynch?" Thomas said, holding the head aloft. "Can you not hear your own words? This is Satan?"

They did not answer. He set the horrible artifact back into the box.

"I'm as responsible as you," Thomas told them. "Yes, I spoke to the possibility of Satan visiting some despot tucked away in a remote wasteland, and that misled you. But isn't it just as possible Satan would have desired to meet and appraise a different kind of tyrant, say, the head of Helios? And because we met with Cooper at his research complex, does that mean another one of us must be Satan, perhaps even you, Brian? No, I think not."

"Fine, I flew off the curve," said Foley. "One wild deduction should not impeach our search."

"This entire endeavor is a wild deduction," Thomas said. "We've seduced ourselves with our own knowledge. We're no closer to knowing Satan than when we began. We are finished."

"Surely not yet," said Mustafah. "There's still so much to know."

Their faces all registered that sentiment.

"I can no longer justify the hardships and danger," said Thomas.

"You don't need to justify anything," challenged Vera. "This has been our choice from the start. Look at us."

Despite their ordeals and the assault of time, they were not the spectral figures Thomas had first collected in the Metropolitan Museum of Art and sparked to action. Their faces were bronzed with exotic suns, their skin toughened by winds and the cold, their eyes lit with adventure. They had been waiting to die, and his call to arms had saved their lives.

"Clearly the group wants to keep going," said Mustafah.

"I'm just starting in with new Olmec evidence," Gault explained.

"And the Swedes are developing a new DNA test," said Vera. "I'm in daily contact. They think it suggests a whole new species branch. It's just a matter of months."

"And there was another ghost transmission from the interior," said Parsifal. "From the Helios expedition. The date code was August 8, almost four months ago, I know. But that's still a full month more recent than anything else we've managed to receive. The digital string needs enhancement, and it's only a partial communication, something about a river. It's not much. But they're alive. Or were. Just months ago. We can't just cut loose from them, Thomas. They're depending on us."

Parsifal's remark was not meant to be cruel, but it drove Thomas's chin down to his chest. Week by week, his face had been growing more hollowed. Haunted, it seemed, by what he had put in motion.

"And what about you?" January asked more gently. "This has been your quest since before any of us came to know you."

"My quest," Thomas murmured. "And where has that brought us?"

"The hunt," said Mustafah, "has intrinsic value. You knew that in the beginning. Whether we ever sighted our prey, much less brought him to earth, we were learning about ourselves. By fitting our own foot into Satan's tracks, we've come that much closer to dispelling ancient illusions. Touching the reality of what we really are."

"Illusion? Reality?" said Thomas. "We've lost Lynch to the jungle. Rau to his madness. And Branch to his quest. And sent a young woman to her death in the center of the earth. I've taken you from your families and homes. And every day we continue brings new risks."

"But, Thomas," said Vera, "we volunteered."

"No," he said, "I can no longer justify it."

"Then leave," came de l'Orme's voice.

Out the window behind his head, dark thunderheads were piling for an afternoon storm. His face was positively radiant with the reflected flames. His tone was stern. "You may hand the torch on," he told Thomas, "but you may not extinguish it."

"We're too damned close, Thomas," January said.

"Close to what?" Thomas asked. "Among us, we have over five hundred years of combined scholarship and experience. And where have we gotten with it in a year and a half of searching?" He dropped the strand of Lynch's teeth into the box, like so many rosary beads. "That one of us is Satan. My friends, we've looked into the dark water so long it has become a mirror."

A streak of lightning lanced between two limestone towers in the middle distance. Its thunder cracked through the room. Down below, the hired drivers and nurses fled for the cars just as a mountain squall attacked.

"You can't stop us, Thomas," said de l'Orme. "We have our own resources. We have our own imperatives. We'll follow the path you opened to us, wherever it may lead."

Thomas closed the box and rested his fingers on the cardboard.

"Follow it then," he said. "This pains me to say. But from this day on you follow your path without the blessing and imprimatur of the Holy Father. And you follow it without me. My friends, I lack your strength. I lack your conviction. Forgive me my doubt. May God bless you." He picked up the box.

"Don't go," whispered January.

"Good-bye," he said to them, and walked into the storm.

*It had ceased to be a
blank space of delightful
mystery. . . .*

—JOSEPH CONRAD,
Heart of Darkness

23

THE SEA

BENEATH THE MARIANA AND
YAP TRENCHES, 6,010 FATHOMS

The sea stretched on. They had been walking for twenty-one days. Ike kept them on a short leash. He set the pace, resting every half hour, circulating among them like Gunga Din, filling their water bottles, congratulating them on their endurance. "Man, where were you guys when I needed you on Makalu?" he would say.

Next to Ike, the strongest was Troy, the forensics kid, who'd probably been watching *Sesame Street* at the time Ike was battling his Himalayan peaks. He did a fine job trying to be Ike-like, solicitous and useful. But he was wearing down, too. Sometimes Ike posted him at the front, a place of trust, his way of honoring the boy.

Ali decided the best help she could be was to walk with Twiggs, whom everyone else wanted to hogtie and leave. From the moment he woke, the man whined and begged and committed petty thefts. The microbotanist was a born panhandler. Only Ali could deal with him. She treated him like a teenage novitiate with pimples. When Pia or Chelsea marveled at her patience, Ali explained that if it wasn't Twiggs, it would be someone else. She had never seen a tribe without a scapegoat.

Their tents were history. They slept on thin sleeping pads as a pretense of their former civilization. Only three of them had sleeping bags, because the three pounds of weight had proven too much for the rest. When the temperature cooled, they pressed together and draped the bags over their collective body. Ike rarely slept with them. Usually he took his shotgun and wandered away, returning in the morning.

On one such morning, before Ike came in from his night patrolling, Ali woke and walked down to the sea to clean her face. A boggy mist had come in off the water, but she could see to place her feet on the phosphorescent sand. Just as she was about to skirt a large boulder, she heard noises.

The sounds were delicate and bony. Instantly she knew this was not English, probably not human. She listened more keenly, then gently worked ahead several more steps to the flank of the boulder and kept herself hidden.

There seemed to be two figures down there. In silence she listened to the voices murmur and click and slowly dial her into a different horizon of existence. There was no question they were hadals.

She was breathless. One sounded little different from the water lightly lapping against the shore. The other was less joined at the vowels, more cut and dried at the edges of his word strings. They sounded polite or old. She stepped from around the rock to see them.

There weren't two, but three. One was a gargoyle similar to those that Shoat and Ike had killed. It was perched upon the very skin of the water, hands flat, while its wings fanned languidly up and down. The other two appeared to be amphibians, or close to it, like fishermen who have no memory but the sea, half man, half fish. One lay on his side on the sand, feet in the water, while the other drifted in repose. They had the sleek heads and large eyes of seals, but with sharpened teeth. Their flesh was slick and white, with small black hairs fletching their backs.

She had been afraid they would flee.

Abruptly she was afraid they would not.

One of the amphibians stirred and twisted to see her, showing his thick pizzle. It was erect. He'd been stroking himself, she realized. The gargoyle flexed his mouth like a baboon, and the dental arcade looked vicious.

"Oh," Ali said foolishly.

What had she been thinking, to come here alone?

They watched her with the composure of philosophers in a glen. One of the amphibians went ahead and finished his thought in their soft language, still looking at her.

Ali considered running back to the group. She set one foot behind her to turn and go. The gargoyle cut the briefest of side glances at her.

"Don't move," muttered Ike.

He was hunkered on top of the boulder to her left, balanced on the balls of his feet. The pistol in one hand hung relaxed.

The hadals didn't speak anymore. They had that peculiar Oriental ease with long silences. The one went on stroking himself with apelike bemusement, not at all self-conscious or purposeful. There was nothing to hear but the water licking sand, and the skin sound of the one fondling himself.

After a while, the gargoyle cast one more glance at Ali, then pushed forward against the water's surface and departed on slow wings, never rising more than a few inches above the sea. He diagonaled into the mist and was gone.

By the time Ali brought her attention back to the amphibians, one had vanished. The last one—the masturbator—reached a state of boredom and quit. He slid below the water, and it was as if he had been drawn into a mouth. The lips of the sea sealed over him.

"Did that really happen?" Ali asked in a low voice. Her heart was pounding. She started forward to verify the handprints in the sand, to confirm the reality.

"Don't go near that water," Ike warned her. "He's waiting for you."

"He's still there?" Her Zen hadals, lurking? But they were so pacific.

"You want to back up, please. You're making me nervous, Sister."

"Ike," she suddenly bubbled, "you can understand them?"

"Not a word. Not these."

"There are others?"

"I keep telling you, we're not alone."

"But to actually see them . . ."

"Ali, we've been passing among them the whole time."

"Ones like those?"

"And ones you don't want to know about."

"But they looked so peaceful. Like three poets."

Ike tsk'ed.

"Then why didn't they attack us?" she said.

"I don't know. I'm trying to figure it out. It's almost like they knew me." He hesitated. "Or you."

Branch lagged, weary.

He kept cutting their trail, but their spoor wandered, or else he did. It was likely him, he knew. Insect bites had made him sick, and the best thing would be to find a burrow and wait until the fever passed. With so much human presence around, he didn't trust the burrowing, though.

To stop would be to attract predators from many miles around. If one found him convalescing in a cubbyhole, it would be all over. And so Branch kept on his feet.

A lifetime of wounds hampered his pace. Delirium sapped his attention. He felt very old. It seemed as though he'd been voyaging since the beginning of time.

He came to a narrow sinkhole with a skinny rivulet trickling down. Rifle across his back, Branch roped into the abyss. At the bottom, he pulled the line and coiled it and moved on. He was new to this region, but was not a neophyte.

He came upon a woman's skeleton. Her long black hair lay by the skull, which was unusual, because it made good cordage when braided. That it had been left told him there were many more such humans available. That was good. Predators would be less prone to hunt him.

Through the day, Branch found more evidence of humans: whole skeletons, ribs, a footprint, a dried patch of urine, or the distinctive smell of *H. sapiens* in hadal dung. Someone had scratched his name on the wall, along with a date. One date from only two weeks before gave him hope.

Then he found the blubbery pile of survival suits, of which a number had been speared or hacked. To a hadal, the neoprene suits would seem like supernatural skins or even live animals. He rummaged through the pile and dressed in one that was whole and fit.

Shortly afterward, Branch found the rolls of paper with Ali's maps. He raced through them in chronological order. At the end, someone else's hand had scrawled in Walker's treachery at the sea, and the group's dispersal. It all came together for him, why this band had become separated and vulnerable, why Ike was nowhere to be found among them. Branch saw now where he needed to go, that subterranean sea. From there he might find more signs. Ali's chronicle made perfect sense to him. He took the maps and went on.

A day later, Branch realized he was being stalked.

He could actually smell them on the airstream, and that disturbed him. It meant they had to be close, for his nose was not keen. Ike would have sensed them long before. Again he felt old.

He had the same two choices every animal does, fight or flight. Branch ran.

Three hours later he reached the river. He saw the trail leading along the water, but it was too late for that. He faced around, and there were four of them fanning out in the talus above, as pale as larvae.

A slender spear—reed tipped with obsidian—shattered on the rock next to him. Another pierced the water. It would have been easy to shoot the one youngster nearing on his left. That still would have left three, and the same necessity for what he now did.

The leap was clumsy, impaired by his rifle and the tube of maps wrapped in waterproofing. He had meant to strike open water, but his right foot caught a stone. He heard his right knee snap. He clung to the rifle, but dropped the maps on shore. Momentum alone carried him into the current. The current sucked him under.

For as long as he could hold his breath, Branch let the river have him. At last he triggered the survival suit and felt its bladders fill. He was buoyed to the surface like a cork.

The fastest hadal was still tracking him alongside the river. The moment Branch's head popped above water, the hadal made a hurried cast.

The spear lodged deep just as Branch fired a burst from underwater, and the water chopped upward in long rooster tails. The hadal spun, was killed, and hit the water flat.

The river flowed on, taking him around bends and crooks, away from the danger.

For the next five days, Branch had the dead hadal for company as they both drifted to the sea. The river was like a mother, impartial to her children's differences. He drank her water. His fever cooled.

The spear fell out of him eventually.

Parasitic eels gently sucked at him. They took his blood, but his wound stayed clean. Somewhere along the way, he got his knee back in joint.

With all that pain, it was no wonder he dreamed so much as he drifted to the sea.

Back along the riverbank, a monstrosity, painted and inked and ridged with scars, picked up the tube of maps. He unrolled them from the waterproofing and pinned their corners with rocks while hadals gathered around. They had no eye for such things. But Isaac could see the care and detail the cartographer had lavished on these pages.

"There is hope," he said in hadal.

For days they had been remarking on a nebulous gleam the color of milk, occupying the rump of their horizon. They thought it might be a cloudbank or steam from a waterfall or perhaps a beached iceberg. Ali feared they were suffering collective hunger delusions, for they'd begun stumbling on the trail and talking to themselves. No one imagined a seaside fortress carved from phosphorescent cliffs.

Five stories high, its walls were as smooth as Egyptian alabaster. It had been whittled from solid rock. Beerstone, Twiggs told them. The Romans used to quarry it in ancient Britain. Westminster Abbey was made of it. A creamy white calcite, it came out of the ground as soft as soap and over the years dried to a hardness perfect for sculpting. He adored it for its pollen residues.

Long ago, hadals had skinned away the face of this wall, denuding its softer stone to cut out a complex of rooms and ramparts and statues, all of one piece. Not one block or brick had been added to it, a single huge monument.

Three times as broad as it was tall, the dwelling was empty and largely in collapse. It breasted the sea and was clearly a bulwark anchoring the commerce of some great vanished empire. You could see what was left of stone docks and pier slips submerged an inch beneath the water.

Even weak with hunger, they were beguiled. They wandered through the warren of rooms looking across the night sea and, to the fortress's rear, onto the crags below. Stairs had been cut into the cliff sides, seemingly thousands of them, leading off into new depths.

Whoever—or whatever—the hadals had built this defensive monster against, it was not humans. Ali estimated the fortress dated back at least fifteen thousand years, probably more. "Man was still chipping flint in caves while this hadal civilization was engaged in riverine trade across thousands of miles. I doubt we were much of a threat to them."

"But where did they go?" Troy asked. "What could have destroyed them?"

As they wandered through the crumbling hulk, they encountered a people from another time. The fortress rooms and parapets were built to *Homo* scale, with ceilings planed at a remarkably standard six feet.

The walls held traces of engraved images and script and glyphs, and Ali pronounced the writings even older than what they had seen before. She was sure no epigrapher had ever laid eyes on such script.

Deep in the cavernous interior stood a freestanding column, rising twenty meters into a large domed chamber in the heart of the building. A high platform separated them from the spire's base. They made a complete circuit around the immense room, following the narrow walkway and shining their lights on the spire's upper section. There were no doors or stairways leading onto the platform.

"The spire could be a king's tomb," said Ali.

"Or a castle keep," said Troy.

"Or a good old-fashioned phallic symbol," said Pia, who was there because her lover, the primatologist Spurrier, trusted Gitner even less than he trusted Ike. "Like a Siva rock, or a pharaoh's obelisk."

"We need to find out," Ali said. "It could be relevant." Relevant, she did not say, to her search for the missing Satan.

"What do you propose, growing wings?" asked Spurrier. "There are no stairs."

With a pencil-thin beam of light, Ike traced a set of handholds carved into the upper half of the platform's circular wall. He opened his hundred-pound pack and laid out the contents, and they all took a peek.

"You're still carrying rope?" marveled Ruiz. "How many coils do you have in there?"

Ali saw a pair of clean socks. After all these months?

"Look at all those MREs," said Twiggs. "You've been holding out on us."

"Shut up, Twiggy," Pia said. "It's his food."

"Here, I've been waiting," said Ike. He handed around the food packets. "That's the last of them. Happy Thanksgiving." And it was, November 24.

They were ravenous. With no further ceremony, the vestiges of the Jules Verne Society opened the pouches and heated the ham and pineapple slices and filled their pinched stomachs. They made no attempt to ration themselves.

Ike occupied himself uncoiling one of his ropes. He declined the meal, but accepted some of their M&M's, though only the red ones. They didn't know what to make of that, their battle-scarred scout fussing over bits of candy.

"But they're no different from the yellow and blue ones," Chelsea said.

"Sure they are," Ike said. "They're red."

He tied one end of the rope to his waist. "I'll trail the rope," he said. "If there's anything up there, I'll fix the line and you can come take a look."

Armed with his headlamp and their only pistol, Ike stood on Spurrier's and Troy's shoulders and gave a hop to reach the lowest handhold. From there it was only another twenty feet to the top. He spidered up, grabbed the edge of the platform, and started to pull himself over. But he stopped. They watched him not move for a whole minute.

"Is something wrong?" asked Ali.

Ike pulled himself onto the platform and looked down at them. "You better see this for yourself."

He knotted loops in the rope to make them a ladder. One by one, they climbed up, weak, needing help. It was going to take more than one meal to restore their strength.

Between themselves and the tower, ninety feet in, a ceramic army awaited them. Lifeless, yet alive.

They were hadal warriors made of glazed terra-cotta. Facing out toward intruders, they numbered in the hundreds, arranged in concentric circles around the tower, each statue bearing a weapon and a ferocious expression. Some still wore armor made of thin jade plates stitched with gold links. On most, time had stretched or broken the gold, and the plates had tumbled to their feet, leaving the hadal mannequins naked.

It was hard not to speak in a whisper. They were awestruck, intimidated. "What have we stumbled into?" asked Pia.

Some brandished war clubs edged with obsidian chips, pre-Aztec. There were atlatls—spear throwers—and stone maces with iron chains and handles. Some of the weaponry carried Maori-type geometrics, but had to predate Maori culture by fourteen thousand years. Spears and arrows made of abyssal reed had been fletched not with bird feathers but with fish spines.

"It's like the Qin tomb in China," said Ali. "Only smaller."

"And seven times older," said Troy. "And hadal."

They entered the circles of sentinels tentatively, setting their feet carefully, like t'ai chi students, so as not to disturb the scene. Those with film left took pictures. Ike drew his pistol and stalked from one to another, culling facts meaningful only to him. Ali simply wandered. Troy joined her, dazed.

"These furrows in the floor, they're filled with mercury," he said, pointing to the network cut into the stone deck. "And it's moving, like blood. What could be the meaning?"

It was fair to guess by the details that the statues had been built true to life. In that case, the warriors had averaged an extraordinary five feet ten inches—fifteen eons ago. As Troy pointed out, it was always a mistake to generalize too much from the looks of an army, for armies tended to recruit the healthiest and fittest specimens in a population. Even so, during the same Neolithic period the average *H. sapiens* male had stood five to eight inches shorter.

"Next to these guys, Conan the Barbarian would have been nothing more than a mesomorphic runt leading a bunch of human pipsqueaks," Troy said. "It kind of makes you wonder. With their physical size and this level of social organization and wealth, why didn't the hadals just invade us?"

"Who says they didn't?" asked Ali. She went on studying the statues. "What intrigues me is how flexed the cranial base is. And how straight the jaws are. Remember that head Ike brought in? The skull fit differently on the neck. I distinctly remember that. It extended forward, like a chimp's. And the jaw had a pronounced thrust forward."

"I saw that, too," Troy said. "Are you thinking what I am?"

"Reversal?"

"Exactly. I mean, possibly." Troy opened his hands. "I mean, I don't know, Ali."

In lay terms, a straight jaw—orthognathicism—was an evolutionary climb above the more primitive trait of a jutting jaw. Anthropology did not deal in terms of evolutionary ascent, however, any more than it recognized evolutionary decline. A straight jaw was called a "derived" trait. Like all traits, it expressed an adaptation to environmental pressures. But evolutionary pressures were in constant flux, and could lead to new traits that sometimes resembled primitive ones. This was called reversal. Reversal was not a going backward, but rather a seeming to do so. It was not a return to the primitive trait, but a new derived trait that mimicked the primitive trait. In this case the hadals had evolved a straight jaw fifteen or twenty thousand years ago, as seen on these statues, but had apparently derived a jutting jaw that was highly simian and primitive in its look. For whatever reason, *H. hadalis* seemed to be in reversal.

For Ali, the significance lay in what this meant to hadal speech and cognition. A straight jaw provided a wider range of consonants, and an erect neck-skull structure—basicranial flexion—meant a lower larynx or voice box, and that meant more vowel range. The fact that fifteen-thousand-year-old hadal statues had straight jaws and an erect head, and Ike's trophy head did not, suggested problems with modern hadal speech, and possibly with his cognition. Ali remembered Troy's remarks about symmetry in the hadal brain, too. What if subterranean conditions had evolved Haddie from a creature capable of sculpting this fortress, firing these terra-cotta warriors, and plying the sea and rivers, into a virtual beast? Ike had said hadals could no longer read hadal script. What if they had lost their ability to reason? What if Satan was nothing more than a savage cretin? What if the Gitners and Spurriers of the world were right, and *H. hadalis* deserved no better treatment than a vicious dog?

Troy was troubled. "How could they reverse so quickly, though? Call it twenty thousand years. That's not time enough for such a pronounced evolution, is it?"

"I can't explain it," Ali said. "But don't forget, evolution is an answer to environment, and look at the environment. Radioactive rock. Chemical gases. Electromagnetic surges. Gravitational anomalies. Who knows? Simple inbreeding may be to blame."

Ike was just ahead with Ruiz and Pia, examining three figures waving swords of fire, looking them in the face as if checking his own identity. "Is something wrong?" Ali asked.

"They're not like this anymore," Ike said. "They're similar, but they've changed."

Ali and Troy looked at each other.

"How do you mean?" Ali thought he would speak to some of the physical differences she and Troy had noticed.

Ike raised his hands to the entire tableaux. "Look at this. This is—this was—greatness. Magnificence. In all my time among them, there was never any hint of that. Magnificence? Never."

They spent the rest of the first day and the next exploring. Flowstone oozed from doorways, collapsing sections. Deeper in, they found a wealth of relics, most of them human. There were ancient coins from Stygia and Crete mixed with American buffalo nickels and Spanish doubloons minted in Mexico City. They found Coke bottles, Japanese baseball cards, and a flintlock. There were books written in dead languages, a set of samurai armor, an Incan mirror, and, beneath that, figurines and clay tablets and bone carvings from civilizations long forgotten. One of their strangest discoveries was an armillary, a Renaissance-era teaching device with metal spheres inside one another to depict planetary revolutions. "What in God's name is a hadal doing with something like this?" Ruiz wanted to know.

What kept drawing them back was the circular platform with its army surrounding the stone spire. However priceless the human artifacts were, scattered through the fortress, they were mundane compared with the tower display. On the second morning, Ike found a series of hidden nubbins on the tower itself. Using these, he made a daring, unprotected ascent to the top of the column.

They watched him balance atop the spire. For the longest time he just stood there. Then he called down for them to turn off their lights. They sat in the darkness for half an hour, bathed by the faintly incandescent floor.

When he roped down again, Ike looked shaken.

"We're standing on their world," he said. "This whole platform is a giant map. The spire was built as a viewing station."

They glanced around at their feet, and all they saw were wiggling cutmarks on a flat, unpainted surface. But through the afternoon, Ike led them one at a time up the ropes and they saw with their own eyes. By the time he took Ali up for her view, Ike had made the trip six times and was becoming familiar with parts of the map. Ali found the top flat and small, just three feet square. Apparently no one but Ike had felt comfortable standing on top, so he had rigged a pair of loops for people to sit in while hanging alongside. Ali hung beside Ike, sixty feet up, while her night vision adapted.

"It's like a giant sand mandala, but without the sand," Ike said. "It's weird how I keep running across pieces of mandalas down here. I'm talking about places like sub-Iran or under Gibraltar. I thought Haddie must have kidnapped a bunch of monks and put them to work decorating. But now I see."

And so did she. In a giant circle all around her, the platform beneath them began to radiate ghostly colors.

"It's some kind of pigment worked into the stone," said Ike. "Maybe it was visible at ground level at one time. I like the idea of an invisible map, though. Probably commoners like us would never have had access to this knowledge. Only the elite would have been permitted to come up here and get the whole picture."

The longer she waited, the more her vision adjusted. Details clarified. The incisions flowing with mercury became tiny rivers veining across the surface. Lines of turquoise and red and green intertwined and branched in wild patterns: tunnels.

"I think that big stain mark is our sea," said Ike.

The black shape lay quite close to the tower base. Paths threaded in from far-flung regions. If this was reality, then there were whole worlds down here. Whether they had once been known as provinces or nations or frontiers, the gaping cavities stood like air sacs within a great round lung.

"What's happening?" Ali gasped. "It's coming alive."

"Your eyes are still catching up," Ike said. "Just wait. It's three-dimensional."

The flatness suddenly swelled with contours and depth. The color lines no longer overlapped but had levels all their own, dipping and rising among other lines.

"Oh," Ali murmured, "I feel like I'm falling,"

"I know. It opens and opens and opens. It's all in the art. Somehow, Himalayan cultures must have plagiarized it a long time ago. Now the Buddhists use it just to draw blueprints for Dharma palaces. Meditate long enough, and the geometrics turn into an optical illusion of a building. But here you get the original intent. A map of the whole inner earth."

Even the black blot of the sea had dimensions. Ali could see its flat surface and, underneath it, the jagged contours of its floor. The river lines looked suspended in midspace.

"I'm not sure how to read this thing. There's no north-south, no scale," said Ike. "But there's a definite logic here. Look at the coastline of our sea. You can pretty much see how we came."

It was different from the way she had been drawing her own maps. Lacking compass bearings, the maps she continued to make were projections of her westward desire, essentially a straight line with bends. These lines were more languorous and full. Now she could see how tightly she had been disciplining her fear of this space. The subterranean world was practically infinite, more like the sky than the earth.

The sea was shaped like an elongated pear. Ali tried in vain to distinguish any features along the right-hand route Walker had taken. Other than extrapolating that rivers intersected his route, she couldn't read its hazards.

"This spire must represent the map's center, this fortress," Ali said. "An X to mark the spot. But it's not actually touching the sea. In fact the sea is some distance away."

"That had me stumped, too," Ike said. "But you see how all the lines converge here, at the spire? We've all looked outside and there isn't that kind of convergence. The trail we came on continues following the shoreline. And one path leads down from the back, a single path. Now I'm thinking we're just a spot on one of many roads." He pointed to where a single green line departed from the sea. "That spot on that road."

If Ike was right, and if the map's proportions were true, then their party had covered less than a fifth of the sea's circumference.

"Then what could this spire represent?" Ali asked.

"I've been thinking about it. You know the adage, all roads lead to . . ." He let her finish it.

"Rome?" she breathed.

Could it be?

"Why not?" he said.

"The center of ancient hell?"

"Can you stand on top for a minute?" Ike asked her. "I'll hold your legs."

Ali worked her knees onto the meter-wide apex, and then got to her feet. From that extra height, she saw all the lines drawing in toward her feet. Abruptly she had the sensation of enormous power. It was as if, for a moment, the entire world fused in her. The center was here, and it could only be the one center, their destination. Now she understood why Ike had descended so shaken.

"While you're up there," Ike said, his hands firm upon her legs, "tell me if you see the map differently."

"The lines are more distinct," she said. With nothing to hold on to, nothing at her back or front, the panorama surged in toward her. The great web of lines seemed to be lifting higher. Suddenly it was as if she were not looking down, but up.

"Dear God," she said.

The spire had become the pit.

She was seeing the world from deep within.

Her head began spinning.

"Get me down," she pleaded, "before I fall."

"I have something to show you," Ike said to her that night. *More?* she thought. The afternoon's revelations had exhausted her. He seemed happy.

"Can't it wait until tomorrow?" she asked. She was tired. Hours had passed, and she was still reeling from the map's optical illusion. And she was hungry.

"Not really," he said.

They had made camp within the colonnaded entry, where a stream of pure water issued from an eroded spout. Their hunger was telling. Another day of explorations had weakened them. The ones who had climbed atop the spire were weakest. They lay on the ground, mostly curled around their empty stomachs. Pia was holding Spurrier, who suffered from migraines. Troy sat with Ike's pistol facing the sea, his head slumped, halfway to sleep. From here on, things were going to get no better.

Ali changed her mind. "Lead on," she said.

She took Ike's hand and got to her feet. He led her inside and to a secret passage. It contained its own flight of carved stairs.

"Go slow," he said. "Save your strength."

They reached a tower jutting above the fortress. They had to crawl through another hidden duct to more stairs. As they climbed up the final stretch of narrow steps, she saw a rich, buttery light above. He let her go in first.

In a room overlooking the sea, Ike had lit scores of oil lamps. They were small clay leaves that cupped the oil and fed it along a groove to the flame at one tip.

"Where did you find these?" she asked. "And where did the oil come from?"

In one corner stood three large earthenware amphorae that might well have been salvaged from an ancient Greek shipwreck.

"It was all buried in storage vaults under the floor. There's got to be fifty more of these jars down there," he said. "This must have been something like a lighthouse. Maybe there were others like it farther along the shore, a system of relay stations."

A single lamp might have been enough to let her see her fingertips. In their hundreds, the lamps turned the room to gold. She wondered how it would have looked to hadal ships drifting upon the black sea twenty thousand years ago.

Ali sneaked a look at Ike. He had done this for her. The light was hurting his eyes a little, but he didn't shield them from her.

"We can't stay here," he said, wiping at his tears. "I want you to come with me." He was trying not to squint. What was beautiful to her was painful to him. She was tempted to blow out some of the lamps to ease his discomfort, but decided he might be insulted.

"There's no way out," she said. "We can't go on."

"We can." He gestured at the endless sea. "It's not hopeless, the paths go on."

"And what about the others?"

"They can come, too. But they've given up. Ali, don't give up." He was fervent. "Come with me."

This was for her alone, like the light.

"I'm sorry," she said. "You're different. I'm like them, though. I'm tired. I want to stay here."

He twisted his head away.

"I know you think I'm being complacent," she said.

"We don't have to die," Ike said. "No matter what happens to them, we don't have to die here." He was adamant. It did not escape her that he spoke to her as "we."

"Ike," she said, and stopped. She had fasted in her day, and knew it was too soon for the euphoria to be addling her. But her sense of contentment was rich.

"We can get out of here," he urged.

"You've brought us as far as we can go," she said. "You've done everything we set out to do. We've made our discoveries. We know that a great empire once existed down here. Now it's over."

"Come with me, Ali."

"We have no food."

His eyes shifted ever so slightly, a side glance, nothing more. He said nothing, but something about his silence contradicted her. He knew where there was food? It jarred her.

His canniness darted before her like a wild animal. *I am not you,* it said. Then his glance straightened and he was one of them again.

She finished. "I'm grateful for what you've accomplished for us. Now we just want to come to terms with where we've gotten in our lives. Let us make our peace," she said. "You have no reason to stay here anymore. You should go."

There, she thought. All of her nobleness in a cup. Now it was his turn. He would resist gallantly. He was Ike.

"I will," he said.

A frown spoiled her brow. "You're leaving?" she blurted, and immediately wished she hadn't. But still, he was leaving them? Leaving her?

"I thought about staying," he said. "I thought how romantic it would be. I imagined how people might find us ten years from now. There would be you. And there would be me."

Ali blinked. The truth was, she'd imagined the same scene.

"And they would find me holding you," he said. "Because that's what I would do after you died, Ali. I would hold you in my arms forever."

"Ike," she said, and stopped again. Suddenly she was incapable of more than monosyllables.

"That would be legal, I think. You wouldn't be Christ's bride after you died, right? He could have your soul. I could have what was left."

That was a bit morbid, yet nonetheless the truth. "If you're asking my permission," she said, "the answer is yes." Yes, he could hold her. In her imagination, it had been the other way around. He had died first and she had held him. But it was all the same concept.

"The problem is," he continued, "I thought about it some more. And to put it bluntly, I decided it was a pretty raw deal for me."

She let her gaze drift around the glowing room.

"I'd get you," he answered himself, "too late."

Good-bye, Ike, she thought. It was just a matter of saying the words now.

"This isn't easy," he said.

"I know." *Vaya con Dios.*

"No," he said. "I don't think you do."

"It's okay."

"No, it's not," he said. "It would break my heart. It would kill me." He licked his lips. He took the leap. "To have waited too late with you."

Her eyes sprang upon him.

Her surprise alarmed him. "I should be able to say it, if I'm going to stay," he defended himself. "Can't I even say that much?"

"Say what, Ike?" Her voice sounded far away to her.

"I've said enough."

"It's mutual, you know." Mutual? That was the best she could offer?

"I know," he said. "You love me, too. And all God's creatures." He crossed himself, gently mocking.

"Stop," she said.

"Forget it," he said, and his eyes closed in that marauded face.

It was up to her to break this impasse.

No more ghosts. No more imagination. No more dead lovers: her Christ, his Kora.

As her hand reached out, it was like watching herself from a great distance. They might have been someone else's fingers, except they were hers. She touched his head.

Ike recoiled from her touch. Instantly, Ali could see how sure he was she pitied him. Once upon a time, with a face untarnished and young, that might not have been a consideration. But he was wary and filled with his own repulsiveness. Naturally he would distrust a touch.

Ali had not done this forever, it seemed. It could have felt clumsy or foolish or false. If she had contrived it in any way, given the slightest thought to it beforehand, it would have failed. Which was not to say her hands were steady as she opened her buttons and slid her shoulders bare. She let the clothing drop, all of it.

Nude, she felt the warmth of the lamps on her flesh. From the corner of her eye, she saw the light from twenty eons ago turn her into gold.

As they moved into each other, she thought that here was one hunger at least that no longer had to go begging.

Chelsea's scream woke them.

It had become her habit to wash her hair at the edge of the sea early each morning.

"Another fish in the water," Ali murmured to Ike. She had been dreaming of orange juice and birdsong—a mourning dove—and the smell of oak smoke on the hill-country air. Ike's arms fit around her just so. It was a shame to spoil the new day with a false alarm.

Then more shouts rose up to them in the tower. Ike lifted from the floor and leaned out the window, his back dented and pockmarked and striped with text and images and old violence.

"Something's happened," he said, and grabbed his clothes and knife.

Ali followed him down the stairs, the last to reach the group gathered on the shore. They were shivering. It wasn't cold, but they had less fat on them these days. "Here's Ike," someone said, and the group parted.

A body was floating upon the sea. It lay there as quiet as the water.

"It's not hadal," Spurrier was saying.

"He was a big guy," said Ruiz. "Could he be one of Walker's soldiers?"

"Walker?" said Twiggs. "Here?"

"Maybe he fell off one of the rafts and drowned. And then floated here."

He had glided in to shore like a ship with no crew, headfirst, faceup, bleached dead white by the sea. His limp arms wafted in the current. The eyes were gone.

"I thought it was driftwood and started out to get it," Chelsea said. "Then it got closer."

Ike waded into the water and hunched over the body with his back to them. Ali thought she saw the glint of his knife. After a minute he returned to them, towing the body.

"It's one of Walker's, all right," he said.

"A coincidence," said Ruiz. "He was bound to drift ashore somewhere."

"Here, though, of all places? You'd think he would have sunk. Or rotted. Or been eaten."

"He's been preserved," Ike said.

Ali saw what the others seemed not to see, an incision in one of the man's thighs where Ike had probed.

"You mean something in the water?" said Pia.

"No," Ike said. "They did it some other way."

"The hadals?" said Ruiz.

"Yes," Ike said.

"The currents. Chance . . ."

"He was delivered to us."

The group needed a long minute to absorb the fact.

"But why?" asked Troy.

"It must be a warning," Twiggs said.

"They're telling us to go home?" Ruiz laughed.

"You don't understand," Ike quietly told them. "It's an offering."

"They're making a sacrifice to us?"

"I guess if you want to put it that way," Ike said. "They could have eaten him themselves."

They fell silent.

"They're giving us a dead man for food?" whimpered Pia. "To eat?"

"The question is why," Ike said, staring across the dark sea.

Twiggs was affronted. "They think we're cannibals?"

"They think we probably want to live."

Ike did a horrible thing. He did not push the body back out to sea. Instead he waited.

"What are you waiting for?" Twiggs demanded. "Get rid of it."

Ike didn't say anything. He just waited some more.

It was appalling, the temptation.

Finally Ruiz said, "You've misjudged us, Ike."

"Don't insult us," Twiggs said.

Ike ignored him. He waited for the group. Another minute passed. They glared at him. Nobody wanted to say yes and nobody wanted to say no, and he wasn't going to say it for them. Even Ali did not reject the idea out of hand.

Ike was patient. The dead soldier bobbed slightly beside him. He was patient, too.

They were all thinking similar thoughts, she was sure, wondering what it would taste like and how long it would last and who would do the deed. In the end, Ali took it one step further, and that was their answer. "We could eat him," she said. "But when he was finished, what then?"

Ike sighed.

"Exactly," said Pia after a few seconds.

Ruiz and Spurrier closed their eyes. Troy shook his head ever so slightly.

"Thank heavens," said Twiggs.

They languished in the fortress, too weak to do much except shuffle outside to pee. They shifted about on their sleeping pads. It was not comfortable, lying around on your own bones.

So this is famine, thought Ali. A long wait for the ultimate poverty. She had always prided herself on her gift for transcending the moment. You gave up your worldly attachments, but always with the knowledge you could return to them. There was no such thing with starving. Deprivation was monotonous.

Before their strength dwindled anymore, Ali and Ike shared two more nights in the tower room among the lighted lamps. On November 30, they descended to the makeshift camp with finality. After that she was too light-headed to climb the stairs again.

The starvation made them very old and very young. Twiggs, especially, looked aged, his face hollowed and jowls hanging. But also they resembled infants, curled in upon their stomachs and sleeping more and more each day. Except for Ike, who was like a horse in his need to stay on his feet, their catnaps reached twenty hours.

Ali tried to force herself to work, to stay clean, say her prayers, and continue to draw her day maps. It was a matter of getting God's daily chaos in order.

On the morning of December 2, they heard animal noises coming from the beach. Those who could sit struggled upright. Their worst fear was coming true. The hadals were coming for them.

It sounded like wolves loping into position. You could hear whispered snatches of words. Troy began to totter off in search of Ike, but his legs wouldn't work well enough. He sat down again.

"Couldn't they wait?" Twiggs moaned softly. "I just wanted to die in my sleep."

"Shut up, Twiggs," hissed one of the geologists. "And turn out those lights. Maybe they don't know we're here."

The man got to his feet. In the preternatural glow of stone, they all watched him stagger across to a porthole near the doorway. With the stealth of an intruder, he cautiously lifted his head to the opening. And slid back down again.

"What did you see?" Spurrier whispered.

The geologist was silent.

"Hey, Ruiz." Finally, Spurrier crawled over. "Christ, the back of his head's gone!"

At that instant the assault commenced.

Huge shapes poured in, monstrous silhouettes against the gleaming stone.

"Oh, dear God!" screamed Twiggs.

If not for his cry in English, they would have been shredded with gunfire.

Instead there was a pause.

"Hold your fire," a voice commanded. "Who said 'God'?"

"Me," pleaded Twiggs. "Davis Twiggs."

"That's impossible," said the voice.

"It could be a trap," warned a second.

"It's just us," said Spurrier, and shined his light on his own face.

"Soldiers," cried Pia. "Americans!"

Lights snapped on throughout the room.

Shaggy mercenaries ranged right and left, still crouched, ready to shoot. It was hard to say who was more surprised, the debilitated scientists or the tattered remains of Walker's command.

"Don't move, don't move," the mercenaries shouted at them. Their eyes were rimmed with red. They trusted nothing. Their rifle barrels darted like hummingbirds, searching for enemy.

"Get the colonel," said a man.

Walker was carried in, seated on a rifle held on each side by soldiers. To Ali, he looked starved, until she saw his blood. The knifed-open rags of his pant legs showed dozens of bits of obsidian embedded in the flesh and bone. It was pain that had hollowed his face out. His faculties were unimpaired, though. He took in the room with a raptor's eye.

"Are you sick?" Walker demanded.

Ali saw what he saw, gaunt men and women barely able to sit. They looked like scarecrows.

"Just very hungry," said Spurrier. "Do you have food?"

Walker considered them. "Where's the rest of you?" he said. "I recall more than just nine of you."

"They went home," said Chelsea, prone beside her chessboard. She was looking at Ruiz's body. Now they could see that the geologist had been sniped through the eye.

"They're going back the way we came," said Spurrier.

"The physicians, too?" Walker said. For a moment he was hopeful.

"It's just us now," said Pia. "And you."

He surveyed the room. "What is this place, a shrine?"

"A way station," Pia said. Ali hoped she would stop there. She didn't want Walker to know about the circular map, or the ceramic soldiers.

"We found it two weeks ago," Twiggs volunteered.

"And you're still here?"

"We ran out of food."

"It looks defensible," Walker said to a lieutenant in burned clothing. "Set your perimeters. Secure the boats. Bring in the supplies and our guest. And remove that body."

They set Walker on the ground against one wall. They were careful, but laying his legs out was an agony for him.

Mercenaries began arriving from the beach with heavy loads of Helios food and supplies. Not one retained the look of the immaculate crusaders Walker had assiduously groomed. Their uniforms were in rags. Some were missing their boots. There were leg wounds and head injuries. They stank of cordite and old blood. Their beards and greasy locks made them look like a motorcycle gang.

Their veneer of religious vocation had rubbed away, leaving tired, angry, frightened gunmen. The rough way they dumped the wetbags and boxes spoke volumes. Their escape attempt was not going well.

After a few minutes, Walker returned his attention to the scientists. "Tell me," he said, "how many people did you lose along the way?"

"None," said Pia. "Until now."

Walker made no apology as the geologist Ruiz was dragged from the room by the heels. "I'm impressed," he said. "You managed to come hundreds of miles through a wilderness without a single casualty. Unarmed."

"Ike knows what he's doing," said Pia.

"Crockett's here?"

"He's exploring," Troy quickly inserted. "He goes off days at a time. He's looking for Cache V. For food."

"He's wasting his time." Walker turned his head to the black lieutenant. "Take five men," he said. "Locate our friend. We don't need any more surprises."

The soldier said, "You don't hunt that man, sir. Our troops have had enough, the last month."

"I will not have him roaming at large."

"Why are you doing this?" Ali demanded. "What's he done to you?"

"It's what I've done to him that's the problem. Crockett's not the sort to forgive and forget. He's out there watching us right now."

"He'll run off. There's nothing here for him anymore. He said we've given up."

"Then why the tears?"

"You don't have to do this," Ali told him softly.

Walker grew brisk. "No live catches, Lieutenant, do you hear me? Crockett's first commandment."

"Yes sir," the lieutenant breathed out. He tagged five of his men and they started into the building.

After the search team left, Walker closed his eyes. A soldier pulled a knife from his boot sheath and slit open a box of MREs and gestured at the scientists. It was up to Troy to feebly carry packets to his comrades. Twiggs kissed his, then tore it open with his teeth.

Ali's first bite of processed military spaghetti was delicious. She made her bites small. She sipped her water.

Twiggs vomited. Then started over again.

The room was beginning to fill up. More wounded were brought in. Two men mounted a machine gun at the window. All told, including herself and her comrades, Ali counted fewer than twenty-five people remaining from the original hundred and fifty who had started the journey.

Walker opened his bloodshot eyes. "Bring everything inside," he ordered. "The boats, too. They're vulnerable, and they announce our presence."

"But there's twelve of them out there." Fifteen less than they'd started with, Ali realized. What had happened out there?

"Bring them in," said Walker. "We're going to fort up a few days. This is the answer to our prayers, a toehold in this evil place."

The soldier's pig eyes disagreed. He threw his salute. Walker's hold was slipping.

"How did you find us?" Pia asked.

"We saw your light," said Walker.

"Our light?"

Ike's oil lamps, thought Ali. It had been her secret with him. A beacon to the world.

"You found Cache V," said Spurrier.

"Haddie got half," said Walker.

"Call it the devil's due," said a voice, and Montgomery Shoat entered the room.

"You? You're still alive?" said Ali. She couldn't hide her distaste. Being abandoned by the soldiers was one thing. But Shoat was a fellow civilian, and had known Walker's dirty scheme. His betrayal felt worse.

"It's been quite the excursion," said Shoat. He had a black eye and yellow bruises along one cheek, obviously from a beating. "Haddie's been picking us to pieces for weeks. And the boys have been working double-time to fit me in. I'm starting to think we may not complete our grand tour of the sub-Pacific."

Walker was in no mood for a court jester. "Is this coastline inhabited?"

"I've only seen three of them," Ali said.

"Three villages?"

"Three hadals."

"That's all? No villages?" Walker's black beard parted in a smile. "Then we've lost them, thank the Lord. They'll never be able to track us across open water. We're safe. We have food for another two months. And we have Shoat's homing device."

Shoat wagged a finger at the colonel. "Ah-ah," he said. "Not yet. You agreed. Three more days to the west. Then we'll talk about retreat."

"Where's the girl?" asked Ali. As more of the mercenaries came in, she saw the clawed hands and hadal ears and pieces of male and female genitalia dangling from their belts and rucksacks and rifles. Yeats's poem echoed in her mind: *The center cannot hold; . . . The blood-dimmed tide is loosed, and everywhere the ceremony of innocence is drowned. . . .*

"I misjudged her," Walker rasped. He needed morphine. Ali suspected what the soldiers had probably done with it.

"You killed her," Ali said.

"I should have. She's been useless to me." He gestured, and two soldiers dragged the feral girl in and tied her to the wall nearby.

The first thing Ali noticed was her smells. The girl had a raw odor, fecal and musky and layered with sweat. Her hair smelled like smoke and filth. Blood and snot streaked the duct tape.

"What has been done to this child?"

"She's been an ungodly temptation to my men," Walker answered.

"You allowed your men—"

Walker peered at her. "So righteous? You're no different, though. Everyone wants something from this creature. Go ahead, extract your glossary from her, Sister. Just don't leave this room without permission."

Troy stood and draped his jacket on the girl's shoulders. The girl backed away from his chivalry, then opened her legs as far as the ropes would allow, and pumped her groin at him. Troy backed away.

"I wouldn't fall in love with that one, boy." Walker laughed. *"Ferae naturae.* She's wild by nature."

Ali and Troy went to feed the girl.

"What you doing?" a soldier demanded.

"Taking off this duct tape," Ali said. "How else can she eat?"

The soldier gave a hard yank at the tape, and snatched his hand away. The girl all but garroted herself on the wire, lunging for him. Ali fell back. Laughter sprinkled the room. "All yours," he said.

The feeding needed caution. Ali spoke to her with a low voice, enunciating their names, and trying to disarm her. The food was noxious to the girl, but she took it. At one point she spit the applesauce out and made some elaborate complaint, which emerged with extraordinary softness. It wasn't just the volume that was soft, but the formal delivery. For all her ferocity, the girl sounded almost pious. She seemed to be speaking to the food, or discoursing on it. Her temperament was sophisticated, not savage.

When she was done, the girl lay back on the rock floor and closed her eyes. There was no transition between the meal and sleeping. She took what she could get.

Two days passed. Ike still did not show himself. Ali sensed he was somewhere close, but the search teams came up empty.

The soldiers beat Shoat senseless, trying to pry loose the secret of his homing-device code. His stubbornness drove them to a fury, and they only stopped when Ali placed her body across Shoat's. "Kill him and you'll never learn the code," she told them. Nursing Shoat added to her duties, for she was already taking care of Walker and several other soldiers. But someone had to do it. They were still God's creatures.

Walker wavered in and out of fever. He railed in tongues in his sleep. The soldiers exchanged dark looks. The room filled with deadly intent, and Ali grew more and more concerned. The only good news was that Ike was nowhere to be found.

On the second night, Troy bravely tried to stop a mercenary from taking the girl outside to some waiting friends. The soldiers gave him a pistol-whipping that would have gone on but for the girl's laughter, and her strangeness made them lose interest in hitting Troy. Much later she was returned to the room, sweaty and with her mouth duct-taped. Still bleeding himself, Troy helped Ali bathe the girl with a bottle of water.

"She's carried children," Troy observed in a low voice. "Have you seen that?"

"You're mistaken," Ali said.

But there among the tattooed zebra lines and hatchmarks hid the stretch marks of pregnancy. Her areolae were dark. Ali had missed the signs.

On the third night, the mercenaries came for the girl again. Hours later she was returned, semiconscious. While she and Troy washed the girl, Ali quietly hummed a tune. She wasn't even aware of it until Troy said, "Ali, look!"

Ali raised her eyes from the yellowing bruises on the child's pelvic saddle. The girl was staring at her with tears running down her cheeks. Ali lifted the hum into words. "Through many dangers, toils and snares, I have already come," she softly sang. "'Tis grace that brought me safe thus far, And grace will lead me home."

The girl began sobbing. Ali made the mistake of taking the child in her arms. The kindness triggered a terrible storm of kicking and thrashing and rejection. It was a horrible enlightening moment, for now Ali knew the girl had once had a mother who had sung that song.

All night Ali spent with the captive, watching her. In her fourteen years the girl had experienced more of womanhood than Ali had in thirty-four. She had been married, or mated. She appeared to have borne a child. And so far she had kept her sanity through brutal mass rapes. Her inner strength was amazing.

Next morning Twiggs needed to go to the bathroom for his first time since the starvation. Being Twiggs, he did not ask the soldiers' permission to leave the room. One of the mercenaries shot him dead.

That spelled the end of what little freedom the rest of them had. Walker ordered the scientists bound, wired, and removed to a deeper room. Ali was not surprised. For some time now, she had known their execution was imminent.

And darkness was upon the
face of the Deep

—GENESIS 1:2

24
TABULA RASA

The hotel suite was dark except for the blue flicker of the TV.

It was a riddle: television on, volume off, in a blind man's room. Once upon a time, de l'Orme might have orchestrated such a contradiction just to confound his visitors. Tonight he had no visitors. The maid had forgotten to turn off her soaps.

Now the screen showed the Times Square ball as it descended toward the deliriously happy mob.

De l'Orme was browsing his Meister Eckhart. The thirteenth-century mystic had preached such strange things with such common words. And in the bowels of the Dark Ages, so boldly.

God lies in wait for us. His love is like a fisherman's hook. No fish comes to the fisherman that is not caught on his hook. Once it takes the hook, the fish is forfeit to the fisherman. In vain it twists hither and thither—the fisherman is certain of his catch. And so I say of love. The one who hangs on this hook is caught so fast that foot and hand, mouth, eyes and heart are bound to be God's. And the more surely caught, the more surely you will be freed.

No wonder the theologian had been condemned by the Inquisition and excommunicated. God as dominatrix! More dizzying still, man freed of God. God freed of God. And then what? Nothingness. You penetrated the darkness and emerged into the same light you had left in the first place. Then who leave in the first place? de l'Orme wondered why. For the journey itself? Is that the best we have to do with ourselves? These were his thoughts when the phone rang.

"Do you know my voice, yes or no?" asked the man on the far end.

"Bud?" said de l'Orme.

"Great . . . my name," Parsifal mumbled.

"Where are you?"

"Huh-uh." The astronaut sounded sluggish. Drunk. The Golden Boy?

"Something's troubling you," de l'Orme said.

"You bet. Is Santos with you?"

"No."

"Where is he?" Parsifal demanded. "Or do you even know?"

"The Koreas," said de l'Orme, not exactly certain which one. "Another set of hadals has surfaced. He's recording some of the artifacts they brought with them. Emblems of a deity stamped into gold foil."

"Korea. He told you that?"

"I sent him, Bud."

"What makes you so sure he's where you sent him?" Parsifal asked.

De l'Orme took his glasses off. He rubbed his eyes and opened them, and they were white, with no retina or pupil. Distant fireworks streaked his face with sparks of color. He waited.

"I've been trying to call the others," Parsifal said. "All night, nothing."

"It's New Year's Eve," said de l'Orme. "Perhaps they're with their families."

"No one's told you." It was an accusation, not a question.

"I'm afraid not, whatever it is."

"It's too late. You really don't know? Where have you been?"

"Right here. A touch of the flu. I haven't left my room in a week."

"Ever heard of *The New York Times*? Don't you listen to the news?"

"I gave myself the solitude. Fill me in, if you please. I can't help if I don't know."

"Help?"

"Please."

"We're in great danger. You shouldn't be at that phone."

It came out in a tangle. There had been a great fire at the Metropolitan Museum's Map Room two weeks ago. And before that, a bomb explosion in an ancient cliffside temple library at Yungang in China, which the PLA was blaming on Muslim separatists. Archives and archaeological sites in ten or more countries had been vandalized or destroyed in the past month.

"I've heard about the Met, of course. That was everywhere. But the rest of this, what connects them?"

"Someone's trying to erase our information. It's like someone's finishing business. Wiping out his tracks."

"What tracks? Burning museums. Blowing up libraries. What purpose could that serve?"

"He's closing shop."

"He? Who are you talking about? You don't make sense."

Parsifal mentioned several other events, including a fire at the Cambridge Library housing the ancient Cairo *genizah* fragments.

"Gone," he said. "Burned to the ground. Defaced. Blown to pieces."

"Those are all places we've visited over the last year."

"Someone has been erasing our information for some time now," said Parsifal. "Until recently they've been small erasures mostly, an altered manuscript here, a photo negative disappearing there. Now the destruction seems more wholesale and spectacular. It's like someone's trying to finish business before clearing out of town."

"A coincidence," said de l'Orme. "Book burners. A pogrom. Anti-intellectuals. The lumpen are rampant these days."

"It's no coincidence. He used us. Like bloodhounds. Turned us loose on his own trail. Had us hunt him. And now he's backtracking."

"He?"

"Who do you think?"

"But what does it accomplish? Even if you were right, he merely erases our footnotes, not our conclusions."

"He erases his own image."

"Then he defaces himself. What does that change?" But even as he spoke, de l'Orme felt wrong. Were those distant sirens or alarms tripping in his own head?

"It destroys our memory," said Parsifal. "It wipes clean his presence."

"But we know him now. At least we know everything the evidence has already shown. Our memory is fixed."

"We're the last testimony," said Parsifal. "After us, it's back to tabula rasa."

De l'Orme was missing pieces of the puzzle. A week behind closed doors, and it was as if the world had changed orbit. Or Parsifal had.

De l'Orme tried to arrange the information. "You're suggesting we've led our foe on a tour of his own clues. That it's an inside job. That Satan is one of us. That he—or she?—is now revisiting our evidence and spoiling it. Again, why? What does he accomplish by destroying all the past images of himself? If our theory of a reincarnated line of hadal kings is true, then he'll reappear next time with a different face."

"But with all his same subconscious patterns," said Parsifal. "Remember? We talked about that. You can't change your fundamental nature. It's like a fingerprint. He can try to alter his behavior, but five thousand years of human evidence has made him identifiable. If not to us, then to the next Beowulf gang, or the next. No evidence, no discovery. He becomes the invisible man. Whatever the hell he is."

"Let him rampage," de l'Orme said. He was speaking as much to Parsifal's agitation as about their hadal prey. "By the time he finishes his vandalism, we'll know him better than he knows himself. We're close."

He listened to Parsifal's hard breathing on the other end. The astronaut muttered inaudibly. De l'Orme could hear wind lashing the telephone booth. Close by, a sixteen-wheel truck blatted down through lower gears. He pictured Parsifal at some forlorn pit stop along an interstate.

"Go home," de l'Orme counseled.

"Whose side are you on? That's what I really called about. Whose side are you on?"

"Whose side am I on?"

"That's what this whole thing is about, isn't it?" Parsifal's voice trailed off. The wind invaded. He sounded like a man losing mind and body to the storm.

"Your wife has to be wondering where you are."

"And have her end up like Mustafah? We've said good-bye. She'll never see me again. It's for her own good."

There was a bump, and then scratching at de l'Orme's window. He drew back into his presumption of darkness, put his spine against the corduroy sofa. He listened. Claws raked at the glass. And there, he tracked it, the beat of wings. A bird. Or an angel. Lost among the skyscrapers.

"What about Mustafah?"

"You have to know."

"I don't."

"He was found last Friday, in Istanbul. What was left of him was floating in the underground reservoir at Yerebatan Sarayi. You really don't know? He was killed the same day a bomb was found in the Hagia Sofia. We're part of the evidence, don't you see?"

With great, concentrated precision, de l'Orme laid his glasses on the side table. He felt dizzy. He wanted to resist, to challenge Parsifal, to make him retract this terrible news.

"There's only one person who can be doing this," said Parsifal. "You know it as well as I do."

There was a minute of relative silence, neither man speaking. The phone filled with blizzard gales and the beep-beep of snowplows setting off to battle the drifted highways. Then Parsifal spoke again. "I know how close you two were." His lucidity, his compassion, cemented the revelation.

"Yes," de l'Orme said.

It was the worst falseness he could imagine. The man's obsession had guided them. And now he had disinherited them, body and spirit. No, that was wrong, for they'd never been included in his inheritance to begin with. From the start, he had merely exploited them. They had been like livestock to him, to be ridden to death.

"You must get away from him," said Parsifal.

But de l'Orme's thoughts were on the traitor. He tried to configure the thousands of deceptions that had been perpetrated on them. A king's audacity! Almost in admiration, he whispered the name.

"Louder," said Parsifal. "I can't hear you over the wind."

"Thomas," de l'Orme said again. What magnificent courage! What ruthless deception! It was dizzying, the depths of his plotting. What had he been after then? Who was he really? And why commission a posse to hunt himself down?

"Then you've heard," shouted Parsifal. His blizzard was getting worse.

"They've found him?"

"Yes."

De l'Orme was astounded. "But that means we've won."

"Have you lost your mind?" said Parsifal.

"Have you lost yours? Why are you running? They've caught him. Now we can interview him directly. We must go to him immediately. Give me the details, man."

"Caught him? Thomas?"

De l'Orme heard Parsifal's confusion, and he felt equally dumbfounded. Even after so many months spent treating the hadal as a common man, Satan's mortality did not come naturally. How could one *catch* Satan? Yet here it was. They had accomplished the impossible. They had transcended myth.

"Where is he? What have they done with him?"

"Thomas, you mean?"

"Yes, Thomas."

"But Thomas is dead."

"Thomas?"

"I thought you said you knew."

"No," groaned de l'Orme.

"I'm sorry. He was a great friend to us all."

De l'Orme digested the consequences, but still he didn't understand. "They killed him?"

"They?" shouted the astronaut. Was Parsifal not hearing him, or were they stumbling on each other's meaning?

"Satan," enunciated de l'Orme. His thoughts raced. They'd killed the hadal Caesar? Didn't the fools know Satan's value? In his mind's eye, de l'Orme saw some frightened young soldier with a high school education emptying his rifle clip into the shadows, and Thomas tumbling from the darkness into the light, dead.

But still de l'Orme did not understand.

"Yes, Satan," said Parsifal. His voice was growing indistinguishable from the noise of his tempest. "You do understand. My same conclusion. Mustafah. Now Thomas. Satan. Satan killed them."

De l'Orme frowned. "You said they found him, though. Satan."

"No. Thomas," clarified Parsifal. "They found Thomas. A Bedouin goatherder came on him this afternoon. He was lying among the rocks near St. Catherine's monastery. He had fallen—or been pushed—from one of the cliffs on Mount Sinai. It's obvious who killed him. Satan did. He's hunting us down, one by one. He knows our patterns. Our daily lives. Our hiding places. While we were profiling him, the bastard was profiling us."

At last de l'Orme understood what Parsifal was telling him. Thomas was not the deceiver. It was someone even closer to him.

"Are you still there?" asked Parsifal.

De l'Orme cleared his throat. "What have they done with Thomas's body?" he asked.

"Whatever desert monks do to their dead. Probably not much in the way of preservation. They want to get him into the ground as soon as possible. He'll be buried on Wednesday. There at the monastery." He paused. "You're not going, are you?"

So much to plan. So little, really. De l'Orme knew exactly what needed to happen next.

"It's your head," said Parsifal.

De l'Orme set the phone back in its cradle.

She woke in her bed to ancient dreams, that she was young again and beaux pursued her. The many became few. The few became one. In her dreams she was alone, like now, but alone differently, an ache in men's hearts, a memory that would never end. And this one man would never stop searching for her, even if she was lost in herself, even if she grew old.

She opened her eyes and the room was awash in moonbeams.

The coarse linen curtains stirred with a breeze. Crickets sang in the grass off her porch. The window had come open.

A tiny light looped and spiraled in the room, a firefly.

"Vera," said a man from the dark corner.

She jerked, and the glasses flew from her fingers.

A burglar, she thought. But a burglar who knew her name? Who spoke it so sadly?

"Who is it?" she said.

"I have been watching you sleep," he said. "In this light, I see the little girl your father must have loved."

He was going to kill her. Vera could hear the determination in his tenderness.

A form rose in the moon shadows. Released of his weight, the wicker chair creaked in its weave, and he stepped forward.

"Who are you?" she asked.

"Parsifal didn't call you?"

"Yes."

"Didn't he tell you?"

"Tell me what?"

"Who I am."

A winter chill settled on her.

Parsifal had called yesterday, and she had cut short his roadside augury. The sky is falling, that's all she could make of his nonsense. Indeed, his burst of paranoid advice and omens had finally accomplished what Thomas had failed to do: convinced her their quest for the monster was a monster itself.

It had struck her that their search for the king of darkness was autogenetic, brought to life from nothing more real than their idea of it. In retrospect, their search had been feeding on itself for months, on its own clues and predictions and fancy scholarship. Now it was beginning to feed on them. Just as Thomas had warned, the quest had become dangerous. Their enemies were not the tyrants and would-be tyrants, the C.C. Coopers of the world, or their fabled Satan of the underworld. Rather, the enemy was their own overheated imaginings.

She had hung up on Parsifal. Repeatedly. He had called back several times, ranting and raving, sounding like a Yankee carpetbagger trying to scare her off the plantation. I'm staying put, she told him.

He had been right then.

Her wheelchair sat next to her nightstand. She did not try to talk him out of the murder. She did not question his method or test for his sadism. Maybe he would be swift and businesslike. *So you die in bed after all,* she thought to herself.

"Did he sing songs to you?" the man asked.

Vera was trying to arrange her courage and thoughts. Her heart was racing. She wanted to be calm.

"Parsifal?"

"Your father, I meant."

His question distracted her. "Songs?"

"Before you went to sleep."

It was an invitation. She took it. She closed her eyes and threw herself into the search. It meant ignoring the crickets and penetrating her jackhammer heartbeat and descending into remembrances she had thought were gone forever. But there he was, and yes, it was night, and he was singing to her. She laid her head back on the pillow, and his words made a blanket and his voice promised shelter. Papa, she thought.

The floorboard squeaked.

Vera regretted that. If not for the sound, she would have stayed with the song. But the wood returned her to the room. Up through the heart she came, back into the land of crickets and moonbeams.

She opened her eyes and he was there, barehanded, with the firefly spinning a crooked halo high above his head. He was reaching for her like her lover. And then his face entered the light and she said, "You?"

ST. CATHERINE'S MONASTERY, JABAL MUSA (MT. SINAI)

De l'Orme arranged the cups and placed the loaf of bread. The abbot had provided him a meditation chamber, the sort enjoyed for thousands of years by men and women seeking spiritual wisdom.

Santos would be charmed. He loved coarseness and simplicity. The wine jug was clay. The table's planks had been hewn and nailed at least five centuries ago. No curtain in the window. No glass, even. Dust and insects were your prayer mates. Like words from the Bible, a bolt of sunlight stabbed the darkness of his cell. De l'Orme felt its warmth upon his face. He felt it travel east to west across his cheeks. He felt it setting.

It was cool this high, especially compared with the desert heat on his ride in. The road was no longer so good. De l'Orme had suffered its potholes. Because tourists no longer came here in such abundance, there was less reason to maintain the asphalt. The Holy Lands didn't pull them in like they used to. The revelation of hell as a common network of tunnels had achieved what hell itself could not, the end of spiritual fear. The death of God at the hands of existentialism and materialism had been grievous enough. Now the death of Supreme Evil had turned the landscape of afterlife into a cheap haunted house. From Moses to Mohammed to Augustine, the carnies had been good for their day, but no one was buying it anymore.

Along with the road that led to its high walls, St. Catherine's was falling into disrepair. De l'Orme had listened to the scandalized abbot tell how a number of the monks had turned idiorhythmic, acquiring property in the now-abandoned tourist village, eating meat, putting icons and mirrors and rugs in their monastic apartments. Such corruption led to disobedience, of course. And what was a monastery without obedience? Even the shapeless bramble tree in St. Catherine's courtyard, said to be Moses' burning bush, was dying.

De l'Orme drew a lungful of the evening breeze, breathing the incense like oxygen. He could smell an almond tree nearby, even now, in winter. Someone was growing a small pot of basil. And there was a sweet odor, ever so faint: the bodies of dead saints.

Anthropologists called it second burial, this practice of disinterring their dead after several years and adding the bones and skulls of monks to the monastery's collection. The charnel house was jokingly called the University. The dead go on teaching through their memory, so went the tradition. And what will you teach them, Thomas? de l'Orme wondered. Grace? Forgiveness? Or a warning against the darkness?

Evening vespers was beginning. Remarkably, a caged parakeet had been allowed into the courtyard. Its song matched the monks' *Kyrie Eleison*, the notes of a tiny angel.

At moments like this, de l'Orme longed to return to the cloth, or at least to the hermit's cell. If you let it be just as it was, the world was a surfeit of riches. Hold still, and the entire universe was your lover. But it was too late for that.

Santos arrived in a Jeep that rattled on the corrugated dirt. He disturbed a herd of goats, you could hear the bells and scurry of hooves. De l'Orme listened. Santos was alone. His stride was powerful and wide.

The parakeet stopped. The *Kyrie Eleisons* did not. De l'Orme let him find his own way.

After a few minutes, Santos put his head inside de l'Orme's chamber. "There you are," he said.

"Come in," said de l'Orme. "I didn't know if you'd make it before nightfall."

"Here I am," said Santos. "And look, you have our supper. I brought nothing."

"Sit, you must be tired."

"It was a long trip," Santos admitted.

"You've been busy."

"I came as quickly as I could. Is he buried, then?"

"Today. In the cemetery."

"It was good?"

"They treated him as one of their own. He would have been pleased."

"I didn't like him much. But you loved him, I know. Are you all right?"

"Certainly," said de l'Orme. He made himself rise and opened his arms and gave Santos an embrace. The smell of the younger man's sweat and the barren Mosaic desert was good. Santos had the sun trapped in his pores, it seemed.

"He led a full life," Santos sympathized.

"Who knows what more he might have discovered?" said de l'Orme. He gave the broad back a tap and they parted the embrace. De l'Orme sat carefully on his three-legged wooden stool. Santos lowered his satchel to the floor and took the stool de l'Orme had arranged on the far side of the table.

"And now? Where do we go from here? What do we do?"

"Let's eat," said de l'Orme. "We can discuss tomorrow over our meal."

"Olives. Goat cheese. An orange. Bread. A jug of wine," Santos said. "All the makings for a Last Supper."

"If you wish to mock Christ, that's your business. But don't mock your food," de l'Orme said. "You don't need to eat if you're not hungry."

"Just a little joke. I'm famished."

"There should be a candle, too," said de l'Orme. "It must be dark. But I had no matches."

"It's still twilight," said Santos. "There's light enough. I prefer the atmosphere."

"Then pour the wine."

"What could have brought him here, I wonder," said Santos. "You told me Thomas had finished with the search."

"It's clear now, Thomas was never going to be finished with the search."

"Was there something here he was looking for?" De l'Orme could hear Santos's puzzlement. He was really asking why de l'Orme had instructed him to come all this way.

"I thought at first he had come for the Codex Sinaiticus," de l'Orme answered. Santos would know that the Codex was one of the oldest manuscripts of the New Testament. It totaled three thousand volumes, only a few of which still remained in this library. "But now I think otherwise."

"Yes?"

"I believe Satan lured him here," de l'Orme answered.

"Lured him? How?"

"Perhaps with his presence. Or a message. I don't know."

"He has a sense of theater, then," Santos remarked between bites of food. "The mountain of God."

"So it appears."

"You're not hungry?"

"I have no appetite tonight."

The monks were hard at work in the church. Their deep chant reverberated through the stone. Lord have mercy. Christ have mercy. Lord have mercy. *Domine Deus.*

"Are you crying for Thomas?" Santos suddenly asked.

De l'Orme made no move to wipe away the tears flowing down his cheeks. "No," he said. "For you."

"Me? But why? I'm here with you now."

"Yes."

Santos grew quieter. "You're not happy with me."

"It's not that."

"Then what? Tell me."

"You are dying," said de l'Orme.

"But you're mistaken." Santos laughed with relief. "I'm perfectly well."

"No," said de l'Orme. "I poisoned your wine."

"What a terrible joke."

"No joke."

Just then Santos clutched his stomach. He stood, and his wooden stool cracked on the slabs. "What have you done?" he gasped.

There was no drama to it. He did not fall to the floor. Gently he knelt on the stone and laid himself down. "Is it true?" he asked.

"Yes," said de l'Orme. "Ever since Bordubor I've suspected you of mischief."

"What?"

"It was you who defaced the carving. And who killed that poor guard."

"No." Santos's protest was little more than a respiration.

"No? Who, then? Me? Thomas? There was no one else. But you."

Santos groaned. His beloved white shirt would be soiled from the floor, de l'Orme imagined.

"It is you who have set about dismantling your image among man," he continued.

The respiration threaded up from the floor.

"I can't explain how you were able to choose me so long ago," said de l'Orme. "All I know is that I was your pathway to Thomas. I led you to him."

Santos rallied, for the space of one breath. ". . . all wrong," he whispered.

"What's your name?" asked de l'Orme.

But it was too late.

Santos, or Satan, was no more.

He had meant to keep his vigil over the body all night. Santos weighed too much for him to lift onto the cot, and so when the air grew cold and he could not stay awake any longer, de l'Orme wrapped the blanket around himself and lay on the floor beside the corpse. In the morning he would explain his murder to the monks. Beyond that, he didn't care.

And so he fell asleep, shoulder to shoulder with his victim.

The incision across his abdomen woke him.

The pain was so sudden and extreme, he registered it as a bad dream, nothing to panic about.

Then he felt the animal climb inside his chest wall, and realized it was no animal but a hand. It navigated upward with a surgeon's dexterity. He tried to flatten himself, palms against the stone, but his head arched back and his body could not retreat, *could not*, from that awful trespass.

"Santos!" he gasped with his one and only sac of air.

"No, not him," murmured a voice he knew.

De l'Orme's eyes stared into the night.

They did it this way in Mongolia. The nomad makes a slit in the belly of his sheep and darts his hand inside and reaches high through all the slippery organs and drives straight to the beating heart. Done properly, it was considered an all but painless death.

It took a strong hand to squeeze the organ to stillness. This hand was strong.

De l'Orme did not fight. That was one other advantage to the method. By the time the hand was inside, there was nothing more to fight. The body itself cooperated, shocked by the unthinkable violation. No instinct could rehearse a man for such a moment. To feel the fingers wrap around your heart . . . He waited while his slaughterer held the chalice of life.

It took less than a minute.

He rolled his head to the left and Santos was there beside him, as cold as wax, de l'Orme's own creation. His horror was complete. He had sinned against himself. In the name of goodness he had killed goodness. Year upon year he had received the young man's goodness, and he had rebuked and tested it and never believed such a thing could be real. And he had been wrong.

His mouth formed the name of love, but there was no air left to make the word.

To a stranger, it might have seemed de l'Orme now gave himself to the sacrifice. He gave a small heave, and it drove the arm deeper. Like a puppet, he reached for the hand that manipulated him, and it was a phantom within the bones of his chest. Gently he laid his own hands above his heart. His defenseless heart.

Lord have mercy.

The fist closed.

In his last instant, a song came to him. It surged upon his hearing, all but impossible, so beautiful. A child monk's pure voice? A tourist's radio, a bit of opera? He realized it was the parakeet caged in the courtyard. In his mind, he saw the moon rise full above the mountains. But of course the animals would wake to it. Of course they would offer their morning song to such a radiance. De l'Orme had never known such light, even in his imagination.

BENEATH THE SINAI PENINSULA

Through the wound, entrance.

Through the veins, retreat.

His quest was done.

In the nature of true searching, he had found himself. Now his people needed him as they gathered in their desolation. It was his destiny to lead them into a new land, for he was their savior.

Down he sped.

Down from the Egypt eye of the sun, in from the Sinai, away from their skies like a sea inside out, their stars and planets spearing your soul, their cities like insects, all shell and mechanism, their blindness with eyes, their vertiginous plains and mind-crushing mountains. Down from the billions who had made the world in their own human image. Their signature could be a thing of beauty. But it was a thing of death. Their presence had become the world, and their presence was the presence of jackals that strip the muscle from your legs even as you try to outrun them.

The earth closed over him. With each twist and bend, it sealed shut behind him. It resurrected senses long buried.

Solitude! Quiet! Darkness was light.

Once again he could hear the planet's joints and lifeblood. Stirrings in the stone. Ancient events. Here, time was like water. The tiniest creatures were his fathers and mothers. The fossils were his children. It made him into remembrance itself.

He let his bare palms ricochet upon the walls, drawing in the heat and the cold, the sharp and the smooth. Plunging, galloping, he pawed at the flesh of God. This magnificent rock. This fortress of their being. This was the Word. Earth.

Moment by moment, step by step, he felt himself becoming prehistoric. It was a blessed release from human habits. In this vast, capillaried monastery, through these openings and fretted spillways and yawning chthonic fistulae, drinking from pools of water older than mammal life altogether, memory was simply memory. It was not something to be marked on calendars or stored in books or labeled in graphs or drawn on maps. You did not memorize memory any more than you memorized existence.

He remembered his way deeper by the taste of the soil and by the drag of air currents that had no cardinal direction. He left behind the cartography of the Holy Land and its entry caves through Jebel el Lawz in the elusive Midian. He forgot the name of the Indian Ocean as he passed beneath it. He felt gold, soft and serpentine, standing from the walls, but no longer recognized it as gold. Time passed, but he gave up counting it. Days? Weeks? He lost his memory even as he gained it.

He saw himself and did not know it was himself. It was in a sheet of black obsidian. His image rose up as a black silhouette within the blackness. He went to it and laid his hands on the volcanic glass and stared at his face reflecting back. Something about the eyes seemed familiar.

Onward he hurtled, weary, yet refreshed. The depths gave flesh to his strength. Occasional animals provided him the gift of their meat. More and more, he witnessed life in the darkness, heard its chirps and rustling. He found evidence of his refugees and, long before them, of hadal nomads and religious travelers. Their markings on the walls filled him with grief for the lost glory of his empire.

His people had fallen from grace, steeply and deep and for so long they were hardly aware of their own descent. Yet now, even in their emptiness and misery, they were being pursued in the name of God, and that could not be. For they were God's children, and had lived in the wilderness long enough to wash their sins into amnesty. They had paid for their pride or independence or whatever else it was that had offended the natural order, and now, after an exile of a hundred eons, they had been returned to their innocence.

For God to continue punishing them was wrong. To allow them to be hunted into extinction was a sacrilege. But then, from the very beginning, his people had challenged the notion that God ever showed mercy. They were his lie. They were his sin. It had always been a false hope that God might deliver them from His own wrath into love. No, deliverance had to come from some other soul.

The dead have no rights.

—THOMAS JEFFERSON,
near the end of his life

25

PANDEMONIUM

January 5

The end began with a small thing Ali spied on the ground. It could have been an angel lying there, invisible to all but her, telling her to be ready. Not missing a step, she landed her foot on the message and crushed it to bits. It was probably unnecessary. Who else would have read so much in a red M&M?

Not much later, while crouched awkwardly in the shadowy nook designated their latrine, Ali discovered another red candy, this time lodged in a crack in the wall above their sewage. Squatting above the pool of muck, her wrists roped tight by the mercenaries, Ali could still get the fingers of one hand down the crack. Expecting a note, she felt a hard, smooth knob. What she slid from the stone was a knife, black for night work, with a blood gutter and utilitarian weight. Even the handle looked cruel.

"What are you doing in there?" the guard called. Ali slipped the knife into her clothing, and the guard returned her to the little side room that was their dungeon. Heart knocking in her ears, Ali took her place beside the girl. She was afraid, but joyous. Here was her chance.

And now? Ali wondered. Would there be another sign? Should she cut her ropes now or wait? And what did Ike think she was capable of? He had to know there were limits. She was a woman of God.

Three mercenaries stalked ten feet apart through the terra-cotta army surrounding the spire. "This is a waste of time," said one. "He's gone. If I was him, I'd be gone."

"What are we doing anyway, stuck here? The colonel wants more fight?"

"It's a deathwatch, man. He wants us to hold his hand while he rots. And the whole time we're feeding prisoners. I didn't see no grocery on the way in."

"The best target's the one standing still. We're just beautiful, man. Sitting ducks."

"My very thoughts."

There was a pause. They were still feeling one another out.

"So what's the word?"

"Desperate times, man. Desperate measures. The colonel's eating our time. The civilians are eating our food. And the dying are dead. It's called limited resources."

"Makes sense to me."

"So who else is in?"

"You two make twelve. Plus the mope, Shoat. He won't let go of the code for his homing device."

"Give me an hour with Shoat, I'll give you his code. And his mama's phone number."

"You're wasting your time. He gives that up, he knows he's dead. We just have to wait until he activates the box. Then he's dog food."

"When do we do it?"

"Pack your toothbrush. Soon, real soon."

"Ow," barked one. "Fucking statues."

"Be glad they ain't real."

"Hang on, girls. What have we here?"

"Coins! Look at this."

"These are handmade. See the cut edges? They're old."

"Fuck old. This stuff's gold."

"About time. And there's more this way."

"And over here, too. About time we found some booty."

The three separated, plucking coins from the ground with all the elegance of chickens in a yard. They worked farther and farther apart from one another.

Finally the one with a backward Raiders cap got down into a duck-walk with his rifle across his lap, which freed both hands to snatch at the treasure. "Hey, guys," he called, "my pockets are full. Rent me some space in your ruck."

Another minute passed. "Hey," he yelled again, and froze. "Guys?" His hands opened. The coins dropped. Slowly he reached for his rifle.

Too late, he heard the tinkling of jade.

The Chinese had a special word, *ling-lung,* to describe the musical jingling that jade jewelry made as aristocrats walked by. There was no telling what the hadals might have called it twenty eons earlier. But as the statue next to him came alive, the sound was identical.

The mercenary started to rise. The proto-Aztec war club met him on the downstroke. His head popped clear with surgical neatness. Obsidian really was sharper than modern scalpels. The statue shed its jade armor and became a man. Ike socketed the club back into its terra-cotta hands, and hefted the rifle. Fair exchange, he thought.

The mutineers carried the rafts down to the sea and loaded them with the expedition supplies. This was done in full view of their commander, whom they had bound into a wire cocoon and hung raving from the wall. "Neither death, nor life, nor angels, nor principalities, nor powers, nor things present, nor things to come, nor height, nor depth, nor any other creature shall be able to separate us from the vengeance of God," he shouted at them.

In their side room the prisoners could hear Walker. Love, not vengeance, thought Ali, lying on the floor. The colonel had it wrong. The quotation was Romans, and it had to do with the love of God, not His vengeance. A moot point.

Their guard left to help load the getaway vessels. He knew the civilians weren't going anywhere.

The time had come. Ike had given her all the advantage he could. She was going to have to improvise from here on.

Ali drew out the knife.

Troy lifted his head. She laid it against her wrist bonds and the blade was sharp. The rope practically disintegrated. She rolled to face Troy.

Spurrier heard them and looked over. "What are you doing?" he hissed. "Are you crazy?"

She flexed her wrists and shoulders and got to her knees to unravel the wire leashing her neck to the wall.

"If you make them mad, they won't take us with them," Spurrier said.

She frowned at him. "They're not taking us with them."

"Of course they are," Spurrier said. But she had shattered his hope. "Just wait."

"They'll be back," Ali said. "And we don't want to be here."

Troy had the knife, and went over to Chelsea and Pia and Spurrier.

"Get away from me," Spurrier said.

Pia grabbed Ali's hands and pulled her close. She stared at Ali, eyes wild. Her breath smelled like something buried. Beside her, Spurrier said, "We shouldn't make them mad, Pia."

"Stay, then," Ali said.

"What about her?" Troy was kneeling by the captive girl. Her eyes were on his, unwavering, watchful.

The girl might bolt for the entrance or start screaming or even turn on her liberators. On the other hand, leaving her was a death sentence. "Bring her," said Ali. "Leave the tape on her mouth, though. And keep her hands tied. And the wire around her neck, too."

Troy had the knife blade under her rope, ready to cut. He hesitated. The girl's eyes flickered to Ali. Tinged with jaundice, her eyes were cat-like. "You keep her tied, Troy. That's all I'll say."

Spurrier refused to escape. "Fools," he hissed.

Pia started out the door, then turned back. "I can't," she said to Ali.

"You can't stay here," said Ali.

"How can I leave him?"

Ali grasped Pia's arm to pull her, then let go.

"I'm sorry," Pia said. "Be careful." Ali kissed her forehead.

The fugitives stole from the room into the interior fortress. They had no lights, but the walls' luminescence fostered their progress.

"I know a place," Ali told them. They followed her without question. She found the stairs Ike had shown her.

Chelsea was limping badly from whatever the mercenaries had done. Ali helped her, and Troy helped the girl. At the top of the stairs, Ali led them through Ike's secret entrance into the lighthouse room.

It was dark in the room, except for one tiny flame. Someone had pried open the floor vault and emptied it. And left a single clay lamp burning. Ali lowered herself into the vault, and helped Chelsea descend. Troy lowered the captive girl. Ali was surprised at how light she was.

"Ike's been here," she said.

"It feels like a tomb," said Chelsea. She had started shivering. "I don't want to be here."

"It was a storage vault with jars," Ali said. "They were filled with oil. Ike's taken them somewhere."

"Where is he now?"

"Stay here," she said. "I'll find him."

"I'll go with you," said Troy, but reluctantly. He didn't want to leave the girl. He had developed some kind of obsession with her during the past few days. Ali looked at Chelsea: she was in terrible shape. Troy would have to stay with them. Ali tried to think the way Ike would.

"Wait in here," she said. "Keep low. Don't make any sounds. We'll come back for you when it's safe."

The tiny flame lit their drawn faces. Ali wanted to remain here with them, safe with the light. But Ike was out there, and he might need her.

"Take the knife," Troy said.

"I wouldn't know what to do with it," Ali said.

She cherished Troy's and Chelsea's looks of hope. "See you soon," she said.

Their rafts rocked on the seiche. You couldn't feel or hear the tremors, but deeper designs were stirring the sea with swells. The food and gear were lashed with muleskinner knots. They had the chain gun mounted, the spotlights on. It was going to be heavy going for eleven men, but their cornucopia promised months of sustenance and would lighten as they exited.

Half of the soldiers waited on the rafts while half went back to tidy up. They had drawn straws for the wet work. It was disgusting to them that Shoat asked to watch.

You didn't leave witnesses alive, not even the walking dead. Long before they died of starvation, any one of the survivors might pen some damning deposition. Things like that could haunt you. It might be ten years before any colonist found this fortress, but why risk the testimony of ghosts? That was what had confounded them about the colonel. He'd treated this as a calling, when all along it was just a crime.

They worked from front to back and kept it professional. Each of their wounded comrades got a well-placed mercy shot behind the eyes. Walker they left alive, strung to the wall, babbling scripture. Fuck him. In a million years, he wasn't going anywhere.

All that remained were the civilians in the side room. Two entered. "What's this bull?" one shouted.

Spurrier looked up, shielding Pia. "They ran away. We could have gone with them," he said. "But look, we stayed."

"Dumb fuck," the other soldier said.

They rolled two fragmentation grenades into the room and hugged the outer wall, then hosed what was left with a clip each. They returned to the front room. It was quiet, now that the wounded had finished pleading. Only Walker still moaned.

"That sucked," said one of the mercenaries.

"You ain't seen nothing yet," Shoat said. He was just finishing inserting another of his homing capsules into the wall.

"What are you talking about?"

"Visualize whirled peas," Shoat said.

"Hey, Shoat," called another. "Why keep stringing those homers? We ain't ever coming back this way."

"He who plants a tree, plants posterity," Shoat pronounced.

"Shut up, mope."

They watched from just below the water. Others occupied the heights, camouflaged with powdered rock, stone-still. Their composure was reptilian. Or insect. A matter of clans. Isaac had arranged them just so.

Had the mercenaries thought to illuminate the cliffside, they might have detected a faint pulse, the ripple of many lungs respiring. Their lights on the water simply ricocheted off the oscillating surface. The humans thought they were alone.

The party of executioners appeared at the fortress gate, in no hurry. They walked with heavy legs, like peasants at the end of the day. Until you've done it, you have no idea: Killing is a form of gravity.

"Vengeance will be mine," Walker's mad voice bellowed from the fortress.

"Have a nice day," someone muttered.

The flicker of fire coruscated through the doorway. Someone had started a bonfire with the last of the scientists' papers.

"We're going home, boys," the lieutenant called to his men as he welcomed them.

The lance that impaled him bore a beautiful example of Solutrean Ice Age technology. The flint blade was long and leaf-shaped, with exquisite pressure flaking and a smear of toxic poison milked from abyssal rays.

It was a classic impalement, driving straight up from the water and penetrating the lieutenant's anus precisely, pithing him the way, long ago, the lieutenant had readied frogs in junior high school science lab.

No one suspected. The lieutenant stayed erect, or nearly so. His head bowed slightly, but otherwise his eyes stayed open, the smile pinned wide.

"Made in the shade, Lewt," one of the soldiers replied to him.

Down at the far end of the line of boats, a shooter called Grief sat straddling the rubber pontoon. He heard a sound like oil separating and turned and the sea was sliding open. There was just enough time to see a wall-eyed happy face before he was seized and pulled under. The water sealed shut above his heels.

The mercenaries spread out across the sand, angling for different boats beached along the shore. Two carried their rifles by the handle-sight. One draped his, cruciform, across his shoulders.

"Let's go, *pendejos*," called one of the boat men. "I can feel their ghosts."

It was said that Roman slingers could hit a man-sized target at 185 meters. For the record, the stone that cored Boom-Boom Jefferson was slung from 235 meters. His neighbor heard the watermelon-like thump through Boom-Boom's chest wall, and looked to see the once-notorious center for the Utah Jazz stiffen and drop like a huge tree deciding it was time.

Ten seconds had passed.

"Haddie!" cried the neighbor.

They'd been through this before, so the surprise was not surprising. They knew to react with no thought, to simply pull the trigger and make noise and light. They had no targets yet, but you didn't wait for targets, not with the hadals. In the first few moments, firepower was your one chance at jumbling their puzzle pieces and turning the picture around.

And so they fired at the cliff walls. They fired at the sand. They fired at the water. They fired at the sky. They tried not to fire on one another, but that was the collateral risk.

Their special loads gave spectacular results. The Lucifer rounds struck rock and shattered into splinters of brilliant light, July Fourth with intent to kill. They plowed the sand, blew up the water in arcing gouts. High overhead, the ceiling sparkled with lethal constellations, and bits of stone rained down.

It worked.

Haddie quit.

For a minute.

"Hold fire," yelled a man. "Count out. I'm one."

"Two," yelled another.

"Three."

There were only seven left.

The mercenaries closest to the boats raced downshore. Three forged back toward the fortress through molasses-thick sand.

"I'm hit."

"The lieutenant's dead."

"Grief?"

"Gone."

"Boom-Boom?"

"Is it over? Did Haddie leave?" This had been the pattern for weeks, hit and run. The hadals owned the night in a place where night was forever.

"Fucking Haddie. How'd they find us?"

Huddled just inside the fortress gate, Shoat took in the scene and converted the odds. He had not quite left when the attack began, and saw no reason to announce his good health. He touched the pouch containing his homing device. It was like a talisman to him, a source of comfort and great power. A way to make this dangerous world vanish.

With a few simple taps on the keypad, he could eliminate the threat altogether. The hadals would turn into illusions. But so would the mercenaries, and they were still useful to him. Among other things, Shoat didn't enjoy paddling. He held his apocalypse pouch and considered: Use you now or use you later? Later, he decided. No harm in waiting a few minutes more to see how the dust settled out there. It seemed the hadals might have driven home their point, so to speak, and boogied back into the darkness.

"What should we do?" shouted a soldier.

"Leave. We got to leave," yelled another. "Everybody get onto the boats. We're safe on the water."

Several of the rafts were drifting unmanned. The chain gunner was paddling his own boat back to shore. "Let's go, let's go!" he shouted to three comrades crouched against the fortress wall.

Uncertain, the three landbound men stood and peered around for any more ambushers. Seeing no one, they snapped fresh clips into their rifles and tried to prepare themselves for the sprint. The soldiers in the boats kept waving at them to come along.

"A hundred meters," one of the trapped mercenaries estimated. "I did that in nine-point-nine once."

"Not in sand you didn't."

"Watch me."

They offloaded their packs and shed every extra ounce, their grenades and knives and lights and inflatable vests.

"Ready?"

"Nine-point-nine? You're really that slow?"

They were ready.

"Set."

A woman's cry fell upon them from the highest reaches of the fortress. Everyone heard it. Even Ali, winding her way down through the fortress, stopped to listen, and knew that Troy had disobeyed her.

The mercenaries looked up. It was the feral girl, leaning from the window of the tower overlooking the sea. With the tape pulled from her mouth, she unleashed a second call from deep in her throat. Her ululation echoed upon them. It felt like their own hearts lifting across the waters.

She could have been calling to the earth or the sea. Or invoking God.

As if summoned, the sand came to life.

Ali reached a window in time to see.

Midway between the fortress and the water, a patch of beach bulged and grew into a small mountain. The hump rose up and took on the dimensions of an animal. The sand guttered from its shoulders and he became a man. The mercenaries were too astounded to lay waste to him.

He was not muscular the way an athlete or bodybuilder is. But the flesh on him stretched in ropy plates. It seemed to have grown on his bones out of need, and then grown some more, with little symmetry. Ali stared down at him.

His bulk and height and the silver bands on his arms evinced pedigree of some sort. He was imposing, as tall as most of the mercenaries, even majestic. For an instant she wondered if this barbaric deformity might not be the Satan she was seeking.

The mercenaries' spotlights fixed his details for all to see. Ali was close enough to recognize him as a warrior simply from the distribution of his scars. It was a forensic fact that primitive fighters classically presented their left side in battle. From foot to shoulder this barbarian's left hemisphere showed twice the old injuries as his right. His left forearm had been sliced and broken from parrying blows. The calcific growth sprouting from his head had a fluted texture, and the tip of one horn had been snapped in battle.

In his right hand he carried a samurai sword stolen in the sixteenth century. With his ferocious eyes and earth-painted skin, he could have been one of the terra-cotta statues inside the fortress keep. A demon guarding the sanctum. Then he spoke, and it was London-accented. "Will you beg, lad?" he said to his first kill. She had heard this voice over the radio. She had seen Ike's eyes grow wide at the remembrance of him.

Isaac shook the sand from his body and faced the fortress, oblivious to his enemies. He searched the heights, dragging masses of air in through his nostrils to catch a scent. He smelled something. Then he called back to the girl, and there was no question what was happening.

They had stolen the beast's daughter. Now hell wanted her back.

Before the soldiers could pull their triggers, the trap closed. Isaac leaped on the first soldier and snapped his neck.

The main raft pitched upward and dawdled on edge, its occupants windmilling into the black water.

More lances harpooned up through the raft floors, and a desperate man machine-gunned his own feet.

Spotlights slewed.

Strobes auto-activated.

Obsidian hailed down on hadals and humans alike. The last of Walker's outfit faced their own weapons here and there, taken from their dead comrades over the past months. Those who could figure out the safety mechanisms and triggers wreaked as much havoc on their own kind as on the soldiers. Many simply used the rifles as clubs.

The three soldiers trapped near the fortress tried for the doorway, but hadals pounced from the walls and blocked their way. Backed against the wall, one bellowed "Remember the Alamo!" and his partner, a macho from Miami, said, "Fuck the Alamo, *viva la Raza,*" and nailed him through his brainpan. The third soldier shot the gang-banger on principle, then sucked the barrel and triggered his last round. The hadals were properly impressed by the suicides.

Out on the water, the chain gun hosed arcs of light into the black horizon. When the belt feed finally jammed, the lone last gunner grabbed a paddle and set out across the sea. In the silence that followed, you could hear his dogged flight, stroke by stroke, like the beating of wings.

Inside the fortress, Colonel Walker was feasted upon alive. They didn't bother cutting him down from the wall, but simply carved pieces off while he raved scripture.

High in the honeycombed fortress, Ike raced in search of Ali. The minute he'd heard the wild girl cry out, he'd started his race. Still dripping water from his hiding place at the edge of the sea, he sprinted up stairs and down corridors.

He might have known Ali would use his knife to free the others. Of course a nun wouldn't know when to let well enough alone. If only she had done as he'd meant and left the others hog-tied to their fates, her disappearance would have been immaculate. This storm of hadals would have swept through like a summer shower. They would have had their washing of spears, then gone on and left Ike hidden with Ali, none the wiser. Instead the People were now combing this cliff structure, hunting for their property, that feral girl. They would not stop until they got what they wanted, he knew, and that would include Ali now. One way or another, that girl would betray her, no matter what kindness Ali had shown her.

He had to find Ali first, and take it from there.

The hadal assault had been crystallizing for days. In their ignorance, Walker and his mercenaries had failed to see the signs. But tucked in a cubbyhole in the cliffs, Ike had been watching hadals arrive almost from the hour Walker landed, and their strategy was clear. They would wait for the soldiers to begin departing on boats, and during the transition from land to sea, they would attack. Anticipating all of that, Ike had arranged diversions and scouted hiding places and selected what parts of the human depot he wanted for himself. In addition to Ali, he wanted two hundred pounds of military rations and a raft. They didn't need more. Two hundred pounds would feed her to the surface. And he would live off the land.

Ike's one hope was his disguise. The hadals did not know he was operating on their fringe, dressed like them, in powdered rock and ochre and rags of the human enemy. For months he had been eating as they ate, harvesting creatures of all kinds, feeding on the meat, warm or cold, raw or jerked. He had their smell now, and some of their strengths. His spoor was hadal spoor. His sweat tasted like hadal sweat. They would not be looking for him. Yet.

He reached the tower stairs and dashed to the top. Embellished like the savage, rigged with war gear, all but naked, Ike burst into the room.

Chelsea was perched in the window, legs out, waiting as if for a bus ride.

To her, what entered was a hadal beast. Chelsea tipped herself outward just as Ike yelled, "Wait!" In the final instant she heard him.

"Ike?" she said. But there was no getting back from gravity what she had given. She tumbled from the window.

Ike didn't waste a second glance. He went straight to the vault in the floor, and it was empty. Ali had left. Troy and the girl were nowhere to be seen.

The great circle was wrapping him again. That was the way. Everyone had a circle. He had lost a woman once, and now was losing Ali. Was that his fate, to play Orpheus to his own heart?

He had almost surfaced from the maze with Ali, and now the maze was beginning all over again. *God help me,* he thought. He looked down, and it seemed that the new labyrinth was growing from his feet, extending in Daedelian twists, his next million miles. Start from scratch, he told himself. It was the old paradox. He had to lose his path in order to find it.

Ali had left no clues. He looked. No footprints. No blood trail. No blaze marks with her fingernails.

He ranged the room, trying to get a sense of things. Who had been here. When. What had motivated their leaving. Little came to him. Maybe she had taken Troy and the girl with her, though it seemed unlikely Ali would have left Chelsea alone. It came to Ike. Ali had gone searching for him.

The realization was not immaterial. It meant Ali would be looking for him in places she thought he might be. If he could anticipate her guess-work, then he might yet find her. But the prospect was bleak. She wouldn't know to look in the cliffside pockets, two hundred feet off the deck, or in his hideout, burrowed among sand worms and tuber clams. She'd be looking throughout the fortress, now swarming with hadals.

Ike weighed his options. Discretion was safer, but a waste of precious time. He could creep and steal through the building, but this was a race, not hide-and-seek. The only alternative was to reveal himself and hope she would do the same.

"Ali!" he yelled. He went to the doorway and shouted her name and listened, then went to the window and shouted again.

Far below, hadals crouching around their human windfall glanced up at him. The boats were being stripped. Supplies were being looted. Rifles were chattering in long, random bursts, all for the noise and fireworks.

Some of the bigger mercenaries were under the knife, he saw, providing impressive strings of meat that would be cured over heat sources or pickled in brine. At least two had been captured alive and were being bound for transport. Chelsea's body was in use by a pack of skinny fighters pretending she was a live captive. Clan leaders often gave deceased property to their followers as a vicarious experience, a way of amplifying their own prestige.

There were a good hundred or more hadals on the beach, probably that many more wending through the fortress proper. It was a huge number of warriors to bring together in one place. Already Ike had counted eleven different clans. They had laid their trap well; it suggested a knowledge of humans that was extraordinary.

Ike darted his head out the window. Hadals were scaling the fortress face, all merging toward him. He took quick, careful aim at the amphorae he had strung along the fortress crown, and fired three times, each time rupturing a clay vessel and igniting its oil. In sheets of flame, the oil poured down the wall. The hadals scrambled right and left on the vertical face. Some jumped, but several were caught in the first phase.

The blue flames curdled down the stone in diminishing streams.

A storm of arrows and stones rattled against the wall outside his window. Some arced inside. He had their attention now.

Ike could hear more scurrying up the tower stairs, and calmly stepped to the doorway. He put a single shot through the mass of amphorae roped above the landing. Oil from twenty jars gushed down the stairs, a cataract of fire. Hadal screams guttered up.

Ike went to the rear window and called Ali's name again. This time he saw a single tiny light working down the corkscrew trail, a half-mile deep. That would be human, he knew. But which human? He reached for his stolen M-16. He'd shot the clip dry, but its sniperscope still worked. He thumbed the On switch and swung it through the depths and found the light. It was Troy down there, with the feral girl. Ike smeared his cheek against the rifle stock. Ali was nowhere to be seen.

That was when he heard her.

Her echo seemed to rise up inside his skull, and through the flames in the landing and from deep within the building. He put his ear against the stone. Her voice was still vibrating, coming through the walls.

"Oh, dear God," she suddenly groaned, and his heart twisted in his chest.

They had her.

"Just wait," she pleaded. This time her voice was more distinct. She was trying to be courageous, he knew her. And he knew them.

Then she said something that froze him. She spoke the name of God. In hadal.

There was no mistaking it. She placed the clicks and glottal halt and words just right. Ike was stunned. Where could she have learned that? And what effect would it have? He waited, head tight against the stone.

Ike was wild with fear for her. He was helpless here. He had no idea where she was, on the floor below or in some deeper room. Her voice seemed to be coming from throughout the fortress. He wanted to run in search of her, but didn't dare leave this one sweet spot on the wall. He lifted his ear, and her voice ended. He set it back on the planed stone, and she was there again. "Here," she said. "I have this."

"Keep talking," he murmured, hoping to unravel her location.

Instead she started playing a flute.

He recognized that sound. It was that bone flute Ike had discarded months ago on the river. Ali must have kept it as a memento or artifact. Her effort was little more than a few toots and a whistle. Did she really think that would speak to them?

"Well, Ike," she suddenly said. But she was talking to herself. Saying good-bye.

Ike got to his feet. What was happening?

He rushed to the opposite window as a group emerged from the gateway. Ali was in their center. As they crossed the beach, she was tied and limping, but alive.

"Ali," he shouted.

She looked up at his voice.

Abruptly a simian shape reared up in the window, toes scraping for purchase on the sill. Ike tumbled backward, but it had him, ripping long furrows with its nails. Ike pulled the pink sling across his chest and slid his shotgun underarm, from back to hand, and pulled the trigger.

When he saw her again, Ali was on one of the rafts, and not alone. The raft was moving away from the beach, drawn from beneath by amphibians. She sat in the prow, looking up at him. Ali's captor turned to follow her glance, but was too distant for Ike to identify. He reached for the night scope and panned across the water, in vain. The raft had passed around the cliffside.

That was all Ike had time for.

He was the last of their enemy, and they were climbing the walls to get him. Quickly now, Ike fished above the window. The primacord lay where he'd tucked it in a niche. Stealing a demolition kit from the mercenaries had been disgracefully simple. He'd had days to place the C-4 and hide the wires and rig the heavy jars of oil. With two deft motions, he spliced the leads to the hell box and gave the handle a sharp twist and a pull-out and a push-in.

The fortress seemed to melt in upon itself. The amphorae of oil erupted like sunlight along the crown of the building, even as the crown shattered to rubble.

There had never been such pure golden light in this benighted cavity. For the first time in 160 million years, the chamber became visible in its entirety, and it was like the inside of a womb, with the matrix of stress fractures for veins.

Ali got one good look, then closed her eyes to the heat. In her mind, she imagined Ike sitting in the raft across from her, wearing a vast grin while the pyre reflected off the lenses of his glacier glasses. That put a smile on her face. In death, he had become the light. Then the darkness heaved in again, and the figure was not Ike but this other mutilated being, and Ali was more afraid than ever.

26

THE PIT

BENEATH THE YAP AND PALAU TRENCHES

She had been stalking him for two days, gaining insights as long and winding as the trail into the great pit. The human was limping. He had a wound, possibly several. Time and again he exhibited fear.

Was he in true flight or not, though? She didn't know this human well. In the brief moments she'd seen him in action, he'd seemed more adept than the others. But outwardly he appeared to be wearing down. The tortuous path was catching up with her, too.

She licked the wall where he had leaned, and his taste quickened her decision. She still lacked information, but was hungry, and his salt and meat were suddenly too tempting. She gave in to her stomach. It was time to make the kill. She began to close the gap.

It took another day of careful pursuit. She nursed their distance, careful not to startle him. There were too many hunter tales of animals taking fright and bolting into some abyss, never to be retrieved. Also, she didn't want to run him any more than necessary. That wasted the energy in his flesh, and already she considered his flesh hers.

Finally they reached a squeeze, where boulders had all but choked the passage. She saw him puzzling over the jumble of stone, watched him spy the hole near his feet. He got down and wormed into the pass. She darted forward to hamstring him while his legs were still exposed. As if anticipating her, he drew his legs in quickly. She lowered the knife and squatted down, waiting while his sounds diminished as he went deeper.

At last it grew quiet in there, and she knelt and thrust herself into the opening. The stone felt slightly soapy and amphibian from so many bodies, hadal and animal, slithering through. She prided herself for being nearly as quick horizontally as on her feet. In childhood races through such narrow passages, she had usually won.

The squeeze passage was longer than she'd thought, though not as long as some, which could go on for days. There were legends about those, too. And ghost stories, of whole tribes snaking their way into a thin vein, one behind the other, only to reach the feet of a skeleton that bottlenecked the tunnel. She had no qualms about this one: there was too much fresh animal smell for it to be a cul-de-sac.

The passage tightened, and there was an awkward kink sideways and up. It was the kind of bend that took a contortionist shift. Every now and then she'd encountered these puzzles, where your knees or shoulders might pop out of joint if the move wasn't carefully rehearsed. She was limber and small, and even so it took two false starts to decipher the move. She torqued through on her back, surprised that the larger man had made it through with such facility.

She emerged, knife first.

She was just clambering to her feet when he stepped from behind. He dropped a rope around her throat and pulled. She slashed backward, but he kneed her in the spine and that flattened her. He was fast and strong, noosing her wrists and elbows and cinching the rope tight.

The capture took ten seconds. It was accomplished in complete silence. Only now did she realize who had been stalking whom. The limp, the awkward visibility, the fear—all a ploy. He'd offered himself as a weakling, and she'd fallen for it. She started to screech her outrage, only to taste the rope across her tongue as he finished gagging and trussing her.

It occurred to her that he might be a hadal disguised with human frailties. Then she saw by the faint light of the stone that he was indeed a human, and was indeed wounded. By his markings she read that he had been a captive once, and immediately knew which one. From their legends, she recognized the renegade who had caused so much destruction to her people. He was renowned. Feared and despised. They considered him a devil, and the story of his deception was taught to children as an example of estrangement and disorder.

He spoke to her in pidgin hadal, his clicks and utterances almost impenetrable. His pronunciation was barbaric, and his question was stupid. If she understood correctly, the traitor wanted to know which way the center lay, and that alarmed her, for the People could scarcely bear more harm. He gestured downward in the direction they were already headed. Thinking he might be lost, and could be made more lost, she calmly indicated the opposite direction. He smiled knowingly and patted her head—an egregious if playful insult—and said something in his flat language. Then he tugged at her leash and started her down the trail.

At no time in the mercenaries' captivity had the girl been very concerned. She had been alone among them, and that was like being a shadow to your own body. Her life was simply a part of the greater *sangha*, or community, and without the *sangha* she was essentially dead to herself. That was the way. But now this terrible enemy was bringing her back to life, back into the People's midst, and she knew he meant to use her against the *sangha* in some way. And that would be worse than a thousand deaths.

Ike had spent a week finding the girl, and then another week baiting her. Where the trail led, he could only guess. But she had seemed set on following it, and so Ike trusted it somehow led to where he wanted to go.

For seven months he had been gathering evidence of the hadals' diaspora. Stop, open your senses, and you could feel the whole underworld in motion, almost as if it were draining into a deeper recess. This deepening pit, he felt certain, was that recess. It was reasonable to think it might lead to the center of that mandala map they had found in the fortress. Somewhere down here must lie the hub of all subterranean roads. There he would find an answer to the riddle of the People's vanishing. There he would find Ali. With the girl in hand, Ike felt ready at last to proceed.

Knowing she would try to kill herself rather than abet his invasion, Ike searched the naked girl twice. He ran his fingers along her flesh and found three obsidian flakes embedded subcutaneously—one along the inside of her bicep, the other two on her inner thighs—for just such an emergency. With the knife, he made quick incisions just large enough to extrude the tiny razor blades and rid her of those options.

This was the hostage he'd needed, but also she was a hadal captive who, like himself, had managed to thrive among the hadals. Ike studied her. Virtually every human prisoner he'd encountered down here had been sickly and demented and merely waiting for use as pack animals, meat, or sacrifice, or to bait other humans down. Not this one. As much as one could command her own destiny, she commanded. Thirteen years old, Ike guessed.

The girl was not as imposing as she looked. In fact, she was almost slight. Her secret lay in her stately presence and wonderful self-sufficiency. Ike saw the clan marks around her eyes and along her arms, but didn't recognize the clan. Clearly she had been raised a hadal from early on.

Just as clearly she had been cultivated for important breeding. Her breasts were immaculate and unpainted, two white fruits standing out from the accumulation of tribal symbols covering the rest of her body. In that way, suckling infants were granted peace for their first month or so of life. With time the child would begin learning the way by reading her mother's flesh.

Over the past two weeks he had watched her purify herself with blood and water repeatedly, washing the mercenaries' sins off her body. She smelled clean, and her bruises were healing quickly.

Her only other possession besides the obsidian blades was her trail food, a poorly cured forearm and clawed hand with the Helios wrist-watch still attached. Much of the good meat was gone. She'd been getting down to the bone. Ike had passed the rest of Troy twelve days ago.

His own watch had been ruined in the destruction of the fortress, so he took this one. It was January 14 at 0240 hours, not that time had relevance anymore. The altimeter read 7,950 fathoms. They were over nine miles below sea level, deeper by miles than any recorded human descent. That in itself was significant. For the depth itself held promise of a hadal ark, or stronghold.

Much the way Ali and her handlers—that Jesuit and his bunch—had hypothesized a centralized hadal warlord through sheer deduction, Ike had been piecing together a primary refuge to closet all the vanished hordes. They had to have gone somewhere. It wasn't likely they had scattered to multiple hiding places, or armies and colonists would have been straying across them. He had seen a rendezvous of several clans once, a matter of a few dozen hadals squatting in a chamber. The meeting had lasted many days while they told stories to one another and exchanged gifts. It was a cyclical event, Ike had figured out, part of a nomadic seasonal round dictated by the availability of food or water along an established route.

He'd learned in the Himalayas that there were circles within circles. The circle, or *kor*, around the central temple in Lhasa, for instance, lay within the *kor* around the whole city, which lay within the *kor* around the whole country. He was more than ever convinced that hadals adhered to some ancient *kor* down here, a circle that revisited some traditional asylum or ark.

The fortress had strengthened his theory with its antiquity and its obvious purpose as a way station along a trade route. Above all, the assault on the fortress had sealed his hunch. Against such a small group of human marauders, the hadals had mounted an attack in unusually abundant numbers. More important, they had attacked with an extraordinary variety of clans. Haddie was massing down here in a place they meant to keep secure, a place as old as their racial memory.

And so, rather than return to the sea and try to track Ali's captors at a disadvantage of weeks, Ike chose to keep descending. If he was right, they would all be meeting sooner rather than later, and now he wouldn't be showing up empty-handed. In the meantime, whether it was days or months or years, Ali would need to use her wits and inner strength to survive without him. He could not spare her from what he had suffered at the beginning of his captivity, and he could not afford despair, so he tried to make his memory blank. He tried to forget Ali altogether.

One morning, Ike woke dreaming of Ali. It was the girl, though, her arms bound, straddling him, kneading him through his pants. She was offering herself for his pleasure, her body ripe, chest high. Her loins moved sinuously in a figure-eight, and Ike was tempted, but only for a moment.

"You're a good one," he whispered with genuine admiration. The girl used every advantage, every means. And she utterly despised him. That had been young Troy's downfall, his inability to see past his infatuation. The boy had succumbed to this same seduction, Ike was sure, and that had meant his end.

Ike lifted the girl to one side. It was not her blatant manipulation or her menace that gave him pause, or his dream of Ali. Rather, the girl was familiar to him somehow. He had met her before, and it unsettled him, because it must have been during his captivity and she would have been a young child. But he couldn't remember such a child.

Day by day, they plunged deeper. Ike remembered the geologists' belief that a million years ago a bubble of sulfuric acid had blossomed from the mantle and ravaged these cavities into the upper lithosphere. As they wended into the vast, uneven pit, Ike wondered if this might not have been the very avenue that acid bloom had cut in rising up from the deeps. It appealed to the mountaineer in him, the physical mystery of it. How deep could this pit be? Where did the abyss become unbearable?

The girl finished the arm bone. Ike located a nest of snakes, and that gave them food for another week. A stream of water joined their trail one day, and thereafter they had fresh water. It tasted like the abyssal sea, which suggested the sea leaked into this pit as it was fed by higher rivers.

At 8,700 fathoms—almost ten miles deep—they reached a ledge overlooking a canyon. The stream of water joined others and became a waterfall that leaped into freefall. The stone was shot through with fluorines, providing a ghostly luminescence. They were standing at the rim of a hanging valley, partway up the wall. Their waterfall was one of hundreds threading the walls.

Their path snaked across the shield of olive stone, carved into solid rock, where the natural fissures gave out. Chunks of enormous stalactite bridged a section. Iron chains traversed blank spots.

The climb down took all of Ike's attention. The pathway was old and bordered by a precipice falling a thousand feet to the floor. The girl decided this was her opportunity to terminate the relationship. She abruptly pitched herself off the edge, body and soul. It was a good effort and almost took Ike over with her, but he managed to pull her kicking and thrashing back to safety. For the next three days he had to be on constant guard against any further such episodes.

Near the bottom, fog drifted in big ragged islands, like New Mexico clouds. Ike thought the waterfalls must be feeding the fog. They came to a series of broken columns forming a sprawling course of polygonal stairs. Each column had snapped off at a ninety-degree angle, exposing neat, flat tops. Ike noticed the girl's thighs trembling from the descent, and gave her a rest.

They were eating little, mostly insects and some of the shoots topping reeds that grew by the water. Ike could have gone scavenging, but chose not to. Progress aside, he was using the hunger to make the girl more pliable. They were deep in enemy territory, and he meant to get deeper without her setting off any alarms. He figured hunger was kinder than tightened ropes.

The sound of waterfalls pouring from the walls made a steady thunder. They moved among fins of rock that sliced the fog and menaced them with false trails. They passed skeletons of animals that had grown exhausted in the maze.

The fog had a pulse to it, ebbing and flowing. Sometimes it lowered around their heads or feet. It was only by chance that Ike heard a party of hadals approaching through one such tidal bank of fog.

Ike wasted no time bulldogging his prisoner to the ground before she could make any trouble. They stretched flat, bellies to the stone, and then for good measure he climbed on top of her and clamped one hand over her mouth. She struggled, but quickly ran out of breath. He settled his cheek onto her thick hair, and his eyes ranged beneath the ceiling of fog. Its cold mass hung just inches above the stone.

Suddenly a foot appeared by Ike's head. It seemed to reach down from the fog. He could have grabbed the ankle without reaching. Its toes were long. The foot gripped the stone floor as if shoveling gravity. The arch had flattened wide over a lifetime of travels. Ike looked at his own fingers, and they appeared thin and weak next to that brute testament of cracked and yellow nails and veined weight.

The foot relinquished its hold upon the earth as its mate set down just ahead. The creature walked on, soft as a ballerina. Ike's mind raced. Size sixteen, at least.

The creature was followed by others. Ike counted six. Or seven. Or eight. Were they searching for him and the girl? He doubted it. Probably it was a hunting party, or interceptors, their stone-age equivalent of centurions.

The padding of feet stopped not far ahead. Soon Ike could hear the hadals at the site of a kill, cracking sticks. Bones, he knew. By the sound of it, their prey had been larger than hominid. Then he heard what sounded like strips of carpet being torn. It was skin, he realized. They were rawhiding the dead thing, whatever it was. He was tempted to wait until they left, then go scavenge the remains. But while the fog held, he got the girl on her feet and they made a broad arc around the party.

The panels of stone grew wild with aboriginal scrawl, old and new. The hadal script—cut or painted ten thousand years ago—overlaid images overlaid on other images. It was like text foxing through text in old books, a ghost language.

They continued through the labyrinth, Ike leading his hostage by the rope. Like barbarians approaching Rome, they passed increasingly sophisticated landmarks. They walked beneath eroded archways carved from the bedrock. The trail became a tangle of once smoothly laid pavers buckled by eons of earth movement. Along one untouched portion, the path lay perfectly flat, and they walked for half a mile upon a mosaic of luminous cobbles.

Among these fins of rock, the thunder of waterfalls was muted. The canyon floor would have been flooded if not for canals that cleverly channeled the water along the sides of their path. Here and there the *acequias* had broken down with time and they waded through water. For the most part the system was intact. Occasionally they heard music, and it was water passing through the remains of instruments that were built into the walkway.

They were getting close to the center, Ike could tell from the girl's apprehension. Also, they reached a long bank of human mummies bracketing the trail.

Ike and the girl made their way between them. What was left of Walker and his men had been tied standing up, thirty of them. Their thighs and biceps had been ritually mutilated. They looked barrel-chested because their abdomens had been emptied. The eyes had been scooped out and replaced with marble orbs, round and white. The stone eyes were slightly too large, which gave them a ferocious, bulging, insect stare. Calvino was there, and the black lieutenant, and finally Walker's head. As an act of contempt, they had laced Walker's dried heart into his beard for all to see. If they had respected him as an enemy, it would have been eaten on the spot.

Ike was glad now that he'd starved his prisoner. At full strength, she would have presented a serious challenge to his stealth. As it was, she could barely walk a mile without resting. Soon she could feast and be free, he hoped. And Ali—the visitor in his dreams each night—would be restored to him.

On January 23, the girl attempted to drown herself in one of the canals, leaping into the water and wedging her body under an outcrop. Ike had to drag her out, and it was almost too late. He cut the rope gag and finally got the water out of her lungs. She lay limp by his knees, defeated and ill. Exhausted by their battle, both rested.

Somewhat later she began singing. Her eyes were still closed. It was a song for her own comfort, sung softly, in hadal, with the clicks and intonations of a private verse. At first Ike had no idea what it was, her singing was so small. Then he heard, and it was like being shot through the heart.

Ike rocked back on his heels, disbelieving. He listened more closely. The words were too intricate for his small lexicon. But the tune was there, scarcely a whisper: "Amazing Grace."

The song sent him reeling. It was familiar to her, and beloved, he could tell, as it was to him. This was the last thing he had ever heard from Kora, her singing as she sank into the abyss beneath Tibet so many years ago. It was the very anthem he had cast himself into the darkness for. *I once was lost, but now am found / Was blind, but now I see.* She had put her own words to it, but the tune was identical.

He had taken Isaac's claim of fatherhood to be the truth, but saw no resemblance to that beast at all. Prompted by the song, Ike now recognized Kora's features in the girl. Ike groped for other explanations. Perhaps the girl had been taught the melody by Kora. Or Ali had sung it to her. But for days, he had been carrying a vague, troubling sense of already knowing her.

There was something about her cheekbones and forehead, the way that jaw thrust forward in moments of obstinacy, and the general length of her body. Other details drew his attention, too. Could it really be? So much was the image of her mother. But so much was not, her eyes, the shape of her hands, that jaw.

Wearily she opened her eyes. He had not seen Kora in them because they were not Kora's turquoise eyes. Maybe he was wrong. And yet the eyes were familiar. Then it struck him. She had his eyes. This was his own daughter.

Ike sagged against the wall. Her age was right. The color of her hair. He compared their hands, and she had his same long fingers, his same nails. "God," he whispered. What now?

"Ma. You. Where," he said in his fractured hadal.

She quit singing. Her eyes rode up to his, and her thoughts were easy to read. She saw his daze, and it suggested an opportunity. But when she tried prying herself from the wet stone, her body refused to cooperate.

"Please speak more clearly, animal man," she said politely, in high dialect.

To Ike's ear, she had expressed something like What? He tried again, reversing his question and fumbling for the right syntax and possessive. "Where. You own. Mother. To be."

She snorted, and he knew his attempts sounded like grunting to her. All the while she kept her eyes directed away from his knife with the black blade. That was her object of desire, Ike knew. She wanted to kill him.

This time he traced a sign on the ground, then linked it with another sign. "You," he said. "Mother."

She made a gentle sweeping motion with her fingers, and that was his answer. One did not speak about the dead. They became someone—or something—else. And since you could never be sure who or what form that reincarnation might have taken, it was most judicious to give the dead no mention. Ike let it go at that.

Of course Kora was dead. And if she was not, there would probably be no recognizing what was left. Yet here was their legacy. And he needed her as a pawn to trade away for Ali. That had been his working plan. Suddenly it felt as though the life raft he had crafted from wreckage had just wrecked all over again.

It was excruciating, the appearance of a daughter he had never known, changed into what he had almost been changed into. What was he supposed to do now, rescue her? And what then? Obviously the hadals had taken her in and made her one of them. She had no idea who he was or what world he came from. To be honest, he had little idea himself. What kind of rescue was that?

He looked at the girl's thin, painted back. Since capturing her, he had treated her like chattel. The only thing good to say was that he had not beaten or raped or killed her. *My daughter?* He hung his head.

How could he possibly trade away his own flesh and blood, even for a woman he loved? But if he did not, Ali would remain in their bondage forever. Ike tried to clear his mind. The girl was ignorant of her past. However harsh, she had a life among the hadals. To take her out of here would mean tearing her by the roots from the only people she knew. And to leave Ali meant . . . what? Ali could not possibly know he had survived the fortress explosion, much less that he was searching for her. Likewise, she would never know if he turned around and dragged this child away from the darkness. Indeed, knowing her, even if she did know, Ali would approve. And where would that leave him? He had become a curse. Everyone he loved disappeared.

He considered letting the girl go. But that would only be cowardice on his part. The decision was his to make. He had to make it. It was one or the other, at best. He was too much of a realist to waste a moment imagining the whole happy family could make it out. He was tormented the rest of that night.

When the girl awoke, Ike presented her with a meal of larvae and pallid tubers, and loosened her ropes. He knew it would only complicate matters to restore her strength, and that the slightest guilt at having depleted the child was a dangerous moralism. But he could no longer go on starving his own daughter.

Guessing she would never tell it to him, he asked her name. She averted her eyes at the rudeness. No hadal would give such power to a slave. Soon after he started her downward on the trail, though more slowly in consideration of her fatigue.

The revelation tortured him. After his return to the human side, Ike had vowed to keep his choices black and white. Stick to your code. Stray, and you died. If you couldn't decide a matter in three seconds, it was too complicated.

The simplest thing by far, the safest thing, would have been to cut loose and escape while he could. Ike had never been a believer in predestination. God didn't do it to you, you did it to yourself. But the present situation contradicted him.

The mystery of it weighed on Ike, and their slow descent slowed more. The heaviness he felt had nothing to do with their altitude, now eleven miles deep. To the contrary, as the air pressure thickened, he was engorged with more oxygen, and the effect was a hardy lightness of the kind one felt coming down off a mountain. But now the unwanted effect of so much oxygen in his brain was more thoughts and more questions.

Though he couldn't say exactly how, Ike was certain he must have selected each circumstance leading to his own downfall. And yet what choices had his daughter made to be born in darkness and never know the light or her true father or her own people?

The journey down was a journey of water sounds. Blindfolded, Ali passed the first number of days listening to the sea scythe by as amphibians drew their raft on. The next days were spent descending alongside cascades and behind immense falls. Finally, reaching more even ground, she walked across streams bridged with stones. The water was her thread.

They kept her separate from the two mercenaries who'd been captured alive. But on one occasion her blindfold slipped and she saw them in the perpetual twilight cast by phosphorescent lichen. The men were bound with ropes of braided rawhide, and arrows still projected from their wounds. One looked at Ali with horrified eyes, and she made the sign of the cross for his benefit. Then her hadal escort cinched the blindfold over her eyes again, and they went on. Only later did Ali realize why the mercenaries weren't blindfolded, too. The hadals didn't care if the two soldiers saw the path down, because neither would ever have the opportunity to climb back out.

That was the beginning of her hope. They weren't going to kill her anytime soon. Thinking of the two soldiers' certain fate, she felt guilty for her optimism. But Ali clung to it with a greed she'd never known. It had never occurred to her before how base a thing survival was. There was nothing heroic about it.

Prodded, tugged, carried, pushed, she staggered into a cavity that could have been the center of her being. She wasn't harmed. They didn't violate her. But she suffered.

For one thing, she was famished, not that they didn't try to feed her. Ali refused the meat they offered, though. The monster who led them came to her. "But you have to eat, my dear," he said in perfect King's English. "How else will you finish the *hajj*?"

"I know where the meat came from," she answered. "I knew those people."

"Ah, of course. You're not hungry enough."

"Who are you?" she rasped.

"A pilgrim, like you."

But Ali knew. Before the blindfold, she'd seen him orchestrating the hadals, commanding them, delegating tasks. Even without such evidence, he certainly looked the way Satan might, with his cowled brow and the twist of asymmetrical horns and the script drawn upon his flesh. He stood taller than most of the hadals, and carried more scars, and there was something about his eyes that declared a knowledge of life she didn't want to know.

After that, Ali was given a diet of insects and small fish. She forced it down. The trek went on. Her legs ached at night from striking against rocks. Ali welcomed the pain. It was a way not to mourn for a while. Perhaps if she'd been carrying arrows like the mercenaries were, it would have been possible not to mourn at all. But the reality was always there, waiting. Ike was dead.

At last they reached the remains of a city so old it was more like a mountain in collapse. This was their destination. Ali knew because they finally took off her blindfold and she was able to walk without being guided.

Weary, frightened, mesmerized, Ali picked her way higher. The city was up to its neck in a tropical glacier of flowstone, which spun off a faint incandescence. The result was less light than gloom, and that was enough. Ali could see that the city lay at the bottom of an enormous chasm. A slow mineral flood had all but swallowed much of the city, but many of the structures were erect and honeycombed with rooms. The walls and colonnades were embellished with carved animals and depictions of ancient hadal life, all of it blended in subtle arabesques.

Debauched by time and geological siege, the city was nevertheless inhabited, or at least in use. To Ali's shock, thousands of hadals—tens of thousands, for all she knew—had come to rest in this place. Here lay the answer to where the hadals had gone. From around the world, they had poured down to this sanctuary. Just as Ike had said, they were in flight. This was their exodus.

As the war party threaded through the city, Ali saw toddlers resting against their mothers' thighs, exhausted with flu. She looked, but there were very few infants or aged in the listless mob. Weapons of all types lay on the ground, apparently too heavy to lift.

In their listlessness, the hadals imparted a sense of having reached the end of the earth. It had always been a mystery to Ali why refugees—no matter what race—stopped where they did, why they didn't keep going on.

There was a fine line between a refugee and a pioneer; and it had to do with momentum once you crossed a certain border. Why had these hadals not continued deeper? she wondered.

They climbed a hill in the center of the city. At the top, the remnants of a building stood above the amberlike flowstone. Ali was led into a hallway that spiraled within the ruins. Her prison cell was a library. They left her alone.

Ali looked around, astounded by the treasury. This was to be her hell, then, a library of undeciphered text? If so, they'd matched the wrong punishment with her. They had left a clay lamp for her like those Ike had lit. A small flame twitched at the snout of oil.

Ali started to explore by its light, but wasn't careful enough carrying it, and the flame guttered out. She stood in the darkness, filled with uncertainty, scared and lonely. Suddenly the journey caught up with her, and she simply lay down and fell asleep.

When Ali woke, hours later, a second lamp was flickering in the room's far corner. As she approached the flame, a figure rose against the wall, wrapped in rags and a burlap cloak. "Who are you?" a man's voice demanded. He sounded weary and spiritless, like a ghost. Ali rejoiced. Clearly he was a fellow prisoner. She wasn't alone!

"Who are *you*?" she asked, and folded the man's hood back from his face.

It was beyond belief. "Thomas!" she cried.

"Ali!" he grated. "Can it be?"

She embraced him, and felt the bones of his back and rib cage.

The Jesuit had the same furrowed face as when she'd first met him at the museum in New York. But his brow had thickened and he had weeks of grizzled beard, and his hair was long and gray and thick with filth. Crusted blood matted his hair. His eyes were unchanged. They'd always been deeply traveled.

"What have they done to you?" she asked. "How long have you been here? Why are you in this place?"

She helped the old man sit, and brought water for him to drink. He rested against the wall and kept patting her hand, overjoyed. "It's the Lord's will," he kept repeating.

For hours they exchanged their stories. He had come looking for her, Thomas said, once news of the expedition's disappearance reached the surface. "Your benefactor, January, was tireless in reminding me of the Beowulf group's responsibilities to you. Finally I decided there was only one thing to do. Search for you myself."

"But that's absurd," said Ali. A man his age, and all alone.

"And yet, look," said Thomas.

He'd descended from a tunnel in Javanese ruins, praying against the darkness, guessing at the expedition's trajectory. "I wasn't very good at it," he confessed. "In no time I got lost. My batteries wore down. I ran out of food. When the hadals found me, it was more an act of charity than capture. Who can say why they didn't kill me? Or you?"

Ever since, Thomas had languished among these mounds of text. "I thought they'd leave my bones here among the books," he said. "But now you're here!"

In turn, Ali told of the expedition's sad demise. She related Ike's self-immolation in the hadal fortress. "But are you sure he died?" Thomas asked.

"I saw it myself." Her voice caught. Thomas expressed his condolences.

"It was God's will," Ali recovered. "And it was His will that led us here, to this library. Now we shall attempt to accomplish the work we were meant for. Together we may come closer to the original word."

"You are a remarkable woman," Thomas said.

They set about the task with acute focus, grouping texts and comparing observations. At first delicately, then avidly, they examined the books, leaves, codices, scrolls, and tablets. None of it was shelved neatly. It was almost as if the mass of writings had accumulated here like a pile of snowflakes. Setting the lamp to one side, they burrowed into the largest pile.

The material on top was the most current, some in English or Japanese or Chinese. The deeper they worked, the older the writings were. Pages disintegrated in Ali's fingers. On others, the ink had foxed through layer after layer of writings. Some books were locked tight with mineral seep. But much of it yielded lettering and glyphs. Luckily the room was spacious, because they soon had a virtual tree of languages laid out on the floor, pile by pile of books.

At the end of five days, Ali and Thomas had excavated alphabets no linguist had ever seen. Stepping back from their work, it was obvious to Ali they'd barely made a dent in the heaped writings. Here lay the beginnings of all literature, all history. In a sense, it promised to contain the beginnings of memory, human and hadal both. What might lie at its center?

"We need to rest. We need to pace ourselves," Thomas cautioned. He had a bad cough. Ali helped him to his corner, and forced herself to sit, too. But she was excited.

"Ike told me once, the hadals want to be like us," she said. "But they're already like us. And we're like them. This is the key to their Eden. It won't give them back their ancient regime. But it can bind them, and give them concordance as a people. It can bridge the gap between them and us. This is the beginning of their return to the light. Or at least of the sovereignty of their race. Maybe we can find a mutual language. Maybe we can make a place for them among us. Or they can make a place for us among them. But it all starts here."

The torture of Walker's men began. Their screams drifted up to Ali and Thomas. Periodically the sounds tapered off. After a night of silence, Ali was certain the men had died. But then the screaming started again. With pauses, it would go on for many days.

Before they could continue their scholarship, Ali and Thomas received a visitor. "He's the one I told you about," she whispered to him. "He leads them, I think."

"You might be right about him," Thomas said. "But what does he want with us?"

The monster approached with a plastic tube marked HELIOS. It was badly scratched. Ali immediately recognized her map case. He went directly to her, and she could smell fresh blood on him. His feet were bare. He shook out the roll of maps and opened them. "These came into my possession," he said in his crisp English.

Ali wanted to ask how, but thought better of it. Obviously, Gitner and his band of scientists had failed to escape. "They're mine," she said.

"Yes, I know. The soldiers told me. Also, I've studied the maps, and your authorship is clear. Unfortunately they're not real maps, but only your approximation of things. They show how your expedition proceeded in general. I need more. Details. Detours. Side trips. Diversions. And camps, every camp, every night. Who was in them, who wasn't. I need everything. You have to re-create the entire expedition for me. It's crucial."

Ali glanced at Thomas, fearful. How could she possibly remember it all? "I can try," she said.

"Try?" The monster was smelling her. "But your very existence depends on your memory. I would do more than try."

Thomas stepped forward. "I'll help her," he volunteered.

"Help her quickly, then," the monster said. "Now your life depends on it, too."

On February 11, at 1420 hours and 9,856 fathoms, they reached a cliff overlooking a valley. It was not the bottom of the pit; you could see a gaping hole in the far distance. But it was a geological pause in that abyss they had been following.

Before she tried again to martyr herself, Ike tied his nameless daughter to a horn of rock along the wall. Then he flopped on his stomach along the edge to get a view of the land and sort through his options.

It had the shape and size of a crater, lit with a sienna gloom. Veins of luminous minerals spidered through the encircling walls, and the fog was lambent, flickering like tongues. He could make out the architecture of this enormous hollow, two or three miles across, and its honeycombed walls and the vast, intricate city it cupped.

Five hundred meters beneath his perch, the city occupied the entire floor. It was at once magnificent and destitute. From this height he could clearly see the whole obsolete metropolis.

Spires and pyramids stood in ruins. In the distance, one or two towering structures rose nearly as high as the rim, though their tops had crumbled away. Canals had harrowed the avenues deep, carving meandering canyons. Much was in collapse or flooded or had been overrun with flowstone. Several giant stalactites had grown so heavy they had fallen from the invisible ceiling and speared buildings.

It took Ike time to adjust to the scale of this place. Only then did he begin to distinguish the multitudes. They were so numerous and packed together and enfeebled that all he saw at first was a broad stain upon the floor. But the stain had a slight motion to it, like the slow agitation of glaciers. Here and there, winged creatures launched from cliffside aeries, darting through the fog.

In effect, the refugees were camping not in but atop the old city. He couldn't make out individual figures from this distance, but he guessed there had to be thousands down there. Tens of thousands. He had been right about the sanctuary.

They must have come from throughout the planet to this single place. Even though Ike had guessed they were migrating to a central location, their numbers astounded him. Haddie was a solitary race, as willing to demolish one another as their enemy, prone to wandering in small, paranoid packs. He'd decided there were probably no more than a few thousand left in the entire subplanet. There had to be fifty times that right here. For them to have gathered this way, and in apparent armistice, it had to be like the end of the world.

Their abundance was good news and bad. It all but guaranteed that Ali would end up in the refugee horde, if she was not already among them. Ike had devised no specific gambit, but had been relying on a much smaller mob to deal with. Finding her from a distance was going to be impossible, and infiltrating them a lengthy nightmare. Just locating her could take months. And all the while he would have to tend the hostage, his daughter. The prospect threw him into a downward spiral. He looked at his watch—Troy's watch—and noted the time and date and altitude.

He heard the pad of feet, and started to rise up, knife in hand. He had time to see a rifle butt. Then it axed into his face, he felt it clip his temple, and all the brawl went out of him.

By the time Ike revived, he was bound hand to foot with his own rope. He pried his eyes open. His captor was waiting, seated five feet away, barefoot and in rags, sighting on Ike's face through a U.S. Army night-vision sniperscope. A pair of binoculars hung from his neck. Ike sighed. The Rangers had finally hounded him to earth.

"Wait," Ike said. "Before you shoot."

"Sure," said the man, his face still burrowed behind the rifle and sight.

"Just tell me why." What had he done to deserve their vengeance?

"Why what, Ike?" The executioner lifted his head.

Ike was thunderstruck. This was no Ranger.

"Surprise," Shoat said. "I didn't think it was possible, either, an ordinary joe trumping the great Ike Crockett. But you were easy. Talk about bragging rights. I mug Superman *and* get the girl."

Ike couldn't think of what to say. He looked across at his daughter. Shoat had tightened her bonds. That was significant. He hadn't shot the girl outright.

Bearded and emaciated, Shoat had not lost his daft grin. He was very pleased with himself. "In certain ways," he said, "we're the same guy, you and me. Bottom feeders. We can live off other people's shit. And we always make sure we know where the back door is. Back at the *presidio*, I was ready, just like you."

Ike's face ached from the rifle butt, but what hurt most was his pride. "You tracked me?" he said.

Shoat patted the rifle with the sniperscope. "Superior technology," he said. "I could see you from a mile off, clear as day. And once you netted our little bird, things were even easier. I don't know, Ike, you got slow and you got sloppy. Maybe you're getting old. Anyhoo"—he glanced behind him over the precipice—"we've reached the heart of the matter, haven't we?"

While Shoat talked, Ike gathered the few clues. A rucksack sat against the wall, half empty. Over near the watchful girl, Shoat had scattered the plastic refuse from a single military rations packet. It told Ike he had been unconscious long enough to be tied, and for Shoat to finish a meal.

More important, the man had come alone; there was just one pack and the remains of one MRE. And the MRE meant he was not feeding off the land, probably because he didn't know how to.

Obviously, Shoat had foraged through the destroyed fortress and found a few essentials: the rifle, some MREs. Ike was mystified. The man had his ticket home; why pursue the depths?

"You should have taken a raft or just started walking," Ike said. "You could have been partway out of here."

"I would have, but someone took my most vital asset." He lifted the leather pouch that hung from his neck like an amulet. Everyone knew it held his homing device. "It guarantees my exit. I didn't even know it was gone until I needed it. When I opened the pouch, there was only this." He unlaced the top and shook out a flat jade plate.

Sure enough, Ike saw, someone had stolen his device and replaced it with a piece of antique hadal armor. "Now you want me to guide you out," he guessed.

"I don't think that would work very well, Ike. How far could we get before Haddie found us? Or you did me in."

"What do you want then?"

"My box. That would be nice."

"Even if we found it, what's that do for you now?" With or without his homing device, the hadals could still find the man. And Ike could, too.

Shoat smiled cryptically and aimed the jade plate like a TV remote control. "It lets me change the channel." He made a click sound. "Hate to sound like Mr. Zen, but you're just an illusion, Ike. And the girl. And all of them down there. None of you exists."

"But you do?" Ike wasn't taunting him. This was a key to Shoat's strangeness.

"Yeah. Yeah, I do. I'm like the prime mover. The first cause. Or the last. When all of you are gone, I'll still be around."

Shoat knew something, or thought he did, but Ike couldn't begin to guess what. The man had recklessly followed them into the center of the abyss, and now, surrounded by the enemy, had waylaid his only possible ally in getting out. He could have shot them from a distance at any time over the past several weeks. Instead, he'd saved them for something. There was a logic at work here. Shoat was smart and sane, and dangerous. Ike blamed himself. He'd underestimated the man.

"You've got the wrong guy," Ike said. "I didn't take your box."

"Of course not. I've thought a lot about it. Walker's boys wouldn't have bothered with any tricks. They would have just put a bullet through me.

You would have, too. So it was someone else, someone who needed to keep the theft quiet. Someone who thinks she knows my code. I've got it figured out, Ike. Who it was, and when she took it."

"The girl?"

"You think I'd let that wild animal close to me? No. I mean Ali."

"Ali? She's a nun." Ike snorted to deride the notion. But who else could it be?

"A very bad nun. Don't deny it, Ike. I know she's been playing hide-the-snake with you. I can tell these things, I've got good people sense."

Ike watched him. "So you followed me to follow her."

"Good boy."

"I didn't find her, though."

"Actually, Ike, you did."

Shoat grabbed a loop of rope and dragged him to the edge. He draped his binoculars around Ike's neck, and cautiously loosened the rope binding Ike's hands to his feet, then backed away, aiming his pistol.

"Take a look," Shoat announced. "Someone you know is down there. Her and our two-bit warlord. His satanic majesty. The guy who ran off with her."

Ike wrestled to a sitting position. The news of Ali energized him. His hands were numb from the ropes, but he managed to paw the binoculars into place. He scanned up and down the canals and choked avenues and ruins lit green by the night vision. "Look for a spire, then go left," Shoat instructed.

It took several minutes, even with Shoat describing the landmarks while looking through the rifle scope. "See the pillars?"

"Are those Walker's men?" Two men hung, slumped. Neither was Ali. Yet.

"Just taking a rest," Shoat said. "They've been getting some rough treatment. And there's another prisoner, too. I've seen him with Ali. They keep taking him away, though."

Ike searched higher.

"She's there," Shoat encouraged. "I can see her. Unbelievable, it looks like she's writing in her field book. Notes from the underground?"

Ike went on searching. A hill of flowstone knobbed above the masses, enfolding all but the upper stories of a carved stone building. The walls had collapsed on Ike's side of the building, exposing to view a spacious room with no roof. And there she was, sitting on a chunk of rubble. They had freed her hands and legs; why not? Two stories below, she was surrounded by the hadal nation.

"Locked in?"

"I see her." They hadn't started her rites of passage yet. The branding and shackles and mutilations were usually started in the first few days. Recovery could take years. But Ali looked whole, untouched.

"Good." Shoat yanked the binoculars away. "Now you've got your scent. You know where you need to go."

"You want me to infiltrate an entire city of hadals and steal back your homing device?"

"Give me some credit, man. You're mortal. There are some things even you can't do. Besides, why sneak when you can make a grand entrance?"

"You want me to just walk in and ask for your property?"

"Better you than me."

"Even if Ali has it, then what?"

"I'm a businessman, Ike. I live and die by negotiation. Let's see where we can get with them. A little bit of old-fashioned bartering."

"With them? Down there?"

"You'll be my proxy. My private ambassador."

"They'll never let Ali go."

"All I want is my box."

Ike was truly mystified. "Why would they give it to you?"

"That's what I want to talk to them about." Shoat reached over to his rucksack and pulled out a thin, battered laptop computer embossed with the Helios logo. "Our walkie-talkies are all gone. But I've got a two-way comm device set up with my laptop. We're going to have a video conference."

Shoat opened the lid and turned the machine on. He stepped back, plugging a portable earphone into one ear, and held a small camera/speaker ball in front of his face. On screen, his face rotated and mugged. "Testing, testing," his voice spoke over the computer speaker.

Against the wall, the feral girl grunted, eyes wide with fear, a stranger to such magic.

"Here's what you're going to do, Ike. Take the laptop down into nighttown there. Once you reach Ali, open the laptop up. Make sure the computer's in line of sight, a straight shot from you to me. I don't want to lose transmission. Then get their *presidente* on the horn for me. While you're at it, give this whelp back to them. A good-faith gesture. I'll take it from there."

"What's in it for me?"

Shoat grinned. "That's my man. What would you like? Your life? Or Ali's? Wanna bet I know the answer?"

It was exactly the chance Ike had wanted for her. "All right," he said. "You're the boss."

"Good to have you on board, Ike."

"Cut my ropes."

"Of course." Shoat wagged the knife as if Ike were a naughty child, then tossed it on the ground. "But first we need to understand each other. It's going to take you a while to crawl over here and cut yourself loose. And by that time I'll be locked and loaded in a cozy sniper's nest not too far away. You're going to escort this cannibal down through that rabble and back to her people. And set up my link with their CEO, who-ever that guy is."

Shoat set the computer on the floor and backed toward a tall, jagged hole in the wall. Ike had his eyes on the knife.

"No tricks, no detours, no deceit. The laptop's switched on. Don't turn it off. I want to be able to hear everything you say," Shoat said. "And don't come looking for me. From my cubbyhole, I've got a clear shot all the way down the trail. Screw up, and the fireworks begin. But I won't shoot you, Ike. It's Ali that pays for your sins. I'll kill her first. And next, just to piss them off, their leader. After that I'll work through targets of opportunity. But there's not going to be a bullet for you. I promise. You can live with yourself. You can live with them. Hell can have you back. Are we clear?"

Ike started crawling.

And in the lowest deep, a lower deep
Still threat'ning to devour me opens wide,
To which the Hell I suffer seems a Heav'n.

—JOHN MILTON, *Paradise Lost*

27
SHANGRI-LA

BENEATH THE INTERSECTION OF
THE PHILIPPINE, JAVA, AND PALU TRENCHES

Ike descended into the ancient city, leading his daughter by a rope. The city loomed in the organic twilight, a puzzle of remnants, fused architecture, and eyeless windows.

On the floor of the vast canyon, at the ruins' edge, Ike slung Shoat's laptop computer on one shoulder and bent the plastic candle he had been given, breaking the vial inside. The wand came alive with green light. Even without his sniperscope, Shoat would be able to track his progress through the city.

For the first half-mile or so there was no outright challenge, although animals scuttled along the flowstone. With each step, Ike tried to piece together some alternative to what was already in motion. Shoat's spider-web seemed unbreakable. Ike could practically see the back of his own head through the electronic scope. If only he were the prey, he thought. He could duck the bullet, or take it. But Shoat had clearly pronounced his targets: Ali first. Ike continued through the fossilized city.

News of human trespass was rippling forward through the city. In the penumbra of his green light, shapes that normally would have appeared as silhouettes against the pale glow of stone now lurked as shadows. The candle's neon glow was devastating his night vision. Then again, from the beginning of this doomed expedition, he'd been squandering his nocturnal powers, even eating human food. There was no disguising his origins anymore.

Click language cricketed in the gloom. He could smell hadals crowding the penumbra, musky and smeared with ochre. A rock thrown from the shadows struck him on the arm, not hard, just to goad him.

Winged beasts swept inches overhead. Ike maintained his stoic gait. Several others circled out of reach. He felt warm spittle dribbling down his neck.

A monstrosity came racing from ahead and blocked the way. Squat, encrusted with fluorescent mud, he sported a penis sheath and battle scars and brandished an ax. He flicked his tongue like a reptile and bulged his eyes, all challenge. Ike kept his motions passive and the beast let them pass.

The plastic slicks and mineral convolutions of the city floor began to angle upward. Ike approached that rise in the city's center which he had spied through the binoculars. The camp grew dense with refugees, and the canals were fouled with their raw offal and sewage. They lay on the bare ground, ill and hungry.

In his years of captivity, Ike had never seen a fraction of the traits and styles gathered here. Some had flippers for arms, others feet that were tantamount to hands. There were heads flattened by binding, eye sockets genetically emptied. The variety of body art and clothing was wild. Some went naked, some wore armor or chain mail. He passed eunuchs proudly scalped at the groin, warriors with hair woven with beads and horns woven with scalps, and females bred for their smallness or fatness.

Through it all, Ike kept his expression impassive. He climbed the pathway winding toward the hilltop, and the mass of hadals thickened. Here and there, stripped rib cages arched above ravaged carcasses. In times of such want, he knew, human chattel went first.

Behind him, the girl kept pace. His daughter was his passport. There were no challenges to Ike's advance, and he continued through the city. From the cliffs above, Ike had seen how the pit didn't bottom out, but only paused. And yet the entire race seemed to have rooted here. They showed no signs of taking their nomad spirit deeper. It made him want to plunge farther into the hole, to scale the inverse mountain, just to see what new sights there might be. His curiosity made him sad, because it was unlikely he'd live to see another hour, much less another land.

A pile of ruins projected from the top of the heaped flowstone, and Ike aimed for the highest structure. Climbing higher, Ike and the girl reached Walker's men. The two mercenaries were lashed to broken columns, not with rope, but with their own entrails. Seeing her enemy, the girl capered. Ike let her. One lifted his eyeless face to the jubilation. They had taken his lower jaw off, too. The tongue lay spastic on his throat.

After a minute they continued. They crested the mound. The ruins on the flat top occupied several acres. Hadals lay or sat about on the amorphous folds of stone, but, strangely, had not taken up residence in the crowning structure itself. Again, Ike was struck by their sense of waiting.

The wall on one side of the main building had crumbled, and Ike and the girl clambered up its rubble. Warriors bluffed charges and hooted threats and insults. None came closer than the edges of his light, though, and the effect was a riptide of greenish shadows.

They reached that top floor of the ruins Ike had seen through the binoculars. The roof had caved in or been peeled off, and the result was a high stage open to Shoat's sniperscope. The gallery was more spacious than Ike had expected. In fact, he saw that it was some kind of library, dense with holdings.

Ike stopped in the center of the room. This was where he'd sighted Ali reading, though she was gone now. The floor was flat, but listing, like a ship beginning to sink. This was as good a place as any. It gave him a sense of space, exposed to the equivalent of sky. If he had his choice, Ike didn't want to die in some little tube of a cavity. Let it be in the open. Also, as instructed, he needed to stay in Shoat's line of sight.

While he waited, Ike was furiously gathering information, patching together contingency plans and dead-reckoning trajectories, trying to locate the players and weapons in this new arena, searching for exits and hiding places. It was a matter of habit, not hope.

He found a broken stele and placed the computer on top, at eye level. He opened the lid. The screen was lit with Shoat's face, a miniature Wizard of Oz. "What are they waiting for?" Shoat's voice spoke from the monitor. The feral girl backed away from it. Nearby hadals scurried into the shadows and softly hooted their alarm.

"There's a hadal pace to things," Ike said.

He glanced around. Scores of stone tablets were propped side by side against one wall, codices lay open like long road maps, and scrolls and skins painted with glyphs and script lay in piles. To enhance her readings, they had provided Ali with Helios flashlights taken from the expedition. She was hard on the trail of the mother tongue. Another ten minutes passed. Then Ali was sent out from the jumbled interior. She came to a halt fifteen or twenty feet away. Tears were running down her face. "Ike." She had mourned him. Now she was mourning him all over again. "I thought you were dead. I prayed for you. Then I prayed some more, that if you were somehow alive, you'd know not to come for me."

"I must have missed that last one," Ike said. "Are you okay?" As he'd noted through the binoculars, they hadn't started inscribing her yet, nothing that he could see. She had been among them for over three weeks now. By this time they had usually knocked out the women captives' front teeth and begun other initiations. The fact that Ali bore no ownership marks gave him hope. Maybe a bargain was still possible.

"But I kept hearing Walker's soldiers. Are they dead?"

"Don't mind them. What about you?"

"They've been good to me, considering. Until you showed up, I was thinking there might be a place for me here."

"Don't say that," Ike snapped.

Their seduction of her had begun. No great mystery there. It was the seduction of a storybook land, the seduction of becoming an expatriate. You fell for a place like darkest Africa or Paris or Kathmandu, and soon you had no nation of your own, and you were simply a citizen of time. He'd learned that down here. Among the human captives there were always slaves, the walking dead. And then there were the rare few like him—or Isaac—who had lost their souls to this place.

"But I'm so near to the word. The first word. I can feel it. It's here, Ike."

Their lives were on the line. Shoat's storm was about to rage, and she was talking about primal language? The word was her seduction. She was his. "Out of the question," he said.

"Hi, Ali," Shoat said through the computer. "You've been a naughty girl."

"Shoat?" said Ali, staring at the screen.

"Stay calm," Ike said.

"What are you doing?"

"Don't blame him," Shoat's image said. "He's just the pizza delivery boy."

"Ike, please," she whispered. "What is he up to? Whatever you're doing, I've been given assurances. Let me talk to them. You and I—"

"Assurances? You're still treating them like noble savages."

"I can help save them from this."

"Save them? Look around."

"I have a gift." Ali gestured at the scrolls and glyphs and codices. "The treasure is here, the secrets of their past, their racial memory, it's all here."

"They're illiterate. They're inbred. Starving."

"That's why they need me," she said. "We can bring their greatness to life again. It will take time, but now I know we can do it. The interconnections are braided within their writings. It's as different from modern hadal as ancient Egyptian is from English. But this place is the key, a giant Rosetta stone. All the clues are here, in one place. It's possible I can decipher a civilization twenty thousand years dead."

"We?" said Ike.

"There's another prisoner here. It's the most extraordinary coincidence. I know him. We've started the work."

"You can't return them to what they were. They don't need stories from the golden days." Ike drew the air through his nostrils. "Smell, Ali. That's death and decay. This is the city of the damned, not Shangri-la. I don't know why the hadals have all gathered here. It doesn't matter. They're dying off. That's why they take our women and children. It's why they've kept you alive. You're a breeder. We're stock. Nothing more."

"Folks?" Shoat's tiny voice interrupted. "My meter's running. Let's get this over with."

Ali faced the screen, not knowing he was seeing her through the crosshairs of his scope. "What do you want, Shoat?"

"One, the head honcho. Two, my property. Let's start with One. Patch me through."

She looked at Ike.

"He wants to deal. He thinks he can. Let him try. Who's in charge here?"

"The one I came looking for, Ike. The one you've been looking for. They're one and the same."

"But they're not the same."

"They are. He's the one. I spoke to him. He knows you." Using click language, Ali spoke the hadal name for their mythical god-king. "Older-than-Old," she said in English.

It was a forbidden name, and the feral girl gave a sharp, astonished look at her.

"Him." Ali gestured at the claim mark tattooed on Ike's arm, and he grew cold. "Satan."

His eyes went racing through the hadal shapes lurking in the hollow behind Ali. Could it be? Here?

Suddenly the girl gave a small cry. *"Batr,"* she said in hadal. It caught Ike off guard. Father, she had said. His heart jumped at the address, and he turned to see her face. But she was smelling the shadows. A moment later, Ike caught the scent, too. Except for one glimpse of the fiend as the ancient hadal fortress was being sieged, Ike had not seen this man since the cave system in Tibet.

If anything, Isaac had grown more imposing. Gone was the sticklike ascetic's body. He had put on muscle weight, meaning the hadals had granted him higher status and, with it, greater shares of meat. Calcium outgrowths formed a twisted horn on one side of his painted head, and his eyes had an abyssal bulge. He moved with the grace of a t'ai chi master. From the silver bands cinching his biceps to the protruding demon stare and the antique samurai sword in one hand, Isaac looked born to rule down here, a *caudillo* for the underworld.

"Our renegade," Isaac greeted him. His grin was ravenous. "And bearing gifts? My daughter. And a machine."

The girl bucked forward. Ike hauled her back, making another wrap of rope around his fist. Isaac's lip peeled back over his filed teeth. He said something in hadal too intricate for Ike to understand.

Ike gripped the knife, stifled his fear. This was Ali's Satan? It would be like him to deceive her into thinking he was the khan. To deceive Ike's own daughter into believing in a false father.

"Ali," Ike murmured, "he's not the one." He didn't speak the name of Older-than-Old, even as a whisper. He touched his claim mark to indicate who he meant.

"Of course he is."

"No. He's only a man. A captive like me."

"But they obey him."

"Because he obeys their king. He's a lieutenant. A favorite."

Ali frowned. "Then who is the king?"

Ike heard a faint jingling. He knew that sound from the fortress, the tinkling of jade against jade. Warrior armor, ten thousand years old. Ali turned to peer into the shadows.

A terrible gravity began pulling at Ike, a feeling you got when your holds failed and the depths peeled you away.

"We've missed you," a voice spoke out of the ruins.

As a familiar figure surfaced from the darkness, Ike lowered his knife hand. He let go of his daughter's rope, and she darted from his side. His mind filled. His heart emptied. He gave himself to the abyss.

At last, thought Ike, falling to his knees.

Him.

Shoat hummed tunelessly in his sniper's nest, his rifle nested in a stone groove overlooking the abyss. He kept his eye to the scope, watching the tiny figures play out his script. "Tick-tock," he whispered.

Time to nail the coffin shut and start the long road back out. With the exit tunnel sterilized by synthetic virus, there would be no critters left to dodge or run from. His worst dangers would be solitude and boredom. Basically, he faced a lonely half-year of walking with a diet of Power Bars, which he'd secreted at caches all along the way.

Finding the hadals mobbed together in this foul pit had been a stroke of good luck. Helios researchers had projected it would take upward of a decade for the prion contagion to filter throughout the sub-Pacific network and exterminate the entire abyssal food chain, including the hadals. But now, with his last five capsules taped inside the laptop computer shell, Shoat could eradicate the nuisance population years ahead of schedule. It was the ultimate Trojan horse.

Shoat felt the high of a survivor. Sure, there'd been some rough spots, and there were bound to be more ahead. But overall, serendipity had favored him. The expedition had self-destructed, though not before carrying him deep. The mercenaries had unraveled, but only after he'd largely run out of uses for them. And now Ike had conveyed the apocalypse straight into the heart of the enemy. "And flights of angels sing thee to thy rest," he muttered, setting his eye to the sniper-scope once again.

Just a minute ago, it had seemed Ike was ready to run off. Now, oddly, he was on his knees, groveling in front of some character emerging from the inner building. Now there was a sight, Crockett servile, head glued to the floor.

Shoat wished for a more powerful scope. Who could this be? It would have been interesting to see the hadal's face in detail. The crosshairs would have to do.

Pleased to meet you, Shoat hummed. *Hope you guessed my name.*

"So you've returned to me," the voice said from the shadows. "Stand up."

Ike didn't even raise his head.

She stared down at Ike's bare back, frightened by his subjugation. It upended her universe. He had always seemed the ultimate free spirit, the original rebel. Yet now he knelt in abject surrender, offering no resistance, no protest.

The hadal khan—their rex, or mahdi, or king of kings, however it translated—stood motionless with Ike at his feet. He wore armor made of jade and crystal plates, and under that a Crusader's chain-mail shirt, sleeves short, each link oiled against rust.

She felt sick with realization. This was Satan? This was the one Ike had been seeking, face by face, in all those hadal dead? Not to destroy, as she'd thought, but to worship. Ike kowtowed blankly, his fear—and shame—transparent. He ground his forehead against the flowstone.

"What are you doing?" she said, but not to Ike.

Thomas solemnly opened his arms, and from throughout the city the hadal nations roared up to him. Ali sagged to her knees, speechless. She couldn't begin to fathom the depths of his deceptions. The moment she comprehended one, another cropped up that was more outrageous, from pretending to be her fellow prisoner to manipulating January's group, to posing as human when all along he was hadal.

And yet, even seeing him here, draped in ancient battle gear, receiving the hadal celebration, Ali could not help but see him as the Jesuit, austere and rigorous and humane. It was impossible to simply purge the trust and companionship they'd built over these past weeks.

"Stand up," Thomas ordered, then looked at Ali, and his tone softened. "Tell him, if you please, to get off his knees. I have questions."

Ali knelt beside Ike, her head by his so that they could hear each other over the roar of the hadals' adulation. She ran her hand across his knotted shoulders, over the scars at his neck where the iron ring had cinched his vertebrae.

"Get up," Thomas repeated.

Ali looked up at Thomas. "He's not your enemy," she said. An instinct urged her to advocate for Ike. It had to do with more than Ike's submission and fear. Suddenly she had her own grounds for fear. If Thomas was truly their ruler, then it was he who'd permitted Walker's soldiers to be tortured through all these days. And Ike was a soldier.

"Not in the beginning," Thomas conceded. "In the beginning, when we first brought him in, he was more like an orphan. And I brought him into our people. And our reward? He brings war and famine and disease. We gave him life and taught him the way. And he brought soldiers, and guided colonists. Now he's come home to us. But as our prodigal son, or our mortal enemy? Answer me. Stand up."

Ike stood.

Thomas took Ike's left hand and lifted it to his mouth. Ali thought he meant to kiss the sinner's hand, to reconcile, and she felt hope. Instead he parted Ike's fingers and put the index finger into his mouth. Then he sucked it. Ali blinked at the lewdness of it. The old man took the finger in all the way to the bottom knuckle and wrapped his lips around the root.

Ike looked over at Ali, jaws bunching. Close your eyes, he signaled.

She didn't.

Thomas bit.

His teeth snapped through the bone. He yanked Ike's hand to one side.

Ike's blood slashed across Thomas's jade armor and into Ali's hair. She yelped. His body shivered. Otherwise he gave no reaction except to lower his head in supplication. His arm remained outstretched. More fingers? Ali thought.

"What are you doing?" she cried out.

Thomas looked at her with bloody lips. He removed the finger from his mouth as if it were a fishbone, and wrapped it in Ike's mutilated hand, which he then released. "What would you have me do with this faithless lamb?"

Now Ali saw. Here was the real Satan.

He'd misled her from the start. She'd misled herself. With their systematic study of her maps, and their promising interpretation of the hadal alphabets, glyphs, and history, Ali had tricked herself into thinking she understood the terms of this place. It was the scholar's illusion, that words might be the world. But here was the legend with a thousand faces. Kindly, then angry; giving, then taking. Human, then hadal.

Ike knelt, his head still bent. "Spare this woman," he asked. The pain told in his voice.

Thomas was cold. "So gallant."

"You have uses for her."

Ali was astonished, less by Ike trying to save the day than by the fact her day needed saving. Until a few minutes ago, her safety had seemed a reasonable bet. Now Ike's blood was in her hair. No matter how deeply she penetrated with her scholarship, it seemed, the cruelty of this place was adamant.

"I do," said Thomas. "Many uses." He stroked Ali's hair, and the armor tinkled like chandelier glass. She started at the proprietary gesture.

"She will restore my memory. She'll tell me a thousand stories. Through her, I'll remember all the things time has stolen from me. How to read the old writings, how to dream an empire, how to carry a people to greatness. So much has slid from my mind. What it was like in the beginning. The face of God. His voice. His words."

"God?" she murmured.

"Whatever you want to call him. The *shekinah* who existed before me. The divine incarnate. Before history ever began. At the farthest edge of my memory."

"You saw him?"

"I *am* him. The memory of him. An ugly brute, as I recall. More ape than Moses. But, you see, I've forgotten. It's like trying to remember the moment of my own birth. My first birth as who I am." His voice grew as faint as dust.

First birth? The voice of God? Ali couldn't fathom his tales, and suddenly she didn't want to. She wanted to go home, to leave this awful place. She wanted Ike. But fate had sewn her into the planet's belly. A lifetime of prayers, and here she was, surrounded by monsters.

"Father Thomas," she said, less afraid than unable to use his other name. "Since we first met, I've been faithful to your desires. I left behind my own past and traveled here to restore your past. And I'll stay here, just as we discussed. I'll help master your dead language. That won't change."

"I knew I could count on you." But her devotion was simply one more of his possessions, she saw that now.

Ali folded her hands obediently, trying not to see Ike's blood staining his beard. "You can depend on me until the end of my life. But in return, you must not harm this man."

"Is that a demand?"

"He has his uses, too. Ike can clarify my maps. Fill in my blanks. He can guide you wherever you want me to take you."

Ike's head lifted slightly.

"No," Thomas said, "you don't understand. Ike doesn't know who he is anymore. Do you realize how dangerous that is? He's become an animal for others to use. The armies use him to kill us. The corporations use him to lay bare our territory and to guide murderers who plant it with disease. With plague. And he hides from his own evil by leaping back and forth from one race to the other."

Beside him, the monster Isaac smiled.

"Plague?" said Ali, in part to digress from Thomas's finality. But also because he kept mentioning it, and she had no idea what he meant.

"You've brought desolation onto my people. It follows you."

"What plague?"

Thomas's eyes flashed at her. "No more deceptions," he thundered.

Ali shrank from him.

"My sentiments exactly," a reedy voice piped out from the laptop computer.

Thomas turned his head as if hearing a fly buzzing. He scowled at the computer. "What's this?" he hissed.

"A man called Shoat," Ike said. "He wants to talk with you."

"Montgomery Shoat?" Thomas spoke the name as if expelling a fetid stench. "I know you."

"I don't know how," Shoat said. "But we do have mutual concerns."

Thomas grabbed Ike's arm and spun him face-out to the distant cliffs. "Where is this man? Is he near? Is he watching us?"

"Ah-ah, careful, Ike. Not a word more," Shoat warned. His finger wagged at them from the screen.

Thomas stood rooted behind Ike, motionless except for his head switching from side to side, piercing the twilight. "Join us, please, Mr. Shoat," he said.

"Thanks anyhow," Shoat's image said on the screen. "This is close enough for me."

The surreality was breathtaking, a computer screen in this underworld. The ancient speaking to the modern. Then Ali noticed Ike's eyes darting about. He was gathering in the broken chamber, estimating it.

"You'll be down soon enough, Mr. Shoat," Thomas said to the computer. "Until then, there's something you wanted to talk about?"

"A piece of Helios property has fallen into your hands."

"What does this fool want?" Thomas asked Ike.

"It's a locator. A homing device," Ike said. "He claims it was taken from him."

"I'm lost without it," Shoat said. "Return it to me and I'll be out of your hair."

"That's all you want?" asked Thomas.

Shoat considered. "A head start?"

Thomas's face filled with rage, but he regulated his voice. "I know what you've done, Shoat. I know what Prion-9 is. You're going to show me where you've placed it. Every single location."

Ali glanced at Ike, and he looked equally puzzled.

"Common ground," Shoat enthused, "the basis for every negotiation. I've got information you want, and you've got a guarantee of my safe passage. Quid pro quo."

"You mustn't fear for your life, Mr. Shoat," Thomas stated. "You're going to live a very long time in our company. Longer than you ever dreamed possible."

It was plain to Ali that he was stalling, searching. Beside him, Isaac, too, was scanning the gloom for any evidence of the hidden man. The girl stood at one shoulder, whispering, guiding his examination.

"My homing device," Shoat said.

"I visited your mother recently," Thomas said, as if just remembering a courtesy.

Murmuring to the side, Isaac had begun dispatching hadal warriors. Their fluid shapes were indiscernible from the shadows. They streamed down from the ruins.

"My mother?" Shoat was disconcerted.

"Eva. Three months ago. An elegant hostess. It was at her estate in the Hamptons. We had a long chat about you, Montgomery. She was dismayed to hear about what you've been up to."

"That's not possible."

"Come down, Monty. We have things to talk about."

"What have you done to my mother?"

"Why make this difficult? We're going to find you. In an hour or a week, it doesn't matter. You're not leaving, though."

"I asked you about my mother."

Ike's eyes quit roaming. Ali saw them fix on hers, intent, waiting. She took a breath and tried to still her confusion and fear. She anchored herself to his eyes.

"Quid pro quo?" said Thomas.

"What have you done to her?"

"Where to begin," Thomas said lightly. "In the beginning? Your beginning? You were born by C-section . . ."

"My mother would never share such a—"

Thomas's voice grew hard. "She didn't, Monty."

"Then how . . ." Shoat's voice faded.

"I found the scar myself," Thomas said. "And then I opened it. That wound through which you crept into the world."

Shoat had fallen silent.

"Come down," Thomas repeated. "I'll tell you which landfill I left her in."

Shoat's eyes filled the screen, then backed away. The screen went blank. What now? wondered Ali.

"He's started to run," Thomas said to Isaac. "Bring him to me. Alive."

A look of peace flickered across Ike's face. With Thomas lurking over one shoulder, he raised his eyes to the faraway cliffs. Ali had no idea what he was searching for. She looked around at the dark cliffs, and there it was, a twinkle of light. A momentary north star.

Ike dove.

In the same instant, Thomas ignited.

The hadal armor and Crusader's chain mail and the shirt of gold did nothing to shield him. Normally the round would have punched through his back and then quickened into a fireball and phosphorous shrapnel. But in Thomas, clad in back as well as in front, it found no exit. The heat and fléchettes went wild inside him. His flesh burst into flame. His spine snapped. And yet his fall seemed infinite.

Ali was mesmerized. Flames leaped up from the neck of Thomas's armor, and he drew in a great gasp. The fire poured down his throat. He exhaled, and the flames shot from his mouth. His vocal cords seared, Thomas was silent. There was a soft clatter of jade scales falling to earth as the gold sutures holding them together melted.

The warlord towered above her. It seemed he had to topple. But his will was strong. His eyes fixed on the heights as if to fly. At last his knees sagged. Ali felt herself plucked from the ground.

Ike carried her, racing for a toppled pillar in the gloom. He threw her behind the pillar and leaped to join her as Shoat's havoc commenced in earnest. He was an army unto himself, it seemed. His ammunition struck like lightning bolts, detonating in bursts of white light and raking the library with lethal splinters. Back and forth, he strafed the ruins and hadals fell.

The carved pillar gave cover from incoming rounds, but not from the ricochet of fléchettes. Ike pulled bodies on top of them like sandbags.

Ali cried out as precious codices and inscriptions and scrolls were shredded and burst into fire. Delicate glass globes, etched with writings on the inside through some lost process, shattered. Clay tablets, describing satans and gods and cities ten times older than the Mesopotamian creation myth of Emannu Elish, turned to dust. The conflagration spread into the bowels of the library, feeding on vellum and rice paper and papyrus and desiccated wooden artifacts.

The city itself seemed to howl. The masses fled downhill from the ruins, even as martyrs piled around Thomas in an attempt to protect their lord from further desecration. With a shriek, Isaac launched into the darkness in search of the assassins, and warriors sped after him.

Ali peered around the pillar. Shoat's muzzle flash was still sparkling at the eye of his distant sniper nest. A single shot would have accomplished everything Shoat needed to escape. Instead, his rage had gotten the better of him.

While the chaos still held, Ike went to work transforming Ali. He was rough. The flames, the blood, the destruction of ancient lore and science and histories: it was too much for her. Ike began yanking her clothes away and smearing her with ochre grease from the bodies around them.

He used his knife to cut tanned skins and hair ropes from the dead. He dressed her like them, and stiffened her hair into horn shapes with the gore. Just an hour ago she had been a scholar excavating texts, a guest of the empire. Now she was filthy with death. "What are you doing?" she wept.

"It's over. We're leaving. Just wait."

The shooting stopped.

They'd found Shoat.

Ike stood.

Crouched against the bonfire of writings, while the wounded still thrashed about and minced blindly across the needlelike shrapnel, he pulled Ali to her feet. "Quickly," he said, and draped rags across her head.

They passed near Thomas, who lay heaped with his faithful, burned and bleeding, paralyzed within his armor. His face was singed, but intact. Incredibly, he was still alive. His eyes were open and he was staring all around.

The bullet must have cut his spinal column, Ali decided. He could only move his head. Half-buried with Shoat's other victims, he recognized Ike and Ali as they looked down at him. His mouth worked to denounce them, but his vocal cords had been seared and no sound came.

More hadals arrived to tend their god-king. Ike ducked his head and started down the ramp, towing Ali. They were going to make a clean getaway, it seemed. Then Ali felt her arm grabbed from behind.

It was the feral girl. Her face was streaked with blood, and she was injured and aghast. Immediately she saw their scheme, the hadal disguise, their run for the exit. All she had to do was cry out.

Ike gripped his knife. The girl looked at the black blade, and Ali guessed what she was thinking. Raised hadal, she would immediately suspect the most murderous intention.

Instead, Ike offered the knife to her. Ali watched the girl's eyes cut back and forth from him to her. Perhaps she was recalling some kindness they had done for her, or a mercy shown. Perhaps she saw something in Ike's face that belonged to her, a connection with her own mirror. Whatever her equation, she made her decision.

The girl turned her head away for a moment. When she looked back, the barbarians were gone.

I went down to the
moorings of the mountains;
The earth with its bars
closed behind me forever;
Yet You have brought up my
life from the pit.

—JONAH 2:6

28
THE ASCENT

Like a fish with beautiful green scales, Thomas lay beached on
the stone floor, mouth gaping, wordless, dying, surely. His strings were
cut. Below the neck, he could not move a muscle or feel his body, which
was a mercy, given the scorched wreckage left by Shoat's bullet. And yet
he was in agony.

With every labored breath he could smell the burnt meat on his
bones. Open his eyes, and his assassin hung before him. Close them, and
he could hear his nations stubbornly waiting for his great transition. His
greatest torment was that the fire had seared his larynx and he could not
command his people to disperse.

He opened his eyes and there was Shoat on the cross, teeth bared.
They had done an exquisite job of it, driving the nails through the
holes in his wrists, arranging small ledges for his buttocks and feet
so that he would not hang by his arms and asphyxiate. The crucifix
had been positioned at Thomas's feet so that he could enjoy the
human's agony.

Shoat was going to last for weeks up there. A hank of meat dangled at
his shoulder so that he could feed himself. His elbows had been dislo-

cated and his genitals mutilated; otherwise he was relatively intact. Decorations had been cut into his flesh. His ears and nostrils had been jingle-bobbed. Lest anyone think the prisoner had no owner, the symbol for Older-than-Old had been branded onto his face.

Thomas turned his head away from the grim creation. They could not know that Shoat's presence gave him no pleasure. Each view only enraged him more. It was this man who had been planting the contagion along the Helios expedition's trail, yet Thomas could not interrogate him to learn the insidious details. He could not abort the genocide. He could not warn his children and send them fleeing into the deeper unknown. Finally, most enraging, he could not let go of this ravaged shell and cross into a new body. He could not die and be reborn.

It was not for lack of new receptacles. For days now, Thomas had been surrounded by rings of females in every stage of pregnancy or new motherhood, and the smell of their scented bodies and breast milk was in the air. For a minute he saw not living women, but Stone Age Venuses.

In the hadal tradition, they were overfed and gloriously pampered during their maternity. Like women of any great tribe, they wore wealth upon their naked bodies: plastic poker chips or coins from a dozen nations had been stitched together for necklaces, colored string and feathers and seashells had been woven into their hair. Some were covered in dried mud and looked like the earth itself coming to life.

Their waiting was a form of deathwatch, but also of nativity. They were offering the contents of their wombs for his use. Those with newborns periodically held them aloft, hoping to catch his attention. Each mother's greatest desire was that the messiah would enter her own child, even though it would mean his obliterating the soul already in formation.

But Thomas was holding himself back. He saw no alternative. Shoat's presence was a minute-by-minute reminder that the virus was out there, set to annihilate his people. To try and inhabit a developed mind meant risking his own memory. And what was the use of reincarnating into the body of an infant, if he was helpless to warn about the impending plague? No, he was better residing in this body. As a precaution, he—and January and Branch—had been vaccinated by a military doctor at that Antarctic base many months ago, when the presence of prion capsules was first being revealed. Even racked and paralyzed, this shot, burned shell was at least inoculated against the contagion.

And so their king lay in a body that was a tomb, caught between choices. Death was sorrow. But as the Buddha had once said, birth was sorrow, too. Priests and shamans from throughout the hadal world went on drumming and murmuring. The children went on crying. Shoat went on writhing and mewling. Off to one side, the daughter of Isaac continued her fascination with the computer, tapping at keys endlessly, a monkey with a typewriter.

Thomas closed his eyes against the nightmare he had become.

After a week of climbing, Ike and Ali reached the serpentine sea. The last of the Helios rafts rested near the lip of its discharge, which plunged into a waterfall, miles deep. It circled in an eddy by the shore like a faithful steed. A single paddle was still lashed to one pontoon.

"Climb in," whispered Ike, and Ali gratefully lowered herself onto the rubber flooring. Ike had kept them moving almost constantly since their escape. There had been no time to hunt or forage, and she was weak with hunger.

Ike pushed the raft out from shore, but did not begin paddling. "Do you recognize any of this?" he asked her.

She shook her head.

"The trails go in every direction. I've lost my thread, Ali. I don't know which way to go."

"Maybe this will help," said Ali. She opened a thin leather sack tied around her waist, and drew out Shoat's homing device.

"It *was* you," Ike said. "You stole it."

"Walker's men kept beating Shoat. I thought they might kill him. This seemed like something we might need someday."

"But the code . . ."

"He kept repeating a sequence of numbers in his delirium. I don't know if it was the code or not, but I memorized it."

Ike squatted on his heels beside her. "See what happens."

Ali hesitated. What if it didn't work? She carefully touched the numbers on the keypad and waited. "Nothing's happening."

"Try again."

This time a red light flashed for ten seconds. The tiny display read ARMED. There was a single high-pitched beep, and the display read DEPLOYED. After that the red light died out.

"Now what?" Ali despaired.

"It's not the end of the world," Ike said, and threw the box in the water. He fished out a square coin he'd found on the trail. It was very old, with a dragon on one side and Chinese calligraphy on the other. "Heads, we go left. Tails, right." He gave it a flip.

They climbed away from the luminescent waters of the sea and its rivers and streams into a dead zone separating their worlds. They had bypassed the region on their descent via the Galápagos elevator system, but Ike had dipped into this barrier zone on other travels. It was too deep for photosynthesis to support a surficial food chain, and yet too contaminated by the surface for the subplanetary biosphere to survive. Few animals passed up or down between those worlds, none by accident. Only the desperate crossed through this lifeless, tubular desert.

Ike backed them away from the dead zone, found a cavity that Ali could capably defend, then went hunting. At the end of a week he returned with long strings of dried meat, and she did not ask its source. With these provisions, they reentered the dead zone.

Their progress was hampered by boulder chokes, hadal fetishes, and booby traps. It was also made difficult by their gain in altitude. The air pressure was decreasing as they approached sea level. Physiologically they were climbing a mountain, and simple walking became an exertion. Where the path turned vertical and they had to scale cracks or inside tubes, Ali's lungs sometimes felt near to bursting.

She sat up gasping for air one night. After that, Ike employed an old Himalayan rule of thumb: climb high, sleep low. They would ascend through the tunnels to a high point, then descend a thousand feet or so for the night. In that way, neither of them developed pulmonary or cerebral edema. Nevertheless, Ali suffered headaches and was visited by occasional hallucinations.

They had no way to track time or chart their elevation. She found their ignorance liberating. With no calendar or hour to mark, she was forced into the moment. With every turn, they might see sunlight. But after a thousand turns without an end in sight, she relinquished that preoccupation, too.

Next Thomas heard silence. The plainsong and chants and drumming, the sound of children, the talk of women: it had stopped. All was still. Everywhere the People were asleep, to all appearances exhausted by their vigil and rapture. Their silence was a relief to the ears of a trained monk.

Quiet, he wanted to command the crucified lunatic. *You'll wake them.*

Only then did he hear the hiss of aerosol, the fine mist leaking from

Shoat's laptop computer. Thomas worked the air into his scarred lungs, then worked to thrust it out as a shout or a whistle. His people were never waking, though.

He stared in horror at Shoat. Taking a bite of the meat hanging by his cheek, Shoat stared right back at him.

Ike's beard grew. Ali's golden hair fell almost to her waist. They were not really lost, because they had started their escape with little idea where they were anyway. Ali found comfort in her prayers each morning, but also in her growing closeness with this man. She dreamed of him, even lying in his arms.

One morning she woke to find Ike facing the wall in his lotus position, much the way she'd first seen him. In the blackness of the dead zone, she could make out the faint glow of a circle painted on the wall. It could have represented some aborigine's dreamtime or a prehistoric mandala, but she knew from the fortress that it was a map. She entered Ike's same contemplation, and the lines snaking and crossing one another within the circle took on dimension and direction. Their memory of the wall painting guided them for days to come.

Badly lamed, Branch entered the ruins of the city of the damned. He had given up finding Ike alive. In truth, fevers and delirium and the poison on that hadal spear had harrowed him so that he could barely remember Ike at all. His wanderings wound deeper less from his initial search than because the earth's core had become his moon, subtly pulling him into a new orbit. The myriad pathways had reduced to one in his mind. Now here he was.

All lay still. By the thousands.

In his confusion, he was reminded of a Bosnian night long ago. Skeletons lay tangled in final embrace. Flowstone had absorbed many of the dead back into the plastic floor. The putrescence had become an atmosphere all its own. Currents of stench whipped around building corners like squalls of rowdy ghosts. The one sound, besides the whistle of abyssal wind, was of water in canals slicing away at the city's underbelly.

Branch meandered through the apocalypse.

In the center of the city he came to a hill studded with the ruins of an edifice. He scanned it through his night scope. There was a cross on top, and it held a body. The cross drew him as a childhood relic, a vestige of some Arthurian impulse.

His bad leg, plus the closely packed dead, made the climb arduous. That reminded him of Ike, who had talked about his Himalayas with such love. He wondered if Ike might be somewhere around here, perhaps even on that cross.

The creature on their crucifix had died much more recently than the rest of them, unkindly sustained by a shank of meat. Nearby, a Ranger's sniper rifle lay broken in pieces beside a laptop computer. Branch couldn't say whether he'd been a soldier or a scientist. One thing was certain, this was not Ike. He had been newly marked, and the grimace held a jumble of bad teeth.

As he turned to leave, Branch noticed the corpse of a hadal dressed in a suit of regal jade. Unlike the others, this one was perfectly preserved, at least from the neck up. That curiosity led to another. The man's face looked familiar to him. Bending closer, he recognized the priest. How could he have come to be here? It was he who'd called with information of Ike's innocence, and Branch wondered if he'd descended to save Ike, too. What a shock hell must have been for a Jesuit. He stared at the face, straining to summon the good man's name.

"Thomas," he suddenly remembered.

And Thomas opened his eyes.

NEW GUINEA

They stood stock-still in the mouth of a nameless cave, with the jungle spread before them. All but naked, a little raving, Ali resorted to what she knew, and began to offer a hoarse prayer of thanks.

Like her, Ike was blinded and shaken and afraid, not of the sun above the ropelike canopy, or of the animals, or of whatever waited for him out there. It was not the world that frightened him. Rather, he did not know who he was about to become.

There comes a time on every big mountain when you descend the snows and cross a border back to life. It is a first patch of green grass by the trail, or a waft of the forests far below, or the trickle of snowmelt braiding into a stream. Always before, whether he had been gone an hour or a week or much longer—and no matter how many mountains he had left behind—it was, for Ike, an instant that registered in his whole being. Ike was swept with a sense not of departure, but of advent. Not of survival. But of grace.

Not trusting his voice, he circled Ali with his arms.

HELIOS, INC.
SCIENCE AND RESEARCH EXPEDITION
Sub-Pacific Passage
Bathymetric Contour

ASIA

— Tropic of Cancer

— Equator

— Tropic of Capricorn

AUSTRALIA

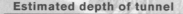

Estimated depth of tunnel

JAVA, PALAU,
AND PHILIPPINE
TRENCHES
(The Pit)
February

8

7

CHALLENGER DEEP
(The Fortress)
November 24

6 CAROLINE TRENCH
(The Sea)
Cache V
October 22

5 MAGELLAN RI
(The Waterfall
Cache IV
September 15

KIRITIMATI
Christmas Island
(The Seamount)
August 23

4

110°E   120°E   130°E   140°E   150°E   160°E   170°E   180°   170°W   160°W